1

Serene was a word you could put to Brooklyn, New York. Especially in the summer of 1912. Somber, as a word, was better. But it did not apply to Williamsburg, Brooklyn. Prairie was lovely and Shenandoah had a beautiful sound, but you couldn't fit those words into Brooklyn. Serene was the only word for it; especially on a Saturday afternoon in summer.

Late in the afternoon the sun slanted down into the mossy yard belonging to Francie Nolan's house, and warmed the worn wooden fence. Looking at the shafted sun, Francie had that same fine feeling that came when she recalled the poem they recite in school.

> *This is the forest primeval. The murmuring*
> *pines and the hemlocks,*
> *Bearded with moss, and in garments green,*
> *indistinct in the twilight,*
> *Stand like Druids of eld.*

The one tree in Francie's yard was neither a pine nor a hemlock. It had pointed leaves which grew along green switches which radiated from the bough and made a tree which looked like a lot of opened green umbrellas. Some people called it the Tree of Heaven. No matter where its seed fell, it made a tree which struggled to reach the sky. It grew in boarded-up lots and out of neglected rubbish heaps and it was the only tree that grew out of cement. It grew lushly, but only in the tenements districts.

You took a walk on a Sunday afternoon and came to a nice neighborhood, very refined. You saw a small one of these trees through the iron gate leading to someone's yard and you knew that soon that section of Brooklyn would get to be a tenement district. The tree knew. It came there first. Afterwards, poor foreigners seeped in and the quiet old brownstone houses were hacked up into flats, feather beds were pushed out on the window sills to air and the Tree of Heaven flourished. That was the kind of tree it was. It liked poor people.

That was the kind of tree in Francie's yard. Its umbrellas curled over, around and under her third-floor fire-escape. An eleven-year-old girl sitting on this fire-escape could imagine that she was living in a tree. That's what Francie imagined every Saturday afternoon in summer.

Oh, what a wonderful day was Saturday in Brooklyn. Oh, how wonderful anywhere! People were paid on Saturday and it was a holiday without the rigidness of a Sunday. People had money to go out and buy things. They ate well for once, got drunk, had dates, made love and stayed up until all hours; singing, playing music, fighting and dancing because the morrow was their own free day. They could sleep late—until late mass anyhow.

On Sunday, most people crowded into the eleven o'clock mass. Well, some people, a few, went to early six o'clock mass. They were given credit for this but they deserved none for they were the ones who had stayed out so late that it was morning when they got home. So they went to this early mass, got it over with and went home and slept all day with a free conscience.

For Francie, Saturday started with the trip to the junkie. She and her brother, Neeley, like other Brooklyn kids, collected rags, paper, metal, rubber, and other junk and hoarded it in locked cellar bins or in boxes hidden under the bed. All week Francie walked home slowly from school with her eyes in the gutter looking for tin foil from cigarette packages or chewing gum wrappers. This was melted in the lid of a jar. The junkie wouldn't take an unmelted ball

Betty Smith

A Tree Grows in Brooklyn

arrow books

Reissued in the United Kingdom in 2000 by Arrow Books

19 20

First published in the United Kingdom in 1944
as *The Tree in the Yard* by William Heinemann Ltd

First published in paperback in the
United Kingdom in 1951 by Penguin

The publishers are unable to locate the copyright holder
for Lewis Hine, but if notified would be pleased to amend
the acknowledgement in any future edition

www.randomhouse.co.uk

Addresses for companies within The Random House Group Limited
can be found at:
www.randomhouse.co.uk/offices.htm

The Random House Group Limited Reg. No. 954009

A CIP catalogue record for this book
is available from the British Library

ISBN 9780099427575

The Random House Group Limited supports The Forest Stewardship
Council® (FSC®), the leading international forest-certification organisation.
Our books carrying the FSC label are printed on FSC®-certified paper.
FSC is the only forest-certification scheme supported by the leading
environmental organisations, including Greenpeace. Our
paper procurement policy can be found at
www.randomhouse.co.uk/environment

Printed and bound in Great Britain by Clays Ltd, St Ives plc

BOOK ONE

of foil because too many kids put iron washers in the middle to make it weigh heavier. Sometimes Neeley found a seltzer bottle. Francie helped him break the top off and melt it down for lead. The junkie wouldn't buy a complete top because he'd get into trouble with the soda water people. A seltzer bottle top was fine. Melted, it was worth a nickel.

Francie and Neeley went down into the cellar each evening and emptied the dumbwaiter shelves of the day's accumulated trash. They owned this privilege because Francie's mother was the janitress. They looted the shelves of paper, rags and deposit bottles. Paper wasn't worth much. They got only a penny for ten pounds. Rags brought two cents a pound and iron, four. Copper was good—ten cents a pound. Sometimes Francie came across a bonanza: the bottom of a discarded wash boiler. She got it off with a can opener, folded it, pounded it, folded it and pounded it again.

Soon after nine o'clock of a Saturday morning, kids began spraying out of all the side streets on to Manhattan Avenue, the main thoroughfare. They made their slow way up the Avenue to Scholes Street. Some carried their junk in their arms. Others had wagons made of a wooden soap box with solid wooden wheels. A few pushed loaded baby buggies.

Francie and Neeley put all their junk into a burlap bag and each grabbed an end and dragged it along the street; up Manhattan Avenue, past Maujer, Ten Eyck, Stagg to Scholes Street. Beautiful names for ugly streets. From each side street hordes of little ragamuffins emerged to swell the main tide. On the way to Carney's, they met other kids coming back empty-handed. They had sold their junk and already squandered the pennies. Now, swaggering back, they jeered at the other kids.

"Rag picker! Rag picker!"

Francie's face burned at the name. No comfort knowing that the taunters were rag pickers too. No matter that her brother would straggle back, empty-handed with his gang and taunt later comers the same way. Francie felt ashamed.

Carney plied his junk business in a tumble-down stable. Turning the corner, Francie saw that both doors were hooked back hospitably and she imagined that the large, bland dial of the swinging scale blinked a welcome. She saw Carney, with his rusty hair, rusty mustache and rusty eyes presiding at the scale. Carney liked girls better than boys. He would give a girl an extra penny if she did not shrink when he pinched her cheek.

Because of the possibility of this bonus, Neeley stepped aside and let Francie drag the bag into the stable. Carney jumped forward, dumped the contents of the bag on the floor and took a preliminary pinch out of her cheek. While he piled the stuff on to the scale, Francie blinked, adjusting her eyes to the darkness and was aware of the mossy air and the odor of wetted rags. Carney slewed his eyes at the dial and spoke two words: his offer. Francie knew that no dickering was permitted. She nodded yes, and Carney flipped the junk off and made her wait while he piled the paper in one corner, threw the rags in another and sorted out the metals. Only then did he reach down in his pants pockets, haul up an old leather pouch tied with a wax string and count out old green pennies that looked like junk too. As she whispered, "thank you," Carney fixed a rusty junked look on her and pinched her cheek hard. She stood her ground. He smiled and added an extra penny. Then his manner changed and became loud and brisk.

"Come on," he hollered to the next one in line, a boy. "Get the lead out!" He timed the laugh. "And I don't mean junk." The children laughed dutifully. The laughter sounded like the bleating of lost little lambs but Carney seemed satisfied.

Francie went outside to report to her brother. "He gave me sixteen cents and a pinching penny."

"That's your penny," he said, according to an old agreement.

She put the penny in her dress pocket and turned the rest of the money over to him. Neeley was ten, a year younger than Francie. But he was the boy; he handled the money. He divided the pennies carefully.

"Eight cents for the bank." That was the rule; half of any money they got from anywhere went into the tin-can bank that was nailed to the floor in the darkest corner of the closet. "And four cents for you and four cents for me."

Francie knotted the bank money in her handkerchief. She looked at her own five pennies realizing happily that they could be changed into a whole nickel.

Neeley rolled up the burlap bag, tucked it under his arm and pushed his way in Cheap Charlie's with Francie right behind him. Cheap Charlie's was the penny candy store next to Carney's which catered to the junk trade. At the end of a Saturday, its cash box was filled with greenish pennies. By an unwritten law, it was a boys' store. So Francie did not go all the way in. She stood by the doorway.

The boys, from eight to fourteen years of age, looked alike in straggling knickerbockers and broken-peaked caps. They stood around, hands in pockets and thin shoulders hunched forward tensely. They would grow up looking like that; standing the same way in other hangouts. The only difference would be the cigarette seemingly permanently fastened between their lips, rising and falling in accent as they spoke.

Now the boys churned about nervously, their thin faces turning from Charlie to each other and back to Charlie again. Francie noticed that some already had their summer hair-cut: hair cropped so short that there were nicks in the scalp where the clippers had bitten too deeply. These fortunates had their caps crammed into their pockets or pushed back on the head. The unshorn ones whose hair curled gently and still babyishly at the nape of the neck, were ashamed and wore their caps pulled so far down over their ears that there was something girlish about them in spite of their jerky profanity.

Cheap Charlie was not cheap and his name wasn't Charlie. He had taken that name and it said so on the store awning and Francie believed it. Charlie gave you a pick for your penny. A board with fifty numbered hooks and a prize hanging from each hook, hung behind the counter. There were a few fine prizes; roller skates, a catcher's mitt, a doll with real hair and so on. The other hooks held blotters, pencils and other penny articles. Francie watched as Neeley bought a pick. He removed the dirty card from the ragged envelope. Twenty-six! Hopefully Francie looked at the board. He had drawn a penny penwiper.

"Prize or candy?" Charlie asked him.

"Candy. What do you think?"

It was always the same. Francie had never heard of anyone winning above a penny prize. Indeed the skate wheels were rusted and the doll's hair was dust filmed as though these things had waited there a long time like Little Boy Blue's toy dog and tin soldier. Someday, Francie resolved, when she had fifty cents, she would take all the picks and win everything on the board. She figured that would be a good business deal: skates, mitt, doll and all the other things for fifty cents. Why the skates alone were worth four times that much! Neeley would have to come along that great day because girls seldom patronized Charlie's. True, there were a few girls there that Saturday . . . bold, brash ones, too developed for their age; girls who talked loud and horseplayed around with the boys—girls whom the neighbors prophesied would come to no good.

Francie went across the street to Gimpy's candy store. Gimpy was lame. He was a gentle man, kind to little children . . . or so everyone thought until that sunny afternoon when he inveigled a little girl into his dismal back room.

Francie debated whether she should sacrifice one of her pennies for a Gimpy Special: the prize bag. Maudie Donavan, her once-in-awhile girl friend, was about to make a purchase. Francie pushed her way in until she was standing behind Maudie. She pretended that she was spending the penny. She held her breath as Maudie, after much speculation, pointed dramatically at a bulging bag in the showcase. Francie would have picked a smaller bag. She looked over her friend's shoulder; saw her take out a few pieces of stale candy and examine her prize—a coarse cambric handkerchief. Once Francie had gotten a small bottle of strong scent. She debated again whether to spend a penny on a prize bag. It was nice to be surprised even if you couldn't eat the candy. But she reasoned she had been surprised by being with Maudie when she made her purchase and that was almost as good.

Francie walked up Manhattan Avenue reading aloud the finesounding names of the streets she passed: Scholes, Meserole, Montrose and then Johnson Avenue. These last two Avenues were where the Italians had settled. The district called Jew Town started at Seigel Street, took in Moore and McKibben and went past Broadway. Francie headed for Broadway.

And what was on Broadway in Williamsburg, Brooklyn? Nothing— only the finest nickel and dime store in all the world! It was big and glittering and had everything in the world in it . . . or so it seemed to an eleven-year-old girl. Francie had a nickel. Francie had power. She could buy practically anything in that store! It was the only place in the world where that could be.

Arriving at the store, she walked up and down the aisles handling any object her fancy favored. What a wonderful feeling to pick something up, hold it for a moment, feel its contour, run her hand over its surface and then replace it carefully. Her nickel gave her this privilege. If a floorwalker asked whether she intended buying anything, she could say, yes, buy it and show him a thing or two. Money was a wonderful thing, she decided. After an orgy of touching things, she made her planned purchase—five cents worth of pink-and-white peppermint wafers.

She walked back home down Graham Avenue, the Ghetto street. She was excited by the filled pushcarts—each a little store in itself— the bargaining, emotional Jews and the peculiar smells of the neighborhood; baked stuffed fish, sour rye bread fresh from the oven, and something that smelled like honey boiling. She stared at the bearded men in their alpaca skull caps and silkolene coats and wondered what made their eyes so small and fierce. She looked into tiny hole-in-the-wall shops and smelled the dress fabrics arranged in disorder on the tables. She noticed the feather beds bellying out of windows, clothes of Oriental-bright colors drying on the fire-escapes and the half-naked children playing in the gutters. A woman, big with child, sat patiently at the curb in a stiff wooden chair. She sat in the hot sunshine watching the life on the street and guarding within herself, her own mystery of life.

Francie remembered her surprise that time when mama told her that Jesus was a Jew. Francie had thought that He was a Catholic. But mama knew. Mama said that the Jews had never looked on Jesus as anything but a troublesome Yiddish boy who would not work at the carpentry trade, marry, settle down and raise a family. And the Jews believed that their Messiah was yet to come, mama said. Thinking of this, Francie stared at the Pregnant Jewess.

"I guess that's why the Jews have so many babies," Francie thought. "And why they sit so quiet . . . waiting. And why they aren't ashamed the way they are fat. Each one thinks that she might be making the real little Jesus. That's why they walk so proud when they're that way. Now the Irish women always look so ashamed. They know that they can never make a Jesus. It will be just another Mick. When I grow up and know that I am going to have a baby, I will remember to walk proud and slow even though I am not a Jew."

It was twelve when Francie got home. Mama came in soon after with her broom and pail which she banged into a corner with that final bang which meant that they wouldn't be touched again until Monday.

Mama was twenty-nine. She had black hair and brown eyes and was quick with her hands. She had a nice shape, too. She worked as a janitress and kept three tenement houses clean. Who would ever believe that mama scrubbed floors to make a living for the four of them? She was so pretty and slight and vivid and always bubbling over with intensity and fun. Even though her hands were red and cracked from the sodaed water, they were beautifully shaped with lovely, curved, oval nails. Everyone said it was a pity that a slight pretty woman like Katie Nolan had to go out scrubbing floors. But what else could she do considering the husband she had, they said. They admitted that, no matter which way you looked at it, Johnny Nolan was a handsome lovable fellow far superior to any man on the block. But he *was* a drunk. That's what they said and it was true.

Francie made mama watch while she put the eight cents in the tin-can bank. They had a pleasant five minutes conjecturing about how much was in the bank. Francie thought there must be nearly a hundred dollars. Mama said eight dollars would be nearer right.

Mama gave Francie instructions about going out to buy something for lunch. "Take eight cents from the cracked cup and get a quarter loaf of Jew rye bread and see that it's fresh. Then take a nickel, go to Sauerwein's and ask for the end-of-the-tongue for a nickel."

"But you have to have a pull with him to get it."

"Tell him that your mother *said*," insisted Katie firmly. She thought something over. "I wonder whether we ought to buy five cents worth of sugar buns or put that money in the bank."

"Oh, Mama, it's *Saturday*. All week you said we could have dessert on Saturday."

"All right. Get the buns."

The little Jewish delicatessen was full of Christians buying Jew rye bread. She watched the man push her quarter loaf into a paper bag. With its wonderful crisp yet tender crust and floury bottom, it was easily the most wonderful bread in the world, she thought, when it was fresh. She entered Sauerwein's store reluctantly. Sometimes he was agreeable about the tongue and sometimes he wasn't. Sliced tongue at seventy-five cents a pound was only for rich people. But when it was nearly all sold, you could get the square end for a nickel if you had a pull with Mr. Sauerwein. Of course there wasn't much tongue to the end. It was mostly soft, small bones and gristle with only the memory of meat.

It happened to be one of Sauerwein's agreeable days. "The tongue came to an end, yesterday," he told Francie. "But I saved it for you because I know your mama likes tongue and I like your mama. You tell her that. Hear?"

"Yes sir," whispered Francie. She looked down on the floor as she felt her face getting warm. She hated Mr. Sauerwein and would *not* tell mama what he had said.

At the baker's, she picked out four buns, carefully choosing those with the most sugar. She met Neeley outside the store. He peeped into the bag and cut a caper of delight when he saw the buns. Although he had eaten four cents worth of candy that morning, he was very hungry and made Francie run all the way home.

Papa did not come home for dinner. He was a free lance singing waiter which meant that he didn't work very often. Usually he spent Saturday morning at Union Headquarters waiting for a job to come in for him.

Francie, Neeley, and mama had a very fine meal. Each had a thick slice of the "tongue," two pieces of sweet-smelling rye bread spread with unsalted butter, a sugar bun apiece and a mug of strong hot coffee with a teaspoon of sweetened condensed milk on the side.

There was a special Nolan idea about the coffee. It was their one great luxury. Mama made a big potful each morning and reheated it for dinner and supper and it got stronger as the day wore on. It was an awful lot of water and very little coffee but mama put a lump of chicory in it which made it taste strong and bitter. Each one was allowed three cups a day *with milk*. Other times you could help yourself to a cup of black coffee anytime you felt like it. Sometimes when you had nothing at all and it was raining and you were alone in the flat, it was wonderful to know that you could have *something* even though it was only a cup of black and bitter coffee.

Neeley and Francie loved coffee but seldom drank it. Today, as usual, Neeley let his coffee stand black and ate his condensed milk spread on bread. He sipped a little of the black coffee for the sake of formality. Mama poured out Francie's coffee and put the milk in it even though she knew that the child wouldn't drink it.

Francie loved the smell of coffee and the way it was hot. As she ate her bread and meat, she kept one hand curved about the cup enjoying its warmth. From time to time, she'd smell the bitter sweetness of it. That was better than drinking it. At the end of the meal, it went down the sink.

Mama had two sisters, Sissy and Evy, who came to the flat often. Every time they saw the coffee thrown away, they gave mama a lecture about wasting things.

Mama explained: "Francie is entitled to one cup each meal like the rest. If it makes her feel better to throw it way rather than to drink it, all right. *I* think it's good that people like us can waste something once in a while and get the feeling of how it would be to have lots of money and not have to worry about scrounging."

This queer point of view satisfied mama and pleased Francie. It was one of the links between the ground-down poor and the wasteful rich. The girl felt that even if she had less than anybody in

Williamsburg, somehow she had more. She was richer because she had something to waste. She ate her sugar bun slowly, reluctant to have done with its sweet taste, while the coffee got ice-cold. Regally, she poured it down the sink drain feeling casually extravagant. After that, she was ready to go to Losher's for the family's semi-weekly supply of stale bread. Mama told her that she could take a nickel and buy a stale pie if she could get one that wasn't mashed too much.

Losher's bread factory supplied the neighborhood stores. The bread was not wrapped in wax paper and grew stale quickly. Losher's redeemed the stale bread from the dealers and sold it at half price to the poor. The outlet store adjoined the bakery. Its long narrow counter filled one side and long narrow benches ran along the other two sides. A huge double door opened behind the counter. The bakery wagons backed up to it and unloaded the bread right on to the counter. They sold two loaves for a nickel, and when it was dumped out, a pushing crowd fought for the privilege of buying it. There was never enough bread and some waited until three or four wagons had reported before they could buy bread. At that price, the customers had to supply their own wrappings. Most of the purchasers were children. Some kids tucked the bread under their arms and walked home brazenly letting all the world know that they were poor. The proud ones wrapped up the bread, some in old newspapers, others in clean or dirty flour sacks. Francie brought along a large paper bag.

She didn't try to get her bread right away. She sat on a bench and watched. A dozen kids pushed and shouted at the counter. Four old men dozed on the opposite bench. The old men, pensioners on their families, were made to run errands and mind babies, the only work left for old worn-out men in Williamsburg. They waited as long as they could before buying because Losher's smelled kindly of baking bread, and the sun coming in the windows felt good on their old backs. They sat and dozed while the hours passed and felt that they were filling up time. The waiting gave them a purpose in life for a little while and, almost, they felt necessary again.

Francie stared at the oldest man. She played her favorite game, figuring out about people. His thin tangled hair was the same dirty gray as the stubble standing on his sunken cheeks. Dried spittle caked the corners of his mouth. He yawned. He had no teeth. She watched, fascinated and revolted, as he closed his mouth, drew his lips inward until there was no mouth, and made his chin come up to almost meet his nose. She studied his old coat with the padding hanging out of the torn sleeve seam. His legs were sprawled wide in helpless relaxation and one of the buttons was missing from his grease-caked pants opening. She saw that his shoes were battered and broken open at the toes. One shoe was laced with a much-knotted shoe string, and the other with a bit of dirty twine. She saw two thick dirty toes with creased gray toenails. Her thoughts ran. . . .

"He is old. He must be past seventy. He was born about the time Abraham Lincoln was living and getting himself ready to be president. Williamsburg must have been a little country place then and maybe Indians were still living in Flatbush. That was so long ago." She kept staring at his feet. "He was a baby once. He must have been sweet and clean and his mother kissed his little pink toes. Maybe when it thundered at night she came to his crib and fixed his blanket better and whispered that he mustn't be afraid, that mother was there. Then she picked him up and put her cheek on his head and said that he was her own sweet baby. He might have been a boy like my brother, running in and out of the house and slamming the door. And while his mother scolded him she was thinking that maybe he'll be president some day. Then he was a young man, strong and happy. When he walked down the street, the girls smiled and turned to watch him. He smiled back and maybe he winked at the prettiest one. I guess he must have married and had children and they thought he was the most wonderful papa in the world the way he worked hard and bought them toys for Christmas. Now his children are getting old too, like him, and *they* have children and nobody wants the old man any more and they are waiting for him to die. But he don't want to die. He wants to keep on living even though he's so old and there's nothing to be happy about anymore."

The place was quiet. The summer sun streamed in and made

dusty, down-slanting roads from the window to the floor. A big green fly buzzed in and out of the sunny dust. Excepting for herself and the dozing old men, the place was empty. The children who waited for bread had gone to play outside. Their high screaming voices seemed to come from far away.

Suddenly Francie jumped up. Her heart was beating fast. She was frightened. For no reason at all, she thought of an accordion pulled out full for a rich note. Then she had an idea that the accordion was closing . . . closing . . . closing. . . . A terrible panic that had no name came over her as she realized that many of the sweet babies in the world were born to come to something like this old man some day. She had to get out of that place or it would happen to her. Suddenly she would be an old woman with toothless gums and feet that disgusted people.

At that moment, the double doors behind the counter were banged open as a bread truck backed up. A man came to stand behind the counter. The truck driver started throwing bread to him which he piled up on the counter. The kids in the street who had heard the doors thrown open piled in and milled around Francie who had already reached the counter.

"I want bread!" Francie called out. A big girl gave her a strong shove and wanted to know who she thought she was. "Never mind! Never mind!" Francie told her. "I want six loaves and a pie not too crushed," she screamed out.

Impressed by her intensity, the counter man shoved six loaves and the least battered of the rejected pies at her and took her two dimes. She pushed her way out of the crowd dropping a loaf which she had trouble picking up as there was no room to stoop over in.

Outside, she sat at the curb fitting the bread and the pie into the paper bag. A woman passed, wheeling a baby in a buggy. The baby was waving his feet in the air. Francie looked and saw, not the baby's foot, but a grotesque thing in a big, worn-out shoe. The panic came on her again and she ran all the way home.

The flat was empty. Mama had dressed and gone off with Aunt Sissy to see a matinee from a ten-cent gallery seat. Francie put the bread and pie away and folded the bag neatly to be used the next time. She went into the tiny, windowless bedroom that she shared with Neeley and sat on her own cot in the dark waiting for the waves of panic to stop passing over her.

After awhile Neeley came in, crawled under his cot and pulled out a ragged catcher's mitt.

"Where you going?" she asked.

"Play ball in the lots."

"Can I come along?"

"No."

She followed him down to the street. Three of his gang were waiting for him. One had a bat, another a baseball and the third had nothing but wore a pair of baseball pants. They started out for an empty lot over towards Greenpoint. Neeley saw Francie following but said nothing. One of the boys nudged him and said,

"Hey! Your sister's followin' us."

"Yeah," agreed Neeley. The boy turned around and yelled at Francie:

"Go chase yourself!"

"It's a free country," Francie stated.

"It's a free country," Neeley repeated to the boy. They took no notice of Francie after that. She continued to follow them. She had nothing to do until two o'clock when the neighborhood library opened up again.

It was a slow, horseplaying walk. The boys stopped to look for tin foil in the gutter and to pick up cigarette butts which they would save and smoke in the cellar on the next rainy afternoon. They took time out to bedevil a little Jew boy on his way to the temple. They detained him while they debated what to do with him. The boy waited, smiling humbly. The Christians released him finally with detailed instructions as to his course of conduct for the coming week.

"Don't show your puss on Devoe Street," he was ordered.

"I won't," he promised. The boys were disappointed. They had expected more fight. One of them took out a bit of chalk from his pocket and drew a wavy line on the sidewalk. He commanded,

"Don't you even step over that line."

The little boy, knowing that he had offended them by giving in too easily, decided to play their way.

"Can't I even put one foot in the gutter, fellers?"

"You can't even *spit* in the gutter," he was told.

"All right." He sighed in pretended resignation.

One of the bigger boys had an inspiration. "And keep away from Christian girls. Get me?" They walked away leaving him staring after them.

"Gol-*lee!*" he whispered rolling his big brown Jewish eyes. The idea that those *Goyem* thought him man enough to be capable of thinking about *any* girl, Gentile or Jew, staggered him and he went his way saying gol-*lee* over and over.

The boys walked on slowly, looking slyly at the big boy who had made the remark about the girls, and wondering whether he would lead off into a dirty talk session. But before this could start, Francie heard her brother say,

"I know that kid. He's a white Jew." Neeley had heard papa speak so of a Jewish bartender that he liked.

"They ain't no such thing as a white Jew," said the big boy.

"Well, if there was such a thing as a white Jew," said Neeley with that combination of agreeing with others, and still sticking to his own opinions, which made him so amiable, "he would be it."

"There never could be a white Jew," said the big boy, "even in supposing."

"Our Lord was a Jew." Neeley was quoting mama.

"And other Jews turned right around and killed him," clinched the big boy.

Before they could go deeper in theology, they saw another little boy turn on to Ainslie Street from Humboldt Street carrying a basket on his arm. The basket was covered with a clean ragged cloth. A stick stuck up from one corner of the basket, and, on it, like a sluggish flag stood six pretzels. The big boy of Neeley's gang gave a command and they made a tightly-packed run on the pretzel seller. He stood his ground, opened his mouth and bawled, "Mama!"

A second story window flew open and a woman clutching a crepe-paperish kimono around her sprawling breasts, yelled out,

"Leave him alone and get off this block, you lousy bastards."

Francie's hands flew to cover her ears so that at confession she would not have to tell the priest that she had stood and listened to a bad word.

"We ain't doing nothing, Lady," said Neeley with that ingratiating smile which always won over his mother.

"You bet your life, you ain't. Not while I'm around." Then without changing her tone she called to her son, "And get upstairs here, you. I'll learn you to bother me when I'm taking a nap." The pretzel boy went upstairs and the gang ambled on.

"That lady's tough." The big boy jerked his head back at the window.

"Yeah," the others agreed.

"My old man's tough," offered a smaller boy.

"Who the hell cares?" inquired the big boy languidly.

"I was just saying," apologized the smaller boy.

"My old man ain't tough," said Neeley. The boys laughed.

They ambled along, stopping now and then to breathe deeply of the smell of Newtown Creek which flowed its narrow tormented way a few blocks up Grand Street.

"God, she stinks," commented the big boy.

"Yeah!" Neeley sounded deeply satisfied.

"I bet that's the worst stink in the world," bragged another boy.

"Yeah."

And Francie whispered yeah in agreement. She was proud of that smell. It let her know that nearby was a waterway, which, dirty though it was, joined a river that flowed out to the sea. To her, the stupendous stench suggested far-sailing ships and adventure and she was pleased with the smell.

Just as the boys reached the lot in which there was a ragged diamond tramped out, a little yellow butterfly flew across the weeds. With man's instinct to capture anything running, flying, swimming or crawling, they gave chase, throwing their ragged caps at it in advance of their coming. Neeley caught it. The boys looked at it briefly, quickly lost interest in it and started up a four-man baseball game of their own devising.

They played furiously, cursing, sweating and punching each other. Every time a stumble bum passed and loitered for a moment, they clowned and showed off. There was a rumor that the Brooklyn's had a hundred scouts roaming the streets of a Saturday afternoon watching lot games and spotting promising players. And there wasn't a Brooklyn boy who wouldn't rather play on the Brooklyn's team than be president of the United States.

After awhile, Francie got tired of watching them. She knew that they would play and fight and show off until it was time to drift home for supper. It was two o'clock. The librarian should be back from lunch by now. With pleasant anticipation, Francie walked back towards the library.

The library was a little old shabby place. Francie thought it was beautiful. The feeling she had about it was as good as the feeling she had about church. She pushed open the door and went in. She liked the combined smell of worn leather bindings, library paste and freshly-inked stamping pads better than she liked the smell of burning incense at high mass.

Francie thought that all the books in the world were in that library and she had a plan about reading all the books in the world. She was reading a book a day in alphabetical order and not skipping the dry ones. She remembered that the first author had been Abbott. She had been reading a book a day for a long time now and she was still in the B's. Already she had read about bees and buffaloes, Bermuda vacations and Byzantine architecture. For all of her enthusiasm, she had to admit that some of the B's had been hard going. But Francie was a reader. She read everything she could find: trash, classics, time tables and the grocer's price list. Some of the reading had been wonderful; the Louisa Alcott books for example. She planned to read all the books over again when she had finished with the Z's.

Saturdays were different. She treated herself by reading a book not in the alphabetical sequence. On that day she asked the librarian to recommend a book.

After Francie had come in and closed the door quietly behind her—the way you were supposed to do in the library—she looked quickly at the little golden-brown pottery jug which stood at the end of the librarian's desk. It was a season indicator. In the fall it held a few sprigs of bittersweet and at Christmas time it held holly. She knew spring was coming, even if there was snow on the ground, when she saw pussy willow in the bowl. And today, on this summer Saturday of 1912, what was the bowl holding? She moved her eyes slowly up the jug past the thin green stems and little round leaves and saw . . . nasturtiums! Red, yellow, gold and ivory-white. A head pain caught her between the eyes at the taking in of such a wonderful sight. It was something to be remembered all her life.

"When I get big," she thought, "I will have such a brown bowl and in hot August there will be nasturtiums in it."

She put her hand on the edge of the polished desk liking the way it felt. She looked at the neat row of freshly-sharpened pencils, the clean green square of blotter, the fat white jar of creamy paste, the precise stack of cards and the returned books waiting to be put back on the shelves. The remarkable pencil with the date slug above its point was by itself near the blotter's edge.

"Yes, when I get big and have my own home, no plush chairs and lace curtains for me. And *no* rubber plants. I'll have a desk like this in my parlor and white walls and a clean green blotter every Saturday night and a row of shining yellow pencils always sharpened for writing and a golden-brown bowl with a flower or some leaves or berries always in it and books . . . books . . . books. . . ."

She chose her book for Sunday; something by an author named Brown. Francie figured she had been reading on the Brown's for months. When she thought she was nearly finished, she noticed that the next shelf started up again with Browne. After that came Browning. She groaned, anxious to get into the C's where there was a book by Marie Corelli that she had peeped into and found thrilling. Would she *ever* get to that? Maybe she ought to read two books a day. Maybe. . . .

She stood at the desk a long time before the librarian deigned to attend to her.

"Yes?" inquired that lady pettishly.

"This book. I want it." Francie pushed the book forward opened at the back with the little card pushed out of the envelope. The librarians had trained the children to present the books that way. It saved them the trouble of opening several hundred books a day and pulling several hundred cards from as many envelopes.

She took the card, stamped it, pushed it down a slot in the desk. She stamped Francie's card and pushed it at her. Francie picked it up but she did not go away.

"Yes?" The librarian did not bother to look up.

"Could you recommend a good book for a girl?"

"How old?"

"She is eleven."

Each week Francie made the same request and each week the librarian asked the same question. A name on a card meant nothing to her and since she never looked up into a child's face, she never did get to know the little girl who took a book out every day and two on Saturday. A smile would have meant a lot to Francie and a friendly comment would have made her so happy. She loved the library and was anxious to worship the lady in charge. But the librarian had other things on her mind. She hated children anyhow.

Francie trembled in anticipation as the woman reached under the desk. She saw the title as the book came up: *If I Were King* by McCarthy. Wonderful! Last week it had been *Beverly of Graustark* and the same two weeks before that. She had had the McCarthy book only twice. The librarian recommended these two books over and over again. Maybe they were the only ones she herself had read; maybe they were on a recommended list; maybe she had discovered that they were sure fire as far as eleven-year-old girls were concerned.

Francie held the books close and hurried home, resisting the temptation to sit on the first stoop she came to, to start reading.

Home at last and now it was the time she had been looking forward to all week: fire-escape-sitting time. She put a small rug on the fire-escape and got the pillow from her bed and propped it against the bars. Luckily there was ice in the icebox. She chipped off a small piece and put it in a glass of water. The pink-and-white peppermint wafers bought that morning were arranged in a little bowl, cracked, but of a pretty blue color. She arranged glass, bowl and book on the window sill and climbed out on the fire-escape. Once out there, she was living in a tree. No one upstairs, downstairs or across the way could see her. But she could look out through the leaves and see everything.

It was a sunny afternoon. A lazy warm wind carried a warm sea smell. The leaves of the tree made fugitive patterns on the white pillow-case. Nobody was in the yard and that was nice. Usually it was pre-empted by the boy whose father rented the store on the ground floor. The boy played an interminable game of graveyard. He dug miniature graves, put live captured caterpillars into little match boxes, buried them with informal ceremony and erected little pebble headstones over the tiny earth mounds. The whole game was accompanied by fake sobbings and heavings of his chest. But today the dismal boy was away visiting an aunt in Bensonhurst. To know that he was away was almost as good as getting a birthday present.

Francie breathed the warm air, watched the dancing leaf shadows, ate the candy and took sips of the cooled water in-between reading the book.

If I were King, Love,
Ah, if I were King. . . .

The story of François Villon was more wonderful each time she read it. Sometimes she worried for fear the book would be lost in the library and she'd never be able to read it again. She had once started copying the book in a two-cent notebook. She wanted to own a book so badly and she had thought the copying would do it. But the penciled sheets did not seem like nor smell like the library book so she had given it up, consoling herself with the vow that when she grew up, she would work hard, save money and buy every single book that she liked.

As she read, at peace with the world and happy as only a little girl could be with a fine book and a little bowl of candy, and all alone in the house, the leaf shadows shifted and the afternoon passed. About four o'clock, the flats in the tenements across from Francie's yard came to life. Through the leaves, she looked into the open uncurtained windows and saw growlers being rushed out and returned overflowing with cool foaming beer. Kids ran in and out, going to and returning from the butcher's, the grocer's and the baker's. Women came in with bulky hock-shop bundles. The man's Sunday suit was home again. On Monday, it would go back to the pawnbroker's for another week. The hock-shop prospered on the weekly interest money and the suit benefited by being brushed and hung away in camphor where the moths couldn't get at it. In on Monday, out on Saturday. Ten cents' interest paid to Uncle Timmy. That was the cycle.

Francie saw young girls making preparations to go out with their fellers. Since none of the flats had bathrooms, the girls stood before the kitchen sinks in their camisoles and petticoats, and the line the arm made, curved over the head while they washed under the arm, was very beautiful. There were so many girls in so many windows washing this way that it seemed a kind of hushed and expectant ritual.

She stopped reading when Fraber's horse and wagon came into the yard next door because watching the beautiful horse was almost as good as reading. The next-door yard was cobblestoned and had a goodlooking stable at the end of it. A wrought-iron double gate separated the yard from the street. At the edge of the cobblestones was a bit of well-manured earth where a lovely rose bush grew and a row of bright red geraniums. The stable was finer than any house in the neighborhood and the yard was the prettiest in Williamsburg.

Francie heard the gate click shut. The horse, a shining brown gelding with a black mane and tail, came into view first. He pulled a small maroon wagon that had *Dr. Fraber, Dentist* and the address painted on the sides in golden letters. This trim wagon delivered nothing and carried nothing. It was driven slowly through the streets all day as an advertisement. It was a dreamily-moving billboard.

Frank, a nice young man with rosy cheeks—like the fabulous youth in the children's song—took the wagon out every morning and brought it back every afternoon. He had a fine life and all the girls flirted with him. All he had to do was to drive the wagon around slowly so that people could read the name and address on it. When it came to a set of plates or the pulling of a tooth, the people would remember the address on the wagon and come to Dr. Fraber.

Frank leisurely removed his coat and donned a leather apron while Bob, the horse, patiently shifted from one foot to the other. Frank then unharnessed him, wiped off the leather and hung the harness up in the stable. Next he washed the horse with a great wet yellow sponge. The horse enjoyed it. He stood there with the sunshine dappling him over and sometimes his hooves struck a spark from the stones as he pawed the ground. Frank squeezed water out on to the brown back and rubbed it down talking to the big horse all the while.

"Steady now, Bob. That's a good boy. Back up there. Whoa now!"

Bob was not the only horse in Francie's life. Her Aunt Evy's husband, Uncle Willie Flittman, also drove a horse. His horse was named Drummer and pulled a milk wagon. Willie and Drummer were not friends the way Frank and his horse were friends. Willie and Drummer lay in wait for each other figuring out injuries to do the other. Uncle Willie reviled Drummer by the hour. To hear him talk, you would think that the horse never slept at night but stood awake in the milk company stable figuring out new torments for his driver.

Francie liked to play a game in which she imagined that people looked like their pets and vice versa. Little white poodles were favorite pets in Brooklyn. The woman who owned a poodle was usually small, plump, white, soiled and with rheumy eyes just like a poodle. Miss Tynmore, the tiny, bright chirping old maid who gave mama music lessons, was just like the canary whose cage hung in her kitchen. If Frank could turn into a horse, he'd look like Bob. Francie had never seen Uncle Willie's horse but she knew what he looked like. Drummer, like Willie, would be small and thin and dark with nervous eyes which showed too much white. He'd be whimpery too, like Aunt Evy's husband. She let her thought go away from Uncle Flittman.

Out on the street, a dozen small boys clung to the iron gate watching the neighborhood's only horse being washed. Francie couldn't see them but she heard them talking. They made up fearful stories about the gentle animal.

"Don't he look still and easy," a boy said. "But that's only a fake. He's layin' his chance for when Frank ain't lookin' then he'll bite him and kick him to death."

"Yeah," said another boy. "I seen him run over a little baby yesterday."

A third boy had an inspiration. "I seen him do number one on a old lady sittin' by the gutter sellin' apples. All over the apples, too," he added as an afterthought.

"They put them blinkers on him so's he can't see how little people is. If he could see how small they is, he would kill them all."

"Them blinkers make him think people is little?"

"Little like pee-wees."

"Gee!"

Each boy as he spoke knew that he was lying. Yet he believed what the other boys said about the horse. Eventually the boys tired of watching gentle Bob just stand there. One of them picked up a stone and threw it at the horse. Bob's skin rippled where it struck him and the boys shivered in anticipation of his going berserk. Frank looked up and spoke to them in a gentle Brooklyn voice.

"You don't want to go and do that now. The horse didn't do nothin' to you."

"Oh, no?" shouted a boy indignantly.

"No," answered Frank.

"Aw, go ——— yourself," came the inevitable *coup de grace* from the smallest boy.

Still gently spoke Frank as he let a rill of water run over the horse's rump: "Do you want to go away from here or do I have to break a couple of vour asses?"

"You and who else?"

"I'll show you who else!" Suddenly Frank swooped down and picked up a loose cobblestone and squared off as if to throw it. The boys backed away hollering out offended retorts.

"I guess this is a free country."

"Yeah. You don't own the streets."

"I'm gonna tell my uncle, the cop, on you."

"Beat it now," said Frank indifferently. He replaced the cobblestone carefully.

The big boys drifted away, tired of the game. But the little boys seeped back. They wanted to see Frank give Bob his oats.

Frank finished washing the horse and stood him under the tree where his head was in the shade. He hung a filled feed bag on his neck, then he went to work washing the wagon, whistling, "Let Me Call You Sweetheart." As if this was a signal, Flossie Gaddis who lived below the Nolans, stuck her head out of the window.

"Hello, there," she called vivaciously.

Frank knew who called. He waited a long time and then answered "Hello" without looking up. He walked around to the other side of the wagon where Floss couldn't see him but her persistent voice followed.

"Done for the day?" she asked brightly.

"Soon. Yeah."

"I guess you're going out sporting, beings it's a Saturday night tonight." No answer. "Don't tell me a goodlooking feller like you ain't got no girl." No answer. "They're running a racket tonight at the Shamrock Club."

"Yeah?" He didn't sound interested.

"Yeah. I got a ticket admitting lady and gent."

"Sorry. I'm all tied up."

"Staying home to keep your old lady company?"

"Maybe."

"Aw, go to hell!" She slammed the window down and Frank breathed a sigh of relief. *That* was over.

Francie felt sorry for Flossie. She never gave up hope no matter how many times she lost out with Frank. Flossie was always running after men and they were always running away from her. Francie's Aunt Sissy ran after men, too. But somehow they ran to meet her halfway.

The difference was that Flossie Gaddis was starved about men and Sissy was healthily hungry about them. And what a difference *that* made.

3

Papa came home at five o'clock. By that time, the horse and wagon had been locked up in Fraber's stable, Francie had finished her book and her candy and had noted how pale and thin the late afternoon sun was on the worn fence boards. She held the sun-warmed, wind-freshened pillow to her cheek a moment before she replaced it on her cot. Papa came in singing his favorite ballad, "Molly Malone." He always sang it coming up the stairs so that everyone would know he was home.

> *In Dublin's fair city,*
> *The girls are so pretty,*
> *Twas there that I first met. . . .*

Francie, smilingly happy, had the door open before he could sing the next line.

"Where's your mother?" he asked. He *always* asked that when he came in.

"She went to the show with Sissy."

"Oh!" He sounded disappointed. He was *always* disappointed if Katie wasn't there. "I work at Klommer's tonight. Big wedding party." He brushed his derby with his coat sleeve before he hung it up.

"Waiting or singing?" Francie asked.

"Both. Have I got a clean waiter's apron, Francie?"

"There's one clean but not ironed. I'll iron it for you."

She set up the ironing board on two chairs and put the iron to heat. She got a square of thick wrinkled duck material with linen tape ties and sprinkled it. While she waited for the iron to get hot, she heated the coffee and poured him a cup. He drank it and ate the sugar bun that they had saved for him. He was very happy because he had a job that night and because it was a nice day.

"A day like this is like somebody giving you a present," he said.

"Yes, Papa."

"Isn't hot coffee a wonderful thing? How did people get along before it was invented?"

"I like the way it smells."

"Where did you buy these buns?"

"Winkler's. Why?"

"They make them better every day."

"There's some Jew bread left, a piece."

"Fine!" He took the slice of bread and turned it over. The Union sticker was on that piece. "Good bread, well made by Union bakers." He pulled the sticker off. A thought struck him. "The Union label on my apron!"

"It's right here, sewn in the seam. I'll iron it out."

"That label is like an ornament," he explained, "like a rose that you wear. Look at my Waiters' Union button." The pale green-and-white button was fastened in his lapel. He polished it with his sleeve. "Before I joined the Union the bosses paid me what they felt like. Sometimes they paid me nothing. The tips, they said, would take care of me. Some places even charged me for the privilege of working. The tips were so big, they said, that they could sell the waiting concession. Then I joined the Union. Your mother shouldn't begrudge the dues. The Union gets me jobs where the boss has to pay me certain wages, regardless of tips. All trades should be unionized."

"Yes, Papa." By now, Francie was ironing away. She loved to hear him talk.

⌒ᕤ

Francie thought of the Union Headquarters. One time she had gone there to bring him an apron and carfare to go to a job. She saw him sitting with some men. He wore his tuxedo all the time. It was the only suit he had. His black derby was cocked jauntily and he was smoking a cigar. He took his hat off and threw the cigar away when he saw Francie come in.

"My daughter," he said proudly. The waiters looked at the thin child in her ragged dress and then exchanged glances. They were different from Johnny Nolan. They had regular waiter jobs during the week and picked up extra money on Saturday night jobs. Johnny had no regular job. He worked at one-night places here and there.

"I want to tell you fellows," he said, "that I got a couple of fine children home and a pretty wife. And I want to tell you that I'm not good enough for them."

"Take it easy," said a friend and patted him on the shoulder.

Francie overheard two men outside the group talking about her father. The short man said.

"I want you to hear this fellow talk about his wife and his kids. It's rich. He's a funny duck. He brings his wages home to his wife but keeps his tips for booze. He's got a funny arrangement at McGarrity's. He turns all his tips over to him and McGarrity supplies him with drinks. He don't know whether McGarrity owes him money or whether he owes McGarrity. The system must work out pretty good for him, though. He's always carrying a load." The men walked away.

There was a pain around Francie's heart but when she saw how the men standing around her father liked him, how they smiled and laughed at what he said and how eagerly they listened to him, the pain lessened. Those two men were exceptions. She knew that everyone loved her father.

Yes, everyone loved Johnny Nolan. He was a sweet singer of sweet songs. Since the beginning of time, everyone, especially the Irish, had loved and cared for the singer in their midst. His brother waiters really loved him. The men he worked for loved him. His wife and children loved him. He was still gay and young and handsome. His wife had not turned bitter against him and his children did not know that they were supposed to be ashamed of him.

Francie pulled her thoughts away from that day when she had visited the Union Headquarters. She listened to her father again. He was reminiscing.

"Take me. I'm nobody." Placidly, he lit up a nickel cigar. "My folks over from Ireland the year the potatoes gave out. Fellow ran a steamship company said he'd take my father to America—had a job waiting for him. Said he'd take the boat fare from his wages. So my father and mother came over.

"My father was like me—never held the one job long." He smoked in silence for awhile.

Francie ironed quietly. She knew that he was just thinking out loud. He did not expect her to understand. He just wanted someone to listen to him. He said practically the same things every Saturday. The rest of the week when he was drinking, he would come and go and say little. But today was Saturday. It was his day to talk.

"My folks never knew how to read or write. I only got to the sixth grade myself—had to leave school when the old man died. You kids are lucky. I'm going to see to it that you get through school."

"Yes, Papa."

"I was a boy of twelve then. I sang in saloons for the drunks and they threw pennies at me. Then I started working around saloons and restaurants . . . waiting on people. . . ." He was quiet awhile with his thoughts.

"I always wanted to be a real singer, the kind that comes out on the stage all dressed up. But I didn't have no education and I didn't know the first way about how to start in being a stage singer. Mind your job, my mother told me. You don't know how lucky you are to have work, she said. So I drifted into the singing waiter business. It's not steady work. I'd be better off if I was just a plain waiter. That's why I drink," he finished up illogically.

She looked up at him as though she were going to ask a question. But she said nothing.

"I drink because I don't stand a chance and I know it. I couldn't drive a truck like other men and I couldn't get on the cops with my build. I got to sling beer and sing when I just want to sing. I drink because I got responsibilities that I can't handle." There was another long pause. Then he whispered, "I am not a happy man. I got a wife and children and I don't happen to be a hard-working man. I never wanted a family."

Again that hurt around Francie's heart. He didn't want her or Neeley?

"What does a man like me want a family for? But I fell in love with Katie Rommely. Oh, I'm not blaming your mother," he said quickly. "If it hadn't been her, it would have been Hildy O'Dair. You know, I think your mother is still jealous of her. But when I met Katie, I said to Hildy, 'You go your way and I'll go mine.' So I married your mother. We had children. Your mother is a good woman, Francie. Don't you ever forget that."

Francie knew that mama was a good woman. She *knew*. And papa said so. Then why did she like her father better than her mother? Why did she? Papa was no good. He said so himself. But she liked papa better.

"Yes, your mother works hard. I love my wife and I love my children." Francie was happy again. "But shouldn't a man have a better life? Maybe someday it will be that the Unions will arrange for a man to work and to have time for himself too. But that won't be in my time. Now, it's work hard all the time or be a bum . . . no in-between. When I die, nobody will remember me for long. No one will say, 'He was a man who loved his family and believed in the Union.' All they will say is, 'Too bad. But he was nothing but a drunk no matter which way you look at it.' Yes, they'll say that."

The room was very quiet. Johnny Nolan threw his half-smoked cigar out of the unscreened window with a bitter gesture. He had a premonition that he was running his life out too fast. He looked at the little girl ironing away so quietly with her head bent over the board and he was stabbed by the soft sadness on the child's thin face.

"Listen!" He went to her and put an arm around her thin shoulders. "If I get a lot of tips tonight, I'll put the money on a good horse that I know is running Monday. I'll put a couple of dollars on him and win ten. Then I'll put the ten on another horse I know and win a hundred. If I use my head and have any kind of luck at all, I'll run it up to five hundred."

Pipe dreams he thought to himself, even while he was telling her about his dream winnings. But oh, how wonderful, he thought, if everything you talked about could come true! He went on talking.

"Then do you know what I'm going to do, Prima Donna?" Francie smiled happily, pleased at his using the nickname he had given her when as a baby, he swore that her crying was as varied and as tuneful as an opera singer's range.

"No. What are you going to do?"

"I'm going to take you on a trip. Just you and me, Prima Donna. We'll go way down south where the cotton blossoms blow." He was delighted with the sentence. He said it again. "Down where the cotton blossoms blow." Then he remembered that the sentence was a line in a song that he knew. He jammed his hands in his pockets, whistled, and started to do a waltz clog like Pat Rooney. Then he went into the song.

> . . . a field of snowy white.
> Hear the darkies singing soft and low.
> I long there to be, for someone waits for me,
> Down where the cotton blossoms blow.

Francie kissed his cheek softly. "Oh, Papa, I love you so much," she whispered.

He held her tight. Again the stab-wound feeling. "Oh, God! Oh, God!" he repeated to himself in almost unendurable agony. "What a hell of a father I am." But when he spoke to her again, it was quietly enough.

"All this isn't getting my apron ironed, though."

"It's all done, Papa." She folded it into a careful square.

"Is there any money in the house, Baby?"

She looked into the cracked cup on the shelf. "A nickel and some pennies."

"Would you take seven cents and go out and get me a dicky and a paper collar?"

Francie went over to the dry-goods store to get her father's Saturday night linen. A dicky was a shirt front made of stiffly starched muslin. It fastened around the neck with a collar button and the vest held it in place. It was used instead of a shirt. It was worn once and then thrown away. A paper collar was not exactly made out of paper. It was called that to differentiate it from a celluloid collar which was what poor men wore because it could be laundered simply by being wiped with a wet rag. A paper collar was made out of thin cambric stiffly starched. It could be used only once.

When Francie got back, papa had shaved, wetted his hair down, shined his shoes and put on a clean undershirt. It was unironed and had a big hole in the back but it smelled nice and clean. He stood on a chair and took down a little box from the top cupboard shelf. It contained the pearl studs that Katie had given him for a wedding present. They had cost her a month's salary. Johnny was very proud of them. No matter how hard up the Nolans were, the studs were never pawned.

Francie helped him put the studs in the dicky. He fastened the wing collar on with a golden collar button, a present that Hildy O'Dair had given him before he became engaged to Katie. He wouldn't part with that either. His tie was a piece of heavy black silk and he tied an expert bow with it. Other waiters wore readymade bows attached to elastics. But not Johnny Nolan. Other waiters wore soiled white shirts or clean shirts indifferently ironed and celluloid collars. But not Johnny. His linen was immaculate, if temporary.

He was dressed at last. His wavy blond hair gleamed and he smelled clean and fresh from washing and shaving. He put his coat on and buttoned it up jauntily. The satin lapels of the tuxedo were threadbare but who would look at that when the suit fitted him so beautifully and the crease in his trousers was so perfect? Francie looked at his well-polished black shoes and noticed how the cuffless trousers came down in the back over the heel, and what a nice break they made across his instep. No other father's pants hung just that way. Francie was proud of her father. She wrapped up his ironed apron carefully in a piece of clean paper saved for that purpose.

She walked with him to the trolley car. Women smiled at him until they noticed the little girl clinging to his hand. Johnny looked like a handsome, devil-may-care Irish boy instead of the husband of a scrubwoman and the father of two children who were always hungry.

They passed Gabriel's Hardware Store and stopped to look at the skates in the window. Mama never had time to do this. Papa talked as though he would buy Francie a pair someday. They walked to the corner. When a Graham Avenue trolley came along, he swung up on to the platform suiting his rhythm to the car's slowing down. As the car started up again, he stood on the back platform holding on to the bar while he leaned way out to wave to Francie. No man had ever looked so gallant as her father, she thought.

4

After she had seen papa off, Francie went up to see what kind of costume Floss Gaddis had for the dance that night.

Flossie supported her mother and brother by working as a turner in a kid glove factory. The gloves were stitched on the wrong side and it was her job to turn them right side out. Often she brought work home to do at night. They needed every cent they could get on account of her brother not being able to work. He had consumption.

Francie had been told that Henny Gaddis was dying but she didn't believe it. He didn't look it. In fact, he looked wonderful. He had clear skin with a beautiful pink color in his cheeks. His eyes were large and dark and burned steadily like a lamp protected from the wind. But he knew. He was nineteen and avid for life and he couldn't understand why he was doomed. Mrs. Gaddis was glad to see Francie. Company took Henny's thoughts off himself.

"Henny, here's Francie," she called out cheerfully.

"Hello, Francie."

"Hello, Henny."

"Don't you think Henny's looking good, Francie? Tell him that he's looking good."

"You're looking good, Henny."

Henny addressed an unseen companion. "She tells a dying man that he's looking good."

"I mean it."

"No, you don't. You're just saying that."

"How you talk, Henny. Look at me—how skinny I am and I never think about dying."

"You won't die, Francie. You were born to lick this rotten life."

"Still and all, I wish I had nice red cheeks like you."

"No, you don't. Not if you know where they come from."

"Henny, you should sit on the roof more," said his mother.

"She tells a dying man he should sit on the roof," reported Henny to his invisible companion.

"Fresh air is what you need, and sunshine."

"Leave me alone, Mama."

"For your own good."

"Mama, Mama, leave me alone! Leave me alone!"

Suddenly he put his head down on his arms and pulled tormented coughing sobs out of his body. Flossie and her mother looked at each other and silently agreed to let him alone. They left him coughing and sobbing in the kitchen and went into the front room to show Francie the costumes.

Flossie did three things each week. She worked on the gloves, she worked on her costumes, and she worked on Frank. She went to a masquerade ball every Saturday night, wearing a different costume each time. The costumes were especially designed to hide her disfigured right arm. As a child, she had fallen into a wash boiler of scalding hot water carelessly left standing on the kitchen floor. Her right arm had been horribly burned and she grew up with its skin withered and purple. She always wore long sleeves.

Since it was essential that a masquerade costume be *décolleté*, she had devised a backless costume, the front cut to display her over-full bust and with one long sleeve to cover that right arm. The judges thought that the one flowing sleeve symbolized something. Invariably, she won first prize.

Flossie got into the costume she was going to wear that night. It resembled the popular conception of what a Klondike dance hall girl wore. It was made of a purple satin sheath with layers of cerise tarleton underskirts. There was a black sequin butterfly stitched over the place where her left breast came to a blunt point. The one sleeve was made of pea green chiffon. Francie admired the costume. Flossie's mother threw open the closet door and Francie looked at the row of brilliantly colored garments.

Flossie had six sheaths of various colors and the same number of tarleton underskirts and at least twenty chiffon sleeves of every color that a person could imagine. Each week, Flossie switched the combinations to make a new costume. Next week the cerise underskirt might froth out from beneath a sky-blue sheath with one black chiffon sleeve. And so on. There were two dozen tightly-rolled, never-used silk umbrellas in that closet; prizes she had won. Flossie collected them for display the way an athlete collects cups. Francie felt happy looking at all the umbrellas. Poor people have a great passion for huge quantities of things.

While Francie was admiring the costumes, she began to grow uneasy. While looking at the brilliant frothing colors, cerise, orange, bright blue, red and yellow, she had a feeling that something was stealthily concealed behind those costumes. It was something wrapped in a long somber cloak with a grinning skull, and bones for hands. And it was hiding behind these brilliant colors waiting for Henny.

5

Mama came home at six with Aunt Sissy. Francie was very glad to see Sissy. She was her favorite aunt. Francie loved her and was fascinated by her. So far, Sissy had led a very exciting life. She was thirty-five now, had been married three times, and had given birth to ten children, all of whom had died soon after being born. Sissy often said that Francie was all of her ten children.

Sissy worked in a rubber factory and was very wild as far as men were concerned. She had roving black eyes, black curling hair, and a high clear color. She liked to wear a cherry-colored bow in her hair. Mama was wearing her jade green hat which made her skin look like cream off the top of the bottle. The roughness of her pretty hands was hidden by a pair of white cotton gloves. She and Sissy came in talking excitedly and laughing as they recalled to each other the jokes they had heard at the show.

Sissy brought Francie a present, a corn cob pipe that you blew into and a rubber hen popped up and swelled over the pipe bowl. The pipe came from Sissy's factory. The factory made a few rubber toys as a blind. It made its big profits from other rubber articles which were bought in whispers.

Francie hoped that Sissy would stay for supper. When Sissy was around, everything was gay and glamorous. Francie felt that Sissy understood how it was with little girls. Other people treated chil-

dren like lovable but necessary evils. Sissy treated them like important human beings. But although mama urged her, Sissy wouldn't
stay. She had to go home, she said, and see if her husband still loved
her. This made mama laugh. Francie laughed too, although she
didn't understand what Sissy meant. Sissy left after promising that
she would come back on the first of the month with the magazines.
Sissy's current husband worked for a pulp magazine house. Each
month he received copies of all their publications: love stories, wild
west stories, detective stories, supernatural stories and what not.
They had shiny colorful covers and he received them from the stock
room tied up in a length of new yellow twine. Sissy brought them
over to Francie just as they came. Francie read them all avidly, then
sold them at half price to the neighborhood stationery store and
put the money in mama's tin-can bank.

After Sissy left, Francie told mama about the old man at Losher's
with the obscene feet.

"Nonsense," said mama. "Old age isn't such a tragedy. If he
was the only old man in the world—yes. But he has other old men
to keep him company. Old people are not unhappy. They don't
long for the things we want. They just want to be warm and have
soft food to eat and remember things with each other. Stop being
so foolish. If there's one thing certain, it's that we all have to get
old someday. So get used to the idea as quickly as you can."

Francie knew that mama was right. Still . . . she was glad when
mama spoke of something else. She and mama planned what meals
they'd make from the stale bread in the week to come.

The Nolans practically lived on that stale bread and what amazing
things Katie could make from it! She'd take a loaf of stale bread,
pour boiling water over it, work it up into a paste, flavor it with salt,
pepper, thyme, minced onion and an egg (if eggs were cheap), and
bake it in the oven. When it was good and brown, she made a sauce
from half a cup of ketchup, two cups of boiling water, seasoning, a
dash of strong coffee, thickened it with flour and poured it over the
baked stuff. It was good, hot, tasty and staying. What was left over,

was sliced thin the next day and fried in hot bacon fat.

Mama made a very fine bread pudding from slices of stale bread, sugar, cinnamon and a penny apple sliced thin. When this was baked brown, sugar was melted and poured over the top. Sometimes she made what she had named *Weg Geschnissen,* which laboriously translated meant something made with bread bits that usually would be thrown away. Bits of bread were dipped into a batter made from flour, water, salt and an egg and then fried in deep hot fat. While they were frying, Francie ran down to the candy store and bought a penny's worth of brown rock candy. This was crushed with a rolling pin and sprinkled on top of the fried bits just before eating. The crystals didn't quite melt and that made it wonderful.

Saturday supper was a red letter meal. The Nolans had fried meat! A loaf of stale bread was made into pulp with hot water and mixed with a dime's worth of chopped meat into which an onion had been cleavered. Salt and a penny's worth of minced parsley were added for flavor. This was made up into little balls, fried and served with hot ketchup. These meat balls had a name, *fricadellen,* which was a great joke with Francie and Neeley.

They lived mostly on these things made from stale bread, and condensed milk and coffee, onions, potatoes, and always the penny's worth of something bought at the last minute, added for fillip. Once in a while, they had a banana. But Francie always longed for oranges and pineapple and especially tangerines which she got only at Christmas.

Sometimes when she had a spare penny, she bought broken crackers. The groceryman would make a toot, which was a poke made of a bit of twisted paper, and fill it with bits of sweet crackers that had been broken in the box and could no longer be sold as whole crackers. Mama's rule was: don't buy candy or cake if you have a penny. Buy an apple. But what was an apple? Francie found that a raw potato tasted just as good and this she could have for free.

There were times though, especially towards the end of a long cold dark winter, when, no matter how hungry Francie was, nothing tasted good. That was big pickle time. She'd take a penny and go down to a store on Moore Street that had nothing in it but fat Jew pickles floating around in a heavy spiced brine. A patriarch with a long white beard, black skull cap and toothless gums presided over the vats with a big forked wooden stick. Francie ordered the same as the other kids did.

"Gimme a penny sheeny pickle."

The Hebrew looked at the Irish child with his fierce red-rimmed eyes, small, tortured and fiery.

"*Goyem! Goyem!*" he spat at her, hating the word "sheeny."

Francie meant no harm. She didn't know what the word meant really. It was a term applied to something alien, yet beloved. The Jew of course did not know this. Francie had been told that he had one vat from which he sold only to Gentiles. It was said that he spat or did worse in this vat once a day. That was his revenge. But this was never proven against the poor old Jew and Francie for one did not believe it.

As he stirred with his stick, muttering curses into his stained white beard, he was thrown into a hysterical passion by Francie asking for a pickle from the bottom of the vat. This brought on eye rollings and clutchings of the beard. Eventually a fine fat pickle, greenish yellow and hard at the ends was fished out and laid on a scrap of brown paper. Still cursing, the Jew received her penny in his vinegar-scarred palm and retired to the rear of his store where his temper cooled as he sat nodding in his beard dreaming of old days in the old country.

The pickle lasted all day. Francie sucked and nibbled on it. She didn't exactly eat it. She just *had* it. When they had just bread and potatoes too many times at home, Francie's thoughts went to dripping sour pickles. She didn't know why, but after a day of the pickle, the bread and potatoes tasted good again. Yes, pickle day was something to look forward to.

6

Neeley came home and he and Francie were sent out for the week-end meat. This was an important ritual and called for detailed instructions by mama.

"Get a five-cent soup bone off of Hassler's. But don't get the chopped meat there. Go to Werner's for that. Get round steak chopped, ten cents worth, and don't let him give it to you off the plate. Take an onion with you, too."

Francie and her brother stood at the counter a long time before the butcher noticed them.

"What's yours?" he asked finally.

Francie started the negotiations. "Ten cents worth of round steak."

"Ground?"

"No."

"Lady was just in. Bought a quarter's worth of round steak ground. Only I ground too much and here's the rest on the plate. Just ten cents' worth. Honestly. I only just ground it."

This was the pitfall Francie had been told to watch against. Don't buy it off the plate no matter what the butcher says.

"No. My mother said ten cents worth of round steak."

Furiously the butcher hacked off a bit of meat and slammed it down on the paper after weighing it. He was just about to wrap it up when Francie said in a trembling voice,

"Oh, I forgot. My mother wants it ground."

"God-damn it to hell!" He hacked up the meat and shoved it into the chopper. Tricked again, he thought bitterly. The meat came out in fresh red spirals. He gathered it up in his hand and was just about to slam it down on the paper when. . . .

"And mama said to chop up this onion in it." Timidly, she pushed the peeled onion that she had brought from home across the counter. Neeley stood by and said nothing. His function was to come along for moral support.

"Jesus!" the butcher said explosively. But he went to work with two cleavers chopping the onion up into the meat. Francie watched, loving the drumbeat rhythm of the cleavers. Again the butcher gathered up the meat, slammed it down on the paper and glared at Francie. She gulped. The last order would be hardest of all. The butcher had an idea of what was coming. He stood there trembling inwardly. Francie said all on one breath,

"And-a-piece-of-suet-to-fry-it-with."

"Son-of-a-bitchin' bastard," whispered the butcher bitterly. He slashed off a piece of white fat, let it fall to the floor in revenge, picked it up and slammed it on the mound of meat. He wrapped it furiously, snatched the dime, and as he turned it over to the boss for ringing up, he cursed the destiny that had made him a butcher.

After the chopped meat deal they went to Hassler's for the soup bone. Hassler was a fine butcher for bones but a bad butcher for chopped meat because he ground it behind closed doors and God knows what you got. Neeley waited outside with the package because if Hassler noticed you had bought meat elsewhere, he'd proudly tell you to go get your bone where you got your other meat.

Francie ordered a nice bone with some meat on it for Sunday soup for five cents. Hassler made her wait while he told the stale joke: how a man had bought two cents' worth of dog meat and how Hassler had asked, should he wrap it up or do you want to eat it here? Francie smiled shyly. The pleased butcher went into the icebox and returned holding up a gleaming white bone with creamy marrow in it and shreds of red meat clinging to the ends. He made Francie admire it.

"After your mama cooks this," he said, "tell her to take the marrow out, spread it on a piece of bread with pepper, salt, and make a nice samwish for you."

"I'll tell mama."

"You eat it and get some meat on your bones, ha, ha."

After the bone was wrapped and paid for, he sliced off a thick piece of liver *wurst* and gave it to her. Francie was sorry that she deceived that kind man by buying the other meat elsewhere. Too bad mama didn't trust him about chopped meat.

It was still early in the evening and the street lights had not yet come on. But already, the horse-radish lady was sitting in front of Hassler's grinding away at her pungent roots. Francie held out the cup that she had brought from home. The old mother filled it halfway up for two cents. Happy that the meat business was over, Francie bought two cents worth of soup greens from the green grocer's. She got an emasculated carrot, a droopy leaf of celery, a soft tomato and a fresh sprig of parsley. These would be boiled with the bone to make a rich soup with shreds of meat floating in it. Fat, homemade noodles would be added. This, with the seasoned marrow spread on bread, would make a good Sunday dinner.

After a supper of fried *fricadellen*, potatoes, smashed pie, and coffee, Neeley went down on the street to play with his friends. Although there was no signal nor agreement, the boys always gathered on the corner after supper where they stood the whole evening, hands in pockets, shoulders hunched forward, arguing, laughing, pushing each other around and jigging in time to whistled tunes.

Maudie Donavan came around to go to confession with Francie. Maudie was an orphan who lived with two maiden aunts who worked at home. They made ladies' shrouds for a living at so much per dozen for a casket company. They made satin tufted shrouds: white ones for dead virgins, pale lavender for the young married, purple for the middle-aged and black for the old. Maudie brought some pieces. She thought Francie might like to make something out of them. Francie pretended to be glad but shuddered as she put the gleaming scraps away.

The church was smoky with incense and guttering candles. The nuns had put fresh flowers on the altars. The Blessed Mother's altar had the nicest flowers. She was more popular with the sisters than either Jesus or Joseph. People were lined up outside the confessionals. The girls and fellows wanted to get it over with before they went out on their dates. The line was longest at Father O'Flynn's cubicle. He was young, kind, tolerant and easy on the penances.

When her turn came, Francie pushed aside the heavy curtain and knelt in the confessional. The old, old mystery took hold as the priest slid open the tiny door that separated him from the sinner and made the sign of the cross before the grilled window. He started whispering rapidly and monotonously in Latin with his eyes closed. She caught the mingled odors of incense, candle wax, flowers, and the good black cloth and shaving lotion of the priest.

"Bless me, Father, for I have sinned. . . ."

Quickly were her sins confessed and quickly absolved. She came out with her head bowed over her clasped hands. She genuflected before the altar, then knelt at the rail. She said her penance using her mother-of-pearl rosary to keep count of the prayers. Maudie, who lived a less complicated life, had had fewer sins to confess and had gotten out sooner. She was sitting outside on the steps waiting when Francie came out.

They walked up and down the block, arms about each other's waists, the way girl friends did in Brooklyn. Maudie had a penny. She bought an ice cream sandwich and treated Francie to a bite. Soon Maudie had to go in. She wasn't allowed out on the street after eight at night. The girls parted after mutual promises were asked and given to go to confession together the following Saturday.

"Don't forget," called Maudie, walking backwards away from Francie, "I called for you this time and it's your turn to call for me next time."

"I won't forget," promised Francie.

There was company in the front room when Francie got home. Aunt Evy was there with her husband, Willie Flittman. Francie liked

Aunt Evy. She looked a lot like mama. She was full of fun and said things to make you laugh like people did in a show and she could mimic anybody in the world.

Uncle Flittman had brought his guitar along. He was playing it and all were singing. Flittman was a thin dark man with smooth black hair and a silky mustache. He played the guitar pretty well considering that the middle finger of his right hand wasn't there. When he came to where he was supposed to use that finger, he'd give the guitar a thumping whack to do for the time when the note should be played. This gave a queer rhythm to his songs. He had nearly reached the end of his repertoire when Francie came in. She was just in time to hear his last selection.

After the music, he went out and got a pitcher of beer. Aunt Evy treated to a loaf of pumpernickel bread and a dime's worth of limburger cheese and they had sandwiches and beer. Uncle Flittman got confidential after the beer.

"Look on me, Kate," he said to mama, "and you look on a man that's a failure." Aunt Evy rolled her eyes up and sighed, pulling in her lower lip. "My children don't respect me," he said. "My wife has no use for me and Drummer, my milk wagon horse, is got it in for me. Do you know what he did to me just the other day?"

He leaned forward and Francie saw his eyes brighten with unshed tears.

"I was washing him in the stable and I was washing under his belly and he went and wet on me."

Katie and Evy looked at each other. Their eyes were dancing with hidden laughter. Katie looked suddenly at Francie. The laughter was still in her eyes but her mouth was stern. Francie looked down on the floor and frowned although she was laughing inside.

"That's what he did. And all the men in the stable laughed at me. Everyone laughs at me." He drank another glass of beer.

"Don't talk like that, Will," said his wife.

"Evy doesn't love me," he said to mama.

"I love you, Will," Evy assured him in her soft tender voice that was a caress in itself.

"You loved me when you married me but you don't love me

now, do you?" He waited. Evy said nothing. "You see, she don't love me anymore," he said to mama.

"It's time we went home," said Evy.

Before they went to bed, Francie and Neeley had to read a page of the Bible and a page from Shakespeare. That was a rule. Mama used to read the two pages to them each night until they were old enough to read for themselves. To save time, Neeley read the Bible page and Francie read from Shakespeare. They had been at this reading for six years and were halfway through the Bible and up to *Macbeth* in Shakespeare's *Complete Works*. They raced through the reading and by eleven, all the Nolans, excepting Johnny, who was working, were in bed.

On Saturday nights Francie was allowed to sleep in the front room. She made a bed by pushing two chairs together in front of the window where she could watch the people on the street. Lying there, she was aware of the nighttime noises in the house. People came in and went to their flats. Some were tired and dragged their feet. Others ran up the stairs lightly. One stumbled, cursing the torn linoleum in the hall. A baby cried half-heartedly and a drunken man in one of the downstairs flats synopsized the wicked life he claimed his wife had led.

At two in the morning, Francie heard papa singing softly as he came up the stairs.

> . . . *sweet Molly Malone.*
> *She drove her wheel barrow,*
> *Through streets wide and narrow,*
> *Crying.* . . .

Mama had the door open on "crying." It was a game papa had. If they got the door opened before he finished the verse, they won. If he was able to finish it out in the hall, he won.

Francie and Neeley got out of bed and they all sat around the table and ate after papa had put three dollars down on the table and given the children each a nickel which mama made them put in the tin-can bank explaining they had already received money that day from the junk. Papa had brought home a paper bagful of food not used at the wedding because some of the guests hadn't come. The bride had divided the unconsumed food among the waiters. There was half of a cold broiled lobster, five stone-cold fried oysters, an inch jar of caviar and a wedge of Roquefort cheese. The children didn't like the lobster and the cold oysters had no taste and the caviar seemed too salty. But they were so hungry that they ate everything on the table and digested it too, during the night. They could have digested nails had they been able to chew them.

After she had eaten, Francie at last faced the fact that she had broken the fast which started at midnight and was to have lasted until after mass next morning. Now she could not receive communion. Here was a real sin to confess to the priest next week.

Neeley went back to bed and resumed his sound sleep. Francie went into the dark front room and sat by the window. She didn't feel like sleeping. Mama and papa sat in the kitchen. They would sit there and talk until daybreak. Papa was telling about the night's work; the people he had seen, what they had looked like and how they spoke. The Nolans just couldn't get enough of life. They lived their own lives up to the hilt but that wasn't enough. They had to fill in on the lives of all the people they made contact with.

So Johnny and Katie talked away the night and the rise and fall of their voices was a safe and soothing sound in the dark. Now it was three in the morning and the street was very quiet. Francie saw a girl who lived in a flat across the street come home from a dance with her feller. They stood pressed close together in her vestibule. They stood embracing without talking until the girl leaned back and unknowingly pressed the bells. Then her father came down in his long underwear and, with quiet but intense profanity, told the fellow what he could go and do to himself. The girl ran upstairs giggling hysterically while the boy friend walked away down the street whistling, "When I Get You Alone, Tonight."

Mr. Tomony who owned the pawnshop came home in a hansom cab from his spendthrift evening in New York. He had never set foot inside his pawnshop which he had inherited along with an efficient manager. No one knew why Mr. Tomony lived in the rooms above the shop—a man with his money. He lived the life of an aristocratic New Yorker in the squalor of Williamsburg. A plasterer who had been in his rooms reported them furnished with statues, oil paintings, and white fur rugs. Mr. Tomony was a bachelor. No one saw him all week. No one saw him leave Saturday evenings. Only Francie and the cop on the beat saw him come home. Francie watched him, feeling like a spectator in a theater box.

His high silk hat was tipped over an ear. The street light picked up the gleam of his silver-knobbed cane as he tucked it under his arm. He swung back his white satin Inverness cape to get some money. The driver took the bill, touched the butt of his whip to the rim of his plug hat and shook the horse's reins. Mr. Tomony watched him drive away as though the cab were the last link in a life that he had found good. Then he went upstairs to his fabulous apartment.

He was supposed to frequent such legendary places as Reisenweber's and the Waldorf. Francie decided to see these places some day. Some day she would go across Williamsburg Bridge, which was only a few blocks away and find her way uptown in New York to where these fine places were and take a good look at the outside. Then she'd be able to place Mr. Tomony more accurately.

A fresh breeze blew in over Brooklyn from the sea. From far away on the north side where the Italians lived and kept chickens in their yards, came the crowing of a rooster. It was answered by the distant barking of a dog and an inquiring whinny from the horse, Bob, comfortably bedded in his stable.

Francie was glad for Saturday and hated to end it by going to sleep. Already the dread of the week to come made her uneasy. She fixed the memory of this Saturday in her mind. It was without fault except for the old man waiting for bread.

Other nights in the week she would have to lie on her cot and from the airshaft hear the indistinct voices of the childlike bride who lived in one of the other flats with her ape-like truck-driver husband. The bride's voice would be soft and pleading, his, rough and demanding. Then there would be a short silence. Then he would start snoring and the wife would cry piteously until nearly morning.

Recalling the sobs, Francie trembled and instinctively her hands flew to cover her ears. Then she remembered it was Saturday; she was in the front room where she couldn't hear sounds from the airshaft. Yes, it was still Saturday and it was wonderful. Monday was a long time away. Peaceful Sunday would come in-between when she would think long thoughts about the nasturtiums in the brown bowl and the way the horse had looked being washed while standing in sunshine and shadow. She was growing drowsy. She listened a moment to Katie and Johnny talking in the kitchen. They were reminiscing.

"I was seventeen when I first met you," Katie was saying, "and I was working in the Castle Braid Factory."

"I was nineteen then," recalled Johnny, "and keeping company with your best friend, Hildy O'Dair."

"Oh, *her*," sniffed Katie.

The sweet-smelling warm wind moved gently in Francie's hair. She folded her arms on the window sill and laid her cheek on them. She could look up and see the stars high above the tenement roofs. After awhile she went to sleep.

BOOK TWO

7

*It was in another Brooklyn summer but twelve years earlier in nine-*teen hundred, that Johnny Nolan first met Katie Rommely. He was nineteen and she was seventeen. Katie worked in the Castle Braid Factory. So did Hildy O'Dair, her best friend. They got along well although Hildy was Irish and Katie came from parents who had been born in Austria. Katie was prettier but Hildy was bolder. Hildy had brassy blond hair, wore a garnet-colored chiffon bow around her neck, chewed sen-sen, knew all the latest songs and was a good dancer.

Hildy had a feller, a beau who took her dancing Saturday nights. His name was Johnny Nolan. Sometimes he waited for Hildy outside the factory. He always brought some of the boys along to wait with him. They stood loafing on the corner, telling jokes and laughing.

One day, Hildy asked Johnny to bring someone for Katie, her girl friend, the next time they went dancing. Johnny obliged. The four of them rode out to Canarsie on the trolley. The boys wore straw katies with a cord attached to the brim and the other end to their coat lapel. The stiff ocean breeze blew the hats off and there was much laughter when the boys pulled the skimmers back by the cords.

Johnny danced with his girl, Hildy. Katie refused to dance with the feller provided for her, a vacuous vulgar boy given to remarks like: "I thought you musta fallen in," when Katie returned from a trip to the ladies' room. However, she let him buy her a beer, and she sat at the table watching Johnny dancing with Hildy and thinking that in all the world, there was nobody like Johnny.

Johnny's feet were long and slender and his shoes were shiny. He danced with his toes pointed in and rocked from heel to toe with beautiful rhythm. It was hot, dancing. Johnny hung his coat over the back of his chair. His trousers settled well on his hips and his white shirt bloused over his belt. He wore a high stiff collar and a polka-dotted tie (which matched the band on his straw hat), baby-blue sleeve garters of satin ribbon shirred on to elastic, which Katie jealously suspected Hildy had made for him. So jealous was she that for the rest of her life she hated that color.

Katie couldn't stop looking at him. He was young, slender and shining with blond curly hair and deep blue eyes. His nose was straight and his shoulders broad and square. She heard the girls at the next table say that he was a nifty dresser. Their escorts said he was a nifty dancer, too. Although he did not belong to her, Katie was proud of him.

Johnny gave her a courtesy dance when the orchestra played "Sweet Rosie O'Grady." Feeling his arms around her and instinctively adjusting herself to his rhythm, Katie knew that he was the man she wanted. She'd ask nothing more than to look at him and to listen to him for the rest of her life. Then and there, she decided that those privileges were worth slaving for all her life.

Maybe that decision was her great mistake. She should have waited until some man came along who felt that way about *her*. Then her children would not have gone hungry; she would not have had to scrub floors for their living and her memory of him would have remained a tender shining thing. But she wanted Johnny Nolan and no one else and she set out to get him.

Her campaign started the following Monday. When the whistle blew dismissal, she ran out of the factory, reached the corner before Hildy did and sang out,

"Hello, Johnny Nolan."

"Hello, Katie, dear," he answered.

After that, she'd manage to get a few words with him each day.

Johnny found that he was waiting around on the corner for those few words.

One day Katie, falling back on a woman's always-respected excuse, told her forelady that it was the time of the month; she didn't feel so good. She got out fifteen minutes before closing time. Johnny was waiting on the corner with his friends. They were whistling "Annie Rooney" to pass the time away. Johnny cocked his skimmer over one eye, put his hands in his pockets and did a waltz clog there on the sidewalk. Passers-by stopped to admire. The cop, walking his beat, called out,

"You're losing time, Sport. You ought to be on the stage."

Johnny saw Katie coming along and stopped performing and grinned at her. She looked mighty fetching in a tight-fitting gray suit, trimmed with black braid from the factory. Intricately whorled and squirled, the braid trimming was designed to call attention to her modest bust already helped out by two rows of ruffles pinned to her corset cover. With the gray suit, she wore a cherry-colored tam pulled over one eye and vici-kid high buttoned shoes with spool heels. Her brown eyes sparkled and her cheeks glowed with excitement and shame as she thought how fresh she must look—running after a feller like that.

Johnny hailed her. The other boys drifted away. What Katie and Johnny said to each other on that special day, they never remembered. Somehow during their aimless but oh-so-significant conversation with its delicious pauses and thrilling undercurrents of emotion, they came to know that they loved each other passionately.

The factory whistle blew and the girls streamed out of the Castle Braid. Hildy came along in a mud-colored brown suit and a black sailor skewered on to her ratted brassy pompadour with an evil-looking hatpin. She smiled possessively when she saw Johnny. But the smile changed to a spasm of hurt, fear and then hate when she saw Katie with him. She rushed down on them pulling her long hatpin from her sailor.

"He's my feller, Katie Rommely," she screamed, "and you can't steal him away."

"Hildy, Hildy," said Johnny in his soft unhurried voice.

"I guess this is a free country," said Katie tossing her head.

"Not free for robbers," yelled Hildy as she lunged at Katie with her hatpin.

Johnny stepped between the girls and got the scratch down his cheek. By this time, a crowd of Castle Braid girls had gathered and were watching them with delighted cluckings. Johnny took each girl by the arm and steered them around the corner. He crowded them into a doorway and imprisoned them there with his arm while he talked to them.

"Hildy," he said, "I'm not much good. I shouldn't have led you on because I see now that I can't marry you."

"It's all her fault," wept Hildy.

"Mine," acknowledged Johnny handsomely. "I never knew what true love was till I met Katie."

"But she's my best friend," said Hildy piteously as though Johnny were committing a kind of incest.

"She's my best girl now and there's nothing more to say about it."

Hildy wept and argued. Finally Johnny quieted her down and explained how it was with him and Katie. He ended by saying that Hildy was to go her way and he'd go his. He liked the sound of his words. He repeated them again, enjoying the drama of the moment.

"So you go your way and I'll go mine."

"You mean, I go my way and you go *her way*," said Hildy bitterly.

Finally Hildy went her way. She walked down the street with her shoulders sagging. Johnny ran after her, and there on the street he put his arms about her and kissed her tenderly in farewell.

"I wish it could have been different with us," he said sadly.

"You wish no such thing," snapped Hildy. "If you did"—she started crying again—"you'd just give her the gate and start going out with me again."

Katie was crying too. After all, Hildy O'Dair had been her best friend. She too kissed Hildy. She looked away when she saw Hildy's tear-wetted eyes so close to hers, grow small with hate.

So Hildy went her way and Johnny went Katie's way.

They kept company for a little while, became engaged, and

were married in Katie's church on New Year's Day, nineteen hundred and one. They had known each other not quite four months when they married.

Thomas Rommely never forgave his daughter. In fact he never forgave any of his daughters for marrying. His philosophy about children was simple and profitable: a man enjoyed himself begetting them, put in as little money and effort into their upbringing as was possible, and then put them to work earning money for the father as soon as they got into their teens. Katie, at seventeen, had only been working four years when she married. He figured that she owed him money.

Rommely hated everybody and everything. No one ever found out why. He was a massive handsome man with iron-gray curly hair covering a leonine head. He had run away from Austria with his bride to avoid being conscripted into the army. Although he hated the old country, he stubbornly refused to like the new country. He understood and could speak English if he wanted to. But he refused to answer when addressed in English and forbade the speaking of English in his home. His daughters understood very little German. (Their mother insisted that the girls speak only English in the home. She reasoned that the less they understood German, the less they would find out about the cruelty of their father.) Consequently, the four daughters grew up having little communion with their father. He never spoke to them except to curse them. His *Gott verdammte* came to be regarded as hello and goodbye. When very angry, he'd call the object of his temper, *Du Russe!* This he considered his most obscene expletive. He hated Austria. He hated America. Most of all he hated Russia. He had never been to that country and had never laid eyes on a Russian. No one understood his hatred of that dimly-known country and its vaguely-known people. This was the man who was Francie's maternal grandfather. She hated him the way his daughters hated him.

Mary Rommely, his wife and Francie's grandmother, was a saint. She had no education; she could not read or write her own name, but she had in her memory over a thousand stories and legends. Some she had invented to entertain her children; others were old folk tales told to her by her own mother and her grandmother. She knew many old-country songs and understood all the wise sayings.

She was intensely religious and knew the life story of every Catholic saint. She believed in ghosts and fairies and all supernatural folk. She knew all about herbs and could brew you either a medicine or a charm—provided you intended no evil with the charm. Back in the old country she had been honored for her wisdom and much sought out for advice. She was a blameless sinless woman, yet she understood how it was with people who sinned. Inflexibly rigid in her own moral conduct, she condoned weaknesses in others. She revered God and loved Jesus, but she understood why people often turned away from these Two.

She had been a virgin when she married and had humbly submitted to her husband's brutal love. His brutality early killed all of her latent desires. Yet she could understand the fierce love hunger that made girls—as people put it—go wrong. She understood how a boy who had been driven from the neighborhood for rape could still be a good boy at heart. She understood why people had to lie and steal and harm one another. She knew of all pitiful human weaknesses and of many cruel strengths.

Yet she could not read or write.

Her eyes were soft brown, limpid and innocent. She wore her shining brown hair parted in the middle and drawn down over her ears. Her skin was pale and translucent and her mouth was tender. She spoke in a low, soft, warmly melodious voice that soothed those who listened. All of her daughters and granddaughters inherited this quality of voice from her.

Mary was convinced that because of some sin she had unwittingly committed in her life, she was mated with the devil himself. She really believed this because her husband told her so. "I am the devil, himself," he told her frequently.

She often looked at him—the way two locks of his hair stood up on either side of his head, the way his cold gray eyes slanted upward at the outer corners, and she sighed and said to herself, "Yes, he is the devil."

He had a way of looking full into her saintly face and in a falsely caressing tone he would accuse Christ of unspeakable things. This always terrified her so much that she'd take her shawl from the nail behind the door, throw it over her head and rush forth into the street where she would walk and walk until concern for her children drove her back into the house.

She went to the public school that the three youngest girls attended and in halting English told the teacher that the children must be encouraged to speak only English; they were not to use a German word or phrase ever. In that way, she protected them against their father. She grieved when her children had to leave school after the sixth grade and go out working. She grieved when they married no-account men. She wept when they gave birth to daughters, knowing that to be born a woman meant a life of humble hardship.

Each time Francie began the prayer, *Hail, Mary, full of grace, the Lord is with thee,* her grandmother's face came before her.

Sissy was the oldest child of Thomas and Mary Rommely. She had been born three months after her parents landed in America. She had never gone to school. At the time when she should have started, Mary did not understand that free education was available for people like them. There were laws about sending children to school but no one sought out these ignorant people in order to enforce the law. By the time the other girls reached school age, Mary had learned about free education. But Sissy was then too big to start in with the six-year-olds. She stayed home and helped her mother.

At ten, Sissy was as fully developed as a woman of thirty and all the boys were after Sissy and Sissy was after all the boys. At twelve, she started keeping steady company with a lad of twenty. Her father nipped that romance by beating up the boy. At fourteen, she was going with a fireman of twenty-five. Because he licked her father, instead of the other way around, this romance ended in the fireman marrying Sissy.

They went to City Hall, where Sissy swore that she was eighteen, and were married by one of the clerks. The neighbors were shocked but Mary knew that marriage was the best thing that could happen to her highly sexed daughter.

Jim, the fireman, was a good man. He was considered educated, having graduated from grammar school. He made good money and wasn't home much. He was an ideal husband. They were very happy. Sissy demanded little from him except a lot of love-making, which made him very happy. Sometimes he was a little ashamed because his wife couldn't read or write. But she was so witty and clever and warmhearted that she made of living a high joyous thing and in time he began to overlook her illiteracy. Sissy was very good to her mother and her younger sisters. Jim gave her a fair household allowance. She was very careful with it and usually had money left over to give her mother.

She became pregnant a month after marriage. She was still a hoyden girl of fourteen in spite of her womanly status. The neighbors were horrified when they watched her skipping rope on the street with other children, heedless of the yet-to-be-born baby who was now an almost unwieldy bulge.

In the hours not devoted to cooking, cleaning, love-making, rope skipping and trying to get into the baseball game with the boys, Sissy made plans for the coming baby. If it were a girl, she was going to call it Mary after her mother. If a boy, it would be named John. For some unknown reason, she had a great affection for the name John. She began calling Jim by the name of John. She said she wanted to name him after the baby. At first, it was an affectionate nickname but soon everyone got to calling him John and many people believed that that was his real name.

The baby was born. It was a girl and a very easy birth. The midwife down the block was called in. Everything went fine. Sissy was in labor only twenty-five minutes. It was a wonderful delivery. The only thing wrong with the whole business was that the baby was born dead. Coincidently, the baby was born and died on Sissy's fifteenth birthday.

She grieved awhile and her grief changed her. She worked harder at keeping her house spotless and clean. She became even more thoughtful of her mother. She stopped being a tomboy. She was convinced that the rope skipping had cost her the child. As she quieted down, she seemed younger and more child-like.

By the time she was twenty, she had had four children, all born dead. Finally she came to the conclusion that her husband was at fault. It wasn't her fault. Hadn't she stopped skipping rope after the first child? She told Jim that she didn't care for him any more since nothing but death grew out of their love-making. She told him to leave her. He argued a little but went finally. At first he sent her money from time to time. Sometimes when Sissy got lonesome for a man, she'd walk past the firehouse where Jim would be sitting outside with his chair tilted against the brick wall. She'd walk slow, smiling and swaying her hips, and Jim would take unauthorized leave, run up to the flat and they'd be very happy together for a half hour or so.

Eventually Sissy met another man who wanted to marry her. What his real name was nobody in her family knew, because she began calling him John right away. Her second marriage was arranged very simply. Divorce was complicated and expensive. Besides she was a Catholic and didn't believe in divorce. She and Jim had been married by a clerk in City Hall. She reasoned that it hadn't been a church, or a real marriage so why let it stand in her way? Using her marriage name and saying nothing about her previous marriage, she was married again in City Hall but by a different clerk.

Mary, her mother, was distressed because Sissy hadn't married in the church. This second marriage provided Thomas with a new implement of torture for his wife. He often told her that he was going to tell a policeman and have Sissy arrested for bigamy. But before he could get around to it, Sissy and her second John had been married four years, she had given birth to four more children, all born dead, and she had decided that this second John wasn't her man either.

She dissolved the marriage very simply by telling her husband, a Protestant, that since the Catholic Church didn't recognize her marriage, she didn't recognize it either and she now announced her freedom.

John Two took it in his stride. He liked Sissy and had been fairly happy with her. But she was like quicksilver. In spite of her terrifying frankness and overwhelming naïveté, he really knew nothing about her and he was tired of living with an enigma. He didn't feel too bad about going away.

Sissy at twenty-four had borne eight children, none of whom had lived. She decided that God was against her marrying. She got a job in a rubber factory where she told everyone she was an old maid (which no one believed), and went home to live with her mother. Between her second and third marriage, she had a succession of lovers all of whom she called John.

After each futile birth, her love of children grew stronger. She had dark moods in which she thought she would go crazy if she didn't have a child to love. She poured out her frustrated maternity on the men she slept with, on her two sisters, Evy and Katie, and on their children. Francie adored her. She had heard it whispered that Sissy was a bad girl but she loved her fiercely just the same. Evy and Katie tried to be mad at their erring sister but she was so good to them that they couldn't hold out against her.

Soon after Francie was eleven, Sissy married for the third time at City Hall. The third John was the one who worked in the magazine company and through him Francie had those fine, new magazines each month. She hoped the third marriage would endure because of the magazines.

Eliza, the second daughter of Mary and Thomas lacked the prettiness and fire of her three sisters. She was plain and dull and indifferent to life. Mary, wanting to give one of her daughters to the church, decided that Eliza was the one. Eliza entered a convent at sixteen. She chose a very rigid order of nuns. She was never permitted to leave the convent walls except on the occasion of her parents' death. She took the name of Ursula and as Sister Ursula she became an unreal legend to Francie.

Francie saw her once when she came out of the convent to attend Thomas Rommely's funeral. Francie was nine at the time. She had just made her first communion and had given herself so whole-heartedly to the church that she thought she might like to be a nun when she grew up.

She awaited Sister Ursula's coming with excitement. Just think of it! An aunt who was a nun! What an honor. But when Sister Ursula stooped to kiss her, Francie saw that she had a fine fringe of hair on her upper lip and chin. This frightened Francie into believing that hair grew on the faces of all nuns who entered the convent at a tender age. Francie decided against sisterhood.

Evy was the third Rommely girl. She, too, had married young. She married Willie Flittman, a handsome, black-haired man with a silky mustache and liquid eyes like an Italian. Francie thought that he had a very comical name and she laughed to herself every time she thought of it.

Flittman wasn't much good. He wasn't exactly a bum, he was just a weak man who whined all the time. *But* he played the guitar. Those Rommely women had a weakness for any kind of man who was by way of being a creator or a performer. Any kind of musical, artistic or story-telling talent was wonderful to them and they felt it their duty to nurture and guard these things.

Evy was the refined one of the family. She lived in a cheap basement flat on the fringes of a very refined neighborhood and studied her betters.

She wanted to be somebody; wanted her children to have advantages she had never had. She had three children; a boy named after his father, a girl named Blossom and another boy called Paul Jones. Her first step towards refinement was to take her children out of the Catholic Sunday School and put them in the Episcopal Sunday School. She had gotten it into her head that the Protestants were more refined than the Catholics.

Evy, loving talent in music and lacking it herself, sought for it avidly in her children. She hoped that Blossom would like to sing and that Paul Jones would want to play the fiddle and Little Willie the piano. But there was no music in the children. Evy took the bull by the horns. They would have to love music whether they wanted to or not. If talent wasn't born in them, maybe it could be shoved in at so much per hour. She bought a second-hand fiddle for Paul Jones and negotiated lessons for him at fifty cents an hour from a man who called himself Professor Allegretto. He taught little Flittman fearsome scrapings and at the end of the year gave him the piece called "Humoresque." Evy thought it was wonderful when he got a piece to play. It was better than playing the scales all the time . . . well, a little better. Then Evy got more ambitious.

"Beings," she said to her husband, "that we've got the fiddle for Paul Jones, little Blossom could take lessons too and both could practice on the same fiddle."

"At different times, I hope," replied her husband sourly.

"What do you think," she answered indignantly.

So fifty cents more a week was scraped up and folded into Blossom's reluctant hand and she was sent off to take fiddle lessons, too.

It so happened that Professor Allegretto had a very slight peculiarity concerning his girl pupils. He made them take off their shoes and stockings and stand in their bare feet on his green carpet while they sawed away. Instead of beating time or correcting their fingering, he spent the hour in a revery staring at their feet.

Evy was watching Blossom getting ready for a lesson one day. She noticed that the child removed her shoes and stockings and washed her feet carefully. Evy thought that commendable but a little strange.

"And why do you wash your feet now?"

"For my fiddle lessons."

"You play with your hands, not your feet."

"I feel ashamed standing in front of the professor with dirty feet."

"He can see through your shoes maybe?"

"I don't think so because he always makes me take my shoes and stockings off."

This made Evy jump. She knew nothing of Freud and her scanty knowledge of sex did not include any of its deviations. But her common sense told her that Professor Allegretto should not charge fifty cents an hour and not attend to his work. Blossom's musical education was terminated then and there.

Upon being questioned, Paul Jones said that he had never been asked to take anything off but his hat when he went for a lesson. He was allowed to continue. In five years, he could play the fiddle almost as well as his father, who had never taken a lesson in his life, could play the guitar.

Aside from his music, Uncle Flittman was a dull man. At home, his only topic of conversation was the way Drummer, the milk wagon horse, treated him. Flittman and the horse had been feuding for five years and Evy hoped that one of them would get the decision soon.

Evy really loved her husband although she could not resist mimicking him. She'd stand in the Nolan kitchen and pretend that she was the horse, Drummer, and she'd give a good imitation of Uncle Flittman trying to put the feedbag on the horse.

"The horse is standing at the curb like this," Evy leaned over until her head was dangling at her knees. "Will comes along with the feedbag. He's just about to put it on, when up goes the horse's head." Here Evy would jerk her head high and whinny like a horse. "Will waits. The horse's head goes down again. You'd think he never could get it up in the air. The horse makes out like he's got no bones." Evy's head lolled alarmingly. "Comes Will with the feedbag, up goes the head."

"*Then* what happens?" asked Francie.

"*I* go down and put the feedbag on the horse. That's what happens."

"Does he let you?"

"Does he let me," Evy reported to Katie, then turned to Francie. "Why he runs up on the sidewalk to meet me and sticks his head in the feedbag before I can lift it up, even. Does he let me," she murmured indignantly. She turned again to Katie. "You know, Kate, sometimes I think my man is jealous the way the horse, Drummer, likes me."

Katie stared at her a moment with her mouth open. Then she started to laugh. Evy laughed and Francie laughed. The two Rommely girls and Francie who was half a Rommely stood there laughing about a secret they shared concerning the weakness of a man.

Those were the Rommely women: Mary, the mother, Evy, Sissy, and Katie, her daughters, and Francie, who would grow up to be a Rommely woman even though her name was Nolan. They were all slender, frail creatures with wondering eyes and soft fluttery voices.

But they were made out of thin invisible steel.

8

The Rommelys ran to women of strong personalities. The Nolans ran to weak and talented men. Johnny's family was dying out. The Nolan men grew handsomer, weaker and more beguiling with each generation. They had a way of falling in love but of ducking marriage. That was the main reason why they were dying out.

Ruthie Nolan had come from Ireland with her handsome young husband soon after their marriage. They had four sons born a year apart. Then Mickey died at thirty and Ruthie carried on. She managed to get Andy, Georgie, Frankie, and Johnny through the sixth grade. As each boy reached the age of twelve, he had to leave school to go out to earn a few pennies.

The boys grew up, handsome, able to play music, to dance and to sing and with all the girls crazy for them. Though the Nolans lived in the shabbiest house in Irish Town, the boys were the dressiest in the neighborhood. The ironing board was kept set up in the kitchen. One or the other was always pressing pants, smoothing out a tie or ironing a shirt. They were the pride of Shantytown, the tall, blond, good-looking Nolan lads. They had quick feet in shoes that were kept highly polished. Their trousers hung just so and their hats set jauntily on their head. But they were all dead before they were thirty-five—all dead, and of the four, only Johnny left children.

Andy was the eldest and the handsomest. He had red-gold wavy hair and finely molded features. He had consumption, too. He was engaged to a girl named Francie Melaney. They kept putting off the marriage waiting for him to get better, only he never did get better.

The Nolan boys were singing waiters. They had been the Nolan Quartette until Andy got too sick to work. They became the Nolan Trio then. They didn't earn much and spent most of that on liquor and horse-racing bets.

When Andy took to his bed for the last time, the boys bought him a genuine swansdown pillow that cost seven dollars. They wanted him to have a luxury before he died. Andy thought it was a wonderful pillow. Andy used it two days, then there was a last great gush of blood which stained the fine new pillow a rusty brown and Andy died. His mother keened over the body for three days. Francie Melaney made a vow that she would never marry. The three remaining Nolan boys swore that they would never leave their mother.

Six months later, Johnny married Katie. Ruthie hated Katie. She had hoped to keep all of her fine boys home with her until either she or they died. So far all had avoided marriage. But that girl—that girl, Katie Rommely! She did it! Ruthie was sure that Johnny had been tricked into marriage.

Georgie and Frankie liked Katie but thought it was a dirty trick for Johnny to skip out and leave them to take care of their mother. They made the best of it, however. They looked around for a wedding present and decided to give Katie the fine pillow they had bought for Andy and which he had used so briefly. The mother sewed a new ticking over it to hide the ugly stain that had been the past part of Andy's life. The pillow thus passed on to Johnny and Katie. It was considered too good for ordinary use and only brought out when one of them was sick. Francie called it "the sick pillow." Neither Katie nor Francie knew that it had been a death pillow.

About a year after Johnny's marriage, Frankie, whom many thought even handsomer than Andy, wavered home after a drinking party one night and stumbled over some taut wire that a bucolic Brooklynite had strung around a square foot of grass before his house stoop. The wire was held up by sharp little sticks. As Frankie stumbled, one of the sticks pierced his stomach. He got up somehow and went home. He died during the night. He died alone and without the priest's last absolution for all of his sins. For the rest of her days, his mother had a mass said once a month for the repose of his soul which she knew wandered about in Purgatory.

In little more than a year, Ruthie Nolan had lost three sons; two by death and one by marriage. She grieved for the three. Georgie, who never left her, died three years later when he was twenty-eight. Johnny, twenty-three, was the only Nolan boy left at the time.

These were the Nolan boys. All died young. All died sudden or violent deaths brought on by their own recklessness or their own bad way of living. Johnny was the only one who lived past his thirtieth birthday.

And the child, Francie Nolan, was of all the Rommelys and all the Nolans. She had the violent weaknesses and passion for beauty of the shanty Nolans. She was a mosaic of her grandmother Rommely's mysticism, her tale-telling, her great belief in everything and her compassion for the weak ones. She had a lot of her grandfather Rommely's cruel will. She had some of her Aunt Evy's talent for mimicking, some of Ruthie Nolan's possessiveness. She had Aunt Sissy's love for life and her love for children. She had Johnny's sentimentality without his good looks. She had all of Katie's soft ways and only half of the invisible steel of Katie. She was made up of all of these good and these bad things.

She was made up of more, too. She was the books she read in the library. She was of the flower in the brown bowl. Part of her life was made from the tree growing rankly in the yard. She was the bitter quarrels she had with her brother whom she loved dearly. She was Katie's secret, despairing weeping. She was the shame of her father staggering home drunk.

She was all of these things and of something more that did not come from the Rommelys nor the Nolans, the reading, the observing, the living from day to day. It was something that had been born into her and her only—the something different from anyone else in the two families. It was what God or whatever is His equivalent puts into each soul that is given life—the one different thing such as that which makes no two fingerprints on the face of the earth alike.

9

Johnny and Katie were married and went to live on a quiet side street in Williamsburg called Bogart Street. Johnny chose the street because its name had a thrilling dark sound. They were very happy there the first year of their marriage.

Katie had married Johnny because she liked the way he sang and danced and dressed. Womanlike, she set about changing all those things in him after marriage. She persuaded him to give up the singing waiter business. He did so, since he was in love and anxious to please her. They got a job together taking care of a public school and they loved it. Their day started when the rest of the world went to bed. After supper, Katie put on her black coat with the big leg-o-mutton sleeves, lavishly trimmed with braid—her last loot from the factory—and threw a cherry wool fascinator over her head (a "noobie" she called it), and she and Johnny set off for work.

The school was old and small and warm. They looked forward to spending the night there. They walked arm-in-arm; he in his patent leather dancing shoes and she in her high laced kid boots. Sometimes when the night was frosty and full of stars, they ran a little, skipped a little and laughed a lot. They felt very important using their private key to get into the school. The school was their world for a night.

They played games while they worked. Johnny sat at one of the desks and Katie pretended she was a teacher. They wrote messages to each other on the blackboards. They pulled down the maps which rolled up like shades and pointed out foreign countries with the rubber-tipped pointer. They were filled with wonder at the thought of strange lands and unknown languages. (He was nineteen and she was seventeen.)

They liked best to clean the assembly room. Johnny dusted the piano and, while doing so, ran his fingers over the keys. He picked out some chords. Katie sat in the front row and asked him to sing. He sang to her; sentimental songs of the time: "She May Have Seen Better Days," or "I'm Wearin' My Heart Away For You." People living nearby would be coaxed out of their midnight sleep by the singing. They'd lie in their warm beds, listening drowsily and murmur to each other,

"That feller, whoever he is, is losing time. He's losing time. He ought to be in a show."

Sometimes Johnny went into one of his dances on the little platform that he pretended was a stage. He was so graceful and handsome, so loving, so full of the grandness of just living, that Katie, watching him, thought she would die of being happy.

At two, they went into the teachers' lunch room where there was a gas plate. They made coffee. They kept a can of condensed milk in the cupboard. They enjoyed the boiling hot coffee which filled the room with a wonderful smell. Their rye bread and bologna sandwiches tasted good. Sometimes after supper, they'd go into the teachers' rest room where there was a chintz-covered couch and lie there for awhile with their arms about each other.

They emptied the wastebaskets, last thing, and Katie salvaged the longer bits of discarded chalk and the pencils that were not too stubby. She took them home and saved them in a box. Later when Francie was growing up, she felt very rich having so much chalk and so many pencils to use.

At dawn, they left the school scrubbed, shiny, warm and ready for the daytime janitor. They walked home watching the stars fade from the sky. They passed the baker's where the smell of freshly-baked rolls came up to them from the baking room in the basement. Johnny ran down and bought a nickel's worth of buns hot from the oven. Arriving home, they had a breakfast of hot coffee and warm sweet buns. Then Johnny ran out and got the morning *American* and read the news to her, with running comments, while she cleaned up their rooms. At noon, they had a hot dinner of pot roast and noodles or something good like that. After dinner they slept until it was time to get up for work.

They earned fifty dollars a month which was good pay for people of their class in those days. They lived comfortably and it was a good life they had . . . happy and full of small adventures.

And they were so young and loved each other so much.

In a few months, to their innocent amazement and consternation, Katie found out that she was pregnant. She told Johnny that she was "that way." Johnny was bewildered and confused at first. He didn't want her to work at the school. She told him she had been that way for quite a while without being sure and had been working and had not suffered. When she convinced him that it was good for her to work, he gave in. She continued working until she got too unwieldy to dust under the desks. Soon she could do little more than go along with him for company and lie on the gay couch no longer used for love-making. He did all the work now. At two in the morning, he made clumsy sandwiches and overboiled coffee for her. They were still very happy although Johnny was getting more and more worried as the time wore on.

Towards the end of a frosty December night, her pains started. She lay on the couch, holding them back not wanting to tell Johnny until the work was finished. On the way home, there was a tearing pain that she couldn't keep back. She moaned and Johnny knew that the baby was on the way. He got her home and put her to bed without undressing her, and covered her warmly. He ran down the block to Mrs. Gindler, the midwife and begged her to hurry. That good woman drove him crazy by taking her time.

She had to take dozens of curlers out of her hair. She couldn't find her teeth and refused to officiate without them. Johnny helped her search and they found them at last in a glass of water on the ledge outside the window. The water had frozen around the teeth and they had to be thawed before she could put them in. That done, she had to go about making a charm out of a piece of blessed palm taken from the altar on Palm Sunday. To this, she added a medal of the Blessed Mother, a small blue bird feather, a broken blade from a penknife and a sprig of some herb. These things were tied together with a bit of dirty string from the corset of a woman who had given birth to twins after only ten minutes of labor. She sprinkled the whole business with holy water that was supposed to have come from a well in Jerusalem from which it was said that Jesus had once quenched His thirst. She explained to the frantic boy that this charm would cut the pains and assure him of a fine, well-born baby. Lastly she grabbed her crocodile satchel—familiar to everyone in the neighborhood and believed by all the youngsters to be the satchel in which they had been delivered, kicking, to their mothers—and she was ready to go.

Katie was screaming in pain when they got to her. The flat was filled with neighbor women who stood around praying and reminiscing about their own child-bed experiences.

"When I had my Wincent," said one, "I . . ."

"I was even smaller than her," said another, "and when . . ."

"They didn't expect me to come through it," proudly declared a third, "but . . ."

They welcomed the midwife and shooed Johnny out of the place. He sat on the stoop and trembled each time Katie cried out. He was confused, it had happened so suddenly. It was now seven in the morning. Her screams kept coming to him even though the windows were closed. Men passed on their way to work, looked at the window from behind which the screams were coming and then looked at Johnny huddled on the stoop and a somber look came over their faces.

Katie was in labor all that day and there was nothing that Johnny could do—nothing that he could do. Towards night, he couldn't stand it any longer. He went to his mother's house for comforting. When he told her that Katie was having a baby, she nearly raised the roof with her lamentations.

"Now she's got you good," she wailed. "You'll never be able to come back to me." She would not be consoled.

Johnny hunted up his brother, Georgie, who was working a dance. He sat drinking, waiting for Georgie to finish, forgetting that he was supposed to be at the school. When Georgie was free for the night, they went to several all-night saloons, had a drink or two at each place and told everyone what Johnny was going through. The men listened sympathetically, treated Johnny to drinks and assured him that they had been through the same mill.

Towards dawn, the boys went to their mother's house where Johnny fell into a troubled sleep. At nine, he woke up with a feeling of coming trouble. He remembered Katie and, too late, he remembered the school. He washed and dressed and started for home. He passed a fruit stand which displayed avocados. He bought two for Katie.

He had no way of knowing that during the night, his wife in great pain, and after nearly twenty-four hours of labor, gave bloody birth to a fragile baby girl. The only notable thing about the birth was that the infant was born with a caul which was supposed to indicate that the child was set apart to do great things in the world. The midwife surreptitiously confiscated the caul and later sold it to a sailor from the Brooklyn Navy Yard for two dollars. Whoever wore a caul would never die by drowning, it was said. The sailor wore it in a flannel bag around his neck.

While he drank and slept the night away, Johnny did not know that the night had turned cold and the school fires which he was supposed to tend had gone out and the water pipes had burst and flooded the school basement and the first floor.

When he got home, he found Katie lying in the dark bedroom. The baby was beside her on Andy's pillow. The flat was scrupulously clean; the neighbor women had attended to that. There was a faint odor of carbolic acid mixed with Mennen's talcum powder. The midwife had gone after saying, "That will be five dollars and your husband knows where I live."

She left and Katie turned her face to the wall and tried not to cry. During the night, she assured herself that Johnny was working at the school. She had hoped that he would run home for a moment during the two o'clock eating period. Now it was late morning and he should be home. Maybe he had gone to his mother's to snatch some sleep after the night's work. She made herself believe that no matter what Johnny was doing, it was all right and that his explanation would set her mind at ease.

Soon after the midwife left, Evy came over. A neighbor's boy had been sent for her. Evy brought along some sweet butter and a package of soda crackers and made tea. It tasted so good to Katie. Evy examined the baby and thought it didn't look like much but she said nothing to Katie.

When Johnny got home, Evy started to lecture him. But when she saw how pale and frightened he looked and when she considered his age—just twenty years old, she choked up inside, kissed his cheek, told him not to worry and made fresh coffee for him.

Johnny hardly looked at the baby. Still clutching the avocados, he knelt by Katie's bed and sobbed out his fear and worry. Katie cried with him. During the night, she had wanted him with her. Now she wished she could have had that baby secretly and gone away somewhere and when it was over come back and tell him that everything was fine. She had had the pain; it had been like being boiled alive in scalding oil and not being able to die to get free of it. She had had the pain. Dear God! Wasn't that enough? Why did *he* have to suffer? *He* wasn't put together for suffering but *she* was. She had borne a child but two hours ago. She was so weak that she couldn't lift her head an inch from the pillow, yet it was she who comforted him and told him not to worry, that she would take care of him.

Johnny began to feel better. He told her that after all it was nothing; that he had learned that a lot of husbands had been "through the mill."

"I've been through the mill, now, too," he said. "And now I'm a man."

He made a big fuss over the baby then. At his suggestion, Katie agreed to name her Francie, after the girl, Francie Melaney, who had never married his brother, Andy. They thought it would help to mend her broken heart if she were made godmother. The child would have the name *she* would have carried had Andy lived: Francie Nolan.

He fixed the avocados with sweet oil and pickled vinegar and brought the salad in to Katie. She was disappointed at the flat taste. Johnny said you had to get used to it, like olives. For his sake and because she was touched by his thinking of her, Katie ate the salad. Evy was urged to try some. She did and said that she'd sooner have tomatoes.

While Johnny was in the kitchen drinking coffee, a boy came from the school with a note from the principal which said that Johnny was fired because of neglect. He was told to come around and get what money was due him. The note ended by telling Johnny not to ask for a recommendation. Johnny's face got pale as he read it. He gave the kid a nickel for bringing the note and a message saying he would be around. He destroyed the note and said nothing about it to Katie.

Johnny saw the principal and tried to explain. The principal told Johnny that since he knew the baby was coming, he should have been more careful of his job. As a kindly afterthought, he told the boy that he wouldn't have to pay the damage caused by the burst pipes; the Board of Education would see to that. Johnny thanked him. The principal paid him from his own pocket after Johnny had signed a voucher turning over the coming pay check to the principal. All in all, the principal did the best he could according to the way he saw things.

Johnny paid the midwife and gave the landlord the next month's rent. He got a little frightened when he realized that now there was a baby and that Katie wouldn't be strong enough to do much for quite some time, and that they were out of a job. He consoled himself finally with the thought that the rent was paid and that they were safe for thirty days. Surely something would turn up in that time.

In the afternoon, he walked over to tell Mary Rommely about the new baby. On the way there, he stopped at the rubber factory and asked for Sissy's foreman. He asked the man to tell her about the baby and would she stop over after work? The foreman said he would, winked, poked Johnny in the ribs and said, "Good for you, Mac." Johnny grinned and gave him ten cents with instructions:

"Buy a good cigar and smoke it on me."

"I'll do that, Mac," promised the foreman. He pumped Johnny's hand and again promised to tell Sissy.

Mary Rommely wept when she heard the news. "The poor child! The poor little one," she lamented. "Born into this world of sorrow; born for suffering and hardship. Ai, there'll be a little happiness, but more of hard work. Ai, ai."

Johnny was all for telling Thomas Rommely but Mary begged him not to just yet. Thomas hated Johnny Nolan because he was Irish. He hated the Germans, he hated Americans, he hated the Russians, but he just couldn't stand the Irish. He was fiercely racial in spite of his stupendous hatred of his race and he had a theory that marriage between two of alien races would result in mongrel children.

"What would I get if I mated a canary with a crow?" was his argument.

After Johnny had escorted his mother-in-law over to his house, he went out looking for work.

Katie was glad to see her mother. With the memory of her own birth pangs still lingering, she had knowledge now of what her mother had suffered when she, Katie, was born. She thought of her mother bearing seven children, bringing them up, watching three of them die, and knowing that those who lived were doomed to hunger and hardship. She had a vision that the same cycle was destined for her less than day-old child. She became frantic with worry.

"What do *I* know?" Katie asked her mother. "I can't teach her anything more than I, myself, know and I know so little. You are poor, Mother. Johnny and I are poor. The baby will grow up to be poor. We can't be any more than we are this day. Sometimes I think that the year past was the best we will ever know. As the years go by and Johnny and I get older, nothing will grow better. All we have now is that we are young and strong enough to work and that will go from us as time passes."

Then the real truth came to her. "I mean," she thought, "that *I* can work. I can't count on Johnny. I'll always have to look after him. Oh, God, don't send me any more children or I won't be able to look after Johnny and I've *got* to look after Johnny. He can't look after himself." Her mother interrupted her thoughts. Mary was saying:

"What did we have in the old country? Nothing. We were peasants. We starved. Well, then, we came over here. It wasn't so much better except that they didn't take your father for the military the way they would do in the old country. But otherwise, it's been harder. I miss the homeland, the trees and broad fields, the familiar way of living, the old friends."

"If you could expect nothing better, why did you come to America?"

"For the sake of my children whom I wished to be born in a free land."

"Your children haven't done so well, Mother." Katie smiled bitterly.

"There is here, what is not in the old country. In spite of hard unfamiliar things, there is here—hope. In the old country, a man can be no more than his father, providing he works hard. If his father was a carpenter, he may be a carpenter. He may not be a teacher or a priest. He may rise—but only to his father's state. In the old country, a man is given to the past. Here he belongs to the future. In this land, he may be what he will, if he has the good heart and the way of working honestly at the right things."

"That is not so. Your children have not done better than you."

Mary Rommely sighed. "That may be my fault. I knew not how to teach my daughters because I have nothing behind me excepting that for hundreds of years, my family has worked on the land of some overlord. I did not send my first child to the school. I was ignorant and did not know at first that the children of folk like us were allowed the free education of this land. Thus, Sissy had no chance to do better than me. But the other three . . . you went to school."

"I finished the sixth grade, if that is what is called education."

"And your Yohnny" (she could not pronounce "j"), "did too. Don't you see?" Excitement came into her voice. "Already, it is starting—the getting better." She picked up the baby and held it high in her arms. "This child was born of parents who can read and write," she said simply. "To me, this is a great wonder."

"Mother, I am young. Mother, I am just eighteen. I am strong. I will work hard, Mother. But I do not want this child to grow up just to work hard. What must I do, Mother, what must I do to make a different world for her? How do I start?"

"The secret lies in the reading and the writing. You are able to read. Every day you must read one page from some good book to your child. Every day this must be until the child learns to read. Then *she* must read every day, I know this is the secret."

"I will read," promised Katie. "What is a good book?"

"There are two great books. Shakespeare is a great book. I have heard tell that all the wonder of life is in that book; all that man has learned of beauty, all that he may know of wisdom and living are on those pages. It is said that these stories are plays to be acted out on the stage. I have never spoken to anyone who has seen this great thing. But I heard the lord of our land back in Austria say that some of the pages sing themselves like songs."

"Is Shakespeare a book in the German?"

"It is of the English. I so heard our lord of the land tell his young son who was setting out for the great university of Heidelberg long ago."

"And what is the other great book?"

"It is the Bible that the Protestant people read."

"We have our own Bible, the Catholic one."

Mary looked around the room furtively. "It is not fitting for a good Catholic to say so but I believe that the Protestant Bible contains more of the loveliness of the greatest story on this earth and beyond it. A much-loved Protestant friend once read some of her Bible to me and I found it as I have said.

"That is the book, then, and the book of Shakespeare. And every day you must read a page of each to your child—even though you yourself do not understand what is written down and cannot sound the words properly. You must do this that the child will grow up knowing of what is great—knowing that these tenements of Williamsburg are not the whole world."

"The Protestant Bible and Shakespeare."

"And you must tell the child the legends I told you—as my mother told them to me and her mother to her. You must tell the fairy tales of the old country. You must tell of those not of the earth who live forever in the hearts of people—fairies, elves, dwarfs and such. You must tell of the great ghosts that haunted your father's people and of the evil eye which a *hex* put on your aunt. You must teach the child of the signs that come to the women of our family when there is trouble and death to be. And the child must believe in the Lord God and Jesus, His Only Son." She crossed herself.

"Oh, and you must not forget the Kris Kringle. The child must believe in him until she reaches the age of six."

"Mother, I know there are no ghosts or fairies. I would be teaching the child foolish lies."

Mary spoke sharply. "You do not *know* whether there are not ghosts on earth or angels in heaven."

"I *know* there is no Santa Claus."

"Yet you must teach the child that these things are so."

"Why? When I, myself, do not believe?"

"Because," explained Mary Rommely simply, "the child must have a valuable thing which is called imagination. The child must have a secret world in which live things that never were. It is necessary that she *believe*. She must start out by believing in things not of this world. Then when the world becomes too ugly for living in, the child can reach back and live in her imagination. I, myself, even in this day and at my age, have great need of recalling the miraculous lives of the Saints and the great miracles that have come to pass on earth. Only by having these things in my mind can I live beyond what I *have* to live for."

"The child will grow up and find out things for herself. She will know that I lied. She will be disappointed."

"That is what is called learning the truth. It is a good thing to learn the truth one's self. To first believe with all your heart, and then not to believe, is good too. It fattens the emotions and makes them to stretch. When as a woman life and people disappoint her, she will have had practice in disappointment and it will not come so hard. In teaching your child, do not forget that suffering is good too. It makes a person rich in character."

"If that is so," commented Katie bitterly, "then we Rommelys are rich."

"We are poor, yes. We suffer. Our way is very hard. But we are better people because we know of the things I have told you. I could not read but I told you of all of the things I learned from living. You must tell them to your child and add on to them such things as you will learn as you grow older."

"What more must I teach the child?"

"The child must be made to believe in heaven. A heaven, not filled with flying angels with God on a throne"—Mary articulated her thoughts painfully, half in German and half in English—"but a heaven which means a wondrous place that people may dream of—as of a place where desires come true. This is probably a different kind of a religion. I do not know."

"And then, what else?"

"Before you die, you must own a bit of land—maybe with a house on it that your child or your children may inherit."

Katie laughed. "*Me own land*? A house? We're lucky if we can pay our rent."

"Even so." Mary spoke firmly. "Yet you must do that. For thousands of years, our people have been peasants working the land of others. This was in the old country. Here we do better working with our hands in the factory. There is a part of each day that does not belong to the master but which the worker owns himself. That is good. But to own a bit of land is better; a bit of land that we may hand down to our children . . . that will raise us up on the face of the earth."

"How can we ever get to own land? Johnny and I work and we earn so little. Sometimes after the rent is paid and the insurance there is hardly enough left for food. How could we save for land?"

"You must take an empty condensed milk can and wash it well."

"A can . . . ?"

"Cut off the top neatly. Cut strips down into the can the length of your finger. Let each strip be so wide." She measured two inches with her fingers. "Bend the strips backward. The can will look like a clumsy star. Make a slit in the top. Then nail the can, a nail in each strip, in the darkest corner of your closet. Each day put five cents in it. In three years there will be a small fortune, fifty dollars. Take the money and buy a lot in the country. Get the papers that say it is yours. Thus you become a landowner. Once one has owned land, there is no going back to being a serf."

"Five cents a day. It seems a little. But where is it to come from? We haven't enough now and with another mouth to feed. . . ."

"You must do it thus: You go to the green grocer's and ask how much are carrots the bunch. The man will say three cents. Then look about until you see another bunch, not so fresh, not so large. You will say: May I have this damaged bunch for two cents? Speak strongly and it shall be yours for two cents. That is a saved penny that you put in the star bank. It is winter, say. You bought a bushel of coal for twenty-five cents. It is cold. You would start a fire in the stove. But wait! Wait one hour more. Suffer the cold for an hour. Put a shawl around you. Say, I am cold because I am saving to buy land. That hour will save you three cents' worth of coal. That is three cents for the bank. When you are alone at night, do not light the lamp. Sit in the darkness and dream awhile. Reckon out how much oil you saved and put its value in pennies in the bank. The money will grow. Someday there will be fifty dollars and somewhere on this long island is a piece of land that you may buy for that money."

"Will it work, this saving?"

"I swear by the Holy Mother it will."

"Then why haven't you ever saved enough money to buy land?"

"I did. When we first landed, I had a star bank. It took me ten years to save that first fifty dollars. I took the money in my hand and went to a man in the neighborhood of whom it was said that he dealt fairly with people who bought land. He showed me a beautiful piece of earth and told me in my own language; 'This is thine.'

He took my money and gave me a paper. I could not read. Later, I saw men building the house of another on my land. I showed them my paper. They laughed at me with pity in their eyes. It was that the land had not been the man's to sell. It was . . . how do you say it in the English . . . a schwindle."

"Swindle."

"Ai. People like us, known as greenhorns from the old country, were often robbed by men such as he because we could not read. But you have education. First you will read on the paper that the land is yours. Only then will you pay."

"And you never saved again, Mother?"

"I did. All over again. The second time it was harder because there were the many children. I saved, but when we moved your father found the bank and took the money. He would not buy land with it. He was always one for birds so he bought a rooster and many hens with the money and put them in the back yard."

"I seem to remember those chickens," said Katie, "a long, long time ago."

"He said the eggs would bring much money in the neighborhood. Ah, what dreams men have! The first night twenty starving cats came over the fence and killed and ate many chickens. The second night, the Italians climbed the fence and stole more. The third day the policeman came and said it was against the law to keep chickens in a yard in Brooklyn. We had to pay him five dollars not to take your father to the station house. Your father sold the few chickens that were left and bought canary birds which he could own without fear. Thus I lost the second savings. But I am saving again. Maybe sometime . . ." She sat in silence for awhile. Then she got up and put on her shawl.

"It grows dark. Your father will be coming home from his work. Holy Mary watch over thee and the child."

Sissy came over right from work. She didn't even take time to brush the gray rubber powder from her hair bow. She went into choking hysterics over the baby, pronouncing it the most beautiful baby in the world. Johnny looked skeptical. The baby looked blue and wizened to him and he felt that there must be something wrong with it. Sissy washed the baby. (It must have been bathed a dozen times the first day.) She rushed out to the delicatessen store and beguiled the man into letting her open a charge account until Saturday payday. She bought two dollars' worth of delicacies: sliced tongue, smoked salmon, creamy-white slices of smoked sturgeon and crisp rolls. She bought a sack of charcoal and made the fire roar. She brought a tray of supper into Katie, then she and Johnny sat in the kitchen and ate together. The house smelled of warmth, good food, sweet powder and a stronger candy-like smell that came from a hard chalkish disc that Sissy wore in an imitation-silver filigree heart on a chain around her neck.

Johnny studied Sissy as he smoked an after-supper cigar. He wondered what criterion people used when they applied the tags "good" and "bad" to their fellowmen. Take Sissy. She was bad. But she was good. She was bad where the men were concerned. But she was good because wherever she was, there was life, good, tender, overwhelming, fun-loving and strong-scented life. He hoped that his newly-born daughter would be a little like Sissy.

When Sissy announced that she was going to stay the night, Katie looked worried and said there was but the one bed which she and Johnny shared. Sissy declared that she was willing to sleep with Johnny if he could guarantee her a fine baby like Francie. Katie frowned. She knew Sissy was joking of course. Yet there was something true and direct about Sissy. She started to give her a lecture. Johnny cut the whole thing short by saying he had to get over to the school.

He couldn't bring himself to tell Katie that he had lost their job. He hunted up his brother, Georgie, who was working that night. Fortunately, they needed another man to wait on table and sing in-between. Johnny got the job and was promised another for the following week. He drifted back into the singing waiter business and from that time on never worked at any other job.

Sissy got into bed with Katie and they talked most of the night away. Katie told of her worry about Johnny and her fears of the future. They talked about Mary Rommely; what a good mother she was to

Evy and Sissy and Katie. They spoke of their father, Thomas Rommely. Sissy said he was an old rip and Katie said Sissy ought to show more respect. Sissy said, "Oh, fudge!" and Katie laughed.

Katie told Sissy of the talk she had had with their mother that day. The idea of the bank so fascinated Sissy, that she got up—even though it was the middle of the night—emptied out a can of milk into a bowl and made the bank then and there. She tried to crawl into the narrow crowded closet to nail it down but her voluminous nightgown got her tangled up. She pulled it off and crawled naked into the closet. All of her couldn't fit into the closet. The large luminous naked back end of her stuck out as she crouched on her knees hammering the bank to the floor. Katie had such a fit of giggling that she was afraid she'd bring on a hemorrhage. The loud banging at three o'clock in the morning woke the other tenants. They pounded on the ceiling from below and on the floor from above. Sissy threw Katie into another spasm of giggles by mumbling from the closet that the tenants had a nerve raising such a racket when there was a sick woman in the house. "How can anybody sleep?" she asked, giving the last nail a terrific bang.

The bank in place, she put on her nightgown again, started off the land account by putting a nickel in the bank and got back into bed. She listened excitedly while Katie told her about the two books. She promised that she would get the two books; they would be her christening present to the baby.

Francie spent her first night on earth sleeping snugly between her mother and Sissy.

The next day, Sissy set about getting the two books. She went to a public library and asked the librarian how she could get a Shakespeare and a Bible for keeps. The librarian couldn't help her out on the Bible but said there was a worn-out copy of Shakespeare in the files, about to be discarded which Sissy could have. She bought it. It was a tattered old volume containing all the plays and sonnets. It had intricate footnotes and detailed explanations as to the playwright's meaning. There was a biography and picture of the author and steel-cut engravings illustrating scenes from each play. It was printed in small type, two columns to the page on thin paper. It cost Sissy twenty-five cents.

The Bible, while a little harder to come by, was cheaper in the long run. In fact, it cost Sissy nothing. It had a name, *Gideon*, on the front.

A few days after buying the volume of Shakespeare, Sissy woke up one morning and nudged her current lover, with whom she was spending the night in a quiet family hotel.

"John," (she called him John although his name was Charlie), "what's that book on the dresser?"

"A Bible."

"A Protestant Bible?"

"That's right."

"I'm going to hook it."

"Go ahead. That's why they put it there."

"No!"

"Yeah!"

"No kidding!"

"People swipe it, read it, reform and repent. They bring it back and buy another one, too, so that other people can swipe, read and reform. In that way, the firm that puts out the books loses nothing."

"Well, here's one they're not going to get back." She wrapped it up in a hotel towel that she was also swiping.

"Say!" A cold fear enveloped her John. "You might read it and reform and then I'd have to go back to my wife." He shuddered and put his arms around her. "Promise me that you won't reform."

"I won't."

"How do you know you won't?"

"I never listen to what people tell me and I can't read. The only way I know what is right and wrong is the way I feel about things. If I feel bad, it's wrong. If I feel good, it's right. And I feel good being here with you." She threw her arm across his chest and exploded a kiss in his ear.

"I sure wish we could get married, Sissy."

"So do I, John. I know we could hit it off. For awhile, any-how," she added honestly.

"But I'm married and that's the hell of the Catholic religion. No divorce."

"I don't believe in divorce anyhow," said Sissy who always remarried without the benefit of a divorce.

"You know what, Sissy?"

"What?"

"You got a heart of gold."

"No kidding?"

"No kidding." He watched her snap a red silk garter over the sheer lisle stocking she had pulled up over her shapely leg. "Give us a kiss," he begged suddenly.

"Have we time?" she asked in a practical way. But she pulled the stocking off again.

That's how the library of Francie Nolan was started.

10

Francie wasn't much of a baby. She was skinny and had a blue look and didn't thrive. Katie nursed her doggedly although the neighbor women told her that her milk was bad for the child.

Francie was put on the bottle soon enough because Katie's milk stopped suddenly when the child was three months old. Katie worried. She consulted her mother. Mary Rommely looked at her, sighed but said nothing. Katie went to the midwife for advice. The woman asked her a foolish question.

"Where do you buy your fish of a Friday?"

"Paddy's market. Why?"

"You wouldn't be after seeing an old woman in there buying a codfish head for her cat, would you now?"

"Yes. I see her every week."

"She did it! She dried up your milk on you."

"Oh, no!"

"She put the eye on you."

"But why?"

"Jealous she is because you're too happy with that pretty Irish lad of yours."

"Jealous? An old woman like that?"

"A witch she is. I knew her back in the old country. Sure and didn't she come over on the same boat as meself. When she was young she was in love with a wild County Kerry boy. And didn't he go and get her that way and he wouldn't go to the priest with her when her old father went after him. He slipped away on a boat for America in the dead of the night. Her baby died when it was born. Then she sold her soul to the devil and he did give her the power of drying up the milk of cows and nanny goats and of girls married to young boys."

"I remember she looked at me in a funny way."

"'Twas then she put the eye on you."

"How can I get my milk back?"

"I'll tell you what you must do. Wait until the moon is full. Then make a little image out of a lock of your curling hair, a cutting from your finger nail and a bit of rag sprinkled with holy water. Christen it Nelly Grogan, and that's the witch's name and stick three rusty pins in it. That will spoil her power over you and sure your milk will be flowing again like the River Shannon. That will be a quarter."

Katie paid her. When the moon was full, she made the little doll and stabbed it and stabbed it. She remained dry. Francie sickened on the bottle. In desperation, Katie called Sissy in for advice. Sissy listened to the witch story.

"A witch my foot," she said scornfully. "It was Johnny who did it and it wasn't with an eye."

In that way Katie knew that she was pregnant again. She told Johnny and he started to worry. He had been fairly happy back in the singing waiter business and he worked pretty often, was steady, didn't drink too much and brought home most of his money. The news that a second child was on the way made him feel trapped. He was only twenty and Katie was eighteen. He felt that they were both so young and so defeated already. He went out and got drunk after he heard the news.

The midwife came around later to see how the charm had worked. Katie told her that the charm had failed since she was pregnant and the witch was not to blame. The midwife lifted her skirt and dug down into a capacious pocket made in her petticoat. She brought up a bottle of evil-looking dark brown stuff.

"Sure and there is nothing to worry about," she said. "A good dose of this night and morning for three days and you'll come around again." Katie shook her head negatively. "You're not afraid of what the priest would be saying to you if you did it?"

"No. It's just that I couldn't kill anything."

"It wouldn't be killing. It don't count until you've felt life. You're not after feeling it move, are you?"

"No."

"There!" she slammed her fist on the table triumphantly. "I'll only be charging you a dollar for the bottle."

"Thank you, I don't want it."

"Don't be foolish. You're just a bit of a girl and have trouble enough with the one you do be having already. And your man is pretty but not the steadiest boy in the world."

"The way my man is, is my own business and my baby is no trouble."

"I'm only after trying to help you out."

"Thank you and goodbye."

The midwife returned the bottle to her petticoat pocket and got up to go. "When your time comes, you know where I live." At the door, she gave a last bit of optimistic advice. "If you keep running up and down the stairs, maybe you'll have a miscarriage."

That fall in the false warmth of a Brooklyn Indian summer, Katie sat on the stoop and held her sickly baby against the bigness which was another child soon to be born. Pitying neighbors stopped to commiserate over Francie.

"You'll never raise that one," they told her. "Her color ain't good. If the good Lord takes her, it will be for the best. What good is a sickly baby in a poor family? There is too many children on this earth already and no room for the weak ones."

"Don't say that," Katie held her baby tightly. "It's not better to die. Who wants to die? Everything struggles to live. Look at that tree growing up there out of that grating. It gets no sun, and water only when it rains. It's growing out of sour earth. And it's strong because its hard struggle to live is making it strong. My children will be strong that way."

"Aw, somebody ought to cut that tree down, the homely thing."

"If there was only one tree like that in the world, you would think it was beautiful," said Katie. "But because there are so many, you just can't see how beautiful it really is. Look at those children." She pointed to a swarm of dirty children playing in the gutter. "You could take any one of them and wash him good and dress him up and sit him in a fine house and you would think he was beautiful."

"You've got fine ideas but a very sick baby, Katie," they told her. "This baby will live," said Katie fiercely. "I'll *make* it live."

And Francie lived, choking and whimpering her way through that first year.

Francie's brother was born a week after her first birthday.

This time Katie was not working when the pains came. This time she bit her lip and did not scream out in her agony. Helpless in her pain, she was capable still of laying the foundation for bitterness and capability.

When the strong healthy boy, howling at the indignity of the birth process, was put to her breast, she felt a wild tenderness for him. The other baby, Francie, in the crib next her bed, began to whimper. Katie had a flash of comtempt for the weak child she had borne a year ago, when she compared her to this new handsome son. She was quickly ashamed of her contempt. She knew it wasn't the little girl's fault. "I must watch myself carefully," she thought. "I am going to love this boy more than the girl but I mustn't ever let her know. It is wrong to love one child more than the other but this is something that I cannot help."

Sissy begged her to call the boy after Johnny but Katie insisted that the boy had a right to a name all his own. Sissy got very angry and told Katie a thing or two. Finally Katie, more in anger than in truth, accused Sissy of being in love with Johnny. Sissy answered, "maybe," and Katie shut up. She was a little afraid that if they quarreled further, she would find out that it was so about Sissy loving Johnny.

Katie called the boy Cornelius after a noble character she had seen a handsome actor represent on the stage. As the boy grew up, the name was changed into Brooklynese and he was known as Neeley.

Without devious reasoning or complicated emotional processes, the boy became Katie's whole world. Johnny took second place and Francie went to the back of her mother's heart. Katie loved the boy because he was more completely hers than either Johnny or Francie. Neeley looked exactly like Johnny. Katie would make him into the kind of man Johnny should have been. He would have everything that was good about Johnny; she would encourage that. She would stamp out all of the things that were bad about Johnny as they came up in the boy, Neeley. He would grow up and she would be proud of him and he would take care of her all of her days. He was the one that she had to see through. Francie and Johnny would get by somehow, but she would take no chances with the boy. She'd see to it that he more than got by.

Gradually, as the children grew up, Katie lost all of her tenderness although she gained in what people call character. She became capable, hard and far-seeing. She loved Johnny dearly but all the old wild worship faded away. She loved her little girl because she felt sorry for her. It was pity and obligation towards her that she felt rather than love.

Johnny and Francie felt the growing change in Katie. As the boy grew stronger and handsomer, Johnny grew in weakness and went further and further down hill. Francie felt the way her mother thought about her. She grew an answering hardness against her mother and this hardness, paradoxically enough, brought them a little closer together because it made them more alike.

By the time Neeley was a year old, Katie had stopped depending on Johnny. Johnny was drinking heavily. He worked when he was offered one-night jobs. He brought home his wages but kept his tips for liquor. Life was going too swiftly for Johnny. He had a wife and two babies before he was old enough to vote. His life was finished before it had a chance to begin. He was doomed and no one knew it better than Johnny Nolan.

Katie had the same hardships as Johnny and she was nineteen, two years younger. It might be said that she, too, was doomed. Her life, too, was over before it began. But there the similarity ended.

Johnny knew he was doomed and accepted it. Katie *wouldn't* accept it. She started a new life where her old one left off.

She exchanged her tenderness for capability. She gave up her dreams and took over hard realities in their place.

Katie had a fierce desire for survival which made her a fighter. Johnny had a hankering after immortality which made him a useless dreamer. And that was the great difference between these two who loved each other so well.

11

Johnny celebrated his voting birthday by getting drunk for three days.
When he was coming out of it, Katie locked him in the bedroom
where he couldn't get anything more to drink. Instead of sobering
up, he started to get delirium tremens. He wept and begged by
turns for a drink. He said he was suffering. She told him it was a
good thing, that suffering would harden him, would teach him
such a lesson that he'd stop drinking. But poor Johnny just
wouldn't harden. He softened into a wailing, screaming banshee.

Neighbors banged on her door and told her to do something
for the poor man. Katie's mouth set in a hard cold line and she
called out to them to mind their own business. But even as she
defied the neighbors, she knew that they would have to move as
soon as the month was up. They couldn't live in the neighborhood
after the way Johnny was disgracing them.

In the late afternoon, his tortured cries unnerved Katie.
Crowding the two babies in the buggy she went over to the factory
and had Sissy's long-suffering foreman get her away from her
machine. She told Sissy about Johnny, and Sissy said she'd come
over and fix him up as soon as she could get away.

Sissy consulted a gentleman friend about Johnny. The friend
gave her instructions. Accordingly, she bought a half pint of good

whiskey, concealed it between her full breasts and laced her corset cover and buttoned her dress over it.

She went over to Katie's and told her that if she could be left alone with Johnny she'd get him out of it. Katie locked Sissy in the bedroom with Johnny. She went back into the kitchen and spent the night with her head on her arms on the table, waiting.

When Johnny saw Sissy, his poor mixed-up brain unscrambled for a minute and he grabbed her arm. "You're my friend, Sissy. You're my sister. For God's sake give me a drink."

"Take it slow, Johnny," she said in her soft comforting voice. "I've got a drink right here for you."

She unbuttoned her waist releasing a cascade of foaming white embroidered ruffles and dark pink ribbon. The room filled up with the sweet scent of the warm strong sachet she used. Johnny stared as she undid an intricate bow and loosened her corset cover. The poor fellow remembered her reputation and misunderstood.

"No, no, Sissy. Please!" he moaned.

"Don't be a dockle, Johnny. There's a time and a place for everything and this isn't the time." She pulled out the bottle.

He grabbed it. It was warm from her. She let him take a long drink, then she dug the bottle out of his clutching fingers. He quieted down after the drink; got sleepy and begged her not to go away. She promised. Without bothering to tie up her ribbons or button her waist, she lay on the bed beside him. She put her arm under his shoulders and he rested his cheek on her bare warm-scented breast. He slept and tears came from under his closed lids and they were warmer than the flesh they fell on.

She lay awake, holding him in her arms and staring into the darkness. She felt towards him as she would have felt towards her babies had they only lived to know her warm love. She stroked his curling hair and smoothed his cheek gently. When he moaned in his sleep, she soothed him with the kind of words she would have spoken to her babies. Her arm cramped and she tried to move it. He woke up for a moment, clutched her tightly and begged her not to leave him. When he spoke to her, he called her mother.

〜

Whenever he woke up and got afraid, she gave him a swallow of whiskey. Towards morning he woke. His head was clearer but he said it hurt. He jerked away from her and moaned.

"Come back to mama," she said in her soft fluttering voice.

She opened her arms wide and once more he crept into them and rested his cheek on her generous breast. He wept quietly. He sobbed out his fears and his worries and his bewilderment at the way things were in the world. She let him talk, she let him weep. She held him the way his mother should have held him as a child (which she never did). Sometimes Sissy wept with him. When he had talked himself out, she gave him what was left of the whiskey and at last he fell into a deep exhausted sleep.

She lay very still for a long time not wanting him to feel her withdrawing from him. Towards dawn, his tight holding of her hand relaxed; peace came into his face and made it boyish again. Sissy put his head on the pillow, expertly undressed him and put him under the covers. She threw the empty whiskey bottle down the airshaft. She figured that what Katie didn't know couldn't possibly bother her. She tied her pink ribbons carelessly and adjusted her waist. She closed the door very softly when she went out.

Sissy had two great failings. She was a great lover and a great mother. She had so much of tenderness in her, so much of wanting to give of herself to whoever needed what she had, whether it was her money, her time, the clothes off her back, her pity, her understanding, her friendship or her companionship and love. She was mother to everything that came her way. She loved men, yes. She loved women too, and old people and especially children. How she loved children! She loved the down-and-outers. She wanted to make everybody happy. She had tried to seduce the good priest who heard her infrequent confessions because she felt sorry for him. She thought he was missing the greatest joy on earth by being committed to a life of celibacy.

She loved all the scratching curs on the street and wept for the gaunt scavenging cats who slunk around Brooklyn corners with their sides swollen looking for a hole in which they might bring forth their young. She loved the sooty sparrows and thought that the very grass that grew in the lots was beautiful. She picked bouquets of white clover in the lots believing they were the most beautiful flowers God ever made. Once she saw a mouse in her room. The next night she set out a tiny box for him with cheese crumbs in it. Yes, she listened to everybody's troubles but no one listened to hers. But that was right because Sissy was a giver and never a taker.

When Sissy came into the kitchen, Katie looked at Sissy's disordered clothing with swollen and suspicious eyes.

"I'm not forgetting," she said with pitiful dignity, "that you are my sister. And I hope you remembered that, too."

"Don't be such a *heimdickischer* ass," said Sissy, knowing what Katie meant. But she smiled deeply into Katie's eyes. Katie was suddenly reassured.

"How's Johnny?"

"Johnny will be fine when he wakes up. But for Christ's sweet sake, don't nag him when he wakes up. Don't nag him, Katie."

"But he's got to be told. . . ."

"If I hear that you nag him, I'll get him away from you. I swear it. Even though I am your sister."

Katie knew that she meant it and was a little frightened. "I won't then," she mumbled. "Not this time."

"Now you're growing up into a woman," approved Sissy as she kissed Katie's cheek. She felt sorry for Katie as well as for Johnny.

Katie broke down then and cried. She made hard ugly noises because she hated herself for crying, yet couldn't help it. Sissy had to listen, to go through again all she had gone through with Johnny, only this time from Katie's angle. Sissy handled Katie differently than she had handled Johnny. She had been gentle and maternal with Johnny because he needed that. Sissy acknowledged the steeliness that was in Katie. She hardened to that steeliness as Katie finished her story.

"And now you know it all, Sissy. Johnny's a drunk."

"Well everybody's *something*. We all got a tag of some kind. Take me now: I never took a drink in my life. But do you know," she stated with honest and consummate ignorance, "that there are some people who talk about me and call *me* a bad woman? Can you imagine that? I admit that I smoke a Sweet Caporal once in awhile. But bad. . . ."

"Well, Sissy, the way you carry on with men makes people . . ."

"Katie! *Don't* nag! All of us are what we have to be and everyone lives the kind of life it's in him to live. You've got a good man, Katie."

"But he drinks."

"And he always will until he dies. There it is. He drinks. You must take that along with the rest."

"What rest? You mean the not working, the staying out all night, the bums he has for friends?"

"You married him. There was something about him that caught your heart. Hang on to that and forget the rest."

"Sometimes, I don't know why I married him."

"You lie! You know why you married him. You married him because you wanted him to sleep with you but you were too religious to take a chance without a church wedding."

"How you talk. The whole thing was that I wanted to get him away from someone else."

"It was the sleeping. It always is. If it is good, the marriage is good. If it is bad, the marriage is bad."

"No. There are other things."

"What other things? Well, maybe there are," conceded Sissy. "If there are other good things too, that's so much velvet."

"You're wrong. That might be important to you, but . . ."

"It's important to everybody or should be. Then all marriages would be happy."

"Oh, I admit that I liked the way he danced, how he sang a song . . . the way he looked . . ."

"You're saying what I'm saying but you're using your own words."

How can you win out with a person like Sissy, thought Katie. She's got everything figured out her way. Maybe her way is a good way to figure things out. I don't know. She is my own sister but people talk about her. She is a bad girl and there is no getting around that. When she dies, her soul will wander through Purgatory through all eternity. I have often told her that and she always answers that it wouldn't wander alone. If Sissy dies before I do, I must have masses said for the repose of her soul. Maybe after awhile she'll get out of Purgatory because even if they say she is bad, she is good to all the people in the world who are lucky enough to run across her. God will have to take that into consideration.

Suddenly Katie leaned over and kissed Sissy on the cheek. Sissy was astonished because she could not know Katie's thoughts.

"Maybe you're right, Sissy, maybe you're wrong. With me it comes down to this: Aside from his drinking, I love everything else about Johnny and I will try to be good to him. I will try to overlook . . ." She said no more. In her heart, Katie knew that she was not the overlooking kind.

Francie lay awake in the wash basket set up near the kitchen range. She lay sucking her thumb and listening to the conversation. But she learned nothing from it being but two years old at the time.

12

Katie was ashamed to stay in the neighborhood after Johnny's great
spree. A good many of the neighbors' husbands were no better
than Johnny, of course, but that was no standard for Katie. She
wanted the Nolans to be *better* and not as good as anybody. Too
there was the question of money. Although it was no question
because they had very little and now there were two children. Katie
looked around for a place where she could work for their rent. At
least, they'd have a roof over their heads.

She found a house where she would get rent free in return for
keeping it clean. Johnny swore that he wouldn't have his wife a janitress. Katie told him in her new crisp hard way that it was janitor or
no home, as it was harder and harder each month to get the rent
money together. Johnny finally gave in after promising that he
would do all the janitor work until he got a steady job when they
would move again.

Katie packed their few belongings; a double bed, the babies'
crib, a busted-down baby buggy, a green plush parlor suit, a carpet
with pink roses, a pair of parlor lace curtains, a rubber plant and a
rose geranium, a yellow canary in a gilt cage, a plush picture album,
a kitchen table and some chairs, a box of dishes and pots and pans,
a gilt crucifix with a music box in its base that played "Ave Maria"
when you wound it up, a plain wooden crucifix that her mother

had given her, a wash basket full of clothes, a roll of bedding, a pile of Johnny's sheet music and two books, the Bible and the *Complete Works of Wm. Shakespeare.*

There was such a little bit of stuff that the ice man could load it all on his wagon and his one shaggy horse could pull it. The four Nolans rode along on the ice wagon to their new home.

The last thing Katie did in their old home after it had been stripped bare and had that look of a near-sighted man with his glasses off, was to rip up the tin-can bank. It had three dollars and eighty cents in it. Out of that she knew regretfully, she would have to give the ice man a dollar for moving them.

The first thing she did in the new home, while Johnny was helping the ice man carry in the furniture, was to nail down the bank in a closet. She put two dollars and eighty cents back in it. She added a dime from the few pennies in her worn purse. That was the dime she wasn't going to give to the ice man.

In Williamsburg, it was the custom to treat the movers to a pint of beer when they had completed their job. But Katie reasoned: "We'll never see *him* again. Besides, the dollar is enough. Think of all the ice he'd have to sell to make a dollar."

While Katie was putting up the lace curtains, Mary Rommely came over and sprinkled the rooms with holy water to drive out any devils that might be lurking in the corners. Who knows? Protestants might have been living there before. A Catholic might have died in the rooms without the last absolution of the church. The holy water would purify the home again so that God might come in if He chose.

The baby Francie crowed with delight as her grandmother held up the cruet and the sun shone through it and made a small fat rainbow on the opposite wall. Mary smiled with the child and made the rainbow dance.

"*Schoen! Schoen!*" she said.

"Shame! Shame!" repeated Francie and held out her two hands.

Mary let her hold the half-filled cruet while she went to help Katie. Francie was disappointed because the rainbow went away.

She thought it must be hidden in the bottle. She poured the holy water out into her lap expecting a rainbow to come slithering from the bottle. Later Katie noticed that she was wet and paddled her softly telling her that she was too big to wet her pants. Mary explained about the holy water.

"Ai, the child has but blessed herself and a spanking comes from the blessing."

Katie laughed then. Francie laughed because her mama wasn't mad anymore. Neeley exposed his three teeth in a baby laugh. Mary smiled at them all and said it was good luck to start life in a new home with laughter.

They were settled by supper time. Johnny stayed with the children while Katie went to the grocery store to establish credit. She told the grocer she had just moved into the neighborhood and would he trust her with a few groceries until Saturday payday? The grocer obliged. He gave her a bag of groceries and a little book in which he jotted down her indebtedness. He told her she was to bring the book along each time she came to "trust." With that little ceremony, Katie's family was assured of food until the next money came in.

After supper, Katie read the babies to sleep. She read a page of the introduction to Shakespeare and a page of begats from the Bible. That was as far as she had gotten to date. Neither the babies nor Katie understood what it was all about. The reading made Katie very drowsy but doggedly she finished the two pages. She covered the babies carefully, then she and Johnny went to bed too. It was only eight o'clock but they were tired out from moving.

The Nolans slept in their new home on Lorimer Street which was still in Williamsburg but almost near where Greenpoint began.

13

Lorimer Street was more refined than Bogart Street. It was peopled by letter carriers, firemen and those store owners who were affluent enough not to have to live in the rooms in back of the store.

The flat had a bathroom. The tub was an oblong wooden box lined with zinc. Francie couldn't get over the wonder of it when it was filled with water. It was the largest body of water she had seen up to that time. To her baby eyes, it seemed like an ocean.

They liked the new home. Katie and Johnny kept the cellar, halls, the roof, and the sidewalk before the house spotlessly clean in return for their rent. There was no airshaft. There was a window in each bedroom and three each in the kitchen and front room. The first autumn there was pleasant. The sun came in all day long. They were warm that first winter, too. Johnny worked fairly steadily, did not drink much and there was money for coal.

When summer came, the children spent most of the day outdoors on the stoop. They were the only children in the house, so there was always room on the stoop. Francie, who was going on four, had to mind Neeley, who was going on three. She sat for long hours on the stoop with her thin arms hugging her thin legs and with her straight brown hair blowing in the slow breeze that came laden with the salt smell of the sea, the sea which was so near-by and which she had never seen. She kept an eye on Neeley as he scrambled up and down the steps. She sat, rocking to and fro, wondering about many things: what made the wind blow and what was grass and why Neeley was a boy instead of a girl like her.

Sometimes Francie and Neeley sat regarding each other with steady eyes. His eyes were the same as hers in shape and depth but his were a bright clear blue and hers a dark clear gray. There was steady unbroken communication between the two children. Neeley spoke very little and Francie spoke a lot. Sometimes Francie talked and talked until the genial little boy fell asleep sitting upright on the steps with his head against the iron rail.

Francie did "stitching" that summer. Katie bought her a square of goods for a penny. It was the size of a lady's handkerchief and had a design outlined on it: a sitting Newfoundland dog with his tongue lolling out. Another penny bought a small reel of red embroidery cotton and two cents went for a pair of small hoops. Francie's grandmother taught her how to work the running stitches. The child became adept at stitching. Women passing would stop and cluck in pitying admiration at the tiny girl, a deep line already showing at the inner edge of her right eyebrow, pushing the needle in and out of the taut material while Neeley hung over her to watch the bright sliver of steel disappear like magic and then come back up again through the cloth. Sissy gave her a fat little cloth strawberry for cleaning the needle. When Neeley got restless, Francie let him push the needle through the strawberry for awhile. You were supposed to stitch a hundred or so of these squares and then sew them together to make a bedspread. Francie heard that some ladies had actually made a bedspread that way and that was Francie's great ambition. But though she worked intermittently on the square all summer, autumn found it only half done. The bedspread had to be saved for the future.

The fall came again, winter, spring and summer. Francie and Neeley kept getting bigger, Katie kept working harder and Johnny worked a little less and drank a little more with each season. The reading went on. Sometimes Katie skipped a page when she was tired at night, but most of the time she stuck with it. They were in "Julius

Caesar" now and the stage direction "Alarum" confused Katie. She thought it had something to do with fire engines and whenever she came to that word, she shouted out "clang-clang." The children thought it was wonderful.

Pennies accumulated in the tin-can bank. Once it had to be ripped open and two dollars taken out to pay the druggist the time Francie ran a rusty nail into her knee. A dozen times one prong was unfastened and a nickel fished out with a knife to provide Johnny with car-fare to get to a job. But the rule was that he had to put ten cents back out of his tip money. So the bank profited.

On the warm days, Francie played alone on the streets or on the stoop. She yearned for playmates but did not know how to make friends with the other little girls. The other youngsters avoided her because she talked funny. Owing to Katie's nightly reading, Francie had a queer way of saying things. Once, when taunted by a youngster, she had retorted, "Aw, you don't know what you're saying. You're jus' full of soun' 'n' furry siggaflying nothing."

Once, trying to make friends with a little girl she said,

"Wait here and I'll go in and begat my rope and we'll play jumping."

"You mean you'll *git* your rope," the little girl corrected.

"No. I'll begat my rope. You don't git things. You begat things."

"What's that—begat?" asked the little girl who was just five years old.

"Begat. Like Eve begat Cain."

"You're buggy. Ladies don't git canes. Only men git canes when they can't walk good."

"Eve begat. She begat Abel too."

"She gits or she don't git. You know what?"

"What."

"You talk just like a Wop."

"I do not talk like no Wop," cried Francie. "I talk like . . . like . . . God talks."

"You'll be struck down dead saying a thing like that."

"I won't neither."

"Nobody home upstairs in your house." The little girl tapped her forehead.

"There is so."

"Why do you talk like that then?"

"My mother reads those things to me."

"Nobody home upstairs in your *mother's* house," corrected the little girl.

"Well anyhow, my mother ain't a dirty slob like your mother." That was the only reply Francie could think of.

The little girl had heard this many times. She was shrewd enough not to debate it. "Well, I'd sooner have a dirty slob for a mother than a crazy woman. And I'd rather have no father than a drunken man for my father."

"Slob! Slob! Slob!" shouted Francie passionately.

"Crazy, crazy, crazy," chanted the little girl.

"Slob! Dirty slob," screamed Francie sobbing in her impotence.

The little girl skipped away, her fat curls bouncing in the sun and sang in a clear high voice: "Sticks and stones will break my bones but names will never hurt me. When I die, you will cry for all the names you called me."

And Francie did cry. Not for all the names called but because she was lonesome and nobody wanted to play with her. The rougher children found Francie too quiet and the better behaved ones seemed to shun her. Dimly, Francie felt that it wasn't all her fault. It had something to do with Aunt Sissy who came to the house so often, the way Sissy looked and the way the men in the neighborhood looked after Sissy when she passed. It had something to do with the way papa couldn't walk straight sometimes and walked sideways down the street when he came home. It had something to do with the way neighbor women asked her questions about papa and mama and Sissy. Their wheedling offhand questions did not deceive Francie. Had not mama warned her: "Don't let the neighbors pick on you."

So in the warm summer days the lonesome child sat on her stoop and pretended disdain for the group of children playing on the sidewalk. Francie played with imaginary companions and made believe that they were better than real children. But all the while her heart beat in rhythm to the poignant sadness of the song the children sang while walking around in a ring with hands joined.

> *Walter, Walter Wildflower.*
> *Growing up so high.*
> *As we are all young ladies*
> *And very sure to die.*
> *Excepting Lizzie Wehner*
> *Who is the finest flower.*
> *Hide, hide, hide for shame.*
> *Turn your back and*
> *Tell your beau's name.*

They paused while the chosen girl, after much coaxing, finally whispered a boy's name. Francie wondered what name she'd give if they ever asked her to play. Would they laugh if she whispered Johnny Nolan?

The little girls whooped when Lizzie whispered a name. Again they joined hands and walked around in a circle genially advertising the boy.

> *Hermy Bachmeier*
> *Is a fine young man.*
> *He comes to the door*
> *With his hat in his hand.*
> *Down comes she*
> *All dressed in silk.*
> *Tomorrow, tomorrow,*
> *The wedding shall begin.*

The girls stopped and clapped their hands joyously. Then without motivation, there was a change in mood. The girls went around the ring slower and with lowered heads.

> *Mother, Mother, I am sick.*
> *Send for the doctor,*

Quick, quick, quick!
Doctor, Doctor, shall I die?
Yes, my darling,
By and by.
How many coaches shall I have?
Enough for you and
Your family, too.

In other neighborhoods there were different words to the song but essentially it was the same game. No one knew where the words had come from. Little girls learned them from other little girls and it was the most frequently played game in Brooklyn.

There were other games. There were jacks that two little girls could play together sitting on the steps of a stoop. Francie played jacks by herself, first being Francie and then her opponent. She'd talk to the imaginary player. "I'm for threesies and you're for twosies," she'd say.

Potsy was a game that the boys started and the girls finished. A couple of boys would put a tin can on the car track and sit along the curb and watch with a professional eye as the trolley wheels flattened the can. They'd fold it and put it on the track again. Again it was flattened, folded and flattened again. Soon there was a flat heavy square of metal. Numbered squares were marked off on the sidewalk and the game was turned over to the girls who hopped on one foot pushing the potsy from square to square. Who ever got through the squares with the least number of hops won the game.

Francie made a potsy. She put a can on the tracks. She watched with a professional frown as the car ran over it. She shuddered in delighted horror when she heard the scrunch. Would the motorman be mad, she wondered, if he knew that she was making his trolley car work for her? She made the squares but could only write one and seven. She hopped through a game ardently wishing someone were playing with her as she was sure she won with less hops than any other little girl in the world.

Sometimes there was music in the streets. This was something that Francie could enjoy without companions. A three-piece band came around once a week. They wore ordinary suits but funny hats, like a motorman's hat only the top was squashed in. When Francie heard the children shouting, "Here comes the Bettelbubbers," she'd run out on the street, sometimes dragging Neeley with her.

The band consisted of a fiddle, drum and cornet. The men played old Viennese airs and if they didn't play well, they at least played loud. Little girls waltzed with each other, round and round on the warm summer sidewalks. There were always two boys who did a grotesque dance together, mimicking the girls and bumping into them rudely. When the girls got angry, the boys would bow with great exaggeration (being sure their buttocks would bump another dancing couple), and apologize in flowery language.

Francie wished she could be one of the brave ones who took no part in the dancing but stood close to the horn-blower sucking noisily on big dripping pickles. This made saliva flow into the horn which made the cornet player very angry. If provoked enough, he'd let out a string of oaths in German ending up with something that sounded like *Gott verdammte Ehrlandiger Jude*. Most Brooklyn Germans had a habit of calling everyone who annoyed them a Jew.

Francie was fascinated by the money angle. After two songs, the fiddle and horn carried on alone while the drummer went around hat in hand ungraciously accepting the pennies doled out to him. After canvassing the street, he'd stand on the curb's edge and look up at the house windows. Women wrapped two pennies in a bit of newspaper and tossed them down. The newspaper was essential. Any pennies thrown loose were considered fair game by the boys and they scrambled for them, picked them up and ran off down the street with an angry musician after them. For some reason, they wouldn't try to get the wrapped pennies. They'd pick them up sometimes and hand them to the musicians. It was some sort of code that made them agree as to whose pennies were whose.

If the musicians got enough, they'd play another song. If the take was meager, they'd move on hoping for greener fields. Francie, usually dragging Neeley along, often followed the musicians from stop to stop, street to street, until it got dark and time for the musicians to disband. Francie was but one of a crowd as many children followed the band Pied Piper fashion. Many of the little girls towed baby brothers and sisters along, some in homemade wagons, others in busted-down baby buggies. The music cast such a spell over them that they forgot about home and eating. And the little babies cried, wet their pants, slept, woke to cry again, wet their pants again and went to sleep again. And "The Beautiful Blue Danube" played on and on.

Francie thought the musicia s had a fine life. She made plans. When Neeley got bigger, he would play the hot-hot (his name for an accordion) and she would bang a tambourine on the street and people would throw them pennies and they'd get rich and mama wouldn't have to work anymore.

Although she followed the band, Francie liked the organ grinder better. Every once in a while a man came around lugging a small organ with a monkey perched atop it. The monkey wore a red jacket with gold braid and a red pill box hat strapped under his chin. His red pants had a convenient hole in them so that his tail could stick out. Francie loved that monkey. She'd give him her precious penny-for-candy just for the happiness of seeing him tip his hat to her. If mama was around, she'd come out with a penny that should have gone into the tin-can bank and give it to the man with sharp instructions not to mistreat his monkey; and if he did and she found out, she would report him. The Italian never understood a word she said and always made the same answer. He pulled off his hat, bowed humbly with a little crook of the leg and called out eagerly, "*Si, Si.*"

The big organ was different. When that came around it was like a *fiesta*. The organ was pulled by a dark curly-haired man with very white teeth. He wore green velveteen pants and a brown corduroy jacket from which hung a red bandana handkerchief. He wore one hoop earring. The woman who helped him pull the organ wore a swirling red skirt and a yellow blouse and large hoop earrings.

The music tinkled out shrilly, a song from *Carmen* or *Il Trovatore*. The woman shook a dirty, be-ribboned tambourine and listlessly punched it with her elbow in time to the music. At the end of a song, she'd twirl suddenly showing her stout legs in dirty white cotton stockings and a flash of multi-colored petticoats.

Francie never noticed the dirt and the lassitude. She heard the music and saw the flashing colors and felt the glamor of a picturesque people. Katie warned her never to follow the big organ. Katie said that those organ grinders who dressed up so were Sicilians. And all the world knew that the Sicilians belonged to the Black Hand and that the Black Hand Society always kidnapped little children and held them for ransom. They took the child and left a note saying to leave a hundred dollars in the cemetery and signed it with the black imprint of a hand. That's what mama said about those organ grinders.

For days after the organ grinder had been around, Francie played organ grinder. She hummed what she recalled of Verdi and bumped her elbow on an old pie tin pretending it was a tambourine. She ended the game by drawing an outline of her hand on paper and filling it in with black crayon.

Sometimes Francie wavered. She didn't know whether it would be better to be a band when she grew up or an organ grinder lady. It would be nice if she and Neeley could get a little organ and a cute monkey. All day they could have fun with him for nothing and go around playing and watching him tip his hat. And people would give them a lot of pennies and the monkey could eat with them and maybe sleep in her bed at night. This profession seemed so desirable that Francie announced her intentions to mama but Katie threw cold water on the project telling her not to be silly; that monkeys had fleas and she wouldn't allow a monkey in one of her clean beds.

Francie toyed with the idea of being a tambourine lady. But then she'd have to be a Sicilian and kidnap little children and she didn't want to do that, although drawing a black hand was fun.

There was always the music. There were songs and dancing on the Brooklyn streets in those long ago summers and the days should have been joyous. But there was something sad about those summers, something sad about the children, thin in body but with the baby curves still lingering in their faces, singing in sad monotony as they went through the figures of a ring game. It was sad the way they were still babies of four and five years of age but so precocious about taking care of themselves. "The Blue Danube" that the band played was sad as well as bad. The monkey had sad eyes under his bright red cap. The organ grinder's tune was sad under its lilting shrillness.

Even the minstrels who came in the back yards and sang,

> *If I had my way,*
> *You would never grow old.*

were sad, too. They were bums and they were hungry and they didn't have talent for song-making. All they had in the world was the nerve to stand in a back yard with cap in hand and sing loudly. The sad thing was in the knowing that all their nerve would get them nowhere in the world and that they were lost as all people in Brooklyn seem lost when the day is nearly over and even though the sun is still bright, it is thin and doesn't give you warmth when it shines on you.

14

Life was pleasant in Lorimer Street and the Nolans would have kept on living there if it hadn't been for Aunt Sissy and her big but mistaken heart. It was Sissy's business with the tricycle and the balloons that ruined and disgraced the Nolans.

One day Sissy was laid off from work and decided to go over and look after Francie and Neeley while Katie was working. A block before she got to their house, her eyes were dazzled by the sun glinting off the brass handlebar of a handsome tricycle. It was a kind of vehicle that you don't see nowadays. It had a wide leather seat, big enough for two little children, with a back to it and an iron steering bar leading to the small front wheel. There were two larger wheels in the back. There was a handlebar of solid brass on top the steering rod. The pedals were in front of the seat and a child sat in it at ease, pedaled it while leaning back in the seat and steered it with the handlebars which lay across the lap.

Sissy saw that tricycle standing there unattended in front of a stoop. She didn't hesitate. She took the tricycle, pulled it around to the Nolan house, got the children out and gave them a ride.

Francie thought it was wonderful! She and Neeley sat in the seat and Sissy pulled them around the block. The leather seat was warm from the sun and had a rich and expensive smell. The hot sun danced on the brass handlebar and it looked like living fire. Francie thought that if she touched it, it would burn her hand surely. Then something happened.

A small crowd bore down on them headed by a hysterical woman and a bawling boy. The woman rushed at Sissy yelling "Robber!" She grabbed the handlebars and pulled. Sissy held on tightly. Francie almost got thrown out. The cop on the beat came rushing up.

"What's this? What's this?" Thus he took over.

"This lady is a robber," reported the woman. "She stole my little boy's tricycle."

"I didn't steal it, Sergeant," said Sissy in her soft appealing voice. "It was just standing there and standing there so I borrowed it to give the kids a ride. They never rode in such a fine tricycle. You know what a ride means to a kid. It's just *heaven*." The cop stared at the mute children in the seat. Francie grinned at him in trembling panic. "I was only going to ride them once around the block and then take it back. *Honest*, Sarge."

The cop let his eyes rest on Sissy's well-shaped bust which was not spoiled any by the tight waists that she liked to wear. He turned to the harassed mother.

"Why do you want to be so stingy for, Lady?" he said. "Let her give the kids a ride around the block. It ain't no skin off your teeth." (Only he didn't say "teeth" to the snickering delight of the youngsters clustered around.) "Let her give them a spin and I'll see that you get the bike back safe."

He was the law. What could the woman do? The cop gave the bawling kid a nickel and told him to shut up. He dispersed the crowd very simply by telling them he'd send for the pie wagon and take them all down to the station house if they didn't twenty-three skidoo.

The crowd scattered. The cop, swinging his club, gallantly escorted Sissy and her charges around the block. Sissy looked up at him and smiled into his eyes. Whereupon he stuck his club in his belt and insisted on pulling the bike for her. Sissy trotted along beside him on her tiny high-heeled shoes and cast a spell over him with her soft fluttering voice. They walked around the block three times, the cop pretending not to notice the hands that went up to hide smiles as the people saw a fully-uniformed officer of the law so engaged. He talked warmly to Sissy, mostly about his wife who was a good woman, you understand, but you know, a kind of invalid.

Sissy said she understood.

After the bike episode, people talked. They talked enough about Johnny coming home drunk once in awhile and about how the men looked at Sissy. Now they had this to add on. Katie thought of moving. It was getting like Bogart Street where the neighbors knew too much about the Nolans. While Katie was thinking about looking for another place, something else happened and they had to move right away. The thing that finally drove them from Lorimer Street was stark raw sex. Only it was very innocent looked at in the right way.

One Saturday afternoon, Katie had an odd job at Gorling's, a large department store in Williamsburg. She fixed coffee and sandwiches for the Saturday night supper that the boss gave the girls in lieu of overtime money. Johnny was at Union Headquarters waiting for a job to find him. Sissy wasn't working that day. Knowing that the children would be left alone locked in the rooms, she decided to keep them company.

She knocked at the door calling out that she was Aunt Sissy. Francie opened the door on the chain to make sure before she let her in. The children swarmed over Sissy smothering her with hugs. They loved her. To them, she was a beautiful lady who always smelled sweet, wore beautiful clothes and brought them amazing presents.

Today she brought a sweet-smelling cedar cigar box, several sheets of tissue paper, some red and some white, and a jar of paste. They sat around the kitchen table and went to work decorating the box. Sissy outlined circles on the paper with a quarter and Francie cut them out. Sissy showed her how to make them into little paper cups by molding the circles around the end of a pencil. When they had a lot of cups made, Sissy drew a heart on the box cover. The bottom of each red cup was given a dab of paste and the cup was pasted on the penciled heart. The heart was filled in with red cups. The rest of the lid was filled in with white. When the top was finished it looked like a bed of closely-packed white carnations with a heart of red ones. The sides were filled in with white cups and the inside lined with red tissue. You never could tell it had been a cigar box, it was that beautiful. The box took up most of the afternoon.

Sissy had a chop suey date at five and she got ready to leave. Francie clung to her and begged her not to go. Sissy hated to leave, yet she didn't want to miss her date. She searched in her purse for something to amuse them in her absence. They stood at her knee helping her look. Francie spied a cigarette box and pulled it out. On the cover was a picture of a man lying on a couch, knees crossed, one foot dangling in the air and smoking a cigarette which made a big smoke ring over his head. In the ring was a picture of a girl with her hair in her eyes and her bust popping out of her dress. The name on the box was *American Dreams*. It was out of the stock at Sissy's factory.

The children clamored for the box. Sissy reluctantly let them have it after explaining that the box contained cigarettes and was only to hold and to look at and not under any circumstances to be opened. They must not touch the seals, she said.

After she left, the children amused themselves for a time by staring at the picture. They shook the box. A dull swishing mysterious sound resulted.

"They is snakes in there and not zingarettes," decided Neeley.

"No," corrected Francie. "Worms are in there. Live ones."

They argued, Francie saying the box was too small for snakes and Neeley insisting that they rolled-up snakes like herring in a glass jar. Curiosity grew to such a pitch that Sissy's instructions were forgotten. The seals were so lightly pasted, it was a simple matter to pull them off. Francie opened the box. There was a sheet of soft dulled tin foil over the contents. Francie lifted the foil carefully. Neeley prepared to crawl under the table if the snakes became active. But there were neither snakes, worms nor cigarettes in the box and its contents were very uninteresting. After trying to devise

some simple games, Francie and Neeley lost interest, clumsily tied
the contents of the box to a string, trailed the string out of the window and finally secured the string by shutting the window on it.
They then took turns jumping on the denuded box and became so
absorbed in breaking it into bits that they forgot all about the string
hanging out of the window.

Consequently, there was a great surprise waiting for Johnny when
he sauntered home to get a fresh dicky and collar for his evening's job.
He took one look and his face burned with shame. He told Katie
when she came home.

Katie questioned Francie closely and found out everything.
Sissy was condemned. That night after the children had been put to
bed and Johnny was away working, Katie sat in her dark kitchen
with blushes coming and going. Johnny went about his work with a
dull feeling that the world had come to an end.

Evy came over later in the evening and she and Katie discussed
Sissy.

"That's the end, Katie," said Evy, "the very end. What Sissy does
is her own business until her own business makes a thing like this happen. I've got a growing girl, so have you, we mustn't let Sissy come
into our homes again. She's bad and there's no getting around it."

"She's good in many ways," temporized Katie.

"You say that after what she did to you today?"

"Well . . . I guess you're right. Only don't tell Mother. She
doesn't know how Sissy lives and Sissy is her eye-apple."

When Johnny came home, Katie told him that Sissy was never
to come to their house again. Johnny sighed and said he guessed
that was the only thing to do. Johnny and Katie talked away the
night, and in the morning they had their plans all made for moving
when the end of the month came.

Katie found a janitor place on Grand Street in Williamsburg. She
took up the tin-can bank when they moved. There was a little over
eight dollars in it. Two had to go to the movers, the rest was put
back when the can was nailed down in the new home. Again Mary

Rommely came and sprinkled the flat with holy water. Again there was the settling process and the establishing of trust or credit at the neighborhood stores.

There was resigned regret that the new flat was not as nice as their Lorimer Street home. They lived on the top floor instead of the ground floor. There was no stoop as a store occupied the street floor of the house. There was no bathroom and the toilet was in the hall and shared by two families.

The only bright spot was that the roof was theirs. By an unwritten agreement, the roof belonged to the people who lived on the top floor as the yard belonged to the people who lived on the first floor. Another advantage was that there was no one living overhead to make vibrations on the ceiling and cause the Welsbach gas mantle to crumble into powder.

While Katie was arguing with the movers, Johnny took Francie up on the roof. She saw a whole new world. Not far away was the lovely span of the Williamsburg Bridge. Across the East River, like a fairy city made of silver cardboard, the skyscrapers loomed cleanly. There was the Brooklyn Bridge further away like an echo of the nearer bridge.

"It's pretty," said Francie. "It's pretty the same way pictures of in-the-country are pretty."

"I go over that bridge sometimes when I go to work," Johnny said.

Francie looked at him in wonder. *He* went over that magic bridge and still talked and looked like always? She couldn't get over it. She put out her hand and touched his arm. Surely the wonderful experience of going over that bridge would make him *feel* different. She was disappointed because his arm felt as it had always felt.

At the child's touch, Johnny put his arm around her and smiled down at her. "How old are you, Prima Donna?"

"Six going on seven."

"Why you'll be going to school in September."

"No. Mama said I must wait until next year till Neeley's old enough so we can start together."

"Why?"

"So we can help each other against the older kids who might lick us if there was only one."

"Your mother thinks of everything."

Francie turned around and looked at the other roofs. Near-by was one with a pigeon coop on it. The pigeons were safely locked up. But the pigeon owner, a youth of seventeen, stood on the edge of the roof with a long bamboo stick. It had a rag on the end and the boy stood waving the stick in circles. Another flock of pigeons was flying around in a circle. One of them left the group to follow the flying rag. The boy lowered the stick cautiously and the silly pigeon followed the rag. The boy grabbed him and stuck him in the coop. Francie was distressed.

"The boy stole a pigeon."

"And tomorrow someone will steal one of his," said Johnny.

"But the poor pigeon, taken away from his relations. Maybe he's got children." Tears came into her eyes.

"I wouldn't cry," said Johnny. "Maybe the pigeon wanted to get away from his relatives. If he doesn't like the new coop, he'll fly back to the old one when he gets out again." Francie was consoled.

They didn't say anything for a long time. They stood hand-in-hand on the roof's edge looking across the river to New York. Finally Johnny said, as if to himself, "Seven years."

"What Papa?"

"Your mama and I have been married seven years already."

"Was I here when you got married?"

"No."

"I was here, though, when Neeley came."

"That's right." Johnny went back to thinking aloud. "Married seven years and we've had three homes. This will be my last home."

Francie didn't notice that he said *my* last home instead of *our* last home.

BOOK THREE

15

Four rooms made up the new flat. They led one into the other and were called railroad rooms. The high narrow kitchen faced on the yard which was a flagstone walk surrounding a square of cement-like sour earth out of which nothing could possibly grow.

Yet, there was this tree growing in the yard.

When Francie first saw it, it was only up to the second story. She could look down on it from her window. It looked like a packed crowd of people of assorted sizes, standing umbrella-protected in the rain.

There was a lean clothes pole in the back of the yard from which six washlines on pulleys connected with six kitchen windows. The neighborhood boys kept themselves in pocket money by climbing the poles to replace a washline when it slipped off a pulley. It was believed that the boys climbed the pole in the dead of night and sneaked the line off the pulley to guarantee the next day's dime.

On a sunny windy day, it was pretty to see the lines filled, the square white sheets taking the wind like the sails of a story-book boat and the red, green and yellow clothes straining at the wooden pins as though they had life.

The pole stood against a brick wall which was the windowless side of the neighborhood school. Francie found that no two bricks were alike when she looked real close. It was a soothing rhythm the way they were put together with crumbly thin lines of white mortar. They glowed when the sun shone on them. They smelled warm and porous when Francie pressed her cheek against them. They were the first to receive the rain and they gave off a wet clay odor that was like the smell of life itself. In the winter, when the first snow was too delicate to last on the sidewalks, it clung to the rough surface of the brick and was like fairy lace.

Four feet of the school yard faced on Francie's yard and was segregated from it by an iron mesh fence. The few times Francie got to play in the yard (it was preempted by the boy who lived on the ground floor who would let no one in it while he was there), she managed to be there at recess time. She watched the horde of children playing in the yard. Recess consisted of getting several hundred children herded into this small, stone-paved enclosure and then getting them out again. Once in the yard, there was no room for games. The children milled about angrily and raised their voices in one steady, monotonous shrieking which continued unabated for five minutes. It was cut off, as if with a sharp knife, when the end-of-recess bell clanged. For an instant after the bell there was dead silence and frozen motion. Then the milling changed to pushing. The children seemed as desperately anxious to get in as they had been to get out. The high shrieking changed to subdued wailing as they fought their way back.

Francie was in her yard one mid-afternoon when a little girl came out alone into the school yard and importantly clapped two blackboard erasers together to free them from chalk dust. To Francie, watching, her face close to the iron mesh, this seemed the most fascinating occupation ever devised. Mama had told her that this was a task reserved for teachers' pets. To Francie, pets meant cats, dogs and birds. She vowed that when she was old enough to go to school, that she would meow, bark and chirp as best she could so that she would be a "pet" and get to clap the erasers together.

On this afternoon, she watched with a heart full of admiration in her eyes. The clapper, aware of Francie's admiration, showed off. She clapped the erasers on the brick wall, on the stone walk and as a finale, behind her back. She spoke to Francie.

"Want to see 'em real close?"

Francie nodded shyly. The girl brought an eraser close to the mesh. Francie poked a finger through to touch the vari-colored felt layers blended together by a film of powdered chalk. As she was about to touch this soft beautifulness, the little girl snatched it away and spat full in Francie's face. Francie closed her eyes tightly to keep the hurt bitter tears from spilling out. The other girl stood there curiously, waiting for the tears. When none came, she taunted:

"Why don't you bust out crying, you dockle? Want I should spit in your face again?"

Francie turned and went down into the cellar and sat in the dark a long time waiting until the waves of hurt stopped breaking over her. It was the first of many disillusionments that were to come as her capacity to feel things grew. She never liked blackboard erasers after that.

The kitchen was living room, dining room and cooking room. There were two long narrow windows in one wall. An iron coal-range was recessed in another wall. Above the stove the recess was made of coral-colored bricks and creamy white plaster. It had a stone mantelpiece and a slate hearthstone on which Francie could draw pictures with chalk. Next to the stove was a water boiler which got hot when the fire was going. Often on a cold day, Francie came in chilled and put her arms around the boiler and pressed her frosty cheek gratefully against its warm silveriness.

Next to the boiler was a pair of soapstone washtubs with a hinged wooden cover. The partition could be removed and the two thrown into one for a bath tub. It didn't make a very good bath tub. Sometimes when Francie sat in it, the cover banged down on her head. The bottom was rubbly and she came out of what should have been a refreshing bath, all sore from sitting on that wet roughness. Then there were four faucets to contend with. No matter how the child tried to remember that they were inflexibly there and wouldn't give way, she would jump up suddenly out of the soapy water and get her back whacked good on a faucet. Francie had a perpetual angry welt on her back.

Following the kitchen, there were two bedrooms, one leading into the other. An airshaft dimensioned like a coffin was built into the bedrooms. The windows were small and dingy gray. You could open an airshaft window, maybe, if you used a chisel and hammer. But when you did, you were rewarded with a blast of cold dank air. The airshaft was topped by a miniature, slant-roofed skylight whose heavy, opaque, wrinkled glass was protected from breakage by heavy, iron netting. The sides were corrugated iron slats. This arrangement supposedly supplied light and air to the bedrooms. But the heavy glass, iron fencing and dirt of many years refused to filter the light through. The openings in the sides were choked with dust, soot and cobwebs. No air could come in, but, stubbornly enough, rain and snow could get in. On stormy days, the wooden bottom of the airshaft was wet and smoky and gave out a tomb-y smell.

The airshaft was a horrible invention. Even with the windows tightly sealed, it served as a sounding box and you could hear everybody's business. Rats scurried around the bottom. There was always the danger of fire. A match absently tossed into the airshaft by a drunken teamster under the impression that he was throwing it into the yard or street would set the house afire in a moment. There were vile things cluttering up the bottom. Since this bottom couldn't be reached by man (the windows being too small to admit the passage of a body), it served as a fearful repository for things that people wanted to put out of their lives. Rusted razor blades and bloody cloths were the most innocent items. Once Francie looked down into the airshaft. She thought of what the priest said about Purgatory and figured it must be like the airshaft bottom only on a larger scale. When Francie went into the parlor, she passed through the bedrooms shuddering and with her eyes shut.

The parlor or front room was The Room. Its two high narrow windows faced on the exciting street. The third floor was so high up that street noises were muted into a comforting sound. The room was a place of dignity. It had its own door leading into the hall. Company could be admitted without having to walk through the bedrooms from the kitchen. The high walls were covered with a somber wall paper, dark brown with golden stripes. The windows had inside shutters of slatted wood which telescoped into a narrow space on either side. Francie spent many happy hours pulling out these hinged shutters and watching them fold back again at a touch of her hand. It was a never-tiring miracle that that which could cover a whole window and blot out light and air, could still meekly compress itself in its little closet and present an innocently paneled front to the eye.

A low parlor stove was built into a black marble fireplace. Only the front half of the stove was in view. It looked like a giant halved melon with the round side out. It was made of numerous isinglass windows with just enough thin carved iron to form a framework. At Christmas time, the only time Katie could afford to have a fire in the parlor, all of the little windows glowed and Francie felt a great joy sitting there, feeling the warmth and watching the windows change from rosy red to amber as the night wore on. And when Katie came in and lit the gas, chasing the shadows away and paling the light in the stove windows, it was like a great sin that she committed.

The most wonderful thing about the front room was the piano. This was a miracle that you could pray for all your life and it would never come to pass. But there it stood in the Nolan parlor, a real true miracle that had come without a wish or a prayer. The piano had been left there by the previous tenants who could not afford to pay to have it moved.

Piano-moving in those days was a project. No piano could be gotten down those narrow steep stairs. Pianos had to be bundled up, roped and hoisted out of the windows with an enormous pulley on the roof and with much shouting, arm-waving and brass-hatting on the part of the boss mover. The street had to be roped off, the policemen had to keep the crowds back and children had to play hooky from school when there was a piano moving. There was always that great moment when the wrapped bulk swung clear of the window and twisted dizzily in the air for a moment before it righted itself. Then began the slow perilous descent while the children cheered hoarsely.

It was a job that cost fifteen dollars, three times what it cost to move all the rest of the furniture. So the owner asked Katie could she leave it and would Katie mind it for her? Katie was glad to give her the promise. Wistfully the woman asked Katie not to let it get damp or cold, to leave the bedroom doors open in winter so a little heat would get through from the kitchen and prevent warping.

"Can you play it?" Katie asked her.

"No," said the woman sorrowfully. "No one in the family can play. I wish I could."

"Why did you ever buy it?"

"It was in a rich house. The people were selling it cheap. I wanted it so much. No, I couldn't play it. But it was so beautiful . . . It dresses up the whole room."

Katie promised to take good care of it until the woman could afford to send for it but as things turned out, the woman never did send for it and the Nolans had this beautiful thing for always.

It was small and made of black polished wood that glowed darkly. The front of thin veneers was cut out to make a pretty pattern and there was old-rose silk behind this fretted wood design. Its lid did not fold back in sections like other uprights. It just turned back and rested against the designed wood like a lovely, dark, polished shell. There was a candle holder on either side. You could put pure white candles in them and play by the candlelight which threw dreamy shadows over the creamy ivoried keys. And you could see the keys again in the dark cover.

When the Nolans walked into the front room on their first possessive tour of inspection, the piano was the only thing that Francie saw. She tried to get her arms around it but it was too big. She had to be content to hug the faded-rose brocade stool.

Katie looked at the piano with dancing eyes. She had noticed a white card in the flat window below which said, "Piano Lessons." Katie had an idea.

Johnny sat on the magic stool, which turned around and went up or down according to your size, and played. He couldn't play, of course. He couldn't read notes in the first place but he knew a few chords. He could sing a song and strike a chord now and then and really it sounded as though he were singing to music. He struck a minor chord, looked into the eyes of his oldest child and smiled a crooked smile. Francie smiled back, her heart waiting in anticipation. He struck the minor chord again; held it. To its soft echo, he sang in his clear true voice:

> *Maxwellton's braes are bonny,*
> *Whe' early fae's the dew.*
> (Chord—chord.)
> *An' 't was there that Annie Laurie,*
> *Gied me her promise true.*
> (Chord—chord—chord—chord.)

Francie looked away, not wanting papa to see her tears. She was afraid he'd ask her why she was crying and she wouldn't be able to tell him. She loved him and she loved the piano. She could find no excuse for her easy tears.

Katie spoke. Her voice had some of the old soft tenderness in it which Johnny had been missing in the last year or so. "Is that an Irish song, Johnny?"

"Scotch."

"I never heard you sing it before."

"No, I guess not. It's just a song I know. I never sing it because it's not the kind of song people want to hear at the rackets where I work. They'd sooner hear 'Call Me Up Some Rainy Afternoon.' Except when they're drunk. Then nothing but 'Sweet Adeline' will do."

They were quickly settled in the new place. The familiar furniture looked strange. Francie sat on a chair and was surprised that it felt the same as it had in Lorimer Street. *She* felt different. Why didn't the chair feel different?

The front room looked pretty after papa and mama got it fixed up. There was a bright green carpet which had great pink roses. There were starched cream-colored lace curtains for the windows, a table with a marble top for the center of the room and a three-piece green plush parlor suit. A bamboo stand in the corner held a plush-covered album in which were pictures of the Rommely sisters as babies lying on their stomachs on a fur rug, and patient-looking great-aunts standing at the shoulders of seated, big-mustached husbands. Little souvenir cups stood on the small shelves. The cups were pink and blue and had gold-encrusted designs of blue forget-me-nots and red American beauty roses. There were phrases like *Remember Me* and *True Friendship* painted in gold. The tiny cups and saucers were memories of Katie's old girl friends and Francie was never permitted to play house with them.

On the bottom shelf stood a curly, bone-white conch shell with a delicate rosy interior. The children loved it dearly and had given it an affectionate name: Tootsy. When Francie held it to her ear, it sang of the great sea. Sometimes for the delight of his children Johnny listened to the shell, then held it dramatically at arm's length, looked at it meltingly and sang:

> *Upon the shore I found a shell.*
> *I held it to my ear.*
> *I listened gladly while it sang,*
> *A sea song sweet and clear.*

Later, Francie saw the sea for the first time when Johnny took them to Canarsie. The sea was remarkable only in that it sounded like the tiny sweet roar of Tootsy, the conch shell.

16

The neighborhood stores are an important part of a city child's life. They are his contact with the supplies that keep life going; they hold the beauty that his soul longs for; they hold the unattainable that he can only dream and wish for.

Francie liked the pawnshop almost the best—not for the treasures prodigiously thrown into its barred windows; not for the shadowy adventure of shawled women slipping into the side entrance, but for the three large golden balls that hung high above the shop and gleamed in the sun or swayed languorously like heavy golden apples when the wind blew.

There was a bakery store to one side of it which sold beautiful charlotte russes with red candied cherries on their whipped cream tops for those who were rich enough to buy.

On the other side was Gollender's Paint Shop. There was a stand in front of it from which was suspended a plate with a dramatically mended crack across it and a hole bored into the bottom from which hung a heavy rock suspended on a chain. This proved how strong *Major's Cement* was. Some said the plate was made of iron and painted to resemble cracked China. But Francie preferred to believe it was a real plate that had been broken and then made whole again by the miracle of the cement.

The most interesting store was housed in a little shanty which had been there when the Indians prowled through Williamsburg. It looked queer among the tenements with its tiny small-paned windows, clapboards and steep slanting roof. The store had a great small-paneled bay window behind which a dignified man sat at a table and made cigars—long thin dark-brown ones which sold four for a nickel. He chose the outside leaf very carefully from a hand of tobacco and filled it expertly with bits of tobacco of mixed browns and rolled it all very beautifully so that it was tight and thin and the ends had squared corners. A craftsman of the old school, he scorned progress. He refused to have gaslight in his store. Sometimes when the days grew dark early and he still had a lot of cigars to finish, he worked by candlelight. He had a wooden Indian outside his store which stood in a threatening stance on a wooden block. He held a tomahawk in one hand and a hand of tobacco in the other. He wore Roman sandals with the lacings coming to his knees, a short skirt of feathers and a war bonnet all of which were painted in bright reds, blues and yellows. The cigar maker gave him a fresh coat of paint four times a year and carried him inside when it rained. The neighborhood children called the Indian "Aunt Maimie."

One of Francie's favorite stores was the one which sold nothing but tea, coffee and spices. It was an exciting place of rows of lacquered bins and strange, romantic, exotic odors. There were a dozen scarlet coffee bins with adventurous words written across the front in black China ink: Brazil! Argentine! Turkish! Java! Mixed Blend! The tea was in smaller bins: beautiful bins with sloping covers. They read: Oolong! Formosa! Orange Pekoe! Black China! Flowering Almond! Jasmine! Irish Tea! The spices were in miniature bins behind the counter. Their names marched in a row across the shelves: cinnamon—cloves—ginger—all-spice—ball nutmeg—curry—pepper corns—sage—thyme—marjoram. All pepper when purchased was ground in a tiny pepper mill.

There was a large hand-turned coffee grinder. The beans were put into a shiny brass hopper, and the great wheel was turned with two hands. The fragrant grounds pattered down into a scarlet box that was shaped like a scoop at the back.

(The Nolans ground their coffee at home. Francie loved to see mama sitting debonairly in the kitchen with the coffee mill clutched between her knees, grinding away with a furious turn of her left wrist and looking up to talk sparklingly to papa while the room filled up with the rich satisfying odor of freshly-ground coffee.)

The tea man had a wonderful pair of scales: two gleaming brass plates which had been rubbed and polished daily for more than twenty-five years until now they were thin and delicate and looked like burnished gold. When Francie bought a pound of coffee or an ounce of pepper she watched while a polished silver block with the weight mark was placed in one scale and the fragrant purchase was conveyed gently by means of a silver-like scoop into the other. Francie, watching, held her breath while the scoop dropped in a few more grains or gently eased some out. It was a beautiful peaceful second when both golden plates were stilled and stood there in perfect balance. It was as if nothing wrong could happen in a world where things balanced so stilly.

The mystery of mysteries to Francie was the Chinaman's one-windowed store. The Chinaman wore his pigtail wound around his head. That was so he could go back to China if he wanted to, mama said. Once he cut it off, they would never let him return. He shuffled back and forth silently in his black felt slippers and listened patiently to instructions about shirts. When Francie spoke to him, he folded his hands in the wide sleeves of his nankeen shirt coat and kept his eyes on the ground. She thought that he was wise and contemplative and listened with all his heart. But he understood nothing of what she said, having little English. All he knew was *tickee* and *shirtee*.

When Francie brought her father's soiled shirt there, he whisked it under the counter, took a square of mysteriously textured paper, dipped a thin brush into a pot of India Ink, made a few strokes and gave her this magic document in exchange for a common dirty shirt. It seemed a wonderful barter.

The inside of the store had a clean, warm but fragile scent, like odorless flowers in a hot room. He did the washing in some mysterious recess and it must have been in the dead of night because all day, from seven in the morning until ten at night, he stood in the store at his clean ironing board pushing a heavy black iron back and forth. The iron must have had a tiny gasoline arrangement inside it to keep it hot. Francie did not know this. She thought it part of the mystery of his race that he could iron with an iron never heated on a stove. She had a vague theory that the heat came from something he used in place of starch in the shirts and collars.

When Francie brought a ticket and a dime back and pushed them across the counter, he gave her the wrapped shirt and two lichee nuts in exchange. Francie loved these lichee nuts. There was a crisp easily broken shell and the soft sweet meat inside. Inside the meat was a hard stone that no child had ever been able to break open. It was said that this stone contained a smaller stone and that the smaller stone contained a smaller stone which contained a yet smaller stone and so on. It was said that soon the stones got so small you could only see them with a magnifying glass and those smaller ones got still smaller until you couldn't see them with anything but they were always there and would never stop coming. It was Francie's first experience with infinity.

The best times were when he had to make change. He brought out a small wooden frame strung with thin rods on which were blue, red, yellow and green balls. He slid the balls up the brass rods, pondered swiftly, clicked them all back into place and announced "dirty-nine cent." The tiny balls told him how much to charge and how much change to give.

Oh, to be a Chinaman, wished Francie, and have such a pretty toy to count on; oh, to eat all the lichee nuts she wanted and to know the mystery of the iron that was ever hot and yet never stood on a stove. Oh, to paint those symbols with a slight brush and a quick turn of the wrist and to make a clear black mark as fragile as a piece of a butterfly wing! That was the mystery of the Orient in Brooklyn.

17

Piano lessons! Magic words! As soon as the Nolans were settled, Katie called on the lady whose card announced piano lessons. There were two Miss Tynmores. Miss Lizzie taught piano and Miss Maggie cultivated the voice. The charge was twenty-five cents per lesson. Katie proposed a bargain. She'd do one hour's cleaning work for the Tynmores in exchange for a lesson each week. Miss Lizzie demurred, claiming her time had more value than Katie's time. Katie argued that time was time. Finally she got Miss Lizzie to agree that time was time and arrangements were made.

The history-making day of the first lesson arrived. Francie and Neeley were instructed to sit in the front room during the lesson and to keep their eyes and ears open. A chair was placed for the teacher. The children sat side by side on the other side of the piano, Katie nervously adjusted and readjusted the seat and the three sat waiting.

Miss Tynmore arrived on the dot of five. Although she only came from downstairs, she was formally attired in street clothes. A taut spotted veil was stretched over her face. Her hat was the breast and wing of a red bird tormentingly pierced by two hatpins. Francie stared at the cruel hat. Mama took her into the bedroom and whispered that the bird wasn't a bird at all just some feathers glued together and that she mustn't stare. She believed mama, yet her eyes kept going back to the tormented effigy.

Miss Tynmore brought everything with her but the piano. She had a nickel alarm clock and a battered metronome. The clock said five o'clock. She set it for six and stood it on the piano. She took the privilege of using up part of the precious hour. She removed her pearl-gray, skin-tight kid gloves, blew into each finger, smoothed and folded them and placed them on the piano. She undid her veil and threw it back over her hat. She limbered up her fingers, glanced at the clock, was satisfied she had taken enough minutes, started the metronome, took her seat and the lesson began.

Francie was so fascinated by the metronome that she found it hard to listen to what Miss Tynmore said and to watch the way she placed mama's hands on the keys. She weaved dreams in time to the soothing monotonous clicking. As for Neeley, his round blue eyes rolled back and forth following the little swinging rod until he hypnotized himself into unconsciousness. His mouth relaxed and his blond head rolled over on his shoulder. A little bubble came and went as he breathed moistly. Katie dared not wake him lest Miss Tynmore catch on that she was teaching three for the price of one.

The metronome clicked on dreamily; the clock ticked querulously. Miss Tynmore, as if not trusting the metronome, counted, *one*, two, three; *one*, two, three. Katie's work-swollen fingers struggled doggedly with her first scale. Time passed and it grew dark in the room. Suddenly the alarm clock rang out shatteringly. Francie's heart jumped and Neeley fell off his chair. The first lesson was ended. Katie's words tumbled over each other in gratitude.

"Even if I never take another lesson, I could go on with what you taught me today. You are a good teacher."

Miss Tynmore, while pleased by the flattery, nevertheless told Katie what was what. "I won't charge extra for the children. I just want you to know you're not fooling me." Katie blushed and the children looked down on the floor, ashamed of being found out. "I will permit the children to stay in the room."

Katie thanked her. Miss Tynmore stood up and waited. Katie verified the time she was to do Miss Tynmore's housework. Still she waited. Katie felt that something was expected of her. Finally she inquired,

"Yes?"

Miss Tynmore flushed a shell pink and spoke proudly. "The ladies . . . where I give lessons . . . well . . . they offer me a cup of tea afterwards." She put her hand to her heart and explained vaguely, "Those stairs."

"Would you sooner take coffee?" Katie asked. "We have no tea."

"Gladly!" Miss Tynmore sat down in relief.

Katie rushed out to the kitchen and heated the coffee which was always standing on the stove. While it was warming, she put a sugar bun and a spoon on a round tin tray.

In the meantime, Neeley had fallen asleep on the sofa. Miss Tynmore and Francie sat exchanging stares. Finally Miss Tynmore asked,

"What are you thinking about, little girl?"

"Just thinking," Francie said.

"Sometimes I see you sitting on the gutter curb for hours. What do you think of then?"

"Nothing. I just tell myself stories."

Miss Tynmore pointed at her sternly. "Little girl, you'll be a story writer when you grow up." It was a command rather than a statement.

"Yes ma'am," agreed Francie out of politeness.

Katie came in with the tray. "This may not be as refined as you're used to," she apologized, "but it's what we have in the house."

"It's very good," stated Miss Tynmore daintily. Then she concentrated on trying not to wolf it down.

To tell the truth, the Tynmores lived on the "tea" they got from their pupils. A few lessons a day at a quarter a lesson did not make for prosperity. After paying their rent, there was little left to eat on. Most of the ladies served them weak tea and soda crackers. The ladies knew what was polite and would come through with a cup of tea but they had no intention of supplying a meal and paying a quarter, too. So Miss Tynmore came to look forward to the hour at the Nolans. The coffee was heartening and there was always a bun or a bologna sandwich to sustain her.

After each lesson, Katie taught the children what she had been taught. She made them practice half an hour each day. In time, all three of them learned to play the piano.

When Johnny heard that Maggie Tynmore gave voice lessons, he figured that he could do no less than Katie. He offered to repair a broken sash cord in one of the Tynmore windows in exchange for two voice lessons for Francie. Johnny, who had never even seen a sash cord in all his life, got a hammer and screw driver and took the whole window frame out of its case. He looked at the broken rope and that was as far as he could go. He experimented and got nowhere. His heart was willing but his skill was nil. In attempting to get the window back in to keep out the cold winter rain that was blowing into the room while he was figuring out about the sash cord, he broke a pane of glass. The deal fell through. The Tynmores had to get a regular window man in to fix it. Katie had to do two washings free for the girls to make up for it and Francie's voice lessons were abandoned forever.

18

School days were eagerly anticipated by Francie. She wanted all of the things that she thought came with school. She was a lonely child and she longed for the companionship of other children. She wanted to drink from the school water fountains in the yard. The faucets were inverted and she thought that soda water came out instead of plain water. She had heard mama and papa speak of the school room. She wanted to see the map that pulled down like a shade. Most of all, she wanted "school supplies": a notebook and· tablet and a pencil box with a sliding top filled with new pencils, an eraser, a little tin pencil sharpener made in the shape of a cannon, a pen wiper and a six-inch, soft wood, yellow ruler.

Before school, there had to be vaccination. That was the law. How it was dreaded! When the health authorities tried to explain to the poor and illiterate that vaccination was a giving of the harmless form of smallpox to work up immunity against the deadly form, the parents didn't believe it. All they got out of the explanation was that germs would be put into a healthy child's body. Some foreign-born parents refused to permit their children to be vaccinated. They were not allowed to enter school. Then the law got after them for keeping the children out of school. A free country? they asked. You should live so long. What's free about it, they reasoned when the law forces you to educate your children and then endangers their lives to get them into school? Weeping mothers brought bawling children to the health center for inoculation. They carried on as though bringing their innocents to the slaughter. The children screamed hysterically at the first sight of the needle and their mothers, waiting in the anteroom, threw their shawls over their heads and keened loudly as if wailing for the dead.

Francie was seven and Neeley six. Katie had held Francie back wishing both children to enter school together so that they could protect each other against the older children. On a dreadful Saturday in August, she stopped in the bedroom to speak to them before she went off to work. She awakened them and gave instructions.

"Now when you get up, wash yourselves good and when it gets to be eleven o'clock, go around the corner to the public health place, tell them to vaccinate you because you're going to school in September."

Francie began to tremble. Neeley burst into tears.

"You coming with us, Mama?" Francie pleaded.

"I've got to go to work. Who's going to do my work if I don't?" asked Katie covering up her conscience with indignation.

Francie said nothing more. Katie knew that she was letting them down. But she couldn't help it, she just couldn't help it. Yes, she should go with them to lend the comfort and authority of her presence but she knew she couldn't stand the ordeal. Yet, they had to be vaccinated. Her being with them or somewhere else couldn't take that fact away. So why shouldn't one of the three be spared? Besides, she said to her conscience, it's a hard and bitter world. They've got to live in it. Let them get hardened young to take care of themselves.

"Papa's going with us then," said Francie hopefully.

"Papa's at Headquarters waiting for a job. He won't be home all day. You're big enough to go alone. Besides, it won't hurt."

Neeley wailed on a higher key. Katie could hardly stand that. She loved the boy so much. Part of her reason for not going with them was that she couldn't bear to see the boy hurt . . . not even by a pin prick. Almost she decided to go with them. But no. If she went she'd lose half a day's work and she'd have to make it up on Sunday morning. Besides, she'd be sick afterwards. They'd manage somehow without her. She hurried off to her work.

Francie tried to console the terrified Neeley. Some older boys had told him that they cut your arm off when they got you in the Health Center. To take his mind off the thing, Francie took him down into the yard and they made mud pies. They quite forgot to wash as mama had told them to.

They almost forgot about eleven o'clock, the mud pie making was so beguiling. Their hands and arms got very dirty playing in the mud. At ten to eleven, Mrs. Gaddis hung out the window and yelled down that their mother had told her to remind them when it was near eleven o'clock. Neeley finished off his last mud pie, watering it with his tears. Francie took his hand and with slow dragging steps the children walked around the corner.

They took their place on a bench. Next to them sat a Jewish mama who clutched a large six-year-old boy in her arms and wept and kissed his forehead passionately from time to time. Other mothers sat there with grim suffering furrowed on their faces. Behind the frosted glass door where the terrifying business was going on, there was a steady bawling punctuated by a shrill scream, resumption of the bawling and then a pale child would come out with a strip of pure white gauze about his left arm. His mother would rush and grab him and with a foreign curse and a shaken fist at the frosted door, hurry him out of the torture chamber.

Francie went in trembling. She had never seen a doctor or a nurse in all of her small life. The whiteness of the uniforms, the shiny cruel instruments laid out on a napkin on a tray, the smell of antiseptics, and especially the cloudy sterilizer with its bloody red cross filled her with tongue-tied fright.

The nurse pulled up her sleeve and swabbed a spot clean on her left arm. Francie saw the white doctor coming towards her with the cruelly-poised needle. He loomed larger and larger until he seemed to blend into a great needle. She closed her eyes waiting to die. Nothing happened, she felt nothing. She opened her eyes slowly, hardly daring to hope that it was all over. She found to her agony, that the doctor was still there, poised needle and all. He was staring at her arm in distaste. Francie looked too. She saw a small white area on a dirty dark brown arm. She heard the doctor talking to the nurse.

"Filth, filth, filth, from morning to night. I know they're poor but they could wash. Water is free and soap is cheap. Just look at that arm, nurse."

The nurse looked and clucked in horror. Francie stood there with the hot flamepoints of shame burning her face. The doctor was a Harvard man, interning at the neighborhood hospital. Once a week, he was obligated to put in a few hours at one of the free clinics. He was going into a smart practice in Boston when his internship was over. Adopting the phraseology of the neighborhood, he referred to his Brooklyn internship as going through Purgatory when he wrote to his socially prominent fiancée in Boston.

The nurse was a Williamsburg girl. You could tell that by her accent. The child of poor Polish immigrants, she had been ambitious, worked days in a sweatshop and gone to school at night. Somehow she had gotten her training. She hoped some day to marry a doctor. She didn't want anyone to know she had come from the slums.

After the doctor's outburst, Francie stood hanging her head. She was a dirty girl. That's what the doctor meant. He was talking more quietly now asking the nurse how that kind of people could survive; that it would be a better world if they were all sterilized and couldn't breed anymore. Did that mean he wanted her to die? Would he do something to make her die because her hands and arms were dirty from the mud pies?

She looked at the nurse. To Francie, all women were mamas like her own mother and Aunt Sissy and Aunt Evy. She thought the nurse might say something like:

"Maybe this little girl's mother works and didn't have time to wash her good this morning," or, "You know how it is, Doctor, children *will* play in dirt." But what the nurse actually said was, "I know. Isn't it terrible? I sympathize with you, Doctor. There is no excuse for these people living in filth."

A person who pulls himself up from a low environment via the boot-strap route has two choices. Having risen above his environment, he can forget it; or, he can rise above it and never forget it and keep compassion and understanding in his heart for those he has left behind him in the cruel up climb. The nurse had chosen the forgetting way. Yet, as she stood there, she knew that years later she would be haunted by the sorrow in the face of that starveling child and that she would wish bitterly that she had said a comforting word then and done something towards the saving of her immortal soul. She had the knowledge that she was small but she lacked the courage to be otherwise.

When the needle jabbed, Francie never felt it. The waves of hurt started by the doctor's words were racking her body and drove out all other feeling. While the nurse was expertly tying a strip of gauze around her arm and the doctor was putting his instrument in the sterilizer and taking out a fresh needle, Francie spoke up.

"My brother is next. His arm is just as dirty as mine so don't be surprised. And you don't have to tell him. You told me." They stared at this bit of humanity who had become so strangely articulate. Francie's voice went ragged with a sob. "You don't have to tell him. Besides it won't do no good. He's a boy and he don't care if he is dirty." She turned, stumbled a little and walked out of the room. As the door closed, she heard the doctor's surprised voice.

"I had no idea she'd understand what I was saying." She heard the nurse say, "Oh, well," on a sighing note.

Katie was home for lunch when the children got back. She looked at their bandaged arms with misery in her eyes. Francie spoke out passionately.

"Why, Mama, why? Why do they have to . . . to . . . say things and then stick a needle in your arm?"

"Vaccination," said mama firmly, now that it was all over, "is a very good thing. It makes you tell your left hand from your right. You have to write with your right hand when you go to school and that sore will be there to say, uh-uh, not this hand. Use the other hand."

This explanation satisfied Francie because she had never been able to tell her left hand from her right. She ate, and drew pictures with her left hand. Katie was always correcting her and transferring the chalk or the needle from her left hand to her right. After mama explained about vaccination, Francie began to think that maybe it was a wonderful thing. It was a small price to pay if it simplified such a great problem and let you know which hand was which. Francie began using her right hand instead of the left after the vaccination and never had trouble afterwards.

Francie worked up a fever that night and the site of the injection itched painfully. She told mama who became greatly alarmed. She gave intense instructions.

"You're not to scratch it, no matter how it bites you."

"Why can't I scratch it?"

"Because if you do, your whole arm will swell up and turn black and drop right off. So don't scratch it."

Katie did not mean to terrify the child. She, herself, was badly frightened. She believed that blood-poisoning would set in if the arm were touched. She wanted to frighten the child into not scratching it.

Francie had to concentrate on not scratching the painfully itching area. The next day, shots of pain were shooting up the arm. While preparing for bed, she peered under the bandage. To her horror, the place where the needle had entered was swollen, dark-green and festering yellowly. And Francie had not scratched it! *She knew she had not scratched it.* But wait! Maybe she had scratched it in her sleep the night before. Yes, she must have done it then. She was afraid to tell mama. Mama would say, "I told you and I told you and still you wouldn't listen. Now look."

It was Sunday night. Papa was out working. She couldn't sleep. She got up from her cot and went into the front room and sat at the window. She leaned her head on her arms and waited to die.

At three in the morning she heard a Graham Avenue trolley grind to a stop on the corner. That meant someone was getting off. She leaned out the window. Yes, it was papa. He sauntered down the street with his light dancer's step whistling "My Sweetheart's the Man in the Moon." The figure in its tuxedo and derby hat, with a rolled-up waiter's apron in a neat packet under its arm, seemed like life itself to Francie. She called to him when he got to the door. He looked up and tipped his hat gallantly. She opened the kitchen door for him.

"What are you doing up so late, Prima Donna?" he asked. "It's not Saturday night, you know."

"I was sitting at the window," she whispered, "waiting for my arm to drop off."

He choked back a laugh. She explained about the arm. He closed the door leading into the bedrooms and turned up the gas. He removed the bandage and his stomach turned over at sight of the swollen festering arm. But he never let her know. He never let her know.

"Why, Baby, that's nothing at all. Just nothing at all. You should have seen my arm when I was vaccinated. It was twice as swollen and red, white and blue instead of green and yellow and now look how hard and strong it is." He lied gallantly for he had never been vaccinated.

He poured warm water into a basin and added a few drops of carbolic acid. He washed the ugly sore over and over again. She winced when it stung but Johnny said that stinging meant curing. He sang a foolish sentimental song in a whisper as he washed it.

> *He never cares to wander from his own fireside.*
> *He never cares to ramble or to roam . . .*

He looked around for a clean bit of cloth to serve as a bandage. Finding none, he took off his coat and shirt dicky, pulled his undershirt off over his head and dramatically ripped a strip of cloth from it.

"Your good undershirt," she protested.

"Aw, it was all full of holes anyhow."

He bandaged the arm. The cloth smelled of Johnny, warm and cigarish. But it was a comforting thing to the child. It smelled of protection and love.

"There! You're all fixed up, Prima Donna. Whatever gave you the idea your arm was going to drop off?"

"Mama said it would if I scratched it. I didn't mean to scratch it but I guess I did while I was sleeping."

"Maybe." He kissed her thin cheek. "Now go back to bed." She went and slept peacefully the rest of the night. In the morning, the throbbing had stopped and in a few days the arm was normal again.

After Francie had gone to bed, Johnny smoked another cigar. Then he undressed slowly and got into Katie's bed. She was sleepily aware of his presence and in one of her rare impulses of affection, she threw her arm across his chest. He removed it gently and edged as far away from her as he could. He lay close to the wall. He folded his hands under his head and lay staring into the darkness all the rest of that night.

19

Francie expected great things from school. Since vaccination taught her instantly the difference between left and right, she thought that school would bring forth even greater miracles. She thought she'd come home from school that first day knowing how to read and write. But all she came home with was a bloody nose gained by an older child slamming her head down on the stone rim of the water trough when she had tried to drink from the faucets that did not gush forth soda water after all.

Francie was disappointed because she had to share a seat and desk (meant only for one) with another girl. She had wanted a desk to herself. She accepted with pride the pencil the monitor passed out to her in the morning and reluctantly surrendered it to another monitor at three o'clock.

She had been in school but half a day when she knew that she would never be a teacher's pet. That privilege was reserved for a small group of girls . . . girls with freshly-curled hair, crisp clean pinafores and new silk hairbows. They were the children of the prosperous storekeepers of the neighborhood. Francie noticed how Miss Briggs, the teacher, beamed on them and seated them in the choicest places in the front row. These darlings were not made to share seats. Miss Briggs' voice was gentle when she spoke to these fortune-favored few, and snarling when she spoke to the great crowd of unwashed.

Francie, huddled with other children of her kind, learned more that first day than she realized. She learned of the class system of a great Democracy. She was puzzled and hurt by teacher's attitude. Obviously the teacher hated her and others like her for no other reason than that they were what they were. Teacher acted as though they had no right to be in the school but that she was forced to accept them and was doing so with as little grace as possible. She begrudged them the few crumbs of learning she threw at them. Like the doctor at the health center, she too acted as though they had no right to live.

It would seem as if all the unwanted children would stick together and be one against the things that were against them. But not so. They hated each other as much as the teacher hated them. They aped teacher's snarling manner when they spoke to each other.

There was always one unfortunate whom the teacher singled out and used for a scapegoat. This poor child was the nagged one, the tormented one, the one on whom she vented her spinsterly spleen. As soon as a child received this dubious recognition, the other children turned on him and duplicated the teacher's torments. Characteristically, they fawned on those close to teacher's heart. Maybe they figured they were nearer to the throne that way.

Three thousand children crowded into this ugly brutalizing school that had facilities for only one thousand. Dirty stories went the rounds of the children. One of them was that Miss Pfieffer, a bleached blond teacher with a high giggle, went down to the basement to sleep with the assistant janitor those times when she put a monitor in charge and explained that she had to "step out to the office." Another, passed around by little boys who had been victims, was that the lady principal, a hard-bitten, heavy cruel woman of middle years who wore sequin-decorated dresses and smelled always of raw gin, got recalcitrant boys into her office and made them take down their pants so that she could flay their naked buttocks with a rattan cane. (She whipped the little girls through their dresses.)

Of course, corporal punishment was forbidden in the schools.

But who, outside, knew? Who would tell? Not the whipped children, certainly. It was a tradition in the neighborhood that if a child reported that he had been whipped in school, he would receive a second home-whipping because he had not behaved in school. So the child took his punishment and kept quiet, leaving well enough alone.

The ugliest thing about these stories was that they were all sordidly true.

Brutalizing is the only adjective for the public schools of that district around 1908 and '09. Child psychology had not been heard of in Williamsburg in those days. Teaching requirements were easy: graduation from high school and two years at Teachers Training School. Few teachers had the true vocation for their work. They taught because it was one of the few jobs open to them; because it was better paying than factory work; because they had a long summer vacation; because they got a pension when they retired. They taught because no one wanted to marry them. Married women were not allowed to teach in those days, hence most of the teachers were women made neurotic by starved love instincts. These barren women spent their fury on other women's children in a twisted authoritative manner.

The cruelest teachers were those who had come from homes similar to those of the poor children. It seemed that in their bitterness towards those unfortunate little ones, they were somehow exorcizing their own fearful background.

Of course, not all of the teachers were bad. Sometimes one who was sweet came along, one who suffered with the children and tried to help them. But these women did not last long as teachers. Either they married quickly and left the profession, or they were hounded out of their jobs by fellow teachers.

The problem of what was delicately called "leaving the room" was a grim one. The children were instructed to "go" before they left home in the morning and then to wait until lunch hour. There was supposed to be a time at recess but few children were able to take advantage of that. Usually the press of the crowd prevented a child's getting near the washrooms. If he was lucky enough to get there (where there were but ten lavatories for five hundred children), he'd find the places pre-empted by the ten most brutalized children in the school. They'd stand in the doorways and prevent entrance to all comers. They were deaf to the piteous pleas of the hordes of tormented children who swarmed before them. A few exacted a fee of a penny which few children were able to pay. The overlords never relaxed their hold on the swinging doors until the bell clanged the end of recess. No one ever ascertained what pleasure they derived from this macabre game. They were never punished since no teacher ever entered the children's washrooms. No child ever snitched. No matter how young he was, he knew that he mustn't squeal. If he tattled, he knew he would be tortured almost to death by the one he reported. So this evil game went on and on.

Technically, a child was permitted to leave the room if he asked permission. There was a system of coy evasion. One finger held aloft meant that a child wished to go out but a short time. Two fingers meant desire for a longer stay. But the harassed and unfeeling teachers assured each other that this was just a subterfuge for a child to get out of the classroom for a little while. They *knew* the child had ample opportunity at recess and at lunch time. Thus they settled things among themselves.

Of course, Francie noted, the favored children, the clean, the dainty, the cared-for in the front seats, were allowed to leave at any time. But that was different somehow.

As for the rest of the children, half of them learned to adjust their functions to the teachers' ideas of such things and the other half became chronic pants-wetters.

It was Aunt Sissy who fixed up the leaving-the-room business for Francie. She had not seen the children since Katie and Johnny had told her she was not to visit the house again. She was lonesome for them. She knew they had started school and she just *had* to know how they were getting along.

It was in November. Work was slack and Sissy was laid off. She sauntered down the school street just as school was letting out. If the children reported meeting her, it would seem like an accident, she figured. She saw Neeley first in the crowd. A bigger boy snatched his cap off, trampled on it and ran away. Neeley turned to a smaller boy and did the same to *his* cap. Sissy grabbed Neeley's arm but with a raucous cry, he twisted loose and ran down the street. With poignancy, Sissy realized that he was growing up.

Francie saw Sissy and put her arms around her right there on the street and kissed her. Sissy took her into a little candy store and treated her to a penny chocolate soda. Then she made Francie sit down on a stoop and tell her all about school. Francie showed her the primer and her homework book with block letters in it. Sissy was impressed. She looked long into the child's thin face and noticed that she was shivering. She saw that she was inadequately dressed against the raw November day in a threadbare cotton dress, ragged little sweater and thin cotton stockings. She put her arm around her and held her close to her own life warmth.

"Francie, baby, you're trembling like a leaf."

Francie had never heard that expression and it made her thoughtful. She looked at the little tree growing out of the concrete at the side of the house. There were still a few dried leaves clinging to it. One of them rustled dryly in the wind. Trembling like a leaf. She stored the phrase away in her mind. Trembling. . . .

"What's the matter?" Sissy asked. "You're ice cold."

Francie wouldn't tell at first. But after being coaxed, she buried her shame-hot face in Sissy's neck and whispered something to her.

"Oh, my," said Sissy. "No wonder you're cold. Why didn't you ask to. . . ."

"Teacher never looks at us when we raise our hands."

"Oh, well. Don't worry about it. It could happen to anyone. It happened to the Queen of England when she was a little girl."

But had the Queen been so shamed and sensitive about it? Francie wept quietly and rackingly, tears of shame and fear. She was afraid to go home, afraid that mama would make scornful shame of her.

"Your mama won't scold you . . . such an accident could happen to any little girl. Don't say I told you but your mama wet her pants when she was little and your grandma did too. It's nothing new in the world and you're not the first one it happened to."

"But I'm too big. Only babies do that. Mama'll make shame on me in front of Neeley."

"Tell her right out before she finds out for herself and promise never to do it again. She won't shame you then."

"I can't promise because it might happen again because teacher don't let us go."

"From now on, your teacher will let you leave the room any time you have to. You believe Aunt Sissy, don't you?"

"Y-e-e-es. But how do you know?"

"I'll burn a candle in church about it."

Francie was consoled with the promise. When Francie went home, Katie did a little routine scolding but Francie was armored against it in the light of what Sissy had told her about the cycle of wetting.

The next morning, ten minutes before school started, Sissy was in that classroom confronting the teacher.

"There's a little girl named Francie Nolan in your room," she started out.

"*Frances* Nolan," corrected Miss Briggs.

"Is she smart?"

"Y-e-e-es."

"Is she good?"

"She had better be."

Sissy brought her face closer to Miss Briggs. Her voice went a tone lower and was gentler than before, but for some reason Miss Briggs backed away. "I just asked you is she a good girl?"

"Yes, she is," said Teacher hurriedly.

"I happen to be her mother," lied Sissy.

"No!"

"Yes!"

"Anything you want to know about the child's work, Mrs. Nolan . . ."

"Did it ever occur to you," lied Sissy, "that Francie's got kidney trouble?"

"Kidney what?"

"The doctor said that if she wants to go and some people don't let her go, she's liable to drop right down dead from overloaded kidneys."

"Surely you're exaggerating."

"How would you like her to drop dead in this room?"

"Naturally, I wouldn't, but . . ."

"And how would you like to get a ride to the station house in the pie wagon and stand up in front of this here doctor and the judge and say you wouldn't let her leave the room?"

Was Sissy lying? Miss Briggs couldn't tell. It was the most fantastic thing. Yet, the woman spoke these sensational things in the calmest, softest voice she had ever heard. At this moment, Sissy happened to look out of the window and saw a burly cop sauntering by. She pointed.

"See that cop?" Miss Briggs nodded. "That's my husband."

"Frances' father?"

"Who else?" Sissy threw open the window and yelled, "Yoo, hoo, Johnny."

The astonished cop looked up. She blew him a great kiss. For a split second, he thought it was some love-starved old-maid teacher gone crazy. Then his native masculine conceit assured him that it was one of the younger teachers who had long had a crush on him and had finally screwed up enough courage to make a passionate overture. He responded to the occasion, blew her a return kiss with a ham-y fist, tipped his hat gallantly and sauntered off down his beat whistling "At the Devil's Ball." "Sure I'm a divil amongst the ladies," he thought. "I am that. And me with six kids at home."

Miss Briggs' eyes bugged out in astonishment. He had been a handsome cop and *strong*. Just then, one of the little golden girls came in with a beribboned box of candy for Teacher. Miss Briggs gurgled with pleasure and kissed the child's satin pink cheek. Sissy had a mind like a freshly-honed razor. In a flash, she saw which way the wind blew; she saw it blew against children like Francie.

"Look," she said. "I guess you don't think we got lots of money."

"I'm sure I never . . ."

"We're not people that put on. Now Christmas is coming," she bribed.

"Maybe," conceded Miss Briggs, "I haven't always seen Frances when she raised her hand."

"Where does she sit that you don't see her so good?" Teacher indicated a dark back seat. "Maybe if she sat up front more, you could see her better."

"The seating arrangements are all set."

"Christmas is coming," warned Sissy coyly.

"I'll see what I can do."

"See, then. And see that you see good." Sissy walked to the door, then turned. "Because not only is Christmas coming, but my husband who is a cop will come up here and beat hell out of you if you don't treat her right."

Francie had no more trouble after that parent-teacher conference. No matter how timorously her hand went up, Miss Briggs happened to see it. She even let her sit in the first row, first seat for awhile. But when Christmas came and no expensive Christmas present came with it, Francie was again relegated to the dark back of the room.

Neither Francie nor Katie ever learned of Sissy's school visit. But Francie was never shamed again in that way and if Miss Briggs did not treat her with kindness, at least she didn't nag at her. Of course, Miss Briggs knew that what that woman had told her was ridiculous. Yet, what was the use of taking chances? She didn't like children but she was no fiend. She wouldn't want to see a child drop dead before her eyes.

A few weeks later, Sissy had one of the girls in her shop write a post-card message for her to Katie. She asked her sister to let by-gones be by-gones and permit her to come to the house at least to see the children once in a while. Katie ignored the card.

Mary Rommely came over to intercede for Sissy. "What is there that is bitter between you and your sister?" she asked Katie.

"I cannot tell you," replied Katie.

"Forgiveness," said Mary Rommely, "is a gift of high value. Yet its cost is nothing."

"I have my own ways," said Katie.

"Ai," agreed her mother. She sighed deeply and said no more.

Katie wouldn't admit it, but she missed Sissy. She missed her reckless good sense and her clear way of straightening out troubles. Evy never mentioned Sissy when she came to see Katie and after that one attempt at reconciliation, Mary Rommely never mentioned Sissy's name again.

Katie got news of her sister through the official accredited family reporter, the insurance agent. All of the Rommelys were insured by the same company and the same agent collected the nickels and dimes from each of the sisters weekly. He brought news, carried gossip, and was the round robin messenger of the family. One day he brought news that Sissy had given birth to another child which he had been unable to insure since it had lived but two hours. Katie felt ashamed of herself at last for being so bitter against poor Sissy.

"Next time you see my sister," she told the collector, "tell her not to be such a stranger." The collector relayed the message of forgiveness and Sissy came back into the Nolan family again.

20

Katie's campaign against vermin and disease started the day her children entered school. The battle was fierce, brief, and successful.

Packed closely together, the children innocently bred vermin and became lousy from each other. Through no fault of their own, they were subjected to the most humiliating procedure that a child could go through.

Once a week, the school nurse came and stationed herself with her back to the window. The little girls lined up and when they came to her, turned round, lifted their heavy braids and bent over. Nurse probed about the hair with a long thin stick. If lice or nits were in evidence, the little one was told to stand aside. At the end of the examination, the pariahs were made to stand before the class while Nurse gave a lecture about how filthy those little girls were and how they had to be shunned. The untouchables were then dismissed for the day with instructions to get "blue ointment" from Knipe's Drug Store and have their mothers treat their head. When they returned to school, they were tormented by their peers. Each offender would have an escort of children following her home, chanting:

"Lousy, ye'r lousy! Teacher said ye'r lousy. Hadda go home, hadda go home, hadda go home because ye'r lousy."

It might be that the infected child would be given a clean bill next examination. In that case, she, in turn, would torment those found guilty, forgetting her own hurt at being tormented. They learned no compassion from their own anguish. Thus their suffering was wasted.

There was no room in Katie's crowded life for additional trouble and worry. She wouldn't accept it. The first day that Francie came home from school and reported that she sat next to a girl who had bugs walking up and down the lanes of her hair, Katie went into action. She scrubbed Francie's head with a cake of her coarse strong yellow scrubwoman's soap until her scalp tingled with rawness. The next morning, she dipped the hair brush into a bowl of kerosene oil, brushed Francie's hair vigorously, braided it into braids so tight that the veins on Francie's temples stuck out, instructed her to keep away from lighted gas jets and sent her off to school.

Francie smelled up the whole classroom. Her seat sharer edged as far away from her as possible. Teacher sent a note home forbidding Katie to use kerosene on Francie's head. Katie remarked that it was a free country and ignored the note. Once a week she scrubbed Francie's head with the yellow soap. Every day she anointed it with the kerosene.

When an epidemic of mumps broke out in the school, Katie went into action against communicable diseases. She made two flannel bags, sewed a bud of garlic in each one, attached a clean corset string and made the children wear them around their necks under their shirts.

Francie attended school stinking of garlic and kerosene oil. Everyone avoided her. In the crowded yard, there was always a cleared space around her. In crowded trolley cars, people huddled away from those Nolan children.

And it worked! Now whether there was a witch's charm in the garlic, whether the strong fumes killed the germs or whether Francie escaped contracting anything because infected children gave her a wide berth, or whether she and Neeley had naturally strong constitutions, is not known. However, it was a fact that not once in all the years of school were Katie's children ever sick. They never so much as came down with a cold. And they never had lice.

Francie, of course, became an outsider shunned by all because of her stench. But she had become accustomed to being lonely. She was used to walking alone and to being considered "different." She did not suffer too much.

21

Francie liked school in spite of all the meanness, cruelty, and unhappiness. The regimented routine of many children, all doing the same thing at once, gave her a feeling of safety. She felt that she was a definite part of something, part of a community gathered under a leader for the one purpose. The Nolans were individualists. They conformed to nothing except what was essential to their being able to live in their world. They followed their own standards of living. They were part of no set social group. This was fine for the making of individualists but sometimes bewildering to a small child. So Francie felt a certain safety and security in school. Although it was a cruel and ugly routine, it had a purpose and a progression.

School was not all unrelieved grimness. There was a great golden glory lasting a half hour each week when Mr. Morton came to Francie's room to teach music. He was a specialized teacher who went around to all the schools in that area. It was holiday time when he appeared. He wore a swallow-tailed coat and a puffed-up tie. He was so vibrant, gay and jolly—so intoxicated with living—that he was like a god come from the clouds. He was homely in a gallant vital way. He understood and loved children and they worshipped him. The teachers adored him. There was a carnival spirit in the room on the day of his visit. Teacher wore her best dress and wasn't quite so mean. Sometimes she curled her hair and wore perfume. That's what Mr. Morton did to those ladies.

He arrived like a tornado. The door burst open and he flew in with his coattails streaming behind him. He leaped to the platform and looked around smiling and saying, "well-well," in a happy voice. The children sat there and laughed and laughed out of happiness and Teacher smiled and smiled.

He drew notes on the blackboard; he drew little legs on them to make them look as though they were running out of the scale. He'd make a flat note look like humpty-dumpty. A sharp note would rate a thin beet-like nose zooming off it. All the while he'd burst into singing just as spontaneously as a bird. Sometimes his happiness was so overflowing that he couldn't hold it and he'd cut a dance caper to spill some of it out.

He taught them good music without letting them know it was good. He set his own words to the great classics and gave them simple names like "Lullaby" and "Serenade" and "Street Song" and "Song for a Sunshine Day." Their baby voices shrilled out in Handel's "Largo" and they knew it merely by the title of "Hymn." Little boys whistled part of Dvorak's *New World Symphony* as they played marbles. When asked the name of the song, they'd reply "Oh, 'Going Home.' " They played potsy, humming "The Soldiers' Chorus" from *Faust* which they called "Glory."

Not as well loved as Mr. Morton, but as much admired, was Miss Bernstone, the special drawing teacher who also came once a week. Ah, she was from another world, a world of beautiful dresses of muted greens and garnets. Her face was sweet and tender, and, like Mr. Morton, she loved the vast hordes of unwashed and unwanted children more than she loved the cared-for ones. The teachers did not like *her*. Yes, they fawned on her when she spoke to them and glowered at her when her back was turned. They were jealous of her charm, her sweetness and her lovely appeal to men. She was warm and glowing and richly feminine. They knew that she didn't sleep alone nights as they were forced to do.

She spoke softly in a clear singing voice. Her hands were beautiful and quick with a bit of chalk or a stick of charcoal. There was magic in the way her wrist turned when she held a crayon. One wrist twist and there was an apple. Two more twists and there was a child's sweet hand holding the apple. On a rainy day, she wouldn't give a lesson. She'd take a block of paper and a stick of charcoal and sketch the poorest, meanest kid in the room. And when the picture was finished, you didn't see the dirt or the meanness; you saw the glory of innocence and the poignancy of a baby growing up too soon. Oh, Miss Bernstone was grand.

These two visiting teachers were the gold and silver sun-splash in the great muddy river of school days, days made up of dreary hours in which Teacher made her pupils sit rigid with their hands folded behind their back while she read a novel hidden in her lap. If all the teachers had been like Miss Bernstone and Mr. Morton, Francie would have known plain what heaven was. But it was just as well. There had to be the dark and muddy waters so that the sun could have something to background its flashing glory.

22

Oh, magic hour when a child first knows it can read printed words!

For quite a while, Francie had been spelling out letters, sounding them and then putting the sounds together to mean a word. But one day, she looked at a page and the word "mouse" had instantaneous meaning. She looked at the word and the picture of a gray mouse scampered through her mind. She looked further and when she saw "horse," she heard him pawing the ground and saw the sun glint on his glossy coat. The word "running" hit her suddenly and she breathed hard as though running herself. The barrier between the individual sound of each letter and the whole meaning of the word was removed and the printed word meant a thing at one quick glance. She read a few pages rapidly and almost became ill with excitement. She wanted to shout it out. She could read! She could read!

From that time on, the world was hers for the reading. She would never be lonely again, never miss the lack of intimate friends. Books became her friends and there was one for every mood. There was poetry for quiet companionship. There was adventure when she tired of quiet hours. There would be love stories when she came into adolescence and when she wanted to feel a closeness to someone she could read a biography. On that day when she first knew she could read, she made a vow to read one book a day as long as she lived.

She liked numbers and sums. She devised a game in which each number was a family member and the "answer" made a family grouping with a story to it. Naught was a babe in arms. He gave no trouble. Whenever he appeared you just "carried" him. The figure 1 was a pretty baby girl just learning to walk, and easy to handle; 2 was a baby boy who could walk and talk a little. He went into family life (into sums, etc.) with very little trouble. And 3 was an older boy in kindergarten, who had to be watched a little. Then there was 4, a girl of Francie's age. She was almost as easy to "mind" as 2. The mother was 5, gentle and kind. In large sums, she came along and made everything easy the way a mother should. The father, 6, was harder than the others but very just. But 7 was mean. He was a crotchety old grandfather and not at all accountable for how he came out. The grandmother, 8, was hard too, but easier to understand than 7. Hardest of all was 9. He was company and what a hard time fitting *him* into family life!

When Francie added a sum, she would fix a little story to go with the result. If the answer was 924, it meant that the little boy and girl were being minded by company while the rest of the family went out. When a number such as 1024 appeared, it meant that all the little children were playing together in the yard. The number 62 meant that papa was taking the little boy for a walk; 50 meant that mama had the baby out in the buggy for an airing and 78 meant grandfather and grandmother sitting home by the fire of a winter's evening. Each single combination of numbers was a new set-up for the family and no two stories were ever the same.

Francie took the game with her up into algebra. X was the boy's sweetheart who came into the family life and complicated it. Y was the boy friend who caused trouble. So arithmetic was a warm and human thing to Francie and occupied many lonely hours of her time.

23

School days went along. Some were made up of meanness, brutality and heartbreak; others were bright and beautiful because of Miss Bernstone and Mr. Morton. And always, there was the magic of learning things.

Francie was out walking one Saturday in October and she chanced on an unfamiliar neighborhood. Here were no tenements or raucous shabby stores. There were old houses that had been standing there when Washington maneuvered his troops across Long Island. They were old and decrepit but there were picket fences around them with gates on which Francie longed to swing. There were bright fall flowers in the front yard and maple trees with crimson and yellow leaves on the curb. The neighborhood stood old, quiet and serene in the Saturday sunshine. There was a brooding quality about the neighborhood, a quiet, deep, timeless, shabby peace. Francie was as happy as though, like Alice, she had stepped through a magic miror. She was in an enchanted land.

She walked on further and came to a little old school. Its old bricks glowed garnet in the late afternoon sun. There was no fence around the school yard and the school grounds were grass and not cement. Across from the school, it was practically open country—a meadow with goldenrod, wild asters and clover growing in it.

Francie's heart turned over. This was it! This was the school she wanted to go to. But how could she get to go there? There was a strict law about attending the school in your own district. Her parents would have to move to that neighborhood if she wanted to go to that school. Francie knew that mama wouldn't move just because *she* felt like going to another school. She walked home slowly thinking about it.

She sat up that night waiting for papa to come home from work. After Johnny had come home whistling his "Molly Malone" as he ran up the steps, after all had eaten of the lobster, caviar, and liverwurst that he brought home, mama and Neeley went to bed. Francie kept papa company while he smoked his last cigar. Francie whispered all about the school in papa's ear. He looked at her, nodded, and said, "We'll see tomorrow."

"You mean we can move near that school?"

"No, but there has to be another way. I'll go there with you tomorrow and we'll see what we can see."

Francie was so excited she couldn't sleep the rest of the night. She was up at seven but Johnny was still sleeping soundly. She waited in a perspiration of impatience. Each time he sighed in his sleep, she ran in to see if he was waking up.

He woke about noon and the Nolans sat down to dinner. Francie couldn't eat. She kept looking at papa but he made her no sign. Had he forgotten? Had he forgotten? No, because while Katie was pouring the coffee, he said carelessly,

"I guess me and the prima donna will take a little walk later on."

Francie's heart jumped. He had not forgotten. He had not forgotten. She waited. Mama had to answer. Mama might object. Mama might ask why. Mama might say she guessed she'd go along too. But all mama said was, "All right."

Francie did the dishes. Then she had to go down to the candy store to get the Sunday paper; then to the cigar store to get papa a nickel Corona. Johnny had to read the paper. He had to read every column of it including the society section in which he couldn't possibly be interested. Worse than that, he had to make comments to mama on every item he read. Each time he'd put the paper aside, turn to mama and say, "Funny things in the papers nowadays. Take this case," Francie would almost cry.

Four o'clock came. The cigar had long since been smoked, the paper lay gutted on the floor, Katie had tired of having the news analyzed and had taken Neeley and gone over to visit Mary Rommely.

Francie and papa set out hand in hand. He was wearing his only suit, the tuxedo and his derby hat and he looked very grand. It was a splendid October day. There was a warm sun and a refreshing wind working together to bring the tang of the ocean around each corner. They walked a few blocks, turned a corner and were in this other neighborhood. Only in a great sprawling place like Brooklyn could there be such a sharp division. It was a neighborhood peopled by fifth and sixth generation Americans, whereas in the Nolan neighborhood, if you could prove *you* had been born in America, it was equivalent to a Mayflower standing.

Indeed, Francie was the only one in her classroom whose parents were American-born. At the beginning of the term, Teacher called the roll and asked each child her lineage. The answers were typical.

"I'm Polish-American. My father was born in Warsaw."

"Irish-American. Me fayther and mither were born in County Cork."

When Nolan was called, Francie answered proudly: "I'm an American."

"I *know* you're American," said the easily exasperated teacher. "But what's your nationality?"

"American!" insisted Francie even more proudly.

"Will you tell me what your parents are or do I have to send you to the principal?"

"My parents are American. They were born in Brooklyn."

All the children turned around to look at a little girl whose parents had *not* come from the old country. And when Teacher said, "Brooklyn? Hm. I guess that makes you American, all right," Francie was proud and happy. How wonderful was Brooklyn, she thought, when just being born there automatically made you an American!

Papa told her about this strange neighborhood: how its families had been Americans for more than a hundred years back; how they were mostly Scotch, English and Welsh extraction. The men worked as cabinet makers and fine carpenters. They worked with metals: gold, silver and copper.

He promised to take Francie to the Spanish section of Brooklyn some day. There the men worked as cigarmakers and each chipped in a few pennies a day to hire a man to read to them while they worked. And the man read fine literature.

They walked along the quiet Sunday street. Francie saw a leaf flutter from a tree and she skipped ahead to get it. It was a clear scarlet with an edging of gold. She stared at it, wondering if she'd ever see anything as beautiful again. A woman came from around the corner. She was rouged heavily and wore a feather boa. She smiled at Johnny and said.

"Lonesome, Mister?"

Johnny looked at her a moment before he answered gently,

"No, Sister."

"Sure?" she inquired archly.

"Sure," he answered quietly.

She went her way. Francie skipped back and took papa's hand.

"Was that a bad lady, Papa?" she asked eagerly.

"No."

"But she *looked* bad."

"There are very few bad people. There are just a lot of people that are unlucky."

"But she was all painted and . . ."

"She was one who had seen better days." He liked the phrase. "Yes, she may have seen better days." He fell into a thoughtful mood. Francie kept skipping ahead and collecting leaves.

They came upon the school and Francie proudly showed it to papa. The late afternoon sun warmed its softly-colored bricks and the small-paned windows seemed to dance in the sunshine. Johnny looked at it a long time, then he said,

"Yes, this is the school. This is it."

Then, as whenever he was moved or stirred, he had to put it

into a song. He held his worn derby over his heart, stood up straight looking up at the school house and sang:

> *School days, school days,*
> *Dear old golden rule days.*
> *Readin' 'n writin' 'n 'rithmetic . . .*

To a passing stranger, it might have looked silly—Johnny standing there in his greenish tuxedo and fresh linen holding the hand of a thin ragged child and singing the banal song so un-self-consciously on the street. But to Francie it seemed right and beautiful.

They crossed the street and wandered in the meadow that folks called "lots." Francie picked a bunch of goldenrod and wild asters to take home. Johnny explained that the place had once been an Indian burying ground and how as a boy, he had often come there to hunt arrowheads. Francie suggested they hunt for some. They searched for half an hour and found none. Johnny recalled that as a boy, he hadn't found any either. This struck Francie as funny and she laughed. Papa confessed that maybe it hadn't been an Indian cemetery after all; maybe someone had made up that story. Johnny was more than right because he had made up the whole story himself.

Soon it was time to go home and tears came into Francie's eyes because papa hadn't said anything about getting her into the new school. He saw the tears and figured out a scheme immediately.

"Tell you what we'll do, Baby. We'll walk around and pick out a nice house and take down the number. I'll write a letter to your principal saying you're moving there and want to be transferred to this school."

They found a house—a one-story white one with a slanting roof and late chrysanthemums growing in the yard. He copied the address carefully.

"You know that what we are going to do is wrong?"

"Is it, Papa?"

"But it's a wrong to gain a bigger good."

"Like a white lie?"

"Like a lie that helps someone out. So you must make up for the wrong by being twice as good. You must never be bad or absent or late. You must never do anything to make them send a letter home through the mails."

"I'll always be good, Papa, if I can go to that school."

"Yes. Now I'll show you a way to go to school through a little park. I know right where it is. Yes sir, I know right where it is."

He showed her the park and how she could walk through it diagonally to go to school.

"That should make you happy. You can see the seasons change as you come and go. What do you say to that?"

Francie, recalling something her mother had once read to her answered, "My cup runneth over." And she meant it.

When Katie heard of the plan, she said: "Suit yourself. But I'll have nothing to do with it. If the police come and arrest you for giving a false address, I'll say honestly that I had nothing to do with it. One school's as good or as bad as another. I don't know why she wants to change. There's homework no matter what school you go to."

"It's settled then," Johnny said. "Francie, here's a penny. Run down to the candy store and get a sheet of writing paper and an envelope."

Francie ran down and ran back. Johnny wrote a note saying Francie was going to live with relatives at such and such an address and wanted a transfer. He added that Neeley would continue living at home and wouldn't require a transfer. He signed his name and underlined it authoritatively.

Tremblingly, Francie handed the note to her principal next morning. That lady read it, grunted, made out the transfer, handed her her report card and told her to go; that the school was too crowded anyhow.

Francie presented herself and documents to the principal of the new school. He shook hands with her and said he hoped she'd be happy in the new school. A monitor took her to the classroom. The teacher stopped the work and introduced Francie to the class.

Francie looked out over the rows of little girls. All were shabby but most were clean. She was given a seat to herself and happily fell into the routine of the new school.

The teachers and children here were not as brutalized as in the old school. Yes, some of the children were mean but it seemed a natural child-meanness and not a campaign. Often the teachers were impatient and cross but never naggingly cruel. There was no corporal punishment either. The parents were too American, too aware of the rights granted them by their Constitution to accept injustices meekly. They could not be bulldozed and exploited as could the immigrants and the second generation Americans.

Francie found that the different feeling in this school came mostly from the janitor. He was a ruddy white-haired man whom even the principal addressed as *Mister* Jenson. He had many children and grandchildren of his own, all of whom he loved dearly. He was father to all children. On rainy days when children came to school soaked, he insisted that they be sent down to the furnace room to dry out. He made them take off their wet shoes and hung their wet stockings on a line to dry. The little shabby shoes stood in a row before the furnace.

It was pleasant down in the furnace room. The walls were white-washed and the big red-painted furnace was a comforting thing. The windows were high up in the walls. Francie liked to sit there and enjoy the warmth and watch the orange and blue flames dancing an inch above the bed of small black coals. (He left the furnace door open when the children were drying out.) On rainy days, she left earlier and walked to school slower so that she would be soaking wet and rate the privilege of drying in the furnace room.

It was unorthodox for Mr. Jenson to keep the children out of class to dry but everyone liked and respected him too much to protest. Francie heard stories around the school concerning Mr. Jenson. She heard that he had been to college and knew more than the principal did. They said he had married and when the children came, had decided that there was more money in being a school engineer than in being a school teacher. Whatever it was, he was liked and respected. Once Francie saw him in the principal's office. He was in his clean striped overalls sitting there with his knees crossed and talking politics. Francie heard that the principal often came down to Mr. Jenson's furnace room to sit and talk for a few moments while he smoked a pipeful of tobacco.

When a boy was bad, he wasn't sent to the principal's office for a licking; he was sent down to Mr. Jenson's room for a talking to. Mr. Jenson never scolded a bad boy. He talked to him about his own youngest son who was a pitcher on the Brooklyn team. He talked about democracy and good citizenship and about a good world where everyone did the best he could for the common good of all. After a talk with Mr. Jenson, the boy could be counted upon not to cause any more trouble.

At graduation, the children asked the principal to sign the first page of their autograph book out of respect to his position but they valued Mr. Jenson's autograph more and he always got the second page to sign. The principal signed quickly in a great sprawling hand. But not Mr. Jenson. He made a ceremony out of it. He took the book over to his big roll-top desk and lit the light over it. He sat down, carefully polished his spectacles and chose a pen. He dipped it in ink, squinted at it, wiped it off and re-dipped it. Then he signed his name in a fine steel-engraving script and blotted it carefully. His signature was always the finest in the book. If you had the nerve to ask him, he'd take the book home and ask his son, who was with the Dodgers, to sign it too. This was a wonderful thing for the boys. The girls didn't care.

Mr. Jenson's handwriting was so wonderful that he wrote out all the diplomas by request.

Mr. Morton and Miss Bernstone came to that school, too. When they were teaching, Mr. Jenson would often come in and squeeze himself into one of the back seats and enjoy the lesson too. On a cold day, he'd have Mr. Morton or Miss Bernstone come down to his furnace room for a hot cup of coffee before they went on to the next school.

He had a gas plate and coffee-making equipment on a little table. He served strong, hot black coffee in thick cups and these visiting teachers blessed his good soul.

Francie was happy in this school. She was very careful about being a good girl. Each day, as she passed the house whose number she claimed, she looked at it with gratitude and affection. On windy days, when papers blew before it, she went about picking up the debris and depositing it in the gutter before the house. Mornings after the rubbish man had emptied the burlap bag and had carelessly tossed the empty bag on the walk instead of in the yard, Francie picked it up and hung it on a fence paling. The people who lived in the house came to look on her as a quiet child who had a queer complex about tidiness.

Francie loved that school. It meant that she had to walk forty-eight blocks each day but she loved the walk, too. She had to leave earlier in the morning than Neeley and she got home much later. She didn't mind except that it was a little hard at lunch time. There were twelve blocks to come home and twelve to go back—all in the hour. It left little time for eating. Mama wouldn't let her carry a lunch. Her reason was:

"She'll be weaned away from her home and family soon enough the way she's growing up. But while she's still a child she has to act like a child and come home and eat the way children should. Is it my fault that she has to go so far to school? Didn't she pick it out herself?"

"But Katie," argued papa, "it's such a good school."

"Then let her take the bad along with this good."

The lunch question was settled. Francie had about five minutes for lunch—just time enough to report home for a sandwich which she ate walking back to school. She never considered herself put upon. She was so happy in the new school that she was anxious to pay in some way for this joy.

It was a good thing that she got herself into this other school. It showed her that there were other worlds beside the world she had been born into and that these other worlds were not unattainable.

24

Francie counted the year's passing not by the days or the months but by the holidays that came along. Her year started with the Fourth of July because it was the first holiday that came along after school closed. A week before the day, she began accumulating firecrackers. Every available penny went for packets of small crackers. She hoarded them in a box under the bed. At least ten times a day, she'd take the box out, re-arrange the fireworks and look long at the pale red tissue and white corded stem and wonder about how they were made. She smelled the thick bit of punk which was given gratis with each purchase and which, when lit, smoldered for hours and was used to set off the firecrackers.

When the great day came, she was reluctant to set them off. It was better to have them than to use them. One year when times were harder than usual and pennies could not be had, Francie and Neeley hoarded paper bags and on the day, filled them with water, twisted the tops shut and dropped them from the roof on to the street below. They made a nice plop which was almost like a firecracker. Passers-by were irritated and looked up angrily when a bag just missed them but they did nothing about it, accepting the fact that poor children had a custom of celebrating the Fourth that way.

The next holiday was Halloween. Neeley blackened his face

with soot, wore his cap backwards and his coat inside out. He filled one of his mother's long black stockings with ashes and roamed the streets with his gang swinging his homely blackjack and crying out raucously from time to time.

Francie, in company with other little girls, roamed the streets carrying a bit of white chalk. She went about drawing a large quick cross on the back of each coated figure that came by. The children performed the ritual without meaning. The symbol was remembered but the reason forgotten. It may have been something that had survived from the middle ages when houses and probably individuals were so marked to indicate where plague had struck. Probably the ruffians of that time so marked innocent people as a cruel joke and the practice had persisted down through the centuries to be distorted into a meaningless Halloween prank.

Election Day seemed the greatest holiday of all to Francie. It, more than any other time, belonged to the whole neighborhood. Maybe people voted in other parts of the country too, but it couldn't be the way it was in Brooklyn, thought Francie.

Johnny showed Francie an Oyster House on Scholes Street. It was housed in a building that had been standing there more than a hundred years before when Big Chief Tammany himself skulked around with his braves. Its oyster fries were known throughout the state. But there was something else that made this place famous. It was the secret meeting place of the great City Hall politicians. The party sachems met here in secret pow-wow in a private dining room and over succulent oysters, they decided who'd be elected and who mowed down.

Francie often passed by the store, looked at it and was thrilled. It had no name over its door and its window was empty save for a potted fern and a half curtain of brown linen run on brass rods along the back of it. Once Francie saw the door open to admit someone. She had a glimpse of a low room dimly lit with dulled red-shaded lamps and thick with the smoke of cigars.

Francie, along with the other neighborhood children, went through some of the Election rites without knowing their meaning or reason. On Election night, she got in line, her hands on the shoulders of the child in front, and snake-danced through the streets singing,

> *Tammany, Tammany,*
> *Big Chief sits in his teepee,*
> *Cheering braves to victory,*
> *Tamma-nee, Tamma-nee.*

She was an interested listener at the debates between mama and papa on the merits and faults of the party. Papa was an ardent Democrat but mama just didn't care. Mama criticized the party and told Johnny he was throwing his vote away.

"Don't say that, Katie," he protested. "By and large the party does a lot of good for the people."

"I can just imagine," sniffed mama.

"All they want is a vote from the man of the family and look what they give in exchange."

"Name one thing *they* give."

"Well, you need advice on a legal matter. You don't need a lawyer. Just ask your Assemblyman."

"The blind leading the blind."

"Don't you believe it. They may be dumb in many ways but they know the City's statues backward and forward."

"Sue the City for something and see how far Tammany will help you."

"Take Civil Service," said Johnny starting on another angle. "They know when the examinations for cops, firemen or letter carriers are coming up. They'll always put a voter wise if he's interested."

"Mrs. Lavey's husband took the examination for letter carrier three years ago. He's still working on a truck."

"Ah! That's because he's a Republican. If he was a Democrat, they'd take his name and put it on the top of the list. I heard about a teacher who wanted to be transferred to another school. Tammany fixed it up."

"Why? Unless she was pretty."

"That's not the point. It was a shrewd move. Teachers are educating future voters. This teacher, for instance, will always say a good word for Tammany to her pupils whenever she can. Every boy has to grow up to vote, you know."

"Why?"

"Because it's a privilege."

"Privilege! Humpf!" sneered Katie.

"Now, for instance, if you had a poodle and it died, what would you do?"

"What would I do with a poodle in the first place?"

"Can't you make out like you have a dead poodle just for the sake of conversation?"

"All right. My poodle's dead. Now what?"

"You go around to Headquarters and the boys will take it away for you. Suppose Francie wanted to get working papers but was too young."

"They'd get them, I suppose."

"Certainly."

"Do you think that's right to fix it so little children can work in factories?"

"Well, supposing you had a bad boy who played hooky from school and was getting to be a loafer hanging around street corners but the law wouldn't let him work. Wouldn't it be better if he got faked working papers?"

"In that case, yes," conceded Katie.

"Look at all the jobs they get for voters."

"You know how they get them, don't you? They inspect a factory and overlook the fact that they're violating the factory laws. Naturally, the boss pays back by letting them know when they need men and Tammany gets all the credit for finding jobs."

"Here's another case. A man has relatives in the old country but he can't get them over here on account of a lot of red tape. Well, Tammany can fix that up."

"Sure, they get them foreigners over here and see to it that they start in on their citizenship papers and then tell them they must vote the Democratic ticket or go back where they came from."

"No matter what you say, Tammany's good to the poor people. Say a man's been sick and can't pay his rent. Do you think the organization would let the landlord dispossess him? No sir. Not if he's a Democrat."

"I suppose the landlords are all Republicans, then," Katie said.

"No. The system works both ways. Suppose the landlord has a bum for a tenant who gives him a punch in the nose instead of the rent. What happens? The organization dispossesses him for the landlord."

"For what Tammany gives to the people, it takes from them double. You wait until us women vote." Johnny's laugh interrupted her. "You don't believe we will? That day will come. Mark my words. We'll put all those crooked politicians where they belong—behind iron bars."

"If that day ever comes when women vote, you'll go along to the polls with me—arm in arm—and vote the way I do." He put his arm around her and gave her a quick hug.

Katie smiled up at him. Francie couldn't help noticing that mama was smiling sidewise, the way the lady did in the picture in the school auditorium, the one they called *Mona Lisa*.

Tammany owed much of its power to the fact that it got the children young and educated them in the party ways. The dumbest ward heeler was smart enough to know that time, no matter what else it did, passed, and that the school boy of today was the voter of tomorrow. They got the boys on their side and the girls, too. A woman couldn't vote in those days but the politicians knew that the women of Brooklyn had a great influence on their men. Bring a little girl up in the party way and when she married, she'd see to it that her man voted the straight Democratic ticket. To woo the children, the Mattie Mahony Association ran an excursion for them and their parents each summer. Although Katie had nothing but contempt for the Organization, she saw no reason why they shouldn't take advantage of the good time. When Francie heard that they were going, she was as excited as only a ten-year-old, who had never been on a boat before, could be.

Johnny refused to go and couldn't see why Katie wanted to go. "I'm going because I like life," was her strange reason.

"If that racket's life, I wouldn't take it with coupons," he said.

But he went anyhow. He figured the boat trip might be educational and he wanted to be on hand to educate the children. It was a hot sweltering day. The decks teemed with kids, wild with excitement, racing up and down and trying to fall into the Hudson River. Francie stared and stared at the moving water until she worked up the first headache of her life. Johnny told his children how Hendrick Hudson had sailed up that same river so long ago. Francie wondered whether Mr. Hudson got sick to his stomach like she did. Mama sat on deck looking very pretty in her jade green straw hat and a yellow dotted-swiss dress that she had borrowed from Aunt Evy. People around her were laughing. Mama was a vivid conversationalist and people liked to hear her talk.

Soon after noon, the boat docked at a wooded glen upstate and the Democrats got off the boat and took over. The kids ran around spending their tickets. The week before, each child had been given a strip of ten tickets labeled "hot dog," "soda water," "merry-go-round" and so on. Francie and Neeley had each been given a strip but Francie had been tempted by some shrewd boys into gambling her tickets in a marble game. They had told her how she might possibly win fifty strips and have a grand day on the excursion. Francie was a poor marble player and quickly lost her tickets. Neeley, on the other hand, had three strips. He had been lucky. Francie asked mama could she have one of Neeley's tickets. Mama seized the opportunity to give her a lecture on gambling.

"You had tickets but you thought you could be smart and get something you weren't entitled to. When people gamble, they think only of winning. They never think of losing. Remember this: Someone has to lose and it's just as apt to be you as the other fellow. If you learn this lesson by giving up a strip of tickets, you're paying cheap for the education."

Mama was right. Francie *knew* she was right. But it didn't make her happy at all. She wanted to go on the merry-go-round like the other kids. She wanted a drink of soda. She was standing disconsolately near the hot dog stand watching other children stuff themselves when a man paused to speak to her. He wore a policeman's uniform only with more gold on it.

"No tickets, little girl?" he asked.

"I forgot them," lied Francie.

"Sure and I was no good at marbles meself as a boy." He pulled three strips from his pocket. "We count on makin' up a certain number of losses each year. But it's seldom the girls are the losin' ones. They hang on to what they have be it ever so little." Francie took the tickets, thanked him and was backing off when he asked, "Would that be your mother sittin' over there in the green hat?"

"Yes." She waited. He said nothing. Finally she asked, "Why?"

"Do you be sayin' your prayers to the Little Flower each night askin' that you grow up half as pretty as your mother. Do that now."

"And that's my papa next to my mama." Francie waited to hear him say that papa was good-looking, too. He stared at Johnny and said nothing. Francie ran off.

Francie was instructed to report back to her mother at half hour intervals during the day. At the next interval when Francie came back, Johnny was over at the free beer keg. Mama teased her.

"You're like Aunt Sissy—always talking to men in uniform."

"He gave me extra tickets."

"I saw." Katie's next words were casual enough. "What did he ask you?"

"He asked was you my mama." Francie did not tell her what he said about mama being pretty.

"Yes, I thought he was asking that." Katie stared at her hands. They were rough and red and cut into with cleansing fluids. She took a pair of mended cotton gloves from her purse. Although it was a hot day, she pulled them on. She sighed. "I work so hard, sometimes I forget that I'm a woman."

Francie was startled. It was the nearest thing to a complaint she had ever heard from mama. She wondered why mama was ashamed of her hands all of a sudden. As she skipped away, she heard mama ask the lady next to her,

"Who's that man over there—the one in the uniform looking this way?"

"That would be Sergeant Michael McShane. It's funny you don't know who he is seein' that it's from your own precinct he is."

The day of joy went on. There was a keg of beer set up at the end of each long table and it was free to all good Democrats. Francie was caught up in the excitement and tore around, screamed and fought like the other children. Beer flowed like a Brooklyn gutter after a rainstorm. A brass band played doggedly. It played "The Kerry Dancers" and "When Irish Eyes Are Smiling" and "Harrigan, That's Me." It played "The River Shannon" and New York's own folk song, "The Sidewalks of New York."

The conductor announced each selection: "Mattie Mahony's Band will now play. . . ." Each song ended with the band members shouting in unison, "Hurray for Mattie Mahony." With each glass of beer drawn, the attendants said, "Compliments of Mattie Mahony." Each event was labeled, "The Mattie Mahony Foot Race," "The Mahony Peanut Race" and so on. Before the day was over, Francie was convinced that Mattie Mahony was a very great man indeed.

Late in the afternoon, Francie got the idea that she ought to find Mr. Mahony and thank him personally for a very nice time. She searched and searched, and asked and asked and a strange thing happened. No one knew Mattie Mahony; no one had ever seen him. Certainly he was not at the picnic. His presence was felt everywhere but the man was invisible. Some man told her that maybe there was no Mattie Mahony; it was just the name they gave to whatever man was head of the organization.

"I been votin' the straight ticket for forty years," he said. "Seems like the candidate was always the same man, Mattie Mahony; or else it was a different man but with the same name. I don't know who he is, Girlie. All I know is that I vote the straight Democratic ticket."

The trip home down the moonlit Hudson was notable only for the many fights that broke out among the men. Most of the children were sick and sunburnt and fretful. Neeley fell asleep on mama's lap. Francie sat on the deck and listened to mama and papa talking.

"Do you happen to know Sergeant McShane?" Katie asked.

"I know who he is. They call him the Honest Cop. The party has its eye on him. It wouldn't surprise me if he was put up for Assemblyman."

A man sitting near-by leaned forward and touched Johnny's arm. "Police Commissioner is more like it, Mac," he said.

"What about his life?" Katie asked.

"It's like one of those Alger stories. He came from Ireland twenty-five years ago with nothing but a trunk small enough to be carried on his back. He worked as a dock walloper, studied nights and got on the force. He kept on studying and taking examinations and finally got to be Sergeant," said Johnny.

"I suppose he's married to an educated woman who helped him?"

"Matter of fact, no. When he first came over, an Irish family took him in and kept him till he got on his feet. The daughter of the family married a bum who ran out on her after the honeymoon and got himself killed in a brawl. Well, the girl was going to have a baby and you couldn't make the neighbors believe she had ever been married. Seems like the family would be disgraced but McShane married her and gave the child his name to kind of repay the family. It wasn't a love marriage, exactly, but he's been very good to her, I hear."

"Did they have children together?"

"Fourteen, I heard."

"Fourteen!"

"But he only raised four. Seemed like they all died before they grew up. They were all born with consumption, you know, inherited it from their mother who had it from a girl."

"He's had more than his share of trouble," mused Johnny. "And he's a good man."

"She's still alive, I suppose."

"But very sick. They say she hasn't long to live."

"Oh, those kind hang on."

"Katie!" Johnny was startled by his wife's remark.

"I don't care! I don't blame her for marrying a bum and having a child by him. That's her privilege. But I do blame her for not taking her medicine when the time came due. Why did she put her troubles off on to a good man?"

"That's no way to talk."

"I hope she dies and dies soon."

"Hush, Katie."

"Yes, I do. So that he can marry again—marry a cheerful healthy woman who'll give him children that can live. That's every good man's right."

Johnny said nothing. A nameless fear had grown within Francie while she listened to her mother talking. Now she got up and went over to papa, took his hand and pressed it hard. In the moonlight, Johnny's eyes flew open in startled surprise. He pulled the child to him and held her tightly. But all he said was,

"Look how the moon walks on the water."

Soon after the picnic, the organization began to prepare for Election Day. They distributed shiny white buttons with Mattie's mug on them to the neighborhood kids. Francie got some and stared long at the face. Mattie had grown so mysterious to her, that he took the place of someone like the Holy Ghost—he was never seen but his presence was felt. The picture was of a bland-faced man with roached hair and handlebar mustaches. It looked like the face of any small-time politician. Francie wished she could see him—just once in the flesh.

There was a lot of excitement about these buttons. The children used them for trading purposes, for games and coin of the realm. Neeley sold his top to a boy for ten buttons. Gimpy, the candy-store man, redeemed fifteen of Francie's buttons for a penny's worth of candy. (He had an arangement with the Organization whereby he got the money back for the buttons.) Francie went around looking for Mattie and found him all over. She found boys playing pitch games with his face. She found him flattened out on a car track to make a miniature potsy. He was in the debris of Neeley's pocket. She peered down the sewer and saw him floating face upward. She found him in the sour soil at the bottoms of gratings. She saw Punky Perkins, next to her in church, drop two buttons in the plate in lieu of the two pennies his mother had given him. She saw him go into the candy store and buy four Sweet Caporal cigarettes with the two cents after mass. She saw Mattie's face everywhere but she never saw Mattie.

The week before Election she went around with Neeley and the boys gathering "'lection" which was what they called the lumber for the big bonfires which would be lighted Election night. She helped store the lection in the cellar.

She was up early on Election Day and saw the man who came and knocked on the door. When Johnny answered, the man said,

"Nolan?"

"Yes," admitted Johnny.

"At the polls, eleven o'clock." He checked Johnny's name on his list. He handed Johnny a cigar. "Compliments of Mattie Mahony." He went on to the next Democrat.

"Wouldn't you go anyhow without being told?" Francie asked.

"Yes, but they give us each a time so that the voting is staggered . . . you know, not everyone coming in a bunch."

"Why?" persisted Francie.

"'Cause," Johnny evaded.

"I'll tell you why," broke in mama. "They want to keep tabs on who's voting and how. They know when each man's due at the polls and God help him if he doesn't show up to vote for Mattie."

"Women don't know anything about politics," said Johnny lighting up Mattie's cigar.

Francie helped Neeley drag their wood out on Election night. They contributed it to the biggest bonfire on the block. Francie got in line with the other children and danced around the fire Indian fashion, singing "Tammany." When the fire had burned down to embers, the boys raided the pushcarts of the Jewish merchants and stole potatoes which they roasted in the ashes. So cooked, they were called "mickies." There weren't enough to go around and Francie didn't get any.

She stood on the street watching the returns come in on a bed sheet stretched from window to window of a house on the corner. A magic lantern across the street threw the figures on the sheet.

Each time new returns came in, Francie shouted with the other kids,

"Another country heard from!"

Mattie's picture appeared on the screen from time to time and the crowd cheered itself hoarse. A Democratic president was elected that year and the Democratic governor of the state was re-elected, but all that Francie knew was that Mattie Mahony got in again.

After Election, the politicians forgot their promises and enjoyed an earned rest until New Year, when they started work on the next Election. January second was Ladies' Day at Democratic Head-quarters. On that day and no other, ladies were received into this strictly masculine precinct and treated to sherry wine and little seeded cakes. All day, the ladies kept calling and were received gallantly by Mattie's henchmen. Mattie himself never showed up. As the ladies went out, they left their little decorated cards with their names written on them in the cut-glass dish on the hall table.

Katie's contempt for the politicians did not interfere with her making her yearly call. She put on her brushed and pressed gray suit with all the braid on it and tilted her jade green velvet hat over her right eye. She even gave the penman, who set up temporary shop outside headquarters, a dime to make a card for her. He wrote *Mrs. John Nolan* with flowers and angels crawling out of the capitals. It was a dime that should have gone into the bank, but Katie figured she could be extravagant once a year.

The family awaited her homecoming. They wanted to hear all about the call.

"How was it this year?" asked Johnny.

"The same as always. The same old push was there. A lot of women had new clothes which I bet they bought on time. Of course, the prostitutes were the best dressed," said Katie in her forthright way, "and like always, they outnumbered the decent women two to one."

25

Johnny was one for taking notions. He'd take a notion that life was too much for him and start drinking heavier to forget it. Francie got to know when he was drinking more than usual. He walked straighter coming home. He walked carefully and slightly sidewise. When he was drunk, he was a quiet man. He didn't brawl, he didn't sing, he didn't grow sentimental. He grew thoughtful. People who didn't know him thought that he was drunk when he was sober, because sober, he was full of song and excitement. When he was drunk, strangers looked on him as a quiet, thoughtful man who minded his own business.

Francie dreaded the drinking periods—not on moral grounds but because papa wasn't a man she knew then. He wouldn't talk to her or to anybody. He looked at her with the eyes of a stranger. When mama spoke to him, he turned his head away from her.

When he got over a drinking time, he'd take a notion that he had to be a better father to his children. He felt that he had to teach them things. He'd stop drinking for awhile, take a notion to work hard and devote all his spare time to Francie and Neeley. He had the same idea that Katie's mother, Mary Rommely, had about education. He wanted to teach his children all that he knew so that at fourteen or fifteen, they would know as much as he knew at thirty. He figured they could go on from there picking up their own knowledge and according to his calculations when they reached thirty, they would be twice as smart as he had been at thirty.

He felt that they needed lessons in—for what passed in his mind—geography, civics and sociology. So he took them over to Bushwick Avenue.

Bushwick Avenue was the high-toned boulevard of old Brooklyn. It was a wide, tree-shaded avenue and the houses were rich and impressively built of large granite blocks with long stone stoops. Here lived the big-time politicians, the monied brewery families, the well-to-do immigrants who had been able to come over first-class instead of steerage. They had taken their money, their statuary and their gloomy oil paintings and had come to America and settled in Brooklyn.

Automobiles were coming into use but most of these families still clung to their handsome horses and magnificent carriages. Papa pointed out and described the various equipages to Francie. She watched in awe as they rolled by.

There were small lacquered dainty ones lined with tufted white satin, with a large fringed umbrella that was used by fine and delicate ladies. There were adorable wicker ones with a bench along each side on which lucky children sat while they were pulled along by a Shetland pony. She stared at the capable-looking governesses who accompanied these children—women from another world, in capes and starch-stringed bonnets who sat sideways on the seat to drive the pony.

Francie saw practical black two-seaters drawn by a single high-stepping horse controlled by dandified young men in kid gloves with edges turned back to look like inverted cuffs.

She saw staid family vehicles drawn by dependable looking teams. These coaches did not impress Francie very much because every undertaker in Williamsburg had a string of them.

Francie liked the hansom cabs best. How magic they were with only two wheels and that funny door that closed by itself when a passenger sat back in the seat! (Francie thought in her innocence that the doors were meant to protect the passenger from flying horse manure.) If I were a man, thought Francie, that's the job I'd like to have, driving one of them. Oh, to sit high up in the back with a brave whip in a socket close to hand. Oh, to wear such a great coat with large buttons and a velvet collar and a squashed-down high hat with a ribbon cockade in the band! Oh, to have such an expensive-looking blanket folded over her knees! Francie imitated the drivers' cry under her breath.

"Kerridge, sir? Kerridge?"

"Anybody," said Johnny, carried away by his personal dream of Democracy, "can ride in one of those hansom cabs, provided," he qualified, "they got the money. So you can see what a free country we got here."

"What's free about it if you have to *pay?*" asked Francie.

"It's free in this way: If you have the money you're allowed to ride in them no matter who you are. In the old countries, certain people aren't free to ride in them, even if they have the money."

"Wouldn't it be more of a free country," persisted Francie, "if we could ride in them free?"

"No."

"Why?"

"Because that would be Socialism," concluded Johnny triumphantly, "and we don't want that over here."

"Why?"

"Because we got Democracy and that's the best thing there is," clinched Johnny.

There were rumors that New York City's next Mayor would come from Bushwick Avenue, Brooklyn. The idea stirred Johnny. "Look up and down this block, Francie, and show me where our future Mayor lives."

Francie looked, then had to hang her head and say, "I don't know, Papa."

"There!" announced Johnny as though he were blowing a trumpet fanfare. "Someday that house over there will have two lamp posts at the bottom of the stoop. And no matter where you roam in this great city," he orated, "and you come across a house with two lamp posts, you'll know that the Mayor of the greatest City in the world lives there."

"What will he need two lamp posts for?" Francie wanted to know.

"Because this is America and in a country where such things are," concluded Johnny vaguely but very patriotically, "you know that the government is by the people, for the people, of the people and shall not perish from the face of the earth the way it does in the old countries." He began to sing under his breath. Soon he was carried away by his feeling and started to sing louder. Francie joined in. Johnny sang:

> *You're a grand old flag,*
> *You're a high-flying flag,*
> *And forever in peace may you wave . . .* *

People stared at Johnny curiously and one kind lady threw him a penny.

Francie had another memory about Bushwick Avenue. It was tied up with the scent of roses. There were roses . . . roses . . . Bushwick Avenue. Streets emptied of traffic. Crowds on the sidewalk, the police holding them back. Always the scent of roses. Then came the cavalcade: mounted policemen and a large open motorcar in which was seated a genial, kindly-looking man with a wreath of roses around his neck. Some people were weeping with joy as they looked at him. Francie clung to papa's hand. She heard people around her talking:

"Just think! He was a Brooklyn boy, too."

"*Was?* You dope, he *still* lives in Brooklyn."

"Yeah?"

"Yeah. And he lives right here on Bushwick Avenue."

"Look at him! Look at him!" a woman cried out. "He did such a great thing and he's still an ordinary man like my husband only better looking."

"It musta been cold up there," said a man. "It wonders me he didn't freeze his whatzis off," said a bawdy boy.

A cadaverous-looking man tapped Johnny on the shoulder. "Mac," he inquired, "do you actually believe there's a pole up there sticking out on top of the world?"

---

*Lyrics by George M. Cohan

"Sure," answered Johnny. "Didn't he go up there and turn around and hang the American flag on it?"

Just then a small boy hollered out, "Here he comes!"

"Aw-w-w-w-w!"

Francie was thrilled by the sound of admiration that swayed the crowd when the car came past where they were standing. Carried away by the excitement, she yelled out shrilly:

"Hurray for Dr. Cook! Hurray for Brooklyn!"

26

Most children brought up in Brooklyn before the first World War remember Thanksgiving Day there with a peculiar tenderness. It was the day children went around "ragamuffin" or "slamming gates," wearing costumes topped off by a penny mask.

Francie chose her mask with great care. She bought a yellow Chinaman one with sleazy rope mandarin mustaches. Neeley bought a chalk-white death head with grinning black teeth. Papa came through at the last minute with a penny tin horn for each, red for Francie, green for Neeley.

What a time Francie had getting Neeley into his costume! He wore one of mama's discarded dresses hacked off ankle length in the front to enable him to walk. The uncut back made a dirty dragging train. He stuffed wadded newspapers in the front to make an enormous bust. His broken-out brass-tipped shoes stuck out in front of the dress. Lest he freeze, he wore a ragged sweater over the ensemble. With this costume, he wore the death mask and one of papa's discarded derbies cocked on his head. Only it was too big and wouldn't cock and rested on his ears.

Francie wore one of mama's yellow waists, a bright blue skirt and a red sash. She held the Chinaman mask on by a red bandanna over her head and tied under her chin. Mama made her wear her zitful cap (Katie's own name for a wool stocking cap) over her headgear because it was a cold day. Francie put two walnuts for decoys in her last year's Easter basket and the children set out.

The street was jammed with masked and costumed children making a deafening din with their penny tin horns. Some kids were too poor to buy a penny mask. They had blackened their faces with burnt cork. Other children with more prosperous parents had store costumes: sleazy Indian suits, cowboy suits and cheesecloth Dutch maiden dresses. A few indifferent ones simply draped a dirty sheet over themselves and called it a costume.

Francie got pushed in with a compact group of children and went the rounds with them. Some storekeepers locked their doors against them but most of them had something for the children. The candy-store man had hoarded all broken bits of candy for weeks and now passed it out in little bags for all who came begging. He had to do this because he lived on the pennies of the youngsters and he didn't want to be boycotted. The bakery stores obliged by baking up batches of soft doughy cookies which they gave away. Children were the marketers of the neighborhood and they would only patronize those stores that treated them well. The bakery people were aware of this. The green grocer obliged with decaying bananas and half-rotted apples. Some stores which had nothing to gain from the children neither locked them out nor gave them anything save a profane lecture on the evils of begging. These people were rewarded by terrific and repeated bangings of the front door by the children. Hence the term, slamming gates.

By noon, it was all over. Francie was tired of her unwieldy costume. Her mask had crumpled. (It was made of cheap gauze, heavily starched and dried in shape over a mold.) A boy had taken her tin horn and broken it in two across his knee. She met Neeley coming along with a bloody nose. He had been in a fight with another boy who wanted to take his basket. Neeley wouldn't say who won but he had the other boy's basket besides his own. They went home to a good Thanksgiving dinner of pot roast and home-made noodles and spent the afternoon listening to papa reminisce how he had gone around Thanksgiving Day as a boy.

It was at a Thanksgiving time that Francie told her first organized lie, was found out and determined to become a writer.

The day before Thanksgiving, there were exercises in Francie's room. Each of four chosen girls recited a Thanksgiving poem and held in her hand a symbol of the day. One held an ear of dried-up corn, another a turkey's foot, meant to stand for the whole turkey. A third girl held a basket of apples and the fourth held a five-cent pumpkin pie which was the size of a small saucer.

After the exercises, the turkey foot and corn were thrown into the wastebasket. Teacher set aside the apples to take home. She asked if anyone wanted the little pumpkin pie. Thirty mouths watered; thirty hands itched to go up into the air but no one moved. Some were poor, many were hungry and all were too proud to accept charitable food. When no one responded, Teacher ordered the pie thrown away.

Francie couldn't stand it; that beautiful pie thrown away and she had never tasted pumpkin pie. To her it was the food of covered wagon people, of Indian fighters. She was dying to taste it. In a flash she invented a lie and up went her hand.

"I'm glad someone wants it," said Teacher.

"I don't want it for myself," lied Francie proudly. "I know a very poor family I'd like to give it to."

"Good," said Teacher. "That's the real Thanksgiving spirit."

Francie ate the pie while walking home that afternoon. Whether it was her conscience or the unfamiliar flavor, she didn't enjoy the pie. It tasted like soap. The Monday following, Teacher saw her in the hall before class and asked her how the poor family had enjoyed the pie.

"They liked it a whole lot," Francie told her. Then when she saw Teacher there looking so interested, she embellished the story. "This family has two little girls with golden curls and big blue eyes."

"And?" prompted Teacher.

"And . . . and . . . they're twins."

"How interesting."

Francie was inspired. "One of them has the name Pamela and the other Camilla." (These were names that Francie had once chosen for her non-existent dolls.)

"And they are very, very poor," suggested Teacher.

"Oh, very poor. They didn't have anything to eat for three days and just would have died the doctor said, if I didn't bring them that pie."

"That was such a tiny pie," commented Teacher gently, "to save two lives."

Francie knew then, that she had gone too far. She hated whatever that thing was inside her that made her invent such whoppers. Teacher bent down and put her arms around Francie. Francie saw that there were tears in her eyes. Francie went to pieces and remorse rose in her like bitter flood waters.

"That's all a big lie," she confessed. "I ate the pie myself."

"I know you did."

"Don't send a letter home," begged Francie, thinking of the address she didn't own. "I'll stay after school every day for . . ."

"I'll not punish you for having an imagination."

Gently, Teacher explained the difference between a lie and a story. A lie was something you told because you were mean or a coward. A story was something you made up out of something that might have happened. Only you didn't tell it like it was; you told it like you thought it should have been.

As Teacher talked, a great trouble left Francie. Lately, she had been given to exaggerating things. She did not report happenings truthfully, but gave them color, excitement and dramatic twists. Katie was annoyed at this tendency and kept warning Francie to tell the plain truth and to stop romancing. But Francie just couldn't tell the plain undecorated truth. She had to put something to it.

Although Katie had this same flair for coloring an incident and Johnny himself lived in a half-dream world, yet they tried to squelch these things in their child. Maybe they had a good reason. Maybe they knew their own gift of imagination colored too rosily the poverty and brutality of their lives and made them able to endure it. Perhaps Katie thought that if they did not have this faculty, they would be clearer-minded; see things as they really were, and seeing them loathe them and somehow find a way to make them better.

Francie always remembered what that kind teacher told her. "You know, Francie, a lot of people would think that these stories that you're making up all the time were terrible lies because they are not the truth as people see the truth. In the future, when something comes up, you *tell* exactly how it happened but *write down for yourself the way you think it should have happened. Tell* the truth and *write* the story. Then you won't get mixed up."

It was the best advice Francie ever got. Truth and fancy were so mixed up in her mind—as they are in the mind of every lonely child—that she didn't know which was which. But Teacher made these two things clear to her. From that time on, she wrote little stories about things she saw and felt and did. In time, she got so that she was able to speak the truth with but a slight and instinctive coloring of the facts.

Francie was ten years old when she first found an outlet in writing. What she wrote was of little consequence. What was important was that the attempt to write stories kept her straight on the dividing line between truth and fiction.

If she had not found this outlet in writing, she might have grown up to be a tremendous liar.

27

Christmas was a charmed time in Brooklyn. It was in the air, long before it came. The first hint of it was Mr. Morton going around the schools teaching Christmas carols, but the first sure sign was the store windows.

You have to be a child to know how wonderful is a store window filled with dolls and sleds and other toys. And this wonder came free to Francie. It was nearly as good as actually having the toys to be permitted to look at them through the glass window.

Oh, what a thrill there was for Francie when she turned a street corner and saw another store all fixed up for Christmas! Ah, the clean shining window with cotton batting sprinkled with star dust for a carpet! There were flaxen-haired dolls and others which Francie liked better who had hair the color of good coffee with lots of cream in it. Their faces were perfectly tinted and they wore clothes the like of which Francie had never seen on earth. The dolls stood upright in flimsy cardboard boxes. They stood with the help of a bit of tape passed around the neck and ankles and through holes at the back of the box. Oh, the deep blue eyes framed by thick lashes that stared straight into a little girl's heart and the perfect miniature hands extended, appealingly asking, "Please, won't *you* be my mama?" And Francie had never had a doll except a two-inch one that cost a nickel.

And the sleds! (Or, as the Williamsburg children called them, the sleighs.) There was a child's dream of heaven come true! A new sled with a flower someone had dreamed up painted on it—a deep blue flower with bright green leaves—the ebony-black painted runners, the smooth steering bar made of hard wood and gleaming varnish over all! And the names painted on them! "Rosebud!" "Magnolia!" "Snow King!" "The Flyer!" Thought Francie, "If I could only have one of those, I'd never ask God for another thing as long as I live."

There were roller skates made of shining nickel with straps of good brown leather and silvered nervous wheels, tensed for rolling, needing but a breath to start them turning, as they lay crossed one over the other, sprinkled with mica snow on a bed of cloud-like cotton.

There were other marvelous things. Francie couldn't take them all in. Her head spun and she was dizzy with the impact of all the seeing and all the making up of stories about the toys in the shop windows.

The spruce trees began coming into the neighborhood the week before Christmas. Their branches were corded to hold back the glory of their spreading and probably to make shipping easier. Vendors rented space on the curb before a store and stretched a rope from pole to pole and leaned the trees against it. All day they walked up and down this one-sided avenue of aromatic leaning trees, blowing on stiff ungloved fingers and looking with bleak hope at those people who paused. A few ordered a tree set aside for the day; others stopped to price, inspect and conjecture. But most came just to touch the boughs and surreptitiously pinch a fingerful of spruce needles together to release the fragrance. And the air was cold and still, and full of the pine smell and the smell of tangerines which appeared in the stores only at Christmas time and the mean street was truly wonderful for a little while.

There was a cruel custom in the neighborhood. It was about the trees still unsold when midnight of Christmas Eve approached. There was a saying that if you waited until then, you wouldn't have to buy a tree; that "they'd chuck 'em at you." This was literally true.

At midnight on the Eve of our dear Saviour's birth, the kids gathered where there were unsold trees. The man threw each tree in turn, starting with the biggest. Kids volunteered to stand up against the throwing. If a boy didn't fall down under the impact, the tree was his. If he fell, he forfeited his chance at winning a tree. Only the roughest boys and some of the young men elected to be hit by the big trees. The others waited shrewdly until a tree came up that they could stand against. The little kids waited for the tiny, foot-high trees and shrieked in delight when they won one.

On the Christmas Eve when Francie was ten and Neeley nine, mama consented to let them go down and have their first try for a tree. Francie had picked out her tree earlier in the day. She had stood near it all afternoon and evening praying that no one would buy it. To her joy, it was still there at midnight. It was the biggest tree in the neighborhood and its price was so high that no one could afford to buy it. It was ten feet high. Its branches were bound with new white rope and it came to a sure pure point at the top.

The man took this tree out first. Before Francie could speak up, a neighborhood bully, a boy of eighteen known as Punky Perkins, stepped forward and ordered the man to chuck the tree at him. The man hated the way Punky was so confident. He looked around and asked;

"Anybody else wanna take a chanct on it?"

Francie stepped forward. "Me, Mister."

A spurt of derisive laughter came from the tree man. The kids snickered. A few adults who had gathered to watch the fun, guffawed.

"Aw g'wan. You're too little," the tree man objected.

"Me and my brother—we're not too little together."

She pulled Neeley forward. The man looked at them—a thin girl of ten with starveling hollows in her cheeks but with the chin still baby-round. He looked at the little boy with his fair hair and round blue-eyes—Neeley Nolan, all innocence and trust.

"Two ain't fair," yelped Punky.

"Shut your lousy trap," advised the man who held all power in that hour. "These here kids is got nerve. Stand back, the rest of yous. These kids is goin' to have a show at this tree."

The others made a wavering lane. Francie and Neeley stood at one end of it and the big man with the big tree at the other. It was a human funnel with Francie and her brother making the small end of it. The man flexed his great arms to throw the great tree. He noticed how tiny the children looked at the end of the short lane. For the split part of a moment, the tree thrower went through a kind of Gethsemane.

"Oh, Jesus Christ," his soul agonized, "why don't I just give 'em the tree, say Merry Christmas and let 'em go. What's the tree to me? I can't sell it no more this year and it won't keep till next year." The kids watched him solemnly as he stood there in his moment of thought. "But then," he rationalized, "if I did that, all the other would expect to get 'em handed to 'em. And next year nobody a-tall would buy a tree off of me. They'd all wait to get 'em handed to 'em on a silver plate. I ain't a big enough man to give this tree away for nothin'. No, I ain't big enough. I ain't big enough to do a thing like that. I gotta think of myself and my own kids." He finally came to his conclusion. "Oh, what the hell! Them two kids is gotta live in this world. They *got* to get used to it. They got to learn to give and to take punishment. And by Jesus, it ain't give but *take, take, take* all the time in this God-damned world." As he threw the tree with all his strength, his heart wailed out, "It's a God-damned, rotten, lousy world!"

Francie saw the tree leave his hands. There was a split bit of being when time and space had no meaning. The whole world stood still as something dark and monstrous came through the air. The tree came towards her blotting out all memory of her ever having lived. There was nothing—nothing but pungent darkness and something that grew and grew as it rushed at her. She staggered as the tree hit them. Neeley went to his knees but she pulled him up fiercely before he could go down. There was a mighty swishing sound as the tree settled. Everything was dark, green and prickly. Then she felt a sharp pain at the side of her head where the trunk of the tree had hit her. She felt Neeley trembling.

When some of the older boys pulled the tree away, they found Francie and her brother standing upright, hand in hand. Blood was coming from scratches on Neeley's face. He looked more like a baby than ever with his bewildered blue eyes and the fairness of his skin made more noticeable because of the clear red blood. But they were smiling. Had they not won the biggest tree in the neighborhood? Some of the boys hollered "Horray!" A few adults clapped. The tree man eulogized them by screaming,

"And now get the hell out of here with your tree, you lousy bastards."

Francie had heard swearing since she had heard words. Obscenity and profanity had no meaning as such among those people. They were emotional expressions of inarticulate people with small vocabularies; they made a kind of dialect. The phrases could mean many things according to the expression and tone used in saying them. So now, when Francie heard themselves called lousy bastards, she smiled tremulously at the kind man. She knew that he was really saying, "Goodbye—God bless you."

It wasn't easy dragging that tree home. They had to pull it inch by inch. They were handicapped by a boy who ran alongside yelping, "Free ride! All aboard!" who'd jump on and make them drag him along. But he got sick of the game eventually and went away.

In a way, it was good that it took them so long to get the tree home. It made their triumph more drawn out. Francie glowed when she heard a lady say, "I never saw such a big tree!" A man called after them, "You kids musta robbed a bank to buy such a big tree." The cop on their corner stopped them, examined the tree, and solemnly offered to buy it for ten cents—fifteen cents if they'd delivered it to his home. Francie nearly burst with pride although she knew he was joking. She said she wouldn't sell it for a dollar, even. He shook his head and said she was foolish not to grab the offer. He went up to a quarter but Francie kept smiling and shaking her head, "no."

It was like acting in a Christmas play where the setting was a street corner and the time, a frosty Christmas Eve and the characters, a kind cop, her brother and herself. Francie knew all the dialogue. The cop gave his lines right and Francie picked up her cues happily and the stage directions were the smiles between the spoken lines.

They had to call up to papa to help them get the tree up the narrow stairs. Papa came running down. To Francie's relief, he ran down straight and not sidewise which proved that he was still sober.

Papa's amazement at the size of the tree was flattering. He pretended to believe that it wasn't theirs. Francie had a lot of fun convincing him although she knew all the while that the whole thing was make believe. Papa pulled in front and Francie and Neeley pushed in back and they began forcing the big tree up the three narrow flights of stairs. Johnny was so excited that he started singing, not caring that it was rather late at night. He sang "Holy Night." The narrow walls took up his clear sweet voice, held it for a breath and gave it back with doubled sweetness. Doors creaked open and families gathered on the landings, pleased and amazed at the something unexpected being added to that moment of their lives.

Francie saw the Tynmore girls standing together in their doorway, their gray hair in crimpers, and ruffled, starched nightgowns showing under their voluminous wrappers. They added their thin poignant voices to Johnny's. Floss Gaddis, her mother and her brother, Henny, who was dying of consumption, stood in their doorway. Henny was crying and when Johnny saw him, he let the song trail off; he thought maybe it made Henny too sad.

Flossie was in costume waiting for an escort to take her to a masquerade ball which started soon after midnight. She stood there in her Klondike-dance-hall-girl costume with sheer black silk stockings, spool-heeled slippers, one red garter fastened under a knee and swinging a black mask in her hand. She smiled into Johnny's eyes. She put her hand on her hip and leaned seductively—or so she thought—against the door jamb. More to make Henny smile than anything else, Johnny said,

"Floss, we got no angel for the top of this Christmas tree. How about you obliging?"

Floss was all ready to make a dirty reply about the wind blowing her drawers off if she was up that high. But she changed her mind. There was something about the big proud tree, now so humble in its being dragged; something about the beaming children; something about the rare good will of the neighbors and the way the lights looked turned low in the halls, that made her ashamed of her unspoken reply. All she said was:

"Gee, ain't you the kidder, Johnny Nolan."

Katie stood alone on the top of the last flight of steps with her hands clasped before her. She listened to the singing. She looked down and watched their slow progress up the stairs. She was thinking deeply.

"They think this is so good," she thought. "They think it's good—the tree they got for nothing and their father playing up to them and the singing and the way the neighbors are happy. They think they're mighty lucky that they're living and that it's Christmas again. They can't see that we live on a dirty street in a dirty house among people who aren't much good. Johnny and the children can't see how pitiful it is that our neighbors have to make happiness out of this filth and dirt. My children must get out of this. They must come to more than Johnny or me or all these people around us. But how is this to come about? Reading a page from those books every day and saving pennies in the tin-can bank isn't enough. Money! Would that make it better for them? Yes, it would make it easy. But no, the money wouldn't be enough. McGarrity owns the saloon standing on the corner and he has a lot of money. His wife wears diamond earrings. But her children are not as good and smart as my children. They are mean and greedy towards others because they have the things to taunt poor children with. I have seen the McGarrity girl eating from a bag of candy on the street while a ring of hungry children watched her. I saw those children looking at her and crying in their hearts. And when she couldn't eat any more, she threw the rest down the sewer rather than give it to them. Ah, no, it isn't the money alone. The McGarrity girl wears a different hair bow each day and they cost fifty cents apiece and that would feed the four of us here for one day. But her hair is thin and pale red. My Neeley has a big hole in his zitful cap and it's stretched out of shape but he has thick, deep golden hair that curls. My Francie wears no hair bow but her hair is long and shining. Can money buy things like that? No. That means there must be something bigger than money. Miss Jackson teaches at the Settlement House and she has no money. She works for charity. She lives in a little room there on the top floor. She only has the one dress but she keeps it clean and pressed. Her eyes look straight into yours when you talk with her. When you listen to her, it's like you used to be sick but hearing her voice, it's making you well again. She knows about things—Miss Jackson. She understands about things. She can live in the middle of a dirty neighborhood and be fine and clean and like an actress in a play; someone you can look at but who is too fine to touch. There is that difference between her and Mrs. McGarrity who has so much money but is too fat and acts in a dirty way with the truck drivers who deliver her husband's beer. So what is this difference between her and this Miss Jackson who has no money?"

An answer came to Katie. It was so simple that a flash of astonishment that felt like pain shot through her head. Education! That was it! It was education that made the difference! Education would pull them out of the grime and dirt. Proof? Miss Jackson was educated, the McGarrity wasn't. Ah! That's what Mary Rommely, her mother had been telling her all those years. Only her mother did not have the one clear word: education!

Watching the children struggling up the stairs with their tree, listening to their voices, still so baby-like, she got these ideas about education.

"Francie is smart," she thought. "She must go to High School and maybe beyond that. She's a learner and she'll be somebody someday. But when she gets educated, she will grow away from me. Why, she's growing away from me now. She does not love me the way the boy loves me. I feel her turn away from me. She does not understand me. All she understands is that I don't understand her. Maybe when she gets education, she will be ashamed of me—the way I talk. But she will have too much character to show it. Instead she will try to make me different. She will come to see me and try to make me live in a better way and I will be mean to her because I'll know she's above me. She will figure out too much about things as she grows older; she'll get to know too much for her own happiness. She'll find out that I don't love her as much as I love the boy. I cannot help it that this is so. But she won't understand that. Sometimes I think she knows that now. Already she is growing away from me; she will fight to get away soon. Changing over to that far-away school was the first step in her getting away from me. But Neeley will never leave me, that is why I love him best. He will cling to me and understand me. I want him to be a doctor. He *must* be a doctor. Maybe he will play the fiddle, too. There is music in him. He got that from his father. He has gone further on the piano than Francie or me. Yes, his father has the music in him but it does him no good. It is ruining him. If he couldn't sing, those men who treat him to drinks wouldn't want him around. What good is the fine way he can sing when it doesn't make him or us any better? With the boy, it will be different. He'll be educated. I must think out ways. We'll not have Johnny with us long. Dear God, I loved him so much once— and sometimes I still do. But he's worthless . . . worthless. And God forgive me for ever finding it out."

Thus Katie figured out everything in the moments it took them to climb the stairs. People looking up at her—at her smooth pretty vivacious face—had no way of knowing about the painfully articulated resolves formulating in her mind.

They set the tree up in the front room after spreading a sheet to protect the carpet of pink roses from falling pine needles. The tree stood in a big tin bucket with broken bricks to hold it upright. When the rope was cut away, the branches spread out to fill the whole room. They draped over the piano and it was so that some of the chairs stood among the branches. There was no money to buy tree decorations or lights. But the great tree standing there was enough. The room was cold. It was a poor year, that one—too poor for them to buy the extra coal for the front room stove. The room smelled cold and clean and aromatic. Every day, during the week the tree stood there, Francie put on her sweater and zitful cap and went in and sat under the tree. She sat there and enjoyed the smell and the dark greenness of it.

Oh, the mystery of a great tree, a prisoner in a tin wash bucket in a tenement front room!

Poor as they were that year, it was a very nice Christmas and the children did not lack for gifts. Mama gave each of them a pair of long woolen drawers, drop seat style, and a woolen shirt with long sleeves and itchy insides. Aunt Evy gave them a joint present; a box of dominoes. Papa showed them how to play. Neeley didn't like the game so papa and Francie played together and he pretended to be disgusted when he lost.

Granma Mary Rommely brought over something very nice that she had made herself. She brought each a scapular. To make it, she cut out two small ovals of bright red wool. On one, she embroidered a cross of bright blue yarn and on the other, a golden heart crowned with brown thorns. A black dagger went through the heart and two drops of deep red blood dripped from the dagger point. The cross and heart were very tiny and made with microscopic stitches. The two ovals were stitched together and attached to a piece of corset string. Mary Rommely had taken the scapulars to be blessed by the priest before she brought them over. As she slipped the scapular over Francie's head, she said "*Hieliges Weihnachten.*" Then she added, "May you walk with the angels always."

Aunt Sissy gave Francie a tiny package. She opened it and found a tiny matchbox. It was very fragile and covered with crinkly paper with a miniature spray of purple wisteria painted on the top. Francie pushed the box open. It held ten discs individually wrapped in pink tissue. The discs turned out to be bright golden pennies. Sissy explained that she had bought a bit of gold paint powder, mixed it with a few drops of banana oil and had gilded each penny. Francie loved Sissy's present the best of all. A dozen times within the hour of receiving it, she slid open the box slowly, gaining great pleasure from holding the box and looking at it and watching the cobalt blue paper and the clean wafer-thin wood of the inside of the box appear. The golden pennies wrapped in the dream-like tissue were a never-tiring miracle. Everyone agreed that the pennies were too beautiful to be spent. During the day, Francie lost two of her pennies somewhere. Mama suggested they'd be safest in the tin-can bank. She promised that Francie could have them back when the bank was opened. Francie was sure that mama was right about the pennies being safest in the bank, yet it was a wrench to let those golden pennies drop down into the darkness.

Papa had a special present for Francie. It was a post card with a church on it. Powdered isinglass was pasted on the roof and it glistened more brightly than real snow. The church window panes were made of tiny squares of shiny orange paper. The magic in this card was that when Francie held it up, light streamed through the paper panes and threw golden shadows on the glistening snow. It was a beautiful thing. Mama said that since it wasn't written on, Francie could save it for next year and mail it to someone.

"Oh no," said Francie. She put both hands over the card and held it to her chest.

Mama laughed. "You must learn to take a joke, Francie, otherwise life will be pretty hard on you."

"Christmas is no day for lessons," said papa.

"But it is a day for getting drunk, isn't it," she flared up.

"Two drinks is all I had, Katie," Johnny pleaded. "I was treated for Christmas."

Francie went into the bedroom and shut the door. She couldn't bear to hear mama scolding papa.

Just before supper, Francie distributed the gifts she had for them. She had a hat pin holder for mama. She had made it with a penny test tube bought at Knipe's drug store. She had covered it with a sheath of blue satin ribbon ruffled at the sides. A length of baby ribbon was sewn to the top. It was meant to hang on the side of the dresser and hold hat pins.

She had a watch fob for papa. She had made it on a spool which had four nails driven into the top. It took two shoe laces. These were worked over and around the nails and a thick braided fob kept growing out of the bottom of the spool as she worked it. Johnny had no watch but he took an iron faucet washer, attached the fob to it and wore it in his vest pocket all day pretending it was a watch. Francie had a very fine present for Neeley: a five-cent shooter which looked like an oversize opal rather than a marble. Neeley had a boxful of "miggies," small brown and blue speckled marbles made of clay which cost a penny for twenty. But he had no good shooter and couldn't get into any important games. Francie watched him as he crooked his forefinger and cradled the marble in it with his thumb behind it. It looked nice and natural that way and she was glad she had got it for him rather than the nickel pop-gun she had first thought of buying.

Neeley shoved the marble in his pocket and announced that he had presents, too. He ran into the bedroom, crawled under his cot and came out with a sticky bag. He thrust it at mama, saying "*You* share them out." He stood in a corner. Mama opened the bag. There was a striped candy cane for each one. Mama went into ecstasies. She said it was the prettiest present she had ever had. She kissed Neeley three times. Francie tried very hard not to be jealous because mama made more fuss over Neeley's present than hers.

It was in that same week that Francie told another great lie. Aunt Evy brought over two tickets. Some Protestant organization was giving a celebration for the poor of all faiths. There would be a decorated Christmas tree on the stage, a Christmas play, carol singing and a gift for each child. Katie couldn't see it—Catholic children at a Protestant party. Evy urged tolerance. Mama finally gave in and Francie and Neeley went to the party.

It was in a large auditorium. The boys sat on one side and the girls on the other. The celebration was fine except that the play was religious and dull. After the play, church ladies went down the aisle and gave each child a gift. All the girls got checker boards and all the boys got lotto games. After a little more singing, a lady came out on the stage and announced a special surprise.

The surprise was a lovely little girl, exquisitely dressed, who came from the wings carrying a beautiful doll. The doll was a foot high, had real yellow hair and blue eyes that opened and shut with real eyelashes. The lady led the child forward and made a speech.

"This little girl is named Mary." Little Mary smiled and bowed. The little girls in the audience smiled up at her and some of the boys who were approaching adolescence whistled shrilly. "Mary's mother bought this doll and had clothes made for it just like the clothes little Mary is wearing."

Little Mary stepped forward and held the doll high in the air. Then she let the lady hold it while she spread her skirt and made a curtsey. It was true, saw Francie. The doll's lace-trimmed blue silk dress, pink hair bow, black patent leather slippers and white silk socks duplicated exactly the clothes of the beautiful Mary.

"Now," said the lady, "this doll is named Mary after the kind little girl who is giving her away." Again the little girl smiled graciously. "Mary wants to give the doll to some poor little girl in the audience who is named Mary." Like wind on growing corn, a rippling murmur came from all the little girls in the audience. "Is there any poor little girl in the audience named Mary?"

There was a great hush. There were at least a hundred Marys in that audience. It was that adjective "poor" that struck them dumb. No Mary would stand up, no matter how much she wanted the doll, and be a symbol of all the poor little girls in the audience. They began whispering to each other that they weren't poor and had better dolls home and better clothes than that girl, too, only they didn't feel like wearing them. Francie sat numb, longing for that doll with all her soul.

"What?" said the lady. "No Marys?" She waited and made her announcement again. No response. She spoke regretfully. "Too bad there are no Marys. Little Mary will have to take the doll home again." The little girl smiled and bowed and turned to leave the stage with the doll.

Francie couldn't stand it, she couldn't stand it. It was like when the teacher was going to throw the pumpkin pie in the wastebasket.

She stood up and held her hand high in the air. The lady saw it and stopped the little girl from leaving the stage.

"Ah! We do have a Mary, a very bashful Mary but a Mary just the same. Come right up on the stage, Mary."

Feverish with embarrassment, Francie walked up the long aisle and on to the stage. She stumbled on the steps and all the girls snickered and the boys guffawed.

"What is your name?" asked the lady.

"Mary Frances Nolan," whispered Francie.

"Louder. And look at the audience."

Miserably, Francie faced the audience and said loudly, "Mary Frances Nolan." All the faces looked like bloated balloons on thick strings. She thought that if she kept on looking, the faces would float away up to the ceiling.

The beautiful girl came forward and put the doll in Francie's arms. Francie's arms took a natural curve around it. It was as if her arms had waited and grown so just for that doll. The beautiful Mary extended her hand for Francie to shake. In spite of embarrassment and confusion, Francie noticed the delicate white hand with the tracery of pale blue veins and the oval nails that glowed like delicate pink sea shells.

The lady talked as Francie backed awkwardly to her seat. She said: "You have all seen an example of the true Christmas spirit. Little Mary is a very rich little girl and received many beautiful dolls for Christmas. But she was not selfish. She wanted to make some poor little Mary, who is not as fortunate as herself, happy. So she gave the doll to that poor little girl who is named Mary, too."

Francie's eyes smarted with hot tears. "Why can't they," she thought bitterly, "just give the doll away without saying I am poor and she is rich? Why couldn't they just give it away without all the talking about it?"

That was not all of Francie's shame. As she walked down the aisle, the girls leaned towards her and whispered hissingly, "Beggar, beggar, beggar."

It was beggar, beggar, beggar, all the way down the aisle. Those girls felt richer than Francie. They were as poor as she but they had something she lacked—pride. And Francie knew it. She had no compunctions about the lie and getting the doll under false pretenses. She was paying for the lie and for the doll by giving up her pride.

She remembered the teacher who had told her to write her lies instead of speaking them. Maybe she shouldn't have gone up for the doll but should have written a story about it instead. But no! No! *Having* the doll was better than any story about having a doll. When they stood to sing the "Star-spangled Banner" in closing, Francie put her face down close to the doll's face. There was the cool delicate smell of painted china, the wonderful unforgettable smell of a doll's hair, the heavenly feel of new-gauze doll's clothes. The doll's real eyelashes touched her cheek and she trembled in ecstasy. The children were singing:

> *O'er the land of the free,*
> *And the home of the brave.*

Francie held one of the doll's tiny hands tightly. A nerve in her thumb throbbed and she thought the doll's hand twitched. She almost believed the doll was real.

She told mama the doll had been given to her as a prize. She dared not tell the truth. Mama hated anything that smacked of charity and if she knew, she'd throw the doll away. Neeley didn't snitch on her. Francie now owned the doll but had yet another lie on her soul. That afternoon she wrote a story about a little girl who wanted a doll so much that she was willing to give over her immortal soul to Purgatory for eternity if she could have the doll. It was a strong story but when Francie read it over, she thought, "that's all right for the girl in the story but it doesn't make me feel any better."

She thought of the confession she would have to make the next Saturday. She resolved that no matter what penance Father gave her, she would triple it voluntarily. Still she felt no better.

Then she remembered something! Maybe she could make the lie a truth! She knew that when Catholic children received Confirmation, they were expected to take some saint's name for a middle name. What a simple solution! She would take the name of Mary when she was confirmed.

That night, after the page from the Bible and the page from Shakespeare had been read, Francie consulted mama.

"Mama, when I make my Confirmation, can I take Mary for a middle name?"

"No."

Francie's heart sunk. "Why?"

"Because when you were christened, you were named Francie after Andy's girl."

"I know."

"But you were also named Mary after my mother. Your real name is Mary Frances Nolan."

Francie took the doll to bed with her. She lay very still so as not to disturb it. She woke up from time to time in the night and whispered "Mary" and touched the doll's infinitesimal slipper with a light finger. She trembled at feeling the thin soft bit of smooth leather.

It was to be her first and her last doll.

28

The future was a near thing to Katie. She had a way of saying, "Christmas will be here before you know it." Or, at the beginning of vacation, "School will be starting up before you know it." In the spring when Francie discarded her long drawers and joyously flung them away, mama made her pick them up again saying, "You'll need them soon enough again. Winter will be here before you know it." What was mama talking about? Spring had just started. The winter would never come again.

A small child has little idea of the future. Next week is as far ahead as his future stretches and the year between Christmas and Christmas again is an eternity. So time was with Francie up until her eleventh year.

Between her eleventh and twelfth birthday, things changed. The future came along quicker; the days seemed shorter and the weeks seemed to have less days in them. Henny Gaddis died and this had something to do with it. She had always heard that Henny was going to die. She heard about it so much that she finally got to believe he would die. But that would be a long, long time away. Now the long time had come. The something which had been a future was now a present and would become a past. Francie wondered whether someone had to die to make that clear to a child. But no, Grandfather Rommely had died when she was nine, a week after she made her first Communion and as she remembered, Christmas still had seemed far away at that time.

Things were changing so fast for Francie now, that she got mixed up. Neeley, who was a year younger than she, grew suddenly and got to be a head taller. Maudie Donavan moved away. When she returned on a visit three months later, Francie found her different. Maudie had developed in a womanly way during those three months.

Francie, who *knew* mama was always right, found out that she was wrong once in a while. She discovered that some of the things she loved so much in her father were considered very comical to other people. The scales at the tea store did not shine so brightly any more and she found the bins were chipped and shabby looking.

She stopped watching for Mr. Tomony to come home on Saturday nights from his New York jaunts. All of a sudden she thought it was silly that he lived so and went to New York and came home longing for where he had been. He had money. Why didn't he just go over to New York and live there if he liked it so much?

Everything was changing. Francie was in a panic. Her world was slipping away from her and what would take its place? *Still, what was different anyhow?* She read a page from the Bible and Shakespeare every night the same as always. She practiced the piano every day for an hour. She put pennies in the tin-can bank. The junk shop was still there; the stores were all the same. Nothing was changing. *She was the one who was changing.*

She told papa about it. He made her stick out her tongue and he felt her wrist. He shook his head sadly and said,

"You have a bad case, a very bad case."

"Of what?"

"Growing up."

Growing up spoiled a lot of things. It spoiled the nice game they had when there was nothing to eat in the house. When money gave out and food ran low, Katie and the children pretended they were explorers discovering the North Pole and had been trapped by a blizzard in a cave with just a little food. They had to make it last till help came. Mama divided up what food there was in the cupboard and called it rations and when the children were still hungry after a meal, she'd say, "Courage, my men, help will come soon." When some money came in and mama bought a lot of groceries, she bought a little cake as celebration, and she'd stick a penny flag in it and say, "We made it, men. We got to the North Pole."

One day after one of those "rescues" Francie asked mama:

"When explorers get hungry and suffer like that, it's for a *reason*. Something big comes out of it. They discover the North Pole. But what big thing comes out of us being hungry like that?"

Katie looked tired all of a sudden. She said something Francie didn't understand at the time. She said, "You found the catch in it."

Growing up spoiled the theater for Francie—well, not the theater exactly, but the plays. She found she was becoming dissatisfied with the way things just happened in the nick of time.

Francie loved the theater dearly. She had once wanted to be a hand-organ lady, then a school teacher. After her first Communion, she wanted to be a nun. At eleven, she wanted to be an actress.

If the Williamsburg kids knew nothing else, they knew their theater. In those days, there were many good stock companies in the neighborhood: Blaney's, Corse Payton's and Phillip's Lyceum. The Lyceum was just around the corner. Local residents called it first "The Lyce," and then changed that into "The Louse." Francie went there every Saturday afternoon (except when it was closed for the summer) when she could scrape up a dime. She sat in the gallery and often waited in line an hour before the show opened in order to get a seat in the first row.

She was in love with Harold Clarence, the leading man. She waited at the stage door after the Saturday matinee and followed him to the shabby brownstone house where he lived untheatrically in a modest furnished room. Even on the street, he had the stiff-legged walk of the old-time actor and his face was baby pink as though he still had juvenile grease paint on it. He walked stiff-leggedly and leisurely, looking neither to right nor left and smoking an important-looking cigar which he threw away before he entered the house, as his land-lady did not permit the great man to smoke in her rooms. Francie stood at the curb, looking down reverently at the discarded butt. She took the paper ring off it and wore it for a week, pretending it was his engagement ring to her.

One Saturday, Harold and his company put on *The Minister's Sweetheart* in which the handsome village minister was in love with Gerry Morehouse, the leading lady. Somehow, the heroine had to seek work in a grocery store. There was a villainess, also in love with the handsome young minister, and out to get the heroine. She swaggered into the store in her un-village-like furs and diamonds and regally ordered a pound of coffee. There was a dreadful moment when she uttered the fatal words, "Grind it!" The audience groaned. It had been planted that the delicate beautiful heroine wasn't strong enough to turn the great wheel. It had also been planted that her job was contingent on her being able to grind coffee. She struggled like anything but couldn't get the wheel to go round even once. She pleaded with the villainess; told her how much she needed the job. The villainess repeated, "Grind it!" When all seemed lost, Handsome Harold entered with his pink face and his clerical garb. Taking in the situation, he threw his wide minister's hat clear across the stage in a dramatic but unseemly gesture, stepped stiff-leggedly to the machine and ground the coffee and thus saved the heroine. There was an awed silence as the odor of freshly-ground coffee permeated the theater. Then bedlam broke loose. Real coffee! Realism in the theater! Everyone had seen coffee ground a thousand times but on the stage it was a revolutionary thing. The villainess gnashed her teeth and said, "Foiled again!" Harold embraced Gerry, making her face upstage, and the curtain came down.

During intermission, Francie did not join the other kids in the interim pastime of spitting down on the plutocrats in the thirty-cent orchestra seats. Instead, she pondered over the situation at curtain. All very well and good that the hero came in the nick of time to grind the coffee. If he hadn't dropped in, what then? The heroine would have been discharged. All right and so what? After she got hungry enough, she'd go out and find another job. She'd go out scrubbing floors like mama or graft chop suey off of her men friends like Floss Gaddis did. The grocery store job was important only because it said so in the play.

She wasn't satisfied with the play she saw the following Saturday, either. All right. The long lost lover came home just in time to pay the mortgage. What if he had been held up and couldn't make it? The landlord would have to give them thirty days to get out—at least that's how it was in Brooklyn. In that month something might turn up. If it didn't and they had to get out, well, they'd have to make the best of it. The pretty heroine would have to get on piece work in the factory; her sensitive brother would have to go out peddling papers. The mother would have to do cleaning by the day. But they'd live. You betcha they'd live, thought Francie grimly. It takes a lot of doing to die.

Francie couldn't understand why the heroine didn't marry the villain. It would solve the rent problem and surely a man who loved her so much that he was willing to go through all kinds of fuss because she wouldn't have him wasn't a man to ignore. At least, he was around while the hero was off on a wild goose chase.

She wrote her own third act to that play—what would happen *if*. She wrote it out in conversations and found it a remarkably easy way of writing. In a story you had to explain why people were the way they were but when you wrote in conversation you didn't have to do that because the things the people said explained what they were. Francie had no trouble selling herself on dialogue. Once more she changed her mind about what profession she'd follow. She decided she wouldn't be an actress after all. She'd be a writer of plays.

29

*In the summer of that same year, Johnny got the notion that his chil-*dren were growing up ignorant of the great ocean that washed the shores of Brooklyn. Johnny felt that they ought to go out to sea in a ship. So he decided to take them for a rowboat ride at Canarsie and do a little deep sea fishing on the side. He had never gone fishing and he'd never been in a rowboat. But that's the idea he got.

Weirdly tied up with this idea, and by a reasoning process known only to Johnny, was the idea of taking Little Tilly along on the trip. Little Tilly was the four-year-old child of neighbors whom he had never met. In fact, he had never seen Little Tilly but he got this idea that he had to make something up to her on account of her brother Gussie. It all tied up with the notion of going to Canarsie.

Gussie, a boy of six, was a murky legend in the neighborhood. A tough little hellion, with an over-developed underlip, he had been born like other babies and nursed at his mother's great breasts. But there, all resemblance to any child, living or dead, ceased. His mother tried to wean him when he was nine months old but Gussie wouldn't stand for it. Denied the breast, he refused a bottle, food or water. He lay in his crib and whimpered. His mother, fearful that he would starve, resumed nursing him. He sucked contentedly, refusing all other food, and lived off his mother's milk until he was nearly two years old. The milk stopped then because his mother was with child again. Gussie sulked and bided his time for nine long months. He refused cow's milk in any form or container and took to drinking black coffee.

Little Tilly was born and the mother flowed with milk again. Gussie went into hysterics the first time he saw the baby nursing. He lay on the floor, screaming and banging his head. He wouldn't eat for four days and he refused to go to the toilet. He got haggard and his mother got frightened. She thought it wouldn't do any harm to give him the breast just once. That was her big mistake. He was like a dope fiend getting the stuff after a long period of deprivation. He wouldn't let go.

He took all of his mother's milk from that time on and Little Tilly, a sickly baby, had to go on the bottle.

Gussie was three years old at this time and big for his age. Like other boys, he wore knee pants and heavy shoes with brass toe tips. As soon as he saw his mother unbutton her dress, he ran to her. He stood up while nursing, an elbow on his mother's knee, his feet crossed jauntily and his eyes roving around the room. Standing to nurse was not such a remarkable feat as his mother's breasts were mountainous and practically rested in her lap when released. Gussie was indeed a fearful sight nursing that way and he looked not unlike a man with his foot on a bar rail, smoking a fat pale cigar.

The neighbors found out about Gussie and discussed his pathological state in hushed whispers. Gussie's father got so that he wouldn't sleep with his wife; he said that she bred monsters. The poor woman figured and figured on a way to wean Gussie. He *was* too big to nurse, she decided. He was going for four. She was afraid his second teeth wouldn't come in straight.

One day she took a can of stove blackening and the brush and closed herself in the bedroom where she copiously blackened her left breast with the stove polish. With a lipstick she drew a wide ugly mouth with frightening teeth in the vicinity of the nipple. She buttoned her dress and went into the kitchen and sat in her nursing rocker near the window. When Gussie saw her, he threw the dice, with which he had been playing, under the washtubs and trotted over for feeding. He crossed his feet, planted his elbow on her knee and waited.

"Gussie want tiddy?" asked his mother wheedlingly.

"Yup!"

"All right. Gussie's gonna get nice tiddy."

Suddenly she ripped open her dress and thrust the horribly made-up breast into his face. Gussie was paralyzed with fright for a moment, then he ran away screaming and hid under the bed where he stayed for twenty-four hours. He came out at last, trembling. He went back to drinking black coffee and shuddered every time his eyes went to his mother's bosom. Gussie was weaned.

The mother reported her success all over the neighborhood. It started a new fashion in weaning called, "Giving the baby the Gussie."

Johnny heard the story and contemptuously dismissed Gussie from his mind. He was concerned about Little Tilly. He thought she had been cheated out of something very important and might grow up thwarted. He got a notion that a boat ride off the Canarsie shore might wipe out some of the wrong her unnatural brother had done her. He sent Francie around to ask could Little Tilly go with them. The harassed mother consented happily.

The next Sunday, Johnny and the three children set out for Canarsie. Francie was eleven years old, Neeley ten and Little Tilly well past three. Johnny wore his tuxedo and derby and a fresh collar and dicky. Francie and Neeley wore their everyday clothes. Little Tilly's mother, in honor of the day, had dressed her up in a cheap but fancy lace dress trimmed with dark pink ribbon.

On the trolley ride out, they sat in the front seat and Johnny made friends with the motorman and they talked politics. They got off at the last stop which was Canarsie and found their way to a little wharf on which was a tiny shack; a couple of water-logged rowboats bobbed up and down on the frayed ropes which held them to the wharf. A sign over the shack read:

"Fishing tackle and boats for rent."

Underneath was a bigger sign which said:

FRESH FISH TO TAKE HOME FOR SALE HERE.

Johnny negotiated with the man and, as was his way, made a

friend of him. The man invited him into the shack for an eye opener saying that he himself only used the stuff for a night cap.

While Johnny was inside getting his eyes opened, Neeley and Francie pondered how a night cap could also be an eye opener. Little Tilly stood there in her lace dress and said nothing.

Johnny came out with a fishing pole and a rusty tin can filled with worms in mud. The friendly man untied the rope from the least sorry of the rowboats, put the rope in Johnny's hand, wished him luck and went back to his shack.

Johnny put the fishing stuff into the bottom of the boat and helped the children in. Then he crouched on the wharf, the bit of rope in his hand and gave instructions about boats.

"There is always a wrong and a right way to get on a boat," said Johnny, who had never been on any boat except an excursion boat once. "The right way is to give the boat a shove and then jump in it before it drifts out to sea. Like this."

He straightened up, pushed the boat from him, leaped . . . and fell into the water. The petrified children stared at him. A second before, papa had been standing on the dock above them. Now he was below them in the water. The water came to his neck and his small waxed mustache and derby hat were in the clear. His derby was still straight on his forehead. Johnny, as surprised as the children, stared at them a moment before he said:

"Don't any of you damned kids dare to laugh!"

He climbed into the boat almost upsetting it. They didn't dare laugh aloud but Francie laughed so hard inside that her ribs hurt. Neeley was afraid to look at his sister. He knew that if their eyes met, he'd burst out laughing. Little Tilly said nothing. Johnny's collar and dicky were a sodden paperish mess. He stripped them off and threw them overboard. He rowed out to sea waveringly, but with silent dignity. When he came to what he thought was a likely spot, he announced that he was going to "drop anchor." The children were disappointed when they discovered that the romantic phrase simply meant that you threw a lump of iron attached to a rope overboard.

Horrified, they watched papa squeamishly impale a muddy worm on the hook. The fishing started. It consisted in baiting the hook, casting it dramatically, waiting awhile, pulling it up minus worm and fish and starting the whole thing over again.

The sun grew bright and hot. Johnny's tuxedo dried to a stiff wrinkled greenish outfit. The children started to get a whopping case of sunburn. After what seemed hours, papa announced to their intense relief and happiness that it was time to eat. He wound up the tackle, put it away, pulled up the anchor and made for the wharf. The boat seemed to go in a circle which made the wharf get further away. Finally they made shore a few hundred yards further down. Johnny tied up the boat, told the children to wait in it and went ashore. He said he was going to treat them to a nice lunch.

He came back after a while walking sideways, carrying hot dogs, huckleberry pie and strawberry pop. They sat in the rocking boat tied to the rotting wharf, looked down into the slimy green water that smelled of decaying fish, and ate. Johnny had had a few drinks ashore which made him sorry that he had hollered at the kids. He told them they could laugh at his falling into the water if they wanted to. But somehow, they couldn't bring up a laugh. The time was past for that. Papa was very cheerful, Francie thought.

"This is the life," he said. "Away from the maddening crowd. Ah, there's nothing like going down to the sea in a ship. We're getting away from it all," he ended up cryptically.

After their amazing lunch, Johnny rowed them out to sea again. Perspiration poured down from under his derby and the wax in the points of his mustache melted causing the neat adornment to change into disorganized hair on his upper lip. He felt fine. He sang lustily as he rowed:

Sailing, sailing, over the bounding main.

He rowed and rowed and kept going around in a circle and never did get out to sea. Eventually his hands got so blistered that he didn't feel like rowing any more. Dramatically he announced that he was going to pull for the shore. He pulled and pulled and finally made it by rowing in smaller and smaller circles and making the circles come near the wharf. He never noticed that the three children were pea green in the spots where they were not beet red from the sunburn. If he had only known it, the hot dogs, huckleberry pie, strawberry pop and worms squirming on the hook weren't doing them much good.

At the wharf, he leaped to the dock and the children followed his example. All made it excepting Tilly who fell into the water. Johnny threw himself flat on the dock, reached in and fished her out. Little Tilly stood there, her lace dress wet and ruined, but she said nothing. Although it was a broiling hot day, Johnny peeled off his tuxedo jacket, knelt down and wrapped it around the child. The arms dragged in the sand. Then Johnny took her up in his arms and strode up and down the dock patting her back soothingly and singing her a lullaby. Little Tilly didn't understand a thing of all that happened that day. She didn't understand why she had been put into a boat, why she had fallen into the water or why the man was making such a fuss over her. She said nothing.

When Johnny felt that she was comforted, he set her down and went into the shack where he had either an eye opener or a night cap. He bought three flounders from the man for a quarter. He came out with the wet fish wrapped in a newspaper. He told his children that he had promised to bring home some fresh-caught fish to mama.

"The principal thing," said papa, "is that I am bringing home fish that were caught at Canarsie. It makes no difference who caught them. The point is that we went fishing and we're bringing home fish."

His children knew that he wanted mama to think he caught the fish. Papa didn't ask them to lie. He just asked them not to be too fussy about the truth. The children understood.

They boarded one of those trolley cars that had two long benches facing each other. They made a queer row. First there was Johnny in green wrinkled salt-stiff pants, an undershirt full of big holes, a derby hat and a disorderly mustache. Next came Little Tilly swallowed up in his coat with salt water dripping from under it and forming a brackish pool on the floor. Francie and Neeley came next. Their faces were brick red and they sat very rigid trying not to be sick.

People got on the car, sat across from them and stared curiously. Johnny sat upright, the fish in his lap, trying not to think of the holes in his exposed undershirt. He looked over the heads of the passengers pretending to study an Ex-Lax advertisement.

More people got on, the car got crowded but no one would sit next to them. Finally one of the fish worked its way out of the sodden newspaper and fell on the floor where it lay slimily in the dust. It was too much for Little Tilly. She looked into the fish's glazed eye, said nothing but vomited silently and thoroughly all over Johnny's tuxedo jacket. Francie and Neeley, as if waiting for that cue, also threw up. Johnny sat there with two exposed fish in his lap, one at his feet and kept staring at the ad. He didn't know what else to do.

When the grisly trip was ended, Johnny took Tilly home feeling that his was the responsibility of explaining. The mother never gave him a chance to explain. She screamed when she saw her dripping be-fouled child. She snatched the coat off, threw it into Johnny's face and called him a Jack-the-Ripper. Johnny tried and tried to explain but she wouldn't listen. Little Tilly said nothing. Finally Johnny got a word in edgewise.

"Lady, I think your little girl has lost her speech."

Whereupon the mother went into hysterics. "You did it, you did it," she screamed at Johnny.

"Can't you make her say something?"

The mother grabbed the child and shook her and shook her. "Speak!" She screamed. "Say something." Finally Little Tilly opened her mouth, smiled happily and said,

"T'anks."

Katie gave Johnny a tongue lashing and said that he wasn't fit to have children. The children in question were alternating between the chills and hot flashes of a bad case of sunburn. Katie nearly cried when she saw the ruin of Johnny's only suit. It would cost a dollar to get it cleaned, steamed and pressed and she knew it would never be the same again. As for the fish, they were found to be in an advanced state of decay and had to be thrown into the garbage can.

The children went to bed. Between chills and fever and bouts of nausea, they buried their heads under the covers and laughed silently and bed-shakingly at the remembrance of papa standing in the water.

Johnny sat at the kitchen window until far into the night trying to figure out why everything had been so wrong. He had sung many a song about ships and going down to the sea in them with a heave ho and a heave to. He wondered why it hadn't turned out the way it said in songs. The children should have returned exhilarated and with a deep and abiding love for the sea and he should have returned with a fine mess of fish. Why, oh why hadn't it turned out the way it did in a song? Why did there have to be his blistered hands and his spoiled suit and sunburn and rotting fish and nausea? Why didn't Little Tilly's mother understand the intention and over-look the result? He couldn't figure it out—he couldn't figure it out.

The songs of the sea had betrayed him.

30

"Today, I am a woman," wrote Francie in her diary in the summer when she was thirteen. She looked at the sentence and absently scratched a mosquito bite on her bare leg. She looked down on her long thin and as yet formless legs. She crossed out the sentence and started over. "Soon, I shall become a woman." She looked down on her chest which was as flat as a washboard and ripped the page out of the book. She started fresh on a new page.

"Intolerance," she wrote, pressing down hard on the pencil, "is a thing that causes war, pogroms, crucifixions, lynchings, and makes people cruel to little children and to each other. It is responsible for most of the viciousness, violence, terror and heart and soul breaking of the world."

She read the words over aloud. They sounded like words that came in a can; the freshness was cooked out of them. She closed the book and put it away.

That summer Saturday was a day that should have gone down in her diary as one of the happiest days of her life. She saw her name in print for the first time. The school got out a magazine at the end of the year in which the best story written in composition class from each grade was published. Francie's composition called "Winter Time" had been chosen as the best of the seventh grade work. The magazine cost a dime and Francie had had to wait until Saturday to get it. School closed for the summer the day before and Francie worried that she wouldn't get the magazine. But Mr. Jenson said he'd be working around on Saturday and if she brought the dime over, he'd give her a copy.

Now in the early afternoon, she stood in front of her door with the magazine opened to the page of her story. She hoped someone would come along to whom she could show it.

She had shown it to mama at lunch time but mama had to get back to work and didn't have time to read it. At least five times during lunch, Francie mentioned that she had a story published. At last mama said,

"Yes, yes. I know. I saw it all coming. There'll be more stories printed and you'll get used to it. Now don't let it go to your head. There are dishes to be washed."

Papa was at Union Headquarters. He wouldn't see the story till Sunday but Francie knew he'd be pleased. So she stood on the street with her glory tucked under her arm. She couldn't let the magazine out of her hands even for a moment. From time to time she'd glance at her name in print and the excitement about it never grew less.

She saw a girl named Joanna come out of her house a few doors away. Joanna was taking her baby out for an airing in its carriage. A gasp came up from some housewives who had stopped to gossip on the sidewalk while going to and fro about their shopping. You see, Joanna was not married. She was a girl who had gotten into trouble. Her baby was illegitimate—bastard was the word they used in the neighborhood—and these good women felt that Joanna had no right to act like a proud mother and bring her baby out into the light of day. They felt that she should have kept it hidden in some dark place.

Francie was curious about Joanna and the baby. She had heard mama and papa talking about them. She stared at the baby when the carriage came by. It was a beautiful little thing sitting up happily in its carriage. Maybe Joanna *was* a bad girl but certainly she kept her baby sweeter and daintier than these good women kept theirs. The baby wore a pretty frilled bonnet and a clean white dress and bib. The carriage cover was spotless and showed much loving handiwork in its embroidery.

Joanna worked in a factory while her mother took care of the baby. The mother was too ashamed to take it out so the baby got an airing only on week-ends when Joanna wasn't working.

Yes, Francie decided, it was a beautiful baby. It looked just like Joanna. Francie remembered how papa had described her that day he and mama were talking about her.

"She has skin like a magnolia petal." (Johnny had never seen a magnolia.) "Her hair is as black as a raven's wing." (He had never seen such a bird.) "And her eyes are deep and dark like forest pools." (He had never been in a forest and the only pool he knew was where each man put in a dime and guessed what the Dodgers score would be and whoever guessed right got all the dimes.) But he had described Joanna accurately. She was a beautiful girl.

"That may be," answered Katie. "But what good is her looks? They're a curse to the girl. I heard that her mother was never married but had two children just the same. And now the mother's son is in Sing Sing and her daughter has this baby. There must be bad blood all along the line and no use getting sentimental about it. Of course," she added with a detachment of which she was astonishingly capable at times, "it's none of my business. I don't need to do anything about it one way or the other. I don't need to go out and spit on the girl because she did wrong. Neither do I have to take her in my house and adopt her because she did wrong. She suffered as much pain bringing that child into the world as though she *was* married. If she's a good girl at heart, she'll learn from the pain and the shame and she won't do it again. If she's naturally bad, it won't bother her the way people treat her. So, if I was you, Johnny, I wouldn't feel too sorry for her." Suddenly she turned to Francie and said, "Let Joanna be a lesson to *you*."

On this Saturday afternoon, Francie watched Joanna walk up and down and wondered in what way she was a lesson. Joanna acted proud about her baby. Was the lesson there? Joanna was only seventeen and friendly and she wanted everybody to be friendly with her. She smiled at the grim good women but the smile went away when she saw that they answered her with frowns. She smiled at the little children playing on the street. Some smiled back. She smiled at Francie. Francie wanted to smile back but didn't. Was the lesson that she mustn't be friendly with girls like Joanna?

The good housewives, their arms filled with bags of vegetables and brown paper parcels of meat, seemed to have little to do that afternoon. They kept gathering into little knots and whispered to each other. The whispering stopped when Joanna came by and started up when she had passed.

Each time Joanna passed, her cheeks got pinker, her head went higher and her skirt flipped behind her more defiantly. She seemed to grow prettier and prouder as she walked. She stopped oftener than needed to adjust the baby's coverlet. She maddened the women by touching the baby's cheek and smiling tenderly at it. How dare she! How dare she, they thought, act as though she had a right to all that?

Many of these good women had children which they brought up by scream and cuff. Many of them hated the husbands who lay by their sides at night. There was no longer high joy for them in the act of love. They endured the love-making rigidly, praying all the while that another child would not result. This bitter submissiveness made the man ugly and brutal. To most of them the love act had become a brutality on both sides; the sooner over with, the better. They resented this girl because they felt this had not been so with her and the father of her child.

Joanna recognized their hate but wouldn't cringe before it. She would not give in and take the baby indoors. Something *had* to give. The women broke first. They couldn't endure it any longer. They had to do something about it. The next time Joanna passed, a stringy woman called out:

"Ain't you ashamed of yourself?"

"What for?" Joanna wanted to know.

This infuriated the woman. "What for, she asks," she reported to the other women. "I'll tell you what for. Because you're a disgrace and a bum. You got no right to parade the streets with your bastard where innocent children can see you."

"I guess this is a free country," said Joanna.

"Not free for the likes of you. Get off the street, get off the street."

"Try and make me!"

"Get off the street, you whore," ordered the stringy woman.

The girl's voice trembled when she answered. "Be careful what you're saying."

"We don't have to be careful what we say to no street walker," chipped in another woman.

A man passing by stopped a moment to take it in. He touched Joanna's arm. "Look, Sister, why don't you go home till these battle-axes cool off? You can't win with them."

Joanna jerked her arm away. "You mind your own business!"

"I meant it in the right way, Sister. Sorry." He walked on.

"Why don't you go with him," taunted the stringy woman. "He might be good for a quarter." The others laughed.

"You're all jealous," said Joanna evenly.

"She says we're jealous," reported the interlocutor. "Jealous of what, you?" (She said "you" as though it were the girl's name.)

"Jealous that men like me. That's what. Lucky you're married already," she told the stringy one. "You'd never get a man otherwise. I bet your husband spits on you—afterwards. I bet that's just what he does."

"Bitch! You bitch!" screamed the stringy one hysterically. Then, acting on an instinct which was strong even in Christ's day, she picked a stone out of the gutter and threw it at Joanna.

It was the signal for the other women to start throwing stones. One, droller than the rest, threw a ball of horse manure. Some of the stones hit Joanna but a sharp pointed one missed and struck the baby's forehead. Immediately, a thin clear trickle of blood ran down the baby's face and spotted its clean bib. The baby whimpered and held out its arms for its mother to pick it up.

A few women, poised to throw the next stones, dropped them quietly back into the gutter. The baiting was all over. Suddenly the women were ashamed. They had not wanted to hurt the baby. They only wanted to drive Joanna off the street. They dispersed and went home quietly. Some children who had been standing around listening, resumed their play.

Joanna, crying now, lifted the baby from the carriage. The baby continued to whimper quietly as though it had no right to cry out loud. Joanna pressed her cheek to her baby's face and her tears mixed with its blood. The women won. Joanna carried her baby into the house not caring that the carriage stood in the middle of the sidewalk.

And Francie had seen it all; had seen it all. She had heard every word. She remembered how Joanna had smiled at her and how she had turned her head away without smiling back. Why hadn't she smiled back? Why hadn't she smiled back? Now she would suffer—she would suffer all the rest of her life every time that she remembered that she had not smiled back.

Some small boys started to play tag around the empty carriage, holding on to its sides and pulling it way over while being chased. Francie scattered them and wheeled the carriage over to Joanna's door and put the brake on. There was an unwritten law that nothing was to be molested that stood outside the door where it belonged.

She was still holding the magazine with her story in it. She stood next to the braked carriage and looked at her name once more. "Winter Time, by Frances Nolan." She wanted to do something, sacrifice something to pay for not having smiled at Joanna. She thought of her story, she was so proud of it; so eager to show papa and Aunt Evy and Sissy. She wanted to keep it always to look at and to get that nice warm feeling when she looked at it. If she gave it away, there was no means by which she could get another copy. She slipped the magazine under the baby's pillow. She left it open at the page of her story.

She saw some tiny drops of blood on the baby's snowy pillow. Again she saw the baby; the thin trickle of blood on its face; the way it held out its arms to be taken up. A wave of hurt broke over Francie and left her weak when it passed. Another wave came, broke and receded. She found her way down to the cellar of her house and sat in the darkest corner on a heap of burlap sacks and waited while the hurt waves swept over her. As each wave spent itself and a new one gathered, she trembled. Tensely she sat there waiting for them to stop. If they didn't stop, she'd have to die—she'd have to die.

After awhile they came fainter and there was a longer time between each one. She began to think. She was now getting her lesson from Joanna but it was not the kind of lesson her mother meant.

She remembered Joanna. Often at night on her way home from the library, she had passed Joanna's house and seen her and the boy standing close together in the narrow vestibule. She had seen the boy stroke Joanna's pretty hair tenderly; had seen how Joanna put up her hand to touch his cheek. And Joanna's face looked peaceful and dreamy in the light from the street lamp. Out of that beginning, then, had come the shame and the baby. Why? Why? The beginning had seemed so tender and so right. Why?

She knew that one of the women stone-throwers had had a baby only three months after her marriage. Francie had been one of the children standing at the curb watching the party leave for the church. She saw the bulge of pregnancy under the virginal veil of the bride as she stepped into the hired carriage. She saw the hand of the father closed tight on the bridegroom's arm. The groom had black shadows under his eyes and looked very sad.

Joanna had no father, no men kin. There was no one to hold her boy's arm tight on the way to the altar. That was Joanna's crime, decided Francie—not that she had been bad, but that she had not been smart enough to get the boy to the church.

Francie had no way of knowing the whole story. As a matter of fact, the boy loved Joanna and was willing to marry her after—as the saying goes—he had gotten her into trouble. The boy had a family—a mother and three sisters. He told them he wanted to marry Joanna and they talked him out of it.

Don't be a fool, they told him. She's no good. Her whole family's no good. Besides, how do you know you're the one? If she had you she had others. Oh, women are tricky. We know. We are women. You are good and tender-hearted. You take her word for it that you are the man. She lies. Don't be tricked my son, don't be tricked, our brother. If you must marry, marry a good girl, one who won't sleep with you without the priest saying the words that make it right. If you marry this girl, you are no longer my son; you are no longer our brother. You'll never be sure whether the child is yours. You will worry while you are at your work. You'll wonder who slips into your bed beside her after you have left in the morning. Oh yes, my son, our brother, that is how women do. *We* know. *We* are women. *We* know how they do.

The boy had let himself be persuaded. His women folk gave him money and he got a room and a new job over in Jersey. They wouldn't tell Joanna where he was. He never saw her again. Joanna wasn't married. Joanna had the baby.

The waves had almost stopped passing over Francie when she discovered to her fright that something was wrong with her. She pressed her hand over her heart trying to feel a jagged edge under the flesh. She had heard papa sing so many songs about the heart; the heart that was breaking—was aching—was dancing—was heavy laden—that leaped for joy—that was heavy in sorrow—that turned over—that stood still. She really believed that the heart actually did those things. She was terrified thinking her heart had broken inside her over Joanna's baby and that the blood was now leaving her heart and flowing from her body.

She went upstairs to the flat and looked into the mirror. Her eyes had dark shadows beneath them and her head was aching. She lay on the old leather couch in the kitchen and waited for mama to come home.

She told mama what had happened to her in the cellar. She said nothing about Joanna. Katie sighed and said, "So soon? You're just thirteen. I didn't think it would come for another year yet. I was fifteen."

"Then . . . then . . . this is all right what's happening?"

"It's a natural thing that comes to all women."

"I'm not a woman."

"It means you're changing from a girl into a woman."

"Do you think it will go away?"

"In a few days. But it will come back again in a month."

"For how long?"

"For a long time. Until you are forty or even fifty." She mused awhile. "My mother was fifty when I was born."

"Oh, it has something to do with having babies."

"Yes. Remember always to be a good girl because you can have a baby now." Joanna and her baby flashed through Francie's mind. "You mustn't let the boys kiss you," said mama.

"Is that how you get a baby?"

"No. But what makes you get a baby often starts with a kiss." She added, "Remember Joanna."

Now Katie didn't know about the street scene. Joanna happened to pop into her mind. But Francie thought she had wonderful powers of insight. She looked at mama with new respect.

Remember Joanna. Remember Joanna. Francie could never forget her. From that time on, remembering the stoning women, she hated women. She feared them for their devious ways, she mistrusted their instincts. She began to hate them for this disloyalty and their cruelty to each other. Of all the stone-throwers, not one had dared to speak a word for the girl for fear that she would be tarred with Joanna's brush. The passing man had been the only one who spoke with kindness in his voice.

Most women had the one thing in common: they had great pain when they gave birth to their children. This should make a bond that held them all together; it should make them love and protect each other against the man-world. But it was not so. It seemed like their great birth pains shrank their hearts and their souls. They stuck together for only one thing: to trample on some other woman . . . whether it was by throwing stones or by mean gossip. It was the only kind of loyalty they seemed to have.

Men were different. They might hate each other but they stuck together against the world and against any woman who would ensnare one of them.

Francie opened the copybook which she used for a diary. She skipped a line under the paragraph that she had written about intolerance and wrote:

"As long as I live, I will never have a woman for a friend. I will never trust any woman again, except maybe mama and sometimes Aunt Evy and Aunt Sissy."

31

Two very important things happened in the year that Francie was thirteen. War broke out in Europe and a horse fell in love with Aunt Evy.

Evy's husband and his horse, Drummer, had been bitter enemies for eight years. He was mean to the horse; he kicked him and punched him and cursed at him and pulled too hard on the bit. The horse was mean to Uncle Willie Flittman. The horse knew the route and stopped automatically at each delivery. It had been his habit to start up again as soon as Flittman mounted the wagon. Lately, he had taken to starting up the instant Flittman got off to deliver milk. He'd break into a trot and often Flittman had to run more than half a block to catch up with him.

Flittman was through delivering at noon. He'd go home to eat dinner, then bring the horse and wagon back to the stable where he was supposed to wash Drummer and the wagon. The horse had a mean trick. Often when Flittman was washing under his belly, he'd wet on him. The other fellows would stand around waiting for this to happen so that they could have a good laugh. Flittman couldn't stand it so he got in the habit of washing the horse in front of his house. That was all right in the summer but it was a little hard on the horse in the winter. Often, on a bitterly cold day, Evy would go down and tell Willie that it was a mean thing to wash Drummer in the cold and with cold water, too. The horse seemed to know that Evy was taking his part. As she argued with her husband, Drummer would whinny pitifully and lay his head on her shoulder.

One cold day, Drummer took matters into his own hands—or as Aunt Evy said it, into his own feet. Francie listened enchanted while Aunt Evy told the story to the Nolans. No one could tell a story like Evy. She acted out all the parts—even the horse and, in a funny way, she'd put in what she thought each one was secretly thinking at the time. It happened like this according to Evy:

Willie was down on the street washing the shivering horse with cold water and hard yellow soap. Evy was standing at the window watching. He leaned under to wash the horse's belly and the horse tensed. Flittman thought Drummer was going to wet on him again and it was more than the harassed and futile little man could stand. He hauled off and punched the horse in the belly. The horse lifted a leg and kicked him decisively in the head. Flittman rolled under the horse and lay unconscious.

Evy ran down. The horse whinnied happily when he saw her but she paid no attention to him. When he looked over his shoulder and saw that Evy was trying to drag Flittman out from under, he started to walk. Maybe he wanted to help Evy by pulling the wagon clear of the unconscious man or maybe he wanted to finish the job by rolling the wagon over him. Evy hollered out, "Whoa there, boy," and Drummer stopped just in time.

A little boy had gone for a policeman who had gone for the ambulance. The ambulance doctor couldn't make out whether Flittman had a fracture or a concussion. He took him to a Greenpoint Hospital.

Well, there was the horse and wagon full of empty milk bottles to be gotten back to the stables. Evy had never driven a horse but that was no reason why she couldn't. She put on one of her husband's old overcoats, wrapped a shawl around her head, climbed up into the seat, picked up the reins and called out, "Git for home, Drummer." The horse swung his head back to give her a loving look, then set off at a cheerful trot.

It was lucky he knew the way. Evy hadn't the slightest idea where the stables were. He was a smart horse. He stopped at each intersection and waited while Evy looked up and down the cross street. If all was clear, she'd say, "Giddy-yap, boy." If another vehicle was coming she'd say, "Just a minute, boy." In this way they reached the stables without mishap and the horse cantered in proudly to his usual place in the row. Other drivers, washing their wagons, were surprised to see a lady driver. They made such a commotion that the stable boss came running and Evy told him what had happened.

"I saw it coming," the boss said. "Flittman never did like that horse and the horse never liked him. Well, we'll have to take on another man."

Evy, fearful lest her husband lose his job, asked whether she couldn't take his route while he was in the hospital. She argued that the milk was delivered in the dark and no one would ever know. The boss laughed at her. She told him how much they needed that twenty-two-fifty a week. She pleaded so hard, and looked so little and pretty and spunky, that he gave in at last. He gave her the list of customers and told her the boys would load the wagon for her. The horse knew the route, he said, and it wouldn't be too hard. One of the drivers suggested that she take the stable dog along for company and protection against milk thieves. The boss agreed to that. He told her to report to the stables at 2 A.M. Evy was the first milk woman on the route.

She got along fine. The fellows at the stable liked her and said that she was a better worker than Flittman. In spite of her practicalness, she was soft and feminine and the men loved the low and breathless way she had of talking. And the horse was very happy and co-operated as much as he could. He stopped automatically before each house where milk was to be left and never started up again until she was safely in the seat.

Like Flittman, she brought him to her house while she ate her dinner. Because the weather was so cold, she took an old quilt from her bed and threw it over him so he wouldn't catch cold while he waited for her. She took his oats upstairs and heated them for a few minutes in the oven before she fed him. She didn't think ice-cold oats were appetizing. The horse enjoyed the warmed oats. After he finished munching, she treated him to half an apple or a lump of sugar.

She thought it was too cold to wash him on the street. She took him back to the stable for that. She thought the yellow soap was too biting, so she brought along a cake of Sweetheart Soap and a big old bath towel to dry him with. The men at the stable offered to wash the horse and wagon for her but she insisted on washing the horse herself. Two men got into a fight over who should wash the wagon. Evy settled it by saying one could wash it one day and the other, the next day.

She heated Drummer's wash water on a gas plate in the boss's office. She'd never think of washing him in cold water. She washed him with the warm water and the sweet-scented soap and dried him carefully bit by bit with the towel. He never committed an indignity on her while she washed him. He snorted and whinnied happily throughout the washing. His skin rippled in voluptuous delight when Evy rubbed him dry. When she worked around his chest, he rested his tremendous head on her small shoulder. There was no doubt about it. The horse was madly in love with Evy.

When Flittman recovered and reported back for work, the horse refused to leave the stable with him on the wagon seat. They had to give Flittman another route and another horse. But Drummer wouldn't got out with any other driver either. The boss had just about made up his mind to have him sold, when he got an idea. Among the drivers, there was an effeminate young man who talked with a lisp. They put him on Flittman's wagon. Drummer seemed satisfied and consented to go out with the lady-like driver on the seat.

So Drummer took up his regular duties again. But every day at noon, he turned into the street where Evy lived and stood in front of her door. He wouldn't go back to the stables until Evy had come down, given him a bit of apple or some sugar, stroked his nose and called him a good boy.

"He was a funny horse," said Francie after she heard the story.

"He may have been funny," said Aunt Evy, "but he sure knew what he wanted."

32

Francie had started a diary on her thirteenth birthday with the entry:

> Dec. 15. Today I enter my teens. What will the year bring
> forth? I wonder.

The year brought forth little according to the entries which
became sparser as the year wore on. She had been prompted to start a
diary because fictional heroines kept them and filled them with lush
sighing thoughts. Francie thought her diary would be like that, but
excepting for some romantic observations on Harold Clarence, actor,
the entries were prosaic. Toward the end of the year she riffled
through the pages reading an item here and there.

> Jan. 8. Granma Mary Rommely has a pretty carved box that her
> great grandfather made in Austria over a hundred years ago. She
> has a black dress and white petticoat and shoes and stockings in it.
> They are her burying clothes as she doesn't want to be buried in
> a shroud. Uncle Willie Flittman said he wants to be cremated and
> his ashes scattered from the Statue of Liberty. He thinks he'll be
> a bird in the next life and he wants a good start. Aunt Evy said
> he's a bird already, a cuckoo. Mama scolded me for laughing. Is
> cremation better than burying? I wonder.
> Jan. 10. Papa sick today.

March 21. Neeley stole pussy willows from McCarren's Park and gave them to Gretchen Hahn. Mama said he's too young to be thinking about girls. There's time enough, she said.

April 2. Papa hasn't worked for three weeks. There's something wrong with his hands. They shake so much he can't hold anything.

April 20. Aunt Sissy says she's going to have a baby. I don't believe it because she's flat in front. I heard her tell mama she's carrying it in the back. I wonder.

May 8. Papa sick today.

May 9. Papa went to work tonight but had to come home. Said the people didn't need him.

May 10. Papa sick. Had bad nightmares in the daytime and screamed. I had to get Aunt Sissy.

May 12. Papa hasn't worked for over a month. Neeley wants to get his working papers and leave school. Mama said no.

May 15. Papa worked tonight. He said he's going to take charge of things from now on. He scolded Neeley about the working papers.

May 17. Papa came home sick. Some kids were following him on the street and making fun of him. I hate kids.

May 20. Neeley has a paper route now. He won't let me help sell papers.

May 28. Carney did not pinch my cheek today. He pinched something else. I guess I'm getting too big to sell junk.

May 30. Miss Garnder said they are going to publish my winter time composition in the magazine.

June 2. Papa came home sick today. Neeley and I had to help mama get him upstairs. Papa cried.

June 4. I got A on my composition today. We had to write on My Ambition. I only made one mistake. I wrote play-writer and Miss Garnder said the right word was playwright.

June 7. Two men brought papa home today. He was sick. Mama was away. I put papa to bed and gave him black coffee. When mama came home she said that was the right thing to do.

June 12. Miss Tynmore gave me Schubert's Serenade today.

Mama's ahead of me. She got Tannhauser's Evening Star. Neeley says he's ahead of both of us. He can play Alexander's Ragtime Band without notes.

June 20. Went to show. Saw The Girl of the Golden West. It was the best show I ever saw, the way the blood dripped through the ceiling.

June 21. Papa was away for two nights. We didn't know where he was. He came home sick.

June 22. Mama turned my mattress today and found my diary and read it. Everywhere I had the word drunk, she made me cross it out and write sick. It's lucky I didn't have anything against mama written down. If ever I have children I will not read their diaries as I believe that even a child is entitled to some privacy. If mama finds this again and reads it, I hope she will take the hint.

June 23. Neeley says he has a girl. Mama says he's too young. I wonder.

June 25. Uncle Willie, Aunt Evy, Sissy and her John over tonight. Uncle Willie drank a lot of beer and cried. He said the new horse he's got, Bessie, did worse than wet on him. Mama scolded me for laughing.

June 27. We finished the Bible today. Now we got to start all over. We've gone through Shakespeare four times already.

July 1. Intolerance. . . .

Francie put her hand over the entry to hide the words. For a moment, she thought the waves would pass over her again. But the feeling went away. She turned the page and read another entry.

July 4. Sergeant McShane brought papa home today. Papa wasn't arrested as we thought at first. He was sick. Mr. McShane gave Neeley and me a quarter. Mama made us give it back.

July 5. Papa still sick. Will he ever work again? I wonder.

July 6. We started playing the North Pole game today.

July 7. North Pole.

July 8. North Pole.

July 9. North Pole. Expected rescue did not come.

July 10. We opened the tin-can bank today. There was eight dollars and twenty cents in it. My golden pennies had turned black.

July 20. All the money from the tin-can bank is gone. Mama took some washing to do for Mrs. McGarrity. I helped iron but burnt a hole on Mrs. McGarrity's drawers. Mama won't let me iron anymore.

July 23. I got a job at Hendler's Restaurant just for the summer. I wash dishes during the dinner and supper rush. I use gobs of soft soap out of a barrel. On Monday a man comes and collects three barrels of scraps of fat and brings back one barrel of soft soap on Wednesday. Nothing is wasted in this world. I get two dollars a week and my meals. It isn't hard work but I don't like that soap.

July 24. Mama said I'd be a woman before I knew it. I wonder.

July 28. Floss Gaddis and Frank are going to be married as soon as he gets a raise. Frank says that the way President Wilson is running things we'll be in the war before you know it. He says he's marrying because he wants a wife and kids so that when war comes he doesn't have to fight. Flossie says that's not true; it's a case of true love. I wonder. I remember how Flossie used to chase him years ago when he was washing the horse.

July 29. Papa wasn't sick today. He's going to get a job. He said mama has to stop washing for Mrs. McGarrity and I have to give up my job. He says we'll be rich and all go to live in the country. I wonder.

Aug. 10. Sissy says she's going to have a baby soon. I wonder. She's as flat as a pancake.

Aug. 17. Papa has been working for three weeks now. We have wonderful suppers.

Aug. 18. Papa's sick.

Aug. 19. Papa's sick because he lost his job. Mr. Hendler won't take me back in the restaurant. He says I'm not reliable.

Sept. 1. Aunt Evy, Uncle Willie over tonight. Willie sang Frankie and Johnny and put dirty words in it. Aunt Evy stood on a chair and punched him in the nose. Mama scolded me for laughing.

Sept. 10. I started my last year of school. Miss Garnder said if I keep on getting A's on my composition, she might let me write a play for graduation. I have a very beautiful idea. There will be a girl in a white dress and her hair hanging down her back and she will be Fate. Other girls will come out on the stage and tell what they *want* from Life and Fate will tell them what they'll *get*. At the end a girl in a blue dress will spread out her arms and say, "Is life worth living then?" And there will be a chorus that says "yes." Only it will all be in rhyme. I told papa about it but he was too sick to understand. Poor papa.

Sept. 18. I asked mama could I get a Castle Clip and she said no that hair was a woman's crowning beauty. Does that mean she expects me to be a woman soon? I hope so because I want to be my own boss and get my hair cut off if I feel like it.

Sept. 24. Tonight when I took a bath, I discovered that I was changing into a woman. It's about time.

Oct. 25. I will be glad when this book is filled up as I am getting tired of keeping a diary. Nothing important ever happens.

Francie came to the last entry. Only one more blank page left. Well, the sooner she got it filled, the sooner the diary keeping would be over and she wouldn't have to bother with it anymore. She wet her pencil.

Nov. 2. Sex is something that invariably comes into everyone's life. People write pieces against it. The priests preach against it. They even make laws against it. But it keeps going on just the same. All the girls in school have but the one topic of conversation: sex and boys. They are very curious about it. Am I curious about sex?

She studied the last sentence. The line on the inner edge of her right eyebrow deepened. She crossed out the sentence and rewrote it to read: "I am curious about sex."

33

Yes, there was a great curiosity about sex among the adolescent chil-
dren of Williamsburg. There was a lot of talk about it. Among the
younger children there was some exhibitionism (you show me and
I'll show you). A few hypocrites devised such evasive games as
"playing house" or "doctor." A few uninhibited ones did what they
called "play dirty."

There was a great hush-hush about sex in that neighborhood.
When children asked questions, the parents didn't know how to
answer them for the reason that these people did not know the cor-
rect words to use. Each married couple had its own secret words for
things which were whispered in bed in the quiet of night. But there
were few mothers brave enough to bring these words out into the
daylight and present them to the child. When the children grew up,
they in turn invented words which they couldn't tell *their* children.

Katie Nolan was neither a mental nor a physical coward. She tackled every problem masterfully. She didn't volunteer sex information
but when Francie asked questions she answered as best she knew
how. Once when Francie and Neeley were young children, they had
agreed to ask their mother certain questions. They stood before her
one day. Francie was the spokesman.

"Mama, where did we come from?"

"God gave you to me."

The Catholic children were willing to accept that but the next question was a sticker. "How did God get us to you?"

"I can't explain that because I'd have to use a lot of big words that you wouldn't understand."

"Say the big words and see if we understand them."

"If you understood them, I wouldn't have to tell you."

"Say it in some kind of words. Tell us how babies get here."

"No, you're too little yet. If I told you, you'd go around telling all the other children what you know and their mothers would come up here and say I was a dirty lady and there would be fights."

"Well, tell us why girls are different from boys."

Mama thought for awhile. "The main difference is that a little girl sits down when she goes to the bathroom and a little boy stands up."

"But Mama," said Francie. "I stand up when I'm afraid in that dark toilet."

"And I," confessed little Neeley, "sit down when . . ."

Mama interrupted. "Well, there's a little bit of man in every woman and a little bit of woman in every man."

That ended the discussion because it was so puzzling to the children that they decided to go no further with it.

When Francie, as she wrote in her diary, started to change into a woman, she went to mama about her sex curiosity. And Katie told her simply and plainly all that she herself knew. There were times in the telling when Katie had to use words which were considered dirty but she used them bravely and unflinchingly because she knew no other words. No one had ever told her about the things she told her daughter. And in those days, there were no books available for people like Katie from which they could learn about sex in the right way. In spite of the blunt words and homely phrasing, there was nothing revolting in Katie's explanations.

Francie was luckier than most children of the neighborhood. She found out all she needed to know at the time she had to know about it. She never needed to slink into dark hallways with other girls and exchange guilty confidences. She never had to learn things in a distorted way.

If normal sex was a great mystery in the neighborhood, criminal sex was an open book. In all poor and congested city areas, the prowling sex fiend is a nightmarish horror that haunts parents. There seems to be one in every neighborhood. There was one in Williamsburg in that year when Francie turned fourteen. For a long time, he had been molesting little girls, and although the police were on a continual lookout for him, he was never caught. One of the reasons was that when a little girl was attacked, the parents kept it secret so that no one would know and discriminate against the child and look on her as a thing apart and make it impossible for her to resume a normal childhood with her playmates.

One day, a little girl on Francie's block was killed and it had to come out in the open. She had been a quiet little thing of seven, well behaved and obedient. When she didn't come home from school, her mother didn't worry; she thought the child had stopped somewhere to play. After supper, they went looking for her; they questioned her playmates. No one had seen the child since school let out.

A fear wave swept over the neighborhood. Children were called in off the streets and kept behind locked doors. McShane came over with half a dozen policemen and they began combing the roofs and cellars.

The child was found at last, by her loutish seventeen-year-old brother. Her little body was lying across a busted-down doll carriage in the cellar of a near-by house. Her torn dress and undergarments, her shoes and her little red socks were thrown on an ash heap. The brother was questioned. He was excited and stuttered when he answered. They arrested him on suspicion. McShane wasn't stupid. The arrest was a blind to put the killer off guard. McShane knew the killer would feel safe and strike again; and this time, the police would be waiting for him.

Parents went into action. The children were told (and to hell with finding the right words) about the fiend and the horrible things he did. Little girls were warned not to take candy from strangers, not to speak to strange men. Mothers took to waiting in the doorways for their children when school let out. The streets were deserted. It was as if the Pied Piper had led all the children off to some mountain fastness. The whole neighborhood was terrorized. Johnny got so worried about Francie that he got a gun.

Johnny had a friend named Burt who was night watchman at the corner bank. Burt was forty years old and married to a girl half his age of whom he was insanely jealous. He suspected that she took a lover in the nights when he was at the bank. He brooded over this so much that he came to the conclusion that it would be a relief if he knew for sure that this was so. He was willing to exchange soul-destroying suspicion for heart-breaking reality. Accordingly, he slipped home at odd hours during the night while his friend, Johnny Nolan, watched the bank for him. They had signals. When, in the night, poor Burt got so tormented that he had to go home, he asked the cop on the beat to ring the Nolan bell three times. If Johnny was home when the signal came, he jumped out of bed like a fireman, dressed hurriedly and ran to the bank as though his life depended on it.

After the watchman slipped out, Johnny lay on Burt's narrow cot and felt the hard revolver through the thin pillow. He hoped someone would attempt to rob the bank so he could save the money and be a hero. But all the hours of his night watching were without event. There wasn't even the excitement of the watchman catching his wife in adultery. The girl always was sleeping soundly and alone when her husband sneaked into their flat.

When Johnny heard of the rape and murder, he went over to the bank to see his friend, Burt. He asked the watchman whether he had another gun.

"Sure. Why?"

"I'd like the lend of it, Burt."

"Why, Johnny?"

"There's this fellow loose that killed the little girl on our block."

"I hope they ketch him, Johnny. I sure hope they ketch the son-of-a-bitch."

"I have a daughter of my own."

"Yeah, yeah, I know, Johnny."

"So I'd like you to loan me a gun."

"It's against the Sullivan Law."

"It's against some other law for you to go away from the bank and leave me here. How do you know? I may be a robber."

"Aw, no, Johnny."

"I figure if we break one law, we might as well break another."

"All right. All right. I'll lend it." He opened a desk drawer and took out a revolver. "Now I'll show you. When you want to kill somebody, you point it at 'em like this," he pointed it at Johnny, "and pull this thing."

"I see. Let me try it." In his turn, Johnny aimed it at Burt.

"'Course," said Burt, "I ain't never shot off the God-damned thing myself."

"This is the first time I ever held a gun in my hand," explained Johnny.

"Watch out then," said the watchman quietly. "It's loaded!"

Johnny shivered and put the gun down carefully. "Say, Burt, I didn't know. We might have killed each other."

"Jesus, you're right." The watchman shuddered.

"One jerk of a finger and a man is dead," mused Johnny.

"Johnny, you ain't thinking of killing yourself?"

"No, I'm letting the booze do that." Johnny started to laugh but stopped abruptly. As he left with the gun Burt said,

"Let me know if you catch the bastard."

"I'll do that," promised Johnny.

"Yeah. So long."

"So long, Burt."

Johnny gathered his family around him and explained about the gun. He warned Francie and Neeley not to touch it. "This little cylinder holds death for five people in it," he explained dramatically.

Francie thought the revolver looked like a grotesque beckoning finger, a finger that beckoned to death and made it come running. She was glad when papa put it out of sight under his pillow.

The gun lay under Johnny's pillow for a month and was never touched. There were no further outrages in the neighborhood. It seemed that the fiend had moved on. Mothers began to relax. A few, however, like Katie, continued to watch in door or hallway when they knew the children were due home from school. It was the killer's habit to lurk in dark hallways for his victims. Katie felt that it cost nothing to be careful.

When most of the people were lulled into a feeling of security, the pervert struck again.

One afternoon, Katie was cleaning in the halls of the second house away from her own. She heard children in the street and knew that school was out. She wondered whether it was necessary to go back and wait in their hallway for Francie as she had been doing since the murder. Francie was nearly fourteen and old enough to take care of herself. Besides the killer usually attacked little girls of six or seven. Maybe he had been caught in some other neighborhood and was safe in jail. Still. . . . She hesitated, then decided to go home. She'd be needing a fresh bar of soap within the hour and could kill two birds with one stone if she got it now.

She looked up and down the street and grew uneasy when she didn't see Francie among the children. Then she remembered that Francie went further to school and came home a bit later. Once in the flat, Katie decided to heat the coffee and have a cupful. By that time, Francie should be home, and her mind would be at peace. She went into the bedroom to see if the gun was still under the pillow. Of course it was and she felt foolish for looking. She drank the coffee, took her bar of yellow soap and started back for work.

Francie got home at her usual time. She opened the hall door, stared up and down the long narrow hall, saw nothing and closed the solid wood door behind her. Now the hall was darkened. She walked the short length of hall towards the stairs. As she put her foot on the first step, she saw him.

He stepped out from a small recess under the stairs that had an entrance to the cellar. He walked softly but with lunging steps. He was thin and undersized and wore a shabby dark suit with a collarless and tieless shirt. His thick bushy hair grew down on his forehead almost to his eyebrows. He had a beaked nose and his mouth was a thin crooked line. Even in the semi-darkness, Francie was aware of his wet-looking eyes. She took another step, then, as she got a better look at him, her legs turned into cement. She couldn't lift them to take the next step! Her hands clutched two banister spokes and she clung to them. What hypnotized her into being unable to move was the fact that the man was coming towards her with his lower garments opened. Francie stared at the exposed part of his body in paralyzed horror. It was wormy white contrasted with the ugly dark sallowness of his face and hands. She felt the same kind of nausea she had once felt when she saw a swarm of fat white maggots crawling over the putrid carcass of a rat. She tried to scream "mama" but her throat closed over and only air came out. It was like a horrible dream where you tried to scream but no sound came. She couldn't move! She couldn't move! Her hands hurt from gripping the banister spokes. Irrelevantly, she wondered why they didn't snap off in her tight grasp. And now he was coming towards her and she couldn't run! She couldn't run! Please God, she prayed, let some tenant come along.

At this moment, Katie was walking down the stairs quietly with the bar of yellow soap in her hand. When she came to the top of the last flight, she looked down and saw the man coming at Francie and saw that Francie was frozen to the banister spokes. Katie made no sound. Neither one saw her. She turned quietly and ran up the two flights to her flat. Her hand was steady as she took the key from under the mat and opened the door. She took precious time, not aware of what she was doing, to set the cake of yellow soap on the washtub cover. She got the gun from under the pillow, aimed it, and keeping it aimed, put it under her apron. Now her hand was trembling. She put her other hand under her apron and steadied the gun with her two hands. Holding the gun in this way, she ran down the stairs.

The murderer reached the foot of the stairs, rounded it, leaped up the two steps, and, quick as a cat, threw one arm about Francie's neck and pressed his palm to her mouth to prevent her screaming. He put his other arm around her waist and started to pull her away. He slipped and the exposed part of his body touched her bare leg. The leg jerked as though a live flame had been put to it. Her legs came out of the paralysis then and she kicked and struggled. At that, the pervert pressed his body close to hers, pinning her against the banister. He began undoing her clenched fingers, one by one. He got one hand free, forced it behind her back and leaned hard against it while he started to work on her other hand.

There was a sound. Francie looked up and saw her mother running down that last flight of stairs. Katie was running awkwardly, not balancing well on account of having both hands clutched under her apron. The man saw her. He couldn't see that she had a gun. Reluctantly, he loosed his hold and backed down the two steps keeping his wet eyes on Katie. Francie stood there, one hand still gripping the banister spoke. She couldn't get her hand opened. The man got off the steps, pressed his back to the wall and started sliding against it to the cellar door. Katie stopped, knelt on a step, pushed her apron bulge between two banister spokes, stared at the exposed part of his body and pulled the trigger.

There was a loud explosion and the smell of burnt cloth as the hole in Katie's apron smoldered. The pervert's lip curled back to show broken dirty teeth. He put both hands on his stomach and fell. His hands came away as he hit the floor and blood was all over that part of him that had been worm-white. The narrow hall was full of smoke.

Women screamed. Doors banged open. There was the sound of running feet in the halls. People in the streets started pouring into the hall. In a second, the doorway was jammed and no one could get in or out.

Katie grabbed Francie's hand and tried to pull her up the stairs, but the child's hand was frozen to the spoke. She couldn't open her fingers. In desperation, Katie hit Francie's wrist with the gun butt and the numb fingers relaxed at last. Katie pulled her up the steps and through the halls. She kept meeting women coming out of their flats.

"What's the matter? What's the matter?" they screamed.

"It's all right now. It's all right now," Katie told them.

Francie kept stumbling and going to her knees. Katie had to drag her on her knees the length of the last hall. She got her into the flat and onto the couch in the kitchen. Then she put the chain bolt on the door. As she put the gun down carefully next to the bar of yellow soap, her hand accidentally touched the muzzle. She was frightened when she found it warm. Katie knew nothing about guns; she had never shot one before. Now she thought the heat might make the gun go off by itself. She opened the washtub cover and threw the gun into the water in which some soiled clothes were soaking. Because the bar of yellow soap was mixed up with the whole thing, she threw that in after the gun. She went to Francie.

"Did he hurt you, Francie?"

"No, Mama," she moaned. "Only he . . . his . . . I mean it . . . touched my leg."

"Where?"

Francie pointed to a spot above her blue sock. The skin was white and unharmed. Francie looked at it in surprise. She had an idea that the skin would be eaten away there.

"There's nothing the matter with it," mama said.

"But I can still feel where it touched." She moaned and cried out insanely, "I want my leg cut off."

People pounded on the door demanding to know what had happened. Katie ignored them and kept the door bolted. She made Francie swallow a cup of scalding hot black coffee. Then she walked up and down the room. She was trembling now. She didn't know what to do next.

Neeley had been loitering on the street when the shot sounded. When he saw people crowding into the hallway, he, too, worked his way in. He got up on the stairs and looked over the banisters. The pervert was huddled where he had fallen. The crowd of women had torn the trousers from his body and all who could get near were grinding their heels into his flesh. Others were kicking at him and spitting on him. All were shrieking obscenities at him. Neeley heard his sister's name.

"Francie Nolan?"

"Yeah. Francie Nolan."

"You sure? Francie Nolan?"

"I tell you I seen."

"Her mother went and . . ."

"Francie Nolan!"

He heard the ambulance gong. He thought Francie had been killed. He raced up the stairs sobbing. He pounded on the door, screaming, "Let me in, Mama! Let me in!"

Katie let him in. When he saw Francie lying on the couch, he bawled louder. Now Francie started to bawl. "Stop it! Stop it!" Katie screamed. She shook Neeley until he didn't have a sob left in him.

"Run and get your father. Look all over until you find him."

Neeley found papa in McGarrity's saloon. Johnny was just about to settle down to a long afternoon of slow drinking. When he heard Neeley's story, he dropped his glass and ran out with him. They couldn't get back into the house. The ambulance was at the door and four policemen were fighting a way through the crowd trying to get the ambulance doctor in.

Johnny and Neeley went through the next door cellar into the yard, helped each other over the board fence into their own yard and climbed up on the fire escape. When Katie saw Johnny's derby looming up outside the window, she screamed and ran around frantically looking for the gun. Fortunately for Johnny, she had forgotten where she had thrown it.

Johnny ran to Francie, and, big as she was, he picked her up in his arms as though she were a baby. He rocked her and told her to go to sleep. Francie kept insisting that she wanted her leg cut off.

"Did he get her?" asked Johnny.

"No, but I got him," Katie said grimly.

"Did you shoot him with the pistol?"

"With what else?" She showed him the hole in her apron.

"Did you shoot him good?"

"As good as I could. But she keeps talking about her leg. His . . ." her eyes slid towards Neeley, ". . . well, you know, touched her leg." She pointed to the spot. Johnny looked but he saw nothing. "That's too bad it had to happen to her," Katie said. "She's such a one for remembering. She might never get married, remembering."

"We'll fix that leg," promised papa.

He put Francie back on the couch, got the carbolic acid and swabbed the spot with the strong raw stuff. Francie welcomed the burning pain of the acid. She felt that the evil of the man's touch was being seared away.

Someone pounded at the door. They remained quiet and unanswering. They wanted no outsiders in their home at this time. A strong Irish voice called.

"Open up the door. 'Tis the law, now."

Katie opened the door. A policeman walked in followed by an ambulance intern carrying a bag. The cop pointed to Francie.

"This the kid he tried to get?"

"Yes."

"Doc, here, has to make an examination."

"I won't allow it," protested Katie.

"It's the law," he answered quietly.

So Katie and the intern took Francie into the bedroom and the terrified child had to submit to the indignity of an examination. The jaunty intern made a quick and careful examination. He straightened up and started to put his instruments back into the bag. He said,

"She's okay. He never got near her." He took her swollen wrist in his hand. "How did this happen?"

"I had to hit her with the gun to make her let go of the banister," Katie explained. He noticed her bruised knee.

"What's this?"

"That's where I had to drag her along the hall." Then he got to the angry burn just above her ankle. "And what in the name of God is this?"

"That's where her father washed her leg with carbolic acid where that man touched her."

"My God!" exploded the intern. "You trying to give her third degree burns?" He opened the bag again, put cooling salve on the burn and bandaged it neatly. "My God!" he said again, "between the two of you, you did more damage than the criminal." He smoothed down Francie's dress, patted her cheek and said, "You'll be all right, girlie. I'm going to give you something to put you to sleep. When you wake up, just remember that you had a bad dream. That's all it was; a bad dream. Hear?"

"Yes, sir," said Francie gratefully. Again she saw a poised needle. She remembered something from a long time ago. She worried. Was her arm clean? Would he say . . .

"That's a brave girl," he said as the needle jabbed.

"Why, he's on my side," thought Francie hazily. She went to sleep immediately after the hypodermic.

Katie and the doctor came out into the kitchen. Johnny and the cop were sitting at the table. The cop had a bit of pencil clutched in his big paw and he was painfully making small notes in a small notebook.

"Kid all right?" asked the cop.

"Fine," the intern told him, "just suffering from shock and parentinitus." He winked at the cop. "When she wakes up," he said to Katie, "remember to keep telling her that she had a bad dream. Don't talk about it otherwise."

"What do I owe you, Doc?" asked Johnny.

"Nothing, Mac. This is on the city."

"Thank you," whispered Johnny.

The intern noticed Johnny's trembling hands. He pulled a pint flask from his hip pocket and thrust it at Johnny. "Here!" Johnny looked up at him. "Go ahead, Mac," insisted the intern. Gratefully, Johnny took a long swallow. The intern passed the flask to Katie. "You too, Lady. You look as if you need it." Katie took a big drink. The cop spoke up.

"What do you take me for? A orphan?"

When the intern got the flask back from the cop, there was only an inch left in it. He sighed and emptied the bottle. The cop sighed, too, and turned to Johnny.

"Now. Where do you keep the gun?"

"Under my pillow."

"Get it. I got to take it over to the station house."

Katie, forgetting how she had disposed of the gun, went into the bedroom to look under the pillow. She came back, looking worried.

"Why, it's not there!"

The cop laughed. "Naturally. You took it out to shoot the louse."

It took Katie a long time to remember that she had thrown it into the washtub. She fished it out. The cop wiped it off and took out the bullets. He asked Johnny a question.

"You got a permit for this, Mac?"

"No."

"That's tough."

"It's not my gun."

"Who gave it to you?"

"No——Nobody." Johnny didn't want to get the watchman in trouble.

"How'd you get it then?"

"I found it. Yes, I found it in the gutter."

"All oiled and loaded?"

"Honest."

"And that's your story?"

"That's my story."

"It's okay by me, Mac. See that you stick to it."

The ambulance driver hollered from the hall that he was back from taking the man to the hospital and was Doc ready to leave.

"Hospital?" Katie asked. "Then I didn't kill him."

"Not quite," said the intern. "We'll get him on his feet so's he can walk to the electric chair by himself."

"I'm sorry," said Katie. "I meant to kill him."

"I got a statement from him before he passed out," said the cop. "That little kid down the block: he killed her. He was responsible for two other jobs, too. I got his statement, signed and witnessed." He patted his pocket. "I wouldn't be surprised if I got a promotion out of this when the Commissioner hears."

"I hope so," said Katie bleakly. "I hope somebody gets some good out of it."

When Francie woke the next morning, papa was there to tell her that it was all a dream. And as time passed it did seem like a dream to Francie. It left no ugliness in her memories. Her physical terror had blunted her emotional perceptions. The terror on the stairs had been brief—a bare three minutes in time—and terror had served as an anesthetic. The events following were hazy in her mind on account of the unaccustomed hypodermic. Even the hearing in court where she had to tell her story seemed like a part in an unreal play in which her lines were brief.

There was a hearing, but Katie was told beforehand that it was a technicality. Francie remembered little of it except that she told her story and Katie told hers. Few words were needed.

"I was coming home from school," testified Francie, "and when I got in the hall, this man came out and grabbed me before I could scream. While he was trying to drag me off the stairs, my mother came down."

Katie said: "I came down the stairs and saw him there pulling my daughter. I ran up and got the gun (it didn't take long) and I ran down and shot him while he was trying to sneak down the cellar."

Francie wondered whether mama would be arrested for shooting a man. But no, it ended up with the judge shaking mama's hand and hers too.

A lucky thing happened about the newspapers. A soused reporter, going through his nightly routine of calling up the station houses for police blotter news, got the facts of the story but confused the Nolan name with the name of the policeman on the case. There was a half column item in a Brooklyn paper which said that Mrs. O'Leary of Williamsburg had shot a prowler in the hallway of her home. The next day, two of the New York newspapers gave it two inches in which they stated that Mrs. O'Leary of Williamsburg had been shot by a prowler in the hallway of her home.

Eventually, the whole affair faded away into the background. Katie was a neighborhood heroine for awhile but as time passed, the neighborhood forgot the murdering pervert. They remembered only that Katie Nolan had shot a man. And in speaking of her, they said that she's not one to get into a fight with. Why she'd shoot a person just as soon as look at them.

The scar from the carbolic acid never left Francie's leg but it dwindled down to the size of a dime. Francie got used to it in time and as she grew older, she seldom noticed it any more.

As for Johnny, they fined him five dollars for violating the Sullivan Law—having a gun without a permit. And, oh, yes! The watchman's young wife eventually ran away with an Italian a little nearer her own age.

Some days later Sergeant McShane came over looking for Katie. He saw her lugging a can of ashes out to the curb and his heart turned over with pity. He gave her a hand with the ash can. Katie thanked him and looked up at him. She had seen him once since the Mattie Mahony outing, the day he had asked Francie was she her mother. The other time was when he had brought Johnny home, the time when Johnny couldn't get himself home. Katie had heard that Mrs. McShane was now in a sanatorium for incurable tuberculosis patients. She was not expected to live long. "Would he marry again—afterwards?" Katie wondered. "Of course he will," she answered her own question. "He is a fine-looking, upstanding man with a good job and some woman will snap him up." He took off his hat while he spoke to her.

"Mrs. Nolan, the boys down at the station house and myself do be thankin' you for helpin' us out in the catchin' of the murtherer."

"You're welcome," said Katie conventionally.

"And to show their appreciation, what did the boys do but pass the hat for you!" He extended an envelope.

"Money?" she asked.

"It is that."

"Keep it!"

"Sure you'll be needin' it with your man not workin' steady and the childthern needin' this and that."

"That's none of your business, Sergeant McShane. You can see that I work hard and we don't need anything from nobody."

"Just as you say."

He put the envelope back into his pocket, looking at her steadily all the while. "Here's a woman," he thought, "with a trim figure on her and a pretty white-faced skin and black curling hair.

And she's got courage enough and pride for six like her. I'm a middle-aged man of forty-five," his thoughts went on, "and she's but a slip of a girl." (Katie was thirty-one but looked much younger.) "We've both had hard luck when it came to marryin'. That we did." McShane knew all about Johnny and knew that he wouldn't last long the way he was going on. He had nothing but pity for Johnny; he had nothing but pity for Molly, his wife. He wouldn't have harmed either of them. He had never once considered being physically unfaithful to his sickly wife. "But is hoping in my heart harming either one of them?" he asked himself. "Of course, there'll be the waitin'. How many years? Two? Five? Ah, well, I've waited a long time without hope of happiness. Sure and I can wait a bit longer, now."

He thanked her again and said goodbye formally. As he held her hand in the handclasp, he thought, "She'll be my wife, someday, God and she willin'."

Katie could not know what he was thinking. (Or could she?) Maybe. Because something prompted her to call after him.

"I hope that someday you'll be as happy as you deserve to be, Sergeant McShane."

34

When Francie heard Aunt Sissy tell mama that she was going to get a baby, she wondered why Sissy didn't say *have* a baby, like other women said. She found out there was a reason why Sissy said *get* instead of *have*.

Sissy had had three husbands. There were ten tiny headstones in a small plot in St. John's Cemetery in Cypress Hills, belonging to Sissy. And on each stone, the date of death was the same as the date of birth. Sissy was thirty-five, now, and desperate about not having children. Katie and Johnny often talked it over and Katie was afraid that Sissy would kidnap a child someday.

Sissy wanted to adopt a child, but her John wouldn't hear of it.

"I'll not support another man's bastard, see?" was his way of putting it.

"Don't you like children, Lover?" she asked wheedlingly.

"Sure I like children. But they got to be my own and not some other bum's," he answered, unintentionally insulting himself.

In most things, her John was like soft dough in Sissy's hands. But in this one thing, he refused to allow himself to be kneaded her way. If there was to be a child, he kept insisting, it would have to be his and no other man's. Sissy knew he meant it. She even had a kind of respect for his attitude. But she *had* to have a living baby.

By chance, Sissy found out that a beautiful sixteen-year-old girl out in Maspeth had gotten into trouble with a married man and was going to have a baby. Her parents, Sicilians lately come over from the other side, had shut up the girl in a dark room so that the neighbors could not see her shame increase. Her father kept her on a diet of bread and water. He had a theory that this would weaken her so that she and her child would die in childbirth. Lest the kind-hearted mother feed Lucia during his absence, the father left no money in the house when he went to work in the mornings. He brought a bagful of groceries each night when he returned home and watched that no food was sneaked out and set aside for the girl. After the family had eaten, he gave the girl her daily ration of half a loaf of bread and a jug of water.

Sissy was shocked when she heard this story of starvation and cruelty. She thought out a plan. Feeling as they did, she thought the family might be glad to give away the baby when it was born. She decided to have a look at the people. If they seemed normal and healthy, she'd offer to take the baby.

The mother wouldn't let her into the house when she called. Sissy came back the next day with a badge pinned to her coat. She knocked on the door. When it was opened a crack, she pointed to the badge and sternly demanded admittance. The frightened mother, thinking Sissy was from the immigration department, let her in. The mother could not read else she would have seen that the badge said "Chicken Inspector."

Sissy took charge. The mother-to-be was frightened and defiant and also very thin from the starvation diet. Sissy threatened the girl's mother with arrest if she didn't treat the girl better. With many tears and in badly broken English, the mother told of the disgrace and of the father's plan to starve the girl and the unborn child to death. Sissy had a day-long talk with the mother and Lucia, the daughter. It was mostly in pantomime. At last Sissy made it understood that she was willing to take the child off their hands as soon as it was born. When the mother understood finally, she covered Sissy's hand with grateful kisses. From that day, Sissy became the adored and trusted friend of the family.

After her John left for work in the morning, Sissy cleaned up her flat, cooked a potful of food for Lucia and took it over to the

Italian home. She fed Lucia well on a combination Irish-German diet. She had a theory that if the child absorbed such food before birth, it wouldn't be so much of an Italian.

Sissy took good care of Lucia. On nice days, she took her out to the park and made her sit in the sun. During the time of their unusual relationship, Sissy was a devoted friend and a gay companion to the girl. Lucia adored Sissy who was the only one in this new world who had treated her kindly. The whole family (except the father, who didn't know of her existence) loved Sissy. The mother and other children gladly entered into a conspiracy to keep the father in ignorance. They locked Lucia up in her dark room again when they heard the father's step on the stairs.

The family couldn't speak much English and Sissy knew no Italian but as the months passed, they learned some English from her and she learned Italian from them and they were able to talk together. Sissy never told her name so they called her "Statch' Lib'ty" after the lady with the torch which had been the first thing they saw of America.

Sissy took over Lucia, her unborn child and the family. When everything was settled and agreed upon, Sissy announced to her friends and family that she was starting another baby. No one paid any attention. Sissy was always starting babies.

She found an obscure midwife and paid her in advance for the delivery. She gave her a paper on which she had asked Katie to write her name, her John's name and Sissy's maiden name. She told the midwife that the paper was to be turned over to the Board of Health immediately after the birth. The ignorant woman, who could not speak Italian (Sissy had made sure of that when she hired her) assumed that the names handed her were the names of the mother and father. Sissy wanted the birth certificate to be in order.

Sissy was so realistic about her pregnancy by proxy that she simulated morning sickness in the beginning weeks. When Lucia announced that she felt life, Sissy told her husband that *she* felt life.

On the afternoon that Lucia's labor pains started, Sissy went home and got into bed. When her John came home from work, she told him the baby was starting to come. He looked at her. She was as trim as a ballet dancer. He argued, but she was so insistent, that he went and got her mother. Mary Rommely looked at Sissy and said she couldn't possibly be having a baby. For answer, Sissy let out a blood-curdling yell and said that her pains were killing her. Mary looked at her thoughtfully. She didn't know what Sissy had in mind but she did know it was useless to argue with her. If Sissy said she was going to have a baby, she was going to have a baby, and that's all there was to it. Her John protested.

"But look how skinny she is. There's no baby in that belly, see?"

"Maybe it will come from her head. That's big enough as one may see," said Mary Rommely.

"Aw, there don't give such things," said the John.

"Who are you to say?" demanded Sissy. "Didn't the Virgin Mary herself get a baby without a man? If she could do it, I'm sure I could do it easier, being's I'm married and have a man."

"Who knows?" asked Mary. She turned to the harassed husband and spoke gently. "There are a lot of things that men don't understand about." She urged the confused man to forget the whole thing, eat a nice supper which she would cook for him, and then go to bed and get a good night's sleep.

The puzzled man lay beside his wife throughout the night. He couldn't get a good night's sleep. From time to time, he'd rise on his elbow and stare at her. From time to time, he'd run his hand over her flat stomach. Sissy slept soundly all through the night.

When he left for work the next morning, Sissy announced that he'd be a father before he returned that night.

"I give up," shouted the tormented man and went off to his work in the pulp magazine house.

Sissy rushed over to Lucia's house. The baby had been born just an hour after the father had left. It was a beautiful healthy girl. Sissy was so happy. She said Lucia would have to nurse the baby for ten days to give it a start, then she'd take it home. She went out and bought a roasting chicken and a bakery store pie. The mother cooked the chicken Italian style. Sissy trusted a bottle of Chianti wine from the Italian grocer on the block and they all had a fine dinner. It was like a *fiesta* in the house. Everybody was happy. Lucia's stomach was almost flat again. There was no longer any monument to her disgrace. Now all was as it had been before . . . or would be when Sissy took the baby away.

Sissy washed the baby every hour. She changed its shirt and band three times during the day. The diapers were changed every five minutes whether they needed to be or not. She washed Lucia and made her clean and sweet. She brushed and brushed her hair until it glowed like satin. She couldn't do enough for Lucia and the baby. She had to tear herself away when it came time for the father's returning.

The father came home and went into the dark room to give Lucia her daily food pittance. He turned up the gas and found a radiant Lucia and a fat healthy baby sleeping contentedly at her side. He was amazed. All this on bread and water! Then fright grew on him. It was a miracle! Surely the Virgin Mary had intervened for the young mother. She had been known to work such miracles in Italy. Maybe he would be punished for treating his flesh and blood so inhumanly. Contrite, he brought her a plate heaped with spaghetti. Lucia declined it saying she had grown used to bread and water. The mother sided with Lucia and explained that the bread and water had formed the perfect baby. More and more the father believed a miracle had come about. Frantically, he tried to be nice to Lucia, but the family were punishing him. They wouldn't permit him to show any kindness to his daughter.

Sissy was lying peacefully in bed when her John came home that evening. Jokingly, he asked,

"Did you have that baby today?"

"Yes," she said in a weak voice.

"Aw, go on!"

"It was born an hour after you left this morning."

"It was not!"

"I swear!"

He looked around the room. "Where is it, then?"

"In the incubator at Coney Island."

"In the *where?*"

"It was a seven months' baby, you know. Only weighed three pounds. That's why I didn't show."

"You lie, see?"

"As soon as I get my strength back, I'll take you to Coney Island right to the glass case where it is."

"What are you trying to do? Drive me crazy?"

"I'm going to bring it home in ten days. Just as soon as it grows finger nails." She put that in on the spur of the moment.

"*What's* gotten into you, Sissy? You know God-damned well you didn't have a baby this morning."

"I had a baby. It weighed three pounds. They took it to the incubator so that it wouldn't die and I'm going to get it back in ten days."

"I give up! I give up," he shouted and went out and got drunk.

Sissy brought the baby home ten days later. It was a big baby and weighed almost eleven pounds. Her John asserted himself for the last time.

"It seems mighty big for a ten-day-old baby."

"You're a mighty big man yourself, Lover," she whispered. She saw a pleased look come into his face. She put her arms around him. "I'm all right now," she said in his ear, "if you want to sleep with me."

"You know," he said afterwards, "it does look a little like me."

"Especially around the ears," murmured Sissy drowsily.

The Italian family went back to Italy a few months later. They were glad to go because the new world had brought them nothing but sorrow, poverty and shame. Sissy never heard of them again.

Everybody knew that it wasn't Sissy's baby—that it *couldn't* be her baby. But she stuck to her story and since there was no other explanation, people had to accept it. After all, strange things did happen in the world. She christened the child Sarah, but in time everyone called it Little Sissy.

Katie was the only one to whom Sissy told the truth about the origin of the baby. She confided in her when she asked her to write out the names for the birth certificate. Ah, but Francie knew too. Often in the night she had been wakened by the sound of voices and heard mama and Aunt Sissy talking in the kitchen about the baby. Francie vowed always to keep Sissy's secret.

Johnny was the only other person (outside of the Italian family) who knew. Katie told him. Francie heard them talking about it when they thought she was sound asleep. Papa took the part of Sissy's husband.

"That's a dirty trick to play on a man, any man. Somebody ought to tell him. I'll tell him."

"No!" said mama sharply. "He's a happy man. Let him be that way."

"Happy? With another man's child palmed off on him? I don't see it."

"He's crazy for Sissy; he's always afraid she's going to leave him and he'd die if she left him. And you know Sissy. She went from one man to another, one husband to another—always trying to get a child. She was on the verge of leaving this one when the baby happened along. Sissy will be a different woman from now on. Mark my words. She'll settle down at last and make him a much better wife than he deserves to have. Who *is* this John, anyhow?" she interrupted herself. "She'll be a good mother. The child will be her whole world and she won't need to be going after the men any more. So don't monkey around with it, Johnny."

"You Rommely women are too deep for us men," decided Johnny. A thought struck him. "Say! You didn't do that to me, did you?"

In answer, Katie got the children out of bed. She had them stand before him in their long white nightgowns. "Look at them," she commanded. Johnny looked at his son. It was as if he were looking in a trick mirror where he saw himself perfectly but on a smaller scale. He looked at Francie. There was Katie's face all over again (only more solemn) except for the eyes. They were Johnny's eyes. On an impulse, Francie picked up a plate and held it over her heart the way Johnny held his hat when he sang. She sang one of his songs:

> *They called her frivolous Sal.*
> *A peculiar sort of a gal . . .*

She had Johnny's expressions and Johnny's gestures.

"I know, I know," papa whispered. He kissed his children, gave them each a pat on the backside and told them to go back to bed. After they had gone, Katie pulled Johnny's head down and whispered something to him.

"No!" he said in a surprised voice.

"Yes, Johnny," she said quietly. He put his hat on. "Where are you going, Johnny?"

"Out."

"Johnny, please don't come home . . ." she looked towards the bedroom door.

"I won't, Katie," he promised. He kissed her gently and went out.

Francie woke up in the middle of the night wondering what had taken her out of her sleep. Ah! Papa hadn't come home yet. That was it. She never slept soundly until she knew he had come home. Once awake, she started thinking. She thought of Sissy's baby. She thought of birth. Her thoughts went to birth's corollary: death. She didn't want to think of death; how everybody was born but to die. While she was fighting off thoughts of death, they heard papa coming up the stairs singing softly. She shivered when she heard that he was singing the last verse of "Molly Malone." He never sang that verse. *Never!* Why . . . ?

> *She died of a fever,*
> *And no one could save her,*
> *And that's how I lo-ost*
> *Sweet Molly Malone . . .*

Francie didn't stir. It was a rule that when papa came home late, mama was to open the door. She didn't want the children to lose their sleep. The song was coming to an end. Mama didn't hear—she wasn't getting up. Francie jumped out of bed. The song was ended before she reached the door. When she opened it, papa was standing there quietly, his hat in his hand. He was looking straight before him, over her head.

"You won, Papa," she said.

"Did I?" he asked. He walked into the room not looking at her.

"You finished the song."

"Yes, I finished the song, I guess." He sat in the chair by the window.

"Papa. . . ."

"Turn out the light and go back to bed." (The light was kept burning low against his return.) She turned out the light.

"Papa, are . . . are you sick?"

"No. I'm not drunk," he said clearly from the dark. And Francie knew that he spoke the truth.

She went to bed and buried her face in the pillow. She did not know why, but she wept.

35

Once more it was in the week before Christmas. Francie had just had her fourteenth birthday. Neeley, as he put it, was waiting to turn thirteen any moment. It looked as though it wouldn't be such a good Christmas. There was something wrong with Johnny. Johnny wasn't drinking. There had been other times, of course, when Johnny stopped drinking but that was when he was working. Now he wasn't drinking at all and he wasn't working, and the wrong thing about Johnny was that he wasn't drinking but he was acting like he was drinking.

He hadn't spoken to his family in more than two weeks. Francie remembered the last time papa had said anything to her was that night when he came home sober singing the last verse of "Molly Malone." Come to think of it, he hadn't sung since that night either. He came and went without speaking. He stayed out late nights and came home sober and nobody knew where he spent that time. His hands were trembling badly. He could hardly hold the fork when he ate. And suddenly, he looked very old.

Yesterday he had come in while they were eating supper. He looked at them as though he were going to say something. Instead of speaking, however, he closed his eyes for a second and then went into the bedroom. He had no regular hours for anything. He came and went at odd hours of the day and night. When he was home, he spent the time lying on his bed fully clothed with his eyes shut.

Katie went about white and quiet. There was a foreboding about her as though she were carrying tragedy within herself. Her face was thin and there were hollows under her cheeks but her body was fuller.

She had taken on an extra job in this week before Christmas. She got up earlier and worked faster at her flat cleaning and was finished in early afternoon. She rushed down to Gorling's, the department store at the Polish end of Grand Street, where she worked from four to seven, serving coffee and sandwiches to the salesgirls who were not allowed to take the time to go out for supper on account of the Christmas rush. Her family desperately needed that seventy-five cents that she earned each day.

It was nearly seven o'clock. Neeley had come home from his paper route and Francie was back from the library. There was no fire in the flat. They had to wait until mama came home with some money with which to buy a bundle of wood. The children wore their coats and zitful caps as it was very cold in the flat. Francie saw that mama had wash on the line and she pulled it in. The garments had frozen into grotesque shapes and didn't want to come in through the window.

"Here, let me at 'em," said Neeley referring to a frozen suit of underwear. The legs of the long drawers had frozen in a spread out position and Neeley's struggles did no good.

"I'll break the damn thing's legs," said Francie. She whacked it fiercely and it crackled and collapsed. She pulled it in viciously. She looked like Katie at that moment.

"Francie?"

"Huh?"

"You . . . you *cursed*."

"I know it."

"God heard you."

"Oh, shoot!"

"Yes, He did. He sees and He hears everything."

"Neeley, do you believe that He looks right in this little old room?"

"You betcha He does."

"Don't you believe it, Neeley. He's too busy watching all the little sparrows fall and worrying about whether the little buds will burst into flowers to have time to investigate us."

"Don't talk like that, Francie."

"I will so. If He went around looking into people's windows like you say, He'd see how things were here; He'd see that it was cold and that there was no food in the house; He'd see that mama isn't strong enough to work so hard. And He'd see how papa was and He'd do something about papa. Yes, He would!"

"Francie . . ." the boy looked around the room uneasily. Francie saw that he was uneasy.

"I'm getting too big to tease him," she thought. Aloud she said, "All right, Neeley." They talked about other things until Katie came home.

Katie came in with a rush. She had a bundle of wood blocks which she had bought for two cents, a can of condensed milk and three bananas in a bag. She stuffed paper and the wood into the range and had a fire going in no time.

"Well, children, I guess we'll have to have oatmeal for supper tonight."

"Again?" groaned Francie.

"It won't be so bad," said mama. "We have condensed milk and I brought bananas to slice on top."

"Mama," ordered Neeley, "don't mix my condensed milk with the oatmeal. Let it stay on top."

"Slice the bananas and cook them with the oatmeal," suggested Francie.

"I want to eat my banana whole," protested Neeley.

Mama settled the argument. "I'll give you each a banana and you eat it the way you want."

When the oatmeal was cooked, Katie filled two soup plates full, set them on the table, punched two holes in the can of milk and set a banana by each plate.

"Aren't you going to eat, Mama?" asked Neeley.

"I'll eat after. I'm not hungry now." Katie sighed.

Francie said, "Mama, if you don't feel like eating, why don't you play the piano so it's like a restaurant while we're eating."

"It's cold in the front room."

"Light the oil stove," chorused the children.

"All right." Katie took a portable oil stove from the cupboard. "Only you know I don't play so good."

"You play grand, Mama," said Francie sincerely.

Katie was pleased. She knelt to light the oil stove. "What do you want me to play?"

"Come, Little Leaves," called Francie.

"Welcome, Sweet Springtime," shouted Neeley.

"I'll play 'Little Leaves' first," decided mama, "because I didn't give Francie a birthday present." She went into the cold front room.

"I think I'll slice my banana on top of my oatmeal. I'll slice it very thin so that there's a whole lot of it," said Francie.

"I'm going to eat mine whole," decided Neeley, "and slow, so that it lasts a long time."

Mama was playing Francie's song, now. It was one that Mr. Morton had taught the children. She sang to the music:

> *Come, little leaves, said the wind one day.*
> *Come o'er the meadows with me and play.*
> *Put on your dresses of red and gold ...*

"Aw, that's a baby song," interrupted Neeley. Francie stopped singing. When Katie finished Francie's song, she started to play Rubinstein's "Melody in F." Mr. Morton had taught them that song, too, calling it "Welcome, Sweet Springtime." Neeley started to sing:

> *Welcome, sweet springtime, we greet thee in song.*

His voice changed suddenly from tenor to bass on the high note in "song." Francie giggled and soon Neeley was giggling so much that he couldn't sing.

"You know what mama would say if she was sitting here now?" asked Francie.

"What?"

"She'd say, 'spring will be here before you know it.'" They laughed.

"Christmas is coming soon," commented Neeley.

"Remember when we were children," said Francie, who had just finished being thirteen, "how we used to smell if Christmas was coming?"

"Let's see if we can still smell it," Neeley said impulsively. He opened the window a crack and put his nose to it. "Yup."

"What does it smell like?"

"I smell snow. Remember how, when we were kids we used to look up at the sky and holler, 'Feather boy, feather boy, shake down some feathers from the sky."

"And when it snowed, we thought there was a feather boy up there. Let me smell," she asked suddenly. She put her nose to the crack. "Yes, I can smell it. It smells like orange peels and Christmas trees put together." They closed the window.

"I never snitched on you that time you got the doll when you said your name was Mary."

"No," said Francie gratefully. "And I didn't tell on you either, the time you made a cigarette out of coffee grounds and when you smoked it, the paper caught fire and fell on your blouse and burned a big hole in it. I helped you hide it."

"You know," mused Neeley, "mama found that blouse and sewed a patch over the hole and she never asked me about it."

"Mama is funny," said Francie. They pondered awhile over their mother's inscrutable ways. The fire was dying down now but the kitchen was still warm. Neeley sat on top of the far end of the stove where it wasn't so hot. Mama had warned him that he'd get piles from sitting on a hot stove. But Neeley didn't care. He liked his backside to be warm.

The children were almost happy. The kitchen was warm and they were fed and mama's playing made them seem safe and comfortable. They reminisced about past Christmases, or, as Francie put it, they talked about olden times.

While they were talking, someone pounded on the door. "It's papa," said Francie.

"No. Papa always sings coming up the stairs so we know it's him."

"Neeley, papa hasn't sung coming home since that night. . . ."

"Let me in!" shouted Johnny's voice and he beat on the door as though he would break it down. Mama came running out from the front room. Her eyes looked very dark in her white face. She opened the door. Johnny lunged in. They stared at him. They had never seen papa looking like that. He was always so neat and now his tuxedo jacket was dirty as though he had been lying in the gutter and his derby hat was bashed in. He didn't own an overcoat or gloves. His cold red hands were trembling. He lunged to the table.

"No, I'm not drunk," he said.

"Nobody said . . ." began Katie.

"At last I'm through with it. I hate it, I hate it, I hate it!" He pounded the table. They knew he was speaking the truth. "I haven't touched a drop since that night . . ." he broke off suddenly. "But no one would believe me any more. No one. . . ."

"There, Johnny," said mama soothingly.

"What's the matter, Papa?" asked Francie.

"Sh! Don't bother your father," said mama. She spoke to Johnny. "There's coffee left from this morning, Johnny. It's nice and hot and we've got milk tonight. I was waiting until you came home so that we could eat together." She poured coffee.

"We ate already," said Neeley.

"Hush!" mama told him. She put milk into the coffee and sat opposite Johnny. "Drink it, Johnny, while it's hot."

Johnny stared at the cup. Suddenly he pushed it from him and Katie drew a sharp breath as it clattered to the floor. Johnny buried his head in his arms and sobbed shudderingly. Katie went to him.

"What's the matter, Johnny, what's the matter?" she asked soothingly. Finally he sobbed out:

"They threw me out of the Waiters' Union today. They said I was a bum and a drunk. They said they'd never give me another job as long as I live." He controlled his sobs for a moment and his voice was frightened as he said, "as long as I live!" He wept bitterly. "They wanted me to turn in my Union button." He put his hand over the tiny green and white button he wore in his lapel. Francie's throat got tight as she remembered how he often said he wore it like an ornament, a rose. He was so proud to be a Union man. "But I wouldn't give it up," he sobbed.

"That's nothing, Johnny. You just get a good rest and get on your feet again and they'll be glad to take you in. You're a good waiter and the best singer they've got."

"I'm no good any more. I can't sing any more. Katie, they laugh at me now when I sing. The last few jobs I had, they hired me to give the people a laugh. It's come to that, now. I'm finished." He sobbed wildly; he sobbed as though he never could stop.

Francie wanted to run into the bedroom and hide her head under the pillow. She edged toward the door. Mama saw her.

"Stay here!" she said sharply. She spoke to papa again. "Come, Johnny. Rest awhile and you'll feel better. The oil stove is lit and I'll put it in the bedroom and it will be nice and warm. I'll sit with you until you fall asleep." She put her arms around him. Gently, he put her arms away and went into the bedroom alone, sobbing more quietly. Katie spoke to the children. "I'm going to stay with papa for awhile. Keep on talking or doing whatever you were doing." The children stared at her numbly. "What are you looking at me like that for?" her voice broke. "Nothing's the matter." They looked away. She went into the front room to get the oil stove.

Francie and Neeley did not look at each other for a long time. Finally he said, "Do you want to talk about olden times?"

"No," said Francie.

36

Johnny died three days later.

He had gone to bed that night and Katie had sat by him until he went to sleep. Later she slept with Francie so as not to disturb him. Sometime during the night he got up, dressed quietly and went out. He did not return the next night. The second day they began looking for him. They looked all over but Johnny hadn't been in any of his accustomed haunts for a week.

The second night, McShane came over to take Katie to a nearby Catholic Hospital. On the way over he told her, as gently as he could, about Johnny. Johnny had been found early that morning huddled in a doorway. He was unconscious when a cop found him. His tuxedo jacket was buttoned up over his undershirt and the cop saw the St. Anthony's medal around his neck and called up the Catholic Hospital ambulance. There were no marks of identification on him. Later the cop made his report at the station house and gave a description of the unconscious man. In the routine of checking the reports, McShane came across the description. His sixth sense told him who the man was. He went to the hospital and saw that it was Johnny Nolan.

Johnny was still living when Katie got there. He had pneumonia, the doctor told her, and there wasn't a chance. It was merely a question of hours. Already he was in the coma that came before death. They took Katie to him. His bed was in a long corridor-like ward.

There were fifty other beds in the ward. Katie thanked McShane and said goodbye. He went away knowing that she wanted to be alone with Johnny.

There was a screen, connoting dying, around Johnny's bed. They brought a chair for Katie and she sat there all day watching him. He was breathing harshly and there were dried tears on his face. Katie stayed there until he died. He had never opened his eyes. He had not spoken a word to his wife.

It was night when she came home. She decided not to tell the children until the morning. "Let them have a night's sleep behind them," she thought, "one more night of griefless sleep." She told them only that their father was in the hospital and very sick. She said no more. There was something about the way she looked that discouraged the children from asking questions.

Just as dawn came, Francie woke. She looked across the narrow bedroom and saw mama sitting next to Neeley's bed and looking down into his face. Her eyes were dark underneath and she looked as though she had been sitting there all night. When she saw that Francie was awake, she told her to get up and get dressed right away. She shook Neeley gently to awaken him and told him the same thing. She went out into the kitchen.

The bedroom was gray and cold and Francie shivered as she got into her clothes. She waited for Neeley, not wanting to go out to mama alone. Katie was sitting by the window. They came before her and stood waiting.

"Your father is dead," she told them.

Francie stood numb. There was no feeling of surprise or grief. There was no feeling of anything. What mama just said had no meaning.

"You're not to cry for him," ordered mama. Her next words had no sense either. "He's out of it now and maybe he's luckier than we are."

An orderly at the hospital was in the pay of an undertaker whom he notified as soon as a death occurred. This wide-awake undertaker gained an advantage over his competitors in that he went after the business while the others waited for the business to come after them. This enterprising fellow called on Katie early in the morning.

"Mrs. Nolan," he said, surreptitiously referring to the slip of paper on which the orderly had written her name and address, "I sympathize with you in your great grief. I give you a thought: What has come to you has to come to all of us."

"What do you want?" asked Katie bluntly.

"To be your friend." He hurried on before she could misunderstand. "There are details connected with . . . ah . . . the remains, I mean . . ." again a quick look at the slip, "I mean Mr. Nolan. I ask you to look on me as a friend who brings comfort at a time when . . . who will . . . well, I want you to leave everything in my hands."

Katie understood. "How much would you charge for a simple funeral?"

"Now don't you worry about costs," he hedged. "I'll give him a fine funeral. There's no man I respected more than Mr. Nolan." (He had never known Mr. Nolan.) "I'll make it my personal business to see that he gets the best there is. Don't worry about the money."

"I won't. Because there's none to worry about."

He wet his lips. "Aside from the insurance money of course." It was a question, not a statement.

"There's insurance. A little."

"Ah!" He rubbed his hands together happily. "There's where I can be of service. There's red tape connected with collecting insurance. Take a long time before you get the money. Now supposing you (and understand I'm not charging you for this) let me take care of it. You just sign this," he whisked a paper out of his pocket, "turning your policy over to me. I'll advance the money and collect on the policy."

All undertakers gave this "service." It was a trick to ascertain how much insurance there was. Once they knew the amount, the funeral cost eighty per cent of it. They *had* to leave a little money for mourning clothes to keep the people satisfied.

Katie got the policy. As she put it on the table, his practiced eye picked out the amount: two hundred dollars. He appeared not to have looked at the policy. After Katie had signed the paper, he talked of other things for awhile. Finally, as if coming to a decision, he said:

"Tell you what I'll do, Mrs. Nolan. I'll give the departed a first-class four-coach funeral with a nickel handle coffin for one hundred and seventy-five dollars. That's my regular two-hundred-and-fifty-dollar job and I'm not making a penny on it."

"Why are you doing it then for?" asked Katie.

He wasn't at all put out. "I'm doing it because I liked Mr. Nolan. A splendid man and a hard-working man." He noticed the surprised look Katie gave him.

"I don't know," she hesitated. "A hundred and seventy-five . . ."

"That includes the mass, too," he put in hastily.

"All right," said Katie dully. She was tired of talking about it.

The undertaker picked up the policy and pretended to see the amount for the first time. "Say! This is for two hundred," he said in stagey surprise. "That means you got twenty-five dollars coming to you after the funeral is paid." He dug into his pocket stretching his leg out straight before him to do so. "Well, I always say that a little cash comes in handy at a time like this . . . at any time, if you ask me." He chuckled understandingly. "So I'll just advance you the balance out of my own pocket." He put twenty-five dollars in new bills on the table.

Katie thanked him. He wasn't fooling her but she made no protest. She knew that was the way things were done. He was only working at his trade. He asked her to get the death certificate from the officiating doctor.

"And please inform them that I'll call for the re . . . I mean for the depart . . . well, I'll come and get Mr. Nolan."

When Katie went to the hospital again, she was taken to the doctor's office. The priest of the parish was there. He was trying to supply information for the making out of the death certificate. When he saw Katie, he made the sign of the cross in blessing and then shook her hand.

"Mrs. Nolan can tell you more than I can," said the priest.

The doctor asked necessary questions; the full name and place of birth and date of birth and so on. Finally Katie asked *him* a question.

"What are you writing down there—what he died from, I mean."

"Acute alcoholism and pneumonia."

"They said he died of pneumonia."

"That was the direct cause of death. But this acute alcoholism was a definite contributing factor; probably the main cause of death, if you wish the truth."

"I don't want you to write down," said Katie slowly and steadily, "that he died from drinking too much. Write that he died of pneumonia alone."

"Madam, I have to state the entire truth."

"He's dead. What can it mean to you what he died of?"

"The law requires . . ."

"Look," said Katie. "I got two nice children. They're going to grow up to amount to something. It isn't their fault that their father . . . that he died from what you said. It would mean a lot to me if I could tell them that their father died of pneumonia alone."

The priest took a hand in it. "You can do it, Doctor," he said, "without hurt to yourself and with benefit to others. Don't be kicking around of a poor lad that's dead and gone. Write down pneumonia which is no lie, and this lady will be remembering you in her prayers for a long time to come. Besides," he added practically, "it's no skin off your teeth."

All of a sudden, the doctor recalled two things; he remembered that the priest was a member of the hospital board and he remembered that he liked being head doctor at that particular hospital.

"All right," he conceded. "I'll do it. But don't let it get around. It's a personal favor to you, Father." He wrote down "pneumonia" in the blank after "Cause of death."

And it was nowhere on record that John Nolan had died a drunkard.

Katie used the twenty-five dollars to buy mourning clothes. She bought Neeley a new black suit with long pants. It was his first long-pants suit, and pride, pleasure and grief fought in Neeley's heart. For herself, Katie got a new black hat and a three-foot widow's veil according to the custom of Brooklyn. Francie got new shoes which she had been needing for a long time anyhow. It was decided not to buy Francie a black coat as she was growing fast and it wouldn't fit her next winter. Mama said her old green coat would do with a black band around the arm. Francie was glad because she hated black and had worried lest her mother put her in deep mourning. The little money left over after the shopping was finished was put in the tin-can bank.

The undertaker came again to report that Johnny was at his funeral parlor and was being fixed up fine and would be brought home that evening. Katie told him, rather sharply, not to give them the details.

Then the blow fell.

"Mrs. Nolan, I have to have the deed to your lot."

"What lot?"

"The cemetery plot. I need the deed to get the grave opened."

"I thought that was all in the hundred and seventy-five dollars."

"No, no, no! I'm giving you a bargain. The coffin alone cost me . . ."

"I don't like you," said Katie in her blunt way. "I don't like the business you're in. But then," she added with her amazing detachment, "I suppose someone has to bury the dead. How much is a plot?"

"Twenty dollars."

"Where in the world would I get . . ." She stopped short. "Francie, get the screwdriver."

They pried up the tin-can bank. There was eighteen dollars and sixty-two cents in it.

"It's not enough," said the undertaker, "but I'll lay out the rest." He held out his hand for the money.

"I'll get all the money together," Katie told him. "But I'll not turn over the money until I have the deed in my hand."

He fussed and argued and finally went away saying he'd bring back the deed. Mama sent Francie over to Sissy's house to borrow two dollars. When the undertaker came back with the deed, Katie, remembering something her mother had said fourteen years ago read it slowly and carefully. She made Francie and Neeley read it too. The undertaker stood first on one foot, then on the other. When all three Nolans were satisfied that the deed was in order, Katie handed over the money.

"Why should I want to cheat you, Mrs. Nolan?" he asked plaintively as he put the money away carefully.

"Why should anyone want to cheat anybody?" she asked in return. "But they do."

The tin-can bank stood in the middle of the table. It was fourteen years old and its strips were battered.

"Do you want me to nail it back down, Mama?" asked Francie.

"No," said mama slowly. "We won't need it any more. You see, we own a bit of land now." She placed the folded deed on top of the clumsy star bank.

Francie and Neeley remained out in the kitchen all the time the coffin was in the front room. They even slept in the kitchen. They didn't want to see their father in the coffin. Katie seemed to understand and did not insist that they go in and look at their father.

The house was full of flowers. The Waiters' Union, which had thrown Johnny out less than a week before, sent around an enormous pillow of white carnations with a purple ribbon running diagonally across it on which were the words in gold letters: *Our Brother.* The cops from the precinct, in memory of the capture of the murderer, sent a cross of red roses. Sergeant McShane sent a sheaf of lilies. Johnny's mother, the Rommelys and some of the neighbors sent flowers. There were flowers from dozens of Johnny's friends that Katie had never heard of. McGarrity, the saloon keeper, sent a wreath of artificial laurel leaves.

"I'd throw it in the ash can," said Evy indignantly when she read the card.

"No," said Katie gently, "I can't blame McGarrity. Johnny didn't *have* to go there."

(Johnny owed McGarrity over thirty-eight dollars at the time of his death. For some reason, the saloon keeper said nothing to Katie about it. He cancelled the debt silently.)

The flat was sickly with the combined scents of roses, lilies and carnations. Forever after, Francie hated those flowers, but it pleased Katie to know how much people had thought of Johnny.

A few moments before they were to close the coffin lid on Johnny, Katie came out to the kitchen to the children. She put her hands on Francie's shoulders and spoke low.

"I heard some neighbors whispering. They said you won't look at your father because he wasn't a good father to you."

"He *was* a good father," said Francie fiercely.

"Yes, he was," agreed Katie. She waited, letting the children make their own decision.

"Come on, Neeley," said Francie. Hand in hand, the children went in to their father. Neeley looked quickly, then, afraid he would start crying, he ran out of the room. Francie stood there with her eyes on the ground, afraid to look. Finally she lifted her eyes. She couldn't believe that papa wasn't living! He wore his tuxedo suit which had been cleaned and pressed. He had on a fresh dicky and collar and a carefully-tied bow tie. There was a carnation in his lapel and, above it, his Union button. His hair was shining and golden and as curling as ever. One of the locks was out of place and had fallen down on the side of his forehead a little. His eyes were closed as though he were sleeping lightly. He looked young and handsome and well-cared for. She noticed for the first time how finely arched his eyebrows were. His small mustache was trimmed and looked as debonair as ever. All the pain and grief and worry had left his face. It was smooth and boyish-looking. Johnny was thirty-four years old when he died. But he looked younger now; like a boy just past twenty. Francie looked at his hands, crossed so casually over a silver crucifix. There was a circlet of whiter skin on his third finger where he used to wear the signet ring that Katie had given him when they married. (Katie had taken it off to give to Neeley when he grew up.) It was queer to see papa's hands so quiet when she remembered them as always trembling. Francie noticed how narrow and sensitive-looking they were with the long and tapering fingers. She stared steadily at his hands and thought she saw them move. Panic churned up in her and she wanted to run away. But the room was full of people watching her. They would say she was running away because . . . He *had* been a good father. He had! He had! She put her hand on his hair and put the lock back in place. Aunt Sissy came and put her arm around her and whispered, "It's time." Francie stepped back to stand with mama while they closed the lid.

At the mass, Francie knelt on one side of mama and Neeley on the other. Francie kept her eyes on the floor so that she wouldn't have to look at the flower-covered coffin standing on trestles before the altar. Once she stole a look at her mother. Katie was kneeling, staring straight ahead, her face white and quiet under the widow's veil.

When the priest stepped down and walked around the coffin sprinkling holy water at the four corners of it, a woman sitting across the aisle sobbed wildly. Katie, jealous and fiercely possessive even in death, turned sharply to look at the woman who dared weep for Johnny. She looked well at the woman, then turned her head away. Her thoughts were like torn bits of paper blowing around.

"Hildy O'Dair is old for her age," she thought. "It's like powder was sprinkled on her yellow hair. But she's not much older than me . . . thirty-two or three. She was eighteen when I was seventeen. You go your way and I'll go my way. You mean you'll go her way. Hildy, Hildy . . . he's my feller, Katie Rommely . . . Hildy, Hildy . . . but she's my best friend . . . I'm not much good, Hildy . . . I shouldn't have led you on . . . you go your . . . Hildy, Hildy. Let her cry, let her cry," thought Katie. "Someone who loved Johnny should cry for him and I can't cry. Let her. . . ."

Katie, Johnny's mother, and Francie and Neeley rode out to the cemetery in the first coach behind the hearse. The children sat with their backs to the driver. Francie was glad because she couldn't see the hearse which led the procession. She saw the coach which followed. Aunt Evy and Aunt Sissy were in that one alone. Their husbands couldn't come because they were working and Granma Mary Rommely was staying home to mind Sissy's new baby. Francie wished she were riding in the second coach. Ruthie Nolan wept and lamented during the whole of the ride. Katie sat in stony quiet. The carriage was close and smelled of damp hay and stale horse manure. The smell, the closeness, the riding backwards and the tension gave Francie an unfamiliar feeling of sickness.

At the cemetery, there was a plain wooden box standing beside a deep hole. They put the cloth covered casket with its shiny handles into the plain box. Francie looked away when they lowered it into the grave.

It was a gray day and a chill wind was blowing. Little whirls of frozen dust eddied about Francie's feet. A short distance away, at a week-old grave, some men were stripping the withered flowers from the wire frames of the floral pieces heaped on the grave. They worked methodically, keeping the withered flowers in a neat heap and piling up the wire frames carefully. Theirs was a legitimate business. They bought this concession from the cemetery officials and sold the wire frames to the florists who used them over and over again. No one complained because the men were very scrupulous about not tearing off the flowers until they were well withered.

Someone pushed a lump of cold damp earth into Francie's hand. She saw that mama and Neeley were standing at the edge of the grave and dropping their handful of earth into it. Francie walked slowly to the edge, closed her eyes and opened her hand slowly. She heard a soft thud after a second, and that feeling of sickness came back again.

After the burial, the coaches went in different directions. Each mourner was to be taken to his own home. Ruthie Nolan went off with some mourners who lived near her. She didn't even say goodbye. All during the services, she had refused to speak to Katie and the children. Aunt Sissy and Evy got into the carriage with Katie and Francie and Neeley. There wasn't room for five people so Francie had to sit on Evy's lap. They were all very quiet on the way home. Aunt Evy tried to cheer them up by telling some new stories about Uncle Willie and his horse. But no one smiled because no one listened.

Mama made the coach stop at a barber shop around the corner from their house.

"Go in there," she told Francie, "and get your father's cup."

Francie didn't know what she meant. "What cup?" she asked.

"Just ask for his cup."

Francie went in. There were two barbers but no customers. One of the barbers sat on one of the chairs in a row against the wall. His left ankle rested on his right knee and he cradled a mandolin. He was playing "O, Sole, Mio." Francie knew the song. Mr. Morton had taught it to them saying the title was "Sunshine." The other barber was sitting in one of the barber chairs looking at himself in the long mirror. He got down from the chair as the girl came in.

"Yes?" he asked.

"I want my father's cup."

"The name?"

"John Nolan."

"Ah, yes. Too bad." He sighed as he took a mug from the row of them on a shelf. It was a thick white mug with "John Nolan" written on it in gold and fancy block letters. There was a worn-down cake of white soap at the bottom of it and a tired-looking brush. He pried out the soap and put it and the brush in a bigger unlettered cup. He washed Johnny's cup.

While Francie waited, she looked around. She had never been inside a barber shop. It smelled of soap and clean towels and bay rum. There was a gas heater which hissed companionably. The barber had finished the song and started it over again. The thin tinkle of the mandolin made a sad sound in the warm shop. Francie sang Mr. Morton's words to the song in her mind.

> *Oh, what's so fine, dear,*
> *As a day of sunshine.*
> *The storm is past at last.*
> *The sky is blue and clear.*

Everyone has a secret life, she mused. Papa never spoke about the barber shop, yet he had come here three times a week to be shaved.

Fastidious Johnny had bought his own cup, emulating men who were in better circumstances. He wouldn't be shaved with lather from the common cup. Not Johnny. He had come there three times a week—when he had the money—and sat in one of those chairs and looked in that mirror and talked with the barber about—maybe—whether the Brooklyns had a good ball team that year or whether the Democrats would get in as usual. Perhaps he had sung when that other barber played the mandolin. Yes, she was sure that he had sung. Singing had come easier than breathing to him. She wondered if, when he had to wait, he read *The Police Gazette* lying on that bench?

The barber gave her the washed and dried cup. "Johnny Nolan was a fine feller," he said. "Tell the mama that I, his barber, said this."

"Thank you," whispered Francie gratefully. She went out closing the door on the sad sound of the mandolin.

Back in the coach, she held out the cup to Katie. "That's for you to have," said mama. "Neeley will have papa's signet ring."

Francie looked at her father's name in gold and whispered "Thank you" gratefully for the second time in five minutes.

Johnny had been on earth for thirty-four years. Less than a week ago, he had walked on those streets. And now the cup, the ring and two unironed waiter's aprons at home were the only concrete objects left to connote that a man had once lived. There were no other physical reminders of Johnny, as he had been buried in all the clothes he owned with his studs and his fourteen-carat gold collar button.

When they got home, they found that the neighbors had been in and straightened up the flat. The furniture had been put back in place in the front room and the withered leaves and fallen flower petals swept out. The windows had been opened and the rooms aired out. They had brought coal and made a great fire in the kitchen range and put a fresh white cloth on the table. The Tynmore girls had brought up a cake which they had baked themselves and it stood on a plate and was already sliced. Floss Gaddis and her mother had bought a whole lot of sliced bologna. It took two plates to hold it. There was a basket of freshly sliced rye bread and the coffee cups were set out on the table. There was a potful of freshly made coffee warming on the stove and someone had set a pitcher of real cream in the middle of the table. They had done all this while the Nolans were away. Then they had left, locked the door behind them and put the key under the mat.

Aunt Sissy, Evy, mama, Francie, and Neeley sat at the table. Aunt Evy poured out the coffee. Katie sat for a long time looking at her cup. She remembered the last time Johnny had sat at that table. She did what Johnny had done; she pushed the cup away with her arm, put her head down on the table and cried in great ugly tearing sobs. Sissy put her arms around her and spoke in her gentle caressing voice.

"Katie, Katie, don't cry so. Don't cry so, else the child you'll soon be bringing into this world will be a sad child."

37

Katie stayed in bed the day after the funeral and Francie and Neeley wandered around the flat stunned and bewildered. Towards evening, Katie got up and made some supper for them. After they had eaten, she urged the children to go for a little walk, saying they needed the air.

Francie and Neeley walked up Graham Avenue towards Broadway. It was a bitterly cold and a still night but there was no snow. The streets were empty. It was three days after Christmas and children were home playing with their new toys. The street lights were bleak and bright. A small icy wind coming in from the sea blew close to the ground. It whirled bits of dirty papers along the gutters.

They had grown out of childhood in the last few days. Christmas as Christmas had passed unnoticed since their father had died on Christmas day. Neeley's thirteenth birthday had been lost somewhere in those last few days.

They came to the brilliantly-lighted façade of a big vaudeville house. Since they were reading children and read everything they came across, they stopped and automatically read the list of acts playing that week. Underneath the sixth act, was an announcement in large letters.

"Here next week! Chauncy Osborne, Sweet Singer of Sweet Songs. Don't miss him!"

Sweet Singer . . . Sweet Singer . . .

Francie had not shed a tear since her father's death. Neither had Neeley. Now Francie felt that all the tears she had were frozen together in her throat in a solid lump and the lump was growing . . . growing. She felt that if the lump didn't melt soon and change back into tears, she too would die. She looked at Neeley. Tears were falling out of his eyes. Then her tears came, too.

They turned into a dark side street and sat on the edge of the sidewalk with their feet in the gutter. Neeley, though weeping, remembered to spread his handkerchief on the curb so that his new long pants wouldn't get dirty. They sat close together because they were cold and lonesome. They wept long and quietly, sitting there in the cold street. At last, when they could cry no more, they talked.

"Neeley, why did papa have to die?"

"I guess God wanted him to die."

"Why?"

"Maybe to punish him."

"Punish him for what?"

"I don't know," said Neeley miserably.

"Do you believe that God put papa on this world?"

"Yes."

"Then He wanted him to live, didn't He?"

"I guess so."

"Then why did He make him die so quick?"

"Maybe to punish him," repeated Neeley not knowing what else to answer.

"If that's true, what good is it? Papa's dead and he don't know that he's punished. God made papa the way he was and then said to Himself, I dare you to do anything about it. I just bet He said that."

"Maybe you shouldn't talk about God like that," said Neeley apprehensively.

"They say God's so great," said Francie scornfully, "and knows everything and can do everything. If He's so great, why didn't He help papa instead of punishing him like you said?"

"I just said *maybe*."

"If God has charge of all the world," said Francie, "and the sun and the moon and the stars and all the birds and trees and flowers and all the animals and people, you'd think He'd be too busy and too important—wouldn't you—to spend so much time punishing one man—one man like papa."

"I don't think you should talk about God like that," said Neeley uneasily. "He might strike you down dead."

"Then let Him," cried Francie fiercely. "Let Him strike me down dead right here in the gutter where I sit!"

They waited fearfully. Nothing happened. When Francie spoke again, she was quieter.

"I believe in the Lord, Jesus Christ, and His Mother, Holy Mary. Jesus was a living baby once. He went barefooted like we do in the summer. I saw a picture where He was a boy and had no shoes on. And when He was a man, He went fishing, like papa did once. And they could hurt Him too, like they couldn't hurt God. Jesus wouldn't go around punishing people. He *knew* about people. So I will always believe in Jesus Christ."

They made the sign of the cross as Catholics do when mentioning Jesus' name. Then she put her hand on Neeley's knee and spoke in a whisper.

"Neeley, I wouldn't tell anybody but you, but I don't believe in God anymore."

"I want to go home," said Neeley. He was shivering.

When Katie let them in, she saw that their faces were tired, yet peaceful. "Well, they've cried it out," she thought.

Francie looked at her mother, then looked away quickly. "While we were gone," she thought, "she cried and cried until she couldn't cry any more." The weeping wasn't mentioned aloud by any one of them.

"I thought you'd come home cold," said mama, "so I made a warm surprise for you."

"What?" asked Neeley.

"You'll see."

The surprise was "hot chocolate" which was cocoa and condensed milk made into a paste and boiling water stirred into it. Katie poured the thick rich stuff into the cups. "And that's not all," she added. She took three marshmallows from a paper bag in her apron pocket and popped one into each cup.

"Mama!" said the children simultaneously and ecstatically. "Hot Chocolate" was something extra special, usually reserved for birthdays.

"Mama is really somebody," thought Francie as she held her marshmallow down with her spoon and watched the melting white sworls vein the dark chocolate. "She knows we've been crying but she's not asking questions about it. Mama never . . ." Suddenly the right word about mama came to Francie. "Mama never *fumbles*."

No, Katie never fumbled. When she used her beautifully-shaped but worn-looking hands, she used them with surety, whether it was to put a broken flower into a tumbler of water with one true gesture, or to wring out a scrub cloth with one decisive motion—the right hand turning in, and the left out, simultaneously. When she spoke, she spoke truly with the plain right words. And her thoughts walked in a clear uncompromising line.

Mama was saying: "Neeley's getting too big to sleep in the same room with his sister. So I fixed the room your . . ." she barely hesitated over the next word, ". . . father and I used to have. That's Neeley's bedroom now."

Neeley's eyes jumped to his mother's. A room of his own! A dream come true; two dreams come true, long pants and a room . . . His eyes saddened then, as he thought of how these good things had come to him.

"And I'll share *your* room, Francie." Instinctive tact made Katie put it that way instead of saying, "You'll share *my* room."

"I wish I had my own room," thought Francie with a flare of jealousy. "But it's right, I guess that Neeley have it. There are only two bedrooms and he couldn't sleep with mama."

Knowing Francie's thought, Katie said, "And when it gets warm again, Francie can have the front room. We'll put her cot in there and put a nice cover on it in the daytime and it will be like a private sitting room. All right, Francie?"

"All right, Mama."

After awhile, mama said: "We forgot the reading the last few nights but now we'll start again."

"So things will go on just the same," thought Francie, a little surprised, as she took the Bible from the mantelpiece.

"Being," said mama, "that we lost Christmas this year, let's skip the part we're supposed to read and go to the birth of the Baby Jesus. We'll take turns reading. You start, Francie."

Francie read.

. . . and so it was, that, while they were there, the days were accomplished that she should be delivered. And she brought forth her first-born son, and wrapped him in swaddling clothes, and laid him in the manger; because there was no room for them in the inn.

Katie sighed sharply. Francie stopped reading and looked up inquiringly. "It's nothing," said mama. "Go on reading."

"No, it's nothing," Katie thought. "It's the time when I should feel life." Again the unborn child trembled faintly within her. "Was it because he knew of this coming child," she wondered silently, "that he stopped drinking at the last?" She had whispered to him that they were to have another child. Had he tried to be different when he knew? And knowing, did he die in the trying to be a better man? "Johnny . . . Johnny . . ." She sighed again.

And they read, each in turn, of the birth of Jesus, and reading, they thought of Johnny dying. But each kept his thoughts.

When the children were ready to go to bed, Katie did something very unusual. It was unusual because she was not a demonstrative woman. She held the children close to her and kissed them good night.

"From now on," she said, "I am your mother and your father."

38

Just before Christmas vacation ended, Francie told mama that she wasn't going back to school.

"Don't you like school?" mama asked.

"Yes, I do. But I'm fourteen now and I can get my working papers easy."

"Why do you want to go to work?"

"To help out."

"No, Francie. I want you to go back to school and graduate. It's only a few more months. June will be here before you know it. You can get your working papers for this summer. Maybe Neeley, too. But you're both going to high school in the fall. So forget working papers and go back to school."

"But, Mama, how'll we get along till summer?"

"We'll manage."

Katie was not as confident as she sounded. She missed Johnny in more ways than one. Johnny had never worked steadily but there had been the unexpected Saturday or Sunday night job with the three dollars it brought in. Then, too, when things got too terrible, Johnny had had a way of pulling himself together for a little while to get them over the bad places. But now, there was no Johnny.

Katie took stock. The rent was paid as long as she could keep those three tenements clean. There was a dollar and a half a week from Neeley's paper route. That would keep them in coal if they used a fire only at night. But wait! Twenty cents weekly insurance premium had to come out of that. (Katie was insured for a dime a week and each of the children for a nickel.) Well, a bit less coal and a little earlier to bed would take care of that. Clothes? Not to be thought of. Lucky Francie had those new shoes and Neeley the suit. The big question, then, was food. Maybe Mrs. McGarrity would let her do the washing again. That would be a dollar a week. Then she'd get a few outside cleaning jobs. Yes, they'd get along somehow.

They got through to the end of March. By that time Katie was unwieldy. (The baby was due in May.) The ladies for whom she worked winced and looked away as they saw her, big with child, standing at the ironing board in their kitchens; or saw her in an awkward sprawling position on her hands and knees scrubbing their floors. They had to help her out of pity. Soon they realized that they were paying a cleaning woman and doing most of the work themselves anyhow. So, one after another, they told her they didn't need her any more.

A day came when Katie didn't have the twenty cents for the insurance collector. He was an old friend of the Rommelys and knew Katie's circumstances.

"I'd hate to see your policies lapse, Mrs. Nolan. Especially after you kept them up all these years."

"You wouldn't lapse me just because I got behind a little in my payments?"

"*I* wouldn't. But the company would. Look! Why don't you cash in the children's policies?"

"I didn't know you could do that."

"Few people know. They stop paying premiums and the company keeps mum. Time passes and the company just keeps the money already paid in. I'd lose my job if they knew I told you about this. But here's how I look at it: I insured your father and mother and all you Rommely girls and your husbands and children, and, I don't know, but I carried so many messages back and forth among you about birth and sickness and death that I feel like part of the family."

"We couldn't do without you," said Katie.

"Here's what you do, Mrs. Nolan. Cash in your children's policies but keep your own. If anything happens to one of the children, God forbid, you could manage to get them buried. Whereas if something happened to you, also God forbid, they couldn't get you buried without insurance money, now could they?"

"No, they couldn't. I must keep my own policy up. I wouldn't want to be buried as a pauper in Potter's Field. That's something they could never rise above; neither they, nor their children, nor their children's children. So I'll keep my policy and take your advice about the children's. Tell me what I have to do."

The twenty-five dollars that Katie got for the two policies got them through until the end of April. In five more weeks the child would be born. In eight more weeks, Francie and Neeley would graduate from grade school. There were those eight weeks to be gotten through somehow.

The three Rommely sisters sat around Katie's kitchen table in conference.

"I'd help if I could," said Evy. "But you know Will's not been right since that horse kicked him. He's fresh to the boss and doesn't get along with the men and it's gotten so that not a horse will go out with him. They put him on stable work, sweeping out manure and dumping broken bottles. They cut him to eighteen a week and that doesn't go far with three children. I'm looking for odd cleaning jobs myself."

"If I could think of some way," began Sissy.

"No," said Katie firmly. "You're doing enough by taking Mother to live with you."

"That's right," said Evy. "Kate and I used to worry so about her living alone in one room and going out cleaning to make a few pennies."

"Mother's no expense and no trouble," said Sissy. "And my John don't mind having her around. Of course, he only earns twenty a week. And now there's the baby. I wanted to get my old job back but Mother's too old to take care of baby and the house. She's eighty-three now. I could work but I'd have to hire somebody to look after Mother and the baby. If I had a job, I could help you out, Katie."

"You just can't do it, Sissy. There's no way," said Katie.

"There's only one thing to do," said Evy. "Take Francie out of school and let her get working papers."

"But I want her to graduate. My children will be the first ones in the Nolan family to get diplomas."

"You can't eat a diploma," said Evy.

"Haven't you any men friends who could help you?" asked Sissy. "You're a very pretty woman, you know."

"Or will be, when she gets her shape back again," put in Evy.

Katie thought briefly of Sergeant McShane. "No," she said. "I have no men friends. There's always been Johnny and no one else."

"I guess Evy's right then," decided Sissy. "I hate to say it, but you've got to put Francie to work."

"Once she leaves grammar school without graduating, she'll never be able to get into high school," protested Katie.

"Well," sighed Evy, "there's always the Catholic Charities."

"When the time comes," said Katie quietly, "that we have to take charity baskets, I'll plug up the doors and windows and wait until the children are sound asleep and then turn on every gas jet in the house."

"Don't talk like that," said Evy sharply. "You want to live, don't you?"

"Yes. But I want to live for *something*. I don't want to live to get charity food to give me enough strength to go back to get more charity food."

"Then it comes back to this again," said Evy. "Francie's got to get out and work. It's got to be Francie because Neeley is only thirteen and they won't give him his working papers."

Sissy put her hand on Katie's arm. "It won't be so terrible. Francie's smart and reads a lot and that girl will get herself educated somehow."

Evy stood up. "Look! We've got to go." She put a fifty-cent piece on the table. Anticipating Katie's refusal, she spoke belligerently. "And don't think that's a present. I expect to be paid back someday."

Katie smiled. "You needn't holler so. I don't mind taking money from my sister."

Sissy took a short cut. As she leaned over to kiss Katie's cheek in goodbye, she slipped a dollar bill in her apron pocket. "If you need me," she said, "send for me and I'll come, even if it's in the middle of the night. But send Neeley. It's not safe for a girl to walk through those dark streets past the coal yards."

Katie sat alone at the kitchen table far into the night. "I need two months . . . just two months," she thought. "Dear God, give me two months. It's such a little time. By that time, my baby will be born and I'll be well again. By that time, the children will be graduated from public school. When I'm boss of my own mind and my own body, I don't need to ask You for anything. But now my body is boss over me and I've got to ask You for help. Just two months . . . two months . . ." She waited for that warm glow that meant that she had established communication with her God. There was no glow. She tried again.

"Holy Mary, Mother of Jesus, *you* know how it is. You had a child. Holy Mary . . ." She waited. There was nothing.

She placed Sissy's dollar and Evy's fifty-cent piece on the table. "That will get us through three more days," she thought. "After that . . . ?" Not aware of what she did, she whispered; "Johnny, wherever you are, pull yourself together just one more time. One more time. . . ." She waited again and this time the glow came.

And it so happened that Johnny helped them.

McGarrity, the saloon keeper, couldn't get Johnny out of his mind. Not that McGarrity's conscience bothered him; no, nothing like that. He didn't force men to come into his saloon. Aside from keeping the door hinges so well oiled that the slightest touch made them swing open easily, he offered no more inducements than other saloon keepers. His free lunch was no better than theirs and there was no beguiling entertainment other than that spontaneously contributed by his customers. No, it wasn't his conscience.

He missed Johnny. That was it. And it wasn't the money, either, because Johnny always owed him. He had liked having Johnny around because he gave class to the place. It was something, all right, to see that slender young fellow standing debonairly at the bar among the truck drivers and ditch diggers. "Sure," admitted McGarrity, "Johnny Nolan drank more than was good for him. But if he didn't get it here, he would have got it somewhere else. But he wasn't a rummy. He never got to cursing or brawling after he had a few drinks. Yes," decided McGarrity, "Johnny had been all right."

The thing that McGarrity missed was Johnny talking. "How that fellow could talk," he thought. "Why he'd tell me about those cotton fields down south or about the shores of Araby or sunny France just like he'd been there instead of getting the information out of those songs he knew. I sure liked to hear him talk about those far-off places," he mused. "But best of all, I liked to hear him talk about his family."

McGarrity used to have a dream about a family. This dream family lived far away from the saloon; so far that he had to hop a trolley to get home in the early morning after he locked up the saloon. The gentle wife of his dreams waited up for him and had hot coffee and something nice to eat ready. After eating, they'd talk . . . talk about other things than the saloon. He had dream children—clean, pretty, smart children who were growing up sort of ashamed that their father ran a saloon. He was proud of their shame because it meant that he had the ability of begetting refined children.

Well, that had been his dream of marriage. Then he had married Mae. She had been a curvy, sensuous girl with dark red hair and a wide mouth. But after a while of marriage, she turned into a stout blowsy woman, known in Brooklyn as "the saloon type." Married life had been fine for a year or two, then McGarrity woke up one morning and found that it was no good. Mae wouldn't change into his dream wife. She liked the saloon. She insisted that they rent rooms above it. She didn't want a house in Flushing; she didn't want to do housework. She liked to sit in the saloon's back room day and night and laugh and drink with the customers. And the children that Mae gave him ran the streets like hoodlums and bragged about their father owning a saloon. To his grievous disappointment, they were proud of it.

He knew that Mae was unfaithful to him. He didn't care so long as it didn't get around to the extent that men laughed at him behind his back. Jealousy had left him years ago when physical desire for Mae left him. He gradually grew indifferent about sleeping with her or with any other woman. Somehow, good talking had gotten tied up with good sex in his mind. He wanted a woman to talk to, one to whom he could tell all his thoughts; and he wanted her to talk to him, warmly, wisely and intimately. If he could find such a woman, he thought, his manhood would come back to him. In his dumb fumbling way, he wanted union of mind and soul along with union of body. As the years passed, the need of talking intimately with a woman who was close to him became an obsession.

In his business, he observed human nature and came to certain conclusions about it. The conclusions lacked wisdom and originality; in fact, they were tiresome. But they were important to McGarrity because he had figured them out for himself. In the first years of their marriage, he had tried to tell Mae about these conclusions, but all she said was, "I can imagine." Sometimes she varied by saying, "I can *just* imagine." Gradually then, because he could not share his inner self with her, he lost the power of being a husband to her and she was unfaithful to him.

McGarrity was a man with a great sin on his soul. He hated his children. His daughter, Irene, was Francie's age. Irene was a pink-eyed girl and her hair was of such a pale red that it, too, could be called pink. She was mean and stupid. She had been left back so many times that at fourteen she was still in the sixth grade. His son, Jim, ten years old, had no outstanding characteristic excepting that his buttocks were always too fat for his breeches.

McGarrity had another dream; it was that Mae would come to him and confess that the children were not his. This dream made him happy. He felt that he could love those children if he knew they were another man's. Then he could see their meanness and their stupidity objectively; then he could pity them and help them. As long as he knew they were his, he hated them because he saw all of his own and Mae's worst traits in them.

In the eight years that Johnny had been patronizing McGarrity's saloon, he had spoken daily to McGarrity in praise of Katie and the children. McGarrity played a secret game during those eight years. He pretended that *he* was Johnny and that he, McGarrity, was talking so about Mae and his children.

"Want to show you something," Johnny said once, proudly, as he pulled a paper from his pocket. "My little girl wrote this composition in school and got 'A' on it and she's only ten years old. Listen. I'll read it to you."

As Johnny read, McGarrity pretended that it was his little girl who had written the story. Another day, Johnny brought in a pair of crudely-made wood book ends and placed them on the bar with a flourish.

"Want to show you something," he said proudly. "My boy, Neeley, made these in school."

"My boy, Jimmy, made these in school," said McGarrity proudly to himself as he examined the book ends.

Another time, to start him talking, McGarrity had asked, "Think we'll get in the war, Johnny?"

"Funny thing," Johnny had answered. "Katie and I sat up till near morning talking about that very thing. I convinced her finally that Wilson will keep us out of it."

How would it be, McGarrity thought, if he and Mae sat up all night to talk about that, and how would it be if she said, "You're right, Jim." But he didn't know how it would be because he knew that could never happen.

So when Johnny died, McGarrity lost his dreams. He tried to play the game by himself but it didn't work out. He needed someone like Johnny to start him off.

About the time that the three sisters sat in Katie's kitchen talking, McGarrity got an idea. He had more money than he knew how to spend, and nothing else. Maybe through Johnny's children he could buy the way of dreaming again. He suspected that Katie was hard up.

Maybe he could scare up a little easy work for Johnny's kids to do after school. He'd be helping them out . . . God knows he could afford it, and maybe he'd get something in return. Maybe they would talk to him the way they must have talked to their father.

He told Mae he was going up to see Katie about some work for the children. Mae told him, cheerfully enough, that he'd be thrown out on his ear. McGarrity didn't think he'd be thrown out on his ear. As he shaved for the visit, he recalled the day that Katie had come in to thank him for the wreath.

After Johnny's funeral, Katie went around thanking each person who had sent flowers. She had walked straight through McGarrity's front door disdaining the deviousness of the side door marked "Ladies' Entrance." Ignoring the staring men hanging on the bar, she had come straight to where McGarrity was. Seeing her, he had tucked up one bottom end of his apron into the belt, signifying that he was off duty for the moment and had come from behind the bar to meet her.

"I came to thank you for the wreath," she said.

"Oh that," he said, relieved. He thought she had come to bawl him out.

"It was thoughtful of you."

"I liked Johnny."

"I know." She put her hand out. He looked at it dumbly for a moment before he got the idea that she wanted to shake him by the hand. As he wrung her hand, he asked, "No hard feelings?"

"Why?" she answered. "Johnny was free, white and over twenty-one." She had turned then and walked out of the saloon.

No, decided McGarrity, such a woman wouldn't throw him out on his ear if he came with well-meant intentions.

He sat ill at ease on one of the kitchen chairs talking to Katie. The children were supposed to be doing their homework. But Francie, head bent deceptively over her book, was listening to Mr. McGarrity.

"I talked it over with my Missus," dreamed McGarrity, "and she agreed with me that we could use your girl. No hard work, you understand, just making the beds and washing a few dishes. I could use the boy downstairs, peeling eggs and cutting cheese into hunks, you know, for the free lunch at night. He wouldn't be anywhere near the bar. He'd work in the back kitchen. It would be for an hour or so after school and half a day on Saturday. I'd pay each two dollars a week."

Katie's heart jumped. "Four dollars a week," she figured to herself, "and the dollar and a half from the paper route. Both of them could stay in school. There'd be enough to eat. It would get us through."

"What do you say, Mrs. Nolan?" he asked.

"It's up to the children," she answered.

"Well?" He threw his voice in their direction. "What do you say?"

Francie pretended to tear herself away from her book. "What did you say?"

"Would you like to help Mrs. McGarrity around the house?"

"Yes, sir," said Francie.

"And you?" He looked at Neeley.

"Yes, sir," echoed the boy.

"That's settled." He turned to Katie. "Of course it's only temporary until we can get a regular woman to take over the house and kitchen work."

"I'd rather it was temporary, anyhow," said Katie.

"You might be a little short." He worked his hand down into his pocket. "So I'll pay the first week's salary in advance."

"No, Mr. McGarrity. If they earn the money, they'll have the privilege of collecting it and bringing it home themselves at the end of the week."

"All right." But instead of taking his hand from his pocket, he closed it over the thick roll of bills. He thought, "I've got so much money that buys me nothing And they haven't got anything." He had an idea.

"Mrs. Nolan, you know how Johnny and I done business. I gave him credit and he turned his tips over to me. Well, when he died, he was a little ahead." He took out the thick roll of bills. Francie's eyes popped when she saw all that money. McGarrity's idea was to say that Johnny was twelve dollars ahead and to give Katie that sum. He looked at Katie as he took the rubber band off the money. Her eyes narrowed and he changed his mind about the twelve dollars. He knew she'd never believe it. "Of course, it isn't much," he said casually. "Just two dollars. But I figure it belongs to you." He detached two bills and held them out to her.

Katie shook her head. "I know there is no money owing us. If you told the truth, you'd say that Johnny owed you." Ashamed at being caught, McGarrity put the thick roll back in his pocket where it felt uncomfortable against his thigh. "But, Mr. McGarrity, I do thank you for your kind intentions," Katie said.

Her last few words released McGarrity's tongue. He started to talk; he spoke of his boyhood in Ireland, of his mother and father and the many brothers and sisters. He spoke of his dream marriage. He told her everything that had been in his thoughts for years. He didn't run down his wife and children. He left them out of his story entirely. He told about Johnny; how Johnny had spoken daily of his wife and children.

"Take those curtains," McGarrity said, waving a thick hand at the half curtains made of yellow calico with a red rose design. "Johnny told me how you ripped up an old dress of yours and made kitchen curtains out of it. He said it made the kitchen look fine, like the inside of a Gypsy wagon."

Francie, who had abandoned the pretense of study, picked up McGarrity's last two words. "Gypsy wagon," she thought, looking at the curtains with new eyes. "So papa had said that. I didn't think he noticed the new curtains at the time. At least he didn't say anything. But he had noticed. He had said that nice thing about them to this man." Hearing Johnny spoken of so made Francie almost believe that he wasn't dead. "So papa had said things like that to this man." She stared at McGarrity with new interest. He was a short stocky man with thick hands, a short red neck and thinning hair. "Who'd ever guess," thought Francie, "looking at the outside of him, that he was so different inside?"

McGarrity talked for two hours without stopping. Katie listened intently. She was not listening to McGarrity *talking*. She was listening to McGarrity *talking about Johnny*. When he stopped for a second, she gave him little transitional replies, such as "Yes?" or "*Then* what?" or "And then . . . ?" When he fumbled for a word, she offered him one which he accepted gratefully.

And as he talked, a remarkable thing happened. He felt his lost manhood stirring within him. It wasn't the physical fact of Katie in the room with him. Her body was swollen and distorted and he couldn't look at her without wincing inwardly. It wasn't the woman. It was the talking to her that was doing it.

It grew dark in the room. McGarrity stopped talking. He was hoarse and tired. But it was a new peaceful kind of tiredness. He thought, reluctantly, that he had to get back. The saloon would be filling up with men on their way home from work, stopping in for a pre-supper drink. He didn't like Mae behind the bar when a crowd of men were there. He got to his feet slowly.

"Mrs. Nolan," he said fumbling with his brown derby, "could I come up here once in a while to talk?" She shook her head slowly. "Just to talk?" he repeated pleadingly.

"No, Mr. McGarrity," she said as gently as she could.

He sighed and went away.

Francie was glad to be so busy. It kept her from missing papa too much. She and Neeley got up at six in the morning and helped mama with the cleaning for two hours before they got ready for school. Mama couldn't work hard now. Francie polished the brass bell plates in the three vestibules and cleaned each banister spoke with an oiled cloth. Neeley swept out the cellars and swept down the carpeted stairs. Both of them got the filled ash cans up on the curb each day. It had been a problem because the two of them together couldn't so much as budge the heavy cans. Francie got the idea of tipping over the cans, dumping the ashes on the cellar floor, carrying the empty cans up to the curb and then refilling them with coal buckets. It worked fine, even if it meant a lot of trips up and down the cellar. That left only the linoleum-laid halls for mama to scrub. Three of the tenants offered to scrub their own hallways until after Katie had had her baby and that helped a whole lot.

After school, the children had to go to church for "instruction" since both were being confirmed that spring. After instruction, they worked for McGarrity. As he had promised, the work was easy. Francie made up four tumbled beds and washed a few breakfast dishes and swept the rooms. It took less than an hour.

Neeley had the same schedule as Francie, except that his paper route was added on. Sometimes he didn't get home for supper until eight o'clock. He worked in the kitchen back of McGarrity's saloon. His job was to take the shells off four dozen hard-boiled eggs, cut hard cheese into inch cubes and stick a toothpick in each cube, and slice big pickles lengthwise.

McGarrity waited a few days until the children got used to working for him. Then he decided it was time to have them talk to him the way Johnny had. He went into the kitchen, sat down, and watched Neeley working. "He's the spitting image of his father," thought McGarrity. He waited a long time letting the boy get used to him there, then he cleared his throat.

"Make any wooden book ends lately?" he asked.

"No . . . no, sir," stammered Neeley, startled at the odd question.

McGarrity waited. Why didn't the boy start talking? Neeley shelled eggs faster. McGarrity tried again. "Think Wilson will keep us out of the war?"

"I don't know," said Neeley.

McGarrity waited a long time. Neeley thought he was checking up on the way he worked. Anxious to please, the boy worked so fast that he was finished ahead of time. He placed the last shelled egg in the glass bowl and looked up. "Ah! Now he's going to talk to me," thought McGarrity.

"Is that all you want done?" asked Neeley.

"That's all." Still McGarrity waited.

"I guess I'll go, then," ventured Neeley.

"All right, son," sighed McGarrity. He watched the boy walk out of the back door. "If he'd only turn around and say something . . . something . . . personal," thought McGarrity. But Neeley didn't turn around.

McGarrity tried Francie the next day. He came upstairs to the flat, sat down and said nothing. Francie got a little frightened and started sweeping towards the door. "If he comes at me," she thought, "I can run out." McGarrity sat quiet for a long time, thinking he was getting her used to him. He didn't know he was frightening her.

"Write any grade A, number one compositions lately?" he asked.

"No, sir."

He waited awhile. "Do you think we'll get into this war?"

"I . . . I don't know." She edged closer to the door.

He thought, "I'm scaring her. She thinks I'm like that fellow in the hallway." Aloud he said, "Don't be afraid, I'm going. You can lock the door after me, if you want."

"Yes, sir," she said. After he had gone, Francie thought: "I guess he only wanted to talk. But I have nothing to say to him."

Mae McGarrity came up once. Francie was on her knees trying to poke out some dirt from behind the water pipes under the sink. Mae told her to get up and forget it.

"Lord love you, child," she said. "Don't be killing yourself working. This flat will be standing here long after you and I are dead and gone."

She took a mound of rosy jello out of the icebox, cut it in half and slid a portion on another plate. She garnished it liberally with whipped cream, plunked two spoons on the table, sat down and indicated that Francie do the same.

"I'm not hungry," lied Francie.

"Eat anyhow, to be sociable," Mae said.

It was the first time Francie had ever eaten jello and whipped cream. It was so good, she had to remember her manners and not gobble it down. As she ate, she thought, "Why Mrs. McGarrity's all right. Mr. McGarrity's all right, too. Only I guess they aren't all right to each other."

Mae and Jim McGarrity sat alone at a little round table in back of the saloon eating their usual hurried and silent supper. Unexpectedly, she placed her hand on his arm. He trembled at the unexpected touch. His small light eyes looked into her large mahogany-colored ones and saw pity in them.

"It won't work out, Jim," she said gently. Excitement churned up in him. "She knows!" he thought. "Why . . . why . . . *she understands.*"

"There's an old saying," Mae continued. "Money won't buy everything."

"I know," he said. "I'll let them go, then."

"Wait until a couple of weeks after her kid is born. Give them a show." She got up and walked out to the bar.

McGarrity sat there, torn apart by his feelings. "We held a conversation," he thought in wonder. "No names were mentioned and nothing was said exactly in the words. But she knew what I was thinking and I knew what she was thinking." He hurried after his wife. He wanted to hold on to that understanding. He saw Mae standing at the end of the bar. A husky teamster had his arm around her waist and was whispering something in her ear. She had her hand over her mouth to hold back her laughter. As McGarrity came in, the teamster removed his arm sheepishly and moved down to stand with a group of men. As McGarrity went behind the bar, he looked into his wife's eyes. They were blank and had no understanding in them. McGarrity's face fell into the old lines of grievous disappointment as he started his evening's work.

Mary Rommely was getting old. She was no longer able to go about Brooklyn alone. She had a longing to see Katie before her confinement, so she gave the insurance collector a message.

"When a woman gives birth," she told him, "death holds her hand for a little while. Sometimes he doesn't let go. Tell my youngest daughter that I would see her once more before her time comes."

The collector gave the message. The following Sunday, Katie went over to see her mother, taking Francie with her. Neeley begged off, saying he had promised to pitch for the Ten Eycks who were trying to get up a ball game in the lots.

Sissy's kitchen was big and warm and sunny and spotlessly clean. Granma Mary Rommely was sitting by the stove in a low rocker. It was the only piece of furniture she had brought from Austria and it had stood by the hearth in her family's hut for more than a hundred years.

Sissy's husband sat by the window, holding the baby while he gave it its bottle. After Mary and Sissy had been greeted, Francie and Katie greeted him.

"Hello, John," said Katie.

"Hello, Kate," he answered.

"Hello, Uncle John."

"Hello, Francie."

He never said another word during the entire visit. Francie stared at him, wondering about him. The family regarded him as temporary, as they had regarded Sissy's other husbands and lovers. Francie wondered whether he, himself, felt temporary. His real name was Steve but Sissy always referred to him as "my John" and when the family spoke of him, they called him "The John" or "Sissy's John." Francie wondered whether the men in the publishing house where he worked called him John, too. Did he ever protest? Did he ever say, "Look here, Sissy. My name is Steve and not John. And tell your sisters to call me Steve, too."

"Sissy, you're getting stouter," mama was saying.

"It's natural for a woman to put on a little weight after she's had a baby," said Sissy with a straight face. She smiled at Francie. "Would you like to hold the baby, Francie?"

"Oh, yes!"

Without a word, Sissy's tall husband got up, gave over the baby and its bottle to Francie, and still without a word, walked out of the room. No one commented on his going.

Francie sat in his vacated chair. She had never held a baby in her arms before. She touched the baby's soft round cheek with her fingers as she had seen Joanna do. A thrill started at her finger tips, went up her arm, and through her entire body. "When I get big," she decided, "I'll always have a new baby in the house."

While she held the baby, she listened to mama and granma talking and watched Sissy making up a month's supply of noodles. Sissy took a ball of stiff yellow dough, rolled it flat with the rolling pin, then rolled the flat dough up like a jelly roll. With a sharp knife, she cut the roll into paper-thin strips, unwound the strips and hung them on a rack made of slender dowel sticks, which stood before the kitchen stove. This was to dry out the noodles.

Francie felt that there was something different about Sissy. She wasn't the old Aunt Sissy. It wasn't that she was a bit less slender than usual; the being different was something that did not have to do with the way she looked. Francie puzzled over it.

Mary Rommely wanted to hear every word of news and Katie told her everything, starting from the end and working back. First she told of the children working for McGarrity's, and how the money they brought in was keeping them. Then she went back to the day McGarrity had sat in her kitchen and talked about Johnny. She ended up with saying:

"I tell you, Mother, if McGarrity hadn't come along when he did, I don't know what would have happened. I was so low, that just a few nights before that, I had prayed to Johnny to help me. That was foolish. I know."

"Not foolish," said Mary. "He heard you and he helped you."

"A ghost can't help anyone, Mother," said Sissy.

"Ghosts are not always those who pass through closed doors," said Mary Rommely. "Katie has told how her husband used to talk to this saloon man. In all those years of the talking, Yohnny gave away pieces of himself to this man. When Katie called on her man for help, the pieces of him came together in this man, and it was Yohnny within the saloon man's soul that heard and came to her help."

Francie turned it over in her mind. "If that is so," she thought, "then Mr. McGarrity gave us back all those pieces of papa when he talked so long about him. There is nothing of papa in him now. Maybe that's why we can't talk to him the way he wants us to."

When it was time to leave, Sissy gave Katie a shoebox full of noodles to take home. As Francie kissed her grandmother in goodbye, Mary Rommely held her close and whispered in her own language:

"In the month to come, give unto thy mother more than obedience and respect. She will have great need of love and understanding."

Francie didn't understand a word of what her grandmother had said, but she answered, "Yes, Granma."

Going home in the trolley, Francie held the shoebox in *her* lap because mama had no lap now. Francie thought deep thoughts during the ride. "If what granma Mary Rommely said is true, then it must be that no one ever dies, really. Papa is gone, but he's still here in many ways. He's here in Neeley who looks just like him and in mama who knew him so long. He's here in his mother who began him and who is still living. Maybe I will have a boy some day who looks like papa and has all of papa's good without the drinking. And that boy will have a boy. And that boy will have a boy. It might be there is no real death." Her thoughts went to McGarrity. "No one would ever believe there was any part of papa in *him*." She thought of Mrs. McGarrity and how she had made it easy for her to sit down and eat that jello. Something clicked in Francie's mind! She knew all of a sudden what was different about Sissy. She spoke to her mother.

"Aunt Sissy doesn't use that strong sweet perfume any more, does she, Mama?"

"No. She doesn't have to, any more."

"Why?"

"She's got her baby now and a man to look after her and the baby."

Francie wanted to ask more questions but mama had her eyes closed and was leaning her head back against the seat. She looked white and tired and Francie decided not to bother her any more. She'd have to figure it out for herself.

"It must be," she thought, "that this using strong perfume is tied up somehow with a woman wanting a baby and wanting to find a man who can give her a baby and look after it and her too." She put that nugget of knowledge away with all the others that she was continually collecting.

Francie was beginning to get a headache. She didn't know whether it was caused by the excitement of holding the baby, the bouncing trolley car, the idea of papa or the discovery about Sissy's perfume. Maybe it was because she was getting up so early in the mornings now, and being so busy all day. Maybe it was because it was the time in the month when she could look for a headache anyhow.

"Well," Francie decided, "I guess the thing that is giving me this headache is life—and nothing else but."

"Don't be silly," said mama quietly, still leaning back with her eyes closed. "Aunt Sissy's kitchen was too hot. I have a headache, myself."

Francie jumped. Was it getting so that mama could look right into her mind even with her eyes closed? Then she remembered that she had forgotten she was thinking and had said that last thought about life out loud. She laughed for the first time since papa had died and mama opened her eyes and smiled.

39

Francie and Neeley were confirmed in May. Francie was almost four-
teen and a half years old and Neeley was just a year younger. Sissy,
who was an expert seamstress, made Francie's simple white muslin
dress. Katie managed to buy her white kid slippers and a pair of
long white silk stockings. They were Francie's first silk stockings.
Neeley wore the black suit he got for his father's funeral.

There was a legend in the neighborhood that any three wishes
made on that day, would come true. One had to be an impossible
wish, another a wish that you could make come true yourself, and
the third had to be a wish for when you grew up. Francie's impossible wish was that her straight brown hair change into golden curly
hair like Neeley's. Her second wish was that she'd have a nice
speaking voice like mama and Evy and Sissy, and her third wish, for
when she was grown up, was that she'd travel all over the world.
Neeley wished, one: that he'd become very wealthy; two, that he'd
get better marks on his report card; and, three: that he wouldn't
drink like papa when he grew up.

There was an iron-bound convention in Brooklyn that children
must have their picture taken by a regular photographer when they
were confirmed. Katie couldn't afford to have pictures made. She
had to be content with letting Flossie Gaddis, who had a box camera, take a snapshot. Floss posed them on the edge of the sidewalk

and snapped the picture, unaware that a trolley lumbered by at the instant of exposure. She had the snapshot enlarged and framed and presented it to Francie as a Confirmation Day present.

Sissy was there when the picture arrived. Katie held it and they all examined it over her shoulder. Francie had never been photographed before. For the first time, she saw herself as others saw her. She was standing stiff and straight on the edge of the curb, her back to the gutter and her dress blowing sidewise in the wind. Neeley stood close to her, was a head taller, and looked very wealthy and handsome in his freshly pressed black suit. The sun had slanted over the roofs in such a way that Neeley was in the sun and his face was clear and bright, while Francie looked dark and angry in the shadow. Behind both, was the blurred trolley going by.

Sissy said, "I bet that's the only confirmation picture in the world with a trolley car in it."

"It's a good picture," said Katie. "They look more natural standing on the street than in front of the picture-man's cardboard church window." She hung it up over the mantelpiece.

"What name did you take, Neeley?" Sissy asked.

"Papa's. Now, I'm Cornelius John Nolan."

"That's a good name for a surgeon," commented Katie.

"I took mama's name," said Francie importantly. "Now my full name is Mary Frances Katherine Nolan." Francie waited. Mama did *not* say that was a good name for a writer.

"Katie, have you any pictures of Johnny?" Sissy asked.

"No. Just the one of both of us taken on our wedding day. Why?"

"Nothing. Only time passes so, doesn't it?"

"Yes," sighed Katie. "That's one of the few things we can be sure of."

Confirmation was over and Francie didn't have to go to instruction any more. She had an extra hour daily which she was devoting to the novel she was writing to prove to Miss Garnder, the new English teacher, that she *did* know about beauty.

Since her father's death, Francie had stopped writing about birds and trees and My Impressions. Because she missed him so, she had taken to writing little stories about him. She tried to show that, in spite of his shortcomings, he had been a good father and a kindly man. She had written three such stories which were marked "C" instead of the usual "A." The fourth came back with a line telling her to remain after school.

All the children had gone home. Miss Garnder and Francie were alone in the room with the big dictionary in it. Francie's last four compositions lay on Miss Garnder's desk.

"What's happened to your writing, Frances?" asked Miss Garnder.

"I don't know."

"You were one of my best pupils. You wrote so prettily. I enjoyed your compositions. But these last ones . . ." she flicked at them contemptuously.

"I looked up the spelling and took pains with my penmanship and . . ."

"I'm referring to your subject matter."

"You said we could choose our own subjects."

"But poverty, starvation and drunkenness are ugly subjects to choose. We all admit these things exist. But one doesn't write about them."

"What does one write about?" Unconsciously, Francie picked up the teacher's phraseology.

"One delves into the imagination and finds beauty there. The writer, like the artist, must strive for beauty always."

"What is beauty?" asked the child.

"I can think of no better definition than Keats': 'Beauty is truth, truth beauty.' "

Francie took her courage into her two hands and said, "Those stories are the truth."

"Nonsense!" exploded Miss Garnder. Then, softening her tone, she continued: "By truth, we mean things like the stars always being there and the sun always rising and the true nobility of man and mother-love and love for one's country," she ended anti-climactically.

"I see," said Francie.

As Miss Garnder continued talking, Francie answered her bitterly in her mind.

"Drunkenness is neither truth nor beauty. It's a vice. Drunkards belong in jail, not in stories. And poverty. There is no excuse for that. There's work enough for all who want it. People are poor because they're too lazy to work. There's nothing beautiful about laziness.

(Imagine mama lazy!)

"Hunger is not beautiful. It is also unnecessary. We have well-organized charities. No one need go hungry."

Francie ground her teeth. Her mother hated the word "charity" above any word in the language and she had brought up her children to hate it too.

"Now I'm not a snob," stated Miss Garnder. "I do not come from a wealthy family. My father was a minister with a very small salary."

(But it *was* a salary, Miss Garnder.)

"And the only help my mother had was a succession of untrained maids, mostly girls from the country."

(I see. You were poor, Miss Garnder, poor with a maid.)

"Many times we were without a maid and my mother had to do all the housework herself."

(And my mother, Miss Garnder, has to do all her own housework, and yes, ten times more cleaning than *that*.)

"I wanted to go to the state university but we couldn't afford it. My father had to send me to a small denominational college."

(But admit you had no trouble *going* to college.)

"And believe me, you're poor when you go to such a college. I know what hunger is, too. Time and time again my father's salary was held up and there was no money for food. Once we had to live on tea and toast for three days."

(So you know what it is to be hungry, too.)

"But I'd be a dull person if I wrote about nothing but being poor and hungry, wouldn't I?" Francie didn't answer. "*Wouldn't I?*" repeated Miss Garnder emphatically.

"Yes ma'am."

"Now your play for graduation." She took a thin manuscript from her desk drawer. "Some parts are very good indeed; other parts, you've gone off. For instance," she turned a page, "here Fate says: 'And Youth, what is thy ambition?' And the boy answers: 'I would be a healer. I would take the broken bodies of men and mend them.' Now *that's* a beautiful idea, Frances. But you spoil it here. Fate: 'That's what thou would'st be. But see! This is what thou shalt be.' Light shines on old man soldering bottom of ash can. Old Man: 'Ah, once I thought to be a mender of men. Now I'm a mender of . . .' " Miss Garnder looked up suddenly. "You didn't by any chance mean that to be funny, did you, Frances?"

"Oh, no, ma'am."

"After our little talk you can see why we can't use your play for graduation."

"I see." Francie's heart all but broke.

"Now Beatrice Williams has a cute idea. A fairy waves a wand and girls and boys in costume come out and there's one for each holiday in the year and each one says a little poem about the holiday he represents. It's an excellent idea but unfortunately Beatrice cannot make rhymes. Wouldn't you like to take that idea and write the verses? Beatrice wouldn't mind. We can put a note on the program that the idea comes from her. That's fair enough, isn't it?"

"Yes, ma'am. But I don't want to use her ideas. I want to use my own."

"That's commendable, of course. Well, I won't insist." She stood up. "I've taken all this time with you because I honestly believe that you have promise. Now that we've talked things out, I'm sure you'll stop writing those sordid little stories."

Sordid. Francie turned the word over. It was not in her vocabulary. "What does that mean—sordid?"

"What—did—I—tell—you—when—you—don't—know—a— word," sing-songed Miss Garnder drolly.

"Oh! I forgot." Francie went to the big dictionary and looked up the word. Sordid: *Filthy*. Filthy? She thought of her father wearing a fresh dicky and collar every day of his life and shining his worn shoes as often as twice a day. *Dirty*. Papa had his own mug at the barber shop. *Base*. Francie passed that up not knowing exactly what it meant. *Gross*. Never! Papa was a dancer. He was slender and quick. His body wasn't gross. *Also mean and low*. She remembered a hundred and one little tendernesses and acts of thoughtfulness on the part of her father. She remembered how everyone had loved him so. Her face got hot. She couldn't see the next words because the page turned red under her eyes. She turned on Miss Garnder, her face twisted with fury.

"Don't you *ever* dare use that word about us!"

"Us?" asked Miss Garnder blankly. "We were talking about your compositions. Why, Frances!" Her voice was shocked. "I'm surprised! A well-behaved girl like you. What would your mother say if she knew you had been impertinent to your teacher?"

Francie was frightened. Impertinence to a teacher was almost a reformatory offense in Brooklyn. "Please excuse me. Please excuse me," she repeated abjectly. "I didn't mean it."

"I understand," said Miss Garnder gently. She put her arm around Francie and led her to the door. "Our little talk has made an impression on you, I see. Sordid *is* an ugly word and I'm glad you resented my using it. It shows that you understand. Probably you don't like me any more, but please believe that I spoke for your own good. Someday you'll remember what I said and you'll thank me for it."

Francie wished adults would stop telling her that. Already the load of thanks in the future was weighing her down. She figured she'd have to spend the best years of her womanhood hunting up people to tell them that they were right and to thank them.

Miss Garnder handed her the "sordid" compositions and the play, saying, "When you get home, burn these in the stove. Apply the match to them yourself. And as the flames rise, keep saying: 'I am burning ugliness. I am burning ugliness.'"

Walking home from school, Francie tried to figure the whole thing out. She knew Miss Garnder wasn't mean. She had spoken for Francie's good. Only it didn't seem good to Francie. She began to understand that her life might seem revolting to some educated people. She wondered, when she got educated, whether she'd be ashamed of her background. Would she be ashamed of her people; ashamed of handsome papa who had been so lighthearted, kind and understanding; ashamed of brave and truthful mama who was so proud of her own mother, even through granma couldn't read or write; ashamed of Neeley who was such a good honest boy? No! No! If being educated would make her ashamed of what she was, then she wanted none of it. "But I'll show that Miss Garnder," she vowed. "I'll show her I've got an imagination. I certainly will show her."

She started her novel that day. Its heroine was Sherry Nola, a girl conceived, born and brought up in sweltering luxury. The story was called THIS IS I and it was the untrue story of Francie's life.

Francie had twenty pages written now. So far, it ran to minute descriptions of the lush furnishings of Sherry's house, rhapsodies over Sherry's exquisite clothes, and course by course accounts of fabulous meals consumed by the heroine.

When it was finished, Francie planned to ask Sissy's John to take it over to his shop and get it published for her. Francie had a fine dream about how it would be when she presented her book to Miss Garnder. The scene was all worked out in her mind. She went over the dialogue.

FRANCIE
(As she gives book to Miss Garnder.)
I believe you'll find nothing sordid in this. Please consider it as my term's work. I hope you won't mind its being published.
(Miss Garnder's jaw drops open. Francie takes no notice.)
It's a bit easier to read print, don't you think?
(As Miss Garnder reads, Francie stares out window, unconcernedly.)

MISS GARNDER
(After reading.)
Why Frances! This is wonderful!

FRANCIE

What?

(With a start of remembrance.)

Oh, the novel. I dashed it off at odd moments. It doesn't take long to write things of which you know nothing. When you write of actual things, it takes longer, because you have to live them first.

Francie crossed that out. She wouldn't want Miss Garnder to suspect her feelings had been hurt. She rewrote it.

FRANCIE

What?

(Recalling.)

Oh! The novel. I'm glad you like it.

MISS GARNDER

(Timidly.)

Frances, could . . . could I ask you to autograph it for me?

FRANCIE

But of course.

(Miss Garnder uncaps her fountain pen and presents it, pen-point end towards herself, to Francie. Francie writes: "Compliments of M. Frances K. Nolan.")

MISS GARNDER

(Examining autograph.)

What a distinctive signature!

FRANCIE

It's merely my legal name.

MISS GARNDER

(Timidly.)

Frances?

FRANCIE

Please feel as free to speak to me as in the old days.

MISS GARNDER

Could I ask you to write, "To my friend, Muriel Garnder" above your signature?

FRANCIE

(After a barely perceptible pause.)
And why not?
(With a twisted smile.)
I've always written what you asked me to write.
(Writes inscription.)

MISS GARNDER

(Low whisper.)
Thank you.

FRANCIE

Miss Garnder . . . not that it matters, now . . . but would you grade this work . . . just for old times' sake?
(Miss Garnder takes red pencil. Writes large "A Plus" on book.)

It was such a rosy dream that Francie started the next chapter in a fever of excitement. She'd write and write and get it done quickly so the dream could come true. She wrote:

"Parker," Sherry Nola asked her personal maid, "what's cook giving us for dinner tonight?"

"Breast of pheasant under glass, I believe, with hothouse asparagus and imported mushrooms and pineapple mousse, Miss Sherry."

"It sounds horribly dull," observed Sherry.

"Yes, Miss Sherry," agreed the maid respectfully.

"You know, Parker, I'd like to indulge a whim of mine."

"Your whims are the household's commands."

"I'd like to see a lot of simple desserts and choose my dinner from among them. Please bring me a dozen charlotte russe, some strawberry shortcake and a quart of ice cream—make it chocolate, a dozen lady fingers and a box of French chocolates."

"Very good, Miss Sherry."

A drop of water fell on the page. Francie looked up. No, the roof wasn't leaking, it was merely her mouth watering. She was very, very hungry. She went to the stove and looked into the pot. It had a pale bone in it, surrounded by water. There was some bread in the bread box. It was a bit hard but better than nothing. She cut a slice and poured a cup of coffee and dipped the bread into the coffee to soften it. As she ate, she read what she had just written. She made an astonishing discovery.

"Look here, Francie Nolan," she told herself, "in this story you're writing exactly the same thing you wrote in those stories Miss Garnder didn't like. Here, you're writing that you're very hungry. Only you're writing it in a twisted round-about silly way."

Furious with the novel, she ripped the copy-book apart and stuffed it into the stove. When the flames began licking on it, her fury increased and she ran and got her box of manuscripts from under her bed. Carefully putting aside the four about her father, she crammed the rest of them into the stove. She was burning all her pretty "A" compositions. Sentences came out clearer for an instant before a sheet blackened and crumbled. *A giant poplar, tall and high, serene and cool against the sky.* Another: *Softly the blue skies arch overhead. 'Tis a perfect October day.* The end of another sentence . . . *hollyhocks like distilled sunsets and larkspur like concentrate of heaven.*

"I never saw a poplar and I *read* somewhere about the sky arching and I never saw those flowers except in a seed catalogue. And I got A's because I was a good liar." She poked the papers to make them burn faster. As they changed into ashes, she chanted, "I am burning ugliness. I am burning ugliness." As the last flame died away, she announced dramatically to the water boiler, "There goes my writing career."

All of a sudden, she was frightened and lonely. She wanted her father, she wanted her father. He *couldn't* be dead, he just couldn't be. In a little while, he'd come running up the stairs singing, *"Molly Malone."* She'd open the door and he'd say, "Hello, Prima Donna." And she'd say, "Papa, I had a terrible dream. I dreamed you were dead." Then she'd tell him what Miss Garnder had said and he'd find the words to convince her that everything was all right. She waited, listening. Maybe it *was* a dream. But no, no dream lasted that long. It was real. Papa was gone forever.

She put her head down on the table and sobbed. "Mama doesn't love me the way she loves Neeley," she wept. "I tried and tried to make her love me. I sit close to her and go wherever she goes and do whatever she asks me to do. But I can't make her love me the way papa loved me."

Then she saw her mother's face in the trolley car when mama sat with her head back and her eyes closed. She remembered how white and tired mama had looked. Mama *did* love her. Of course she did. Only she couldn't show it in the ways that papa could. And mama *was* good. Here, she expected the baby any minute and she was still out working. Supposing mama died when she had the baby? Francie's blood turned icy at the thought. What would Neeley and she do without mama? Where could they go? Evy and Sissy were too poor to take them. They'd have no place to live. They had no one in all the world but mama.

"Dear God," Francie prayed, "don't let mama die. I know that I told Neeley that I didn't believe in You. But I do! I do! I just *said* that. Don't punish mama. She didn't do anything bad. Don't take her away because I said I didn't believe in You. If You let her live, I'll give You my writing. I'll never write another story again if You'll only let her live. Holy Mary, ask your son, Jesus, to ask God not to let my mother die."

But she felt that her prayer was of no use. God remembered that she had said that she didn't believe in Him and He'd punish her by taking mama as He had taken papa. She became hysterical with terror and thought of her mother as already dead. She rushed out of the flat to look for her. Katie wasn't cleaning in their house. She went into the second house and ran up the three flights of stairs, calling "Mama!" She wasn't in that house. Francie went into the third and last house. Mama wasn't on the first floor. Mama wasn't on the second floor. There was one floor left. If mama wasn't there, then she was dead. She screamed:

"Mama! Mama!"

"I'm up here," came Katie's quiet voice from the third floor. "Don't holler so."

Francie was so relieved that she all but collapsed. She didn't want her mother to know she had been crying. She searched for her handkerchief. Not having it, she dried her eyes on her petticoat and walked up the last flight slowly.

"Hello, Mama."

"Has something happened to Neeley?"

"No, Mama." (She always thinks of Neeley first.)

"Well, hello then," said Katie smiling. Katie surmised that something had gone wrong in school to upset Francie. Well, if she wanted to tell her. . . .

"Do you like me, Mama?"

"I'd be a funny person, wouldn't I, if I didn't like my children."

"Do you think I'm as good-looking as Neeley?" She waited anxiously for mama's answer because she knew that mama never lied. Mama's answer was a long time in coming.

"You have very pretty hands and nice long thick hair."

"But do you think I'm as good-looking as Neeley?" persisted Francie, *wanting* her mother to lie.

"Look, Francie, I know that you're getting at something in a roundabout way and I'm too tired to figure it out. Have a little patience until after the baby gets here. I like you and Neeley and I think you're both nice enough looking children. Now please try not to worry me."

Francie was instantly contrite. Pity twisted her heart as she saw her mother, so soon to bear a child, sprawled awkwardly on her hands and knees. She knelt beside her mother.

"Get up, Mama, and let me finish this hall. I have time." She plunged her hand into the pail of water.

"No!" exclaimed Katie sharply. She took Francie's hand out of the water and dried it on her apron. "Don't put your hands in that water. It has soda and lye in it. Look what it's done to my hands." She held out her shapely but work-scarred hands. "I don't want your hands to get like that. I want you to have nice hands always. Besides, I'm almost finished."

"If I can't help, can I sit on the stairs and watch?"

"If you've nothing better to do."

Francie sat watching her mother. It was so good to be there and know that mama was alive and close by. Even the scrubbing made a safe, pleasant sound. Swish-a-swish-a-swish-a-swish-a went the brush. Slup-a slup-a slup-slup went the rag wiping up. Klunk, flump went the brush and rag as mama dropped them into the pail. Skrunk, skrunk went the pail as mama pushed it to the next area.

"Haven't you any girl friends to talk to, Francie?"

"No. I hate women."

"That's not natural. It would do you good to talk things over with girls your own age."

"Have you any women friends, Mama?"

"No, I hate women," said Katie.

"See? You're just like me."

"But I had a girl friend once and I got your father through her. So you see, a girl friend comes in handy sometimes." She spoke jokingly, but her scrub brush seemed to swish out, you-go-your-way, I'll-go-my-way. She fought back her tears. "Yes," she continued, "you need friends. You never talk to anybody but Neeley and me, and read your books and write your stories."

"I've given up writing."

Katie knew then that whatever was on Francie's mind had to do with her compositions. "Did you get a bad mark on a composition today?"

"No," lied Francie, amazed as always by her mother's guesswork. She got up. "I guess it's time for me to go to McGarrity's now."

"Wait!" Katie put her brush and scrub rag in the pail. "I'm finished for the day." She held out her hands. "Help me to get up."

Francie grasped her mother's hands. Katie pulled heavily on them as she got to her feet clumsily. "Walk back home with me, Francie."

Francie carried the pail. Katie put one hand on the banister and put her other arm around Francie's shoulder. She leaned heavily on the girl as she walked downstairs slowly, Francie keeping time with her mother's uncertain steps.

"Francie, I expect the baby any day now and I'd feel better if you were never very far away from me. Stay close to me. And when I'm working, come looking for me from time to time to see that I'm all right. I can't tell you how much I'm counting on you. I can't count on Neeley because a boy's no use at a time like this. I need you badly now and I feel safer when I know you're nearby. So stay close to me for awhile."

A great tenderness for her mother came into Francie's heart. "I won't ever go away from you, Mama," she said.

"That's my good girl." Katie pressed her shoulder.

"Maybe," thought Francie, "she doesn't love me as much as she loves Neeley. But she needs me more than she needs him and I guess being needed is almost as good as being loved. Maybe better."

40

Two days, Francie came home for lunch and did not return to school in the afternoon. Mama was in bed. After Neeley was told to go back to school, Francie wanted to get Sissy or Evy but mama said it wasn't time, yet.

Francie felt important being in sole charge. She cleaned the flat and looked over the food in the house and planned their supper. Every ten minutes, she plumped up her mother's pillow and asked whether she wanted a drink of water.

Soon after three, Neeley rushed in out of breath, flung his books in a corner and asked whether it was time to run for anybody yet. Katie smiled at his eagerness and said it was no use taking Evy or Sissy away from their own affairs until it was necessary. Neeley went off to work with instructions to ask McGarrity if he could do Francie's work as well as his own since Francie had to stay home with their mother. McGarrity not only agreed, but helped the boy with the free lunch so that Neeley was all finished at four-thirty. They had supper early. The sooner Neeley started with his papers, the quicker he'd be finished. Mama said she didn't want anything except a cup of hot tea.

Mama didn't want the tea after Francie brewed it. Francie worried because she wouldn't eat anything. After Neeley left on his paper route, Francie brought in a bowl of stew and tried to make her mother eat it. Katie lashed out at her; told her to leave her alone; that when she wanted something to eat, she'd ask for it. Francie poured it back into the pot trying to hold back the hurt tears. She had only meant to help. Mama called her again and didn't seem mad anymore.

"What time is it?" asked Katie.

"Five to six."

"Are you sure the clock isn't slow?"

"No, Mama."

"Maybe it's fast, then." She seemed so worried that Francie looked out the front window at Jeweler Woronov's large street clock.

"Our clock's right," reported Francie.

"Is it dark out yet?" Katie had no way of knowing because even at bright noon only a dull gray light filtered through the airshaft window.

"No, it's still light outdoors."

"It's dark in here," said Katie fretfully.

"I'll light the night candle."

Bracketed to the wall was a small shelf holding a plaster statue of the blue-robed Virgin Mary with her hands held out supplicatingly. At the foot of the image, was a thick red glass filled with yellow wax and a wick. Next to it, was a vase holding paper red roses. Francie put a lighted match to the wick. The candlelight glowed dully and ruby red through the thick glass.

"What time is it?" Katie asked after a little while.

"Ten after six."

"You're sure the clock is neither slow nor fast?"

"Just exactly right."

Katie seemed satisfied. But five minutes later, she again demanded the time. It was as if she had an important rendezvous to keep and was fearful of being late.

At half past six, Francie told her the time again and added that Neeley would be home in an hour. "The minute he comes in, send him for Aunt Evy. Tell him not to take the time to walk. Find a nickel carfare for him and tell him, Evy, because she lives closer than Sissy."

"Mama, suppose the baby comes all of a sudden and I don't know what to do?"

"I couldn't be that lucky—to have a baby all of a sudden. What time is it?"

"Twenty-five to seven."

"Sure?"

"I'm sure. Mama, even if Neeley is a boy it would've been better if he stayed with you instead of me."

"Why?"

"Because he's always such a great comfort to you." She said it without malice or jealousy. It was a simple statement of fact. "While I . . . I . . . just don't know the right things to say to make you feel better."

"What time is it?"

"A minute after twenty-five to seven."

Katie was silent for a long time. When she spoke, she said the words quietly, as if speaking to herself. "No, men shouldn't be around at that time. Yet, women make them stand next to them. They want them to hear every moan and groan and see every drop of blood and hear every tear of the flesh. What is this twisted pleasure they get out of making the man suffer along with them? They seem to be taking revenge because God made them women. What time is it?" Without waiting for an answer, she continued: "Before they're married, they'd *die* if a man saw them in curl crimpers or with their corsets off. But when they have a baby, they want him to see them in the ugliest way a woman can be seen. I don't know why. I don't know why. A man thinks of the pain and agony that came to her out of their being together and then it isn't good anymore to him. That's why many men start being unfaithful after the baby. . . ." Katie hardly realized what she was saying. She was missing Johnny so terribly and thinking so, to rationalize his not being there. "Besides, there is this: If you love someone, you'd rather suffer the pain alone to spare them. So keep your man out of the house when your time comes."

"Yes, Mama. It's five after seven."

"See if Neeley's coming."

Francie looked and had to report that Neeley wasn't in sight yet. Katie's mind went back to what Francie had said about Neeley being a comfort.

"No, Francie, it's you who's the comfort to me now." She sighed. "If it's a boy, we'll call him Johnny."

"It will be nice, Mama, when there are four of us again."

"Yes, it will." After that, Katie didn't say anything for awhile. When next she asked the time, Francie told her it was a quarter past seven and that Neeley would be home soon. Katie instructed her to wrap Neeley's nightshirt, toothbrush, a clean towel and a bit of soap in a newspaper, as Neeley was to remain at Evy's house for the night.

Francie made two more trips to the street with the bundle under her arm before she saw Neeley coming. He was running down the street. She ran to meet him; gave him the bundle, carfare and instructions, and told him to hurry.

"How's mama?" he asked.

"Good."

"You sure?"

"Sure. I hear a trolley coming. You better run." Neeley ran.

When Francie got back, she saw that her mother's face was bathed in sweat and that there was blood on her lower lip as though she had bitten through it.

"Oh, Mama, Mama!" She shook her mother's hand and held it to her own cheek.

"Wring a cloth out of cold water and wipe my face," mama whispered. After Francie had done so, Katie went back to what was incompleted in her mind. "Of course, you're a comfort to me." Her mind veered off to something that seemed irrelevant but wasn't. "I've always been meaning to read your A compositions but I never had the time. I've a little time now. Would you like to read one to me?"

"I can't. I burned them all up."

"You thought about them, and wrote them, and handed them in, and got marks on them, and thought about them some more, and then you burned them up. And all through that, I never read one of them."

"That's all right, Mama. They weren't much good."

"It's on my conscience."

"They weren't much good, Mama, and I know you never had the time."

Katie thought, "But I always had time for anything the boy did. I *made* time for him." She continued her thought aloud. "But then, Neeley needs more encouragement. You can go on with what you have inside you, like I can. But he needs so much from outside."

"That's all right, Mama," Francie repeated.

"I couldn't do any different than I did," said Katie. "But it will always be on my conscience just the same. What time is it?"

"Nearly seven-thirty."

"The towel again, Francie." Katie's mind seemed to be trying to clutch at something. "And isn't there one left you can read?"

Francie thought of the four about her father, what Miss Garnder had said about them, and answered, "No."

"Then read something from the Shakespeare book." Francie got the book. "Read about ' 'twas on a night like this,' I'd like to have something pretty in my mind just before the baby comes."

The print was so small that Francie had to light the gas to read. As the light flared up, she had a good look at her mother's face. It was gray and contorted. Mama didn't look like mama. She looked like Granma Mary Rommely in pain. Katie winced away from the light and Francie shut it off quickly.

"Mama, we've read these plays so many times over, that I almost know them by heart. I don't need a light or the book, Mama. Listen!" She recited:

> The moon shines bright!—In such a night as this
> When the sweet wind did gently kiss the trees
> And they did make no noise; in such a night
> Troilus . . .

"What time is it?"

"Seven-forty."

> . . . methinks mounted the Trojan walls,
> And sighed his soul toward the Grecian tents
> Where Cressida lay the night.

"And did you ever find out who Troilus was, Francie? And Cressida?"

"Yes, Mama."

"Someday you must tell me. When I have time to listen."

"I will, Mama."

Katie moaned. Francie wiped the sweat away again. Katie held out her two hands as she had done that day in the hall. Francie took the hands and braced her feet. Katie pulled and Francie thought her arms would come out of their sockets. Then mama relaxed and let go.

So the next hour passed. Francie recited passages she knew by heart—Portia's speech, Marc Antony's funeral oration, "Tomorrow and tomorrow"—the obvious things that are remembered from Shakespeare. Sometimes Katie asked a question. Sometimes she put her hands over her face and moaned. Without knowing she did so, and taking no note of the answer, she kept asking the time. Francie wiped off her face at intervals, and three or four times in that hour, Katie held out her two hands to Francie.

When Evy arrived at half past eight, Francie all but died of pure relief. "Aunt Sissy will be along in half an hour," announced Evy as she rushed into the bedroom. After a look at Katie, Evy pulled the sheet from Francie's cot, knotted one end to Katie's bedpost and put the other end in Katie's hand. "Try pulling on that for a change," she suggested.

"What time is it?" whispered Katie after she had taken a tremendous tug on the sheet; a tug that made the sweat stand out on her face again.

"What do you care," answered Evy, cheerfully. "You're not going any place." Katie started a smile but a pain spasm wiped it off her face. "We can do with a better light," decided Evy.

"But the gas light hurts her eyes," objected Francie.

Evy took the glass globe from the parlor fixture, coated the outside with soap and attached it to the bedroom fixture. When she lit the gas, there was a soft diffused light without glare. Although it was a warm May night, Evy built a fire in the range. She snapped out orders to Francie. Francie rushed around filling the kettle with water and placing it over the flames. She scoured the enameled wash basin and poured a bottle of sweet oil in it and set it on the back of the stove. The soiled clothes were dumped out of the wash basket and it was lined with a ragged but clean blanket and set up on two chairs near the stove. Evy put all the dinner plates in the oven to heat and instructed Francie to put hot plates into the basket, remove them when they cooled and substitute other hot plates.

"Has your mother any baby clothes?" she asked.

"What kind of people do you think we are?" asked Francie scornfully as she displayed a modest layette consisting of four hand-made flannel kimonos, four bands, a dozen hand-hemmed diapers and four threadbare shirts which she and Neeley had worn in turn as babies. "And I made everything myself, excepting the shirts," admitted Francie proudly.

"Hm. I see your mother's looking for a boy," commented Evy, examining the blue feather stitching on the kimonos. "Well, we shall see."

When Sissy arrived, the two sisters went into the bedroom, ordering Francie to wait outside. Francie listened to them talking.

"It's time to get the midwife," Sissy said. "Does Francie know where she lives?"

"I didn't make arrangements," Katie said. "There just isn't five dollars in the house for a midwife."

"Well, maybe Sissy and I can raise the money," began Evy, "if . . ."

"Look," Sissy said. "I bore ten—no—eleven children. You had three and Katie had two. Among us, we had sixteen children. We ought to know enough to bring a baby."

"All right. *We'll* bring the baby," decided Evy.

Then they closed the bedroom door. Now Francie could hear the sound of their voices but couldn't hear what they said. She resented her aunts shutting her out like that, especially when she had been in complete charge until they came. She took the cool plates from the basket, put them into the oven and took out two heated plates. She felt all alone in the world. She wished that Neeley was home so that they could talk about olden times.

Francie opened her eyes with a start. She couldn't have been drowsing, she thought. She just *couldn't* have. She felt the plates in the basket. They were cold. Quickly she substituted hot plates. The basket had to be kept warm for the baby. She listened to the sounds from the bedroom. They had changed since she nodded. There was no more leisurely moving to and fro; no more quiet talking. Her aunts seemed to be running back and forth with quick short steps and their voices came in short sentences. She looked at the clock. Nine-thirty. Evy came out of the bedroom, shutting the door behind her.

"Here's fifty cents, Francie. Go out and get a quarter pound of sweet butter, a box of soda crackers and two navel oranges. Tell the man you want navel. Say they're for a sick lady."

"But all the stores are closed."

"Go down to Jewtown. They're always open."

"I'll go in the morning."

"Do as you're told," said Evy sharply.

Francie went unwillingly. Going down the last flight of stairs, she heard a hoarse guttural scream. She stopped, undecided whether to run back or to continue. She remembered Evy's sharp command and continued down the stairs. As she reached the door, there was another and more agonized scream. She was glad to get out on to the street.

In one of the flats, the ape-like teamster, ordering his unwilling wife to prepare for bed, heard Katie's first scream and ejaculated, "Jesus!" When the second scream came, he said, "I hope to Christ she don't keep me awake all night." His childlike bride wept as she unfastened her dress.

Flossie Gaddis and her mother were sitting in their kitchen. Floss was sewing on another costume, one of white satin intended for her delayed marriage to Frank. Mrs. Gaddis was knitting on a gray sock for Henny. Henny was dead, of course, but all of his life the mother had knit socks for him and she couldn't let go of the habit. Mrs. Gaddis dropped a stitch when the first scream came.

Floss said: "The men have all the fun and women, the pain." The mother said nothing. She trembled when next Katie cried out. "It seems funny," said Floss, "to be making a costume with *two* sleeves."

"Yes."

They worked awhile in silence before Floss spoke again. "I wonder are they worth it? The children, I mean."

Mrs. Gaddis thought of her dead son and her daughter's withered arm. She said nothing. She bent her head over her knitting. She had come around to the place where she dropped a stitch. She concentrated on picking it up.

The spare Tynmore spinsters lay in their hard virginal bed. They groped for each other's hands. "Did you hear it, Sister?" asked Miss Maggie.

"Her time has come," answered Miss Lizzie.

"That's why I didn't marry Harvey—long ago when he asked me. I was afraid of *that*. So afraid."

"I don't know," Miss Lizzie said. "Sometimes I think it's better to suffer bitter unhappiness and to fight and to scream out, and even to suffer that terrible pain, than just to be . . . safe." She waited until the next scream died away. "At least *she* knows she's *living*."

Miss Maggie had no answer.

The flat across the hall from the Nolans was vacant. The remaining flat in the house was occupied by a Polish dock walloper, his wife and their four kids. He was filling a glass from a can of beer on the table when he heard Katie.

"Women!" he grunted contemptuously.

"Shut up, you," snarled his wife.

And all the women in the house tensed each time Katie cried out, and they suffered with her. It was the only thing the women held in common—the sure knowledge of the pain of giving birth.

Francie had to walk a long way up Manhattan Avenue before she found a Jewish Dairy open. She had to go to another store for the crackers and then find a fruit stand that had navel oranges. As she came back, she glanced at the large clock in Knipe's Drug Store, and noted that it was nearly half past ten. She didn't care what time it was except that it seemed so important to her mother.

When she walked into the kitchen, she felt a difference. There was a new quiet feeling and an indefinable smell, new and faintly fragrant. Sissy was standing with her back to the basket.

"What do you think," she said. "You have a baby sister."

"Mama?"

"Your mother's fine."

"So *that's* why I was sent to the store."

"We thought you knew too much already for fourteen," said Evy coming out of the bedroom.

"I just want to know the one thing," said Francie fiercely. "Did mama send me out?"

"Yes, Francie, she did," said Sissy gently. "She said something about sparing those you love."

"All right then," said Francie mollified.

"Don't you want to see the baby?"

Sissy stepped aside. Francie lifted the blanket from the baby's head. The baby was a beautiful little thing with white skin and downy black curls which grew down into a point on her forehead, like mama's. The baby's eyes opened briefly. Francie noticed that they were a milky blue. Sissy explained that all new babies had blue eyes and that probably they'd be dark as coffee beans as she grew older.

"It looks like mama," Francie decided.

"That's what we thought," said Sissy.

"Is it all right?"

"Perfect," Evy told her.

"Not crooked or anything?"

"Certainly not. Where do you get such ideas?"

Francie didn't tell Evy how she was afraid the baby would be born crooked because mama had worked on her hands and knees up to the last minute.

"May I go in and see mama?" she asked humbly, feeling like a stranger in her own home.

"You can bring the plate in to her." Francie took the plate holding two buttered crackers in to her mother.

"Hello, Mama."

"Hello, Francie."

Mama looked like mama again, only very tired. She couldn't raise her head so Francie held the crackers while she ate them. After they were gone, Francie stood holding the empty plate. Mama said nothing. It seemed to Francie that she and mama were strangers again. The closeness of the last few days was gone.

"And you had a boy's named picked out, Mama."

"Yes. But I don't mind a girl, really."

"She's pretty."

"She'll have black curling hair. And Neeley has blond curling hair. Poor Francie got the straight brown hair."

"I *like* straight brown hair," Francie said defiantly. She was dying to know the baby's name but mama seemed like such a stranger now that she didn't like to ask outright. "Shall I write the information out to send to the Board of Health?"

"No. The priest will send it in when she's christened."

"Oh!"

Katie recognized the disappointment in Francie's tone. "But bring in the ink and the book and I'll let you write down her name."

Francie took the Gideon Bible that Sissy had swiped nearly fifteen years ago, from the mantelpiece. She looked at the four entries on the flyleaf. The first three were in Johnny's fine careful hand.

January 1, 1901. Married. Katherine Rommely and John Nolan.

December 15, 1901. Born. Frances Nolan.

December 23, 1902. Born. Cornelius Nolan.

The fourth entry was in Katie's firm back-hand slant.

December 25, 1915. Died. John Nolan. Age, 34.

Sissy and Evy followed Francie in to the bedroom. They, too, were curious as to what Katie would name the baby. Sarah? Eva? Ruth? Elizabeth?

"Write this down." Katie dictated. "May 28, 1916. Born."
Francie dipped her pen in the ink bottle. "Annie Laurie Nolan."

"Annie! Such an ordinary name," groaned Sissy.

"Why, Katie? Why?" demanded Evy patiently.

"A song that Johnny sang once," explained Katie.

As Francie wrote the name, she heard the chords; she heard her
father singing, "*And 'twas there that Annie Laurie.*" . . . Papa . . .
papa. . . .

". . . a song, he said, that belonged to a better world," Katie went
on. "He would have liked the child named after one of his songs."

"Laurie is a pretty name," said Francie.

And Laurie became the baby's name.

41

Laurie was a good baby. She slept contentedly most of the time. When she was awake, she put in the time lying quietly and trying to focus her berry brown eyes on her infinitesimal fist.

Katie nursed the baby, not only because it was the instinctive thing to do, but because there was no money for fresh milk. Since the baby couldn't be left alone, Katie started her work at five in the morning, doing the other two houses first. She worked until nearly nine when Francie and Neeley left for school. Then she cleaned her own house leaving the door of her flat ajar in case Laurie cried. Katie went to bed immediately after supper each night and Francie saw so little of her mother that it seemed as if mama had gone away.

McGarrity didn't fire them after the baby's birth as he had planned. He really needed them now because his business boomed suddenly in that spring of 1916. His saloon was crowded all the time. Great changes were taking place in the country, and his customers, like Americans everywhere, had to get together to talk things over. The corner saloon was their only gathering place, the poor man's club.

Francie, working in the flat above the saloon, heard their raised voices through the thin floor boards. Often she paused in her work and listened. Yes, the world was changing rapidly and this time she knew it was the *world* and not herself. She heard the world changing as she listened to the voices.

It's a fact. They're gonna stop making liquor and in a few years the country will be dry.

    A man that works hard has a right to his beer.

    Tell that to the president and see how far you get.

    This is a people's country. If we don't want it dry, it won't be dry.

    Sure it's a people's country but they're gonna push prohibition down your throat.

    By Jesus, I'll make my own wine, then. My old man used to make it in the old country. You take a bushel of grapes. . . .

G'wan! They'll never give wimmen the vote.

    Don't lay any bets on it.

    If that comes, my wife votes like I do, otherwise I'll break her neck.

    My old woman wouldn't go to the polls and mix in with a bunch of bums and rummies.

    . . . a woman president. That might be.

    They'll never let a woman run the government.

    There's one running it right now.

    Like hell!

    Wilson can't turn around and go to the bathroom 'less he asks Mrs. Wilson if it's okay by her.

    Wilson's an old woman himself.

    He's keeping us out of war.

    That college professor!

    What we need in the White House is a sound politician and *not a school teacher.*

. . . automobiles. Soon the horse will be a thing of the past. That feller out in Dee-troit's making cars so cheap that soon every working man can have one.

    A laborer driving his own car! You should live so long!

Airplanes! Just a crazy fad. Won't last long.

The moving pitchers is here to stay. The thee-ayters is closing up one by one in Brooklyn. Take me: I'd rather see this here Charlie Chaplin any day than this here Corset Payton the wife goes for.

. . . wireless. Greatest thing ever invented. Words come through the air, mind you, without wires. You need a kind of a machine to ketch it and earphones to listen in. . . .

They call it twilight sleep and a woman don't feel a thing when the kid comes. So when this friend tells my wife, she says that it's about time they invented something like that.

What're you talking about! Gaslight's out of date. They're putting 'lectricity even in the cheapest tenements.

Don't know what's got into the youngsters nowadays. They're all dance crazy. Dance . . . dance . . . dance. . . .

So I changed my name from Schultz to Scott. The judge says what do you want to go and do that for? Schultz is a good name. He was German himself, see? Listen, Mac, I says . . . that's just how I talked to him; judge or no judge. I'm through with the old country, I says. After what they done to them Belgian babies, I says, I want no part of Germany. I'm an American now, I says, and I want an American name.

And we're heading straight for war. Man, I can see it coming.

All we got to do is to elect Wilson again this fall. He'll keep us out of war.

Don't bet on them campaign promises. When you got a Democrat president, you got a war president.

Lincoln was a Republican.

But the south had a Democrat president and they was the ones started the Civil War.

I ask you how long we gotta stand for it? The bastards sunk another one of our ships. How many do they gotta sink before we get up enough nerve to go over there and lick hell out of them?

We got to stay out. This country's getting along fine. Let them fight their own wars without dragging us in.

We don't want war.

War's declared, I'll enlist the next day.

You can talk. You're past fifty. They wouldn't take you.

I'd sooner go to jail than to war.

A feller's got to fight for what he thinks is right. I'd be glad to go.

I got nothing to worry about. I got a double hernia.

Let the war come. They'll need us working men then to build their ships and their guns. They'll need the farmer to grow their food. Then watch them come sucking around us. Us laborers will have the God-damned capitalists by the throat. They won't tell us. We'll tell them. By Jesus, we'll make them sweat. War can't come quick enough to suit me.

Like I'm telling you. Everything is machines. I heard a joke the other day. Feller and his wife going around getting food, clothes, everything out of machines. So they come to this baby machine and the feller puts money in and out comes a baby. So the feller turns around and says, give me the good old days.

The good old days! Yeah. I guess they're gone forever.

Fill 'em up again, Jim.

And Francie, pausing in her sweeping to listen, tried to put everything together and tried to understand a world spinning in confusion. And it seemed to her that the whole world changed in between the time that Laurie was born and graduation day.

42

Francie hardly had time to get used to Laurie when graduation night came around. Katie couldn't go to both graduations so it was decided that she go to Neeley's. And that was right. Neeley shouldn't be deprived because Francie had felt like changing schools. Francie understood but felt a bit hurt just the same. Papa would have gone to see her graduate if he were living. They arranged that Sissy go with Francie. Evy would stay with Laurie.

On the last night in June, 1916, Francie walked for the last time to the school she so loved. Sissy, quiet and changed since she got her baby, walked sedately beside her. Two firemen passed and Sissy never so much as noticed and there had been a time when Sissy couldn't resist a uniform. Francie wished Sissy hadn't changed. It made her feel lonesome. Her hand crept into Sissy's and Sissy squeezed it. Francie was comforted. Sissy was still Sissy underneath.

The graduates sat in the front part of the auditorium and the guests in the back. The principal made an earnest speech to the children about how they were going out into a troubled world and about how it would be up to them to build a new world after the war which was sure to come to America. He urged them on to higher education so that they would be better equipped for this world building. Francie was impressed and vowed in her heart that she'd help carry the torch like he said.

Then came the graduation play. Francie's eyes burned with unshed tears. As the diluted dialogue droned on, she thought, "My play would have been better. I would have taken the ash can out. I would have done whatever Teacher said if she had only let me write the play."

After the play, they marched up, got their diplomas and were graduates at last. The oath of allegiance to the flag and the singing of "The Star Spangled Banner" clinched it.

And now came the time of Francie's Gethsemane.

It was the custom to present bouquets to the girl graduates. Since flowers were not allowed in the auditorium, they were delivered to the classrooms where the teachers placed them on the recipient's desk.

Francie had to go back to her room to get her report card; also her pencil box and autograph book from her desk. She stood outside nerving herself for the ordeal, knowing her desk would be the only one without flowers. She was sure, because she hadn't told mama about the custom, knowing there was no money at home for such things.

Deciding to get it over with, she went in and walked straight to the teacher's desk, not daring to look at her own. The air was thick with flower scents. She heard the girls chattering and squealing with delight over their flowers. She heard the exchange of triumphant admiration.

She got her report card: four "A's" and one "C minus." The latter was her English mark. She used to be the best writer in school and here she ended up barely passing English. Suddenly, she hated the school and all the teachers, especially Miss Garnder. And she didn't care about not getting flowers. She didn't care. It was a silly custom, anyway. "I'll go to my desk and get my things," she decided. "And if anyone speaks to me, I'll tell them to shut up. And then I'll walk out of this school forever and not say goodbye to anyone." She raised her eyes. "The desk without flowers on it will be mine." But there were no empty desks! There were flowers on every single one!

Francie went to her desk, reasoning that a girl had placed one of her bouquets there for a moment. Francie planned to pick it up and hand it to the owner saying coolly, "Do you *mind*? I have to get something out of my desk."

She picked up the flowers—two dozen dark red roses on a sheaf of ferns. She cradled them in her arm, the way the other girls did, and pretended for a moment that they were hers. She looked for the owner's name on the card. But her own name was on the card! Her name! The card said: *For Francie on graduation day. Love from Papa.*

Papa!

The writing was in his fine careful hand, in the black ink from the bottle in the cupboard at home. Then it *was* all a dream, a long mixed-up dream. Laurie was a dream, and the working at McGarrity's, and the graduation play, and the bad mark in English. She was waking up now and everything would be all right. Papa would be waiting out in the hall.

But there was only Sissy in the hall.

"Then papa *is dead*," she said.

"Yes," said Sissy. "And it's six months now."

"But he *can't* be, Aunt Sissy. He sent me flowers."

"Francie, about a year ago he gave me that card all written out and two dollars. He said, 'When Francie graduates, send her some flowers for me—in case I forget.' "

Francie started to cry. It wasn't only because she was sure, now, that nothing was a dream; it was because she was unstrung from working too hard and worrying about mama; because she didn't get to write the graduation play; because she got a bad mark in English; because she had been too well prepared not to receive flowers.

Sissy took her to the girls' washroom and pushed her into a booth. "Cry loud and hard," she ordered, "and hurry up. Your mother will be wondering what's keeping us."

Francie stood in the booth, clutching her roses and sobbing. Each time the washroom door opened and chattering announced incoming girls, she flushed the toilet so that the noise of the water would drown out her sobs. Soon she was over it. When she came out, Sissy had a handkerchief wet with cold water to hand her. As Francie mopped her eyes, Sissy asked whether she felt better. Francie nodded yes, and begged her to wait a moment while she said her goodbyes.

She went into the principal's office and shook hands with him. "Don't forget the old school, Frances. Come back and see us sometime," he said.

"I will," promised Francie. She went back to say goodbye to her classroom teacher.

"We'll miss you, Frances," said Teacher.

Francie got her pencil box and autograph book from her desk. She started to say goodbye to the girls. They crowded around her. One put her arm around her waist and two others kissed her cheek. They called out goodbye messages.

"Come to my house to see me, Frances."

"Write to me, Frances, and let me know how you're getting along."

"Frances, we have a telephone now. Ring me up sometime. Ring me up tomorrow."

"Write something in my autograph book, huh, Frances? So's I can sell it when you get famous."

"I'm going to summer camp. I'll put down my address. Write to me. Hear, Frances?"

"I'm going to Girls High in September. You come to Girls High, too, Frances."

"No. Come to Eastern District High with me."

"Girls High!"

"Eastern District!"

"Erasmus Hall High's the best. You come there, Frances, with me and we'll be friends all through high school. I'll never have any other friend but you, if you'll come."

"Frances, you never let me write in your autograph book."

"Me neither."

"Gimme, gimme."

They wrote in Francie's all but empty book. "They're *nice*," Francie thought. "I could have been friends with them all the time. I thought they didn't want to be friends. It must have been me that was wrong."

They wrote in the book. Some wrote small and cramped; others, loose and sprawling. But all the writing was the handwriting of children. Francie read as they wrote:

> *I wish you luck, I wish you joy.*
> *I wish you first, a baby boy.*
> *And when his hair begins to curl,*
> *I wish you then, a baby girl.*
> Florence Fitzgerald.

> *When you are married*
> *And your husband gets cross,*
> *Sock him with the poker,*
> *And get a divorce.*
> Jeannie Leigh.

> *When night draws back the curtain,*
> *And pins it with a star,*
> *Remember I am still your friend,*
> *Though you may wander far.*
> Noreen O'Leary.

Beatrice Williams turned to the last page in the book and wrote:

> *Way back here and out of sight,*
> *I sign my name, just for spite.*

She signed it, *Your Fellow Writer, Beatrice Williams.* "She would say fellow writer," thought Francie still jealous about the play.

Francie got away at last. Out in the hall she said to Sissy, "Just one more goodbye."

"It's taking you the longest time to graduate," protested Sissy good-naturedly.

Miss Garnder sat at her desk in her brilliantly lighted room. She was alone. She wasn't popular and so far no one had been in to say goodbye. She looked up eagerly as Francie entered.

"So you've come to say goodbye to your old English teacher," she said, pleased.

"Yes, ma'am."

Miss Garnder couldn't let it go at that. She *had* to be a teacher. "About your mark: You haven't turned in work this term. I should have failed you. But at the last moment, I decided to pass you so that you could graduate with your class." She waited. Francie said nothing. "Well? Aren't you going to thank me?"

"Thank you, Miss Garnder."

"You remember our little chat?"

"Yes, ma'am."

"Why did you turn stubborn and stop handing in work, then?"

Francie had nothing to say. It was something she couldn't explain to Miss Garnder. She held out her hand. "Goodbye, Miss Garnder."

Miss Garnder was taken aback. "Well—goodbye, then," she said. They shook hands. "In time to come, you'll see I was right, Frances." Francie said nothing. "Won't you?" Miss Garnder asked sharply.

"Yes, ma'am."

Francie went out of the room. She did not hate Miss Garnder anymore. She didn't like her, but she felt sorry for her. Miss Garnder had nothing in all the world excepting a sureness about how right she was.

Mr. Jenson stood on the school steps. He took each child's hand in both of his and said, "Goodbye and God bless you." He added a personal message for Francie. "Be good, work hard, and reflect credit on our school." Francie promised that she would.

On the way home, Sissy said, "Look! Let's not tell your mother who sent the flowers. It will start her to remembering and she's just about getting well after Laurie." They agreed to say that Sissy bought the flowers. Francie removed the card and put it in her pencil box.

When they told mama the lie about the flowers, she said, "Sissy, you shouldn't have spent your money." But Francie could tell that mama was pleased.

The two diplomas were admired and everyone agreed that Francie's was the prettiest on account of Mr. Jenson's fine handwriting.

"The first diplomas in the Nolan family," said Katie.

"But not the last I hope," said Sissy.

"I'm going to see to it that each of my children have three," said Evy, "grade school, high school and college."

"In twenty-five years," said Sissy, "our family will have a stack of diplomas this high." She stood on tiptoe and measured six feet from the ground.

Mama examined the report cards for the last time. Neeley had "B" in conduct, the same in physical education and "C" in all his other subjects. Mama said, "That's good, son." She looked past Francie's "A's" and concentrated on the "C minus."

"Francie! I'm surprised. How did this happen?"

"Mama, I don't want to talk about it."

"And in English, too. Your best subject."

Francie's voice notched up higher as she repeated, "Mama, I don't want to talk about it."

"She always wrote the best compositions in school," explained Katie to her sisters.

"Mama!" It was almost a scream.

"Katie! Stop it!" ordered Sissy sharply.

"All right, then," surrendered Katie, suddenly aware that she was nagging and ashamed of herself.

Evy jumped in with a change of subject. "Do we have that party, or don't we?" she asked.

"I'm putting my hat on," Katie said.

Sissy stayed with Laurie while Evy, mama, and the two graduates went to Scheefly's Ice-Cream Saloon for the party. Scheefly's was crowded with graduation parties. The kids had their diplomas with them and the girls brought their bouquets. There was a mother or a father—sometimes both, at each table. The Nolan party found a free table at the back of the room.

The place was a medley of shouting kids, beaming parents and rushed waiters. Some kids were thirteen, a few fifteen, but most of them Francie's age—fourteen. Most of the boys were Neeley's classmates and he had a great time hollering greetings across the room. Francie hardly knew the girls, nevertheless she waved and called out to them as gaily as though they had been close friends for years.

Francie was proud of mama. The other mothers had graying hair and most of them were so fat that their backsides slopped over the edges of the chair. Mama was slender and didn't look at all like going on thirty-three. Her skin was as smoothly clear and her hair as black and curling as it had ever been. "Put her in a white dress," thought Francie, "with a bunch of roses in her arms, and she'd look like any fourteen-year-old graduate—except for the line between her eyes that cut deeper since papa died."

They ordered. Francie had a mental list of all the soda flavors. She was going down the list so that she could say she had tasted all the kinds of sodas in the world. Pineapple was next and she ordered that. Neeley ordered the old standby, chocolate soda, and Katie and Evy chose plain vanilla ice cream.

Evy made up little stories about the people in the place and kept Francie and Neeley laughing. Francie studied her mother from time to time. Mama wasn't smiling at Evy's jokes. She ate her ice cream slowly and the line between her eyes deepened and Francie knew that she was figuring something out.

"My children," thought Katie, "have more education at thirteen and fourteen than I have at thirty-two. And still it isn't enough. When I think of how ignorant I was at their age. Yes, and even when I was married and had a baby. Imagine. I believed in witch's charms, then— what the midwife told me about the woman in the fish market. They started in 'way ahead of me. They were never that ignorant.

"I got them graduated from grade school. I can't do more for them. All my plans . . . Neeley, a doctor, Francie in college . . . can't work them out now. The baby. . . . Have they enough in them to get somewhere alone? I don't know. The Shakespeare . . . the Bible. . . . They know how to play piano but they've stopped practicing now. I taught them to be clean and truthful and not to take charity. Is that enough, though?

"They'll have a boss to please, soon, and new people to get along with. They'll get into other ways. Good? Bad? They won't sit home with me nights if they work all day. Neeley will be off with his friends. And Francie? Reading. . . . Away to the library . . . a show . . . a free lecture or band concert. Of course, I'll have the baby. The baby. She'll get a better start. When she graduates, the other two might see her through high school. I must do better for Laurie than I did for them. They never had enough to eat, never had right clothes. The best I could do wasn't enough. And now they have to go out to work and they're still little children. Oh, if I could only get them into high school this fall! *Please* God! I'll give twenty years off my life. I'll work night and day. But I can't, of course. No one to stay with the baby."

Her thoughts were broken into by a wave of singing that rolled over the room. Some one started a popular anti-war song and the rest took it up.

> *I didn't raise my boy to be a soldier.**
> *I brought him up to be my pride and joy . . .*

Katie resumed her thoughts. "There is no one to help us. No one." She thought briefly of Sergeant McShane. He had sent a big basket of fruit when Laurie was born. She knew he was retiring from the police force in September. He was going to run for Assemblyman from Queens, his home borough, next Election. Everyone said he'd be sure to get in. She had heard that his wife was very sick, might not live to see her husband elected.

"He'll marry again," thought Katie. "Of course. Some woman who knows all about social life . . . help him . . . the way a politician's wife must." She stared at her workworn hands for a long time, then put them under the table as though she were ashamed of them.

Francie noticed. "She's thinking of Sergeant McShane," she guessed, remembering how mama had put on her cotton gloves that time long ago at the outing when McShane had looked at her. "He likes her," thought Francie. "I wonder does she know it? She must. She seems to know everything. I bet she could marry him if she wanted to.

---

* I Didn't Raise My Boy to Be a Soldier. Words by Alfred Bryan, Music by Al Piantadosi. Copyright 1916 Leo Feist, Inc. Copyright Renewal 1943 Leo Feist, Inc. Used by permission.

But he needn't think I'd ever call him father. My father is dead and no matter who mama marries, he will only be Mr. So-and-So to me."

They were finishing the song.

> *There'd be no wars today,*
> *If mothers all would say,*
> *I didn't raise my boy to be a soldier.*

". . . Neeley," thought Katie. "Thirteen. If war does come here, it will be over before he gets old enough to go, thank God."

Now Aunt Evy was singing softly to them, making up a parody on the song.

> *Who dares to place a mustache on his shoulder.*

"Aunt Evy, you're *terrible*," said Francie as she and Neeley screamed with laughter. Katie jerked out of her thoughts and looked up and smiled. Then the waiter laid down the check and they all grew silent, watching Katie.

"I hope she's not fool enough to tip him," thought Evy.

"Does mama know you're supposed to leave a nickel tip?" thought Neeley. "I hope so."

"Whatever mama does," thought Francie, "it will be the right thing."

It wasn't the custom to tip in the ice-cream saloons except on special parties when you were supposed to leave a nickel. Katie saw that the check was for thirty cents. She had one coin in her old purse, it was a fifty-cent piece which she laid on the check. The waiter took it away and brought back four nickels which he laid in a row. He hovered nearby waiting for Katie to pick up three of them. She looked at the four nickels. "Four loaves of bread," she thought. Four pair of eyes watched Katie's hand. Katie never hesitated once she put her hand on the money. With a sure gesture, she pushed the four nickels toward the waiter.

"Keep the change," she said grandly.

Francie had all she could do not to stand up on her chair and cheer. "Mama is somebody," she kept saying to herself. The waiter scooped up the nickels happily and rushed away.

"Two sodas shot," groaned Neeley.

"Katie, Katie, how foolish," protested Evy. "I bet it's your last money, too."

"It is. But it may be our last graduation, too."

"McGarrity pays us four dollars tomorrow," said Francie, defending her mother.

"And he fires us tomorrow too," added Neeley.

"There'll be no money after that four dollars until they get jobs, then," concluded Evy.

"I don't care," said Katie. "For once I wanted us to feel like millionaires. And if twenty cents can make us feel rich, it's a cheap price to pay."

Evy recalled how Katie let Francie pour her coffee down the sink and said nothing more. There were many things she didn't understand about her sister.

The parties were breaking up. Albie Seedmore, the leggy son of a prosperous grocer, came over to their table.

"Go-to-the-movies-with-me-tomorrow-Francie?" He asked all on a breath. "I'll pay," he added hastily.

(A movie house was letting the graduates attend the Saturday matinee two-for-a-nickel providing they brought their diplomas along as proof.)

Francie looked at her mother. Mama nodded her consent.

"Sure, Albie," accepted Francie.

"See you. Two. Tomorrow." He loped off.

"Your first date," said Evy. "Make a wish." She held out her little finger and crooked it. Francie hooked her little finger into Aunt Evy's.

"I wish I could always wear a white dress and carry red roses and that we could always throw money around like we did tonight," wished Francie.

BOOK FOUR

43

"*You got the idea now,*" *said the forelady to Francie.* "*You'll make a good stemmer in time.*" She went away and Francie was on her own; the first hour of the first day of her first job.

Following the forelady's instructions, her left hand picked up a foot length of shiny wire. Simultaneously her right hand picked up a narrow strip of dark green tissue paper. She touched the end of the strip to a damp sponge, then, using the thumb and first two fingers of each hand as a rolling machine, she wound the paper on the wire. She placed the covered wire aside. It was now a stem.

At intervals, Mark, the pimply-faced utility boy, distributed the stems to the "pet'lers" who wired paper rose petals to them. Another girl strung a calyx up under the rose and turned it over to the "leafer" who pried a unit, three dark glossy leaves on a short stem, from a block of leaves, wired the unit to the stem and turned the rose over to the "finisher," who wound a strip of heavier-textured green paper around the calyx and down the stem. The stem, calyx, rose and leaves were now one and seemed to have grown so.

Francie's back hurt and a shooting pain ran through her shoulder. She must have covered a thousand stems, she figured. Surely it was time for lunch. She turned around to look at the clock and found that she had been working just one hour!

"Clock watcher," commented a girl derisively. Francie looked up, startled, but said nothing.

She got a rhythm to her work and it seemed to come easier. *One.* She set aside the covered wire. *And a half.* She picked up a new wire and a strip of paper. *Two.* She moistened the paper. *Three-four-five-six-seven-eight-nine-ten.* The wire was covered. Soon the rhythm became instinctive, she didn't have to count and it wasn't necessary to concentrate. Her back relaxed and her shoulder stopped aching. Her mind was freed and she started to figure things out.

"This could be a whole life," she thought. "You work eight hours a day covering wires to earn money to buy food and to pay for a place to sleep so that you can keep living to come back to cover more wires. Some people are born and kept living just to come to this. Of course, some of these girls will marry; marry men who have the same kind of life. What will they gain? They'll gain someone to hold conversations with in the few hours at night between work and sleep." But she knew the gain wouldn't last. She had seen too many working couples who, after the children came and the bills piled up, rarely communicated with each other except in bitter snarls. "These people are caught," she thought. "And why? Because" (remembering her grandmother's repeated convictions), "they haven't got enough education." Fright grew in Francie. Maybe it would be so that she'd never get to high school; maybe she'd never have more education than she had at that moment. Maybe all her life she'd have to cover wires . . . cover wires. . . . *One . . . and a half . . . two . . . three-four-five-six-seven-eight-nine-ten.* The same unreasoning terror came on her that had come when, as an eleven-year-old child, she had seen the old man with the obscene feet in Losher's Bakery. In her panic, she speeded up her rhythm so that she'd *have* to concentrate on her work and not have room to think.

"New broom," observed a finisher cynically.

"Trying to make a hit with the boss," was the opinion of a pet'ler.

Soon even the speeding up became automatic and again Francie's mind was free. Covertly, she studied the girls at the long table. There were a dozen of them, Poles and Italians. The youngest looked sixteen and the oldest, thirty, and all were swarthy. For some unaccountable reason, all wore black dresses, evidently not realizing how unbecoming black was to dark skins. Francie was the only one wearing a gingham wash dress and she felt like a silly baby. The sharp-eyed workers noticed her quick stares and retaliated with their own peculiar brand of hazing. The girl at the head of the table started it.

"Somebody at this table is got a dirty face," she announced. "Not me," answered the others one by one. When Francie's turn came they stopped work and waited. Not knowing what to answer, Francie remained silent. "New girl says nothing," summarized the ringleader. "So she's got the dirty face." Francie's face got hot but she worked faster hoping they'd drop the whole thing.

"Somebody is got a dirty neck." It started all over again. "Not me," answered the girls in order. When it came to Francie's turn, she too said, "Not me." But instead of appeasing them, it gave them more material to work on.

"New girl says her neck ain't dirty."

"*She* says!"

"How does she know? Can she see her own neck?"

"Would she admit it if it was dirty?"

"They want me to do something," puzzled Francie. "But what? Do they want me to get mad and curse at them? Do they want me to give up this job? Or do they want to see me cry the way that little girl did long ago when I watched her clean the blackboard erasers? Whatever they want, I won't do it!" She bent her head over the wires and made her fingers fly faster.

The tiresome game went on all morning. The only respites were when Mark, the utility boy, came in. Then they let up on Francie a little in order to work on him.

"New girl, watch out for Mark," they warned her. "He was arrested twice for rape and once for white slavery."

The accusations were crudely ironical considering the obvious effeminacy of Mark. Francie saw how the unfortunate boy flushed a brick red at each taunt and she felt sorry for him.

The morning wore on. When it seemed that it would never end, a bell rang announcing lunch time. The girls dropped their work, hauled out paper bags of lunch, ripped the bags open to form a tablecloth, spread out their onion-garnished sandwiches and started to eat.

Francie's hands were hot and sticky. She wanted to wash them before she ate so she asked her neighbor where the washroom was.

"No spik Eng-leash," answered the girl in exaggerated green-horn dialect.

"Nix verstandt," said another who had been taunting her in idiomatic English all morning.

"What's a washroom?" asked a fat girl.

"Where they make washers," replied a wit.

Mark was collecting boxes. He stood in the doorway, his arms laden, made his Adam's apple go up and down twice, and Francie heard him speak for the first time.

"Jesus Christ died on the cross for people like you," he announced passionately, "and now you won't show a new girl where the terlet is."

Francie stared at him, astonished. Then she couldn't help it—it had sounded so funny—she burst out laughing. Mark gulped, turned and disappeared down the hall. Everything changed then. A murmur ran round the table.

"She laughed!"

"Hey! The new girl laughed!"

"Laughed!"

A young Italian girl linked her arm in Francie's and said, "Come on, new girl. I'll show you the terlet."

In the washroom, she turned on the water for Francie, punched down on the glass bowl of liquid soap and hovered over Francie solicitously while she washed her hands. When Francie would have dried her hands on the snowy, obviously-unused roller towel, her guide snatched her away.

"Don't use that towel, new girl."

"Why? It looks clean."

"It's dangerous. Some of the girls working here is clappy and you'll catch it if you use the towel."

"What'll I do?" Francie waved her wet hands.

"Use your petticoat like we do."

Francie dried her hands on her petticoat eyeing the deadly towel with horror.

Back in the workroom, she found that they had flattened her paper bag and set out the two bologna sandwiches mama had fixed for her. She saw that someone had placed a nice red tomato on her paper. The girls welcomed her back with smiles. The one who had led the taunts all morning, took a long swig out of a whiskey bottle and then passed it to Francie.

"Take a drink, new girl," she ordered. "Them samwishes is dry going down alone." Francie shrank back and declined hastily. "Go ahead! It's only cold tea." Francie thought of the washroom towel and shook her head "no" emphatically. "Ah!" exclaimed the girl. "I know why you don't drink from my bottle. In the terlet, Anastasia scared you. Don't you believe her, new girl. The boss started that clappy talk hisself so's we wouldn't use the towels. That way he saves a couple dollars each week on laundry."

"Yeah?" said Anastasia, "I don't see none of youse using the towel."

"Hell, we only got half a hour for lunch. Who wants to waste time washing hands? Drink up, new girl."

Francie took a long drink from the bottle. The cold tea was strong and refreshing. She thanked the girl and then tried to thank the donor of the tomato. Immediately each girl in turn denied giving it.

"What are you talking about?"

"What termater?"

"Don't see no termater."

"New girl brings a termater for lunch and don't even remember."

So they teased her. But now there was something warmly companionable about the teasing. Francie enjoyed the lunch period and was glad she had found out what they wanted from her. They had just wanted her to laugh—such a simple thing and so hard to find out.

The rest of the day passed pleasantly. The girls told her not to break her neck—that it was seasonable work and they'd all be laid off when the fall orders had been made up. The quicker the orders were finished, the sooner they'd be fired. Francie, pleased at being taken into the confidence of these older, more experienced workers, obligingly slowed down. They told jokes all afternoon and Francie laughed at them all, whether they were funny or just plain dirty. And her conscience bothered her only a little bit when she joined the others in tormenting Mark, the martyr, who didn't know that if he would laugh but once, his troubles in the shop would be over.

It was a few minutes past noon on Saturday. Francie stood at the foot of the Flushing Avenue station of the Broadway El waiting for Neeley. She held an envelope containing five dollars—her first week's pay. Neeley was bringing home five dollars too. They had agreed to arrive home together and make a little ceremony out of giving the money to mama.

Neeley worked as errand boy in a downtown New York broker-age house. Sissy's John had gotten him the job through a friend already working there. Francie envied Neeley. Each day he crossed the great Williamsburg Bridge and went into the strange big city while Francie walked to her work on the north side of Brooklyn. And Neeley ate in a restaurant. Like Francie, he had brought his lunch the first day but the boys made fun of him, calling him the country boy from Brooklyn. After that, mama gave him fifteen cents a day for lunch. He told Francie how he ate in a place called the Automat where you put a nickel in a slot and coffee and cream came out together—not too little, not too much, just a cupful. Francie wished she could ride across the bridge to work and eat in the Automat instead of carrying sandwiches from home.

Neeley ran down the El steps. He carried a flat package under his arm. Francie noticed how he put his feet down at an angle so that the whole foot was on the step instead of just the heel part. This gave him sure footing. Papa had always come down stairs that way. Neeley wouldn't tell Francie what was in the package, saying that would spoil the surprise. They stopped in a neighborhood bank which was just about to close for the day and asked a teller to give them new one-dollar bills in exchange for their old money.

"What do you want new bills for?" asked the teller.

"It's our first pay and we'd like to bring it home in new money," explained Francie.

"First pay, eh?" said the teller. "That takes me back. It certainly takes me back. I remember when I took home my first pay. I was a boy at the time . . . working on a farm in Manhasset, Long Island. Well, sir. . . ." He went off into a biographical sketch while people in line shuffled impatiently. He ended, ". . . and when I turned my first pay over to my mother, the tears stood in her eyes. Yes, sir, the tears stood in her eyes."

He tore the wrapper from a bundle of new bills and exchanged their old money. Then he said, "And here's a present for you." He gave each a fresh-minted gold-looking penny which he took from the cash drawer. "New 1916 pennies," he explained. "The first in the neighborhood. Don't spend them, now. Save them." He took two old coppers from his pocket and put them in the drawer to make up the deficiency. Francie thanked him. As they moved away, she heard the man next in line say as he leaned his elbow on the ledge,

"I remember when I brought my first pay home to my old lady."

As they went out, Francie wondered whether everyone in line would tell about his first pay. "Everyone who works," said Francie, "has this one thing together: They remember about bringing home their first pay."

"Yeah," agreed Neeley.

As they turned a corner, Francie mused, "And the tears stood in her eyes." She had never heard that expression before and it caught her fancy.

"How could that be?" Neeley wanted to know. "Tears have no legs. They can't stand."

"He didn't mean that. He meant it like when people say, 'I stood in bed all day.' "

"But 'stood' is no word that way."

"It is so," countered Francie. "Here in Brooklyn 'stood' is like the past tense of 'stay.' "

"I guess so," agreed Neeley. "Let's walk down Manhattan Avenue instead of Graham."

"Neeley, I have an idea. Let's make a tin-can bank without telling mama and nail it in your closet. We'll start it off with these new pennies and if mama gives us any spending money, we'll each put ten cents in every week. We'll open it Christmas and buy presents for mama and Laurie."

"And for us, too," stipulated Neeley.

"Yeah. I'll buy one for you and you buy one for me. I'll tell you what I want when the time comes."

It was agreed.

They walked briskly, outdistancing loitering kids homeward bound from the junk shops. They looked towards Carney's as they passed Scholes Street and noticed the crowd outside of Cheap Charlie's.

"Kids," said Neeley contemptuously, jingling some coins in his pockets.

"Remember, Neeley, when we used to go out selling junk?"

"That was a long time ago."

"Yeah," agreed Francie. It was, in fact, two weeks since they had dragged their last haul to Carney's.

Neeley presented the flat package to mama. "For you and Francie," he said. Mama unwrapped it. It was a pound box of Loft's peanut brittle. "And I didn't buy it out of my salary, either," explained Neeley mysteriously. They made mama go into the bedroom for a minute. They arranged the ten new bills on the table, then called mama out.

"For you, Mama," said Francie with a grand wave of her hand.

"Oh, my!" said Mama. "I can hardly believe it."

"And that's not all," said Neeley. He took eighty cents in change from his pocket and placed it on the table. "Tips for running errands fast," he explained. "I saved 'em all week. There was more, but I bought the candy."

Mama slid the change across the table to Neeley. "All the tips you make, you keep for spending money," she said.

(Just like papa, thought Francie.)

"Gee! Well, I'll give Francie a quarter out of it."

"No." Mama got a fifty-cent piece from the cracked cup and gave it to Francie. "That's Francie's spending money. Fifty cents a week." Francie was pleased. She hadn't expected that much of an allowance. The children overwhelmed their mother with thanks.

Katie looked at the candy, at the new bills and then at her children. She bit her lip, turned suddenly and went into the bedroom, closing the door after her.

"Is she mad about something?" whispered Neeley.

"No," said Francie. "She's not mad. She just didn't want us to see her start crying."

"How do you know she's going to cry?"

"'Cause. When she looked at the money, I saw that tears stood in her eyes."

44

Francie had been working two weeks when the layoff came. The girls exchanged looks while the Boss explained that it was just for a few days.

"A few days, six months long," explained Anastasia for Francie's information.

The girls were going over to a Greenpoint factory which needed hands for winter orders, poinsettias and artificial holly wreaths. When the layoff came *there,* they'd go on to another factory. And so on. They were Brooklyn migratory workers following seasonal work from one part of the borough to the other.

They urged Francie to go along with them but she wanted to try new work. She figured that since she had to work, she'd get variety in it by changing her job each chance she got. Then, like the sodas, she could say she had tried every work there was.

Katie found an ad in *The World* that said a file clerk was wanted; beginner considered, age sixteen, state religion. Francie bought a sheet of writing paper and an envelope for a penny and carefully wrote an application and addressed it to the ad's box number. Although she was only fourteen, she and her mother agreed that she could pass for sixteen easily. So she said she was sixteen in the letter.

Two days later, Francie received a reply on an exciting letter head: a pair of shears lying on a folded newspaper with a pot of paste nearby.

It was from the Model Press Clipping Bureau on Canal Street, New York, and it asked Miss Nolan to report for an interview.

Sissy went shopping with Francie and helped her buy a grown-up dress and her first pair of high-heeled pumps. When she tried on her new outfit, mama and Sissy swore that she looked sixteen except for her hair. Her braids made her look very kiddish.

"Mama, please let me get it bobbed," begged Francie.

"It took you fourteen years to grow that hair," said mama, "and I'll not let you have it cut off."

"Gee, Mama, you're 'way behind the time."

"Why do you want short hair like a boy?"

"It would be easier to care for."

"Taking care of her hair should be a woman's pleasure."

"But Katie," protested Sissy, "all the girls are bobbing their hair nowadays."

"They're fools, then. A woman's hair is her mystery. Daytimes, it's pinned up. But at night, alone with her man, the pins come out and it hangs loose like a shining cape. It makes her a special secret woman for the man."

"At night, *all* cats are gray," said Sissy wickedly.

"None of your remarks," said Katie sharply.

"I'd look just like Irene Castle if I had short hair," persisted Francie.

"They make Jew women cut off their hair when they marry, so no other man will look at them. Nuns get their hair cut off to prove they're done with men. Why should any young girl do it when she doesn't have to?" Francie was about to reply when mama said, "We'll have no more arguments."

"All right," said Francie. "But when I'm eighteen, I'll be my own boss. Then *you'll* see."

"When you're eighteen, you can shave your scalp for all I care. In the meantime . . ." She wound Francie's two heavy braids around her head and pinned them in place with bone hairpins which she took from her own hair. "There!" She stepped back and surveyed her daughter. "It looks just like a shining crown," she announced dramatically.

"It does make her look at least eighteen," conceded Sissy.

Francie looked in the mirror. She was pleased that she looked so old the way mama had fixed her hair. But she wouldn't give in and say so.

"All my life I'll have headaches carrying this load of hair around," she complained.

"Lucky you, if that's all gives you a life of headaches," said mama.

Next morning, Neeley escorted his sister to New York. As the train came on to the Williamsburg Bridge after leaving Marcy Avenue station, Francie noticed that many people seated in the car rose as if in accord and then sat down again.

"Why do they do that, Neeley?"

"Just as you get on the Bridge, there's a bank with a big clock. People stand up to look at the time so's they know whether they're early or late for work. I betcha a million people look at that clock every day," figured Neeley.

Francie had anticipated a thrill when she rode over that Bridge for the first time. But the ride wasn't half as thrilling as wearing grown-up clothes for the first time.

The interview was short. She was hired on trial. Hours, nine to five-thirty, half an hour for lunch, salary, seven dollars a week to start. First, the Boss took her on a tour of inspection of the Press Clipping Bureau.

The ten readers sat at long sloping desks. The newspapers of all the states were divided among them. The papers poured into the Bureau every hour of every day from every city in every state of the Union. The girls marked and boxed items sought and put down their total and their own identifying number on the top of the front page.

The marked papers were collected and brought to the printer who had a hand press containing an adjustable date apparatus, and racks of slugs before her. She adjusted the paper's date on her press, inserted the slug containing the name, city, and state of the newspaper and printed as many slips as there were items marked.

Then, slips and newspaper went to the cutter who stood before a large slanting desk and slashed out the marked items with a sharp curved knife. (In spite of the letterhead, there wasn't a pair of shears on the premises.) As the cutter slashed out the items, throwing the discarded paper to the floor, a sea of newspaper rose as high as her waist each fifteen minutes. A man collected this waste paper and took it away for baling.

The clipped items and slips were turned over to the paster who affixed the clippings to the slips. Then they were filed, collected and placed in envelopes and mailed.

Francie got on to the filing system very easily. In two weeks, she had memorized the two thousand or so names or headings on the file box. Then she was put into training as a reader. For two more weeks, she did nothing but study the clients' cards which were more detailed than the file box headings. When an informal examination proved that she had memorized the orders, she was given the Oklahoma papers to read. The Boss went over her papers before they went to the cutter and pointed out her mistakes. When she got expert enough not to need checking, the Pennsylvania papers were added. Soon after she was given the New York state papers, and now had three states to read. By the end of August, she was reading more papers and marking more items than any other reader in the Bureau. She was fresh to the work, anxious to please, had strong clear eyes (she was the only reader not wearing glasses), and had developed a photographic eye very quickly. She could take in an item at a glance and note immediately whether it was something to mark. She read between a hundred and eighty and two hundred newspapers a day. The next best reader averaged from a hundred to a hundred and ten papers.

Yes, Francie was the fastest reader in the Bureau—and the poorest paid. Although she had been raised to ten dollars a week when she went on reading, her runnerup received twenty-five dollars a week and the other readers received twenty. Since Francie never became friendly enough with the girls to be taken into their confidence, she had no way of knowing how grossly underpaid she was.

Although Francie liked reading newspapers and was proud to earn ten dollars a week, she was not happy. She had been excited about going to work in New York. Since such a tiny thing as a flower in a brown bowl at the library had thrilled her so, she expected that the great city of New York would thrill her a hundred times more. But it was not so.

The Bridge had been the first disappointment. Looking at it from the roof of her house, she had thought that crossing it would make her feel like a gossamer-winged fairy flying through the air. But the actual ride over the Bridge was no different than the ride above the Brooklyn streets. The Bridge was paved in sidewalks and traffic roads like the streets of Broadway and the tracks were the same tracks. There was no different feeling about the train as it went over the Bridge. New York was disappointing. The buildings were higher and the crowds thicker; otherwise it was little different from Brooklyn. From now on, would all new things be disappointing, she wondered?

She had often studied the map of the United States and crossed its plains, mountains, deserts, and rivers in her imagination. And it had seemed a wonderful thing. Now she wondered whether she wouldn't be disappointed in that, too. Supposing, she thought, she was to walk across this great country. She'd start out at seven in the morning, say, and walk westward. She'd put one foot down in front of the other to cover distance, and, as she walked to the west, she'd be so busy with her feet and with the realization that her footsteps were part of a chain that had started in Brooklyn, that she might think nothing at all of the mountains, rivers, plains, and deserts she came upon. All she'd notice was that some things were strange because they reminded her of Brooklyn and that other things were strange because they were so different from Brooklyn. "I guess there is nothing new, then, in the world," decided Francie unhappily. "If there is anything new or different, some part of it must be in Brooklyn and I must be used to it and wouldn't be able to notice it if I came across it." Like Alexander the Great, Francie grieved, being convinced that there were no new worlds to conquer.

She adapted herself to the split-second rhythm of the New Yorker going to and from work. Getting to the office was a nervous ordeal. If she arrived one minute before nine, she was a free person. If she arrived a minute after, she worried because that made her the logical scapegoat of the Boss if he happened to be in a bad mood that day. So she learned ways of conserving bits of seconds. Long before the train ground to a stop at her station, she pushed her way to the door to be one of the first expelled when it slid open. Out of the train, she ran like a deer, circling the crowd to be the first up the stairs leading to the street. Walking to the office, she kept close to the buildings so she could turn corners sharply. She crossed streets kittycorner to save stepping off and on an extra pair of curbs. At the building, she shoved her way into the elevator even though the operator yelled "Car's full!" And all this maneuvering to arrive one minute before, instead of after nine!

Once she left home ten minutes earlier to have more time. In spite of no need of hurry, she still pushed her way out of the train, flew up the steps, rushed through the streets economically and crowded into a full elevator. She was fifteen minutes early. The big room was echoingly empty and she felt desolate and lost. When the other workers rushed in seconds before nine, Francie felt like a traitor. The next morning, she slept ten minutes longer and returned to her original timing.

She was the only Brooklyn girl in the Bureau. The others came from Manhattan, Hoboken, the Bronx, and one commuted from Bayonne, New Jersey. Two of the oldest readers there, sisters, had originally come from Ohio. The first day Francie worked at the Bureau one of the sisters said to her, "You have a Brooklyn accent." It had sounded like a shocked accusation and made Francie self-conscious of her speech. She took to pronouncing words carefully, lest she say things like "goil" for "girl," and "appermtment" instead of "appointment."

There were but two people in the Bureau to whom she could talk without embarrassment. One was the Boss-manager. He was a Harvard graduate and in spite of a broad "a" which he used indiscriminately, his speech was plain and his vocabulary less affected than those of the readers, most of whom had graduated from high school and had picked up an extensive vocabulary from years of reading. The other person was Miss Armstrong, who was the only other college graduate.

Miss Armstrong was the special city reader. Her desk was isolated in the choicest corner of the room where there was a north and an east window, the best light for reading. She read nothing but the Chicago, Boston, Philadelphia, and New York City newspapers. A special messenger brought her each edition of the New York City newspapers soon after it left the presses. When her papers were read up, she didn't have to pitch in, as the other readers did, and help the girls who were behind. She crocheted or manicured her nails while waiting for the next edition. She was the highest paid, receiving thirty dollars a week. Miss Armstrong was a kindly person and she took a helpful interest in Francie and tried to draw her out in conversation so that she wouldn't feel lonely.

Once in the washroom, Francie overheard a remark about Miss Armstrong being the Boss' mistress. Francie had heard of, but never seen one of those fabulous beings. Immediately, she examined Miss Armstrong closely as a mistress. She saw that Miss Armstrong wasn't pretty; her face was almost simian with its wide mouth and flat thick nostrils, and her figure was merely passable. Francie looked at her legs. They were long, slender and exquisitely molded. She wore the sheerest of flawless silk stockings, and expensively-made high-heeled pumps shod her beautifully-arched feet. "Beautiful legs, then, is the secret of being a mistress," concluded Francie. She looked down at her own long thin legs. "I'll never make it, I guess." Sighing, she resigned herself to a sinless life.

There was a class system in the Bureau engendered by the cutter, printer, paster, paper baler, and delivery boy. These workers, illiterate but sharp-witted, who for some reason called themselves The Club, assumed that the better-educated readers looked down on them. In retaliation, they stirred up as much trouble as possible among the readers.

Francie's loyalties were divided. By background and education, she belonged to The Club class but by ability and intelligence she belonged to the readers' class. The Club was shrewd enough to feel this division in Francie and tried to use her as a go-between. They informed her of trouble-making office rumors, expecting that she would relay them to the readers and create dissension. But Francie wasn't friendly enough with the readers to exchange gossip with them and the rumors died with her.

So one day, when the cutter told her that Miss Armstrong was leaving in September, and that she, Francie, was to be promoted to the city reader job, Francie assumed this to be a rumor invented to arouse jealousy among the readers, all of whom expected the city reading job when and if Miss Armstrong resigned. She thought it was preposterous, that she, a girl of fourteen, with nothing but a grade school education, would be considered eligible to take over the work of a thirty-year-old college graduate like Miss Armstrong.

It was nearing the end of August and Francie was worried because mama hadn't mentioned anything about her going to high school. She wanted desperately to go back to school. All the years of talk about higher education she had heard from her mother, grandmother, and aunts not only made her anxious to get more education, but gave her an inferiority complex about her present lack of education.

She remembered with affection the girls who had written in her autograph book. She wanted to be one of them again. They came out of the same life as she did; they were no further along. Her natural place was going to school with them, not working competitively with older women.

She didn't like working in New York. The crowds continually swarming about her made her tremble. She felt that she was being pushed into a way of life that she wasn't ready to handle. And the things she dreaded worst about working in New York was the crowded El trains.

There had been that time in the train when, hanging from a strap and so tightly wedged in the crowd that she couldn't so much as lower her arm, she had felt a man's hand. No matter how she twisted and squirmed, she couldn't get away from that hand. When she swayed with the crowd as the cars swerved, the hand tightened. She was unable to twist her head to see whose hand it was. She stood in desperate futility, helplessly enduring the indignity. She could have called out and protested but she was too ashamed to call public attention to her predicament. It seemed an eternity before the crowd thinned out enough for her to move to a different part of the car. After that, standing in a crowded train became a dreaded ordeal.

One Sunday, when she and mama brought Laurie over to see granma, Francie told Sissy about the man on the train, expecting that Sissy would comfort her. But her aunt treated it as a great joke.

"So a man pinched you on the El," she said. "I wouldn't let that bother me. It means you're getting a good shape and there are some men who can't resist a woman's shape. Say! I must be getting old! It's been years since anybody pinched me on the El. There was a time when I couldn't ride in a crowd without coming home black and blue," she said proudly.

"Is that anything to brag about?" asked Katie.

Sissy ignored that remark. "The day will come, Francie," she said, "when you're forty-five and have a shape like a bag of horses' oats tied in the middle. Then you'll look back and long for the old days when men *wanted* to pinch you."

"If she does look back," said Katie, "it will be because you put it in her mind and not because it's anything wonderful to remember." She turned to Francie. "As for you, learn to stand in the train without holding on to a strap. Keep your hands down and keep a long sharp pin in your pocket. If you feel a man's hand on you, stick it good with the pin."

Francie did as mama said. She learned to keep her feet without holding to a strap. She kept her hand closed on a long vicious pin in her coat pocket. She hoped someone would pinch her again. She just hoped so, so that she could stab him with the pin. "It's all very well for Sissy to talk about shapes and men, but I don't like to be pinched in the back. And when I get to be forty-five, I certainly hope that I have something nicer to look back on and long for than being pinched by a stranger. Sissy ought to be ashamed. . . .

"What's the matter with me, anyhow? Here I stand criticizing Sissy—Sissy who's been so darn good to me. I'm dissatisfied with my job when I should feel lucky having such interesting work.

Imagine getting *paid* to read when I like to read so much anyhow. And everyone thinks New York is the most wonderful city in the world and *I* can't even get to like New York. Seems like I'm the most dissatisfied person in the whole world. Oh, I wish I was young again when everything seemed so wonderful!"

Just before Labor Day, the Boss called Francie into his private office and informed her that Miss Armstrong was leaving to be married. He cleared his throat and added that Miss Armstrong was marrying him, in fact.

Francie's conception of a mistress broke and scattered. She had believed that men never married their mistresses—that they cast them aside like worn-out gloves. So Miss Armstrong was to become a wife instead of a worn-out glove. Well!

"So we'll need a new city reader," the Boss was saying. "Miss Armstrong herself, suggested that we . . . ah . . . try *you* out, Miss Nolan."

Francie's heart jumped. She, city reader! The most coveted job in the Bureau! There had been truth, then, in The Club's rumors. Another preconceived idea gone. She had always assumed that all rumors were false.

The Boss planned to offer her fifteen a week, figuring he'd get as good a reader as his future wife at half the salary. The girl should be tickled to death, too—a youngster like that . . . fifteen a week. She said she was past sixteen. She looked thirteen. Of course her age was none of his business as long as she was competent. The law couldn't touch him—hiring someone under age. All he'd have to say was that she deceived him as to her true age.

"There's a little raise along with the job," he said benignly. Francie smiled happily and he worried. "Have I put my foot in it?" he thought. "Maybe she didn't expect a raise." He covered his blunder hastily. ". . . a small raise after we see how you work out."

"I don't know . . ." began Francie doubtfully.

"She's over sixteen," decided the boss, "and she's going to hold me up for a big raise." To forestall her, he said, "We'll give you fifteen a week, starting. . . ." He hesitated. No use being too good-natured. ". . . starting the first of October." He leaned back in his chair feeling as gracious as God, Himself.

"I mean, I don't think I'll be here much longer."

"She's working me for more money," he thought. Aloud, he asked, "Why not?"

"I'm going back to school after Labor Day, I think. I meant to tell you as soon as my plans were settled."

"College?"

"High school."

"I'll have to put Pinski on city," he thought. "She's getting twenty-five now, she'll expect thirty and I'm right back where I started. This Nolan is better than Pinski, too. Damn Irma! Where does she get the idea that a woman shouldn't work after marriage? She could keep right on . . . keep the money in the family . . . buy a home with it." He spoke to Francie.

"Oh! I'm sorry to hear that. Not that I don't approve of higher education. But I consider newspaper reading a darn fine education. It's a good live ever-growing contemporary education. While in school . . . it's merely books. Dead books," he said contemptuously.

"I'll . . . I'll have to talk it over with my mother."

"By all means. Tell her what your Boss said about education. And tell her I said," he closed his eyes and took the plunge, "that we'll pay you *twenty* dollars a week. Starting the first of November," he shaved off a month.

"That's an awful lot of money," she said in all honesty.

"We believe in paying our workers well so they stick with us. And . . . ah . . . Miss Nolan, please don't mention your future salary. It's more than anyone else is getting," he lied, "and if they found out . . ." he spread his hands in a gesture of futility. "You understand? No washroom gossip."

Francie felt gracious as she set his mind at ease by assuring him that she'd never betray him in the washroom. The Boss started to sign letters, indicating that the interview was over.

"That's all, Miss Nolan. And we must have your decision the day after Labor Day."

"Yes, sir."

Twenty dollars a week! Francie was stunned. Two months ago, she was glad to earn five dollars a week. Uncle Willie only earned eighteen a week and he was forty. Sissy's John was smart and earned but twenty-two-fifty a week. Few men in her neighborhood earned as much as twenty a week and they had families, too.

"With that money, our troubles would be over," thought Francie. "We could pay rent on a three-room flat somewhere, mama wouldn't have to go out to work and Laurie wouldn't be left alone so much. I gues I'd be mighty important if I could manage something like that.

"But I want to go back to school!"

She recalled the constant harping on education in the family.

Granma: It will raise you up on the face of the earth.

Evy: Each of my three children will get three diplomas.

Sissy: And when mother goes—pray God not for a long time yet—and baby is big enough to start kindergarten, I'm going out to work again. And I'll bank my pay and when Little Sissy grows up, I'll put her in the best college there is.

Mama: And I don't want my children to have the same hard-working life I have. Education will fix it so that their lives are easier.

"Still it's such a good job," thought Francie. "That is, good right now. But my eyes will get worn out from the work. All the older readers have to wear glasses. Miss Armstrong said a reader's only good as long as her eyes hold out. Those other readers were fast, too, when they first started. Like me. But now their eyes. . . . I must save my eyes . . . not read away from the job.

"If mama knew I could get twenty a week, maybe she wouldn't send me back to school and I couldn't blame her. We've been poor so long. Mama is very fair in all things but this money might make her see things in a different way and it wouldn't be her fault. I won't tell her about the raise until after she decides about school."

Francie spoke to mama about school and mama said, yes, they'd have to talk about it. They'd talk about it right after supper that night.

After finishing their supper coffee, Katie announced needlessly (since everybody knew it), that school was opening next week. "I want both of you to go to high school but it's working out that only one of you can start this fall. I'm saving every cent I can out of your pay so that next year, both of you will be back in school." She waited. She waited a long time. Neither of the children answered. "Well? Don't you want to go to high school?"

Francie's lips were stiff as she spoke. So much depended on mama, and Francie wanted her words to make a good impression. "Yes, Mama. I want to go back to school more'n I'll ever want anything in my life."

"I don't want to go," said Neeley. "Don't make me go back to school, Mama. I like to work and I'm going to get a two-dollar raise the first of the year."

"Don't you want to be a doctor?"

"No. I want to be a broker and make lots of money like my bosses. I'll get on to the stock market and make a million dollars some day."

"My son will be a great doctor."

"How do you know? I might turn out like Dr. Hueller on Maujer Street with an office in a basement flat and always wear a dirty shirt like him. Anyhow, I know enough. I don't need to go back to school."

"Neeley doesn't want to go back to school," said Katie. She spoke to Francie almost pleadingly. "You know what that means, Francie." Francie bit her lip. It wouldn't do to cry. She must keep calm. She must keep thinking clearly. "It means," said mama, "*that Neeley has to go back to school.*"

"I won't!" cried Neeley. "I won't go back no matter what you say! I'm working and earning money and I want to keep on. I'm somebody now with the fellers. If I go back to school, I'm just a punk kid again. Besides, you need my money, Mama. We don't want to be poor again."

"You'll go back to school," announced Katie quietly. "Francie's money will be enough."

"Why do you make him go when he doesn't want to," cried Francie, "and keep me out of school when I want to go so much?"

"Yeah," agreed Neeley.

"Because if I don't make him, he'll never go back," said mama, "where you, Francie, will fight and manage to get back somehow."

"Why are you so sure all the time?" protested Francie. "In a year I'll be too old to go back. Neeley's only thirteen. He'll still be young enough next year."

"Nonsense. You'll only be fifteen next fall."

"Seventeen," corrected Francie, "going on eighteen; too old to start."

"What kind of silly talk is that?"

"Not silly. On the job, I'm sixteen. I have to look and act sixteen instead of fourteen. Next year I'll be fifteen in years but two years older in the way I'm living; too old to change back into a school girl."

"Neeley will go back to school next week," said Katie stubbornly, "and Francie will go back next year."

"I hate both of you," shouted Neeley. "And if you make me go back, I'll run away from home. Yes, I will!" He ran out slamming the door.

Katie's face set in lines of misery and Francie felt sorry for her. "Don't worry, Mama. He won't run away. He just said that." The instant relief that came into her mother's face angered Francie. "But I'm the one who'll go away and I won't make a speech about it. When the time comes that you don't need what I earn, I'll leave."

"What's gotten into my children who used to be so good?" asked Katie poignantly.

"Years have gotten into us." Katie looked puzzled. Francie explained: "We never did get working papers."

"But they were hard to get. The priest wanted a dollar for each baptismal certificate and I would have had to go to City Hall with you. I was nursing Laurie every two hours then, and couldn't go. We all figured it was easier for you both to claim to be sixteen and not have all the fuss."

"That part was all right. But saying we were sixteen, we had to *be* sixteen, and you treat us like thirteen-year-old children."

"I wish your father were here. He understood things about you that I can't get to understand." Pain stabbed through Francie. After it passed, she told her mother that her salary was to be doubled on November first.

"Twenty dollars!" Katie's mouth fell open in surprise. "Oh, my!" That was her usual expression when anything astonished her. "When did you know?"

"Saturday."

"And you didn't tell me till now."

"No."

"You thought if I knew that it would fix my mind about you keeping on working."

"Yes."

"But I didn't know when I said it was right for Neeley to go back to school. You can see that I did what I thought was right and the money didn't come into it. Can't you see?" she asked pleadingly.

"No, I can't see. I can only see that you favor Neeley more than me. You fix everything for him and tell me that I can find a way myself. Some day I'll fool you, Mama. I'll do what I think is right for me and it might not be right in your way."

"I'm not worrying, because I know that I can trust my daughter." Katie spoke with such simple dignity that Francie was ashamed of herself. "And I trust my son. He's mad now about doing what he doesn't want to do. But he'll get over it and do well in school. Neeley's a good boy."

"Yes, he's a good boy," conceded Francie, "but even if he was bad, you wouldn't notice it. But where I'm concerned . . ." her voice went ragged on a sob.

Katie sighed sharply but said nothing. She got up and started to clear the table. Her hand reached for a cup, and Francie, for the first time in her life, saw her mother's hand fumble. It trembled and couldn't connect with the cup. Francie put the cup in her mother's hand. She noticed a big crack in the cup.

"Our family used to be like a strong cup," thought Francie. "It was whole and sound and held things well. When papa died, the first crack came. And this fight tonight made another crack. Soon there will be so many cracks that the cup will break and we'll all be pieces instead of a whole thing together. I don't want this to happen, yet I'm deliberately making a deep crack." Her sharp sigh was just like Katie's.

The mother went to the washbasket in which the baby was sleeping peacefully in spite of the bitter talking. Francie saw her mother's still fumbling hands take the sleeping child from the basket. Katie sat in her rocker near the window, held her baby tightly and rocked.

Francie almost went blind with pity. "I shouldn't be so mean to her," she thought. "What has she ever had but hard work and trouble? Now she has to turn to her baby for comfort. Maybe she's thinking that Laurie whom she loves so and who is so dependent on her now, will grow up to turn against her like I'm doing now."

She put her hand awkwardly on her mother's cheek. "It's all right, Mama. I didn't mean it. You're right and I'll do as you say. Neeley must go to school and you and I will see that he gets through."

Katie put her hand over Francie's. "That's my good girl," she said.

"Don't be mad at me, Mama, because I fought you. You, yourself, taught me to fight for what I thought was right and I . . . I thought I was right."

"I know. And I'm pleased that you can and will fight for what you should have. And you'll always come out all right—no matter what. You're like me that way."

"And that's where the whole trouble is," thought Francie. "We're too much alike to understand each other because we don't even understand our own selves. Papa and I were too different persons and we understood each other. Mama understands Neeley because he's different from her. I wish I was different in the way that Neeley is."

"Then everything's all right now between us?" Katie asked with a smile.

"Of course." Francie smiled back and kissed her mother's cheek.

But in their secret hearts, each knew that it wasn't all right and would never be all right between them again.

45

Christmas again. But this year there was money for presents and lots of food in the icebox and the flat was always warm now. When Francie came in off the cold street she thought that the warmth was like a lover's arms around her drawing her into the room. She wondered, incidentally, exactly what a lover's arms felt like.

Francie took comfort out of not returning to school in the realization that the money she earned made life easier for them. Mama had been very fair. When Francie was raised to twenty dollars a week, mama gave her five dollars a week for herself to pay for her carfare, lunches, and clothes. Also, Katie deposited five dollars each week in Francie's name in the Williamsburg Savings Bank—for college, she explained. Katie managed well on the remaining ten dollars and a dollar that Neeley contributed. It wasn't a fortune, but things were cheap in 1916 and the Nolans got along fine.

Neeley had taken to school cheerfully when he found that many of his old gang were entering Eastern District High. He had his old after-school job back at McGarrity's and mama gave him one of the two dollars for pocket money. He was somebody in school. He had more spending money than most boys and he knew *Julius Caesar* backwards, forwards, and upside-down.

When they opened the tin-can bank, there was nearly four dollars in it. Neeley added another dollar, and Francie, five, and they had ten dollars to spend for Christmas presents. The three of them went shopping the afternoon before Christmas, taking Laurie with them.

First they went to buy mama a new hat. In the hat store they stood behind mama's chair while she held the baby in her lap and tried on hats. Francie wanted her to have a jade-green velvet one but there wasn't a hat of that color to be found in Williamsburg. Mama thought she ought to get a black hat.

"We're buying the hat, not you," Francie told her, "and we say, no more mourning hats."

"Try on this red one, Mama," suggested Neeley.

"No. I'll try on that very dark green one in the window."

"It's a new shade," said the woman proprietor, getting it out of the window. "We call it moss green." She set it straight on Katie's brow. With an impatient flick of her hand, Katie tilted the hat over one eye.

"That's it!" declared Neeley.

"Mama, you look beautiful," was Francie's verdict.

"I like it," decided mama. "How much?" she asked the woman. The woman drew a long breath and the Nolans girded themselves for bargaining.

"It's like this . . ." began the woman.

"How much?" repeated Katie inflexibly.

"In New York, ten dollars would you pay for the same merchandise. But. . . ."

"If I wanted to pay ten dollars, I'd go to New York for a hat."

"Is that a way to talk? Exact copy, same hat in Wanamaker's is seven-fifty." Pregnant pause. "I'm going to give you identical hat for five dollars."

"I have exactly two dollars to spend on a hat."

"Get out from my store!" shouted the woman dramatically.

"All right." Katie gathered up the baby and got to her feet.

"You must be so hasty?" The woman pushed her back into the chair. She thrust the hat into a paper bag. "I'm letting you take it home for four-fifty. Believe me, my own mother-in-law shouldn't have it for that price!"

"I believe you," thought Katie, "especially if she's like my mother-in-law." Aloud she said: "The hat's nice but I can only afford two dollars. There are lots of other hat stores and I ought to get one for that—not as good as this one but good enough to keep the wind off my head."

"I want you should listen." The woman made her voice deep and sincere. "They say that by the Jews, money is everything. By me is different. When I got a pretty hat and it goes with a pretty customer, something happens to me here." She put her hand on her heart. "I get so . . . profits is nothing. I give free." She pushed the bag into Katie's hand. "Take the hat for four dollars. That's what it cost me wholesale." She sighed. "Believe me, a business woman I shouldn't be. Better I should be a picture painter."

And the bargaining went on. Katie knew when the price finally reached two-fifty the woman wouldn't go lower. She tested her by pretending she was leaving. But this time the woman made no attempt to stop her. Francie nodded to Neeley. He gave the woman two dollars and fifty cents.

"You shouldn't tell nobody how cheap you got it," warned the woman.

"We won't," promised Francie. "Put the hat in a box."

"Ten cents extra is a box—what it costs me wholesale."

"A bag's good enough," protested Katie.

"This is your Christmas present," said Francie, "and it goes in a box."

Neeley got out another dime. The hat was wrapped in tissue and put in a box. "I give it to you so cheap, you should come back next time you buy a hat. But don't expect such bargains next time." Katie laughed. As they left, the woman said, "Wear it in good health."

"Thank you."

As the door closed on them, the woman whispered bitterly, "*Goyem!*" and spat after them.

On the street Neeley said, "No wonder mama waits five years to buy a new hat if it's all that trouble."

"Trouble?" said Francie. "Why, that's fun!"

Next they went to Seigler's to buy a sweater suit for Laurie's Christmas. When Seigler saw Francie, he let loose a flood of abuse.

"So! At last you come in mine store! Is something maybe, other dry-goods stores ain't got and you come by me? Maybe by other store is dicky penny cheaper but damaged stock, no?" He turned to Katie and explained: "So many years comes this girl by me to buy dickies and paper collars for the papa. Now for a whole year already, she don't come."

"Her father died a year ago," explained Katie.

Mr. Seigler gave his forehead a mighty blow with the flat of his hand. "Oi! By me is so big the mouth, so my foot always goes in," he apologized.

"That's all right," said Katie soothingly.

"It's this way by me: Nobody tells me nothing and I don't know till now."

"That's the way it always is," said Katie.

"And now," he asked briskly, getting down to business, "what can I show you?"

"A sweater suit for a seven months' old baby."

"I got here exzactle size."

He took a blue wool outfit from a box. But when they held it up to Laurie, the sweater reached only to her navel and the leggings went to just below her knees. They measured other sizes and found a two-year-old size that was just right. Mr. Seigler went into ecstasies.

"I'm in dry-goods business twenty years—fifteen on Grand Stritt and five on Graham Am-yer and never *ins leben* do I see a seven months so big." And the Nolans glowed with pride.

There was no bargaining because Seigler's was a one-price store. Neeley counted out three dollars. They put the suit on the baby then and there. She looked cute with the zitful cap pulled down over her ears. The bright blue color brought out the rosiness of her skin. You'd think she understood—the way she acted so pleased, flashing her two-toothed smile about indiscriminately.

"*Ach du Liebschen,*" crooned Seigler, hands clasped prayerfully, "she should wear it in good health." This time the wish was not nullified by his spitting after them.

Mama went home with the baby and her new hat while Neeley and Francie continued their Christmas shopping. They bought small gifts for their Flittman cousins and something for Sissy's baby. Then it was time for their own gifts.

"I'll tell you what I want and you can buy it for me," said Neeley.

"All right. What?"

"Spats."

"Spats?" Francie's voice scaled up.

"Pearl gray ones," he said firmly.

"If that's what you want . . ." she began, dubiously.

"Medium size."

"How do you know the size?"

"I went in and tried them on yesterday."

He gave Francie a dollar and a half and she bought the spats. She had the man wrap them in a gift box. On the street, she presented the package to Neeley while they frowned solemnly at each other.

"From me to you. Merry Christmas," said Francie.

"Thank you," he replied formally. "And now, what do you want?"

"A black lace dance set in the window of that store near Union Avenue."

"Is that ladies' stuff?" asked Neeley uneasily.

"Uh-huh. Twenty-four waist and 32 bust. Two dollars."

"You buy it. I don't like to ask for anything like that."

She bought the coveted dance set—panties and brassiere made of scraps of black lace held together by narrow black satin ribbon. Neeley disapproved and muttered an ungracious, "You're welcome," to her thanks.

They passed the Christmas tree curb market. "Remember the time," said Neeley, "when we let the man chuck the biggest tree at us?"

"Do I! Every time I get a headache, it's in the place where the tree hit me."

"And the way papa sang when he helped us get the tree up the stairs," recalled Neeley.

Several times that day, the name or thought of papa had come up. And each time, Francie had felt a flash of tenderness instead of the old stab of pain. "Am I forgetting him?" she thought. "In time to come, will it be hard to remember anything about him? I guess it's like Granma Mary Rommely says: 'With time, passes all.' The first year was hard because we could say last 'lection he voted. Last Thanksgiving he ate with us. But next year it will be two years ago that he . . . and as time passes it will be harder and harder to remember and keep track."

"Look!" Neeley grabbed her arm and pointed to a two-foot fir tree in a wooden tub.

"It's growing!" she cried out. .

"What did you think? They all have to grow in the beginning."

"I know. Still and all you always see them cut off and get the idea that they grow chopped down. Let's buy it, Neeley."

"It's awful little."

"But it has roots."

When they brought it home, Katie examined the tree and the line between her eyes deepened as she figured something out. "Yes," she said, "after Christmas we'll put it on the fire escape and see that it gets sun and water and, once a month, horse manure."

"No, Mama," protested Francie. "You're not going to put that horse manure over on us."

As small children, gathering horse manure had been one of their most dreaded chores. Granma Mary Rommely kept a row of scarlet geraniums on her window sill and they were strong and bright and clear-colored because once a month either Francie or Neeley had to go out on the streets with a cigar box and fill it with two neat rows of manure balls. On delivery, Granma made payment of two cents. Francie had been ashamed to gather horse manure. Once she had protested to Granma who had answered:

"Ai, the blood runs thin in the third generation. Back in Austria, my good brothers loaded large wagons with the manure and they were strong and honorable men."

"They'd have to be," Francie had thought, "to work with stuff like that."

Katie was saying: "Now that we own a tree, we have to take care of it and make it grow. You can get manure in the dark of night if you're ashamed."

"There's so few horses now—mostly automobiles. It's hard to get," argued Neeley.

"Go on a cobblestoned street where autos don't go and if there isn't any manure, wait for a horse and follow him until there is."

"Gee whiz," protested Neeley, "I'm sorry we ever bought the old tree."

"What's the matter with us," said Francie. "These aren't olden times. We've got money now. All we have to do is give some old kid on the block a nickel and he'll collect it for us."

"Yeah," agreed Neeley, relieved.

"I should think," said mama, "that you'd want to take care of your tree with your own hands."

"The difference between rich and poor," said Francie, "is that the poor do everything with their own hands and the rich hire hands to do things. We're not poor any more. We can pay to have some things done for us."

"I want to stay poor, then," said Katie, "because I like to use my hands."

Neeley, as always, became bored when his mother and sister began one of their figuring-out conversations. To change the subject, he said, "I bet Laurie's as big as that tree." They fished the baby out of her basket and measured her against the tree.

"Exzactle the same height," said Francie, imitating Mr. Seigler.

"I wonder which will grow the fastest?" said Neeley.

"Neeley, we've never had a puppy or a kitten. So let's make a pet out of the tree."

"Aw, a tree can't be a pet."

"Why can't it? It lives and breathes, doesn't it? We'll give it a name. Annie! The tree's Annie and the baby's Laurie and together, they're the song."

"You know what?" asked Neeley.

"No. What?"

"You're crazy. That's what."

"I know it and isn't it wonderful? Today I don't feel like Miss Nolan, supposed to be seventeen and head reader of The Model Press Clipping Bureau. It's like olden times when I had to let you carry the junk money. I feel just like a kid."

"And you are," said Katie. "A kid just turned fifteen."

"Yeah? You won't think so when you see what Neeley bought me for Christmas."

"What you *made* me buy you," corrected Neeley.

"Show mama what you made me buy *you* for Christmas, smarty. Just go on and show her," urged Francie.

When he showed mama, her voice scaled up like Francie's when she said, "Spats?"

"Just to keep my ankles warm," explained Neeley.

Francie showed her dance set and mama let loose her "Oh, my!" of astonishment.

"Do you think that's what fast women wear?" asked Francie hopefully.

"If they do, I'm sure they all come down with pneumonia. Now let's see: What'll we have for supper?"

"Aren't you going to *object*?" Francie was disappointed because mama wasn't making a fuss.

"No. All women go through a black-lace-drawers time. You came to it earlier than most and you'll get over it sooner. I think we'll heat up the soup and have that and soup meat and potatoes. . . ."

"Mama thinks she knows everything," thought Francie resentfully.

They attended mass together Christmas morning. Katie was having a prayer said for the repose of Johnny's soul.

She looked very pretty in her new hat. The baby looked nice, too, in her new outfit. Neeley, wearing his new spats, manfully insisted on carrying the baby. As they passed Stagg Street, some boys hanging out in front of a candy store, hooted at Neeley. His face got red. Francie knew they were making fun of his spats and to save his feelings, she pretended they hooted because he was carrying a baby and she offered to take Laurie. He refused the offer. He knew as well as she did that they were making fun of his spats and he was filled with bitterness at the narrow-mindedness of Williamsburg. He decided to put the spats away in the box when he got home and not wear them again until they moved to a more decent neighborhood.

Francie was wearing her lace pants and freezing. Whenever an icy wind blew her coat apart and went through her thin dress, it was as if she had no underwear on at all. "I wish—oh, how I wish I had my flannel bloomers on," she mourned. "Mama was right. A person could get pneumonia. But I wouldn't give her the satisfaction of letting her know. I guess I'll have to put these lace things away until summer."

Inside the church, they pre-empted a whole front pew by laying Laurie full length on the seat. Several late-comers, thinking there was an empty seat, genuflected at the pew's entrance and prepared to enter. When they saw the baby stretched out over two places, they scowled fiercely at Katie who sat rigid and scowled back twice as fiercely.

Francie thought it was the most beautiful church in Brooklyn. It was made of old gray stone and had twin spires that rose cleanly into the sky, high above the tallest tenements. Inside, the high vaulted ceilings, narrow deepset stained-glass windows and elaborately carved altars made it a miniature cathedral. Francie was proud of the center altar because the left side had been carved by Granpa Rommely more than half a century ago when, as a young fellow lately come from Austria, he had begrudgingly given his tithe of labor to his Church.

The thrifty man had gathered up the bits of gouged-out wood and taken them home. Stubbornly he had fitted and glued the scraps together and carved out three small crucifixes from the blessed wood. Mary gave one to each of her daughters on their wedding day with instructions that the crosses were to be passed on to the first daughter in each succeeding generation.

Katie's crucifix hung high on the wall over the mantelpiece at home. It would be Francie's when she married and she was proud that it had come from the wood of that fine altar.

Today the altar was lovely with banked scarlet poinsettias and fir boughs with the golden points of lighted slender white candles gleaming among the leaves. The thatched *crèche* was inside the altar rail. Francie knew that the tiny hand-carved figures of Mary, Joseph, the kings, and shepherds were grouped about the Child in the manger as they had first been grouped a hundred years ago when they had been brought over from the old country.

The priest entered, followed by the altar boys. Over his other vestments, he wore a white satin chasuble with a golden cross on the front and back. Francie knew that the chasuble was symbolic of the seamless garment, supposedly woven by Mary, that they had removed from Christ before they nailed Him to the cross. It was said that on Calvary, the soldiers, not wishing to divide the garment, had cast dice for it while Jesus was dying.

Absorbed in her thoughts, Francie missed the beginning of the mass. She picked it up now, following the familiar Latin in translation.

To Thee, O God, my God, I will give praise upon the harp. Why art thou sad, my soul, and why dost thou disquiet me, chanted the priest in his deep rich voice.

Hope in God, for I will still give praise to Him, responded the altar boy.

Glory be to the Father and to the Son and to the Holy Ghost.

As it was in the beginning, is now and ever shall be, world without end, Amen, came the response.

I will go unto the altar of God, chanted the priest.

To God, Who giveth joy to my youth, came the response.

Our help is in the name of the Lord.

Who made Heaven and earth.

The priest bowed and recited the *Confiteor.*

Francie believed with all her heart that the altar was Calvary and that again Jesus was offered up as a sacrifice. As she listened to the consecrations, one for His Body and one for His Blood, she believed that the words of the priest were a sword which mystically separated the Blood from the Body. And she knew, without knowing how to explain why, that Jesus was entirely present, Body, Blood, Soul, and Divinity in the wine in the golden chalice and in the bread on the golden plate.

"It's a beautiful religion," she mused, "and I wish I understood it more. No. I don't want to understand it all. It's beautiful because it's always a mystery, like God Himself is a mystery. Sometimes I say I don't believe in God. But I only say that when I'm mad at Him . . . Because I do! I do! I believe in God and Jesus and Mary. I'm a bad Catholic because I miss mass once in awhile and I grumble when, at confession, I get a heavy penance for something I couldn't help doing. But good or bad, I *am* a Catholic and I'll never be anything else.

"Of course, I didn't ask to be born a Catholic no more than I asked to be born an American. But I'm glad it turned out that I'm both these things."

The priest ascended the curved steps to the pulpit. "Your prayers are requested," intoned his magnificent voice, "for the repose of the soul of John Nolan."

"Nolan . . . Nolan . . ." sighed the echoes of the vaulted ceiling.

With a sound like an anguished whisper, nearly a thousand people knelt to pray briefly for the soul of a man only a dozen of them had known. Francie began the prayer for the souls in Purgatory.

Good Jesus, Whose loving heart was ever troubled by the sorrows of others, look with pity on the soul of our dear one in Purgatory. Oh You, Who loved Your own, hear my cry for mercy. . . .

46

"In ten more minutes," announced Francie, *"it will be 1917."*

Francie and her brother were sitting side by side with their stockinged feet inside the oven of the kitchen range. Mama, who had given strict orders to be called five minutes before midnight, was resting on her bed.

"I have a feeling," continued Francie, "that 1917 will be more important than any year we've ever had."

"You say that about every year," claimed Neeley. "First, 1915 was going to be the most important. Then 1916, and now, 1917."

"It *will* be important. For one thing, in 1917 I'll be sixteen for real instead of just in the office. And other important things have started already. The landlord's putting in wires. In a few weeks we'll have 'lectricity instead of gas."

"Suits me."

"Then he's going to rip out these stoves and put in steam heat."

"Gee, I'll miss this old stove. Remember how in olden times," (two years ago!) "I used to sit on the stove?"

"And I used to be afraid you'd catch on fire."

"I feel like sitting on the stove right now."

"Go ahead." He sat on the surface furthest away from the firebox. It was pleasantly warm but not hot. "Remember," Francie went on, "how we did our examples on this hearthstone, and the time papa got us a real blackboard eraser and then the stone was like the blackboard in school, only lying down?"

"Yeah. That was a long time ago. But look! You can't claim 1917's going to be important because we'll have 'lectricity and steam heat. Other flats have had 'em for years. That's nothing important."

"The important thing about this year is that we'll get into the war."

"When?"

"Soon. Next week . . . next month."

"How do you know?"

"I read the papers every day, brother—two hundred of 'em."

"Oh, boy! I hope it lasts 'til I'm old enough to join the navy."

"Who's joining the navy?" They looked around, startled. Mama was standing in the bedroom doorway.

"We're just talking, Mama," explained Francie.

"You forgot to call me," said mama reproachfully, "and I thought I heard a whistle. It must be New Year's now."

Francie threw open the window. It was a frosty night without a wind. All was still. Across the yards, the backs of the houses were dark and brooding. As they stood at the window, they heard the joyous peal of a church bell. Then other bell sounds tumbled over the first pealing. Whistles came in. A siren shrieked. Darkened windows banged open. Tin horns were added to the cacophony. Someone fired off a blank cartridge. There were shouts and cat-calls.

1917!

The sounds died away and the air was filled with waiting. Someone started to sing:

> *Should auld acquaintance be forgot,*
> *And never brought to mind . . .*

The Nolans picked up the song. One by one, the neighbors joined in. And they all sang. But as they sang something disquieting came among them. A group of Germans were singing a round. The German words crowded into "Auld Lang Syne."

> *Ja, das ist ein Gartenhaus,*
> *Gartenhaus,*
> *Gartenhaus.*
> *Ach, du schoenes,*
> *Ach, du schoenes,*
> *Ach, du schoenes Gartenhaus.*

Someone shouted: "Shut up, you lousy heinies!" In answer, the German song swelled mightily and drowned out "Auld Lang Syne."

In retaliation, the Irish shouted a parody of the song across the dark back yards.

> *Yeah, das is a God-damned song,*
> *God-damned song,*
> *God-damned song.*
> *Oh, du lousy,*
> *Oh, du lousy,*
> *Oh, du lousy heinie song.*

Windows could be heard shutting as the Jews and Italians withdrew leaving the fight to the Germans and Irish. The Germans sang lustier and more voices came in until they killed the parody even as they had killed "Auld Lang Syne." The Germans won. They finished their interminable rounds in shouting triumph.

Francie shivered. "I don't like Germans," she said. "They're so . . . so persistent when they want something and they've always got to be ahead."

Once more the night was quiet. Francie grabbed her mother and Neeley. "All together now," she ordered. The three of them leaned out of the window and shouted,

"Happy New Year, everybody!"

An instant of silence, then out of the dark a thick Irish brogue shouted: "Happy New Year, youse Nolans!"

"Now who could that be?" puzzled Katie.

"Happy New Year, you dirty Irish mick!" Neeley screamed back. Mama clapped her hand over his mouth and pulled him away while Francie slammed the window down. All three of them were laughing hysterically.

"*Now* you did it!" gasped Francie, laughing so hard that she cried.

"He knows who we are and he'll come around here and fi . . . fi . . . fight," gurgled Katie so weak from laughing that she had to hold on to the table. "Who . . . who . . . was it?"

"Old man O'Brien. Last week he cursed me out of his yard, the dirty Irish. . . ."

"Hush!" said Mama. "You know that whatever you do when the new year starts, you'll do all year."

"And you don't want to go around saying, dirty Irish mick like a busted record, do you?" asked Francie. "Besides, you're a mick yourself."

"You, too," accused Neeley.

"We're all Irish, except mama."

"And I'm Irish by marriage," she said.

"Well, do us Irish drink a toast on New Year's Eve, or don't we?" demanded Francie.

"Of course," said mama. "I'll mix us a drink."

McGarrity had given the Nolans a bottle of fine old brandy for Christmas. Now Katie poured a small jiggerful of it into each of three tall glasses. She filled the rest of each glass with beaten egg and milk mixed with a little sugar. She grated nutmeg and sprinkled it on the top.

Her hands were steady as she worked although she considered this drinking tonight as something crucial. She worried constantly that the children might have inherited the Nolan love of drink. She had tried to come to an attitude about liquor in the family. She felt that if she preached against it, the children, unpredictable individualists that they were, might consider drinking forbidden and fascinating. On the other hand, if she made light of it, they might consider drunkenness a natural thing. She decided neither to make nothing of it nor much of it; to proceed as though drinking was no more or less than something to be moderately indulged in at seasonal times. Well, New Year's was such a time. She handed each a glass. A lot depended on their reactions.

"What do we drink to?" asked Francie.

"To a hope," said Katie. "A hope that our family will always be together the way it is tonight."

"Wait!" said Francie. "Get Laurie, so she's together with us, too."

Katie got the patient sleeping baby out of her crib and carried her into the warm kitchen. Laurie opened her eyes, lifted her head and showed two teeth in a befuddled smile. Then her head went down on Katie's shoulder and she was asleep again.

"Now!" said Francie holding up her glass. "To being together, always." They clicked glasses and drank.

Neeley tasted his drink, frowned, and said he'd rather have plain milk. He poured the drink down the sink and filled another glass with cold milk. Katie watched, worried, as Francie drained her glass.

"It's good," Francie said, "pretty good. But not half as good as a vanilla ice-cream soda."

"What am I worrying about?" sang Katie inwardly. "After all, they're as much Rommely as Nolan and we Rommelys are not drinking people."

"Neeley, let's go up on the roof," said Francie impulsively, "and see how the whole world looks at the beginning of a year."

"Okay," he agreed.

"Put your shoes on first," ordered mama, "and your coats."

They climbed the shaky wooden ladder, Neeley pushed the opening aside and they were on the roof.

The night was heady and frosty. There was no wind and the air was cold and still. The stars were brilliant and hung low in the sky. There were so many stars that their light made the sky a deep cobalt blue. There wasn't a moon but the starlight served better than moonlight.

Francie stood on tiptoe and stretched her arms wide. "Oh, I want to hold it all!" she cried. "I want to hold the way the night is—cold without wind. And the way the stars are so near and shiny. I want to hold all of it tight until it hollers out, 'Let me go! Let me go!'"

"Don't stand so near the edge," said Neeley, uneasily. "You might fall off the roof."

"I need someone," thought Francie desperately. "I need someone. I need to hold somebody close. And I need more than this holding. I need someone to understand how I feel at a time like now. And the understading must be part of the holding.

"I love mama and Neeley and Laurie. But I need someone to love in a different way from the way I love them.

"If I talked to mama about it, she'd say, 'Yes? Well, when you get that feeling don't linger in dark hallways with the boys.' She'd worry, too, thinking I was going to be the way Sissy used to be. But it isn't an Aunt Sissy thing because there's this understanding that I want almost more than I want the holding. If I told Sissy or Evy, they'd talk the same as mama, although Sissy was married at fourteen and Evy at sixteen. Mama was only a girl when she married. But they've forgotten . . . and they'd tell me I was too young to be having such ideas. I'm young, maybe, in just being fifteen. But I'm older than those years in some things. But there is no one for me to hold and no one to understand. Maybe someday . . . someday. . . ."

"Neeley, if you *had* to die, wouldn't it be wonderful to die now—while you believed that everything was perfect, the way this night is perfect?"

"You know what?" asked Neeley.

"No. What?"

"You're drunk from that milk punch. That's what."

She clenched her hands and advanced on him. "Don't you say that! Don't you ever say that!"

He backed away, frightened at her fierceness. "Tha . . . tha . . . that's all right," he stammered. "I was drunk myself, once."

She lost her anger in curiosity. "Were you, Neeley? Honest?"

"Yeah. One of the fellers had some bottles of beer and we went down the cellar and drank it. I drank two bottles and got drunk."

"What did it feel like?"

"Well, first the whole world turned upside down. Then everything was like—you know those cardboard toots you buy for a penny, and you look in the small end and turn the big end, and pieces of colored paper keep falling around and they never fall around the same way twice? Mostly though, I was very dizzy. Afterwards I vomited."

"Then I've been drunk, too," admitted Francie.

"On beer?"

"No. Last spring, in McCarren's Park, I saw a tulip for the first time in my life."

"How'd you know it was a tulip if you'd never seen one?"

"I'd seen pictures. Well, when I looked at it, the way it was growing, and how the leaves were, and how purely red the petals were, with yellow inside, the world turned upside down and everything went around like the colors in a kaleidoscope—like you said. I was so dizzy I had to sit on a park bench."

"Did you throw up, too?"

"No," she answered. "And I've got that same feeling here on this roof tonight, and I know it's not the milk punch."

"Gee!"

She remembered something. "Mama tested us when she gave us that milk punch. I know it."

"Poor mama," said Neeley. "But she doesn't have to worry about me. I'll never get drunk again because I don't like to throw up."

"And she doesn't have to worry about me, either. I don't need to drink to get drunk. I can get drunk on things like the tulip—and this night."

"I guess it is a swell night," agreed Neeley.

"It's so still and bright . . . almost . . . holy."

She waited. If papa were here with her now. . . .

Neeley sang.

Silent night. Holy night.
All is calm, all is bright.

"He's just like papa," she thought happily.

She looked out over Brooklyn. The starlight half revealed, half concealed. She looked out over the flat roofs, uneven in height, broken once in a while by a slanting roof from a house left over from older times. The chimney pots on the roofs . . . and on some, the shadowing looming of pigeon cotes . . . sometimes, faintly heard, the sleepy cooing of pigeons . . . the twin spires of the Church, remotely brooding over the dark tenements. . . . And at the end of their street, the great Bridge that threw itself like a sigh across the East River and was lost . . . lost . . . on the other shore. The dark East River beneath the Bridge, and far away, the misty-gray skyline of New York, looking like a city cut from cardboard.

"There's no other place like it," Francie said.

"Like what?"

"Brooklyn. It's a magic city and it isn't real."

"It's just like any other place."

"It isn't! I go to New York every day and New York's not the same. I went to Bayonne once to see a girl from the office who was home, sick. And Bayonne isn't the same. It's mysterious here in Brooklyn. It's like—yes—like a dream. The houses and streets don't seem real. Neither do the people."

"They're real enough—the way they fight and holler at each other and the way they're poor, and dirty, too."

"But it's like a dream of being poor and fighting. They don't really feel these things. It's like it's all happening in a dream."

"Brooklyn is no different than any other place," said Neeley firmly. "It's only your imagination makes it different. But that's all right," he added magnanimously, "as long as it makes you feel so happy."

Neeley! So much like mama, so much like papa; the best of each in Neeley. She loved her brother She wanted to put her arms around him and kiss him But he was like mama. He hated people to be demonstrative. If she tried to kiss him, he'd get mad and push her away. So, she held out her hand instead.

"Happy New Year, Neeley."

"The same to you."

They shook hands solemnly.

47

For the little while of the Christmas holidays, it had been almost like old times in the Nolan family. But after New Year's things reverted to the new routine which had grown on them since Johnny's death.

There were no more piano lessons for one thing. Francie hadn't practiced in months. Neeley did his piano playing evenings in the neighborhood ice-cream saloons. He had been expert at rag-time and was becoming even more expert at jazz. He could make a piano talk—so people said—and he was very popular. He played for free sodas. Sometimes Scheefly gave him a dollar on a Saturday night for playing the whole evening. Francie didn't like it and spoke to her mother about it.

"I wouldn't let him, Mama," she said.

"But where's the harm in it?"

"You don't want him to get into the habit of playing for free refreshments like. . . ." She hesitated. Katie picked up the sentence.

"Like your father? No, he'd never be like him. Your father never sang the songs he loved, like 'Annie Laurie' or 'The Last Rose of Summer.' He sang what the people wanted, 'Sweet Adeline' and 'Down by the Old Mill Stream.' Neeley's different. He'll always play what *he* likes and not care two cents whether anyone else likes it."

"You're saying, then, that papa was only an entertainer and that Neeley is an artist."

"Well . . . yes," admitted Katie defiantly.

"I think that's carrying mother love a little too far."

Katie frowned and Francie dropped the subject.

They had stopped reading the Bible and Shakespeare since Neeley started high school. He reported that they were studying *Julius Caesar* and the principal read from the Bible each assembly period and that was enough for Neeley. Francie begged off reading at night because her eyes were tird from reading all day. Katie did not insist, feeling that they were now old enough to read or not— just as they wished.

Francie's evenings were lonely. The Nolans were together only at the supper hour when even Laurie sat up to the table in her high chair. After supper Neeley went out, either to be with his gang or to play at some ice-cream saloon. Mama read the paper and then she and Laurie went to bed at eight o'clock. (Katie was still getting up at five in order to have most of her cleaning done while Francie and Neeley were in the flat with the baby.)

Francie seldom went to the movies because they jumped around so and hurt her eyes. There were no shows to go to. Most of the stock companies had gone out of existence. Besides she had seen Barrymore in Galsworthy's *Justice* on Broadway and she was spoiled for stock companies after that. That past fall she had seen a movie she liked: *War Brides* with Nazimova. She had hoped to see it again but read in the papers that because of the imminence of war, the film had been banned. She had a wonderful memory of journeying to a strange part of Brooklyn to see the great Sarah Bernhardt in a one-act play in a Keith vaudeville house. The great actress was past seventy, but looked half that age from the stage. Francie couldn't understand the French but she gathered that the play was written around the actress' amputated leg. Bernhardt played the part of a French soldier who had lost his leg in the War. Francie caught the word *Boche* from time to time. Francie would never forget the flaming red hair and the golden voice of Bernhardt. She treasured the program in her scrapbook.

But those had been just three evenings out of months and months of evenings.

Spring came early that year and the sweet warm nights made

her restless. She walked up and down the streets and through the park. And wherever she went, she saw a boy and a girl together; walking arm-in-arm, sitting on a park bench with their arms around each other, standing closely and in silence in a vestibule. Everyone in the world but Francie had a sweetheart or a friend. She seemed to be the only lonely one in Brooklyn.

March, 1917. All the neighborhood could think or talk about was the inevitability of war. A widow living in the flats had an only son. She was afraid he'd have to go and would be killed. She bought him a cornet and made him take lessons, figuring he'd be put in an army band and play at parades and reviews only and be kept away from the front. People in the house were tormented almost to death by his incessant fumbling cornet practice. One harassed man, made crafty by desperation, told the mother that he had inside information that the military bands led the soldiers into action and invariably were the first ones killed. The terrified mother pawned the cornet immediately and destroyed the pawn ticket. There was no more dreadful practicing.

Each night at supper Katie asked Francie, "Has the war started yet?"

"Not yet. But any day now."

"Well, I wish it would hurry up and start."

"Do you want war?"

"No, I don't. But if it has to be, the sooner the better. The sooner it starts, the quicker it will end."

Then Sissy created such a sensation that the war was pushed into the background temporarily.

Sissy, who was done with her wild past, and who should have been settling down into the calm that precedes satisfied middle age, threw the family into a turmoil by falling madly in love with the John to whom she had been married for more than five years. Not only that, but she got herself widowed, divorced, married, and pregnant—all in ten days' time.

The Standard Union, Williamsburg's favorite newspaper, was delivered as usual one afternoon to Francie's desk at closing time. As usual, she took it home so that Katie could read it after supper. Francie would bring it back to the office the next morning and read and mark it. Since Francie never read newspapers outside of office hours, she had no way of knowing what was in that particular issue.

After supper, Katie sat by the window to look through the paper. An instant after turning the third page, she exploded her "Oh, my!" of utter astonishment. Francie and Neeley ran to look over her shoulder. Katie pointed to a heading:

HERO FIREMAN LOSES LIFE IN
WALLABOUT MARKET BLAZE.

Underneath in small type was a sub-heading: "Had planned to retire on pension next month."

Reading the item, Francie discovered that the heroic fireman had been Sissy's first husband. There was a picture of Sissy taken twenty years ago—Sissy with a towering crimped pompadour and huge leg-of-mutton sleeves—Sissy, sixteen years old. There was a caption under Sissy's picture: "Widow of heroic fire fighter."

"Oh, my!" repeated Katie. "Then he never married again. He must have kept Sissy's picture all that time and when he died some men must have gone through his stuff and found—Sissy!

"I've got to go over there right away." Katie took off her apron and went to get her hat, explaining, "Sissy's John reads the papers. She told him she was divorced. Now that he knows the truth, he'll kill her. At least throw her out," she amended. "She'll have no place to go with the baby and mother."

"He seems like a nice man," said Francie, "I don't think he'd do that."

"We don't know what all he won't do. We don't know anything about him. He's a stranger in the family and always has been. Pray God I don't get there too late."

Francie insisted on going along and Neeley agreed to stay home with the baby on condition that he be told every single thing that happened.

When they got to Sissy's house, they found her rosy with excitement. Granma Mary Rommely had taken the baby and retired to the front room where she sat in the dark and prayed for everything to come out all right.

Sissy's John gave them his version of the story.

"I'm away working in the shop, see? These here men come to the house and say to Sissy, 'Your husband's just been killed, see?' Sissy thinks they mean me." He turned on Sissy suddenly. "Did you cry?"

"You could hear me on the next block," she assured him. He seemed gratified.

"They ask Sissy what they should do with the body. Sissy asks is there any insurance, see? Well, it turns out there is—for five hundred dollars, paid up ten years ago and still made out in Sissy's name. So what does Sissy go to work and do! She tells them to lay him out in Specht's Funeral Parlor, see? A five-hundred-dollar funeral she orders."

"I had to make the arrangements," apologized Sissy. "I'm his only living relation."

"And that's not all," he went on. "Now they're going to come around and give Sissy a pension. I won't stand for it!" he roared suddenly. "When I marry her," he went on more calmly, "she tells me she's a divorced woman. Now it turns out she's not."

"But there's no divorce in the Catholic Church," insisted Sissy.

"You wasn't married in the Catholic Church."

"I know. So I never considered I was married, and didn't think I had to get a divorce."

He threw his hands up in the air and moaned, "I give up!" It was the same cry of futile despair he had uttered when Sissy had insisted that she had given birth to the baby. "I marry her in good faith, see? And what does she do?" he asked rhetorically. "She turns right around and makes us live in adultery."

"Don't say that!" said Sissy sharply. "We're *not* living in adultery. We're living in bigamy."

"And it's got to stop right now, see? You're widowed from the first one and you're going to get a divorce from the second, and then you're going to marry me again, see?"

"Yes, John," she said meekly.

"And my name ain't John!" he roared. "It's Steve! Steve! Steve!"

With each repetition of his name, he pounded on the table so hard that the blue glass sugar bowl with the spoons hanging around its rim clattered up and down. He pushed a finger into Francie's face.

"And you! From now on I'm Uncle *Steve*, see?"

Francie stared at the transformed man in dumb amazement.

"Well? What do you say?" he barked.

"Hel . . . hel . . . hello, Uncle Steve."

"That's more like it." He was mollified. He took his hat from a nail behind the door and jamed it on his head.

"Where are you going, John . . . I mean, Steve?" asked Katie, worried.

"Listen! When I was a kid, my old man always went out and got ice cream when company came in his house. Well, this is *my* house, see? And *I* got company. So I'm going out and get a quart of strawberry ice cream, see?" He went.

"Isn't he wonderful?" sighed Sissy. "A woman could fall in love with a person like that."

"Looks like the Rommelys have a man in the family at last," commented Katie drily.

Francie went into the dark front room. By the light of the street lamp, she saw her grandmother sitting at the window with Sissy's sleeping baby in her lap and amber rosary beads dangling from her trembling fingers.

"You can stop praying now, Granma," she said. "Everything's all right. He went out for ice cream, see?"

"Glory be to the father, and to the Son and to the Holy Ghost," praised Mary Rommely.

In Sissy's name, Steve wrote to her second husband at his last-known address and put "Please Forward" on the envelope. Sissy asked him to consent to a divorce so that she might remarry. A week later, a fat letter came from Wisconsin. Sissy's second husband informed her that he was well, had obtained a Wisconsin divorce seven years ago, had promptly remarried, settled down in Wisconsin where he had a good job and was the father of three children. He was very happy, he wrote and in belligerently underlined words threatened that he intended to stay that way. He enclosed an old press clipping to prove that she had been legally informed of the divorce action by publication. He enclosed a photostatic copy of the decree (grounds, desertion), and a snapshot of three bouncing children.

Sissy was so happy at being divorced so quickly that she sent him a silver-plated pickle dish as a belated wedding present. She felt that she had to send a letter of congratulation also. Steve refused to write it for her so she asked Francie to do it.

"Write that I hope he'll be very happy," dictated Sissy.

"But Aunt Sissy, he's been married seven years and it's settled by now—whether he's happy or not."

"When you first hear that someone's married, it's polite to wish them happiness. Write it down."

"All right." She wrote it down. "What else?"

"Write something about his children . . . how cute they are . . . something like . . ." The words stuck in her throat. She knew he had sent the picture to prove that Sissy's stillborn children had not been his fault. That hurt Sissy. "Write that I'm the mother of a beautiful healthy baby girl and put a line under healthy."

"But Steve's letter said you were only planning to get married. This man might think it funny that you got a baby so soon."

"Write it like I said," ordered Sissy, "and write that I expect another baby to be born next week."

"Sissy! You don't, really!"

"Of course not. But write it down anyhow."

Francie wrote that down. "Anything else?"

"Say thanks for the divorce paper. Then say I got my own divorce a year before he got it. Only I forgot," she concluded lamely.

"But that's a lie."

"I *did* get the divorce before he did. I got it in my mind."

"All right. All right," surrendered Francie.

"Write that I'm very happy and intend to stay that way and put a line under those words like he did."

"Gosh, Sissy. *Must* you have the last word?"

"Yes. Just like your mother has to have it, and Evy and you, too."

Francie made no more objections.

Steve got a license and married Sissy all over again. This time a Methodist minister performed the ceremony. It was Sissy's first marriage by the Church and at last she believed that she was truly married until death did the parting. Steve was very happy. He loved Sissy and had always been afraid of losing her. She had left her other husbands, casually and with no regrets. He had been afraid that she'd leave him, too, and take with her the baby whom he had grown to love dearly. He knew that Sissy believed in the Church . . . any Church, Catholic, or Protestant; that she'd never walk out on a church marriage. For the first time in their relationship, he felt happy, secure, and masterful. And Sissy discovered that she was madly in love with him.

Sissy came over one evening after Katie had gone to bed. She told her not to get up; that she'd sit in the bedroom and talk to her. Francie was sitting at the kitchen table pasting poems in old note books. She kept a razor blade at the office and cut out poems and stories she liked for her scrapbooks. She had a series of them. One was labeled *The Nolan Book of Classical Poems*. Another, *The Nolan Volume of Contemporary Poetry*. A third was, *The Book of Annie Laurie,* in which Francie was collecting nursery rhymes and animal stories to be read to Laurie when she was old enough to understand.

The voices coming from the dark bedroom made a soothing rhythm. Francie listened as she pasted. Sissy was saying:

". . . Steve, so fine and decent. And when I realized it, I hated myself on account of the others—outside of my husbands, I mean."

"You didn't tell him about the others?" asked Katie apprehensively.

"Do I look like a fool? But I wish with all my heart that he had been the first and only one."

"Woman talks that way," said Katie, "it means she's going into the change of life."

"How do you make that out?"

"If she never had any lovers, she kicks herself around when the change comes, thinking of all the fun she could have had, didn't have, and now can't have. If she had a lot of lovers, she argues herself into believing that she did wrong and she's sorry now. She carries on that way because she knows that soon all her woman-ness will be lost . . . lost. And if she makes believe being with a man was never any good in the first place, she can get comfort out of her change."

"I'm not going into any change of life," said Sissy indignantly. "In the first place I'm too young and in the second place I wouldn't stand for it."

"It has to come to all of us some day," sighed Katie.

There was terror in Sissy's voice. "Not to be able to have children anymore . . . to be half a woman . . . get fat . . . have hair grow on your chin. I'll kill myself first!" she cried passionately. "Anyhow," she added complacently, "I'm nowhere near the change because I'm that way again."

There was a rustle from the dark bedroom. Francie could visualize her mother raising herself on her elbow.

"No, Sissy! No! You can't go through that again. Ten times it's happened—ten children stillborn. And it will be harder this time because you're going for thirty-seven."

"That's not too old to have a baby."

"No, but it's too old to get over another disappointment easily."

"You needn't worry, Katie. This child will live."

"You've said that each time."

"This time I'm sure because I feel that God is on my side," she said with quiet assurance. After a while she said, "I told Steve how I got Little Sissy."

"What did he say?"

"He knew all the while I hadn't given birth to her, but the way I claimed I had, got him mixed up. He said it didn't matter as long as I didn't have her by another man and that since we had her from birth almost he really feels that she's his baby. It's funny how the baby looks like him. She has his dark eyes and the same round chin and the same small ears close to her head like him."

"She got those dark eyes from Lucia and a million people in the world have round chins and small ears. But if it makes Steve happy to think the baby looks like him, that's fine." There was a long silence before Katie spoke again. "Sissy, did you ever get any idea from that Italian family as to who the father was?"

"No." Sissy too, waited a long time before she continued. "You know who told me about the girl being in trouble and where she lived and all?"

"Who?"

"Steve."

"Oh, my!"

Both were quiet for a long time. Then Katie said, "Of course, that was accidental."

"Of course," agreed Sissy. "One of the fellows in his shop told him, he said; a fellow who lived on Lucia's block."

"Of course," Katie repeated. "You know funny things happen here in Brooklyn that have no meaning at all. Like sometimes I'm walking on the street and I think of someone I haven't seen maybe, in five years and I turn a corner and there's that person walking towards me."

"I know," answered Sissy. "Sometimes I'm doing something that I never did before in my life and all of a sudden I have the feeling that I did that same thing before—maybe in another life. . . ." Her voice died away. After awhile she said, "Steve always said he'd never take another man's child."

"*All* men say that. Life's funny," Katie went on. "A couple of accidental things come together and a person could make a lot out of them. It was just an accident that you got to know about that girl. That same fellow must háve told a dozen men in the shop. Steve just mentioned it to you accidentally. It was just by accident that you got in with that family and just accidental that the baby has a round instead of a square chin. It's even less than accidental. It's . . ." Katie stopped to search for a word.

Francie in the kitchen had become so interested that she forgot that she wasn't supposed to be listening. When she knew her mother was groping for a word, she supplied it unthinkingly.

"You mean *coincidental,* Mama?" she called out.

A shocked silence came from the bedroom. Then the conversation was resumed—but this time in whispers.

48

A newspaper lay on Francie's desk. It was an "extra" and had come directly from the presses. The ink was still damp on its headline. The paper had been there five minutes and as yet she had not picked up her pencil to mark it. She stared at the date.

April 6, 1917.

The one-word headline was six inches high. The three letters were smudged at the edges and the word, WAR, seemed to waver.

Francie had a vision. Fifty years from now, she'd be telling her grandchildren how she had come to the office, sat at her reader's desk and in the routine of work had read that war had been declared. She knew from listening to her grandmother that old age was made up of such remembrances of youth.

But she didn't want to recall things. She wanted to live things—or as a compromise, re-live rather than reminisce.

She decided to fix this time in her life exactly the way it was this instant. Perhaps that way she could hold on to it as a living thing and not have it become something called a memory.

She brought her eyes close to the surface of her desk and examined the patterned grain of the wood. She ran her fingers along the groove where her pencils rested, fixing the feel of the groove in her mind. Using a razor blade, she nicked the next dot on one of her pencils and unraveled the paper. She held the raveling in her palm, touched it with her forefinger, and noted its spiraling. She dropped it into the metal wastebasket counting the seconds it took to fall. She listened intently so as not to miss its almost noiseless thud as it hit the bottom. She pressed her finger tips to the damp headline, examined her inked finger tips, then made finger prints on a sheet of white paper.

Not caring about clients who might be mentioned on pages one and two, she detached the front sheet of the newspaper and folded the sheet into a careful oblong, watching the creases come under her thumb. She inserted it into one of the strong manilla envelopes that the Bureau used to mail clippings in.

Francie heard, as if for the first time, the sound the desk drawer made when she opened it to get her purse. She noted the device of the purse's catch—the sound of its click. She felt the leather, memorized its smell and studied the whorlings of the black moiré-silk lining. She read the dates on the coins in her change purse. There was a new 1917 penny which she put in the envelope. She uncapped her lipstick and made a line with it under her finger prints. The clear red color, the texture and the scent of it pleased her. She examined in turn the powder in her compact, the ridges on her nail file, the way her comb was inflexible and the threads of her handkerchief. There was a worn clipping in the purse, a poem she had torn out of an Oklahoma newspaper. It had been written by a poet who had lived in Brooklyn, gone to the Brooklyn public schools and, as a young man, had edited *The. Brooklyn Eagle*. She reread it for the twentieth time handling each word in her mind.

> *I am of old and young, of the foolish as much as the wise;*
> *Regardless of others, ever regardful of others.*
> *Maternal as well as paternal, a child as well as a man,*
> *Stuff'd with the stuff that is coarse, and stuff'd*
>   *with the stuff that is fine.*

The tattered poem went into the envelope. In the mirror of her compact, she looked at the way her hair was braided—how the braids wound around her head. She noticed how her straight black eyelashes were uneven in length. Then her shoes were inspected. She ran her hand down her stockings and for the first time noticed that the silk felt rough instead of smooth. The fabric of her dress was made of tiny cords. She turned back the hem and noticed that the narrow lace edge of her slip was diamond-shaped in design.

"If I can fix every detail of this time in my mind, I can keep this moment always," she thought.

Using the razor blade, she clipped a lock of her hair, wrapped it in the square of paper on which were her finger prints and lipstick mark, folded it, placed it in the envelope and sealed the envelope. On the outside she wrote:

Frances Nolan, age 15 years and 4 months. April 6, 1917.

She thought: "If I open this envelope fifty years from now, I will be again as I am now and there will be no being old for me. There's a long, long time yet before fifty years . . . millions of hours of time. But one hour has gone already since I sat here . . . one hour less to live . . . one hour gone away from all the hours of my life.

"Dear God," she prayed, "let me be *something* every minute of every hour of my life. Let me be gay; let me be sad. Let me be cold; let me be warm. Let me be hungry . . . have too much to eat. Let me be ragged or well dressed. Let me be sincere—be deceitful. Let me be truthful; let me be a liar. Let me be honorable and let me sin. Only let me be *something* every blessed minute. And when I sleep, let me dream all the time so that not one little piece of living is ever lost."

The delivery boy came by and slapped another city paper on her desk. This one had a two-word headline.

WAR DECLARED!

The floor seemed to swerve up, colors flashed before her eyes and she put her head down on the ink-damp paper and wept quietly. One of the older readers, returning from the washroom, paused by Francie's desk. She noticed the headline and the weeping girl. She thought she understood.

"Ah, the war!" She sighed. "You have a sweetheart or a brother, I presume?" she asked in her stilted readerish way.

"Yes, I have a brother," Francie answered truthfully enough.

"My sympathies, Miss Nolan." The reader went back to her desk.

"I'm drunk again," thought Francie, "and this time on a newspaper headline. And this is a bad one—I've got a crying jag."

The war touched the Model Press Clipping Bureau with its mailed finger and made it wither away. First, the client who was the backbone of the business—the man who paid out thousands a year for clippings on the Panama Canal and such—came in the day after the declaration of war and said that since his address would be uncertain for a while, he'd call in person each day for his clippings.

A few days later, two slow-moving men with heavy feet came in to see the Boss. One of them pushed his palm under the Boss' nose and what he saw in that palm made the Boss turn pale. He got a thick stack of clippings from the file box of the most important client. The heavy-footed ones looked them over and returned them to the Boss who put them in an envelope and put the envelope in his desk. The two men went into the Boss' lavatory leaving the door ajar. They waited in there all day. At noon, they sent an errand boy out for a bag of sandwiches and a carton of coffee and they ate their lunch in the lavatory.

The Panama Canal client came in at four-thirty. In slow motion, the Boss handed him the fat envelope. Just as the client put it in his inner coat pocket, the heavy ones strolled out of the lavatory. One of them touched the client on the shoulder. He sighed, took the envelope out of his pocket and surrendered it. The second heavy one touched him on the shoulder. The client clicked his heels together, bowed stiffly and walked out between the two men. The Boss went home with an acute attack of dyspepsia.

That evening, Francie told mama and Neeley how a German spy had been caught right in the office.

The next day, a brisk-looking man came in with a brief case. The Boss had to answer a lot of questions and the brisk man wrote down the answers in spaces provided on a printed form. Then came the sad part. The Boss had to make out a check for nearly four hundred dollars—the balance due on the involuntarily-canceled account. After the brisk man left, the Boss rushed out to borrow money to make the check good.

After that, everything went to pieces. The Boss was afraid to take in new accounts no matter how innocent they seemed. The theatrical season was running out and actor accounts fell off. The deluge of spring-published books which brought in hundreds of seasonal five-dollar author clients and dozens of hundred-dollar publisher clients, had not been a deluge but a mere trickle. Houses were holding off important publications until things settled down a bit. Many research workers canceled their accounts in expectation of being called up in the draft. Even if business had been normal the Bureau couldn't have handled it because the workers began to go.

The government, anticipating a man shortage, threw open Civil Service examinations for women workers in the big Thirty-fourth Street post office. Many of the readers took and passed the examination and were called to work immediately. The manual workers, The Club, left almost in a body to work in war projects plants. They not only tripled their earnings but they received much praise for their unselfish patriotism. The Boss' wife came back to read and he fired all the remaining readers except Francie.

The huge loft echoed with emptiness as the three of them tried to carry on the business alone. Francie and the wife read, filed, and attended to the office work. The Boss slashed impotently at newspapers, printed blurry slips and pasted items askew.

In the middle of June, he gave up. He made arrangements for the sale of his office equipment, broke his lease, and settled the matter of refunds to clients very simply by saying, "Let 'em sue me."

Francie phoned the only other clipping bureau she knew of in New York and asked whether they needed a reader. She was told that they never hired new readers. "We treat our readers right," said an argumentative voice, "and never have to make replacements." Francie thought that was very nice, said so, and hung up.

She spent her last morning at the Bureau marking help wanted ads. She skipped the office jobs knowing she'd have to start as a file clerk again. You didn't stand a chance in an office unless you were a stenographer and typist. Anyhow she preferred factory work. She liked factory people better and she liked keeping her mind free while she worked with her hands. But of course mama wouldn't let her work in a factory again.

She found an ad that seemed a happy combination of factory and office; operating a machine in office surroundings. A Communications Corporation offered to teach girls teletype machine operating and to pay them twelve-fifty a week while they were learning. The hours were five P.M. to one A.M. At least that would give her something to do with her evenings—if she got the job.

When she went to say goodbye to the Boss, he told her that he'd have to owe her the last week's salary. He had her address, he said, and would send it. Francie said goodbye to the Boss, to his wife, and to her final week's pay.

The Communications Corporation had a skyscraper office overlooking the East River in downtown New York. Along with a dozen other girls, Francie filled out an application after presenting a fervent letter of recommendation from her ex-Boss. She took an aptitude test in which she answered questions which seemed silly—which weighs the most, a pound of lead or a pound of feathers, was an example. Evidently she passed the test for she was given a number, a locker key for which she had to pay a quarter deposit, and told to report the next day at five o'clock.

It wasn't quite four when Francie got home. Katie was cleaning in their house and she looked upset when she saw Francie come up the stairs.

"Don't look so worried, Mama. I'm not sick or anything."

"Oh," said Katie relieved. "For a moment I thought you had lost your job."

"I have."

"Oh, my!"

"And I won't get my last week's pay either. But I got another job . . . start tomorrow . . . twelve and a half a week. I'll get a raise in time, I expect." Katie started to ask questions. "Mama, I'm tired. Mama, I don't want to talk. We'll talk about it tomorrow. And I don't want supper. I just want to go to bed." She went upstairs.

Katie sat on the steps and started to worry. Since war started, prices of food and everything else had skyrocketed. In the past month, Katie had not been able to add to Francie's bank account. The ten dollars a week hadn't been enough. Laurie had to have a quart of fresh milk every day and the milk modifier was expensive. Then there had to be orange juice. Now with twelve-fifty a week . . . after Francie's expenses were taken out there'd be less money. Soon it would be vacation. Neeley could work during the summer. But what about the fall? Neeley would return to high school. Francie had to get to high school that fall. How? How? She sat there and worried.

Francie, after a brief glance at the sleeping baby, undressed and got into bed. She folded her hands under her head and stared at the gray patch which was the airshaft window.

"Here I am," she thought, "fifteen years old and a drifter. I've been working less than a year and I've had three jobs already. I used to think it would be fun to go from one job to the other. But now I'm scared. I've been fired from two jobs through no fault of my own. At each job, I worked as best I could. I gave everything I could give. And here I'm starting all over again somewhere else. Only now I'm frightened. This time when the new boss says 'jump once,' I'll jump twice because I'll be afraid of losing the job. I'm scared because they're depending on me here for money. How did we ever get along before I worked? Well, there wasn't Laurie then. Neeley and I were smaller and could do with less and of course, papa helped some.

"Well . . . goodbye college. Goodbye everything for that matter." She turned her face away from the gray light and closed her eyes.

Francie sat at a typewriter in a big room. There was a metal roof fastened over the top of Francie's machine so that she couldn't see the keyboard. An enormous chart of the keyboard diagram was tacked up in front of the room. Francie consulted the chart and felt for the letters under the shield. That was the first day. On the second day she was given a stack of old telegrams to copy. Her eyes went from the copy to the chart as her fingers groped for the letters. At the end of the second day she had memorized the position of the letters on the machine and didn't have to consult the chart. A week later, they took the shield off. It made no difference now. Francie was a touch typist.

An instructor explained the workings of the teletype machine. For a day, Francie practiced sending and receiving dummy messages. Then she was put on the New York–Cleveland wire.

She thought it a wonderful miracle that she could sit at that machine and type and have the words come out hundreds of miles away on a piece of paper on the roller of a machine in *Cleveland, Ohio!* No less miraculous was that a girl typing away in Cleveland made the hammers of *Francie's* machine pound out the words.

It was easy work. Francie would send for an hour, then receive for an hour. There were two fifteen-minute rest periods in the work shift and half an hour for "lunch" at nine o'clock. Her pay had been increased to fifteen a week when she went on a wire. All in all, it wasn't a bad job.

The household adjusted itself to Francie's new schedule. She left home soon after four in the afternoon and got home a little before two in the morning. She pressed the bell button three times before she entered the hallway so that mama could be on the alert and make sure that Francie wouldn't be attacked by someone lurking in the hallways.

Francie slept mornings until eleven o'clock. Mama didn't have to get up so early because Francie was in the flat with Laurie. She started work in her own house first. By the time she was ready for the other two houses, Francie was up and looking after Laurie. Francie had to work on Sunday nights but she had Wednesday night off.

Francie liked the new arrangement. It took care of her lonely evenings, it helped mama out and gave Francie a few hours each day to sit in the park with Laurie. The warm sun did both of them a lot of good.

A plan took shape in Katie's mind and she spoke to Francie about it.

"Will they keep you on night work?" she asked.

"Will they! They're tickled to death. No girl wants to work nights. That's why they push it off on the new girls."

"I was thinking that maybe in the fall you could keep on working nights and go to high school in the daytime. I know it'll be hard but it could be done somehow."

"Mama, no matter what you say, I won't go to high school."

"But you fought to go last year."

"That was last year. That was the right time to go. Now it's too late."

"It's not too late and don't be stubborn."

"But what in the world could I learn in high school now? Oh, I'm not conceited or anything, but after all, I read eight hours a day for almost a year and I learned things. I've got my own ideas about history and government and geography and writing and poetry. I've read too much about people—what they do and how they live. I've read about crimes and about heroic things. Mama, I've read about *everything*. I couldn't sit still now in a classroom with a bunch of baby kids and listen to an old maid teacher drool away about this and that. I'd be jumping up and correcting her all the time. Or else, I'd be good and swallow it all down and then I'd hate myself for . . . well . . . eating mush instead of bread. So I will not go to high school. But I *will* go to college someday."

"But you've got to go through high school before they'll let you in college."

"Four years of high school . . . no, five. Because something would come up to delay me. Then four years of college. I'd be a dried-up old maid of twenty-five before I was finished."

"Whether you like it or not, you'll get to be twenty-five in time no matter what you do. You might as well be getting educated while you're going towards it."

"Once and for all, Mama, I will not go to high school."

"We'll see," said Katie as her jaw settled into a square line.

Francie said nothing more. But the set of her jaw was like her mother's.

However, the conversation gave Francie an idea. If mama thought she could work evenings and go to high school in the day, why couldn't she go to college that way? She studied a newspaper ad. Brooklyn's oldest and most reputable college was advertising summer courses available for college students wishing to take advanced work or to make up or work off conditions, and for high school students wishing to gain advance college credits. Francie thought she might come under the last heading. She wasn't exactly a high school student but she was eligible to be one. She sent for the catalogue.

From the catalogue, she chose three courses with classes meeting in the afternoon. She'd be able to sleep as usual until eleven, attend classes and go straight to work from the college. She chose Beginning French, Elementary Chemistry, and something called Restoration Drama. She figured up the tuition; a little over sixty dollars with laboratory fees. She had one hundred and five dollars in her savings account. She went to Katie.

"Mama, could I have sixty-five dollars of the money you've been saving for me towards college?"

"What for?"

"College, of course." She was deliberately casual for the drama of it. She was rewarded by the way mama's voice scaled up as she repeated after Francie:

"College?"

"Summer school college."

"But-but-but," sputtered Katie.

"I know. No high school. But maybe I can get in if I tell them I don't want a diploma or any grades—that I just want the lessons." Katie got her green hat down from the closet shelf. "Where're you going, Mama?"

"To the bank for the money."

Francie laughed at her mother's eagerness. "It's after hours. The bank's closed. Besides there's no hurry. Registration's a week off yet."

The college was located in Brooklyn Heights, another strange section of great Brooklyn for Francie to explore. As she filled out the registration blank, her pen hovered over the question of previous education. There were three headings with blanks after them: Elementary Schools, High Schools, and Colleges. After a little thought, she crossed out the words and wrote in the space above them, "Privately educated."

"And when you come right down to it, that's no lie," she assured herself.

To her utter relief and astonishment, she was not challenged in any way. The cashier took her money and gave her a receipt for her tuition. She was given a registration number, a pass to the library, a schedule of her classes, and a list of the textbooks she needed.

She followed a crowd to the college bookshop further down the block. She consulted her list and ordered a "Beginning French" and an "Elementary Chemistry."

"New or second-hand?" asked the clerk.

"Why, I don't know. Which am I supposed to have?"

"New," said the clerk.

Someone touched her on the shoulder. She turned and saw a handsome well-dressed boy. He said, "Get second-hand. Serves the same purpose as new and half the price."

"Thank you." She turned to the clerk. "Second-hand," she said firmly. She started to order the two books for the drama course. Again the touch on her shoulder.

"Uh, uh," said the boy negatively. "You can read them in the library before and after classes and when you get cuts."

"Thank you again," she said.

"Any time," he answered and sauntered away.

Her eyes followed him out of the store. "Gosh, he's tall and goodlooking," she thought. "College is certainly wonderful."

She sat in the El train on her way to the office, clutching the two textbooks. As the train grated over the tracks its rhythm seemed to be, college-college-college. Francie started to feel sick. She felt so sick that she had to get off at the next station even though she knew she'd be late for work. She leaned against a penny weighing machine wondering what was the matter with her. It couldn't have been anything she ate because she had forgotten to eat lunch. Then a thunderous thought came to her.

"My grandparents never knew how to read or write. Those who came before them couldn't read or write. My mother's sister can't read or write. My parents never even graduated from grade school. I never went to high school. But I, M. Frances K. Nolan, am now in college. Do you hear that, Francie? *You're in college!*

"Oh gosh, I feel sick."

49

Francie came away from her first chemistry lecture in a glow. In one hour she had found out that everything was made up of atoms which were in continual motion. She grasped the idea that nothing was ever lost or destroyed. Even if something was burned up or left to rot away, it did not disappear from the face of the earth; it changed into something else—gases, liquids, and powders. Everything, decided Francie after that first lecture, was vibrant with life and there was no death in chemistry. She was puzzled as to why learned people didn't adopt chemistry as a religion.

The drama of the Restoration, aside from the time-consuming reading required, was easy to manage after her home study of Shakespeare. She had no worries about that course nor the chemistry course. But when it came to Beginning French, she was lost. It wasn't really *beginning* French. The instructor, working on the knowledge that his students either had taken it before and flunked it, or had already had it in high school, sluffed over the preliminaries and got right down to translation. Francie, shaky enough regarding English grammar, spelling, and punctuation, didn't stand a chance with the French language. She'd never pass the course. All she could do was memorize vocabulary each day and try to hang on.

She studied going back and forth on the El. She studied in her rest periods and ate her meals with a book propped up on the table before her. She typed out her assignments on one of the machines in the instruction room of the Communications Corporation. She was never late or absent and she asked nothing more than to pass at least two of her courses.

The boy who had befriended her in the bookstore became her guardian angel. His name was Ben Blake and he was a most amazing fellow. He was a senior in a Maspeth high school. He was editor of the school magazine, president of his class, played half-back on the football team, and was an honor student. For the past three summers, he had been taking college courses. He would finish high school with more than one year of college work out of the way.

In addition to his school work, he put in his afternoons working for a law firm. He drew up briefs, served summonses, examined deeds and records, and searched out precedents. He was familiar with the state's statutes and was completely capable of trying a case in court. Besides doing so well in school, he earned twenty-five dollars a week. His firm wanted him to come into the office full-time after his graduation from high school, read law with them, and eventually take the bar exam. But Ben was contemptuous of non-college lawyers. He had a great midwestern college picked out. He planned to complete work for an A.B. degree and then enter law school.

At nineteen, his life was planned out in a straight unswerving line. After passing the bar exam, he was all set to take over a country law practice. He believed that a young lawyer had more political opportunities in a small-town practice. He even had the practice picked out. He was to succeed a distant relative, an aged country lawyer who had a well-established practice. He was in constant touch with his future predecessor and received long weekly letters of guidance from him.

Ben planned to take over this practice and await his turn to be county prosecutor. (By agreement, the lawyers in this small county rotated the office among them.) That would be his start in politics. He'd work hard, get himself well-known and trusted, and eventually be elected to the House of Representatives from his state. He'd serve faithfully and be re-elected. Then he'd come back and work himself up to the governship of his state. That was his plan.

The amazing thing about the whole idea was that those who knew Ben Blake were sure that everything would come out the way he planned it.

In the meantime in that summer of 1917, the object of his ambitions, a vast midwestern state, lay dreaming beneath the hot prairie sun—lay dreaming among its great wheat fields and its unending orchards of winesap, Baldwin and northern spy apples—lay dreaming—unaware that the man who planned to occupy its White House as its youngest governor was, at the moment, a boy in Brooklyn.

That was Ben Blake; well-dressed, gay, handsome, brilliant, sure of himself, well-liked by the boys, with all the girls crazy about him—and Francie Nolan tremulously in love with him.

She saw him every day. His fountain pen flashed through her French assignments. He checked her chemistry work and cleared up obscurities in the Restoration plays. He helped her plan her next summer's courses and, obligingly enough, tried to plan out the rest of her life for her.

As the end of summer came near, two things saddened Francie. Soon she wouldn't be seeing Ben every day, and she wasn't going to pass the French course. She took Ben into her confidence about the latter sadness.

"Don't be silly," he told her briskly. "You paid for the course, you sat in class all summer, you're not a moron. You'll pass. Q.E.D."

"No," she laughed, "I'll flunk P.D.Q."

"We'll have to cram you for the final exam, then. We'll need a whole day. Now where can we go?"

"My house?" suggested Francie timidly.

"No. There'd be people around." He thought for a moment. "I know a good place. Meet me Sunday morning at nine, corner Gates and Broadway."

He was waiting for her when she stepped off the trolley. She wondered where in the world he'd take her in *that* neighborhood. He took her to the stage door of a theater given over to Broadway shows on the first lap of the road. He got through the magic door merely by saying, "Morning, Pop," to the white-haired man sitting on a tilted chair in the sun beside the opened door. Francie then discovered that this amazing boy was a Saturday night usher in this theater.

She had never been backstage before and she was so excited that she almost ran a temperature. The stage seemed vast and the roof of the theater house seemed lost—so far away it was. As she walked across the stage, she changed her stride and walked slowly and stiff-leggedly as she remembered Harold Clarence walking. When Ben spoke, she turned slowly, with dramatic intensity, and said in a throaty voice, "You" (pause: then with meaning) "spoke?"

"Want to see something?" he asked.

He pulled the curtain and she saw the asbestos roll up like a giant's shade. He turned on the foots and she walked out on the apron and looked over the thousand dark empty waiting raked seats. She tilted her head and threw her voice to the last row of the gallery.

"Hello, out there!" she called and her voice seemed amplified a hundred times in the dark waiting emptiness.

"Look," he asked good-naturedly, "are you more interested in the theater or your French?"

"Why the theater, of course."

It was true. Then and there she renounced all other ambitions and went back to her first love, the stage.

Ben laughed as he cut off the foots. He brought down the curtain and placed two chairs facing each other. In some way, he had gotten hold of the examination papers for five years back. From them, he had made a master exam paper using the questions asked most frequently and those seldom asked. Most of the day, he drilled Francie in these questions and answers. Then he had her memorize a page from Molière's *Le Tartuffe* and its English translation. He explained:

"There'll be one question in the exam tomorrow that will be absolute Greek to you. Don't attempt to answer it. Do this: State frankly that you can't answer the question but that you are offering in its stead an excerpt from Molière with translation. Then write down what you've memorized and you'll get away with it."

"But suppose they ask for that exact passage in a regular question?"

"They won't. I picked out a very obscure passage."

Evidently she got away with it for she passed the examination in French. True, she passed with the lowest mark but she consoled herself with the idea that passing was passing. She did very well on the chemistry and drama examinations.

Acting on Ben's instructions, she came back for the transcript of her grades a week later and met him by arrangement. He took her to Huyler's for a chocolate soda.

"How old are you, Francie?" he asked over the sodas.

She calculated rapidly. She was fifteen at home, seventeen at work. Ben was nineteen. He'd never speak to her again if he knew she was only fifteen. He saw her hesitation and said,

"Anything you say may be used against you."

She took her courage into her two hands and quavered boldly, "I'm . . . fifteen." She hung her head in shame.

"Hm. I like you, Francie."

"And I love you," she thought.

"I like you as much as any girl I've ever known. But of course, I have no time for girls."

"Not even for an hour say, on Sunday?" she ventured.

"My few free hours belong to my mother. I'm all that she has."

Francie had never heard of Mrs. Blake until that moment. But she hated her because she pre-empted those free hours, a few of which would have made Francie happy.

"But I'll be thinking of you," he continued. "I'll write if I have a moment." (He lived half an hour away from her.) "But if you ever need me—not for any trivial reason, of course—drop me a line and I'll manage to see you." He gave her one of the firm's cards with his full name, Benjamin Franklin Blake, written in the corner.

They parted outside of Huyler's shaking hands warmly. "See you next summer," he called back as he walked away.

Francie stood looking after him until he turned the corner. Next summer! It was only September and next summer seemed a million years away.

She had enjoyed the summer school so much that she wanted to matriculate in the same college that fall but she had no way of raising the more than three hundred dollars required for tuition. In a morning spent in studying catalogues in the Forty-second Street, New York Library, she discovered a college for women in which tuition was free to residents of New York.

Armed with her transcripts, she went over to register. She was told that she couldn't matriculate lacking a high school education. She explained how she had been permitted to go to summer school. Ah! That was different. There courses were given for credit only. No degree was offered in summer courses. She asked couldn't she take courses now without expecting a degree. No. If she were past twenty-five, she might be permitted to enter as a special student and take courses without being a candidate for a degree. Francie regretfully acknowledged that she was not yet past twenty-five. There was an alternative, however. If she was able to pass the entrance or regents' examination, she would be permitted to enroll regardless of high school credits.

Francie took the examinations and flunked everything but chemistry.

"Oh, well! I should have known," she told her mother. "If people could get into college that easy, no one would ever bother with high school. But don't you worry, Mama. I know what the entrance examinations are now, and I'll get the books and study and take those examinations next year. And I'll pass next year. It can be done and I'll do it. You'll see."

Even if she had been able to enter college, it wouldn't have worked out because she was put on the day shift after all. She was now a fast and expert operator and they needed her in the day when the traffic was heaviest. They assured her that she could go back on night work in the summer if she wished. She got her next raise. She was now earning seventeen-fifty a week.

Again the lonely evenings. Francie roamed the Brooklyn streets in the lovely nights of fall and thought of Ben.

("If you ever need me, write and I'll manage to see you.")

Yes, she needed him but she was sure he'd never come if she wrote: "I'm lonely. Please come and walk with me and talk to me." In his firm schedule of life, there was no heading labeled "Loneliness."

The neighborhood seemed the same, yet it was different. Gold stars had appeared in some of the tenement windows. The boys still got together on the corner or in front of a penny candy store of an evening. But now, often as not, one of the boys would be in khaki.

The boys stood around harmonizing. They sang "A Shanty in Old Shantytown" and "When You Wore a Tulip," "Dear Old Girl," "I'm Sorry I Made You Cry," and other songs.

Sometimes the soldier boy led them in war songs: "Over There," "K-K-K-Katy" and "The Rose of No Man's Land."

But no matter what they sang, always they finished off with one of Brooklyn's own folk songs: "Mother Machree," "When Irish Eyes Are Smiling," "Let Me Call You Sweetheart," or "The Band Played On."

And Francie walked past them in the evenings and wondered why all the songs sounded so sad.

50

Sissy expected her baby late in November. Katie and Evy went to a lot of trouble to avoid discussing it with Sissy. They were certain it would be another stillbirth and they reasoned that the less said about it, the less Sissy would have to remember afterward. But Sissy did such a revolutionary thing that they *had* to talk about it. She announced that she was going to have a *doctor* when the baby came and that she was going to a *hospital*.

Her mother and sisters were stunned. No Rommely women had had a doctor at childbirth, ever. It didn't seem right. You called in a midwife, a neighbor woman, or your mother, and you got through the business secretively and behind closed doors and kept the men out. Babies were women's business. As for hospitals, everyone knew you went there only to die.

Sissy told them they were way behind the times; that midwives were things of the past. Besides, she informed them proudly, she had no say in the matter. Her Steve insisted on the doctor and the hospital. And that wasn't all.

Sissy was going to have a Jewish doctor!

"Why, Sissy? Why?" asked her shocked sisters.

"Because Jewish doctors are more sympathetic than Christian ones at a time like that."

"I've nothing against the Jews," began Katie, "but . . ."

"Look! Just because Dr. Aaronstein's people look at a star when they pray and our people look at a cross has nothing to do with whether he's a good doctor or not."

"But I'd think you'd want a doctor of your own faith around at a time of . . ." (Katie was going to say, "death" but checked herself in time) . . . "birth."

"Oh, sugar!" said Sissy contemptuously.

"Like should stick to like. You don't see Jews calling in Christian doctors," said Evy, thinking she had made a telling point.

"Why should they," countered Sissy, "when they and everybody else knows that the Jewish doctors are smarter."

The birth was the same as all the others. Sissy had her usual easy time made easier by the skill of the doctor. When the baby was delivered, she closed her eyes tightly. She was afraid to look at it. She had been so sure that this one would live. But now that the time had come, she felt in her heart that it wouldn't be so. She opened her eyes finally. The baby was lying on a near-by table. It was still and blue. She turned her head away.

"Again," she thought. "Again and again and again. Eleven times. Oh, God, why couldn't You let me have one? Just one out of eleven? In a few years, my time of childbearing will be over. For a woman to die at last . . . knowing that she has never given life. Oh, God, why have You put Your curse on me?"

Then she heard a word. She heard a word that she had never known. She heard the word "oxygen."

"Quick! Oxygen!" she heard the doctor say.

She watched him work over her baby. She saw a miracle that transcended the miracles of the saints her mother had told her about. She saw the dead blue change to living white. She saw an apparently lifeless child draw a breath. For the first time she heard the cry of a child she had borne.

"Is . . . is . . . it alive?" she asked, afraid to believe.

"What else?" The doctor shrugged his shoulders eloquently. "You've got as fine a boy as I've ever seen."

"You're *sure* he'll live?"

"Why not?" Again the shrug. "Unless you let him fall out of a three-story window."

Sissy took his hands and covered them with kisses. And Dr. Aaron Aaronstein was not embarrassed about her emotionalism the way a Gentile doctor would have been.

She named the baby Stephen Aaron.

"I've never seen it to fail," said Katie. "Let a childless woman adopt a baby and bang! A year or two later she's sure to have one of her own. It's as if God recognized her good intentions at last. It's nice that Sissy has two to bring up because it's no good to bring up one child alone."

"Little Sissy and Stevie are just two years apart," said Francie. "Almost like Neeley and me."

"Yes. They'll be company for each other."

Sissy's living son was the great wonder of the family until Uncle Willie Flittman gave them something else to talk about. Willie tried to enlist in the army and was turned down; whereupon he threw up his job with the milk company, came home, announced that he was a failure, and went to bed. He wouldn't get up next morning or the morning after. He said he was going to stay in bed and never get up as long as he lived. All his life he had lived as a failure and now he was going to die as a failure and the sooner the better, he stated.

Evy sent for her sisters.

Evy, Sissy, Katie, and Francie stood around the big brass bed in which the failure had ensconced himself. Willie took one look at the circle of strong-willed Rommely women and wailed, "I'm a failure." He pulled the blanket up over his head.

Evy turned her husband over to Sissy and Francie watched Sissy go to work on him. She put her arms around him and held the futile little fellow to her breast. Sissy convinced him that not all the brave men were in trenches—that many a hero was risking his life daily for his country in a munitions factory. She talked and talked until Willie got so excited about helping to win the war that he jumped out of bed and made Aunt Evy scurry around getting him his pants and shoes.

Steve was foreman now, at a munitions factory on Morgan Avenue. He got Willie a good paying job there with time and a half for overtime.

It was a tradition in the Rommely family that the men keep for themselves any tips or overtime money that they earned. With his first check for overtime work, Willie bought himself a bass drum and a pair of cymbals. He spent all of his evenings (when he didn't have to work overtime) practicing on the drum and cymbals in the front room. Francie gave him a dollar harmonica for Christmas. He fastened it to a stick and attached the stick to his belt so he could play the harmonica like riding a bicycle no hands. He tried to manipulate the guitar, harmonica, drums, and cymbals all at once. He was practicing to be a one-man band.

And so he sat in the front room evenings. He blew into the harmonica, strummed the guitar, thumped the great drum, and clashed the brass cymbals. And he grieved because he was a failure.

51

When it got too cold to go walking, Francie enrolled in two evening classes at the Settlement House—sewing and dancing.

She learned to decode paper patterns and to run a sewing machine. In time she hoped to be able to make her own clothes.

She learned "ballroom" dancing, although neither she nor her partners ever expected to set foot in something called a ballroom. Sometimes her partner was one of the brilliantine-haired neighborhood sheiks who was a snappy dancer and made her watch her steps. Sometimes he was a little old boy of fourteen in knee pants and she made him watch his steps. She loved dancing and took to it instinctively.

And that year began to draw to a close.

"What's that book you're studying, Francie?"

"That's Neeley's geometry book."

"What's geometry?"

"Something you have to pass to get into college, Mama."

"Well, don't sit up too late."

"What news do you bring me of my mother and sisters?" Katie asked the insurance collector.

"Well, for one thing I just insured your sister's babies, Sarah and Stephen."

"But she's had them insured since birth—a nickel a week policy."

"This is a different policy. Endowment."

"What does that mean?"

"They don't have to die to collect. They get a thousand dollars each when they're eighteen. It's insurance to get them through college."

"Oh my! First a doctor and hospital to give birth, then college insurance. What next?"

"Any mail, Mama?" asked Francie as usual when she got home from work.

"No. Just a card from Evy."

"What does she say?"

"Nothing. Except they've got to move again on account of Willie's drumming."

"Where're they moving now?"

"Evy found a one-family house in Cypress Hills. I wonder whether that's in Brooklyn?"

"It's out East New York way—where Brooklyn changes into Queens. It's around Crescent Street, the last stop on the Broadway El. I mean it used to be the last stop until they extended the El to Jamaica."

Mary Rommely lay in her narrow white bed. A crucifix stood out on the bare wall above her head. Her three daughters and Francie, her eldest granddaughter, stood by her bed.

"Ai. I am eighty-five now and I feel that this is my last time of sickness. I wait for death with the courage I gained from living. I will not speak falsely and say to you: 'Do not grieve for me when I go.' I have loved my children and tried to be a good mother and it is right that my children grieve for me. But let your grief be gentle and brief. And let resignation creep into it. Know that I shall be happy. I shall see face to face the great saints I have loved all my life."

Francie showed the snapshots to a group of girls in the recreation room.

"This is Annie Laurie, my baby sister. She's only eighteen months old but she runs all over the place. And you ought to hear her talk!"

"She's cute."

"This is my brother, Cornelius. He's going to be a doctor."

"He's cute."

"This is my mother."

"She's cute. And so young-looking."

"And this is me on the roof."

"The roof's cute."

"*I'm* cute," said Francie with mock belligerence.

"We're all cute." The girls laughed. "Our supervisor's cute— the old wagon. I hope she chokes."

They laughed and laughed.

"What are we all laughing at?" asked Francie.

"Nothing." They laughed harder.

"Send Francie. The last time I asked for sauerkraut he chased me out of the store," complained Neeley.

"You've got to ask for Liberty Cabbage now, you dope," said Francie.

"Don't call each other names," chided Katie absentmindedly.

"Did you know they changed Hamburg Avenue to Wilson Avenue?" asked Francie.

"War makes people do funny things," sighed Katie.

"You going to tell mama?" asked Neeley apprehensively.

"No. But you're too young to go out with that kind of a girl. They say she's wild," said Francie.

"Who wants a tame girl?"

"I wouldn't care only you don't know anything at all about— well—sex."

"I know more than you, anyhow." He put his hand on his hip and squealed in a lisping falsetto: "Oh, Mama! Will I have a baby if a man just kisses me? Will I, Mama? Will I?"

"Neeley! You listened that day!"

"Sure! I was right outside in the hall and heard every word."

"Of all the low things. . . ."

"You listen, too. Many's the time I caught you when mama and Sissy or Aunt Evy were talking and you were supposed to be asleep in bed."

"That's different. I have to find out things."

"Check!"

"Francie! Francie! It's seven o'clock. Get up!"

"What for?"

"You've got to be at work at eight-thirty."

"Tell me something new, Mama."

"You're sixteen years old today."

"Tell me something new. I've been sixteen for two years now."

"You'll have to be sixteen for another year, then."

"I'll probably be sixteen all my life."

"I wouldn't be surprised."

"I *wasn't* snooping," said Katie indignantly. "I needed another nickel for the gas man and I thought you wouldn't care. You look in *my* pocketbook for change many a time."

"That's different," said Francie.

Katie held a small violet box in her hand. There were scented gold-tipped cigarettes in it. One was missing from the full box.

"Well, now you know the worst," said Francie. "I smoked a *Milo* cigarette."

"They smell nice anyway," said Katie.

"Go ahead, Mama. Give me the lecture and get it over with."

"With so many soldiers dying in France and all, the world's not going to fall apart if *you* smoke a cigarette once in a while."

"Gee, Mama, you take all the fun out of things—like not objecting to my black lace pants last year. Well, throw the cigarettes away."

"I'll do no such thing! I'll scatter them in my bureau drawer. They'll make my nightgowns smell nice."

"I was thinking," said Katie, "that instead of buying each other Christmas presents this year, that we put all the money together and buy a roasting chicken and a big cake from the bakery and a pound of good coffee and . . ."

"We have enough money for food," protested Francie. "We don't have to use our Christmas money."

"I mean to give to the Tynmore girls for Christmas. No one takes lessons from them now—people say they're behind the times. They don't have enough to eat and Miss Lizzie's been so good to us."

"Well, all right," consented Francie not very enthusiastically.

"Gee!" Neeley kicked the table leg viciously.

"Don't worry, Neeley," laughed Francie. "You'll get a present. I'll buy you *fawn*-colored spats this year."

"Aw, shut up!"

"Don't say shut up to each other," chided Katie absentmindedly.

"I want to ask your advice, Mama. There was this boy I met in summer school. He said he might write but he never has. I want to know would it look forward if I sent him a Christmas card?"

"Forward? Nonsense! Send the card if you feel like it. I hate all those flirty-birty games that women make up. Life's too short. If you ever find a man you love, don't waste time hanging your head and simpering. Go right up to him and say, 'I love you. How about getting married?' That is," she added hastily with an apprehensive look at her daughter, "when you're old enough to know your own mind."

"I'll send the card," decided Francie.

"Mama, we decided, Neeley and I, that we'd like coffee instead of milk punch."

"All right." Katie put the brandy bottle back in the cupboard.

"And make the coffee very strong and hot and fill the cups with half coffee and half hot milk and we'll toast 1918 in *café au lait*."

"*S'il vous plâit*," put in Neeley.

"Wee-wee-wee," said mama. "*I* know some French words, too."

Katie held the coffeepot in one hand and the saucepan of hot milk in the other and poured both into the cups simultaneously. "I remember," she said, "when there was no milk in the house. Your father would put a lump of butter in his coffee—if we had butter. He said that butter was cream in the first place and just as good in coffee."

Papa . . . !

52

One sunny day in the spring when Francie was sixteen, she walked out of the office at five o'clock and saw Anita, a girl who operated a machine in her row, standing in the doorway of the Communications Building with two soldiers. One, short, stubby, and beaming, held Anita's arm possessively. The other, tall and gangling, stood there awkwardly. Anita detached herself from the soldiers and drew Francie aside.

"Francie, you've *got* to help me out. Joey's on his last leave before his unit goes overseas and we're engaged."

"If you're engaged already you're doing all right and don't need anybody's help," said Francie jokingly.

"I mean help with that other fellow. Joey just *had* to bring him along, darn it. Seems like they're buddies and where one goes the other goes. This other fellow comes from some hick town in Pennsylvania and doesn't know a soul in New York and I *know* he'll stick around and I'll never get to be alone with Joey. You've *got* to help me out, Francie. Three girls turned me down already."

Francie took a speculative look at the Pennsylvania fellow standing ten feet away. He didn't look like much. No wonder the other three girls refused to help out Anita. Then his eyes met hers and he smiled a slow shy smile and somehow, while he wasn't good-looking, he was nicer than good-looking. The shy smile decided Francie.

"Look," she said to Anita, "if I can catch my brother where he works, I'll give him a message for my mother. If he's left, I'll have to go home because my mother will worry if I don't turn up for supper."

"Hurry up, then. Phone him," urged Anita. "Here!" She fished in her pocketbook. "I'll give you the nickel for the call."

Francie phoned from the corner cigar store. It just happened that Neeley was still at McGarrity's. She gave him the message. When she got back, she found that Anita and her Joey had gone. The soldier with the shy smile was all alone.

"Where's 'Nita?" she asked.

"I reckon she's run out on you. She went off with Joe."

Francie was dismayed. She had expected it to be a double date. What in the world was she to do with this tall stranger now?

"I don't blame them," he was saying, "wanting to be alone. I'm an engaged man myself. I know how it is. The last leave—the only girl."

"Engaged, hm?" thought Francie. "At least he wouldn't try any romancing."

"But that's no reason why *you* should be stuck with me," he went on. "If you'll show me where to get the subway to Thirty-fourth Street—I'm a stranger in this city—I'll go back to the hotel room. A person can always write letters I guess, when there's nothing else to do." He smiled his lonely shy smile.

"I've already phoned my folks that I won't be home. So if you'd like. . . ."

"*Like?* Gosh! This is my lucky day. Well, gee, thanks, Miss. . . ."

"Nolan. Frances Nolan."

"My name's Lee Rhynor. It's really Leo but everybody says 'Lee.' I'm sure pleased to meet you, Miss Nolan." He held out his hand.

"And I'm pleased to meet you, Corporal Rhynor." They shook hands.

"Oh, you noticed the stripes." He smiled happily. "I suppose you're hungry after working all day. Any special place you'd like to go for supper . . . I mean dinner?"

"*Supper's* okay. No. No place special. You?"

"I'd like to try some of this here chop suey I heard about."

"There's a nice place up around Forty-second Street. With music."

"Let's go!"

On the way to the subway he said, "Miss Nolan, do you care if I call you Frances?"

"I don't care. Everyone calls me Francie, though."

"Francie!" He repeated the name. "Francie, another thing: Would you mind if I sort of made believe that you were my best girl—just for this evening?"

"Hm," thought Francie, "fast worker."

He took the thought out of her mind. "I guess you think I'm a fast worker but it's this way: I haven't been out with a girl in nearly a year and a few days from now I'll be on a boat heading for France and after that, I don't know what may be. So for these few hours—if you don't mind—I'd consider it a great favor."

"I don't mind."

"Thanks," he indicated his arm. "Hang on, best girl." As they were about to enter the subway, he paused. "Say 'Lee,'" he ordered.

"Lee," she said.

"Say, 'Hello, Lee. It's so good to see you again, dear.'"

"Hello, Lee. It's so good to see you again . . ." she said shyly. He tightened his arm.

The waiter at Ruby's put two bowls of chop suey and a fat pot of tea between them.

"You pour out my tea so it's more homelike," said Lee.

"How much sugar?"

"I don't take sugar."

"Me either."

"Say! We have exactly the same tastes, don't we?" he said.

Both were very hungry and they stopped talking in order to concentrate on the slippery wet food. Every time Francie looked up at him he smiled. Every time he looked down at her he grinned happily. After the chop suey, rice, and tea were all gone, he leaned back and took out a pack of cigarettes.

"Smoke?"

She shook her head. "I tried it once and didn't seem to like it."

"Good. I don't like a girl who smokes."

Then he started to talk. He told her all that he could remember about himself. He told her of his boyhood in a Pennsylvania town. (She remembered the town from reading its weekly newspaper in the press clipping bureau.) He told her about his parents and his brothers and sisters. He spoke of his school days—parties he had gone to—jobs he had worked at—he told her he was twenty-two—how he had come to enlist at twenty-one. He told her about his life at the army camp—how he got to be a corporal. He told her every single thing about himself. Excepting the girl he was engaged to, back home.

And Francie told him of her life. She told only of the happy things—how handsome papa had been—how wise mama was—what a swell brother Neeley was, and how cute her baby sister was. She told him about the brown bowl on the library desk—about the New Year's night she and Neeley had talked on the roof. She didn't mention Ben Blake because he never entered her thoughts. After she had finished, he said:

"All my life I've been so lonely. I've been lonely at crowded parties. I've been lonely in the middle of kissing a girl and I've been lonely at camp with hundreds of fellows around. But now I'm not lonely any more." He smiled his special slow shy smile.

"That's the way it was with me too," confessed Francie, "except I've never kissed any boy. And now for the first time, I'm not lonely either."

The waiter again replenished their almost filled water glasses. Francie knew it was a hint that they had sat there too long. People were waiting for tables. She asked Lee the time. Almost ten o'clock! They had been talking for nearly four hours!

"I have to start for home," she said regretfully.

"I'll take you home. Do you live near the Brooklyn Bridge?"

"No. The Williamsburg."

"I hoped it was the Brooklyn Bridge. I thought that if I ever got to New York, I'd like to walk across the Brooklyn Bridge."

"Why not?" suggested Francie. "I can get a Graham Avenue

trolley from the Brooklyn end that will take me right to my corner."

They took the I.R.T. Subway to Brooklyn Bridge, got out and started to walk across. Halfway over, they paused to look down on the East River. They stood close together and he held her hand. He looked up at the skyline on the Manhattan shore.

"New York! I've always wanted to see it and now I've seen it. It's true what they say—it's the most wonderful city in the world."

"Brooklyn's better."

"It hasn't got skyscrapers like New York, has it?"

"No. But there's a *feeling* about it—Oh, I can't explain it. You've got to live in Brooklyn to know."

"We'll live in Brooklyn some day," he said quietly. And her heart skipped a beat.

She saw one of the cops who patrolled the Bridge coming toward them.

"We'd better move," she said uneasily. "The Brooklyn Navy Yard's right over there and that camouflaged boat anchored there is a transport. The cops are always watching out for spies."

As the cop came up to them Lee said, "We're not going to blow up anything. We're just looking at the East River."

"Sure, sure," said the cop. "Don't I know how it is on a fine May night? Wasn't I young, meself, once and not so long ago as you might think?"

He smiled at them. Lee smiled back and Francie grinned at both of them. The cop glanced at Lee's sleeve.

"Well, so long, General," said the cop. "Give 'em hell when you get over there."

"I'll do that," promised Lee.

The cop went on his way.

"Nice guy," commented Lee.

"Everybody's nice," said Francie happily.

When they got to the Brooklyn side, she said that he was not to take her the rest of the way home. She had often gone home alone late at night when working on the night shift, she explained. He'd get lost if he tried to find his way back to New York from her neighborhood. Brooklyn was tricky that way. You had to live there in order to find your way about, she said.

In truth, she didn't want him to see where she lived. She loved her neighborhood and wasn't ashamed of it. But she felt that to a stranger who didn't know about it the way she did, it might seem a mean and shabby place.

First she showed him where to get the El that would return him to New York. Then they walked over to where she had to get the trolley. They passed a one-window tattoo shop. Inside sat a young sailor with his sleeve rolled up. The tattoo artist sat before him on a stool with his pan of inks near-by. He was pricking out an arrow-pierced heart on the sailor boy's arm. Francie and Lee stopped to stare in the window. The sailor waved at them with his free arm. They waved back. The artist looked up and made signs that they were welcome to enter, Francie frowned and shook her head, "no."

Walking away from the store, Lee said with wonder in his voice. "That fellow was actually getting tattooed! Gosh!"

"Don't you ever *ever* let me catch you getting tattooed," she said with playful severity.

"No, Mother," he answered meekly and they laughed.

They stood on the corner waiting for the trolley. An awkward silence came between them. They stood apart and he kept lighting cigarettes and discarding them before they were half smoked. Finally a trolley came in sight.

"Here comes my car," said Francie. She held out her right hand. "Good night, Lee."

He threw away the cigarette he had just lighted.

"Francie?" He held out his arms.

She went to him and he kissed her.

The next morning, Francie dressed in her new navy blue faille suit with the white georgette crepe blouse and her Sunday patent leather pumps. She and Lee had no date—had made no arrangements to meet again. But she knew he'd be waiting for her at five o'clock. Neeley got up from bed as she was about to leave. She asked him to tell mama she wouldn't be home for supper.

"Francie's got a feller at last! Francie's got a feller at last!" chanted Neeley.

He went to Laurie who was sitting by the window in her high chair. There was a bowl of oatmeal on the chair's tray. The baby was busily engaged in spooning out the oatmeal and dumping it on the floor. Neeley chucked her under the chin.

"Hey! Dopey! At last Francie's got a feller."

A faint line appeared on the inner edge of the child's right eyebrow (the Rommely line, Katie called it) as the two-year-old tried to understand.

"Fran-nee?" she said in a puzzled way.

"Listen, Neeley, I got her out of bed and gave her her oatmeal. It's your job to feed her now. And don't call her dopey."

As she came out of the hallway on the street, she heard her name called. She looked up. Neeley was hanging out of the window in his pajamas. He sang at the top of his voice:

> *There she goes*
> *On her toes,*
> *All dressed up*
> *In her Sunday clothes . . .*

"Neeley, you're terrible! Just terrible!" she called up to the window. He pretended not to understand.

"Did you say he was terrible? Did you say he had a big mustache and a baldy head?"

"You better go feed the baby," she hollered back.

"Did you say you were going to have a baby, Francie? Did you say you were going to have a baby?"

A man passing on the street winked at Francie. Two girls coming by arm-in-arm had a terrific fit of giggling.

"You damned kid!" screamed Francie in impotent fury.

"You cursed! I'm gonna tell mama, I'm gonna tell mama, I'm gonna tell mama you cursed," chanted Neeley.

She heard the trolley coming and had to run for it.

He was waiting for her when she got out of work. He met her with that smile.

"Hello, my best girl." He tucked her arm within his.

"Hello, Lee. It's good to see you again."

". . . dear," he prompted.

"Dear," she added.

They ate at the Automat—another place he had wanted to see. Since smoking wasn't permitted there and Lee couldn't sit still for long without smoking, they didn't linger to talk after coffee and dessert. They decided to go dancing. They found a dime-a-dance place just off Broadway where servicemen were given half rates. He bought a strip of twenty tickets for a dollar and they started to dance.

They had gone but halfway around the floor when Francie discovered that his gangling awkwardness was extremely deceptive. He was a smooth and skillful dancer. They danced, holding each other closely. There was no need for conversation.

The orchestra was playing one of Francie's favorite songs, "Some Sunday Morning."

> *Some Sunday morning,*
> *When the weather's fine.*

She hummed the chorus as the vocalist sang it.

> *Dressed up in gingham,*
> *What a bride I'll be.*

She felt Lee's arm tighten around her.

> *I know my girl friends,*
> *They're gonna envy me.*

Francie was so happy. Once more around the floor, then the vocalist sang the chorus again, this time varying it slightly in honor of the soldiers present.

> *Dressed up in khaki,*
> *What a groom you'll be.*

Her arm tightened around his shoulders and she rested her cheek on his tunic. She had the same thought Katie had had seventeen years ago dancing with Johnny—that she'd willingly accept any sacrifice or hardship if she could only have this man near her for always. And like Katie, Francie gave no thought to the children who might have to help her work out the hardship and sacrifice.

A group of soldiers were leaving the hall. As was the custom, the orchestra cut off the song they were playing and went into "Till We Meet Again." Everyone stopped dancing and sang a farewell to the soldiers. Francie and Lee held hands and sang, even though neither was quite certain of the words.

> *. . . When the clouds roll by*
> *Then I'll come back to you,*
> *Then the skies will seem more blue . . .*

There were cries of "Goodbye, soldier!" "Good luck, soldier!" "Till we meet again, soldier." Then the departing soldiers stood in a group and sang the song. Lee pulled Francie towards the door.

"We'll leave now," he said. "So that this moment will remain a perfect memory."

They walked down the stairs slowly, the song following them. As they reached the street, they waited until the song died away.

> *. . . Pray each night for me,*
> *Till we meet again.*

"Let it be our song," he whispered, "and think of me every time you hear it."

As they walked, it started to rain and they had to run and find shelter in the doorway of a vacant store. They stood in the protected and dark doorway, held each other's hand and watched the rain falling.

"People always think that happiness is a faraway thing," thought Francie, "something complicated and hard to get. Yet, what little things can make it up; a place of shelter when it rains—a cup of strong hot coffee when you're blue; for a man, a cigarette for contentment; a book to read when you're alone—just to be with someone you love. Those things make happiness."

"I'm leaving early in the morning."

"Not for France?" Suddenly she was jolted out of her happiness.

"No, for home. My mother wants me for a day or two before . . ."

"Oh!"

"I love you, Francie."

"But you're engaged. That's the first thing you ever told me."

"Engaged," he said bitterly. "Everybody's engaged. Everybody in a small town is engaged or married or in trouble. There's nothing else to do in a small town.

"You go to school. You start walking home with a girl—maybe for no other reason than that she lives out your way. You grow up. She invites you to parties at her home. You go to other parties— people ask you to bring her along; you're expected to take her home. Soon no one else takes her out. Everybody thinks she's your girl and then . . . well, if you don't take her around, you feel like a heel. And then, because there's nothing else to do, you marry. And it works out all right if she's a decent girl (and most of the time she is) and you're a half-way decent fellow. No great passion but a kind of affectionate contentment. And then children come along and you give them the great love you kind of miss in each other. And the children gain in the long run.

"Yes, I'm engaged all right. But it isn't the same between her and me as it is between you and me."

"But you're going to marry her?"

He waited a long time before he answered.

"No."

She was happy again.

"Say it, Francie," he whispered. "Say it."

She said, "I love you, Lee."

"Francie . . ." there was urgency in his voice, "I may not come back from over there and I'm afraid . . . afraid. I might die . . . die, never having had anything . . . never . . . Francie, *can't* we be together for a little while?"

"We are together," said Francie innocently.

"I mean in a room . . . alone . . . Just till morning when I leave?"

"I . . . couldn't."

"Don't you *want* to?"

"Yes," she answered honestly.

"Then why. . . ."

"I'm only sixteen," she confessed bravely. "I've never been with . . . anybody. I wouldn't know how."

"That makes no difference."

"And I've never been away from home overnight. My mother would worry."

"You could tell her you spent the night with a girl friend."

"She knows I have no girl friend."

"You could think of some excuse . . . tomorrow."

"I wouldn't need to think of an excuse. I'd tell her the truth."

"You *would?*" he asked in astonishment.

"I love you. I wouldn't be ashamed . . . afterwards if I stayed with you. I'd be proud and happy and I wouldn't want to lie about it."

"I had no way of knowing, no way of knowing," he whispered as if to himself.

"*You* wouldn't want it to be something . . . sneaky, would you?"

"Francie, forgive me. I shouldn't have asked. I had no way of knowing."

"Knowing?" asked Francie, puzzled.

He put his arms around her and held her tightly. She saw that he was crying.

"Francie, I'm afraid . . . so afraid. I'm afraid that if I go away

I'll lose you . . . never see you again. Tell me not to go home and I'll stay. We'll have tomorrow and the next day. We'll eat together and walk around or sit in a park or ride on top of a bus and just talk and be with each other. Tell me not to go."

"I guess you have to go. I guess that it's right that you see your mother once more before. . . . I don't know. But I guess it's right."

"Francie, will you marry me when the war's over—*if* I come back?"

"*When* you come back, I'll marry you."

"Will you, Francie? . . . please, will you?"

"Yes."

"Say it again."

"I'll marry you when you come back, Lee."

"And, Francie, we'll live in Brooklyn."

"We'll live wherever you want to live."

"We'll live in Brooklyn, then."

"Only if *you* want to, Lee."

"And will you write to me every day? *Every* day?"

"Every day," she promised.

"And will you write to me tonight when you get home and tell me how much you love me so that the letter will be waiting for me when I get home?" She promised. "Will you promise never to let anyone kiss you? Never to go out with anyone? To wait for me . . . no matter how long? And if I don't come back, never to *want* to marry anyone else?"

She promised.

And he asked for her whole life as simply as he'd ask for a date. And she promised away her whole life as simply as she'd offer a hand in greeting or farewell.

It stopped raining after a while and the stars came out.

53

She wrote that night as she had promised—a long letter in which she poured out all her love and repeated the promises she had given.

She left a little earlier for work to have time to mail the letter from the Thirty-fourth Street post office. The clerk at the window assured her that it would reach its destination that afternoon. That was Wednesday.

She looked for but tried not to expect a letter Thursday night. There hadn't been time—unless he, too, wrote immediately after they had parted. But of course, he had to pack maybe—get up early to make his train. (It never occurred to her that *she* had managed to find time.) There was no letter Thursday night.

Friday, she had to work straight through—a sixteen-hour shift— because the company was short-handed on account of an influenza epidemic. When she got home a little before two in the morning, there was a letter propped against the sugar bowl on the kitchen table. She ripped it open eagerly.

"Dear Miss Nolan:"

Her happiness died. It couldn't be from Lee because he'd write, "Dear Francie." She turned the page and looked at the signature. "Elizabeth Rhynor (Mrs.)" Oh! His mother. Or a sister-in-law. Maybe he was sick and couldn't write. Maybe there was an army rule that men about to go overseas couldn't write letters. He had asked someone to write for him. Of course. That was it. She started to read the letter.

> "Lee told me all about you. I want to thank you for being so nice and friendly to him while he was in New York. He arrived home Wednesday afternoon but had to leave for camp the next night. He was home only a day and a half. We had a very quiet wedding, just the families and a few friends . . ."

Francie put the letter down. "I've been working sixteen hours in a row," she thought, "and I'm tired. I've read thousands of messages today and no words make sense right now. Anyhow, I got into bad reading habits at the Bureau—reading a column at a glance and seeing only one word in it. First I'll wash the sleep out of my eyes, have some coffee, and read the letter again. This time I'll read it right."

While the coffee heated, she splashed cold water on her face thinking that when she came to the part of the letter that said "wedding" she'd go on reading and the next words would be: "Lee was the best man. I married his brother, you know."

Katie lying awake in her bed heard Francie moving about in the kitchen. She lay tense . . . waiting. And she wondered what it was she waited for.

Francie read the letter again.

> ". . . wedding, just the families and a few friends. Lee asked me to write and explain why he hadn't answered your letter. Again thank you for entertaining him so nicely while he was in your city. Yours truly, Elizabeth Rhynor (Mrs.)"

There was a postscript.

> "I read the letter you sent Lee. It was mean of him to pretend to be in love with you and I told him so. He said to tell you he's dreadfully sorry. E.R."

Francie was trembling violently. Her teeth made little biting sounds.

"Mama," she moaned. *"Mama!"*

Katie heard the story. "It's come at last," she thought, "the time when you can no longer stand between your children and heartache. When there wasn't enough food in the house you pretended that you weren't hungry so they could have more. In the cold of a winter's night you got up and put your blanket on their bed so they wouldn't be cold. You'd kill anyone who tried to harm them—I tried my best to kill that man in the hallway. Then one sunny day, they walk out in all innocence and they walk right into the grief that you'd give your life to spare them."

Francie gave her the letter. She read it slowly and as she read, she thought she knew how it was. Here was a man of twenty-two who evidently (to use one of Sissy's phrases) had been around. Here was a girl sixteen years old; six years younger than he. A girl—in spite of bright-red lipstick and grown-up clothes and a lot of knowledge picked up here and there—who was yet tremulously innocent; a girl who had come face to face with some of the evil of the world and most of its hardships, and yet had remained curiously untouched by the world. Yes, she could understand her appeal for him.

Well, what could she say? That he was no good or at best just a weak man who was easily susceptible to whoever he was with? No, she couldn't be so cruel as to say that. Besides the girl wouldn't believe her anyhow.

"Say something," demanded Francie. "Why don't you say something?"

"What can I say?"

"Say that I'm young—that I'll get over it. Go ahead and say it. Go ahead and lie."

"I know that's what people say—you'll get over it. I'd say it, too. But I know it's not true. Oh, you'll be happy again, never fear. But you won't forget. Everytime you fall in love it will be because something in the man reminds you of *him*."

"Mother. . . ."

Mother! Katie remembered. She had called her own mother "mama" until the day she had told her that she was going to marry Johnny. She had said, "Mother, I'm going to marry . . ." She had never said "mama" after that. She had finished growing up when she stopped calling her mother "mama." Now Francie . . .

"Mother, he asked me to be with him for the night. Should I have gone?"

Katie's mind darted around looking for words.

"Don't make up a lie, Mother. Tell me the truth."

Katie couldn't find the right words.

"I promise you that I'll never go with a man without being married first—if I ever marry. And if I feel that I must—without being married, I'll tell you first. That's a solemn promise. So you can tell me the truth without worrying that I'll go wrong if I know it."

"There are two truths," said Katie finally.

"As a mother, I say it would have been a terrible thing for a girl to sleep with a stranger—a man she had known less than forty-eight hours. Horrible things might have happened to you. Your whole life might have been ruined. As your mother, I tell you the truth.

"But as a woman . . ." she hesitated. "I will tell you the truth as a woman. It would have been a very beautiful thing. Because there is only once that you love that way."

Francie thought, "I should have gone with him then. I'll never love anyone as much again. I wanted to go and I didn't go and now I don't want him that way anymore because *she* owns him now. But I wanted to and I didn't and now it's too late." She put her head down on the table and wept.

After a while, Katie said, "I got a letter, too."

Her letter had come several days ago but she had been waiting for the right time to mention it. She decided that this was a good time.

"I got a letter," she repeated.

"Who . . . who wrote?" sobbed Francie.

"Mr. McShane."

Francie sobbed louder.

"Aren't you interested?"

Francie tried to stop crying. "All right. What does he say?" she asked listlessly.

"Nothing. Except he's coming to see us next week." She waited. Francie showed no further sign of interest. "How would you like Mr. McShane for a father?"

Francie's head jerked up. "Mother! A man writes that he's coming to the house. Right away you think things. What makes you think you know everything all the time?"

"I don't *know*. I don't know anything, really. I *just* feel. And when the *feeling* is strong enough, then I just *say* I know. But I don't. Well how would you like him as a father?"

"After the botch I've made of my own life," said Francie bitterly (and Katie didn't smile), "I'm the last person to hand out advice."

"I'm not asking for your advice. Only I'd know better what to do if I knew how my children felt about him."

Francie suspected that her mother's talking about McShane was a trick to divert her thoughts and she was angry because the trick had almost worked.

"I don't know, Mother. I don't know anything. And I don't want to talk about anything any more. Please go away. Please go away and let me alone."

Katie went back to bed.

Well, a person can cry only so long. Then he has to do something else with his time. It was five o'clock. Francie decided it was no use going to bed; she'd have to get up again at seven. She discovered that she was very hungry. She had had nothing to eat since noon the day before, except a sandwich between the day and night shift. She made a pot of fresh coffee, some toast, and scrambled a couple of eggs. She was astonished at how good everything tasted. But while she was eating, her eyes went to the letter and the tears came again. She put the letter in the sink and set a match to it. Then she turned on the faucet and watched the black ashes go down the drain. She resumed her breakfast.

Afterwards she got her box of writing paper from the cupboard and sat down to write a letter. She wrote:

Dear Ben: you said I was to write if ever I needed you. So I'm writing. . . .

She tore the sheet in half.

"No! I don't want to need anybody. I want someone to need *me . . . I want someone to need me.*"

She wept again, but not so hard this time.

54

It was the first time Francie had seen McShane without his uniform. She decided that he looked very impressive in his expensively-tailored double-breasted gray suit. Of course he wasn't as good-looking as papa had been; he was taller and more massive. But he was handsome in his own way, decided Francie, even though his hair was gray. But gosh, he was awful old for mother. True, mother wasn't so young, either. She was going on thirty-five. Still that was much younger than fifty. Anyhow, no woman need be ashamed to have McShane for a husband. While he looked exactly what he was, a shrewd politician, his voice was gentle when he spoke.

They were having coffee and cake. With a pang, Francie noticed that McShane was sitting in her father's place at the table. Katie had just finished telling him all that had happened since Johnny died. McShane seemed amazed at the progress they had made. He looked at Francie.

"So this slip of a girl got herself to college last summer!"

"And she's going again this summer," announced Katie proudly.

"There's wonderful for you!"

"And she works in the bargain and earns twenty dollars a week now."

"All that and good health, too?" he asked in honest amazement.

"The boy is halfway through high school."

"No!"

"And he works at this and that afternoons and evenings. Sometimes he earns as much as five dollars a week outside of school."

"A fine lad. One of the finest of lads. And look at the health of him—would you now."

Francie wondered why he commented so much on the health which they themselves always took for granted. Then she remembered about his own children; how most of them had been born but to sicken and die before they grew up. No wonder he thought healthiness such a remarkable thing.

"And the baby?" he inquired.

"Go get her, Francie," said Katie.

The baby was in her crib in the front room. It was supposed to be Francie's room but all had agreed that the baby needed to sleep where there was air. Francie picked up the sleeping child. She opened her eyes and instantly was ready for anything.

"Bye-bye, Fran-nee? Park? Park?" she asked.

"No, sweet. Just an introduction to a man."

"Man?" said Laurie doubtfully.

"Yes. A great big man."

"Big man!" repeated the child happily.

Francie brought her out to the kitchen. The baby was truly a beautiful thing to see. She had a fresh dewy look in her pink flannel nightgown. Her hair was a mass of soft black curls. Her widely-set-apart dark eyes were luminous and there was a dusky rose color in her cheeks.

"Ah, the baby, the baby," crooned McShane. " 'Tis a rose she is. A wild rose."

"If papa were here," thought Francie, "he'd start to sing, 'My Wild Irish Rose.' " She heard her mother sigh and wondered whether she too, was thinking. . . .

McShane took the baby. The child sat on his knees, stiffened her back away from him and stared at him doubtfully. Katie hoped she wouldn't cry.

"Laurie!" she said. "Mr. McShane. Say Mr. McShane."

The child lowered her head, looked up through her lashes, smiled knowingly and shook her head, "no."

"No may-mane," she stated. "Man!" she shouted triumphantly. "Big man!" She smiled at McShane and said wheedlingly, "Take Laurie bye-bye? Park? Park?" Then she rested her cheek against his coat and closed her eyes.

"*Aroon, aroon,*" McShane crooned.

The child slept in his arms.

"Mrs. Nolan, you're wonderin' why I came tonight. Let your wonderin' be over. I came to ask a personal question." Francie and Neeley got up to leave. "No. Don't be leavin' chilthern. The question would be concernin' you as well as your mother." They sat down again. He cleared his throat. "Mrs. Nolan, time has passed since your husband—God rest his soul. . . ."

"Yes. Two and a half years. God rest his soul."

"God rest his soul," echoed Francie and Neeley.

"And my wife—'tis a year since she's been gone, God rest her soul."

"God rest her soul," echoed the Nolans.

"I have been waitin' many years and now the time has come when 'tis no longer disrespect to the dead to speak out.

"Katherine Nolan, I'm askin' to keep company with you. Object, a weddin' in the fall."

Katie looked quickly at Francie and frowned. What was the matter with mother anyhow? Francie wasn't even *thinking* of laughing.

"I am in a position to take care of you and the three chilthern. With my pension and salary and income from real estate in Woodhaven and Richmond Hill, I have over ten thousand dollars a year. I have insurance, too. I offer to put the boy and girl through college and I promise to be a faithful husband in the future as I was in the past."

"Have you thought this over, Mr. McShane?"

"I don't need to be thinkin'. Sure didn't I make up me mind five years ago when I saw you first at the Mahoney Outin'? 'Twas then I asked the girl if it was her mother you were."

"I am a scrubwoman without education." She stated it as a fact, not an apology.

"Education! And sure, who was it taught *me* to read and write? Nobody but meself."

"But a man like you—in public life—needs a wife who knows social business—who can entertain his influential business friends. I'm not that kind of a woman."

"My office is where I do my business entertainin'. My home is where I live. Now I'm not meanin' you wouldn't be a credit to me— you'd be a credit to a better man: But I'm needin' no woman to help me out in my business. I can handle that meself, thank you. Need I be sayin' I love you . . ." he hesitated before calling her by her first name ". . . Katherine? And is it time you want to think it over?"

"No. I don't need time to think it over. I will marry you, Mr. McShane.

"Not for your income. Although I'm not overlooking that. Ten thousand a year's a lot of money. But so is one thousand to people like us. We've had little money and are well trained in doing without it. It's not for sending the children to college. Your help will make it so easy. But without help at all, I knew we'd manage some way. It's not for your grand public position although it'll be fine to have a husband to be proud of.

"I will marry you because you are a good man and I'd like to have you for my husband."

It was true. Katie had made up her mind to marry him—if he asked her—simply because life was incomplete without a man to love her. It had nothing to do with her love for Johnny. She'd always love him. Her feeling for McShane was quieter. She admired and respected him and she knew she'd be a good wife to him.

"Thank you, Katherine. Sure it's little enough I'm givin' in exchange for a pretty young wife and three healthy chilthern," he said in sincere humility.

He turned to Francie. "As the eldest, do you be approvin'?"

Francie looked at her mother who seemed to be waiting for her to speak. She looked at her brother. He nodded.

"I think my brother and I would like to have you for a. . . ." Tears came into her eyes as she thought of her father and she couldn't say that next word.

"Now, now," said McShane soothingly, "I'll not have you worryin'." He turned to Katie.

"I'm not askin' that the two oldest call me 'father.' They had a father and he as fine a lad as God ever made—the way he was always singin'."

Francie felt her throat tightening.

"And I won't be askin' that they take my name—Nolan bein' the fine name it is.

"But this little one I'm holdin'—the one who never looked on a father's face: Would you be lettin' her call me father, and lettin' me legally adopt her and give her the name that you and I will be carryin' together?"

Katie looked at Francie and Neeley. How would they take it—their sister called McShane instead of Nolan? Francie nodded approval. Neeley nodded approval.

"We will give you the child," said Katie.

"We can't call you 'father,' " said Neeley suddenly. "But we'll call you 'dad,' maybe."

"I'm thankin' you," said McShane simply. He relaxed and smiled at them. "Now I'm wonderin' if I could smoke me pipe?"

"Why you could have smoked anytime without asking," said Katie in surprise.

"I didn't want to be takin' privileges before I was entitled to them," he explained.

Francie took the sleeping baby from him in order to let him smoke.

"Help me put her to bed, Neeley."

"Why?" Neeley was thoroughly enjoying himself and didn't want to leave.

"To fix the blankets in the crib. Somebody's got to do it while I hold her." Didn't Neeley know *anything*? Didn't he know that maybe McShane and mother wanted to be alone for a minute, at least?

In the darkness of the front room, Francie whispered to her brother, "What do you think of it?"

"It's sure a good break for mama. Of course he isn't papa. . . ."

"No. No one will ever be . . . papa. But aside from that, he's a nice man, though."

"Laurie's going to have a mighty easy life all right."

"Annie Laurie McShane! She'll never have the hard times we had, will she?"

"No. And she'll never have the fun we had, either."

"Gosh! We *did* have fun, didn't we, Neeley?"

"Yeah!"

"Poor Laurie," said Francie pityingly.

BOOK FIVE

55

Francie jumped as someone tapped her on the shoulder. Then she relaxed and smiled. Of course! It was one o'clock in the morning, she was through, and her "relief" had come to take over the machine.

"Let me send just one more," begged Francie.

"The way some people like their job!" smiled the "relief."

Francie typed her last message slowly and lovingly. She was glad it was a birth announcement rather than a notification of a death. The message was her farewell. She hadn't told anyone she was leaving. She was afraid she'd break down and cry if she went around saying goodbye. Like her mother, she was afraid of being openly sentimental.

Instead of going directly to her locker, she stopped in the big recreation room where some girls were making the most of their fifteen-minute rest period. They were grouped around a girl at the piano and were singing, "Hello, Central, Give Me No Man's Land."

As Francie walked in, the pianist drifted into another song inspired by Francie's new gray fall suit and her gray suede pumps. The girls sang: "There's a Quaker Down in Quaker Town." A girl put her arm around Francie and drew her into the circle. Francie sang with them.

Down in her heart I know, she's not so slow . . .

"Francie, where'd you ever get the idea for an all-gray outfit?"

"Oh, I don't know—some actress I saw when I was a kid. Don't remember her name but the show was *The Minister's Sweetheart*."

"It's *cute*!"

> *She has that "meet me later" look . . .*
> *My little Quaker down in Quaker town.*

Do-o-o-own To-o-o-o-own, harmonized the girls in a grand finale.

Next they sang, "You'll Find Old Dixieland in France." Francie went over to stand at the great window from which she could see the East River twenty stories below. It was the last time she'd see the river from that window. The last time of anything has the poignancy of death itself. This that I see now, she thought, to see no more this way. Oh, the last time how clearly you see everything; as though a magnifying light had been turned on it. And you grieve because you hadn't held it tighter when you had it every day.

What had granma Mary Rommely said? "To look at everything always as though you were seeing it either for the first or last time: Thus is your time on earth filled with glory."

Granma Mary Rommely!

She had lingered on for months in her last illness. But a time had come when Steve came just before dawn to tell them.

"I'll miss her," he said. "She was a great lady."

"You mean a great woman," said Katie.

Why, puzzled Francie, had Uncle Willie chosen that time to leave his family? She watched a boat glide under the Bridge before she resumed her thoughts. Was it that one less Rommely woman to be accountable to made him feel more free? Had her death given him the idea that there was such a thing as escape? Or was it (as Evy claimed) that he was able in his meanness, to take advantage of the confusion created by granma's funeral to run away from his family? Whatever it was, Willie was gone.

Willie Flittman!

He had practiced desperately until he got so that he could play all the instruments at once. Then as a one-man band he competed with others at a movie house on amateur night. He won the first prize of ten dollars.

He never came home with the prize money and his instruments, and no one in the family had seen him since.

They heard about him now and then. It seemed that he was roaming the streets of Brooklyn as a one-man band and living on the pennies he collected. Evy said he'd be home again when the snow started to fly but Francie, for one, doubted it.

Evy got a job in the factory where he had worked. She earned thirty dollars a week and got along fine, except at night, when, like all Rommely women, she found it hard to get along without a man.

Francie, standing at the window overlooking the river, recalled how always there had been something dreamlike about Uncle Willie. But then, so many things seemed like dreams to her. That man in the hallway that day: Surely that had been a dream! The way McShane had been waiting for mother all those years—a dream. Papa dead. For a long time that had been a dream but now papa was like someone who had never been. The way Laurie seemed to come out of a dream—born the living child of a father five months dead. Brooklyn was a dream. All the things that happened there just *couldn't* happen. It was all dream stuff. Or was it all real and true and was it that she, Francie, was the dreamer?

Well, she'd find out when she got out to Michigan. If there was that same dream feeling about Michigan, then Francie would know that she was the one dreaming.

Ann Arbor!

The University of Michigan was there. And in two more days, she would be on a train heading for Ann Arbor. Summer school was over. She had passed the four subjects she had elected. Crammed by Ben, she had passed the regents' college entrance examinations, too. That meant that she, sixteen and a half years old, could now enter college with half a year's freshman credits behind her.

She had wanted to go to Columbia in New York or Adelphi in

Brooklyn, but Ben said that part of education was adapting oneself to a new environment. Her mother and McShane had agreed. Even Neeley said it would be a good thing for her to go far off to college—she might get rid of her Brooklyn accent that way. But Francie didn't want to get rid of it any more than she wanted to get rid of her name. It meant that she *belonged* some place. She was a Brooklyn girl with a Brooklyn name and a Brooklyn accent. She didn't want to change into a bit of this and a bit of that.

Ben had chosen Michigan for her. He said it was a liberal state college, had a good English department and low tuition. Francie wondered, if it was so good, why he hadn't matriculated there instead of at the university of another midwestern state. He explained that eventually he would practice in that state, enter into its politics and he might as well be classmates with its prominent citizens of the future.

Ben was twenty now. He was in the Reserve Officers' Training Corps of his college and he looked very handsome in his uniform.

Ben!

She looked at the ring on the third finger of her left hand. Ben's high school ring. "M.H.S. 1918." Inside was engraved, "B.B. to F.N." He had told her that while he knew *his* mind, she was too young to know *hers*. He gave her the ring to bind what he called their understanding. Of course, it would be five more years before he'd be in a position to marry, he said. By that time she'd be old enough to know her own mind. Then, if there was still the undertsanding, he'd ask her to accept another kind of ring. Since Francie had five years in which to make up her mind, the responsibility of deciding whether or not to marry Ben did not weigh too heavily upon her.

Amazing Ben!

He had graduated from high school in January, 1918, had entered college immediately, taken a staggering number of courses and had come back to summer school in Brooklyn to take more work, and—as he confessed at the end of the session—to be with Francie again. Now in September, 1918, he was returning to college to start his junior year!

Good old Ben!

Decent, honorable, and brilliant. *He* knew his own mind. *He'd* never ask one girl to marry him and the next day go off and marry another girl. *He'd* never ask her to write out her love and then let someone else read the letter. Not Ben . . . not Ben. Yes, Ben was wonderful. She was proud to have him for a friend. But she thought of Lee.

Lee!

Where was Lee now?

He had sailed away to France on a transport just like the one she now saw slipping out of the harbor—a long boat with its swirls of camouflage and the silent white faces of its thousand soldier passengers, looking from where she stood, like so many white-headed pins in a long awkward pin cushion.

("Francie, I'm afraid . . . so afraid. I'm afraid that if I go away I'll lose you . . . never see you again. Tell me not to go. . . .")

("I guess that it's right that you see your mother once more before . . . I don't know. . . .")

He was with the Rainbow Division—the Division even now pushing into the Argonne Woods. Was he even now lying dead in France under a plain white cross? Who would tell her if he died? Not the woman in Pennsylvania.

("Elizabeth Rhynor [Mrs.]")

Anita had left months ago to work somewhere else and had left no address. No one to ask . . . no one to tell her.

Fiercely she wished he were dead so that the woman in Pennsylvania could never have him. In the next breath she prayed, "Oh God, don't let him be killed and I won't complain no matter who has him. Please . . . Please!"

Oh time . . . time, pass so that I forget!

("You'll be happy again, never fear. But you won't forget.")

Mother was wrong. She *had* to be wrong. Francie wanted to forget. It was four months since she had known him but she couldn't forget. ("Happy again . . . but you'll never forget.") How could she be happy again if she couldn't forget?

Oh Time, Great Healer, pass over me and let me forget.

("Everytime you fall in love it will be because something in the man reminds you of *him*.")

Ben had the same slow smile. But she had thought she was in love with Ben last year—long before she had seen Lee. So that didn't work out.

Lee, Lee!

The recreation period was over and a new bunch of girls came in. It was their recreation period now. They flocked around the piano and started on a sequence of "Smile" songs. Francie knew what would come.

Run, run, you fool, before the waves of hurt start breaking.

But she couldn't move.

They did Ted Lewis' song: "For When My Baby Smiles at Me." From that it was inevitable that they go into, "There Are Smiles That Make You Happy."

And then it came.

Smile the while
You kiss me sad adieu. . . .

(". . . think of me every time you hear it. Think of me. . . .") She ran out of the room. She snatched her gray hat and her new gray purse and gloves from her locker. She ran for the elevator.

She looked up and down the canyon-like street. It was dark and deserted. A tall man in uniform stood in the shadowed doorway of the next building. He walked out of the dark and came towards her with a shy lonely smile.

She closed her eyes. Granma had said that the Rommely women had the power of seeing the ghosts of their beloved dead. Francie had never believed it because she had never seen papa. But now . . . now. . . .

"Hello, Francie."

She opened her eyes. No, he wasn't a ghost.

"I had an idea that you'd feel blue—your last night on the job—so I came to take you home. Surprised?"

"No. I thought you'd come," she said.

"Hungry?"

"Starved!"

"Where do you want to go? Want to get some coffee at the Automat or would you like chop suey?"

"No! *No!*"

"Child's?"

"Yes. Let's go to Child's and have buttercakes and coffee."

He took her hand and drew her arm through his.

"Francie, you seem so strange tonight. You're not mad at me, are you?"

"No."

"Glad I came?"

"Yes," she said quietly. "It's good to see you, Ben."

56

Saturday! The last Saturday in their old home. The next day was Katie's wedding day and they were going straight to their new home from the church. The movers were coming Monday morning for their stuff. They were leaving most of their furniture for the new janitress. They were taking only their personal belongings and the front room furniture. Francie wanted the green carpet with the big pink roses, the cream-colored lace curtains and the lovely little piano. These things were to be installed in the room set aside for Francie in their new home.

Katie insisted on working as usual that last Saturday morning. They laughed when mother set out with her broom and pail. McShane had given her a checking account with a thousand dollars in it as a wedding present. According to Nolan standards, Katie was rich now and didn't have to do another lick of work. Yet, she insisted on working that last day. Francie suspected that she had a sentimental feeling about the houses and wanted to give them a last good cleaning before she left.

Shamelessly, Francie searched for the check book in her mother's purse and examined the only stub in the fabulous folder.

No: *1*
Date: *9-20-18*
To: *Eva Flittman*

For: *Because she's my sister*
Total: *1000.00*
Amt this ck: *200.00*
Bal fwd: *800.00*

Francie wondered why that amount? Why not fifty dollars or five hundred? Why two hundred? Then she understood. Two hundred was the amount Uncle Willie was insured for; what Evy would have collected had he died. No doubt Katie considered Willie as good as dead.

No check had been made out for Katie's wedding dress. She explained that she didn't want to use any of that money for herself until after she had married the giver. In order to buy the dress, she had borrowed the money she had saved for Francie, promising to give her a check for it as soon as the ceremony was over.

On that last Saturday morning, Francie strapped Laurie into her two-wheeled sulky and took her down on the street. She stood on the corner for a long time watching the kids lug their junk up Manhattan Avenue to Carney's junk shop. Then she walked up that way and went into Cheap Charlie's during a lull in business. She put a fifty-cent piece down on the counter and announced that she wanted to take all the picks.

"Aw, now, Francie! *Gee*, Francie," he said.

"I don't have to bother picking. Just give me all the stuff on the board."

"Aw, *lissen!*"

"Then there aren't any prize numbers in that box, are there, Charlie?"

"Christ, Francie, a feller is got to make a living and it comes slow in this business—a penny at a time."

"I always thought those prizes were fake. You ought to be ashamed—fooling little kids that way."

"Don't say that. I give them a penny's worth of candy for each cent they spend here. The pick is just so's it's more interesting."

"And it makes them keep coming back—hoping."

"If they don't go here, they go across to Gimpy's, see? And it's better they come here because I'm a married man," he said virtuously, "and I don't take girls in my back room, see?"

"Oh, well. I guess there's something in what you say. Look! Have you got a fifty-cent doll?"

He dredged up an ugly-faced doll from under the counter. "I only got a sixty-nine-cent doll but I'll let you have it for fifty cents."

"I'll pay for it if you'll hang it up as a prize and let some kid win it."

"But look, Francie: A kid wins it. *All* the kids expect to win then, see? It's a bad example."

"O, for sweet Christ's sake," she said, not profanely but prayerfully, "let somebody win something just *once!*"

"All right! All right! Don't get excited, now."

"I just want one little kid to get something for nothing."

"I'll put it up and I won't take the number out of the box, either, after you go. Satisfied?"

"Thanks, Charlie."

"And I'll tell the winner the doll's name's Francie, see?"

"Oh no, you don't! Not with the face that doll's got."

"You know what, Francie?"

"What?"

"You're getting to be quite a girl. How old are you now?"

"I'll be seventeen in a couple of months."

"I remember you used to be a skinny long-legged kid. Well, I think you'll make a nice-looking woman some day—not pretty, but something."

"Thanks for nothing." She laughed.

"Your kid sister?" he nodded at Laurie.

"Uh-huh."

"First thing you know she'll be lugging junk and coming in here with her pennies. One day they're babies in buggies and the next day they're in here taking picks. Kids grow up quick in this neighborhood."

"*She'll* never lug junk. And she'll never come in here, either."

"That's right. I hear you're moving away."

"Yes, we're moving away."

"Well, the best of luck, Francie."

She took Laurie to the park, lifted her out of the sulky and let her run around on the grass. A boy came by selling pretzels and Francie bought one for a penny. She crumbled it into bits and scattered it on the grass. A flock of sooty sparrows appeared from nowhere and squabbled over the bits. Laurie stumbled about trying to catch them. The bored birds let her get within inches of them before they lifted their wings and took off. The child screamed with delighted laughter each time a bird flew away.

Pulling Laurie along in the sulky, Francie went over for a last look at her old school. It was but a couple of blocks from the park which she visited every day, but for some reason or other, Francie had never gone back to see it since the night she graduated.

She was surprised at how tiny it seemed now. She supposed the school was just as big as it had ever been only her eyes had grown used to looking at bigger things.

"There's the school that Francie went to," she told Laurie.

"Fran-nee went to school," agreed Laurie.

"Your papa came with me one day and sang a song."

"Papa?" asked Laurie, puzzled.

"I forgot. You never saw your papa."

"Laurie saw papa. Man. *Big* man." She thought Francie meant McShane.

"*That's* right," agreed Francie.

In the two years since she had last looked on the school, Francie had changed from a child to a woman.

She went home past the house whose address she had claimed. It looked little and shabby to her now, but she still loved it.

She passed McGarrity's saloon. Only McGarrity didn't own it any more. He had moved away early in the summer. He had confided in Neeley that he, McGarrity, was a man who had his ear to the ground and was therefore in a position to hear prohibition coming. He was getting all set for it, too. He bought a large place on the Hempstead Turnpike out on Long Island and was systematically stocking its cellars with liquor against the day. As soon as prohibition came, he was going to open up what he called a Club. He had the name picked out: The Club Mae-Marie. His wife was going to wear an evening dress and be a hostess, which was right up her alley, McGarrity explained. Francie was sure that Mrs. McGarrity would be very happy as a hostess. She hoped that Mr. McGarrity would be happy some day, too.

After lunch, she went around to the library to turn in her books for the last time. The librarian stamped her card and shoved it back to her without, as was usual, looking up.

"Could you recommend a good book for a girl?" asked Francie.

"How old?"

"She is eleven."

The librarian brought up a book from under the desk. Francie saw the title: *If I Were King*.

"I don't really want to take it out," said Francie, "and I'm not eleven years old."

The librarian looked up at Francie for the first time.

"I've been coming here since I was a little girl," said Francie, "and you never looked at me till now."

"There are so many children," said the librarian fretfully. "I can't be looking at each one of them. Anything else?"

"I just want to say about that brown bowl . . . what it has meant to me . . . the flower always in it."

The librarian looked at the brown bowl. There was a spray of pink wild aster in it. Francie had an idea that the librarian was seeing the brown bowl for the first time, also.

"Oh that! The janitor puts the flowers in. Or somebody. Anything else?" she asked impatiently.

"I'm turning in my card." Francie pushed the wrinkled dog-eared card covered with stamped dates across the desk. The librarian picked it up and was about to tear it in two, when Francie took it back from her.

"I guess I'll keep it after all," she said.

She went out and took a last long look at the shabby little library. She knew she would never see it again. Eyes changed after they looked at new things. If in the years to be, she were to come back, her new eyes might make everything seem different from the way she saw it now. The way it was now was the way she wanted to remember it.

No, she'd never come back to the old neighborhood.

Besides in years to come, there would be no old neighborhood to come back to. After the war, the city was going to tear down the tenements and the ugly school where a woman principal used to whip little boys, and build a model housing project on the site; a place of living where sunlight and air were to be trapped, measured and weighed, and doled out so much per resident.

Katie banged her broom and pail in the corner with that final bang that meant she was through. Then she picked up the broom and pail again and replaced them gently.

As she dressed to go out—she was going for a last-minute fitting of the jade-green velvet dress she had chosen to be married in—she fretted because the weather was so mild for the end of September. She thought it might be too warm to wear a velvet dress. She was angry that the fall was so late in coming that year. She argued with Francie when Francie insisted that fall *was* here.

Francie knew that autumn had come. *Let* the wind blow warm, *let* the days be heat hazy; nevertheless autumn had come to Brooklyn. Francie knew that this was so because now, as soon as night came and the street lights went on, the hot chestnut man set up his little stand on the corner. On the rack above the charcoal fire, chestnuts roasted in a covered pan. The man held unroasted ones in his hand and made little crosses on them with a blunt knife before he put them in the pan.

Yes, autumn had surely come when the hot chestnut man appeared—no matter what the weather said to the contrary.

After Laurie had been tucked into her crib for her afternoon nap, Francie packed a few last things in a wooden Fels-Naptha soap box.

From over the mantelpiece, she took down the crucifix and the picture of her and Neeley on Confirmation Day. She wrapped these things in her First Communion veil and placed them in the box. She folded her father's two waiter's aprons and put them in. She wrapped the shaving cup with the name "John Nolan" on it in gilt block letters, in a white georgette crepe blouse which Katie had put in the "give-away" basket because its lace jabot had torn badly in the wash. It was the blouse Francie had worn that rainy night when she stood in the doorway with Lee. The doll named Mary and the pretty little box which had once held ten gilded pennies, were stowed away next. Her sparse library went into the box: the Gideon Bible, *The Complete Works of Wm. Shakespeare,* a tattered volume of *Leaves of Grass,* the three scrapbooks—*The Nolan Volume of Contemporary Poetry, The Nolan Book of Classical Poems,* and *The Book of Annie Laurie.*

She went into the bedroom, turned back her mattress and took from under it a notebook in which she had kept a desultory diary during her thirteenth year, and a square manila envelope. Kneeling before the box, she opened the diary and read a random entry dated September 24th, three years ago.

> *Tonight when I took a bath, I discovered I was changing into a woman. It's about time!*

She grinned as she packed the diary in the box. She looked at the writing on the envelope.

> *Contents:*
> *1 sealed envelope to be opened in 1967.*
> *1 diploma.*
> *4 stories.*

Four stories, which Miss Garnder had told her to burn. Ah, well. Francie remembered how she had promised God she'd give up writing if He wouldn't let mother die. She had kept her promise. But she knew God a little better, now. She was sure that

He wouldn't care at all if she started to write again. Well, maybe she'd try again some day. She added her library card to the contents of the envelope, made an entry for it on the envelope and put that in the box. Her packing was finished. All her possessions, except her clothes, were in that box.

Neeley came running up the stairs whistling, "At the Darktown Strutters' Ball." He burst into the kitchen peeling off his coat.

"I'm in a hurry, Francie. Have I got a clean shirt?"

"There's one washed but not ironed. I'll iron it for you."

She put the iron on to heat while she sprinkled the shirt and set up the ironing board on two chairs. Neeley got the shoe-shine kit from the closet and proceeded to put a higher shine on his already flawlessly polished shoes.

"Going somewhere?" she asked.

"Yup. Just got time to catch the show. They've got Van and Schenck and boy, can Schenck sing! He sits at the piano like this." Neeley sat at the kitchen table and demonstrated. "He sits sideways and crosses his legs, looking out at the audience. Then he leans his left elbow on the music rack and picks out the tune with his right hand while he sings." Neeley went into a fair imitation of his idol singing, "When You're a Long, Long Way From Home."

"Yup, he's swell. Sings the way papa used to . . . a little."

Papa!

Francie looked for the union label in Neeley's shirt and pressed that first.

("That label is like an ornament . . . like a rose that you wear.")

The Nolans sought for the union label on everything they bought. It was their memorial to Johnny.

Neeley looked at himself in the glass hanging over the sink.

"Do you think I need a shave?" he asked.

"Not for five years, yet."

"Aw, shut up!"

"Don't-say-shut-up-to-each-other," said Francie, imitating her mother.

Neeley smiled and proceeded to scrub his face, neck, arms, and hands. He sang as he washed.

> *There's Egypt in your dreamy eyes,*
> *A bit of Cairo in your style. . . .*

Francie ironed away contentedly.

Neeley was dressed at last. He stood before her in his dark blue double-breasted suit, fresh white shirt with the soft turned-down collar and a polka dot bow tie. He smelled fresh and clean from washing and his curly blond hair gleamed.

"How do I look, Prima Donna?"

He buttoned up his coat jauntily and Francie saw that he wore their father's signet ring.

It was true then—what granma had said: that the Rommely women had the gift of seeing the ghosts of their beloved dead. Francie saw her father.

"Neeley, do you still remember, 'Molly Malone'?"

He put a hand in his pocket, turned away from her and sang.

> *In Dublin's fair city,*
> *The girls are so pretty . . .*

Papa . . . papa!

Neeley had the same clear true voice. And how unbelievably handsome he was! So handsome that, even though he wasn't sixteen years old yet, women turned to look after him with a sigh when he walked down the street. He was so handsome that Francie felt like a dark drab alongside of him.

"Neeley, do you think I'm good-looking?"

"Look! Why don't you make a novena to St. Theresa about it? I think a miracle might fix you up."

"No, I mean it."

"Why don't you get your hair cut off and wear it in curls like the other girls instead of those chunks wound around your head?"

"I have to wait until I'm eighteen on account of mother. But do you think I'm good-looking?"

"Ask me again when you fill out a little more."

"Please tell me."

He examined her carefully, then said, "You'll pass." She had to be satisfied with that.

He had said he was in a hurry, but now he seemed reluctant to go.

"Francie! McShane . . . I mean dad, will be here for supper tonight. I'm working afterwards. Tomorrow will be the wedding and a party in the new house tomorrow night. Monday, I have to go to school. And while I'm there, you'll be getting on that Wolverine train for Michigan. There'll be no chance to say goodbye to you alone. So I'll say goodbye now."

"I'll be home for Christmas, Neeley."

"But it won't be the same."

"I know."

He waited. Francie extended her right hand. He pushed her hand aside, put his arms around her and kissed her on the cheek. Francie clung to him and started to cry. He pushed her away.

"Gee, girls make me sick," he said. "Always so mushy." But his voice was ragged as though he, too, was going to cry.

He turned and ran out of the flat. Francie went out into the hallway and watched him run down the steps. He paused in the well of darkness at the foot of the stairs and turned to look back up at her. Although it was dark, there was brightness where he stood.

So like papa . . . so like papa, she thought. But he had more strength in his face than papa had had. He waved to her. Then he was gone.

Four o'clock.

Francie decided to get dressed first, and then fix supper so that she'd be all ready when Ben came to call for her. He had tickets and they were going to see Henry Hull in *The Man Who Came Back*. It was their last date until Christmas because Ben was leaving for college tomorrow. She liked Ben. She liked him an awful lot. She wished that she could love him. If only he wasn't so sure of himself all the time. If only he'd stumble—just once. If only he needed her. Ah, well. She had five years to think it over.

She stood before the mirror in her white slip. As she curved her arm over her head in washing, she remembered how she had sat on the fire escape when a little girl and watched the big girls in the flats across the yards getting ready for their dates. Was some one watching her as she had once watched?

She looked towards the window. Yes, across two yards she saw a little girl sitting on a fire escape with a book in her lap and a bag of candy at hand. The girl was peering through the bars at Francie. Francie knew the girl, too. She was a slender little thing of ten, and her name was Florry Wendy.

Francie brushed out her long hair, braided it and wound the braids around her head. She put on fresh stockings and white high-heeled pumps. Before she slipped a fresh pink linen dress over her head, she sprinkled violet sachet powder on a square of cotton and tucked it inside her brassiere.

She thought she heard Fraber's wagon come in. She leaned out of the window and looked. Yes, the wagon had come in. Only it wasn't a wagon anymore. It was a small maroon motor truck with the name in gilt letters on the sides and the man making preparations to wash it wasn't Frank, the nice young man with rosy cheeks. He was a little bandy-legged draft-exempt fellow.

She looked across the yards and saw that Florry was still staring at her through the bars of the fire escape. Francie waved and called:

"Hello, Francie."

"My name *ain't* Francie," the little girl yelled back. "It's *Florry*, and you know it, too."

"I know," said Francie.

She looked down into the yard. The tree whose leaf umbrellas had curled around, under and over her fire escape had been cut down because the housewives complained that wash on the lines got entangled in its branches. The landlord had sent two men and they had chopped it down.

But the tree hadn't died . . . it hadn't died.

A new tree had grown from the stump and its trunk had grown along the ground until it reached a place where there were no wash lines above it. Then it had started to grow towards the sky again.

Annie, the fir tree, that the Nolans had cherished with waterings and manurings, had long since sickened and died. But this tree in the yard—this tree that men chopped down . . . this tree that they built a bonfire around, trying to burn up its stump—this tree lived!

It lived! And nothing could destroy it.

Once more she looked at Florry Wendy reading on the fire escape.

"Goodbye, Francie," she whispered.

She closed the window.

THE END

A Tree Grows in Brooklyn

1943

"I, Betty Smith, wrote a novel," the author of A Tree Grows in Brooklyn told a literary gathering, about a year after the book's astounding publishing success. "I had no axe to grind. I just wanted to write, but it seems I didn't know my own strength."

Strength, indeed. When it was published in 1943, this first novel by a little known playwright sold three hundred thousand copies in just six weeks. More than fifty years later, the book is still a perennial bestseller, with more than a million copies sold. It remains a staple on school reading lists, holding its own alongside such other American classics as *Huckleberry Finn* and *The Great Gatsby*. Oprah Winfrey, arbiter of contemporary reading tastes, counts it among the ten books that have deeply affected her life. In 1995, the New York Public Library chose it as one of the "Books of the Century."

Soon after the novel's publication, Smith started hearing from both her fans and detractors. They demanded to know her purpose. At the time, some considered *A Tree Grows in Brooklyn* a daring book, rife with pro-union sentiment and unapologetic compassion for the poor. Others dismissed the book as prurient, although Smith's frank discussions of sexual issues may seem tame to today's reader. One Boston woman, in a letter to Smith, decreed that the author of such a book should live in a stable. Through it all, Smith denied having set out to write a book of "social significance." She wrote about a poor family struggling to stay afloat in turn-of-the-century Brooklyn, she said, because they were "the kind of people I know and the kind of people I like."

Whatever Smith's intentions, in 1943, at the height of the Second World War, *everyone*—from cabbies and salesclerks to society matrons—was reading *A Tree Grows in Brooklyn*. The critics, too, embraced the book. Orville Prescott called it "one of the most dearly beloved and one of the finest books of our day," and the *New York Times* said that Francie Nolan, the heroine of the novel, "is a superb feat of characterization, an imaginative, alert, resourceful child."

It seems inevitable that Betty Smith's enviable success in artfully mining her own childhood experience would call forth some measure of greed. In May 1944, Smith and Harper & Brothers, were hit with a $250,000 damage suit by Mrs. Sadie Grandner of Brooklyn, who claimed to be a cousin of the author and the prototype for the character of Sissy. Grandner's contention of libel, based on the fact that Sissy lives an "immoral" life, seems to have missed the point that Sissy is one of the, if not *the most*, generous and warm-hearted characters in the book.

Smith sold the film rights to *A Tree Grows in Brooklyn* for $55,000, and Twentieth Century Fox released their production in 1945. The movie, which was the directorial debut of Elia Kazan, is noticeably more sentimental than the novel and compresses the action of the book out of cinematic necessity, ending just after Johnny Nolan's death. James Dunn won an Oscar for his portrayal of Johnny, and the film's screenwriters, Frank Davis and Tess Slesinger, were nominated for their work.

James Agee, reviewing the film in *The Nation*, wrote, "I think it a more interesting and likable movie than most. It concentrates on poverty, on some crucial aspects of early puberty, on domestic relationships, and on life in a big city, which are rarely undertaken on the American screen, with considerable enthusiasm, tenderness, discipline, and intelligence. It even presents and accepts the idea, unpopular enough even in contemporary fiction, that some antagonisms and inadequacies are too deeply rooted to be wholly explicable, or curable. It also develops its main love interest between a little girl and her father, and it presents a drunkard, the father, for once without moralizing about him or reforming him."

Agee's appraisal of the film applies equally well to the book. These are no doubt some of the reasons the clear-sighted narrative, which presents humanity in all of its lovable and contemptible intransigence, continues to draw readers. Betty Smith's fictional achievement is the novel's timelessness. Sadly, the extraordinary recognition this first-time novelist enjoyed was never matched with her subsequent novels.

The Old Man and the Sea

Ernest Hemingway

'The best short story Hemingway has written . . . no page of this beautiful master-work could have been done better or differently'
Sunday Times

Set in the Gulf Stream off the coast of Havana, Hemingway's magnificent fable is the story of an old man, a young boy and a giant fish. In a perfectly crafted story, which won for Hemingway the Nobel Prize for Literature, is a unique and timeless vision of the beauty and grief of man's challenge to the elements in which he lives.

'It is unsurpassed in Hemingway's oeuvre. Every word tells and there is not a word too many'
Anthony Burgess

'A quite wonderful example of narrative art. The writing is as taut, and at the same time as lithe and cunningly played out, as the line on which the old man plays the fish'
Guardian

arrow books

Balkan Trilogy

Olivia Manning

Living and working in Rumania, Guy and Harriet Pringle are forced to evacuate to Greece before the steady advance of the German army. *The Balkan Trilogy* is the remarkable portrait of their marriage, a haunting evocation of a vanished way of life and a delightfully ironic comedy of manners in a breaking world.

'She is revealed as the most considerable of our women novelists; *The Balkan Trilogy* itself is, besides being one of the most massive, one of the finest fictional productions that Britain has seen since the war . . . Her gallery of personages is huge, her scene painting superb, her pathos controlled, her humour quiet and civilised'
Anthony Burgess

'So glittering is the overall parade . . . and so entertaining the surface that the triology remains excitingly vivid; it amuses, it diverts and it informs, and to do these things so elegantly is no small achievement'
Frederic Raphael, *Sunday Times*

arrow books

Staying On

Paul Scott

WINNER OF THE BOOKER PRIZE

Tusker and Lucy Smalley stayed on in India. Given the chance to return 'home' when Tusker, once a Colonel in the British Army, retired, they chose instead to remain in the small hill town of Pankot, with its eccentric inhabitants and archaic rituals left over from the days of the Empire. Only the tyranny of their landlady, the imposing Mrs Bhoolabhoy, threatens to upset the quiet rhythm of their days.

Both funny and deeply moving, *Staying On* is a unique, engrossing portrait of the end of an empire and of a forty-year love affair.

'*Staying On* covers only a few months but it carries the emotional impact of a lifetime, even a civilisation'
Philip Larkin, *Chairman of the Booker Prize Judges*

'Certainly his funniest and, I think, his best. It is a first-class book and deserves to be remembered for a long time'
Auberon Waugh, *Evening Standard*

arrow books

To Kill a Mockingbird

Harper Lee

'Shoot all the Bluejays you want, if you can hit 'em, but remember it's a sin to kill a Mockingbird.'

A lawyer's advice to his children as he defends the real mockingbird of Harper Lee's classic novel – a black man charged with the rape of a white girl in the deep South of the thirties.

'No one ever forgets this book'
Independent

'Someone rare has written this very fine novel, a writer of the liveliest sense of life and the warmest, most authentic humour. A touching book; and so funny, so likeable'
Truman Capote

'Her book is lifted . . . into the rare company of those that linger in the memory long after dramas, sagas and sophisticated frolics have coalesced into a blur of half-forgotten fiction'
Bookman

arrow books

THE POWER OF READING

Visit the Random House website and get connected with information on all our books and authors

EXTRACTS from our recently published books and selected backlist titles

COMPETITIONS AND PRIZE DRAWS Win signed books, audiobooks and more

AUTHOR EVENTS Find out which of our authors are on tour and where you can meet them

TEST NEWS on bestsellers, ...rds and new publications

MINISITES with exclusive special features dedicated to our authors and their titles

READING GROUPS Reading guides, special features and all the information you need for your reading group

LISTEN to extracts from the latest audiobook publications

WATCH video clips of interviews and readings with our authors

RANDOM HOUSE INFORMATION including advice for writers, job vacancies and all your general queries answered

Come home to Random House

www.randomhouse.co.uk

BLACKTOP WASTELAND

'The action sequences are superb, the dialogue wouldn't shame Elmore Leonard, and Bug's experiences recall Walter Mosley at his most powerful . . . fantastic'
Sunday Times

'One of those books that explodes out of nowhere and takes the field by storm'
Financial Times

'Spectacular . . . a voice as stark and distinctive as Elmore Leonard's, and a humanity that touches the soul'
Daily Mail

'Sensationally good – new, fresh, real, authentic, twisty, with characters and dilemmas that will break your heart. More than recommended'
Lee Child

'*Blacktop Wasteland* is an urgent, timely, pitch-perfect jolt of American noir. S. A. Cosby is a welcome, refreshing new voice in crime literature'
Dennis Lehane

'Stunning, just . . . stunning. Can't remember the last time I read such a powerful crime novel'
Mark Billingham

'Every once in a while a writer comes along with an incredible voice . . . add S. A. Cosby to that list. Trust me, this guy is gonna be a big name someday'
Steve Cavanagh

'Every now and then, a novelist shows up with a confidence and a swagger that makes it silly to compare him to anyone else. S. A. Cosby, the man behind the wheel of *Blacktop Wasteland*, writes the way his main character drives – with precision and fearlessness, in complete command of the road ahead. The book will leave you breathless, but also desperate to know where Cosby will take us next'
Laura Lippman

'Diamonds and fast cars, trailer park dreams and late night illegal street racing, S. A. Cosby reinvents the American crime novel . . . *Blacktop Wasteland* thrums and races – it's an intoxicating thrill of a ride'
Walter Mosley

'A delicious slice of country gothic wrapped in smart, hard, contemporary neo noir'
Adrian McKinty

'Hard-boiled crime fiction at its very finest. Propulsive, haunting, and richly imagined'
Lou Berney

'An exciting slice of American noir . . . Executed with such relentless power and heart'
Mail on Sunday

'A superb character study wrapped up in a high-octane heist novel . . . a complex and moving take on racial tension and self-destructive masculinity, with blistering action sequences and car chases that fairly roar off the page, this is undoubtedly one of the summer's standout reads'
Guardian

S. A. Cosby is a writer from Southeastern Virginia.
He resides in Gloucester, VA.

Also by S. A. Cosby:

Razorblade Tears

S.A.COSBY

BLACKTOP WASTELAND

HEADLINE

First published in the USA in 2020 by
Flatiron Books

First published in Great Britain in 2020 by
HEADLINE PUBLISHING GROUP

First published as a paperback in Great Britain in 2021 by
HEADLINE PUBLISHING GROUP

3

Cataloguing in Publication Data is available from the British Library

ISBN 978 1 4722 7375 8

Offset in 10.12/14.70 pt Minion Pro by Jouve (UK), Milton Keynes

Printed and bound in Great Britain by Clays Ltd, Elcograf S.p.A.

Headline's policy is to use papers that are natural, renewable and recyclable
products and made from wood grown in well-managed forests and other
controlled sources. The logging and manufacturing processes are expected
to conform to the environmental regulations of the country of origin.

HEADLINE PUBLISHING GROUP
An Hachette UK Company
Carmelite House
50 Victoria Embankment
London EC4Y 0DZ

www.headline.co.uk
www.hachette.co.uk

For my father, Roy Cosby

*Your reach sometimes exceeded your
grasp, but once you got a hold of that
steering wheel, you drove it like you stole it.*

Ride on, wild man. Ride on.

*A father is a man who expects his son
to be as good a man as he was meant
to be.*

FRANK A. CLARK

BLACKTOP
WASTELAND

ONE

Beauregard thought the night sky looked like a painting.

Laughter filled the air only to be drowned out by a cacophony of revving engines as the moon slid from behind the clouds. The bass from the sound system in a nearby Chevelle was hitting him in his chest so hard, it felt like someone was performing CPR on him. There were about a dozen other late-model cars parked haphazardly in front of the old convenience store. In addition to the Chevelle, there was a Maverick, two Impalas, a few Camaros and five or six more examples of the heyday of American muscle. The air was cool and filled with the scent of gas and oil. The rich, acrid smell of exhaust fumes and burnt rubber. A choir of crickets and whippoorwills tried in vain to be heard. Beauregard closed his eyes and strained his ears. He could hear them but just barely. They were screaming for love. He thought a lot of people spent a large part of their life doing the same thing.

The wind caught the sign hanging above his head from the arm of a pole that extended twenty feet into the air. It creaked as the breeze moved it back and forth.

CARTER SPEEDE MART the sign proclaimed in big black letters set against a white background. The sign was beginning to yellow with age. The letters were worn and chipped. The cheap paint flaking away like dried skin. The second "E" had disappeared from the word

"SPEEDEE." Beauregard wondered what had happened to Carter. He wondered if he had disappeared too.

"Ain't none of y'all motherfuckers ready for the legendary Olds! Y'all might as well go on back home to your ugly wives and try and get some Tuesday night pussy. For real though, y'all ain't got nothing for the legendary Olds! She does 60 in second. Five hundred dollars line to line. Huh? Y'all mighty quiet. Come on, the Olds done sent many a boy home with his pockets lighter. I done outrun more cops than the Duke boys in the Olds! You ain't just beating the Olds, home-boy!" a guy named Warren Crocker crowed. He was strutting around his '76 Oldsmobile Cutlass. It was a beautiful car. A dark green body with chrome Mag rims and chrome trim that ran across its surface like liquid lightning. Smoked-out glass and LED lights emitted an ethereal bluish glow like some bioluminescent sea creature.

Beauregard leaned against his Duster as Warren pontificated about the invincibility of the Oldsmobile. Beauregard let him talk. Talk didn't mean anything. Talk didn't drive the car. Talk was just noise. He had $1,000 in his pocket. It was all the profits from the last two weeks at the garage after most of the bills had been paid. He was $800 short on the rent for the building that housed his business. It had come down to a choice between the rent or glasses for his young-est. Which wasn't really a choice at all. So, he had reached out to his cousin Kelvin and asked him to find out where the nearest street race was being held. Kelvin still knew some guys who knew some guys who knew where the money races could be found.

That was how they found themselves just outside of Dinwiddie County ten miles from the fairgrounds where legally sanctioned drag races were held. Beauregard closed his eyes again. He listened to Warren's car idle. Under the sound of the boasting and dick swing-ing, Beau heard an unmistakable ticking.

Warren had a bad valve in his engine. That left two possibilities. He knew about it but thought it was an acceptable defect that could be overcome by the sheer power of his motor. Maybe he had a nitrous boost on it and didn't care about one funky valve. Or he didn't know it was bad and was just talking a lot of shit.

Beau nodded at Kelvin. His cousin had been milling through the crowd, trying to drum up a big money race. There had already been four contests, but no one was willing to put up more than $200. That wasn't gonna cut it. Beau needed at least a $1,000 bet. He needed someone who would look at the Duster and see an easy payday. Look at its stripped-down exterior and assume it was a pushover.

He needed an asshole like Warren Crocker.

Crocker had already won one race, but that had taken place before Beauregard and Kelvin arrived. Ideally, he would have liked to watch the man drive before he made the bet. See how he handled the wheel. How he navigated the cracked asphalt on this stretch of Route 83. But beggars can't be choosers. It had taken them an hour and a half to get out here, but they had come because Beauregard knew no one in Red Hill County would race him. Not in the Duster.

Kelvin moved in front of Warren as he was preening around his car. "My man over there got ten friends that say he can be doing 70 in second while you still trying to drag your ass out of first," he said. He let his booming voice fill the night. All the chatter ceased. The crickets and the whippoorwills were working themselves into a frenzy.

"Or is all you do is talk?" Beauregard asked.

"Oooooh shit," someone from the crowd that had gathered said. Warren stopped strutting and leaned on the roof of his car. He was tall and thin. His dark skin appeared blue in the glow of the moonlight.

"Well, that's a bold statement, motherfucker. You got the paper to back it up?" he said.

Beauregard pulled his wallet out and fanned ten $100 bills out like a deck of cards in his large hands.

"The question is, do you have the balls to back it up?" Kelvin said. He sounded like a Quiet Storm DJ. He grinned like a lunatic at Warren Crocker. Crocker tucked his tongue into the inside of his cheek.

Seconds ticked by and Beauregard felt a hollow opening blossom in his chest. He could see the gears working in Warren's head and for a moment he thought he was gonna pass. But Beauregard knew he wouldn't. How could he? He had talked himself into a corner and his pride wouldn't let him back down. Besides, the Duster didn't look that impressive. It was clean, and the body was free of rust, but the red candy apple paint was not showroom ready and the leather seats had a few rips and cracks.

"Alright. From here to the oak tree that's split down the middle. Sherm can hold the money. Unless you want to go for pinks?" Warren said.

"No. Let him hold the money. Who you want to call it?" Beauregard asked.

Sherm nodded at another guy. "Me and Jaymie will call it. You want your boy to go too?" he said. He squeaked when he talked.

"Yeah," Beauregard said. Kelvin, Sherm and Jaymie hopped in Sherm's car. A primer-covered Nova. They took off for the split tree a quarter mile down the road. Beauregard hadn't seen any other drivers since they arrived. Most people avoided this stretch and used the four-lane highway that snaked its way from the interstate up through Shepherd's Corner proper. Progress had left this part of town behind. It was abandoned just like the store. A blacktop wasteland haunted by the phantoms of the past.

He turned and got in the Duster. When he started the car, the engine sounded like a pride of angry lions. Vibrations traveled up from the motor through the steering wheel. He tapped the gas a few times. The lions became dragons. He flicked on the headlights. The double yellow line down the middle of the road came alive. He grabbed the gearshift and put it into first. Warren pulled out of the parking lot and Beauregard took a position next to him. One of the other guys that was in the crowd walked up and stood between them. He held his arm up and reached for the sky. Beauregard glanced at the stars and the moon again. Out of the corner of his eye, he saw Warren put on a seat belt. The Duster didn't have seat belts. His father used to say if they ever wrecked the only thing seat belts would do was make it hard for the undertaker to get them out the car.

"You ready?" the guy standing between them yelled.

Warren gave him a thumbs-up.

Beauregard nodded.

"ONE, TWO . . . THREE!" the guy screamed.

The secret ain't about the motor. That's part of it, yeah, but that ain't the main thing. The real thing, the thing most people don't want to talk about, is how you drive. If you drive like you scared, you gonna lose. If you drive like you don't want to have to rebuild the whole engine, you gonna lose. You gotta drive like don't nothing else matter except getting to that line. Drive like you fucking stole it.

Beauregard heard his Daddy's voice every time he drove the Duster. Sometimes he heard it when he was driving for crews. In those moments, it offered him bitter pearls of wisdom. Nonsensical chatter that reminded him not to end up like his Daddy. A ghost without a grave.

Beauregard slammed the gas pedal to the floor. Wheels spun, and white smoke plumed up from the rear of the Duster. G-forces pressed against his chest, crushing his sternum. Warren's car jumped off the line and the front two wheels left the road. Beauregard jammed the car into second as the Duster's front wheels grabbed the road like a pair of eagle's talons.

The trees on both sides of the road were shimmering blurs as he tore down through the night. He glanced at the speedometer. 70 mph.

Beauregard hit the clutch and shifted into third. There were no numbers on the gearshift knob. It was an old 8-ball his Daddy had fixed to fit on top of the shifter. He didn't need numbers. He knew what gear he was in by feel. By sound. The car shivered like a wolf shaking its pelt.

90 mph.

The leather-covered steering wheel crackled in his grip. He could see Sherm's car up ahead idling on the side of the road. He shifted into fourth gear. The motor went from a roar to the war cry of a god. The duals were the trumpets that heralded his arrival. He had the pedal flat against the floorboard. The car seemed to contort itself and leap forward like a snake about to strike. The speedometer hit 105 mph.

The Duster had passed Warren like he was mired in glue. The old bisected oak tree was rapidly receding in his side mirror. He could see Kelvin pumping both his fists in the rearview mirror. Beauregard popped the clutch and downshifted until he was back in first. He slowed down even more, executed a three-point turn and headed back to the old convenience store.

Beauregard pulled back into the parking lot with Warren right on his heels. A few minutes behind him were Sherm, Kelvin and Jaymie. Beauregard got out, walked around to the front of the car and leaned back against the hood.

"That old Duster got some get-up-and-go!" said a heavyset brother with a wide nose and beads of sweat gathering on his forehead. He was leaning against a black and white Maverick, Ford's answer to the Duster.

"Thanks," Beauregard said.

Sherm, Jaymie and Kelvin got out of the Nova. Kelvin trotted over to the Duster and held out his left hand. Beauregard slapped the palm without looking.

"You whupped his ass like a runaway slave," Kelvin said. A deep laugh erupted from his chest.

"That bad valve fucked him up. Look at that exhaust. He's burning oil," Beauregard said. A plume of black smoke was trailing from the exhaust of the Olds. Sherm came over and handed Beauregard two wads of money. His original thousand and Warren's roll.

"What you got under the hood on that thing?" Sherm asked.

"Two rockets and a comet," Kelvin said. Sherm chuckled.

Warren finally got out of the Oldsmobile. He stood by the car with his arms crossed. His face was twisted into a snarl. "You giving him my money after he jumped off the line?" he asked.

The boisterous crowd became deathly quiet. Beauregard didn't move off the hood, didn't look at Warren. His voice cut through the night like a razor.

"You saying I cheated?"

Warren uncrossed his arms, then crossed them again. He swiveled his large head on his thin neck.

"I'm just saying you was two lengths ahead before he got to three. That's all I'm saying," Warren said. He put his hands in the pockets of his baggy jeans. Then he took them out again. He didn't seem to know where to put them. His initial bravado was evaporating.

"I ain't gotta cheat to beat you. By the sound of that leaky valve, your motor gonna seize up tighter than virgin pussy any day now. Your driveshaft and rear end too heavy. That's why you pop up when you take off," Beauregard said. He pushed off the hood and turned to face Warren. Warren was peering at the night sky. He was studying his feet. He was doing everything except looking at Beauregard.

"Yo, man, you lost. Just take the L and admit the Olds ain't as legendary as you thought," Kelvin said. This elicited a few guffaws from the crowd. Warren shifted on the balls of his feet. Beauregard closed the distance between them in three strides.

"So why don't you tell me how I cheated again," he said.

Warren licked his lips. Beauregard wasn't as tall as he was, but he was twice as wide. All broad shoulders and wiry muscle. Warren took a step back. "I'm just saying," he said. His voice was as thin as crepe paper.

"You just saying. You just saying but you ain't saying shit," Beauregard said. Kelvin got between them.

"Come on, Bug, let's go. We got our money," he said.

"Not until he takes it back," Beauregard said. A few other drivers had crowded around them. Kelvin thought they were two seconds away from chanting "Fight! Fight!" like they were back in school.

"Yo, man, take it back," Kelvin said.

Warren twisted his head left and right. He wouldn't look directly at Beauregard or the crowd gathering around them. "Look, maybe I was wrong. I'm just saying—" he started to say but Beauregard held up his hand. Warren's mouth closed with an audible plop.

"Don't say 'you just saying' again. And don't say you was wrong. Take. It. Back," Beauregard said.

"Don't let him punk you, man!" someone yelled from the crowd.

Kelvin turned and faced Warren. He spoke in low tones. "Don't let these boys get your face fucked up. My cousin takes this shit seriously. Take it back and you can go home with all your teeth."

Beauregard had his hands down by his sides. He clenched and unclenched them at steady intervals. He watched Warren's eyes. They kept peering around like he was looking for a way out that didn't entail taking back what he said. Beauregard knew he wasn't going to take it back. He couldn't. Guys like Warren fed off their own arrogance. It was like oxygen for them. They couldn't back down any more than they could stop breathing.

Headlights lit up the parking lot. Then blue lights flashed off the weathered exterior of the SpeeDee Mart.

"Ah shit, it's the sex lights," Kelvin said. Beauregard saw a red unmarked cop car parking diagonally across the SpeeDee Mart exit. A few guys were walking slowly toward their cars. Most of them were just standing still.

"Sex lights?" the sweaty brother said.

"Yeah, cuz when you see them, you're fucked," Kelvin said. Two deputies got out of the car and pulled out their flashlights. Beauregard held up his hand to shield his eyes.

"So, what we got here, fellas? A little night racing? But I don't see no NASCAR signs. You see any NASCAR signs, Deputy Hall?" the deputy that wasn't Hall said. He was a blondish white guy with a chin so square he probably had to study geometry to learn how to shave.

"Nah, Deputy Jones, I don't see no NASCAR signs. Why don't you boys get out your IDs and have a seat on the pavement here?" Deputy Hall said.

"We ain't doing nothing but parking here, officer," the sweaty brother said. Deputy Jones whirled around. He dropped his hand to his gun.

"Did I ask you a goddamn thing? Get your ass on the ground. All of you get out your IDs and get on the ground." There were about twenty of them in the crowd and about fifteen cars. But they were all black and the two cops were white, and had guns. Everyone pulled out their wallets and sat down on the pavement. Beauregard sat on a sprig of scrub grass that had broken through the concrete. He grabbed his driver's license out of his wallet. The cops started at opposite ends and worked their way to the middle of the group.

"Anybody got any warrants? Child support, assault, shoplifting?" Deputy Hall asked. Beauregard tried to see what county they were from, but they kept the light in his eyes. Deputy Jones stopped in front of him.

"You got any warrants?" he asked as he took Beauregard's license. "No."

Deputy Jones shined the flashlight on Beauregard's license. There was a patch on the deputy's shoulder that said POLICE.

"What county you from?" Beauregard asked. Deputy Jones shone the flashlight's beam in Beauregard's face.

"Fuck You County, population of one," Deputy Jones said. He handed Beauregard his license. He turned and spoke into the radio on his shoulder. Deputy Hall was doing the same thing. The whip-poorwills and frogs and crickets had resumed their concert. Minutes ticked by as the two deputies conferred with whoever was on the other end of their radios.

"Alright, fellas, here's the deal. Some of you got warrants. Some of you don't. But that don't matter. We don't need y'all tearing up and down our roads here in Shepherd's Corner. So, we're gonna let you go on down the road. But to discourage you from coming back, we gonna get you to pay the racing tax," Deputy Hall said.

"What the hell is a racing tax?" the sweaty brother asked. Deputy Jones pulled out his gun and put the barrel against the sweaty brother's cheek. Beauregard felt his stomach tighten.

"Everything in your wallet, fat boy. Or do you want to be a victim of police brutality?" Deputy Jones asked.

"You heard the man. Empty your pockets, gents," Deputy Hall said. A soft breeze began to blow. The wind caressed Beauregard's face. The scent of honeysuckle traveled on that breeze. The deputies filed up and down the men sitting in a row and grabbed the money out of their hands. Deputy Jones came to Beauregard.

"Empty those pockets, son."

Beauregard looked up at him. "Take me in. Arrest me. But I ain't giving you my money."

Deputy Jones put his gun against Beauregard's cheek. The harsh smell of gun oil wafted up his nose and stuck to the back of his throat.

"Maybe you didn't hear what I said to your friend over there."

"He ain't my friend," Beauregard said.

"You want to catch a bullet? You trying to commit suicide by cop?" Deputy Jones said. His eyes glistened in the moonlight.

"No. I just ain't giving you my money," Beauregard said.

"Bug, let it go," Kelvin said. Deputy Jones shot him a glance. He pointed his gun at Kelvin.

"He's your friend, isn't he? You should listen, Bug," Deputy Jones said. He grinned, exposing a row of crooked brown teeth. Beauregard pulled out his roll of money and the one he had won from Warren. Deputy Jones snatched them out of his hands.

"Good boy," Deputy Jones said.

"Alright, fellas, go on and get out of here. And don't come back to

Shepherd's Corner," Deputy Hall said. Beauregard and Kelvin got up. The crowd dispersed amid a smattering of muffled complaints. The night was filled with the howl of Chargers and Chevelles and Mustangs and Impalas coming to life. Kelvin and Beauregard climbed into the Duster. The cops had moved, and cars were leaving as fast as they legally could. Warren was sitting in the Olds staring straight ahead.

"Move along, Warren," Deputy Hall said.

Warren rubbed his hands across his face. "It won't start," he mumbled.

"What?" Deputy Hall said.

Warren's hands flew away from his face. "It won't start!" he said. Kelvin laughed as he and Beauregard pulled out of the parking lot.

Beauregard turned left and headed down the narrow road.

"Interstate is that way," Kelvin said.

"Yeah. The town is this way. So are the bars," Beauregard said.

"How we getting a drink with no money?" Kelvin said.

Beauregard stopped and backed the Duster into the entrance of an old logging road. He killed the lights and let the car idle.

"Those weren't real cops. They didn't have no county insignia on their uniforms. And that gun was a .38. Cops haven't carried .38s for twenty fucking years. And they knew his name," Beauregard said.

"Motherfucker. We got played," Kelvin said. He punched the dashboard. Beauregard glared at him. Kelvin ran his hand over the dash, smoothing down the leather. "Shit, sorry, man. So, what we doing here?"

"Warren said his car wouldn't start. He the only one that stayed behind," Beauregard said.

"You think he was the snitch?"

"Ain't no snitch. He in with them. He stayed behind to get his cut. None of us was from here that was racing. I'm thinking somebody like Warren gonna want a drink to celebrate," Beauregard said.

"All that shit he was saying about you cheating was just a show."

Beauregard nodded. "Didn't want me to leave. Give his crew time to get there. He ran a few races to get people in. Probably was checking for how much money was on the table. Then when I dropped that grip, he texted them."

"Son of a bitch. Huh. Dr. King would be so proud. Whites and blacks working together," Kelvin said.

"Yeah," Beauregard said.

"You think he really coming this way? I mean he can't be that stupid, can he?" Kelvin asked.

Beauregard didn't speak. He drummed his fingers on the steering wheel. He figured not everything Warren had said and done was for show. He really was a conceited ass. Guys like that never think they can get caught. They always think they're one step ahead of everyone.

"I used to run into guys like him when I was driving for crews. He ain't from around here. He sounds like he from somewhere north of Richmond. Maybe Alexandria. Guys like that can't wait till they get home to celebrate. And he wants to celebrate. Cuz he thinks he won. He thinks he fooled us good. He wants to get to the nearest place that sells alcohol and get his drink on. He'll be by himself cuz his partners can't go walking around in their fake uniforms. He'll be in there talking big shit like he was before. He can't help himself."

"You really think so, don't you?" Kelvin said. Beauregard didn't answer. He couldn't go home without that money. A thousand wasn't enough to pay the rent but it beat a blank. His instincts told him that Warren was gonna go into town and get his drink on. He trusted his instincts. He had to.

Minutes ticked by and Kelvin checked his watch.

"Man, I don't think he—" Kelvin started to say. A car shot past them. A bright green paint job that sparkled in the moonlight.

"The legendary Olds," Beauregard said. He pulled out behind the Oldsmobile. They followed him through the flat plains and the gentle slopes of slight hills. The moonlight gave way to porch lamps and landscape lighting as they passed single-story houses and mobile homes. They sailed through a curve so sharp it could slice cheese and downtown Shepherd's Corner came into view. A collection of drab concrete and brick buildings illuminated by pale streetlamps. A library, a pharmacy and a restaurant lined the street. Near the end of the sidewalk was a wide brick building with a sign over the front door that said DINO'S BAR AND GRILL.

Warren turned right and drove around to the back of Dino's. Beauregard parked the Duster on the street. He reached into the back seat and grabbed a crescent wrench. No one was on the sidewalk or loitering outside Dino's front door. There were a few cars in front of the Duster. The deep tribal thump of a hip-hop beat seeped through Dino's walls.

"Stay here. You see anybody coming, hit the horn," Beauregard said.

"Don't kill him, man," Kelvin said. Beauregard didn't make any promises. He got out and hurried down the sidewalk and across Dino's parking lot. He stopped at the back corner of the building. Peeping around the corner he saw Warren standing next to the Oldsmobile. He was taking a piss. Beauregard ran across the parking lot. His footsteps were hidden by the music coming from the bar.

Warren started to turn just as Beauregard hit him with the wrench. He slammed the tool into Warren's trapezius muscle. Beauregard heard a wet crack like when his grandfather would snap chicken wings at the dinner table. Warren crumpled to the ground as piss sprayed across the side of the Oldsmobile. He rolled onto his side and Beauregard hit him again in his ribs. Warren rolled onto his back. A trickle of blood flowed out of his mouth and down his chin. Beauregard knelt beside him. He took the wrench and laid it across Warren's mouth like a gag. He gripped both ends of it and pressed down with all his weight. Warren's tongue squirmed around the handle of the wrench like a plump pink worm. Blood and spit ran from the sides of his mouth down his cheeks.

"I know you got my money. I know you and them rent-a-cops was working together. Y'all travel around setting up races and pop the fools who show up. None of that matters to me. I know you got my money. Now I'm going to move this wrench, and if you say anything about anything other than my money, I'm going to break your jaw in seven places," Beauregard said. He didn't yell, and he didn't scream. He straightened up and moved the wrench. Warren coughed and turned his head to the side. He spit a globule of pinkish saliva and it landed on his chin. He took a few deep gasps and more blood-spit flowed across his chin.

"My back pocket," he wheezed. Beauregard rolled him over and Warren wailed. It was a high animalistic moan. Beauregard thought he could hear the soft clicking of his shattered clavicle bones rubbing together. He pulled out a wad of cash. He flipped through it quickly.

"There's only 750. Where's my thousand? Where's yours? Where's the rest?" Beauregard asked.

"My . . . . mine was a dummy roll," Warren said.

"This is your cut," Beauregard said. Warren nodded weakly. Beauregard sucked his teeth. He stood and pocketed the money. Warren closed his eyes and swallowed hard.

Beauregard put the wrench in his back pocket and stomped on Warren's right ankle right at the joint. Warren screamed but there was no one around to hear except for Beauregard.

"Take it back," Beauregard said.

"What . . . what the fuck, man, you broke my fucking ankle."

"Take it back or I'll break the other one."

Warren rolled onto his back again. Beauregard saw dark patches that spread from his crotch to his knees. His dick was still hanging out of his pants like a bloodworm. The smell of piss wafted up Beauregard's nose.

"I take it back. You not a cheater, okay? Fuck, you not a cheater," he said. Beauregard saw tears slip from the corners of Warren's eyes.

"Alright then," Beauregard said. He nodded his head then turned and walked back to the Duster.

TWO

The motion-activated lights on the roof of the garage flicked on as Beauregard pulled up in front of the building. He stopped and let Kelvin hop out of the Duster to open one of the three roll-up doors. Beauregard swung the car around and backed it into the garage. Echoes from the motor reverberated through the cavernous interior. Beauregard shut off the car. He ran his wide, thick-fingered hands over his face. He twisted around in his seat and grabbed the wrench off the back seat. It still had Warren's blood and a bit of his skin on it. He'd have to soak it in water and bleach before putting it back in his toolbox.

He got out and headed for the office. A pale blue light flashed overhead from a flickering fluorescent fixture. He went to a mini-fridge behind his desk and grabbed two beers. He dropped the wrench on the desk. The sound of metal against metal clanged against his ears. Kelvin came in and sat down in a folding chair in front of the desk. Beauregard tossed him a beer. They opened them in unison and raised their bottles. Beauregard killed most of his beer in one loud gulp. Kelvin sipped his twice before putting it on the desk.

"Guess I'm gonna have to cuss Jerome the fuck out," Kelvin said. Beauregard finished his beer.

"Nah. It ain't his fault. Them boys probably go up and down the East Coast doing this shit," he said.

"It's still fucked up, though. I can ask around again. Maybe down in Raleigh? Or Charlotte?" Kelvin asked.

Beauregard shook his head. He finished his beer and tossed it in the trash can. "You know I can't go that far out. Not for some maybe money. Anyway, the rent is due by the twenty-third. I didn't really want to ask Phil for another extension. Not getting that contract with Davidson's construction company really put us in a bad spot," Beauregard said.

Kelvin sipped his beer. "You thought about talking to Boonie?" he asked.

Beauregard fell into his swivel chair. He put his boots up on the desk. "I've thought about it," he said.

Kelvin finished his beer. "All I'm saying is we been open three years and then Precision comes along and it's like people forgot we was here. Maybe Red Hill ain't big enough for two mechanic shops. Or at least not a black one," he said.

"I don't know. We was in the running for that Davidson's contract. Twenty years ago, we wouldn't even have been in the goddamn conversation. I just couldn't go as low as Precision," Beauregard said.

"That's why I'm saying you might want to talk to Boonie. Nothing too big. Just something to keep us afloat until . . . I don't know, until more people move to Red Hill who don't know how to change their oil," Kelvin said.

Beauregard picked up the wrench. He grabbed a rag from the pile sitting in a plastic bin next to his desk and began wiping the blood off it.

"I said I'm thinking about it."

"Alright, well, I'm gonna get up the road. Christy is off tonight and since Sasha is working I'm gonna go by and say heyyyyy," he said, singing the word "hey" until he hit a falsetto.

Beauregard smirked. "One of them girls is gonna cut your thing off and mail it to you," he said.

"Man, whatever. They gonna dip it in bronze and put that thing on a pedestal," Kelvin said as he rose from his chair. "Catch you in the morning?"

"Yeah," Beauregard said. He set the wrench down again. Kelvin gave him a two-finger salute and left through the office door. Beauregard swung around and planted his feet on the floor. 750. That was worse than having a grand. That's not even considering the gas it took to get out to Shepherd's Corner. Phil Dormer had told him last month that he wouldn't be able to give him another extension.

"Beau, I know times are tight right now. I get it. But my boss has told me we can't extend you any more credit or time on this loan. Look, maybe we can refinance it—"

"I'm only one year away from paying it off," Beauregard said. Phil frowned.

"Well, that's true but you're also technically three months behind. And per your loan agreement once you're 120 days behind the loan becomes delinquent. I don't want that to happen, Beau. Refinance and you'll have more years, but you won't lose the building," Phil had said. Beauregard heard what he was saying. He saw the pained look on his face. And in a perfect world, he would have believed that Phil really was concerned about his livelihood. The world was far from perfect. Beauregard knew that Phil was saying all the right words. He also knew that the lot he sat on was right next to a development. They were building Red Hill's first fast food restaurant. The old Tastee Freez didn't count. They had closed ten years ago. They were never fast but they had made one hell of a milkshake.

Beauregard got up and put the keys to the Duster on the hook in the corkboard and grabbed the keys to his truck. He locked up the garage and headed home.

The sun was just peeking over the horizon as he backed into the street. Beauregard drove past the municipal offices of Red Hill County out to the wide-open fields. He always thought it was funny a county with "hill" in its name had a terrible paucity of actual hills. He passed Grove Lane. His daughter lived down there. The sky was streaked with gold and red as he turned down Market Drive. Two more turns down two more side roads and he was pulling down the dirt lane to his double-wide.

Beauregard parked next to Kia's little blue two-door Honda. He never drove the thing, he just kept it running. He was an American Muscle kind of guy. The house was quiet as he stepped up onto the porch. He made his way through the rectangular house, passing the room where his sons slept. The sun spilled through the blinds as rays of light filled the double-wide. His and Kia's room was at the end of the trailer. Beauregard slipped into the room and sat down on the foot of their bed. Kia was sprawled across it like a piece of origami art. Beauregard touched her soft, exposed thigh. Her caramel-colored leg twitched. She didn't turn over but spoke to him with her face still buried in her pillow.

"How'd it go?" she mumbled into the pillow.

"I won but the guy didn't want to pay. It got a little messy."

She turned over then. "What you mean he ain't wanna pay? What kind of shit is that?" she asked.

She was propped up on one elbow. The sheet that had barely covered her had fallen away. Her hair was sticking off her head in strange geometric patterns. Beauregard kneaded the flesh on her thigh.

"You didn't get arrested, did you?" she asked.

Yeah, by some fake-ass cops, he thought.

He took his hand off her leg. "No, but the guy, he didn't have all the money he said he had. The whole thing was messed up. I'm still 800 short," he said. He let it sit there between them for a while. Kia pulled the sheet up and drew her knees up to her chest.

"What about that contract to work on them trucks from the construction company?" she asked. Beauregard moved closer to her. His shoulder brushed against hers.

"We didn't get it. Precision got the contract. And then we had to get those glasses for Darren. And last month I had to give Janice money for Ariel's cap and gown. It's been a slow couple of months," Beauregard said. Actually, it had been a slow year. Kia knew this, but neither one of them liked saying it out loud.

"Can we get an extension?" she asked. Beauregard stretched out beside her. She didn't lie back but instead wrapped her arms around her knees and squeezed them. Beauregard stared up at the ceiling. The fan spun on a shaky axis. The globe on the light of the ceiling fan had the image of a Rottweiler.

They'd had that damn fan for five years and it never failed to give him the creeps. But Kia loved the damn thing. One thing he'd learned about marriage was that a novelty fan was not the hill you wanted to die on if you could help it.

"I don't know," he said. She ran a hand through her tousled hair. A few minutes went by and then she lay back against Beauregard. Her skin was cool to the touch and smelled like roses. She had showered before bed. He snaked one arm around her midsection and laid his hand on her belly.

"What if we can't get an extension?" Kia asked.

Beauregard stroked her belly. "I might have to sell something. Maybe the hydraulic lift. Or the second tire-changing machine. Which is why I got the damn loan in the first place," he said. He didn't mention going to talk to his Uncle Boonie.

Almost as if on cue, Kia turned on her side and touched his face.

"You thinking about it, ain't you?" she asked.

"Thinking about what?"

"Going to Boonie. Looking for a job. You know that's not an option, right? You were blessed. We all was. You never got caught and you got out and you opened the garage. That's a blessing, baby," she said. Her light eyes searched his dark ones. They'd been together since he was nineteen and she was eighteen. Married since they both were twenty-three. Almost fifteen years together. She knew him about as well as anyone did.

A lot of couples liked to say they couldn't lie to each other. That their partner could spot their falsehoods from a mile away. That line of thinking was a one-way street between him and Kia. He knew when she had gone out drinking with her girls. He knew when she had eaten the last chocolate chip cookie. Her face was an open book and he had read every page a long time ago. He hated lying to her, but the ease with which he could do it never failed to shock him. Then again, he did have a lot of practice with mendacity.

"No. I'm not thinking of it. Did it cross my mind? Yeah. Just like buying a lottery ticket crossed my mind," he said. He hugged her close to him and closed his eyes.

"It's gonna be alright. I'll figure out something," he said.

"I got a call from the dentist yesterday. Javon might need braces," she said. Beauregard squeezed her tight but didn't say anything.

"What are we gonna do, baby? I can try to pick up some extra shifts at the hotel," she said.

"That ain't gonna buy braces," he said. Silence enveloped them both. Then Kia cleared her throat.

"You know you could sell—" But Beauregard cut her off midsentence.

"The Duster ain't for sale," he said. Kia laid her head on his chest. He slipped his arm around her shoulders and watched the blades on the ceiling fan spin until he drifted off to sleep.

"Daddy. Daddy. Daddy."

Beauregard opened his eyes. It seemed like he had just closed them five seconds ago. Darren was standing by the bed. He was holding his favorite toy. A twelve-inch-tall Batman action figure. His tiny brown hand gripped the Caped Crusader in one hand and a rapidly disintegrating biscuit in the other.

"Hey, Stink," Beauregard said. His youngest got Kia's eyes and his complexion. Powerful green eyes that contrasted with his dark chocolate skin.

"Mama say come get your food before she gotta take us to Aunt Jean," Darren said. A smile flickered across his lips. Beauregard figured Kia had used colorful language when she had instructed Darren to wake him. Whenever anyone cursed, Darren was overcome with the giggles. They didn't subside quickly either. Judging by the slight grin on his son's face, Kia had probably cussed him out nearly an hour ago.

"I guess I better get my ass up then," Beauregard said. Darren exploded in a shower of giggles. Beauregard hopped out of bed and grabbed Darren around the waist. He hoisted the boy off the ground and headed for the kitchen, making airplane noises as he went.

"Bout time you get your ass up," Kia said, but there was no malice behind it. It was more for Darren's benefit than anything else. Darren howled with laughter again.

"Oooooh, you said bad words," Darren whimpered between deep breaths. "You going down there!" he exclaimed. Javon was sitting at the small table, lost in his ear buds. Beauregard thought Javon could have passed for his twin when he was that age. Slim and tall with sleepy eyes. He put Darren down and gently plucked Javon on the ear. Javon snapped his head up and pulled out his ear buds.

"Good morning to you too," Beauregard said.

"Y'all finish your biscuits so we can go to Aunt Jean's," Kia said. Beauregard grabbed a biscuit and dipped it in the gravy that was in a bowl on the table. He plopped the whole thing in his mouth.

"I knew I married you for some reason," he said through a mouthful of bread. Kia snorted.

"It wasn't the biscuits," she said as she slipped by him to put her plate in the sink. He saw her in his mind as the young girl she had been when they first met. She had been dancing on the hood of Kelvin's car to a funky go-go song. Her wild hair in braids and wearing a black jumper with a white T-shirt. They had all been hanging out at the basketball court in the park near the high school. He had been a teenage ex–juvenile detainee with a two-year-old daughter. She had been an eighteen-year-old high school senior. Three weeks later, they were exchanging promise rings. Four years later, they were married and expecting Javon.

"Can I go to the shop with you today?" Javon asked. Beauregard and Kia exchanged a glance.

"Not today," Beauregard said. A long time ago, when he had worked in a different industry, he had taken great pains to make sure his private and professional lives never shared the same space. He didn't want that world to touch his family. He didn't want it to sully them with its filth. He was three years removed from that place, but he knew it still had teeth. He didn't want it to reach out and bite his boys or Kia. He kept them away from the shop just in case someone from that world came knocking.

Javon popped in his ear buds and got up from the table. He went and stood by the door. Beauregard knew the boy wanted to hang out with him. He liked cars and he was good with his hands. He hoped Javon would still be interested in cars by the time it was safe enough for him to come by the garage.

"Come on, Darren, let's go," Kia said. She stood on her tiptoes and kissed Beauregard on the lips. He could taste peppermint on her breath. He slipped an arm around her waist and returned her kiss tenfold.

"Eww," Darren said. He stuck his tongue out and rolled his eyes.

"Watch your mouth, boy," Kia said after she had pulled away from Beauregard.

"I'll call you on your lunch break," Beauregard said.

"You better," she said. She and the boys left. School was out, and Kia worked the ten-to-six shift at the Comfort Inn over in Gloucester. Javon wasn't quite old enough to watch out for himself and his little brother, so while Beauregard and Kia were working, she took the boys to her sister's place. Jean Brooks ran a hair salon from the back of her house. The boys got to play with their cousins the way Beauregard used to play with Kelvin and his brother Kaden at his Aunt Mara's house. Kaden had been dead for seven years. He'd been murdered when he was just twenty-three years old in a motel robbery. Word on the street had been that it had been a setup. Kaden and his buddy had been lured to a motel in Church Hill by some party girls they had met in the club. Church Hill was one of the roughest neighborhoods in the city of Richmond. It was so bad the postal service had stopped delivering mail there. They had gone there expecting some casual sex and some bomb-ass weed. What they had gotten were two bullets to the head and a closed-casket funeral.

When Kelvin and Beauregard had found the two guys that had popped Kaden and his friend, they had tried to shift blame to the girls. Then they had blamed each other. Finally, they had cried for their mothers.

Beauregard slipped out of his underwear and padded down to the bathroom. He was going to take a shower and head to the garage after making a few stops. As he turned on the water, he heard a chirping coming from the bedroom. It was his cell phone. Kia had taken it out of his pants and put it on the nightstand. He ran to the room and picked it up off the nightstand's scarred surface. He recognized the number.

"Hello," he said.

"Hello, is this Mr. Beauregard Montage?" a slightly nasal voice asked.

"Yes, it is, Mrs. Talbot," he said.

"Hello, Mr. Montage. It's Gloria Talbot at Lake Castor Convalescent Home," she said.

"I know," Beauregard said.

"Oh yes, I'm sorry. Mr. Montage, I'm afraid we have a problem with your mother," Mrs. Talbot said.

"Has she verbally abused another aide?" he asked.

"No, it's—"

"Has she peed on someone on purpose again?" he asked.

"No, it's nothing like—"

"Did she call 10 On Your Side again and tell them the staff was beating her?" he asked.

"No, no, Mr. Montage, it's not her behavior . . . this time. It appears there is a problem with her Medicaid paperwork. We were hoping you could come by in the next few days to discuss it," Mrs. Talbot said.

"What kind of problem?"

"I think it's best if we discuss it face to face, Mr. Montage."

Beauregard closed his eyes and took a deep breath.

"Okay, I can come in a few hours," he said.

"That would be fine, Mr. Montage. We will see you then. Goodbye," Mrs. Talbot said. The line went dead.

After his shower, he put on fresh jeans and a button-down short-sleeve shirt with his name over the breast pocket and MONTAGE MOTORS over the other. He made himself a cup of coffee and stood in front of the sink taking quick sips. The house was as quiet as it ever got. Through the window over the sink he could see his backyard. A wooden shed to the right and a basketball hoop to the left. Their property went back into the woods for nearly two hundred yards. Two does were walking across the yard. They stopped every few moments to nibble at the grass. It was so quiet around the house this time of day that the does didn't seem skittish. They were taking their time, like shoppers at a flea market.

Beauregard finished his coffee. Once upon a time, he had dreamed of living in a house like this one. A house with running water and a roof that didn't leak like a sieve. A house where everyone had their own room and there wasn't a slop bucket in the corner. He put the coffee cup in the sink. He didn't know what was sadder. That his dreams had been so modest or that they had been so prophetic. That was in the days before his father had disappeared. Seeing him again had taken over the top spot on his wish list. But after all these years, he had learned to accept that some dreams don't come true.

He grabbed his keys and his phone and walked out of the house. It was only ten and it was already as hot as hell. When he stepped off the porch, he could feel the sun beating down on him like he owed it money. He hopped in his truck and revved up the engine to get the AC cranking. He backed up, turned around and drove down the driveway, leaving a cloud of dust in his wake.

He hit the main highway, but instead of turning left toward the garage, he turned right toward the outskirts of town. He cut through Trader Lane and drove past the desiccated husks of several deserted houses. A little bit farther up the road, he passed the abandoned Clover Hill Industrial Park. Years ago, the Powers That Be of Red Hill County tried to reinvent the former farming community as a mecca for manufacturing. They offered fat tax breaks to the corporations, and in turn the corporations offered the town hundreds of jobs. For a while it was a mutually beneficial relationship. Right up until the 2008 recession hit. This was right about the same time the corporations realized they could ship their plants overseas and cut expenses by half while doubling profits.

The empty buildings stood like forgotten monoliths to a lost civilization. The ice plant, the insulation plant, the flag factory and the elastic plant were hardly discernible anymore. Mother Nature was reclaiming her land with steady, implacable persistence. The pine trees and the dogwoods and the honeysuckle and the kudzu were slowly but surely enveloping the old buildings in an arboreal embrace. Beauregard's mother had worked at the elastic plant from the time it opened until its untimely demise. Which just happened to be two years before her retirement, but only a week after she had been diagnosed with breast cancer. A month later, he had taken his first job. Boonie had set him up with a crew out of Philly who needed a driver. Since he had been the new guy, his cut had only been five grand. That was the going rate, or so they had told him. He had only been seventeen so he didn't really question it. That was a mistake. He would learn that the going rate was a full share or nothing at all. He didn't really dwell on it too much. A mistake is a lesson, unless you make the same mistake twice.

As he got closer to the county line, fields of corn and beans began to dominate the landscape. Residential encroachment hadn't yet reached this part of town. Eventually some enterprising developer would drop a dozen or so narrow rectangular boxes out here and call it a trailer court.

He rolled through a narrow curve and spotted the sign. A five-foot-wide saw blade attached to a three-foot-tall metal pole. RED HILL METALS was spelled out on the sign with sections of rebar painted bright red. The saw blade had been painted white, but the paint was peeling like a bad sunburn. Beauregard turned down the gravel driveway. The driveway was buffeted on both sides by enormous blue and white hydrangeas. At the end of the driveway was a set of fifteen-foot-tall chain-link gates. As Beauregard approached, the gates began to roll on large metal caster wheels. Boonie had attached a motion sensor to the gate a few years ago. He'd gotten tired of having to stop working every time someone pulled up with their mama's old wood stove. Rusted razor wire topped the gate and the equally tall fence that was attached to it. Two dark-skinned men nodded at Beauregard as he drove past them. They were both wielding massive reciprocating saws. A mangled AMC Gremlin appeared to be their intended target.

Beauregard drove over the ten-foot-wide scale that was embedded in the ground, took a hard left and parked in front of the main office. He got out of the truck and immediately started sweating. The heat had gone from volcano to Hell in the span of twenty minutes. Metallic screams of agony filled the air as the two compactors crushed cars, trucks and the occasional washing machine. Cubes of steel and iron were stacked across the yard like giant dominoes. A graveyard of vehicles rose up from behind the office building as they waited their turn in the maw of Chompy Number One and Chompy Number Two. Kaden had named them on a summer day long ago.

Beauregard's Daddy had taken him, Kaden and Kelvin out riding in the Duster that day. "Gotta go see ya Uncle Boonie for a minute, then we can go to the Tastee Freez. Y'all want some whiskey with your milkshakes?" his father had asked with a wink.

"Yeah!" Kelvin had spoken up. Of course it was Kelvin. He had even raised his hand.

Beauregard's father had laughed so hard he had started coughing.

"Boy, your Mama would have both our asses in a sling. Maybe in a few years."

When they had pulled into the yard the three of them had leaned over the front seat to watch the belching, groaning claw crane drop a car into the crusher. It tumbled trunk over hood before slamming into the compactor.

"Chompy Number One, finish him!" Kaden had howled. Beauregard's Daddy had told Boonie and the names had stuck. They'd never had that shot of whiskey, though.

The word "OFFICE" was spelled out on the door using lengths of copper tubing. Beauregard knocked three times on the door in quick succession. You never knew what kind of business was being conducted in there, so it was best to knock.

"Come on in," a raspy voice said. Boonie was sitting behind his desk. A slab of iron on four wide metal cylinders. A ragged AC wheezed from the window over his shoulder. It was making more noise than cool air. A smattering of file cabinets and shelves ran along the walls. Boonie smiled.

"Bug! How the hell you doing? Boy, I ain't seen you in what? Six months? A year?" Boonie said.

"Ain't been that long. Just been busy at the shop."

"Aw, I'm just fucking with you, boy. I know you working your ass off over there. I ain't mad atcha. I just . . . just seems like you ain't around like you used to be," Boonie said. He took off his oil-stained baseball cap and fanned himself. His iron gray flattop contrasted with his coal black skin.

"I know. How things been around here?"

"Aw, ya know. Steady. People never run out of junk."

Beauregard sat down in a folding chair next to the desk. "Yeah, always got shit to throw away."

"How you been? How's Kia and the boys?"

"They alright. Darren had to get some glasses and now Javon

gotta have some special kind of braces. Kia doing alright. Coming up on five years at the hotel. Anything else going on?" he said.

Boonie replaced his hat and cocked his head at Beauregard. "You asking?" he said.

Beauregard nodded his head.

"Not that I ain't glad to see you cuz you know I am, but I thought you was done," Boonie said.

"I've just hit a rough patch. Things been kind of tough ever since Precision opened up," Beauregard said.

Boonie entwined his fingers and laid them on his prodigious belly.

"Well, I wish I had something, but things have really dried up these last few years. The Italians got pushed out by the Russians, and the Russians only using their own crews. Shit, Bug, it's been real quiet. Them Russians coming through sounding like Ivan Koloff trying to be all scary and shit," Boonie said. He made a face like he had bitten into a rotten apple.

Beauregard let his hands hang between his knees and lowered his head.

"You ever thought about going out West? I hear there's still some work out that way for a fella who know his way around a steering wheel."

Beauregard grunted. "My Daddy went out West and didn't never come back," he said.

Boonie sighed. "Your Daddy . . . your Daddy was one of a kind. I only seen two other men who could handle a car under the hood or behind the wheel like Ant Montage. You one of them. The other one is locked up in Mecklenburg. Your Daddy was as good a driver as he was a friend. And he was a damn good driver," Boonie said. He pushed his baseball cap back on his head and stared at the aluminum beams in the ceiling.

Beauregard knew he was seeing it in his mind. Seeing him and his father flying down the road moving moonshine or speeding away from a bank robbery on the streets of Philadelphia, hooting and hollering all the way.

"You still think he might come back?" Beauregard said.

"Huh?"

"Daddy. You still think he might show up on my doorstep one day? Carrying a basketball and bottle of Jack so we can go catch up," Beauregard said.

Boonie blew some air between his full lips. "Men like your Daddy, like me, like you used to be, we don't die in hospital beds. Ant wasn't perfect. He loved driving, drinking, and women, in that order. He lived life at 100 miles per hour. Men like that, well, they go out on their own terms, usually with a bang. But I tell you what, if he did go out that way, you can bet your ass he took some boys with him. You look so much like him. It's like he spit you out. But you different. Your Daddy, he just won't the settling down type. That made things hard for him and your Mama. How is Ella these days?"

"She doing. She over at the nursing home. Her cancer done slowed down but she still smoking like she got a bad ring in her engine," Beauregard said.

"Damn. That cancer, boy, it just takes 'em down inch by inch. Louise went down so fast. Doctor told her she had it in March, she was gone by September. How long your Mama had it?" Boonie asked.

"Since '95." Beauregard said. He thought his mother was going to outlive them all. Unlike Mrs. Boonie, she was too mean to die.

"Ella was always tough as shoe leather," Boonie said. He smiled at his own joke.

"Well, I guess I should get on down the road, Boonie." Beauregard stood.

"Hey, hold up, let's have a drink real quick," Boonie said. He swiveled in his chair and grabbed a mason jar out of one of the drawers in the filing cabinet directly behind him.

"It's 11 o'clock."

Boonie unscrewed the lid. Two shot glasses had magically

appeared on the desk as well. "Hey, like Alan Jackson says, it's five o'clock somewhere. I'm sure glad we been able to catch up," Boonie said.

He filled both glasses. Beauregard picked up a glass and clinked it against the one Boonie was holding. The shine was smooth as the glass it was held in. A warm tingle wound its way down his throat.

"Alright. Well, keep me in mind if you hear anything," Beauregard said.

"You sure?" Boonie asked.

"What?"

Boonie put the mason jar back in the drawer.

"Just saying maybe it's a good thing I ain't got nothing. Like I said, you different from your Daddy. You don't live for this. It ain't all you got," he said.

Beauregard knew Boonie meant well. Nowadays he was a connect. A guy who could put you in touch with some other guys. He also hired out Chompy One and Two as garbage disposals. They disposed of the kind of garbage that bled and cried for its mama before it died. He was the guy who could help you move your loot without charging an exorbitant finder's fee. He was also Beauregard's de facto godfather. Boonie had helped him refurbish the Duster. He'd given Kia away at their wedding because her father was doing twenty to life in Coldwater for killing her mother. Boonie was the third person to hold Javon when he was born. Boonie did all the things Anthony Montage should have done. So Beauregard knew he meant well. But Boonie didn't have a daughter graduating from summer school next month. He didn't have two sons who seemed to grow six inches every night. Or a wife who wanted a house with a foundation before she died. Or a business that was one month from going under.

"Yeah, I'm sure," he said.

He left.

THREE

Kelvin rolled up to the shop around eleven. Bug wasn't there yet, so he went across the street to the 7-Eleven and got a chicken salad sandwich and a soda. He slipped into a weathered booth and ate his sandwich and sipped his soda. Most 7-Elevens didn't have a place to eat but this one had once been a diner. When the Egyptian family that owned the 7-Eleven bought the building they had kept the booths. It was a scorcher today. Not for the first time, he contemplated cutting off his braids. But he knew he had an odd-shaped head with a few too many indentations to rock the bald look. By the time he finished his food, Bug still hadn't arrived, so he walked back across the road and opened up the garage. They had a transmission to put in for Lulu Morris that was going to be a bitch. Shane Helton had dropped his truck off complaining of a shimmy in the steering column. Kelvin thought it might be the rack and pinion. Bug was of the opinion it was just the velocity boot on the driver side. Bug was probably right, but a velocity boot was only 300 bucks. A rack and pinion was at least 1500.

He hoped to God it was the rack and pinion.

Kelvin raised the three garage doors on the three repair bays and turned on the overhead air handler. Whistling, he drove Shane's truck onto the hydraulic lift. As he was hopping out, he saw a faded blue Toyota pull up to the first bay door. The car stopped and a short thin white man got out and walked into the garage. He stopped just in front of the tire changer. He had longish brown hair and a scraggly brown beard. His muddy brown eyes darted from side to side.

"Beauregard?" he asked with an inquisitive inflection at the end.

"Nah, I'm Kelvin. He ain't in yet. Can I help you with something?" The man licked his dry lips.

"I really need to talk to Beauregard," he said.

"Well, as he ain't here can I help you?" Kelvin asked.

The man ran his hand through his hair. He stepped a little closer to Kelvin. He smelled like cigarettes and old sweat.

"Just tell him my brother Ronnie is looking for him. Wants to talk to him, patch things up, maybe have some work for him," the man said.

"Ronnie who?" Kelvin asked.

"Ronnie Sessions. He know him. They used to work together," the man said.

Kelvin sighed. He knew who Ronnie Sessions was, or at least he had heard the name. Ronnie was a crazy-ass good ol' boy from Queen County down on the back heel of the state. Ronnie was known for two things: his twenty-three Elvis tattoos, and stealing anything that wasn't nailed down with titanium fasteners. Last Kelvin had heard, Ronnie was doing five years up in Coldwater on a burglary charge. Robbed a marina or something. This was after he screwed Beauregard over on a job.

Bug had not been pleased.

So Kelvin couldn't imagine why in the hell Ronnie wanted to be within one hundred feet of Bug. Let alone tell him he was back in town. Maybe he had a fetish for getting his teeth kicked down his throat.

"Alright, I'll tell him," Kelvin said. Ronnie's brother nodded his head up and down rapidly then turned and headed for his car. He stopped halfway and turned back around.

"Hey, you wouldn't be holding, would you?" he asked.

"Why would you think I'm holding? Because I'm black?" Kelvin asked.

The man frowned. "Nah. It's just most everybody in Red Hill be holding. I was just asking," he said. He got in his car and slammed the door. He tried to spin his tires on the gravel but the car stalled. He started it again and eased out of the parking lot.

Kelvin chuckled. He hit the "up" button on the lift and raised Shane's truck until he could walk under without ducking. "He gonna spin tires like I offended him. Motherfuckers will look high and low for a reason to feel disrespected," he muttered as he began inspecting the undercarriage of the truck.

The Lake Castor Convalescent Home took great pains to not look like a nursing home. The front of the building had an elaborate brick portico that covered the automatic doors at the entrance. Lush green boxwood shrubs that appeared to have been trimmed with lasers lined the sidewalk like verdant sentries. The brick carport had a pair of flying buttresses at each end. The whole campus seemed more like a small community college with a decent alumni organization than a nursing home. Beauregard stepped through the automatic doors and was smacked in the face by the pungent scent of urine. All that fancy architecture couldn't do anything about the smell of piss.

A blond receptionist smiled at him as he entered the building. He didn't return it.

"Hello, sir, can I help?" she asked.

"I'm going to see Mrs. Talbot," he said without breaking his stride. He was intimately familiar with the patient coordinator's office. He had hoped that putting his mother in the nursing home might make his life just a tiny bit easier. She could yell at the staff not putting her drink on a coaster or being too rough wiping her ass. The fact that she only had one coaster or that her hemorrhoids were inflamed never seemed to cross her mind. Instead putting her in the home made her meaner and in turn made his life harder. In the two years she had been in Lake Castor, he had been called in for corrective-action meetings at least thirty times.

Ella Montage was not a model patient.

In the beginning, he had smoothed things over with an extra payment here or donating a piece of equipment there. A few times he had even straight up handed the administrator an envelope. The money had been rolling in and he had still had some savings from the jobs he had worked. Those days were long over now. He wondered if this was the day they finally rolled his mother out to that lovely exposed aggregate sidewalk and told him to take her. He could see the administrator telling him she didn't have to go home but she had to get the hell out of there.

He knocked on Mrs. Talbot's door then checked his watch. Almost noon. Kelvin was probably already at work but it would take two of them to get Lulu's transmission out.

"Please come in," Mrs. Talbot said. Beauregard did as he was told. The slim and neat woman sat at a glass-top desk. She had her hair pulled back in a severe bun with a pair of decorative chopsticks jutting out of the back of her head. She stood and extended her hand.

"Mr. Montage."

Beauregard gripped her hand lightly and shook it.

"Mrs. Talbot."

She gestured toward the chair and Beauregard sat down. It struck him how many times his life had been changed by sitting across from someone at a desk.

"Mr. Montage, I am glad you could come in today to discuss this issue," Mrs. Talbot said.

"You didn't make it sound like I had much of a choice."

Mrs. Talbot pursed her lips. "Mr. Montage, I'll get right to the point. There is a discrepancy with your mother's Medicaid coverage."

"No, there isn't," he said.

Mrs. Talbot blinked a few times. "I'm sorry?" she said.

Beauregard shifted in his seat. "You said there's a discrepancy.

That makes it sound like some books ain't adding up. My Mama's Medicaid ain't got no discrepancy. Now is there something wrong with her coverage?" he asked.

Mrs. Talbot's face reddened and she leaned forward in her chair. Beauregard knew that he sounded like an asshole, but he didn't like the way she had framed the situation. Mrs. Talbot didn't like his mother and Beauregard couldn't really say he blamed her. At the same time, it was no need to make it sound like his mother was a thief. Cruel, insensitive, manipulative, yes. Thief, no. The Montage men held down the thievery crown in his family.

"I'm sorry, I used a poor choice of words. Let me phrase it this way. Your mother kept up a life insurance policy that she didn't declare when she entered the facility that now puts her over the asset limit for Medicaid assistance," Mrs. Talbot said.

Beauregard's mouth went dry. "Can't she just cancel it? Or cash it out?"

Mrs. Talbot pursed her lips again. "Well, she can cash it out but it's only fifteen thousand dollars. The discrep—um, the mistake was noted by Medicaid two months ago. They immediately ceased subsidizing her care. As it stands now, she has an outstanding balance of . . ." She touched a tablet sitting on her desk. "Forty-eight thousand three hundred and sixty dollars. She could cash out but that would leave her owing—"

"Thirty-three thousand three hundred and sixty," Beauregard said.

Mrs. Talbot blinked hard. "Yes. The facility is requesting that payment in full by the end of next month. If you and your family can't find the resources to pay the outstanding debt, Mrs. Montage will have to leave the facility. I'm sorry," she said. She didn't sound sorry to Beauregard. She sounded positively delighted.

"Do you know if my mother has agreed to cancel the policy?" he asked. His mouth was so dry he felt like he could spit sand.

"She has been made aware of the situation, but she insists this is an inheritance for her grandchildren," Mrs. Talbot said. The arch of her eyebrows told him she didn't believe that any more than he did. His mother tolerated her grandchildren. No, that policy was all about control. His mother reveled in being in control. Whether it was not allowing him to get his license unless he broke up with Ariel's mom or holding on to a life insurance policy, Ella Montage liked having leverage. She might quote the Bible from time to time but that was her religion.

"Let me go talk to her. Could you print me something with the date the money has to be paid on it and I'll pick it up on my way out," he said.

"Of course, Mr. Montage. If you like, I could also print you up a list of nearby facilities and their waiting lists."

"Yeah, sure," he said. He didn't need to see a list of other places. If his mother got kicked out of here, she would probably be dead before a bed opened up somewhere else.

Beauregard got up and headed for his mother's room. As he walked down the hallway, he thought about what Boonie had said. A quiet, dignified death in one of these dimly lit rooms didn't seem so bad. That is, until you realized that no death is dignified. It's a messy process. The Grim Reaper sneaks up behind you and squeezes you until shit fills your adult diaper and an artery bursts in your chest. He works his bony fingers in your guts and makes your own cells eat you alive from the inside. He skull fucks you until your brain retreats inside itself and you forget how to even breathe. He guides the hand of a man you've wronged and aims his gun at your face. There is no dignity in death. Beauregard had seen enough people die to realize that. There's only fear and confusion and pain.

The door to his mother's room was open wide. A CNA was standing next to the bed. He heard his mother's three-pack-a-day voice loud and clear. The CNA could too, and by the way her neck and shoulders were knotted up, she didn't like what she was hearing.

"I've been pushing that 'call' button for forty-five minutes. You girls up there with ya nose buried in a phone while I'm sitting in piss. I've pissed myself. Do you know how that feels? Do you understand that? I'm sitting here in a puddle of piss." She paused to take a deep hit of oxygen from her nasal cannula. "No, you don't, but don't worry, one day you will. You all cute and pretty now but one day you gonna be right here like I am and I hope somebody lets you sit in your own piss like your privates in a stew," she said.

"I'm sorry, Mrs. Montage. We just so short-staffed today," the CNA said. She sounded genuinely apologetic. That was a mistake. Ella was like a lioness on the Serengeti. She could sense weakness.

"Oh, I'm sorry, chile. You're short-staffed. I'll try to die more quietly," Ella said.

The CNA made a wet strangled noise and rushed out of the room. She brushed past Beauregard mumbling to herself. He caught the words "miserable" and "witch."

"Hey, Mama," Beauregard said. He stepped just inside the door.

Ella appraised him from top to bottom with a gentle flick of her eyes. "You getting skinny. I never thought that girl knew how to cook," she said.

"Kia cooks just fine, Mama. How you feeling?"

"Ha! I'm dying. Other than that, I'm feeling great," she said.

Beauregard inched farther into the room. "You ain't going nowhere," he said.

"Get my cigarettes out that drawer," she said.

"Mama, you don't need them cigarettes. Didn't you just say you was dying?"

"Yeah, so a cigarette ain't gonna hurt nothing," Ella said.

"Have you been smoking with your oxygen on? You know you could blow this place up, right?" Beauregard asked.

His mother shrugged. "I probably be doing most of the people here a favor," she said. Beauregard had to chuckle at that one. That was the thing about his mother. She could be emotionally manipulative one minute then making you laugh the next. It was like getting hit in the face with a pie that had a padlock in it. When he was a kid, she had combined that acerbic wit with her looks to pretty much get whatever she wanted. All children think their mother is beautiful, but Beauregard had noticed fairly early on that other people thought his mother was beautiful too. Long coal black hair like an oil slick ran down her back to her waist. Skin the color of coffee with too much cream told the story of her varied ancestry. Her light gray irises gave her almond-shaped eyes an otherworldly appearance.

Cashiers always seemed to have extra change if she was short at the grocery store. Cops always seemed to give her a warning even if she was doing the speed of light through a school zone. People always seemed to want to do what Ella Montage told them to do. Even if she was telling them to go fuck themselves. Everybody except his Daddy. She once told him that his father was the only man to ever put her in her place.

"I loved him for it. Hated him too," she would say between puffs on her omnipresent dark brown More cigarette. He could remember sitting on her lap as she told him over and over again how they met. He never got fairy tales as a kid. He got Sturm and Drang epics set against the backdrop of sultry country nights. Eventually he realized his mother considered it some kind of weird therapy. She had her very own captive eight-year-old psychologist.

The cancer and its subsequent treatments had taken her hair first. She wore a black scarf now. Then it withered her skin. The stoma in her throat stared at him like the mouth of some strange parasite. A lamprey eel that was trying to crawl out of her neck. Only the gray eyes remained untouched. So light they sometimes appeared blue. Smart eyes that never forgot anything they ever saw. And they never let you forget it either.

"Mama, why didn't you tell me about this policy?"

Ella fixed those cool eyes on him. "Because it wasn't none of your damn business."

Ella stretched her thin arm out to the drawer beside her bed and pulled out a pack of More cigarettes and a lighter. She lit one up and inhaled deeply. A thin trail of smoke leaked out of the hole in her throat and encircled her head like a dirty halo. Beauregard rubbed his hand over his face. A long sigh hissed out of his mouth.

"Mama, that policy counts as an asset. That asset counts against your Medicaid. Now you're behind on your payments to the nursing home. Do you hear what I'm saying? They talking about kicking you out of here," he said.

"And you and Little Miss Big Booty don't want me dirtying up your fancy double-wide, right? You know she never brings the boys up here to see me? I've seen Ariel more than I've seen Darren and Javon and her mama don't even like black people anymore," Ella said. Beauregard grabbed a metal chair from the corner and sat down close to his mother's bed.

"That ain't just on Kia. We've both been real busy and I'm sorry for that. Mama, look, you know I asked you when you first got sick to come live with us. You said no. You said you didn't want to live under my roof, under my rules. 'What it look like, a mother letting her child tell her what to do?' Remember saying that? Now it's just . . . you need a lot of help now. More than we can give you." He reached out and touched his mother's free hand. The skin felt like crepe paper. Ella took another drag on her cigarette and moved her hand to her lap.

"You said it but you didn't mean it," she said. Her voice was a low sharp rasp. Beauregard leaned back in the chair and stared up at the acoustical tiles in the ceiling. He'd gone down this particular road a thousand times over the years. He didn't need a map or a signpost to see where it was headed.

"Mama, we going to have to get rid of that policy. Ain't no way around that because you ain't got anywhere else to go," Beauregard said. Ella took another long deep drag off her cigarette.

"If your Daddy was here, I wouldn't need to be in no nursing home. If he hadn't walked out on me when I needed him the most I wouldn't be here sitting in my own piss. I'd be in my own house with my own husband. But when it came to handling his responsibilities we both know Anthony Montage was about as useful as a white crayon, don't we?" Ella asked. Beauregard let the question hang in the air between them.

"He left me too, Mama," he said. His deep baritone had dropped four octaves. The words seemed to emanate from his chest, not his mouth. If Ella heard him she wasn't in the mood to acknowledge it.

"He should have never walked out on me. Goddamn black bastard. He promised me he would always take care of me," Ella mumbled. Beauregard saw her eyes begin to glisten. He stood up and put the chair back.

"I gotta go, Mama," he said. Ella waved her cigarette toward the door.

Beauregard walked out of the room, down the hall and out of the nursing home. He would have to ask Mrs. Talbot how his mother was getting cigarettes. He couldn't stand watching her smoke. It didn't revolt him. He just couldn't stand watching her do that to herself. He was more disturbed by her eyes welling up with tears. He could count on one hand how many times he'd actually seen his mother cry. She gave up her tears as sparingly as she gave out compliments. If she was weeping, she was in terrible pain. Either spiritually or physically or both. Ella Montage was not an easy woman to love but seeing the reality of her fragility pierced him in places that were soft and frightened. It was like someone had shot him in the stomach then shoved their thumb in the hole.

By the time he got to the garage, it was lunchtime. Kelvin was sitting at his desk eating a cheeseburger with the radio turned up to eleven. A Stevie Wonder song was warbling through the busted speakers. Kelvin had his feet up on the desk as he bobbed his head in time with the music.

"Get your feet down," Beauregard said as he entered the office.

"Well, look what the cat dragged in. I figure I could put my feet up since I was the only employee who had actually done some work to-day," he said between bites. When Beauregard didn't laugh, he moved his feet and put the burger down. "Hey, you alright?" Kelvin said.

"Just got done talking to Mama," Beauregard said.

Kelvin sucked in a breath. "Aw man, Aunt Ella being her usual wonderful self?" Kelvin said.

Beauregard grabbed a beer out of the mini-fridge. Even though he had chided Boonie for day drinking, he needed something after dealing with his mother.

"There was some mix-up with her insurance and they might be kicking her out the home. Unless I can pay it off," Beauregard said. His head was beginning to throb.

"Did you, um, go see Boonie?" Kelvin asked.

"Yeah. He ain't got nothing. So I'm right where I started. Nah, ac-tually it's worse cuz I gotta pay the nursing home," Beauregard said. He killed half the beer with one sip.

"That's one of the perks of having your own business. Beer for lunch," Kelvin said.

Beauregard chuckled. "I see you got Shane's truck up on the rack. What was it?" he said.

"Fucking velocity boot. I was hoping it was the rack and pinion. Don't worry, I already ordered it," Kelvin said.

Beauregard finished his beer. "Alright, let's get on this damn transmission," he said as he tossed his beer in the trash.

"Oh hey, a guy came by saying Ronnie Sessions was looking for you. I think it was Ronnie's brother. He never did get you straight about that thing with the horse, did he?" Kelvin asked. Beauregard sighed. He was sighing an awful lot these days.

"No, he didn't."

Ronnie Fucking Sessions. The mastermind behind what Bug liked to think of as the Fucking Horse Job.

Ronnie had approached him one night out at Wonderland. The way Ronnie had told it, some fancy-ass horse breeder out of Fairfax was selling a healthy young thoroughbred to some famous trainer in Kentucky.

One of the farmhands at the breeder's ranch was buying Oxy-Contin from Ronnie's cousin and had let the cat out of the proverbial bag while making small talk during a transaction. Ronnie had come sidling up to Beauregard to help him steal the horse and sell it to another trainer in South Carolina so he could put him out to stud. Beauregard had taken the job, then set about planning it out because, as Ronnie said, he was an idea man. Beauregard was the details guy. Beauregard had gone out to Fairfax and studied the breeder's farm, the horse trailer, the hitch on the trailer, the weight of the horse, everything. He ended up building an exact replica of the horse trailer, right down to the fist-sized dent on the right side. Put the equivalent of the horse's weight in sandbags in the trailer. When the boys towing the trailer stopped to get something to eat at the same diner they always stopped at when transporting a horse for the breeder, Beauregard and Ronnie were waiting. The fellas parked around the back of the diner and went inside. Beauregard and Ronnie parked next to them, towing their fake trailer covered in a tarp. Under the weak sodium arc lights in the parking lot of the diner Beauregard and Ronnie switched the trailers. It was just past midnight in the middle of nowhere in the Roanoke Valley when they pulled out of the parking lot and hopped on the interstate headed for South Carolina.

"Goddamn if that won't work just like a fucking magic trick!" Ronnie had said as they jumped on I-85.

Unfortunately, what Beauregard didn't know, what no one outside of the breeder and his vet knew, was that the horse had a fairly serious medical condition. A condition that required a certain type of medication. Medication that was in the pocket of one of the boys they had left behind at the diner. Rich Man's Folly was as dead as Dillinger when Ronnie and Beauregard had reached South Carolina.

Beauregard had not been pleased.

"I ain't got nothing to say to Ronnie Sessions," Beauregard said. It was a simple sentence but Kelvin felt the weight of the ominous intent that clung to it like a shadow.

By the time they got the transmission out, the heat in the shop had reached Saharan levels. They were both soaked in sweat despite the air running at full strength. The transmission had fought them every step of the way. Beauregard had busted one of the knuckles on his right hand after it slipped off of a socket wrench. Kelvin wiped his face with a red shop rag. Beauregard had the sickly sweet scent of transmission fluid so far up his nose it felt like it was infecting his brain. Kelvin looked at his watch.

"Shit, it's almost five. You want to call it for today? That torque converter is all the way fucked anyway," he said.

"Yeah. But we gotta get here early tomorrow. I wanna get both of them outta here so we can get paid. I owe Snap-on a grip and the light bill is two weeks past due," Beauregard said.

"Damn, do you ever feel like Jean Valjean?" Kelvin asked. Beauregard squinted at him. "Cynthia likes the movie. Anyway, I'm gonna get gone. See you in the morning," Kelvin said.

Beauregard grabbed his own rag and began to wipe his hands. He only succeeded in moving the dirt and grease to different locations. Kelvin headed for the door. Halfway there he stopped.

"Hey, Bug. We gonna be alright. You'll figure something out. You always do," Kelvin said.

"Yeah. See ya tomorrow," Beauregard said.

After Kelvin left, he started closing down the shop. He turned off all the lights except for the one in his office. He lowered the roll-up doors. Turned off the air compressor and the overhead air handler. On his way back to his office he stopped by the Duster. He ran his hand over the hood. The metal was warm to the touch. Like it was alive. His father had left the car at his own mother's house when he went West. It had sat in the backyard for five years while Beauregard was in juvenile detention. When he got out, his grandmother Dora Montage had handed him the keys and the title.

"Your Mama wanted to sell it to Bartholomew for scrap. I wouldn't let her do it. Her name might be on the title but this car belongs to you," she had said.

Beauregard remembered how strange it felt hearing Boonie's Christian name. He walked around the front of the car and got in the driver's seat. He ran his hands over the steering wheel.

His father was dead. He was sure of that now. Probably buried in a shallow grave or chopped up and tossed in a river by the same kind of men he had worked for as a driver. Just another job to killers who didn't care he had a son who loved his bad jokes. Anthony Montage always seemed so full of life it was difficult to accept the fact he was dead. Beauregard had no doubt that if his father was alive he would have come back by now. Most of the folks around here who wanted him dead were either in prison or the ground. When he hadn't shown up for Grandma Dora's funeral, Beauregard had finally believed he was gone. Kia wanted him to sell the Duster. He could probably get at least twenty-five grand for it if he spruced up the paint job. That was never going to happen. She didn't understand that the Duster was his father's tombstone. Beauregard let his head rest against the steering wheel. He sat that way for a long time.

Finally he got out, turned off the light in the office, and headed home. He had forgotten to call Kia. He called on his cell as he was pulling out of the parking lot. She answered on the first ring.

"Hey, I'm sorry I didn't call on your break. But we closed up a little early so I'm headed to get the boys," he said.

"They wouldn't let me work a double. They actually cut me a little early so I already got the boys. We at the house," she said. There was a pause. "Beau, there are guys here. They were waiting when we pulled up. They said they friends of yours. I told them to wait on the porch," she said.

Beauregard gripped the steering wheel so hard his hand ached. "What they look like?" he said. His tongue felt thick and unsuited to his mouth.

"They white. One got long brown hair. The other one got a bunch of Elvis tattoos running up and down his arm," she said.

Beauregard's vision got blurry for a second. He gripped the steering wheel even harder. "Alright. I'm a be there in like ten minutes."

"You want me to tell them you on your way? I told them you wouldn't be home till seven. They said they was gonna wait."

"No. I'll talk to them when I get there. Just give the boys something to eat and I'll be there in a minute," he said.

"Okay. Love ya."

"Love you too," he croaked. He hung the phone up and put it in the cup holder.

Beauregard stopped at the intersection of Town Road and John Byrd highway. He reached over and opened the glove box. There were no cars behind him and only a few passing him in the other lane at the stop sign. Lying there in the glove box mute as a stone was a Smith and Wesson .45 caliber semiautomatic. Beauregard rooted around in the glove box and found the clip. He took out the gun and the clip and slammed the clip home. He had gotten a concealed carry permit when he had opened the shop. Back then, a lot of people paid him in cash.

Beauregard thought about the clichéd scene in every crime movie where the main character who has gotten out of the "Life" buries his weapons under a hundred pounds of concrete only to have to dig them up when his enemies come knocking at his door.

He understood the appeal of the symbolism for filmmakers. It was just unrealistic. You were never out of the Life completely. You were always looking over your shoulder. You always kept a gun within reach, not buried under cement in your basement. Having a gun nearby was the only way you could pretend to relax. He had a gun in every room of the house. They were like good friends who were always down to do bad things.

Beauregard didn't know why Ronnie Sessions had come knocking at his door but he was going to have his friends Mr. Smith and Mr. Wesson ask him.

FOUR

Beauregard saw a faded blue Toyota sitting behind Kia's Honda as he parked his truck. He slipped the .45 into his waistband near the small of his back. He could feel the butt of the gun and the textured cross pattern on the grip against his skin. He got out and walked toward his house. Two men were sitting in the white plastic lawn chairs arranged on the porch. He didn't recognize the one with the long hair. He figured he was Ronnie's brother. They both stood when they saw him approaching. Ronnie stepped down off the porch first and extended his hand.

"Beau, how the hell are you, man? Long time no speak," he said. He was almost as tall as Beau so that put him around five eight or nine. He was thin but wiry. Veins pressed against the skin of his left forearm and bicep. He had a full sleeve on his right arm from his hands to his shoulder. The tattoo was a time line of the history of Elvis Presley. On his shoulder were images of gold-blazer-wearing Elvis. On his bicep and tricep were multiple Elvises from the sixties. The forearm was fat Elvises in the sequined white jumpsuit wearing Polynesian leis. The images continued until they reached the back of his hand. There in full color was an Elvis with a halo and wings. Angel Elvis. Ronnie was wearing a black T-shirt with cut-off sleeves. That was all Beauregard had ever seen him wear. It didn't matter if it was 100 degrees or 0. Beauregard wondered if he even owned a shirt with sleeves.

Beauregard grabbed Ronnie's left hand with his right. At the same time he reached behind him and slipped the .45 from his waistband. He put the barrel against Ronnie's stomach.

"Why are you at my house? My children in there. My wife. Why would you come here? We ain't got nothing to talk about. So now you gonna leave," he said. He spoke softly so that only Ronnie could hear him. His brother was standing on the second step on the porch just out of earshot.

"Hey, now hold on, Beau, I ain't mean no disrespect. Goddamn, man," Ronnie said. His blue eyes were open wide. His black goatee had more gray in it than Beauregard remembered. His temples had gone white too, giving him a redneck George Clooney look.

"Go, Ronnie. I don't want my family to see me splatter your guts all over the driveway. How did you even find my house?" Beauregard asked.

"Marshall Hanson told me where you stay. Look, man, I didn't know the goddamn thing had horse diabetes or whatever the hell it was," Ronnie said.

"But you should have known, Ronnie. That's the problem. Now leave."

"Beau, just wait a minute."

"My boys are here. My boys, Ronnie. What we did ain't got nothing to do with them. I don't bring that shit around my kids," Beauregard said.

"Come on now, Beau, just hear me out."

Beauregard pressed the barrel into Ronnie's stomach. Ronnie winced.

"I got a line on a job, Beau. A big one. One that can set us up for a long time. A long goddamn time," he said.

Beauregard eased up on the gun just a hair. Sweat dripped into his eyes. It was almost sundown and the heat hadn't slacked off at all. He felt like he was standing in an oven. Beauregard looked over Ronnie's shoulder and saw Kia peeking through the front window. The window of their house. He remembered the day the company brought the double-wide down. He and Kia had held hands as they watched the crew set the trailer on cinder blocks.

Beauregard pulled the gun away from Ronnie's stomach. He clicked the safety into place with his thumb. He let go of Ronnie's hand.

"What kind of job?" Beauregard said. The words tasted sour in his mouth. The fact that he was even entertaining this fool for one second told him how much his back really was against the wall.

"Can you put the gun away so we can talk? You gonna like what I have to say," Ronnie asked.

Beauregard eased up a little more.

"Come on, at least hear me out. Cuz I need ya, man. I need the Bug."

Beauregard put the gun back in his waistband. He looked over Ronnie's shoulder again. Kia was gone. "Meet me at my shop in thirty minutes," he said.

"Alright, alright, that's what's good, man. You won't regret it," Ronnie said. He motioned for his brother, who hustled over to the car and hopped inside. Ronnie got in the passenger side. Beauregard went to his window and squatted down on his haunches.

"I lost $3,800. That's the cost of retrofitting the trailer and my time. So what you got better replace that first. And Ronnie? Don't ever come to my house again. I'll shoot you next time. No questions asked, just a bullet in your guts," Beauregard said. He stood.

"I gotcha, bruh. Sorry, it's just I'm . . . uh, I'm just really hyped about this. You gonna get your money back and then some. I know I owe you, man," he said. Beauregard didn't say anything so Ronnie thumped his brother on the shoulder.

"Let's go, Reggie," he said.

The Toyota backed out of the yard and took off down the dirt lane like a bat out of hell.

———

Kia was pacing a hole in the floor. Beauregard went through the living room and sat at the kitchen table. Kia came and sat down across from him.

"What was all that about?" she asked.

"Just some guys with some work for me," he said.

"What kind of work?"

He took her hand and closed his fingers around it. "The nursing home called today. They say Mama owes them $48,000. Something went wrong with her Medicaid. With everything else going, I think I should just hear them out."

"No. NO. Why the hell does your Mama owe them that much? Bug, I don't mean to sound evil, but that's on your Mama. We got our own problems," Kia said.

"That's why I'm gonna hear them out," he said. Kia pulled her hand out of his grasp.

"No. I'm not gonna let you do this. I can't. Do you know what it's like laying in bed waiting for somebody to call and tell me to come identify your body because you got killed on a job? Yeah, the money was good, but I can't take you coming in here with a bullet in your shoulder and a head full of broken glass. Going up to Boonie's when you should be in a hospital."

Beauregard reached out to stroke her cheek. She flinched but did not pull away.

"We don't have any choice. We right behind it. If this is legit it might give us some breathing room," he said.

Kia inhaled, held it for a second, and let out a long breath. "Sell the Duster. It's worth at least twenty-five thousand. God knows you've put enough money in it."

"You know that's not an option." His voice was low. Dark.

"Why, because it belonged to your Daddy? I don't want you to end up like him. You holding on to that car like he was some kind of saint when everybody know he was a snitch," Kia said. Beauregard stopped stroking her cheek.

"Bug, I'm sorry. I shouldn't—"

Beauregard slammed his fist down on the table. Two jelly jars at the far end fell off and shattered on the floor.

"The Duster ain't for fucking sale," he said. He got up and stalked out the front door. The whole house shook when he slammed it.

Ronnie and Reggie were sitting in front of the garage when he got there. Beauregard didn't speak to them when he got out of the truck. He went to the door, unlocked it and stepped inside. They got the hint after a few minutes and followed him. He was sitting behind his desk by the time they got to the office. Ronnie sat and Reggie leaned against the door frame.

"Talk," Beauregard said.

"Damn, right to the point, huh? Alright. So I got this little piece I mess with. She lives over in Cutter County near Newport News. She works at a jewelry store. The manager is this big bull dyke who probably got a strap-on pecker bigger than yours and mine put together. Anyway, she been trying to get down Jenny's pants. That's her name, Jenny. So one night a couple of weeks ago, this carpet licker took Jenny out for drinks and let it drop they were getting in a shipment of diamonds. Diamonds that ain't on no manifest. Jenny said she was talking about giving her one of the diamonds. You know, because she all sweet on her and shit. Now this the part when you ask how much we talking about," Ronnie said.

Beauregard took the gun out of his waistband and put it on the desk between them.

"How much we talking about, Ronnie." His tone was flat as a pancake.

Ronnie ignored his apparent disinterest. He knew the next words out of his mouth would change that. "Five hundred thousand dollars' worth. I know a boy out of DC who says he will give us fifty cents on the dollar for them. That's $250,000 split three ways. Eighty grand, Beau. That can buy a lot of motor oil."

"It's $83,333.33. My cut would be $87,133.33. You owe me, re-member," Beauregard said.

Ronnie sniffed hard. "Yeah, I remember."

Beauregard leaned forward and put his elbows on the desk. "How many people know about this other than you, me, Jenny, your brother back there and the fence?" he asked.

Ronnie frowned. "Well, Quan knows," he said.

"Who is Quan?"

"He's the third guy. I met him upstate. He's good for this."

"When you trying to do this?" Beauregard asked.

"Next week," Ronnie said without hesitation.

Beauregard got up and grabbed a beer out of the mini-fridge, then sat down again. He popped the top off with the edge of the desk. "That ain't gonna work. Next week the Fourth of July. Traffic on the roads gonna be heavy as shit. Plus it's supposed to be nice. In the mid-eighties. Cops are out heavy in that kind of weather." He took a long swig and killed half the bottle. "Plus we would need to go check it out. Plan routes. Get the layout of the store. Things like that," Beauregard said.

"So how long you thinking?" Ronnie asked. Beauregard hadn't offered him a beer, but he wanted one. Badly.

"At least a month. Depending on the route," Beauregard said. He finished his beer.

"A month? That's not gonna work. I need this like yesterday, man," Ronnie said.

Beauregard tossed his beer in the trash can in the corner. "See, that's why that damn horse died. You always in a rush," he said. Ronnie didn't say anything. He rubbed the palms of his hands over his thighs. He pushed the heels down into his thick-corded quadriceps.

"Look, man, can we split the difference and say two weeks?" he said.

"I didn't say I was in. I'm just saying what you would need to do," Beauregard said.

Ronnie leaned back in his chair until the front legs came off the floor. "Bug, I got a guy who is gonna be in DC on the twenty-sixth and gone by the end of the thirty-first. At the most, that gives us three weeks to get ready. And that's pushing it. This gotta move smooth and quick. Like I said, we can get paid. Real money. Not some pissy-ass stick-up money. Real dollars. But we gotta move fast. I need you on this, man. Not just cuz I owe you but because you the best. I ain't never seen nobody do what you can do with four wheels on the road," Ronnie said.

"I ain't some trailer park trick you trying to talk out of her panties, Ronnie. I'm listening to what you have to say. You lucky I'm doing that," he said.

"Alright, Bug. I hear you. I'm just trying to help you out. It looks like you need it," Ronnie said.

"What you mean by that?" Beauregard said.

The way he stared at him made Ronnie's balls climb up somewhere around his ears.

"I didn't mean nothing. Nothing. I noticed you only got the two cars on the lifts, that's all," Ronnie said. Beauregard studied Ronnie's face. His cheeks bloomed with red splotches that worked their way up from his neck. Ronnie's Adam's apple bobbed as he swallowed hard.

"I'll think about it," Beauregard said.

"Alright then. Look, let me leave you my brother's cell phone number. When you make up your mind, give me a call," Ronnie said.

"Go get a burner phone and call the shop tomorrow around noon," Beauregard said. Ronnie nodded his head up and down like he was in a lecture hall. He stood.

"Hey, man, don't think I don't understand what you are doing here. This is legal and ain't nothing wrong with that. I just figured I could give you a little help, that's all," Ronnie said. Beauregard didn't say anything. "Well, talk at you tomorrow, man," Ronnie said. He brushed past Reggie and headed for the door.

"Reggie, we leaving," he said. Reggie jumped like a demon had spoken to him.

"Oh yeah," he said. He slipped out of the office and ran after his brother.

Beauregard waited until he heard their car start, then he got up and cut the lights off for the second time that day. He locked up, hopped in his truck and headed back toward his house. He was passing the Long Street Mart when he saw a pink Ford Mustang idling by the gas pumps. He slammed on the brakes with his left foot while hitting the gas with his right. He swung the steering wheel to the right and the whole truck did a 180-degree turn. It slid into the parking lot sideways. He let it roll until he was behind the Mustang. He got out of the truck and walked up to the driver's side.

She wasn't in the car. That didn't mean the car was empty. A young black guy was in the passenger seat. He had frizzy braids sticking up all over his head like he had thumb-wrestled a light socket. A teardrop was drawn near his left eye. Beauregard thought the lines were too clean to be a jailhouse work of art. He had those small, thin features that teenaged girls loved and grown women avoided like the plague.

"What you want, old man?" the boy asked when he noticed Beauregard.

"Where's Ariel?" Beauregard asked in return.

"Why you asking about my girl, nigga?" the boy asked.

"Because I'm her daddy," Beauregard said. At first the words didn't seem to register. As they sank in, the boy's face broke into a wide platinum-toothed smile.

"Aw shit, man, I thought you was some old dude trying to holla at my girl. My bad, man. She in the store with her fine self," the boy said.

Beauregard thought he was entirely too comfortable talking about how fine Ariel was. "What's your name?" he asked the boy.

"Lil Rip," the boy said.

"No. Your name. What your mama calls you when she mad at you," Beauregard said.

The boy's smile faltered. "William," Lil Rip said.

"William. Nice to meet you. I'm Beauregard. You be nice to my girl, alright?" He squatted and extended his hand through the open car window. Lil Rip stared at it for a second before extending his own hand. Beauregard grabbed it and squeezed as hard as he could. Years of gripping pliers, stretching serpentine belts and pulling apart brake calipers ensured that was quite hard. Lil Rip winced. His lips parted slightly, and a few drops of spittle fell from his mouth.

"Cuz if you don't, if she ever tells me you giving her some problems, you and me are gonna have problems. And you don't want that do you . . . William?" Beauregard asked. He clamped down on Lil Rip's hand even tighter before finally letting it go. Then he straightened up and walked into the store without waiting for an answer. Lil Rip flexed his hand.

"Crazy motherfucker," he said when Beauregard was almost out of earshot.

Ariel was standing in front of the drink cooler. She was sporting a pair of cut-off denim shorts and a black tank top that Beauregard thought was at least one size too small. Her mop of brownish black curls was piled up on the top of her head in a loose bun. Beauregard's dark chocolate genes and her mother's French and Dutch genetic code had given her a light toffee complexion. Her light gray eyes were a gift from her grandmother.

"Hey," he said. She turned, gave him a once-over and then turned back to the drink cooler.

"Hey," she said.

"How's the Mustang holding up?" he asked.

"I'm driving it so it's doing alright, I guess," she said. She grabbed a fruit drink out of the cooler.

"I met your friend. Lil Rip. The one with the teardrop tattoo," Beauregard said.

"It's not a tattoo. He had me draw it for him with my makeup pen," she said. She pushed an errant lock of hair out of her face and then poked out her bottom lip and let out a gust of air. It was her tell when she was upset about something. He had watched her do the same thing in her car seat when he wouldn't let her have another piece of candy.

"What's wrong?"

Ariel shrugged her shoulders. "Nothing. Just getting ready for graduation. Me and the other five dummies who couldn't graduate with the rest of the class."

"You ain't no dummy. You had a lot going on," he said.

"Yeah. Like Mama getting her third DUI and wrecking my car. Of course, that ain't no excuse, according to her and grandma," Ariel said. She shook her bottle of juice lackadaisically in her left hand.

"Don't worry about them. You just concentrate on college and getting that accounting degree," Beauregard said.

Ariel blew air over her bottom lip.

"What?" Beauregard said.

"Since I won't be eighteen until January, Mama has to co-sign for my student loans. She says she don't want to put her name down on nothing like that. She says I should just take classes at J. Sargeant Reynolds and get a job until January," Ariel said.

"I could sign for you," Beauregard said.

"I don't think Kia would like that, do you?" Ariel asked. She put one hand on her hip and kept shaking the bottle of juice. "It's okay. I'll just get a job at the hospital or Walmart or something. Go to school in the spring," she said. Her body language said she was resigned to the fact that college was on hold for now.

But she didn't *sound* resigned to the idea. In fact, she sounded pissed. Beauregard thought she was about to blow up on him. He felt like their conversation was on the verge of devolving into a clichéd confrontation. She would start screaming at him about why he hadn't done more for her. She would ask why he hadn't taken her and raised her in his house. He would respond that he had only been seventeen and fresh out of juvie when he got her mother pregnant. He readied himself to take whatever came out of her mouth. He deserved it. Ariel deserved a better father and a better mother. She deserved a father who wasn't barely treading water. She deserved a mom who wasn't eating OxyContin like Tic Tacs and washing them down with vodka. She didn't deserve a grandmother who took one look at her tawny skin and cranked up Fox News as she tried to pretend her granddaughter wasn't half black.

Ariel didn't scream at him. She didn't ask him anything. She just shrugged her shoulders. "It is what it is, I guess. I gotta get Rip to work," she said.

Beauregard stepped aside. He wanted to ask for a hug. Wrap his arms around her and tell her he was sorry he hadn't been stronger. Apologize for not taking her from that viper's nest of a household. Tell her that every time he went on a job, he gave her mother half his earnings. Let her know he fought for her. Actually, fought her grandfather and her uncles and her mother for her. That he was the reason her Uncle Chad walked with a limp. Pull her close and whisper in her ear that her grandmother filed a restraining order to keep him away. Wouldn't even accept child support from him. That once he got married he filed for custody, but the judge took one look at him and threw the case out of court. Squeeze her tight and say he loved her just as much as he loved Darren and Javon. He wanted to say all those things. Had wanted to say them for a long time. But he didn't. Explanations were like assholes. Everyone has one and they are all full of shit.

"Alright then. Let me know if you have any problems with the Mustang," he said.

Ariel shook her head. "See ya," she said. He watched as she walked up to the counter, paid for her drink and her gas and strolled out of the store. As she stepped across the parking lot it was like he was watching a time-lapse movie in reverse. She was sixteen, then twelve, then five. By the time she got to the car, he could see her in his arms just after she had been born. Her little fists had been balled up like she was ready for a fight. A fight she was destined to lose because the game was rigged, and the points didn't matter.

Through the big picture window he saw her get in the Mustang and tear out of the parking lot spinning tires. Like grandfather, like father, like daughter.

He would tell himself later that he had slept on it. That he had mulled over the pros and cons and finally decided the benefits outweighed the risks. All that was true. However, in his heart he knew that when Ariel told him about skipping college, that was the moment he decided to take the job with Ronnie Sessions and hit the jewelry store.

FIVE

Ronnie rolled over on his back and stared up at the ceiling. The AC in the window of Reggie's trailer was as weak as a chicken. It pushed the heat around but didn't actually condition the air. A trickle of sweat was working its way down his forehead. He hadn't slept at all. He and Reggie had left Beauregard's and went over to Wonderland to score some Percs.

Reggie had $100 left from his disability check. Ronnie had nothing left from the $2,000 he had gotten for running some stolen eels up to Philly for Chuly Pettigrew. Eels were a delicacy in fancy restaurants all over New York and Chicago. Chuly's men had stolen a batch of eels from a fisherman in South Carolina who was now sleeping with the fishes. They weren't worth much in South Carolina, about $70 a pound. But take them up to Philly or New York and some pretentious celebrity chef would cream his linen pants for eel sushi. The guy in Philly had paid $1,000 per pound. There had been 125 pounds of eels in the trunk of the car he and Skunk Mitchell had driven to Philly.

That was $125,500 for some slimy sea worms. Skunk was one of Chuly's main men. Ronnie had done some of his time with one of Chuly's other main guys, Winston Chambers. He'd recommended Ronnie as a good ol' boy who could handle a gun and keep his mouth shut. Everything had gone smooth and less than a week after leaving prison Ronnie had a pocketful of money. Which he promptly blew up like the World Trade Center. That wasn't that surprising or that big of a deal. How he had blown it, however, was quite concerning. Ronnie swung his feet around and moved into a sitting position. He grabbed his T-shirt from the back of the couch he had crashed on and pulled it over his head. Reggie was in his room with a girl they had taken home from Wonderland. She was a big girl, but Ronnie didn't mind. She tried hard to please both of them, but Reggie couldn't get it up and Ronnie was quick on the draw. She didn't seem to mind that and curled up with Reggie after Ronnie had rolled off her.

Ronnie got up and went into the kitchenette and grabbed a beer from the fridge. When he had gotten back from Philly, he had gone down to North Carolina and celebrated a job well done at a strip club Chuly owned just outside of Fayetteville. A strip club that had poker games and craps in the back. Long story short, he had drunk away two hundred dollars, made it rain with a hundred dollars' worth of ones and gambled away the rest. Then he had done something so monumentally stupid he figured he should be the one getting a disability check. He had gotten a marker from Chuly's guy at the club. They let him play and play until Skunk had the guy cut him off. By that time, he was fifteen thousand dollars in the hole.

Skunk had called Chuly, and Chuly had said he had thirty days to get it to them.

"He gave you thirty days cuz he likes you," Skunk had said in that gravelly voice that made his skin crawl. He sounded like he gargled with battery acid.

"What happens if I don't have it in thirty days? You gonna kill me?" Ronnie had asked as they walked him out of the strip club.

Skunk had pushed him into the passenger seat of Reggie's car and closed the door.

"Nah, not at first. First, I'll come get you and take you out to the farm. Cut off a couple of your toes. Let you watch me feed them to the pigs," he said. He tapped the roof of the car and motioned for Reggie to leave.

"Jesus, Ronnie, what you gonna do? He was talking about cutting off your damn toes. I think that fucker would do it too. He got crazy eyes," Reggie said as they barreled out of the parking lot and onto the highway.

"Shut up, Reggie," Ronnie had said. His head had begun to spin and not from the all the alcohol he had drunk.

Ronnie took a sip from his beer. The sun was shining through the small window over the sink. The rays of light found every crack and crusty crevice in the trailer and highlighted them. Ronnie pulled a crumpled pack of cigarettes from his back pocket. He turned on the stove and lit his smoke from the blue flame of the front burner. He had gone to Wonderland last night to find another driver. He had fucked things up with Beauregard. That much was obvious. He might as well as gone to a chicken coop to count hen's teeth. There wasn't one decent driver among all the pill-popping, moonshine-swilling meth head patrons of Wonderland. At least not one he trusted with his life. And none of them had one ounce of the skill Beauregard had. Ronnie heard some noise from Reggie's room. Maybe they could do it without Beauregard. Him, Reggie and Quan. He pushed that thought away. He loved his brother but what little in the way of brains the good Lord had given him was being eaten away by pills and on occasion Mr. Brownstone. Technically Reggie could operate a motor vehicle. He just couldn't drive.

Reggie came stumbling out of the bedroom. He tripped, righted himself, then headed for the fridge.

"I gotta take Ann back up to Wonderland. You wanna go with?" Reggie said. He opened the fridge and pulled out a bottle of orange juice and took off the top.

"Don't drink that. That shit's rancid. I can smell it from here," Ronnie said. He took a drag off his cigarette.

"Might as well finish it. My EBT don't come until next week," Reggie said.

Ronnie took another hit of the beer. When you grew up poor you got used to waiting. Wait for a welfare check in the mail. Wait in line for the poor box from church. Wait for the parishioners to gaze at you with a sour look of pity on their faces. Wait for your brother to outgrow his no-name sneakers so you could take over gluing them back together. Wait, wait, wait. Wait to die so you can finally get out of debt. He was sick to death of waiting.

"So, you coming?" Reggie asked.

"Nah. I gotta find somebody to help me with this thing," Ronnie said.

"You gonna call Bug? He said to call him," Reggie asked.

"I don't think it's gonna happen. Anyway, I didn't get the burner," Ronnie said.

"I did. I got it from the 7-Eleven last night when we left Wonderland," Reggie said. He took a drink from the jug of orange juice.

Ronnie stubbed out his cigarette on the stove top. "When was that?" he asked. He didn't even remember stopping at a store last night. Maybe he was the one who needed to cut back on the moonshine.

"I just told you. When we left Wonderland. Ann wanted something to eat so I stopped," Reggie said.

"Well, that ain't no fucking shock," Ronnie said. Reggie grimaced.

"Hey, she might hear you," Reggie said in a hushed tone.

"And? What she gonna do? Sit on me?" Ronnie asked.

"Why you so mean, Ronnie?" Reggie asked. Ronnie finished his beer. He felt his gorge try to rise but he forced it back down through sheer will.

Hair of the dog my white ass, he thought.

"Where's the phone?"

Reggie jerked his thumb toward the door. "It's in the car. You gonna have to plug it into the charger," he said.

"Wow, thanks. I had no idea I'd have to plug a brand-new phone in to charge. I was only gone five years. I ain't Buck fucking Rogers. You and Big Bertha hang tight for a minute," Ronnie said. He walked out the door and down the rickety steps.

"Who?" Reggie asked as Ronnie went out the door.

Ronnie plugged the phone into the charger then called information and got the number for Montage Motors. He started the car and turned on the AC. The AC in the car was cooler than the one in the damn house.

"Montage Motors," a voice said.

"Hey, Beau? It's Ronnie."

"Yeah."

"So, um . . . that thing. We good to go or you ain't . . . ," Ronnie stammered. He didn't know how much he should say over a cell phone.

"You mean that car you want me to look at? Yeah, I'm good to go," Beauregard said. Ronnie had been slouching to his right. He sat up so fast he bumped his head on the roof.

"Yeah. Yeah, that's what's up. So, when you wanna get up and talk about it?" Ronnie said. His skin felt like he had sat too close to a wood stove. This was happening. He was gonna do it. He was going to be able to keep all his toes.

"I can come take a look at it later today. Where you got the car at?" Beauregard asked.

Ronnie didn't say anything. He was lost. "Um . . . I uh have it out at my brother's place. Over on Fox Hill Road," he said finally.

"Alright. I won't get done around here till seven. I'll see you then. If I call you back and can't get you, just sit tight. I know you been having trouble with that phone. Hope you don't have to trash it," Beauregard said.

Ronnie caught that one. He had to trash the phone. "Alright, alright, alright. See you then," he said. The line went dead. Ronnie got out of the car, threw the phone on the ground and crushed it beneath his black motorcycle boots. He gathered the pieces and carried them back into the trailer. He tossed the remains in the trash. Muffled grunts and groans were coming from Reggie's room. Ronnie flopped back on the couch and grabbed Reggie's cell phone off the coffee table. He called Quan.

"What up?" Quan said.

"The guy I was telling you about is in. We bout to do this. Can you get to my brother's place around seven thirty?" he asked.

"Man, I don't wanna come down to that country-ass, big-mosquito-having redneck town. Why can't y'all come up to Richmond?" Quan asked.

"Cuz I'm the one planning it. You in or you out? I mean if you don't want $80,000 I can always get somebody else," Ronnie said.

"Hold your horses, white boy, I'll be there. Shit. Goddamn mosquitoes driving trucks down there," he said.

"Don't worry, just put a Dixie flag in your back window, you be fine," Ronnie said.

"Fuck you, Ronnie," he said. The line went dead.

He dialed Jenny's number from memory.

"Yeah, what's up?" she asked in that honey-coated husky voice that drove him crazy.

"Hey, we on. You wanna come by tonight and celebrate?" he asked. All he heard was the hum of the open line.

"Celebrate what? Planning a robbery? I don't know, maybe we should call the whole thing off," Jenny said. He could see her in his mind. Sprawled out across her futon in that efficiency apartment over in Taylor's Corner. Her red hair fanning out around her head like a wreath made of fire.

"Come on now, baby girl. We done talked about this. Nobody gonna get hurt. Nobody is gonna get caught. I got it all planned out. Don't back out on me now. I need you. None of this works without you, baby girl," he cooed. He had known Jenny since high school. They'd been on-again off-again for decades. Whenever she got on her feet, they were off. Whenever she found herself adrift, they were back on. They usually made each other feel good for a few weeks. That was a better ratio than some supposedly monogamous couples.

"I only been working there for a few months, Ronnie. Don't you think they gonna be all up in my face if the place gets robbed?" she said.

"Not if you play it cool. Sit on your cut for a few months. Then slip away. We can go down South. Florida. Maybe even the Bahamas. If there's as much as you say, we can be farting through silk the rest of our lives," Ronnie said. He couldn't let her back out now. The thirty days were almost up. The guy in DC who was going to pay them for the stones was waiting. He had gotten Beauregard on board. He would sweet-talk her until she had Type 2 diabetes if he had to, but he couldn't let her back out.

More silence.

"This is what I do, Jenny. You know that. I been doing this since I had hair on my nuts. This is what I do, and I've only taken one fall and that was because of a fucking snitch," he said. That was partly true. He had gotten five years for robbery for stealing a gold-plated cupola from a vacation house out in Stingray Point. But he hadn't gotten caught because of a snitch. He had gotten caught because Reggie hadn't fixed the tail lights on his old truck. When the cops had pulled them over he had taken the whole fall. Reggie wasn't built for doing time. He couldn't be in tight spaces. He freaked out in elevators. He lost his shit in revolving doors. If you yelled at him, he would shut down like a robot who had gotten his plug pulled. So he took the weight. Those three years taught him two things. One: Prison food tasted like wet, piss-soaked cardboard. Two: He was never going back.

"I can't come down tonight. I gotta work today from noon till close. Then tomorrow I open," Jenny said.

Ronnie smiled. She was still in. He could hear her letting herself be talked into it.

"Alright, well, things gonna start moving fast," he said.

"I'll call you when I get off. Maybe you can come by," she said. Ronnie thought she was thinking about white sand beaches and margaritas the size of washtubs.

"No doubt," he said.

"Okay. I gotta go take a shower," she said.

"Thanks for that nice mental image. I'll be filing that away for later," he said.

"Nasty," she said. He could hear the smile on her face.

"Talk to you later, baby girl," he said. They hung up and Ronnie lay back down. He let his boots hang over the arm of the sofa. This was it. The big one. This was the one that you had wet dreams about. This wasn't some stupid-ass sickly horse or some roof trinket. This was the one that let you write your "fuck you" list. He'd told Beauregard there was five hundred thousand dollars' worth of diamonds.

That wasn't exactly true either. Lying in her bed after bumping uglies, Jenny told him it was three times that much. Even after taking a hit from the fence and giving Beauregard his cut plus his goddamn $3,800 and paying off Chuly, he would still be able to use ten-dollar bills for toilet paper. If everything worked out, people would be waiting on him from now on. If he was superstitious like his Mama had been, he might have worried about things falling into place so easily. Getting in the hole one week, then having this jewelry store drop in his lap the next. Things didn't usually work like that for the Sessions family. He didn't let it shake him. He didn't believe in superstitions or religion. His Mama had spent her life watching Sunday morning televangelists and throwing enough salt over her shoulder to season a full-grown hog. She still died broke and lonely on the bathroom floor of a bingo hall in Richmond. That wasn't how he was going out. Not now. He started humming "Money Honey." It was one of the King's lesser-known hits, but it was one of Ronnie's favorites. Because everyone knew in the end it always came down to money, honey.

SIX

Beauregard pulled down the first bay door and locked it while Kelvin shut off the air compressors and the overhead lights. The sun had finally set over Red Hill County, but the heat hadn't subsided at all. A few lightning bugs performed aerial acrobatics near the motion lights. They didn't have enough mass to set off the sensors. Beauregard paused and watched them for a second before closing the other two doors. They reminded him of summers gone by when he would sit on his grandparents' porch playing checkers with his granddad. The old man was a checkers savant. The day Beauregard finally beat him was the day he knew his grandfather was slipping away.

"You wanna go over to Danny's Bar and play some pool? I got a few hours to kill before Sandra gets off work," Kelvin asked.

Beauregard wiped his face with the least dirty rag in his pocket. "Who is Sandra? I thought you was seeing Cynthia and the other one," Beauregard said.

Kelvin grinned. "Met Sandra on Snapchat. She from Richmond. I'm riding up there when she gets off from her job at the tobacco plant," Kelvin said.

"Nah, I got something I gotta do," Beauregard said.

Kelvin raised his eyebrows. "That something got anything to do with Ronnie Sessions?" Kelvin asked.

"Something like that," Beauregard said.

"You want me to go with you?"

Beauregard shook his head. "No. I'm just getting more details. It still might be nothing," Beauregard said.

Kelvin shrugged. "Whatever, man. Let me know. I'll be at Danny's till about ten. If y'all get done. I might be down if it's something worth doing," Kelvin said.

"I'll let you know," Beauregard said. Kelvin walked toward Beauregard and held out his hand. Beauregard slapped it as Kelvin passed him and headed out the door. He heard Kelvin's Nova start up and tear out of the parking lot.

He went and sat in the Duster. The old leather on the seats smelled like tobacco that had been soaked in oil. He could see his Daddy sitting in the same seat he now occupied. He could see himself sitting in the passenger seat. Beauregard didn't dream of his Daddy. He didn't have dreams. He never had nightmares. At least none he could remember. He slipped into a quiet darkness when he slept and then emerged from that blackness when he awoke. Usually to the sounds of Darren and Javon fighting about any and everything.

When his father came to him, it was through memories. Waking dreams that grabbed him by the neck and pulled him into the past. He would see himself and his father as they had been. Sometimes he would see his grandparents or his mother. But mostly he saw his father. Smiling, laughing, sullen or sad. His father working on the Duster. His father coming up behind his mother and wrapping his tree trunk arms around her waist. His father storming out of the trailer and slamming the door so hard the whole structure rocked. His father beating down Solomon Gray with a bar stool. Him and his Daddy sitting on the hood of the Duster under a star-filled night sky looking for Orion's belt. He remembered how his five-year-old self had thought it would look like an actual belt. Whenever he went into these fugue states, he felt like Janus. Looking forward and backwards with equal amounts of trepidation.

Sitting there in the darkened garage, he was transported back to the last day he saw his father. It was hellishly hot that day too. He had waited on the steps of their trailer for his Daddy to come pick him up and go riding. He had known this visit would be a different one. His mother was more agitated than usual. He had overheard her talking to one of her friends about "Anthony done got himself in some shit he won't talk his way out of," but he didn't know what that meant. By the end of that day, he would learn.

His cell phone rang, breaking the spell. He pulled it out of his pocket. It was Kia.

"Hey," he said when he answered it.

"The boys want to spend the night at Jean's. Her neighbor's grandson got dropped off while they were there. I told them it was okay," she said.

"Hey, I'm sorry about yesterday," he said. When he had gotten home last night, she was in the bedroom pretending to be asleep. He had stayed in the living room playing with the boys. When he had finally put them to sleep and gone to lie down, she wasn't pretending anymore. He had left before breakfast. His temper could be like a lightning strike. Kia was like a smoldering forest fire. He knew he had to give her some space to let it burn itself out.

"Yeah, me too. I shouldn't have said what I said."

"I shouldn't have slammed the door like that. You know I'm just trying to do right by you and the boys. And Ariel," he said.

"You wanna do right by us, don't do nothing with them boys that came by yesterday. As far as Ariel goes, you been trying to do for that girl. Ain't your fault her mama a cracked-out bitch," she said.

Beauregard clucked his tongue against the roof of his mouth. "Knowing these boys, it probably ain't nothing too serious," he said.

Kia grunted. "Baby, nobody gets you to drive their aunty to the store. So, don't talk to me like I'm dumb. You wouldn't even be thinking about it if it wasn't something big. And that means it's dangerous," she said.

"I don't wanna argue with you, Kia," Beauregard said.

"And I don't wanna lose you, Bug," she said.

They both went quiet.

"I'll talk to you when I get home. I gotta go," he said.

"Yeah, you will. We need to do a lot of talking," she said. She hung up.

Beauregard put the phone in his pocket and got out of the Duster. The thing about loving someone was that they knew all your pressure points. They knew all the spots that were open and raw. You let them into your heart and they cased the place. They knew what made you feel weak and what ticked you off. Like somebody hanging up on you. He opened his mouth and closed it like a lion then shook his head violently side to side. He had to let that go.

He needed to have his head in the game. Getting ready for a job was like putting on a new coat. You had to make sure it fit. If everything didn't look right he would walk away. Leave that coat on the rack. No matter how much money was on the table. He glanced back at the Duster. The money was important. God knows they needed it. So many people were depending on him. Kia, his Mama, the boys, Ariel, Kelvin. He thought about what Boonie had said. About how he wasn't like his father. That's what he liked to believe. That they were completely different. In some respects that was true. No matter how intense the pressure got, he didn't run out on his family or his friends. He wasn't Anthony Montage. So why did he feel a flutter in his chest like a hornet was trapped in his ribs? If he wasn't like his Daddy, why did he miss the Life?

There were nights he would cruise around and find a race on his own without Kelvin. Mostly young kids with some aftermarket overseas windup toy of a car. Other times he took the Duster and blew it out on a backcountry road. Passing by the trees and the raccoons like a comet running on high-test. He'd get up to 160 before slamming on the brakes and drifting to a stop. No matter how fast he went or how many races he won it didn't compare to driving for a crew. Being behind the wheel with the cops behind you and the road in front of you while everyone around you was wishing they had worn brown pants. It was a high that couldn't be replicated with drugs or drinks. He'd tried both and they didn't come close.

They had never spoken about it, but he was sure if he could talk to his Daddy he would have felt the same way. The words "need for speed" should have been burned onto the Montage family crest. Along with a skull and crossbones.

He locked up the garage and hopped in the truck. As he drove away the sun cast elongated shadows against the front of the garage. Narrow black fingers squeezing the building in their grip.

SEVEN

Beauregard navigated his way down a pothole-filled dirt road that the county in their infinite wisdom had decided to name Chitlin Lane. When Virginia went to a statewide emergency GPS system, they required any road, lane or cul-de-sac with more than three residents to have an actual name. The county administrators decided to fully embrace the stereotypical Southern ethos and name all the side roads with names that sounded like rejected country song titles. They thought it might help tourism. The only problem with that was that Red Hill was no one's destination. It was a place you drove through, not to.

Wild blackberry bushes lined the lane, interspersed with the occasional pine tree or cypress. The black sky was moonless. The truck creaked and groaned as it rolled over the rough terrain. He passed a dilapidated one-story ranch and two newish double-wides similar to his own. Finally, the lane widened into a clearing with a rusty single-wide smack dab in the middle. The blue Toyota was parked near the door beside a tricked-out Bonneville with 24-inch rims and a matte black paint job. Beauregard parked behind the Bonneville, got out and knocked on the door of the trailer.

Ronnie Sessions opened the door and smiled at Beauregard. Beauregard didn't return the smile. Ronnie stepped aside and beckoned for Beauregard to come in.

"Quan just got here. We was about to have some beers. You want one?" Ronnie asked. Beauregard surveyed the living area of the trailer. A huge brown couch covered in threadbare suede uphol-stery dominated the room. It was too big and too ostentatious for the small structure. It had the feel of a yard sale find that was shoe-horned into the single-wide. A heavily scarred wooden coffee table composed of rough-hewn planks of timber sat in front of the couch. An easy chair sat at the head of the coffee table. Sitting in the chair was a chubby black guy with a forest of tiny braids protruding from his scalp. He was wearing a baggy T-shirt that was two sizes too big. On his feet were the latest incarnation of a washed-up basketball player's most enduring legacy. His jeans were so baggy they could have been pantaloons. He had a wide face that was slick with sweat. An unruly goatee covered the lower half of his face and threatened to envelop his mouth.

Across from the couch was a love seat. It was covered in a bright red and yellow floral print. Beauregard thought it looked like a clown had vomited on it. Reggie was sitting there next to a large white woman with a rat's nest of green and blue hair. Whoever had dyed her hair had missed a few places. Blond spots dotted her head like cheetah print. A wooden chair sat at the end of the coffee table nearest to Beauregard.

"No," Beauregard said. He sat down in the wooden chair. Ron-nie grabbed three beers out of the fridge and handed one to Reggie and one to the black man. Beauregard figured he was Quan. Ronnie plopped down on the couch and opened his beer.

"You got somewhere to be?" Beauregard said to the large woman sitting next to Reggie.

She scrunched up her face. "Uh . . . no. I mean not really," she said.

"Yeah, you do," Beauregard said.

The woman turned her head from Beauregard to Reggie then back to Beauregard.

"Huh?" she said.

"Reggie, go on and take her back to Wonderland," Ronnie said.

Reggie opened his mouth, closed it then opened it again. "Come on, girl, I'll take you back," he said finally.

"I thought I was spending the night again?" she whined. Her eyes pleaded with Reggie. Reggie stood.

"Let's go. I'll just crash up there with you," he said. The woman didn't seem like she was going to move at first. She crossed her legs at the ankles and her arms across her ample bosom.

"You deaf? Get the fuck up," Ronnie said. The woman flinched. Huffing and puffing she pulled herself off the love seat and got to her feet. Reggie shot Ronnie a dirty look, but Ronnie was studying the top of his can of beer.

"Let's go, Ann," Reggie said. He headed for the door. She followed him without saying a word.

"I bet people scream 'Godzilla!' when they see her walk into Walmart," Quan said. He tittered at his own joke, then sipped his beer. Beauregard caught his gaze. Neither one of them said anything for a few seconds. Beauregard turned to Ronnie.

"Three things. One: We don't talk to nobody about this but the five people that already know about it. Not no girl you might meet in the club. Not some homie you trying to impress. Not your mama or your daddy. Nobody. Two: When it's done, we stay away from each other. We don't go get drinks to celebrate. We don't go to Atlantic City as a group and hit the slots. We go our separate ways and we stay separate. Three: The day it goes down, we are all straight. Don't get high. Don't pop no Oxy. Don't smoke a blunt. Nothing. If y'all can get down with that, then I'm in. If not, I walk right now," Beauregard said.

Quan and Ronnie exchanged bemused glances.

"Alright, Ethan Hunt. I feel ya," Quan said.

"Hey, man, that works for me," Ronnie said.

Beauregard sat back in his chair and put his hands on his knees. "Then let's get to it," he said.

He listened to Ronnie talk about the job for twenty minutes before he held up his hand and stopped him midsentence.

"You haven't checked the place out, have you? Does your girl know the code to the alarm system? How far from the interstate is the store? How many ways are there other than the interstate to get away? Is there some construction going on down there? How often do the police patrol that part of town? Is there a lock-down system? Who knows the combination to the safe other than the manager?" Beauregard said.

This time it was Ronnie's turn to hold up his hand.

"I get it, okay? We need to do some recon on the place. Jenny can get the alarm code, but the way I figured it, nobody will have a chance to hit the alarm. We get in, we get the diamonds, we get out."

"You have to take more than the diamonds in the safe," Beauregard said. He flexed his left hand. His knuckles popped like knots of green wood in a fireplace.

"Why you say that?" Quan asked.

"Because if you only take the diamonds, the cops will know it was an inside job. And I bet there ain't more than five or six people that work at this store," Beauregard said.

Ronnie stared up at the ceiling.

"That's a good point," he mumbled.

"Man, fuck all this ying-yang. We go in there, blast the ceiling, them motherfuckers do what we say do. Or we ventilate they ass," Quan said.

He reached around to the small of his back and pulled out an enormous nickel-plated semiautomatic pistol. Beauregard thought it might be a Desert Eagle.

Quan held the gun near his face. "I got the gat, so I make the rules," he said. He punctuated each syllable by shaking the gun.

"Put that thing away," Beauregard said.

Quan smiled. "Don't worry, big man, I got the safety on. I know how to handle it," Quan said. He tucked the gun back in his waistband. Beauregard figured it was a miracle of physics that the gun didn't fall to his feet every time he wore those baggy-ass jeans.

"We gonna need new guns too," Beauregard said.

Quan rolled his eyes. "Nigga, this my favorite gun."

"That's why we need new ones. How many bodies on that one? How many robberies? You think the cops don't keep them shell casings?" Beauregard asked.

Quan seemed to ponder this for a moment. "Where we gonna get new pieces from?" Quan asked.

Beauregard rubbed his palms over his thighs. "I know somebody. We can get two pieces for five hundred. But before we get to that I need to go to check the place out."

"Damn, nigga, five hundred? I thought we was the ones doing the robbing," Quan said. Beauregard glared at him. The other man held his gaze. Eventually Quan looked away. Beauregard got up and went into the kitchen. He opened the fridge and grabbed a can of beer. He went back into the living room and sat at the end of the love seat near Quan's chair. He popped the tab and took a long sip. The beer was cold as ice and chilled him all the way to his belly.

"You know, I had this friend who had a Chihuahua. Little nasty ankle biter. Every time I came around, he would bark and bark and bark. Bare his teeth and shit. But if I stomped my feet at him, he would run and hide under the couch," Beauregard said. He set the beer on the coffee table close to the edge.

"Why the fuck you telling me about some dog, man?" Quan asked.

Beauregard didn't respond. Instead he tipped over the can with his right hand. Beer splashed over Quan's sneakers and pants. Cursing, he jumped up out of the chair. At the same time, Beauregard jumped up too. He grabbed Quan's gun from his waistband near the small of his back. Clicked off the safety and let the gun hang loosely by his side. Quan spun to his right until he was facing Beauregard.

Beauregard heard a strangled cough come from the couch as Ronnie choked on his beer.

"Because you remind me of that little dog. You yap and yap and talk a lot of shit, but I think at the first sign of trouble you might just piss your pants. Or run. Or both. Ronnie say you good people. He says he knows you. He trusts you. That's fine. But I don't. You talk like this a movie. It ain't. It's real life. My life. And I ain't putting it in your hands. So, I'm going to check the place out. I'm going to get the car. I'm going to take us to get the guns. You don't like that, then I walk. Cuz I ain't trying to wake up to three hots and a cot because you gonna ball up like a baby when the work goes down," Beauregard said.

He ejected the clip from the Desert Eagle and then racked the slide to eject the one in the chamber. It rolled across the vinyl-covered floor and came to rest against the far wall. He tossed the gun and clip onto the couch next to Ronnie.

"You got a problem with that, we can handle it. Or we can get this money. It's up to you," Beauregard asked. The AC wheezed as it struggled to cool the rectangular box. Quan scowled at Beauregard but didn't say a word for nearly a full minute. He glanced at Ronnie then turned his attention back to Beauregard.

"Oh, we gonna handle it, motherfucker. After. But for now, let's talk about making this money," he snarled. Beauregard sat back down. Quan waited for what he thought was an appropriate amount of time before he sat down as well.

"Alright then. Like I said, I'm gonna go check out the place tomorrow. Ronnie, can you talk to your girl and find out if she knows the alarm code and the combination to the safe? Once I scope the place out, we can go talk to my boy about getting strapped. The two of you should be able to come up with five bills for the pieces," Beauregard said.

"Sure, sure, I can talk to her. You need the address of the store, though," Ronnie said. He dug around in his pocket for a piece a paper. He pulled out an old receipt and grabbed a pen off the coffee table. Beauregard shook his head.

"Don't write nothing down. You said the store is in Cutter County. I think I can find it. We'll meet again in a week to get the guns. That will give me enough time to get some wheels and make some modifications. We'll only use burners from here on out. Keep your mouth shut and your head down," he said.

"What we do with the pieces after we done?" Quan said.

Beauregard tilted his head toward him. "If you don't have to use them, you can keep 'em. If you do, we break 'em down and toss them," he said.

Quan rolled his eyes. "Five hundred down the drain," he said.

"What, you want to make it a family heirloom?" Ronnie asked.

"Just a waste of money. That's all I'm saying," Quan said.

"I don't think you get what's going on here. Armed robbery in the state of Virginia is a Class 5 felony with a mandatory minimum of three years with a maximum of life. That's if no one gets hurt. The guns are just tools. Tools break. Tools get lost. Don't get attached to them," Beauregard said.

"Sound like you talking about people," Ronnie said.

"Same difference," Beauregard said. He stood. "I think that's all we gotta talk about right now."

"What kind of car you gonna get?" Ronnie asked.

"What difference do it make?" Beauregard said.

"It don't. I was just curious," Ronnie said.

"Can you get a BMW like in that movie with the motherfucker from England? The Transformer," Quan said. Beauregard closed his eyes.

"It won't be a BMW," he said. He ground his teeth together. "I'm out." Beauregard turned and headed for the door. He opened it and was just about to step out when he stopped. "You wanna see me after the job, that's fine. But if I see you coming and you ain't smiling and friendly, it ain't going to go well," he said.

He stepped through the door and into the night. A few moments passed, and they heard his truck start. The trailer was silent save for the shuddering AC and the slight hum of the overhead light fixture.

"Hey, man, he takes this shit seriously. I don't think he was trying to disrespect you," Ronnie said finally.

"Man, give me my fucking gun," Quan said.

Beauregard parked his truck next to Kia's car and got out. The air was still stifling hot. The house was dark save for the porch light. Beauregard unlocked the door and made his way through the shadowy interior toward the bedroom.

Kia was spread across the bed like a Botticelli painting. A thin white T-shirt and zebra-striped panties were her only accoutrements. Beauregard took off his boots and let his pants fall to the floor. He pulled his shirt up over his head and let it fall to the floor as well. He eased his body down to the bed, snaked his arm over Kia's stomach.

"That night you came home with that bullet wound, I asked you how much more of this we was supposed to take. You said the juice was worth the squeeze. Do you remember what I said?" she asked.

"You said that was the dumbest shit you had ever heard," Beauregard said. Kia grabbed his hand and pulled his arm tighter around her body. He could feel the warmth from the small of her back against the bottom of his belly.

"But you was right. It was worth it. We got the house. We got the garage. We got out, baby. We got out. And now you wanna go back, and I'm telling you this time the juice ain't worth it," she said. Her voice hitched a few times and Beauregard knew she was crying.

"If there was any other way, I would do it differently," he said. He spoke directly into her ear.

"Sell the garage. Take a job at the tire plant over in Parker County. Start selling vacuum cleaners," she said.

He moved closer to her and squeezed her tight. "It's gonna be alright. I promise," he said.

She squirmed against him and rolled over onto her back. "I shouldn't have said that about your Daddy. I'm sorry. But that's something he would tell your Mama. You can't promise that it's gonna be okay. You don't know that. What if it ain't? Then I have to tell your sons stories about you the way people told you stories about your Daddy. Because memories fade, Bug," she said.

Beauregard ran his index finger down the length of her face and under her chin. He tilted her head up and kissed her cheeks. The salt from her tears lingered in his mouth. He had no rebuttal to her argument. Things might go south. The job might fall apart. Anyone who was in the Life knew that was a possibility, but he didn't dwell on those kinds of thoughts. He had survived this long because he never envisioned himself behind bars. He refused to see that as an option. Five years in juvenile detention had given him focus. Sharpened his mind to a deadly edge. He would never be at the mercy of anyone who controlled his freedom again.

Beyond the vanities of his own ego, he could see that his wife was also right about memories. He thought about his father all the time and yet his Daddy's voice seemed to grow more and more faint. Did he sound the way Beauregard remembered or was there more vibrato in his speech? Did he have a scar on his right hand or left hand? His father's face was becoming blurred around the edges in his mind. Unless he was sitting in the Duster, Anthony Montage was a shade who spoke in whispers. Sitting in the car brought everything back into crystalline clarity. If he went through with this job, would his sons have to sit in the Duster to recall his face? Would they even want to?

"I promise you. We will be fine," he said. He leaned forward and kissed her on her mouth. At first her lips were set in a hard line but slowly they opened, and her tongue slipped into his. His hand slid up her thigh until he touched her in the center of her body. She shuddered and pulled away from him.

"You better keep your promises," she moaned. He crushed his lips against hers again, and they fell against each other in a tangle of arms and legs and groans and sighs.

EIGHT

Jenny awoke to a series of horns and trumpets going off like Judgment Day. Her text message tone echoed through her tiny apartment. The horns reached a crescendo then started at the top of the melody again.

She grabbed her phone off the nightstand. The contact name on the screen said Rock and Roll. Her first text message of the day was from Ronnie "Rock and Roll" Sessions.

Need the alarm codes, the message said.

Jenny stared at her phone and blinked her eyes. Hard.

I don't know what you are talking about. Call me. She typed. She hit send then grabbed her cigarettes and a lighter out of the nightstand. After her third drag off the smoke a set of bird chirps began to emanate from her phone. This was her ringtone. She touched the screen and answered the phone.

"Don't text me shit like that. Jesus."

"Well, good morning to you too," Ronnie said.

"I'm serious, Ronnie. Who do you think the police gonna be looking at with all the eyes they have if we pull this off? I don't need shit like that in my phone records."

"Damn, you woke on the wrong side of the crypt this morning. Sound like you need a good tuning up," Ronnie said.

"You know, your dick ain't the answer to everything," Jenny said.

"If my dick ain't the answer you ain't asking the right questions. But never mind all that. Can you get it?"

"Get what?" Jenny asked.

"The alarm code," Ronnie said. Jenny took a long drag off her cigarette.

"I already know it. Lou Ellen told me what it was the other day."

"How is your girlfriend doing? She get that call from the Cowboys yet about that starting offensive lineman position?" Ronnie asked.

"Not funny, Ronnie. She's nice."

"Don't tell me you're falling for her. She can't be that good at eating pussy."

"You so damn nasty. She's just nice to me. I don't want her to get hurt. I don't want anybody to get hurt. Not Lou Ellen, not you, not me. I just want to get out of here. Get out of Cutter County. Out of Virginia. I want to go somewhere and answer to a new name for the rest of my life. Try to start over. Maybe try not to make so many mistakes this time," Jenny said.

"And we will. All you got to do is exactly what I tell you to do. And before you know it we will be fucking on a bed full of hundred-dollar bills," Ronnie said. Jenny exhaled. A plume of smoke billowed from her nostrils.

"I just don't want to get fucked up behind this," Jenny said.

"Baby girl, you won't. All you got to do is trust me. Is that so hard? Now stop worrying about all that and let's get back to talking about more important things. What you getting into today? Maybe I can come over. I got some Percocets and a case of beer with your name all over them."

"Down, boy. I gotta go into work. You know, that thing people do instead of stealing."

"Well shit. Hey, tell your sugar mama I said hi."

"Bye, Ronnie."

"Wait, what time you get off?"

"About fifteen minutes after you roll off me and go to sleep," Jenny said and hung up the phone.

NINE

Beauregard got up at first light. Kia was curled up next to him like a cat. He slipped out of bed and put on a pair of jeans and a T-shirt. He grabbed a baseball cap out of the dresser drawer and pulled it down over his eyes. Then he kissed Kia on her cheek.

"You leaving early," she said without opening her eyes.

"Gotta get to the shop," he lied. He stroked her cheek with the back of his hand.

"I'm gonna need you to pick the boys up tonight. I'm going with Lakisha Berry to clean up some offices near the courthouse," Kia said.

Beauregard kissed her again. "That's good, boo. I'll get 'em when we close tonight. Love you," he said.

"Love you too," she said. The last part of the sentence disintegrated into a sigh. Beauregard left the house and got into his truck. He turned on the radio and scrolled through the stations until he hit one playing some old-school R&B. Rev. Al Green's trembling falsetto drifted out of the speakers like a cool mist. He headed out of Red Hill and onto Route 60 toward the interstate. Just before hitting the on-ramp he passed the abandoned Tastee Freez. The white aluminum carport that had covered the pick-up window had collapsed but the rest of the building appeared solid. A crowd of thistles and kudzu covered the eastern side of the building. Verdant green weeds had forced their way up between the seams of the pavement in the parking lot. Ellery and Emma Sheridan had run the Tastee Freez for fifty years before Ellery died in 2001. Emma had tried to soldier on without her husband, but Alzheimer's had snatched the remnants of her mind and tossed them to the four winds. The county had stepped in after some customers had pulled up and found Emma making milkshakes and burgers in her birthday suit.

When he had been a kid, Beauregard had loved the Tastee Freez double chocolate milkshake. It was a rare treat on a hot summer day like today. The kind of dessert that made you throw caution to the wind. His Daddy used to joke that if a van pulled up with no windows, Beauregard would jump in the back if they promised him they were taking him to the Tastee Freez. As they had ridden around on what would be the last day he would see his father, the Tastee Freez had been one of their stops. Years later, a legend spread through Red Hill that there were bloodstains on the pavement that no amount of water could wash away.

Beauregard turned the music up and merged onto the interstate. The sounds of Rev. Green did little to drown out the memories of that long-ago day.

Cutter County was seventy miles away from Red Hill County on the other side of the state. Through a combination of chance and design it had begrudgingly become a suburb of the city of Newport News. Most of the residents worked in the city at one of three large employers. The naval shipyard, the Canon manufacturing plant or Patrick Henry Mall. Beauregard could see the effect of those industries on Cutter County. It was like Red Hill's wealthier twin. He had only seen three mobile homes as he drove through town. There were more brick houses on one road than in all of Red Hill. He turned onto Main Street and passed two cleaners, a liquor store, three consignment shops and two medical offices. The traffic was light, but it was all BMWs and Mercedeses with a stray Lexus here and there. For a moment, he was afraid there would be five jewelry stores and he would have to call Ronnie from his personal cell and not a burner. Before he had to suffer that indignity, he spotted a sign for a shopping center that listed VALENTI JEWELERS as one of the tenants. Apparently, the residents of Cutter County needed a wide variety of choices for their dry cleaning, but when it came to jewelry, Valenti's had cornered the market.

Beauregard drove past the shopping center. He turned left at the next cross street and saw a blue sign that indicated the sheriff's office was 3.5 miles away. He followed the road until he passed a small brick building with the Cutter County seal emblazoned on its front door. Beauregard counted two cruisers parked in front of the building. They would have to move quick. The sheriff's office was much closer than he would have liked. He turned around at the end of the street and headed back to the shopping center.

Beauregard pulled in and drove through the empty parking lot. The shopping center was composed of one long L-shaped building divided into individual units. The jewelry store was the last unit at the bottom of the L. It was also closest to the entrance/exit. Beauregard rolled through the parking lot and out of the shopping center. He didn't need to go in the store. That was on Ronnie. His job was to drive. He committed the layout of the shopping center, Main Street and the road to the interstate exit to memory. He noted the one stoplight at the corner of Main and Lafayette. The speed bump at the exit of the parking lot. The coffee shop across the street with the big picture window, which would give any potential witnesses a bird's-eye view to the job. All these and dozens of other details filled his mind. It was like his brain was a sponge absorbing water. The counselor in juvie had told him he had an eidetic memory. Mr. Skorzeny had tried his best to get him to consider going back to school when he got out. Maybe college. Beauregard knew Mr. Skorzeny had meant well. Unlike a lot of the staff at Jefferson Davis Reformatory, he didn't view boys like him as lost causes. What Mr. Skorzeny didn't understand, what he couldn't understand, was that boys like Beauregard didn't have the luxury of options. No father. A mother who was one flat tire and a bad day away from a nervous breakdown, and grandparents who had lived and died in a constant state of abject poverty. For boys like Beauregard, college was the stuff of dreams. Mr. Skorzeny might as well have told him to go to Mars.

Beauregard turned onto Route 60 West and headed back to the interstate. He checked his watch. It was exactly thirteen minutes from the jewelry store to the exit with minimal traffic traveling at 55 mph. He would be going a lot faster than 55 when they left the parking lot. On his way into town, he had noticed the interstate was undergoing some extensive renovations. The road crested just before the exit to Cutter County and became an overpass for nearly a mile. Under that overpass was a single-lane highway that led to Cutter County through the back roads. The concrete median between the northbound and southbound lanes had been demolished. It seemed the state had finally decided to address the god-awful clusterfuck that was Interstate 64 and widen the road to six lanes. A silt fence encircled the gaping maw. Beauregard noticed that the distances between the overpass and the road couldn't have been over twenty feet.

Interesting.

Up ahead Beauregard saw brake lights flash like Christmas decorations. Traffic on Route 60 moved to the left lane then back to the right. Once the box truck in front of him had changed lanes, Beauregard could see what had caused everyone in front of him to hit the brakes. A small boxy car was sitting in the middle of the road with its hazard flashers on. A slim black man with a youngish face was next to the vehicle, frantically waving his arms. A diaphanous plume of steam was billowing from under the hood of the small car.

Vehicles zipped by the man like he was one of those tube men flapping in the air near the entrance to a car dealership. Beauregard started to pass by the man too. As he drove by, he noticed a woman was sitting in the passenger seat. A young white girl with blond hair too bright not to have come from a bottle. The blond hair was plastered to her head. She was panting like a hound dog and her eyes were closed tight.

"Shit," Beauregard breathed. He pulled over to the side of the road and hopped out of his truck. The man came running over before he had closed his door.

"Hey, man, I need help. My car just broke down and my wife is in labor. Piece of shit just died on me. No warning, no nothing. Fucking piece of shit," the man yelled.

"Why you ain't call a rescue squad?" Beauregard asked.

The man cast his eyes downward. "Our cell got cut off a few days ago. I got laid off last month from the shipyard. Look, man, I think the baby is about to come. Can you give us a ride to the hospital?" the man asked.

Beauregard took in the whole scene. The man was breathing hard. The girl in the car was moaning. He recognized that moan. He recognized the quivering lips of the man standing in front of him. They were terrified. The baby was coming, and they didn't know what in the hell they were doing. Fifteen minutes of fun was about to turn into a lifetime of responsibility. The weight of that responsibility was pressing down on them like an anvil on their chests. He was on his way home from casing the site of a job. He needed to get in and get out without being noticed.

The smart thing to do, the professional thing to do, was to get back in his truck and drive away. The girl moaned again. The moan became a scream that Beauregard could hear over the sound of traffic zipping by them on the lonely stretch of road. Ariel had been a breech baby. The doctors had a hell of time getting her out of Janice's uterus. They told him that if she hadn't been delivered in a hospital, she would have probably died.

"Let's get your car out of the road first," he said.

The two of them were able to push the car off to the side of the road without too much difficulty. Beauregard grabbed the young girl and half helped, half carried her to the truck. The man opened the door for her and together they helped her up into the cab. The man hopped in on the passenger side and Beauregard ran around to the driver's side.

"You think you can get us to the hospital before . . ." The man let the statement hang in the air. Beauregard almost smiled.

"Just hold on," he said as he hit the gas.

The nearest hospital was Reed General in Newport News. It was thirty-five minutes away. Beauregard pulled up to the emergency entrance eighteen minutes after picking up the couple. The man hopped out and ran into the emergency room. A few seconds later, a nurse was following him back out pushing a wheelchair. They helped the girl out of the truck and wheeled her into the hospital. The young guy lingered by the door. Beauregard got back into his truck. When he looked up, the guy was trotting over to the window.

"Hey, man, I don't know what to say. I wish I could give you something. I'm just so strapped right now, and Caitlin had to stop working because of the baby. We moved in with her mom and . . ." Without warning, tears began to trickle from the corners of his eyes.

"Hey. Hey. You don't owe me nothing. I just hope everything goes alright," Beauregard said.

The man wiped at his face. He had a close-cropped haircut and the beginnings of a moustache. Beauregard figured he was barely out of his teens.

"Yeah. Me too. Hey look, thanks, man. I don't know what would have happened if you hadn't stopped. Everybody else drove by us like we were shit that they didn't want to get on their shoes. I tell you what, you one driving mofo. I think we got here before we left," the man said. He held his hand out to Beauregard. Beauregard took it and shook it. The guy had a firm grip. A working man's grip.

"Hey, what's your name? If it's a boy, we might name it after you," the man said. Beauregard didn't say anything. He shook the man's hand again.

"Anthony," he said finally. His father's name tasted like a bitter pill that could save your life by almost killing you.

He let go of the man's hand and drove away.

Red Hill County
August 1991

Beauregard could feel the power of the Duster's engine rumbling up through the floorboards, through the seat and out the top of his head. A Buddy Guy cassette was playing in the tape deck. The warbling whine of Buddy's polka-dot guitar erupted from the radio speakers. His Daddy had one hand on the steering wheel while his other hand gripped a brown bag. He alternated between singing along with the cassette and taking swigs from the bottle. Beauregard glanced at the speedometer. They were approaching 90 miles an hour. The trees and the rolling fields looked like pieces of Technicolor taffy as the Duster flew by.

"You know why I wanted to have you come over this weekend, don't ya, Bug?" Anthony said.

Beauregard nodded. "Mama says you going away. For a long time," he said.

His Daddy took another long swig from his bottle. He switched it from his right hand to his left hand while holding the steering wheel steady with his knee. Then he launched it out the window. Beauregard heard it smash against a sign that stated the speed limit on Town Bridge Road was 45 mph.

"Your Mama say anything else?" Anthony asked. Beauregard turned his head and gazed out the window. "That's what I thought. Your Mama . . . your Mama is a good woman. She just can't stand herself for falling for my bullshit. She don't take it out on you, do she, Bug?" Anthony asked.

Beauregard shook his head. He hated lying to his Daddy. But he hated seeing his parents argue more.

"Well, I ain't going away for that long, Bug. A year, maybe two. Just until things cool down," Anthony said.

"Where are you going?" Beauregard asked. He already knew, but he wanted to hear his Daddy say it. Until he said where he was going, it wasn't real.

Anthony cut his eyes at Beauregard. "California. There's work out there for a man that can drive," he said. They slid through a curve without downshifting. Anthony pressed on the brake and the clutch with his feet and let the car drift into the turn then hit the gas before it could stall. Neither one of them spoke for a few minutes. The 340 did all the talking for them.

"Why you gotta go away, Daddy?" Beauregard asked.

Anthony didn't turn his head. He gripped the steering wheel so tight Beauregard could hear it creak. The muscles in Anthony's neck bulged under his dark obsidian skin. The Duster leaped forward as they descended a slight incline. Beauregard felt his stomach float up near his neck.

"Bug, I want you to listen to me here. Really listen. I'm gonna say two things and I don't want you to forget them, alright? Shit, what am I saying, you don't never forget nothing. First thing is I love ya. I done some fucked-up shit in my time but the best thing I ever done was be your Daddy. No matter what nobody ever tells you, including your Mama, don't ever doubt I love ya," Anthony said.

A park-and-ride lot came into view about five hundred feet up ahead. As they approached it, Anthony whipped the steering wheel to the right and the Duster skidded across the gravel until it came to a stop in front of a concrete parking bumper.

"Second: When it comes down to it, don't nobody care about you the way you care about yourself. Don't ever let nobody make you do for them something they wouldn't do for you. You hear me, boy?" Anthony asked.

Beauregard nodded. "I hear ya, Daddy," he said.

"People want you to put up with something for a lifetime they wouldn't put up with for five minutes. I'll be damned if I'm doing that. Hey, look, I know your grandma put her foot in them biscuits but I could use a shake. You want to go to the Tastee Freez?" Anthony asked.

Beauregard knew his Daddy didn't really want a milkshake. He was trying to be nice. He always tried to be nice whenever he did something that hurt him or his Mama.

"Yeah," Beauregard said.

"Alright then. We gonna get you the biggest strawberry shake they got," Anthony said. He put the Duster in gear and spun his tires as they sped out of the park-and-ride.

"Chocolate. My favorite is chocolate," Beauregard whispered.

TEN

Beauregard closed the shop early. He'd let Kelvin go around noon. The morning had been painfully slow. They'd passed the time playing checkers, listening to the radio and shooting the shit.

"You want me to call you tomorrow before I come in?" Kelvin had asked.

"Yeah."

"Just so you know, I told Jamal Paige I would help him out a few days next week. Driving his tow truck for him while he out of town. Just so you know," Kelvin had said.

"That's fine."

"Told him I might be available a few days a week. Until things pick up around here," Kelvin said.

"I understand. You gotta do what you gotta do. It's cool," Beauregard said.

Kelvin had stood there with his hands in the pockets of his coveralls. "I just don't want you to think I'm dipping on you."

"I know you ain't," Beauregard said. But he wouldn't blame Kelvin if he did.

After Kelvin had left, he had sat in his office watching the minute hand on the clock on the wall. It moved languidly. He held on for three more hours, then went over to see Boonie.

The yard was busy. Cars and trucks were moving across the weigh scale at a brisk clip. A cavalcade of rusted iron and crumpled steel was passing through the gates of Red Hill Metals. Beauregard wondered about where some of the items came from. A wrought iron bed frame sat on the back of a lime green pickup sitting in front of him, waiting its turn on the scale. The finials on the headboard were shaped like blackberries. Had children pretended they were real? Had a beautiful woman reached out and grabbed them as she sat astride her lover? Did an old gangster experience the death Boonie said was denied to men like him in that bed?

He got through the gate and went into the office. Boonie was sitting at his desk counting out money to a wide white man wearing a Confederate flag hat. Beauregard stood near the door.

"That's two-fifty, Howard," Boonie said after he had finished counting. He handed the wad of bills to the man, who seemed to hesitate before he grabbed them.

"That motor by itself is worth $200. It weighs damn dear a thousand pounds," the man grumbled.

"Howard, that's the motor out a Gremlin. Now if you want to try your luck somewhere else, go right ahead. But they gonna ask a lot more questions than I do," Boonie said.

Howard stood up and put the money in his pocket. He left without saying a word.

"You wanna bet he's calling me a nigger in his head?" Boonie asked.

Beauregard chuckled. "Hell, he was probably doing that before he sat down," he said.

Boonie swiveled in his chair and locked the safe that sat behind him. "Long as he don't say it out loud. You see that hat he was wearing? Them good ol' boys always telling us to get over slavery, but they can't get over having their ass handed to them by Sherman," Boonie said.

Beauregard sat in the chair Howard had just vacated. "I need a favor," he said.

"I haven't heard anything about any jobs yet," Boonie said.

Beauregard shook his head. "I need a car. I can't pay you up front, but I'll get you on the back end. Doesn't matter what condition the body is in, but the frame gotta be tight," he said.

Boonie leaned back in his chair. It wailed under his weight. "You got a line on something?" he asked.

Beauregard crossed his legs at the ankles. "Something like that," he said. He could feel tremors coming up from the floor as a dually drove by the window. Boonie rocked back and forth in the chair. It cried out for mercy.

"This wouldn't have anything to do with Ronnie Sessions, would it?" Boonie said. Beauregard held his face in check, but the shock registered in his hands. He squeezed them into fists so tight his knuckles popped. They sounded like pieces of glass thrown against a brick wall.

"Why you say that? Did he tell you that?" Beauregard said. His words came out in a slow monotone.

"Nah. But he came in here this morning talking a mile a minute with five rolls of copper that I know he fucking stole and five bags of mulch that I also know he stole, but I can't figure out why. I gave him four for the rolls. They were worth five, but I don't like that boy. He like to play dumb, but he as slick as two eels in a bucketful of snot. He told Samuel he had a job in the works and needed some money for tools. Told him it was a rocking chair job. He wouldn't never have to work again. And now you asking about a car," Boonie said.

He let the statement hang in the air between them. Beauregard didn't say anything. He kept his face placid.

"Well, shit. Just promise me you gonna be careful. Let's go out back. I think I got something for you," Boonie said.

They wandered through the maze-like back lot of Red Hill Metals. Dozens upon dozens of junk cars littered the landscape like the dead husks of some great forgotten creatures. The smell of stagnant rainwater mixed with oil and gas and grease filled the air. Dust devils chased at their feet as they crunched across the gravel. Finally, they came to a dark blue two-door sedan.

"Just got this the other day from Sean Tuttle's old house. '87 Buick Regal GNX. The motor's shot but I don't guess that gonna bother you much. The bones on this ol' boy are rock solid. Transmission was still good too. Sean didn't see himself doing anything with it, so we picked it up. I was gonna start selling parts off it, but I can let you have it for a grand."

Beauregard peered through the driver's window. The interior was torn and busted in multiple places. The headliner was drooping like a stroke victim's cheek. The front bumper had a hole in it the size of an offensive lineman's fist. Pockets of rust covered the hood like some oxidizing eczema. The side mirrors were barely holding on. A good stiff wind would send them flying. It saddened him to see a car in such a state of disrepair. It made his skin crawl to see a car deteriorate like this. There was a part of him that wanted to fix up every junked broke-down rambling wreck he saw. Kia told him he felt about cars the way most people felt about puppies.

"Can you bring it by the shop tomorrow?" Beauregard asked.

"Yeah, I can. Probably shouldn't, though. I know you pressed up against it, Bug, but I don't trust that boy. He so crooked they gonna have to screw him into the ground when he dies," Boonie said.

Beauregard knew Boonie meant well. He knew the old man cared. But Boonie had options. Beauregard didn't. "I'll get you straight after it's all done," he said.

"I know that. Just make sure you straight after it's done. And if that cracker come at you sideways, get at me and we'll make sure he meets Chompy Number One up close and personal like," Boonie said.

He better not come at me sideways, Beauregard thought.

"You know I used to drive too. Got hung up one time, almost didn't get away. Your Daddy said something to me that made me stop driving. Get into the other side of things."

Beauregard wiped his hands on his pants.

"What was that?"

"He told me that I had a wife who loved me. I had the yard. He said, 'Boonie, a man gotta be one thing or another. You either gonna run the yard or you gonna be running in the streets. Man can't be two types of beasts,'" Boonie said.

"Too bad he didn't take his own advice."

"Didn't he, though? Ant wasn't a mechanic who drove. He was a driver who sometimes worked as a mechanic. Love him or hate him, he knew who he was," Boonie said.

"You think I don't know who I am?"

"I think you know. You just don't like it," Boonie said.

He left the scrap yard and headed for his sister-in-law's place to pick up the boys. As Beauregard pulled into Jean's driveway, he wondered, not for the first time, how a single mom could afford such a nice house on a hairdresser's salary. He parked the truck but before he could get to the door of the two-story brick Colonial Darren was already running out the door.

"Daddy, look, Javon made me a tattoo!" Darren said. He rolled up the sleeve of his Captain America T-shirt to show Beauregard the drawing of Wolverine on his arm.

"It's just magic marker. It's not permanent," Javon said. He was walking out behind Darren.

"We should take a picture of it before your Mama makes him wash it off," Beauregard said. The detail in the drawing was uncanny. Javon had even added the iconic "Snikt!" in a thought bubble above Wolverine's head.

"No, I'm never washing it off," Darren wailed. Beauregard scooped him up with one arm and slung him over his shoulder.

"You gonna have to take a bath someday. You can't walk around with a shitty butthole," he said. Darren exploded with laughter. Javon walked past them carrying his backpack and Darren's bag of crayons, coloring books and action figures. He climbed in the truck and put in his ear buds.

"Hey Beau," Jean said. She had appeared at the door like a wraith.

"Hey Jean. How ya doing?" Beauregard said. His sister-in-law crossed her arms. She and Kia had similar features, but Jean had a video model's shape. Full in the hips and the chest with a figure like a Coke bottle.

"Oh, I'm doing alright. You are looking good, though. Being your own boss agrees with you."

"Well, you should know all about that."

"Yeah. I'm used to doing things my own way by myself. When you do it that way, you never get disappointed. At the end of the day, you're always satisfied," Jean said.

Beauregard felt his face get hot. "Well, I'm gonna get on down the road," he said. Jean smiled and faded back into the house. Beauregard carried a still giggling Darren to the truck and put him next to his brother. They backed out of the driveway and headed home.

"Is Aunt Jean lonely doing everything by herself?" Darren asked. He had his hand out the window waving it up and down in the wind.

"I think Aunt Jean is just fine," Beauregard said.

They pulled into their own driveway and Darren was out and running to the house before Beauregard had put the truck into gear. Javon didn't move. During the ride, Darren had fished his Iron Man action figure out of his bag. He was now pitting Iron Man against the geranium Kia kept on the porch.

"Are we gonna be okay?" Javon asked.

Beauregard sat back against the bench seat of the truck. "Why you asking me that?"

"I've heard you and Mama talking," Javon said. He had pulled his ear buds down around his neck.

"We gonna be fine. We might have hit a rough patch, but you ain't gotta worry about that. All you need to do is get ready for the eighth grade," Beauregard said.

"Mama was on the phone the other night saying she might have to get another job because that Precision place opened up," Javon said.

"Listen. Don't you worry about Precision or your mom getting another job. All you gotta worry about is hitting them books and getting through high school," Beauregard said.

"I wish I could just go to work too. I could get a job helping Uncle Boonie. I hate school. It's boring. The only thing I like is art class and I can do that on my own," Javon said. Beauregard drummed his fingers on the steering wheel. He knew Javon was struggling in math. Beauregard had tried to help him. He tried his best to unravel the Pythagorean theorem or scientific notation for Javon but he knew he was a piss-poor teacher. He couldn't seem to explain angles and variables to Javon in a way that made sense to his son. Beauregard just seemed to get it and it was hard to articulate how he got it to someone else. He figured Javon felt the same way about drawing. His son was smart and talented, just in a different way. His Daddy used to say you didn't call a fish dumb because it couldn't climb a tree.

Beauregard held his hand up in front of his son's face.

"You see this grease on my hands? I've washed them five times today and it still won't come all the way off. Don't get me wrong, there is no shame working with your hands for a living. But for me, it was the only choice I had. It don't have to be that way for you. You wanna go to Auto and Diesel school and get a job working on race cars, that's fine. You wanna go to VCU, take art classes and be a graphic designer, hey that's fine too. You wanna be a lawyer or a doctor or a writer, ain't nothing wrong with that either. Education gives you those choices."

Beauregard sat back against the driver's seat.

"Listen, when you're a black man in America you live with the weight of people's low expectations on your back every day. They can crush you right down to the goddamn ground. Think about it like it's a race. Everybody else has a head start and you dragging those low expectations behind you. Choices give you freedom from those expectations. Allows you to cut 'em loose. Because that's what freedom is. Being able to let things go. And nothing is more important than freedom. Nothing. You hear me, boy?" Beauregard said.

Javon nodded his head.

"Alright then. All I want you to worry about is keeping your head in them books. I'll take care of everything else. Now help me get your brother in the house. We don't watch him he'll be out here all night fighting with that damn plant," Beauregard said.

Beauregard got the boys inside and made them their favorite daddy dinner. Cheeseburger casserole with a pitcher of lemon-lime Kool-Aid. Later, after he had put them to bed, he waited up for Kia to get home. A little after eleven, she came stumbling into the house.

"What did you feed the boys?"

"Their favorite," he said.

She collapsed next to him on the couch. In less than five minutes she was asleep. Beauregard got up and carried her to bed. Her lithe body wrapped around him like a snake. He laid her down in the bed and went back out to the living room to cut off the lights. He pulled his key ring out of his pocket. As he was hanging it on the key hook the key to the Duster slipped from the ring. The 8-ball at the end of the chain clattered across the floor. He bent over and picked it up. The letters ATM were scratched into the surface of the plastic resin on the miniature 8-ball. Tomorrow he would start working on the Buick. He'd have to go back up to Cutter County and check the route a few more times. He needed to go over the plan with Ronnie and that Quan character again and again. Boonie was right about Ronnie. He was playing some angle that only he could see. That was his way. It was like he was addicted to being duplicitous. Quan was a wannabe gangsta playing with a grown man's gun. He didn't trust either one of them, not even a little bit. His father had trusted his partners and they had tried to kill him in front of his only son. He had no intention of letting that happen to him.

Beauregard knew there was no honor among thieves. Boys in the game only respected you in direct proportion to how much they needed you divided by how much they feared you. There was no doubt they needed his skill.

And if they weren't a little bit afraid of him then that was their mistake.

ELEVEN

Ronnie and Reggie sat in Reggie's car with the engine idling so hard the doors were rattling like maracas. They were parked on a lonely county service road. A cell phone tower rose out of the woods behind them like the arm of a titanic robot. Beauregard's truck came rumbling down the gravel road, throwing up a hazy cloud of dust. Beauregard pulled up to Reggie's car so that their driver's side windows were parallel to each other. He grabbed a cooler from the passenger seat and passed it to Reggie through the window. Reggie handed the cooler to Ronnie.

"We been out here for almost an hour. I hope you got some beers in here too," Ronnie said. Beauregard ignored him.

"The guy I got 'em from don't live around here. And he stay nervous. Takes a little time to do business with him," Beauregard said. Ronnie grabbed the lid of the cooler.

"Don't open it here," Beauregard said.

"Well can you at least tell us what you got?"

"Six-shot revolvers. Made from pieces of a .38 but with an extended barrel. No serial numbers and no ballistics history. Madness makes them clean. Ghost pieces," Beauregard said.

"'Madness makes them clean.' Where you get that from, some fucked-up fortune cookie?" Ronnie asked.

"Madness is the guy who makes them," Beauregard said.

"Oh. Six-shooters huh? Quan ain't gonna like that," Ronnie said.

"Quan ain't gotta like it. Revolvers don't leave behind shell casings. And if you need more than six shots you in the wrong line of work," Beauregard said. He put the truck in reverse, turned around and flew down the service road.

He didn't really like leaving Ronnie with the guns but he didn't need to get caught with unregistered weapons. Beauregard didn't think Ronnie was dumb enough to use the guns before the job. At least he hoped he wasn't.

When he got to the shop, Kelvin was changing the oil on Esther Mae Burke's ancient Chevy Caprice. He had it up on the lift while Mrs. Burke sat on the bench seat near the door.

"How you doing, Mrs. Burke?" Beauregard asked as he passed her on his way to his office.

"I'm well, Beauregard. Things a little slow around here today?" Mrs. Burke asked. She was a trim, neat little white woman with a helmet of bluish white hair propped up on her head like a rooster comb.

"Things will pick up eventually," Beauregard said.

"My neighbor Louise Keating says them fellas at Precision Auto only charge $19.99 for an oil change. And they top off all your fluids and will even rotate the tires. All for $19.99. I told her if it's that cheap, they probably ain't doing it correctly. I'd rather come here where I know it's done right," Mrs. Burke said.

"Well, we appreciate your business," Beauregard said. He continued to his office.

"I'll keep coming here until you close down, Beauregard," Mrs. Burke yelled. Beauregard didn't break his stride. He went into the office and closed the door behind him. The mountain of bills on the desk had gotten higher. It was like financial plate tectonics. He sat down and began going through them. He divided them into two different piles. Thirty days past due and final notice. He had a credit card with about $200 left on it. He could use that to pay the light bill. But that would burn up his budget for supplies. He wasn't robbing Peter to pay Paul. They had both ganged up on him and were mugging him.

An hour later there was a knock on the door.

"Yeah," Beauregard said. Kelvin came in and shut the door behind him.

"Mrs. Burke told me to tell you if you're here in three months, she will get us to change her brakes," Kelvin said.

"I should thank her for the vote of confidence," Beauregard said.

"So you gonna show me?" Kelvin asked.

"Show you what?"

"Don't play with me, man. Come on, show me what you been working on under that big-ass tarp in the corner," Kelvin said.

Beauregard leaned back in his chair. "It's just a little personal project," he said.

Kelvin laughed. "Bug, I know it's for a job. I just wanna see it. You been working on it day and night for a week and a half. The other night I drove by around three A.M. and the lights were still on. Come on, let me see this masterpiece, then we can lock up and go over to Danny's for some liquid lunch. It's been a pretty slow day," he said.

Beauregard sighed. "Alright, come on," he said.

They went back out into the shop area and walked over to the far corner near the used oil container. He pulled the tarp off the car with a flourish. The body had been painted a dark navy blue. Nothing extravagant, just serviceable. Kelvin noticed the windows and the windshield were slightly opaque.

"You put homemade bulletproof glass in the windows," Kelvin said. It was more a statement than a question.

"Yeah. Fixed up some run-flat tires too," Beauregard said. He opened the driver door and popped the hood. The motor was pristine. Kelvin let out a low whistle.

"V6?" he asked.

"Yeah. I rebuilt it from the top down. Got some extras in there too," Beauregard said.

"Ha, I bet you do. Shit, man, I wish I was driving it. She looks legit. I bet she get up," Kelvin said.

"Yeah. She got some legs. I burnt up all my credit with Bivins Auto Supply getting her straight," Beauregard said. He slammed the hood down and took a step back from the car.

"Feel good, don't it? Getting ready for a job," Kelvin said.

"No," Beauregard lied. It felt better than good. It felt right. It was like he had found a comfortable pair of old shoes that he had thought were lost forever. Intrinsically he knew that was a problem. It shouldn't feel good or right. The list of things that should bring him joy should begin with his wife and children and end with something benign like an upcoming fishing trip or going to a see a legal drag race. But what should be and what was rarely aligned.

"Let's get that beer," he said.

The music in Danny's was as dark as the décor. "Hey Joe" by Jimi Hendrix was pumping through the surround sound. Danny's had a fancy new LED illuminated jukebox, but someone had decided Jimi's old tale of murder and woe was apropos for some day drinking. Beauregard ordered a Bud Light and Kelvin got a rum and Coke.

"You sure you don't need some help on this?" Kelvin asked.

Beauregard sipped his beer. "I'm sure," he said.

Kelvin threw back his drink. The ice cubes clinked together. "Alright. Just saying you keep me in mind," he said.

Beauregard sipped his beer again. "Yeah. I think this is gonna be a one-time thing. Everything goes right we can make some improvements to the shop. Add an auto body department. Compete with Precision for the next round of county contracts," he said.

"Yeah, I hear you. Don't mean we can't do a little something on the side," Kelvin said.

"Actually, that's exactly what it means," Beauregard said. He finished his beer and slid off the bar stool.

"Hey, man, I didn't . . ." Kelvin's voice trailed off.

"I know you didn't," Beauregard said. He leaned forward and put his mouth close to Kelvin's ear. "If anyone asks, I was at the shop all day this coming Monday and Tuesday."

"You didn't even have to tell me that. I already know what time it is," Kelvin said.

Beauregard patted him on the back and headed for the exit. As he approached the door a tall gangly white man stepped through. A mop of unruly brown hair sat on his head like a designer dog. His wide brown eyes were rheumy and bloodshot. The man gave Beauregard a brief glance before sidling up to the bar. As he passed, Beauregard noticed a red birthmark on his neck that bore a passing resemblance to a map of the United States. The birthmark ran in the man's family. His father and his two uncles had sported the exact same birthmark in the exact same place. That was how they had acquired their nicknames. Melvin's father had been Red, and Melvin's uncles were White and Blue. The Navelys had been what passed for bad around Red Hill back in the day.

Melvin Navely sat two seats down from Kelvin at the bar. Beauregard heard him order a gin on the rocks. When he raised the glass to his lips he noticed Melvin's hand was trembling. Beauregard wondered if it was the d.t.'s or seeing him as he entered the bar that made Melvin's hand shake. Despite Red Hill being such a small town, they didn't run into each other all that often. He could count on one hand the number of times he had seen Melvin Navely in the last fifteen years. Did Melvin consciously avoid him? Beauregard thought it was possible. He didn't blame the man.

He wouldn't want to see the person who ran his father down walking around free either.

TWELVE

Monday morning, Beauregard woke up at six. He put on a pair of blue jeans and a black T-shirt. He dug an old pair of sunglasses out of the nightstand. He left his wallet on the nightstand. Kia was lying on her side with her legs tucked up to her chest. He leaned over and kissed her on the cheek. She turned and kissed him back.

"Hey," she said.

He stroked her hair. "I'm heading out," he said.

Kia opened her eyes. "It's today, ain't it?" she asked.

"Yeah. I might not be home till late," Beauregard said.

She sat up and kissed him on the mouth. "You just make sure your ass comes home," she said.

"I will," he said.

They stared at each other and spoke with their eyes.

Don't get killed. Don't get caught.

I won't. I'm built for this. It's all I've ever been good at.

That's not true. You're a good father. A good husband. I love you.

I love you too.

He went in and kissed his boys too. Then he headed for the shop.

Beauregard slipped into the Buick and fired her up. It didn't sound as impressive as the Duster, but it was almost as fast. He had taken it out last night for a test drive. It handled smooth, taking the curves like a tango dancer executing a *balanceo*. He eased her out of the garage, got out and pulled down the roll door, and headed for Reggie's trailer.

Ronnie and Quan came out on the second honk of the horn. They were dressed identically in blue coveralls. They both carried plastic grocery bags with the IGA logo prominently displayed. Ronnie got in the passenger's seat and Quan climbed into the back seat. Ronnie was uncharacteristically quiet. Quan was humming a tune Beauregard recognized as "Regulate" by Warren G and Nate Dogg. He backed up next to Quan's car, then headed down Reggie and Ronnie's driveway. The Buick had tags from another old Buick in Boonie's yard and a counterfeit inspection sticker. Beauregard kept it well under the speed limit as they drove out to Cutter County. They would be fine unless some overeager Johnny Law decided to racially profile them and run the plates.

"Did you get everything I told you to?" Beauregard said.

Ronnie flinched like he had been kicked in the nuts.

"Huh?"

"The ski mask and the grease paint and the surgical gloves," Beauregard said.

"Oh yeah. We paid cash like you said. Got the mask at different stores than the grease paint, on different days."

"Good. You guys both straight?" Beauregard asked

"Yeah. I didn't even have a beer this morning," Ronnie said.

Quan didn't respond.

"Quan?" Beauregard said.

"I'm straight, nigga," Quan said. He spoke clearly and distinctly. His voice was even and clear. He pronounced each syllable with articulation so sharp you could have sliced bread on it.

"This thing got a radio?" Ronnie asked. Beauregard pulled on to Town Bridge Road and headed for the interstate. He had on a pair of black driving gloves with holes over the knuckles. He flexed his right hand and pushed a button on the radio in the center of the console. "Ante Up" by M.O.P. started to fill the car.

"Well, that's appropriate," Ronnie said.

The AC in the car did not work. Beauregard cracked his window and a torrent of wind barreled into the Buick. He felt his heart begin to pound. It felt like a dogfish flopping on a pier. The sky was so dark it looked like dusk. A blanket of clouds obscured the early morning sun. Another old hip-hop song came on the radio and Beauregard felt himself nodding his head before he realized the title of the song. "Mind Playing Tricks on Me" by Houston trio the Geto Boys. He remembered when that song first came out how Kelvin wanted a copy of the tape so bad he convinced Beauregard to hitchhike with him to the mall in Richmond and try and steal one. Beauregard had gone to the arcade and hustled some white college kids on *Pit-Fighter* and earned enough money to buy the tape. Kelvin had asked him why they didn't just take it.

"My Daddy says a risk always gotta be worth the reward. That tape ain't worth getting caught at the door," he had said.

"He told you that?" Kelvin had asked.

"Nah, but I heard him talking to Uncle Boonie."

He knew why that memory had come to him. He didn't need six years of overpriced psychoanalysis to understand his own mind. The diamonds were worth the risk. Even if Ronnie was shady and Quan was shaky. The reward outweighed the risk by a metric ton. Beauregard merged onto the interstate and hit the gas.

The parking lot of the shopping center was nearly empty when they arrived. There were two cars in front of a Chinese restaurant two doors down from the jewelry store. There were five cars in front of the jewelry store itself. The rest of the parking lot was bare. The clouds had cleared, revealing a cerulean sky. Beauregard thought it looked like someone had spilled watercolors across the heavens. He drove past the store and parked so that he was facing the exit. He took a deep breath. "Time to fly," he said as he expelled the breath.

"Huh?" Quan asked.

"Nothing. Check your guns. Make sure they loaded. Put on the makeup. One minute to make sure no heroes get in the mix. Two minutes to open the safe and grab the diamonds and some other pieces out of the display case. One minute to get back here to the car. Four minutes. At five minutes, I'm leaving the parking lot. You hear me?" Beauregard said.

Ronnie and Quan opened their bags and took out cans of white grease paint. They pulled on their latex gloves and light camo hunting masks. They both pulled out their pieces.

"I hear you, man. We'll be back quicker than a hiccup," Ronnie said.

"Quan, you hear me?" Beauregard asked. He studied Quan's reflection in the rearview mirror. A backwoods Grim Reaper was sitting in his car.

"I hear you, man," Quan said, over-enunciating each word.

"Are you fucked up?" Beauregard asked.

Quan shoved the .38 in his pocket.

"Nope."

Beauregard turned around and leaned over the seat. "Look at me."

Quan raised his head. "Nigga, I said I'm straight. Damn, let's just do this," Quan said.

Beauregard rubbed the thumb on his left hand against his forefinger.

"Four minutes. Two hundred and forty seconds. That will give us a two-minute head start on the cops that are three streets over. Get in, get out, get gone," he said. An old Irish bank robber he had worked with on three separate occasions had coined that phrase, but Beauregard never forgot it. That Irishman had been a professional. These boys were not in his league. They weren't even playing the same game.

"I got it," Quan said.

Ronnie adjusted his mask. "Let's shake, rattle and roll," he said. He opened the car door and hopped out. Quan climbed over the seat and followed him after slamming the door shut.

Beauregard watched them hurry across the parking lot. Fifteen steps to the door from where he was parked. He had come back up here a few days ago and counted the steps from the door to the closest parking space. He checked his watch. It was 8:15.

He gripped the steering wheel.

"Time to fly," he whispered.

THIRTEEN

Ronnie felt like he was in a movie. Everything around him seemed electric. Shimmering like scenes coming out of a projector. He had scored a tiny miniscule amount of coke the night before. This morning he had done two lines. Just enough to sharpen his senses. He realized now that had been a mistake. He felt overwhelmed by all the stimuli around him. He thought he could hear his eyelids click when he blinked. His skin felt raw and exposed as a nerve in a broken tooth.

Fuck it. Get this money. Blue suede shoes, motherfuckers, he thought.

Ronnie pushed through the door of the jewelry store with his shoulder. He had his gun in his right hand and his plastic bag in his left. The overhead recessed lights bathed the sales floor in a sepia tone. The display cases were laid out in an upside-down U shape. A long case at the rear of the store served as a sales desk. The cash register sat on the far left side. Two long cases ran the length of the store on both sides. A huge picture window took up most of the front of the store. Jenny was standing behind the desk with a stocky woman in a shaggy crew cut. They were talking to an older white woman in a rainbow-colored sundress. Her long white hair was plaited into two long pigtails. To his right a young black man was leaning over one of the display cases, obviously deep in thought.

"You know what time it is! Get on the floor and shut your goddamn mouths!" Ronnie screamed.

"Get on the ground or they gonna be cleaning your brains off the fucking ceiling tiles!" Quan screamed. At first no one moved. The young black guy didn't even raise his head.

"NOW!" Ronnie screamed. The young man dropped to the floor so quickly he might have stepped through a trap door. The older white woman took longer but she too got down on the floor. Jenny and the heavyset lady, who had to be the manager, also got down on the floor. Ronnie rushed over to the desk. The two of them were on all fours about to lie flat on the floor.

"Come on, Red, you and me going in the back," Ronnie said. The manager hopped up faster than her size would have suggested.

"Don't you touch her!" she said. She put herself between Ronnie and Jenny. Ronnie nearly took a step back. The ferociousness in her voice was palatable. Her eyes were bugging from their sockets and a vein was pulsating in her forehead. As a rule, Ronnie didn't believe in hitting women. He had enough Southern hospitality instilled in him as a kid that he found the idea distasteful. Under normal circumstances he would never put his hands on a lady. However, these were not normal circumstances. Not by a long shot.

Ronnie struck the manager just above her right eye with the butt of the .38. A divot the width of a popsicle stick appeared above her eye. Blood spewed from the wound like water from a broken faucet. The manager fell forward, grabbed at the counter, and fell to the floor. Ronnie grabbed Jenny by the arm and pulled her up to her feet.

"Keep an eye on them!" Ronnie barked.

Quan nodded his head vigorously. Ronnie dragged Jenny into the back room.

Once they were through the door that said EMPLOYEES ONLY, Ronnie pulled Jenny close.

"Did you deactivate the alarm?" he asked.

"I couldn't. Lou Ellen was here when I got here. She was supposed to be off, but she traded with Lisa."

"Fuck. Does the alarm run through the safe?" Ronnie asked.

"How the fuck am I supposed to know?" Jenny said.

Ronnie almost hit a woman for the second time in his life. "Just open the damn thing," he said. Jenny wrenched her arm free and navigated her way through three wide metal worktables and past a large metal desk. She stopped at a large gunmetal gray safe nearly as tall as Ronnie. She punched a few buttons on a keypad on the front of the safe. A green light started flashing on an LED screen on the door. Jenny pulled on the handle.

Nothing happened.

"Try it again!" Ronnie hissed. Jenny punched in the combination again. The green light flashed. She pulled the handle.

Nothing.

"Get out the way," Ronnie said. He pulled on the handle. At first it didn't seem like it was moving. He pulled harder. The door started to open, painfully slow. It was heavy as hell. He put his gun in the pocket of his coveralls, dropped his plastic bag and used both hands to open the door. Inside the safe were six shelves lined in black fabric. On the first shelf were three bundles of cash. Ronnie picked up his bag and threw all three bundles into the former grocery sack. He didn't know the money was going to be in the safe, but he wasn't going to look a gift horse in the mouth. On the next three shelves were ledgers, files and random papers. On the sixth shelf was a nondescript brown box the size of a pencil box. He grabbed it and ripped open the stiff cardboard lid. It flew up and Ronnie was greeted by the prettiest sight his eyes had ever had the pleasure of viewing. The box was full of uncut diamonds. Each one was as big as a good-sized raisin.

"Hello, ladies," Ronnie said. He snapped the lid back down and shoved the box in his bag. "Come on, you gotta lay down beside Indigo Girl out there." He grabbed Jenny by the arm and headed back out to the sales floor. His heart was a hornet in his chest. He tried to will it to calm down, but it was futile. That was alright, the job was almost done. He had done it. He had seen the opportunity and he had grabbed it. Like the King said, ambition was just a dream with a V8 engine. He was gonna ride that V8 all the way to a place with sand by the ton and water so clear you could see a mermaid coming up to give you a kiss.

Ronnie knew something was wrong as soon as he opened the door, but he didn't know what it was until he saw the dyke's reflection in the polarized glass in the door of the shop. She had a handheld howitzer pointed at Quan from the other side of the office door.

Ronnie reached into his right pocket and gripped his gun. He fired through his pocket into the door. Lou Ellen fired her gun as she lost her balance. As she fell she let out a jagged wail. While she was falling she continued to pull the trigger on her gun.

Glass rained down on Quan. One of the shots from the woman behind the counter had whizzed by his head and punched a hole in the picture window in the front of the store. Ronnie saw the brother on the floor pop up and run toward the door. Quan's hand raised reflexively.

The young brother's head snapped back like it was tied to an invisible rope that had been pulled taut. A red mist filled the space between him and Quan. The brother dropped like a wet sheet falling off a clothesline. Quan was blinking frantically. There was something in his eyes.

Ronnie stepped over the brother with half his head missing and grabbed Quan by the arm. He shoved him toward the door. He could hear Jenny screaming. Her sugar mama was howling like a banshee. The old woman on the floor was crying. Ronnie pushed Quan through the door. They hit the sidewalk in a dead sprint. The picture window in the front of the shop exploded. Ronnie didn't look back but he knew the dyke was still shooting at them. He ran toward the Buick with Quan in tow. It wasn't until he got to the car that he realized he was screaming too.

Beauregard opened the passenger door when he saw them run out of the jewelry store. Quan climbed into the back seat and Ronnie jumped into the front. Ronnie had barely closed the door all the way when Beauregard took off, tires squealing and leaving a cloud of gray smoke in his wake. The Buick sailed out of the parking lot doing 40. Beauregard slammed on the brakes and the gas as he twisted the steering wheel to the right. There were only a few cars on the street this time of morning. Beauregard careened around them going up on the sidewalk then back to the street. He ran a red light and Ronnie screamed as he threaded the needle between a jacked-up good ol' boy truck and a short-body delivery van.

Beauregard gripped the steering wheel like it was a life preserver. He could feel the vibrations of the engine radiating through the wheel and up his arms. His heart wasn't pounding. He guessed it wasn't doing more than 70 beats per minute. This was where he belonged. Where he excelled. Some people were meant to pound the keys on a piano or strum the strings of a guitar. A car was his instrument and he was performing a symphony. A coldness filled him. It started in his stomach and spread to his extremities. He knew no matter what happened he would never feel more alive, more present than he felt at this moment. There was truth in that idea and sadness too.

Quan pulled his mask off and tossed it to the floor of the car. He wiped at his eyes while simultaneously spitting repeatedly. There was a hot coppery taste in his mouth. Sirens erupted behind them. He turned and looked out the back window. Two blue and white police cruisers had materialized out of nowhere. The lights were nearly lost in the glare from the sun. Quan wiped his eyes with his sleeve again. He looked at it and noticed the grease paint had a pinkish hue. Blood. It was blood. The guy's blood. He had killed the guy. He had killed someone. Quan dropped his gun to the floor like it was on fire.

The vomit was coming out of his mouth before he even realized he was nauseous.

Beauregard cut his eyes to the left and appraised the cruisers rapidly approaching in his side mirror. During his second recon trip he had driven by the police station once again. It had been near dark and he had counted four cruisers sitting in the parking lot next to the station. Counting the one he had seen parked near the exit made five. A place the size of Cutter County didn't need more than five police cruisers. The two that were chasing them and the one that was likely on patrol were Dodge Charger Pursuit Special Editions. A 340 hp Hemi engine under the hood meant the car could accelerate from 0 to 60 in six seconds. They came equipped with advanced steering and suspension options. A powerful rear suspension camber linkage and wider-than-normal disk brakes gave the car near supernatural handling capabilities.

As his Daddy would have said, them dogs could hunt.

Beauregard had calculated they would have at least two minutes before the cops even knew the store had been robbed once they had left if everything went smooth. Conversely, he had figured they would only have thirty seconds if shit went south. He had heard gunshots as he sat in the Buick. That was a good indicator things had gone pretty far south. The cops showing up in his rearview mirror was not a shock.

A sign near the on-ramp indicated sensible drivers should slow down to 35 mph to access the ramp and merge into traffic.

Beauregard took it doing 60. He held the gas down with his right foot and the brakes with his left. The car drifted in a semicircle before emerging onto the interstate.

"Shit shit shit!" Ronnie howled.

Beauregard let up off the brake and held the gas pedal down to the floor. The Buick leaped forward as the five-speed transmission he had installed engaged. Beauregard merged and cut off a tractor trailer as he slid into the second of the interstate's three lanes. The trucker laid on his horn, but Beauregard only heard it as a faint trumpeting in the distance. The sirens soon overwhelmed the horn. Beauregard glanced in the rearview mirror without moving his head. Drivers were pulling over for the cruisers as they closed in on him. They would be close enough to ram him with their bullbars before he knew it. Beauregard cranked up the radio. "WHAM!" by Stevie Ray Vaughan was on the radio. He must have hit the PBS station. Regular radio didn't play instrumental tunes anymore.

A blue toggle switch was just below the radio. Beauregard pushed it and the engine roared like a cave bear. Nitrous oxide. N_2O. He had installed a plate delivery system on the engine. He'd also adjusted the piston rings so that when the engine heated up from the introduction of the nitro the rings wouldn't fuse shut and crack the pistons.

A lot of work but it would be worth it. The needle on the speedometer was lying all the way to the right. It trembled just above 135. An SUV with a plethora of stickers on the rear window that told the story of a stick figure family and several honor roll students loomed in front of him. Beauregard slammed the steering wheel to the right again and drove on the wide shoulder of the interstate to get around the SUV.

"OH JESUS!" Ronnie screamed.

Orange triangle-shaped road signs warned of construction ahead. Beauregard hazarded a look in the rearview again. The cruisers were still back there but he had at least six car lengths between the Buick and their Chargers. The overpass that carried the interstate over a two-lane intersection rose up in front of him like a pale white whale's back breaching out of the ocean depths. The interstate had narrowed from three lanes to two. When the construction was completed the lanes would widen to four. Two additional lanes were being added to the overpass. The new construction stopped well short of its older cousin. A gap sixty feet wide stretched beyond the end of the concrete and the exposed rebars. Twenty-five feet below this chasm, a mound of reddish clay-infused soil rose ten feet into the air. Orange traffic barrels and neatly stacked steel struts and angle iron occupied the space to the right of the pile of dirt. To its left was the intersection and a single-lane highway that had been closed off by traffic cones.

"Shit, tell me you ain't trying to jump this motherfucker!" Ronnie said over the last notes of Stevie Ray's Stratocaster.

"Put on your neck pillows," Beauregard said. He grabbed his own from his lap with one hand and slipped it around his neck.

Ronnie grabbed the pillows from the floor. He put one on then tossed one to Quan.

"Why we gotta wear these, Bug?" Ronnie asked. Instead of putting on his pillow Quan fell over and lay down in the fetal position.

Beauregard ignored Ronnie's question. He slammed on the brakes and yanked the steering wheel to the left. The Buick did a 180 as a gray cloud of smoke engulfed them. Without a second of hesitation he slammed the car in reverse and stomped on the gas. The wooden pickets that had surrounded the median had been replaced with orange snow fencing.

Ronnie was screaming in his ear. No words, just one long nonsensical wail. They were doing 60, hurtling toward an unfinished section of road.

Backwards.

The police were closing in like wolves chasing a deer.

Then the deer sprouted wings.

Beauregard didn't say hold on. He didn't say watch out. But in his mind, he heard his father's voice.

"She flying now, Bug!"

The Buick sailed off the overpass. It plummeted twenty-five feet like a stone. The trunk slammed into the pile of dirt, but the dirt helped to cushion their fall. The edge of the overpass rapidly receded from Beauregard's vision as they fell. He braced himself by gripping the steering wheel and leaning back in his seat as hard as he could.

The rear bumper took some of the force. The load-leveling shocks he had installed took the rest. He could feel every inch of the steel plating he welded to the chassis stretch to its tensile limit.

The cop car that had been closest to them had slammed on the brakes. The cop car behind hadn't. It crashed into the first one and sent it careening off the edge. It landed nose first into the asphalt. Steam and engine coolant burst from the crumpled hood even as the car fell forward on its roof. Beauregard jerked on the gearshift, dropped the car into drive and extricated himself from the dry dirt pile. Red clay flew fifty feet into the air as the rear tires strained for purchase. Finally, after what seemed like ten years Beauregard felt the rubber meet the road. He slipped by the upside-down cop car and crashed through the traffic cones. He took the road back to Route 314 and turned right.

"I think I done shit my pants," Ronnie mumbled.

The Buick streaked down the single-lane blacktop road. They passed one decrepit work van and then the road was empty. Two miles later Beauregard turned off the blacktop onto an old dirt lane with mud holes deep enough for spelunking. He did his best to navigate the Buick around the holes. The trees lining the lane cast awkward shadows as the sun seemed to rise higher in the sky.

The road ended twenty feet from a wide body of standing water. Beauregard had found the place on his second recon trip. The lane was overgrown now but once it had led to a quarry. Over the years, rainwater had filled it and created a man-made lake. There were no fish in the water but sometimes the local kids would ride down the road to go swimming. Sometimes young lovers would come down the road to engage in awkward couplings as they fumbled their way to ecstasy. Boonie's wrecker sat near the edge of the lake.

Beauregard stopped the Buick. Ronnie and Quan got out and stripped out of their coveralls. Ronnie was wearing his usual attire and Quan had on sweat pants and a baggy blue T-shirt. They tossed the coveralls in the car but not before using them to wipe the grease paint off their faces. Ronnie and Quan ran over to the truck. Beauregard got out and retrieved a short two-by-four from the back seat. One end was covered in what appeared to be ground beef and tomato sauce. He put that end against the gas pedal and wedged the other end into the steering wheel. Beauregard wound down the window and closed the door. Then he reached through the open window and shifted the car into drive. Beauregard jumped back as the car began to rocket forward.

The Buick hit the edge of the lake and for a moment it took flight again. Gravity reached out and snatched it out of the air and pulled it into the water. A spray of stagnant water rained down on Beauregard, but he didn't move. He watched the car sink until it was fully submerged. How long would the engine run underwater? The question popped into his head and he made a mental note to research it later.

"Come on, man, let's go!" Ronnie said.

Beauregard got into the truck and eased it back to the main road. He had borrowed it from Boonie. One of Boonie's guys had followed him to Cutter County last night. The guy had parked at the convenience store two miles down the road. Beauregard had hidden the truck then hoofed it back to the store.

They turned left onto Route 314 and headed for Route 249. Beauregard wanted to avoid the interstate. The old state roads would get them back to Red Hill. It would just take a while.

A state police cruiser shot past them doing at least 100 headed back toward Cutter County. Ronnie put his hand in his pocket as if reaching for the gun that he'd thrown in the lake.

"They're looking for a primer blue Buick. Not a tow truck," Beauregard said.

It took them nearly three hours to get back to Red Hill. Beauregard drove Ronnie and Quan back to Reggie's trailer. He stopped the truck and put it in park. The three of them climbed out of the truck. Ronnie had the box tucked under his arm like a high school textbook. He walked around the front of the truck to the driver side and playfully punched Beauregard in the shoulder.

"Now that was what I call some driving! That's why I needed the Bug! Goddamn, I thought I saw Jesus trying to take the wheel, but you were like nah, Hoss, I got this!" he said. He held up his hand for a high five. Beauregard put his hands in his pockets. Ronnie held his hand up for a few more moments then put it down by his side. Beauregard looked at Ronnie.

"I heard shots. Other people heard them too. That's why the cops got called. What happened in there?" Beauregard asked.

Ronnie shrugged. "That dyke pulled a gun."

"You kill her?"

"Well, I didn't stop and take her pulse."

"What about him? He kill anybody?"

"Man, it got crazy in there. Couldn't be helped."

"How she get the drop on you? I thought he was supposed to be crowd control while you went in the back," Beauregard said. Ronnie had been wondering the same thing but now that they were out and back home he wasn't that concerned about it.

Beauregard walked around him and went over to Quan. He stood well inside the other man's personal space.

"How about it, gangster? What happened in there?"

"Man, what difference it make. We made it," he said. He slurred the words "made it."

"What you say?" Beauregard asked.

"I said—"

Beauregard slapped him so hard it sounded like a rifle shot. Quan did a 180 and slid against the hood of the wrecker. His blue T-shirt got caught on the wire cage over the headlight. Beauregard squatted beside him.

"You fucked-up, ain't ya? I can see it in your eyes. Let me tell you what difference it makes. It's the difference between an armed robbery that they might chase for a few months and first-degree murder that they won't never let go. I told you not to get fucked-up. But you did it anyway. Let me guess. That lady got the drop on you when you zoned out while Ronnie was in the back. You stupid ass." Beauregard stood.

"Don't come back to Red Hill. You're persona non grata now. I don't ever wanna see you again. And you," he said as he turned to face Ronnie.

"I don't wanna see you until you got my money. Then we meet somewhere outside of town. Toss your phones," he said. He squatted down again. He grabbed Quan by his braids.

"I don't think I gotta tell you, don't say nothing to nobody about today. I heard you vomit in the back of the car. I know this gonna be hard for you to live with. But you gonna learn to live with it or you gonna die because of it. You hear me?" he said. Quan nodded. Beauregard got to his feet.

"Last time, Ronnie. After you pay me, don't ever come around me or mines again." Beauregard climbed in the truck and fired it up. Quan extricated himself from the grill and got to his feet. Beauregard backed all the way out of Reggie's driveway.

"I hate that motherfucker," Quan said.

"I don't think he too fond of your ass either. Come on, let's get a beer. In a week, you gonna be eighty grand richer. Then you can hire a boxing trainer," Ronnie said.

"Fuck you, Ronnie," Quan said. He rubbed his face.

"Yeah, yeah. Let's get that beer before Bug come back and give you a matching set," Ronnie said. He headed for the trailer. A few seconds later, Quan followed him.

"I hate that motherfucker," Quan murmured under his breath.

Beauregard drove out to Boonie's, traded the wrecker for his truck and headed to the shop. The sign on the door had been turned to CLOSED. Kelvin must have been at lunch. He unlocked the door, went inside and turned on the lights. The Duster sat in the corner mute as the Sphinx, yet it still spoke to him inside his head.

"We are who we were meant to be."

The voice in his head sounded like his Daddy. That rough, whiskey-soaked melodic voice that haunted his daydreams. But the words belonged to someone far more eloquent that he couldn't recall. He ran his finger over the hood of the Duster. People had been shot. They might even be dead. There was going to be major heat coming down after such a brazen robbery in broad daylight. He had a feeling Ronnie was going to try and fuck him over for his cut. Quan was a fucking train wreck.

But they had gotten away. He still had it. Whatever "it" was.

"We are who we were meant to be," he said.

His words echoed through the garage.

FOURTEEN

"Ms. Lovell, we just want you to know we are sorry about what you have been through," the first cop, whose name was LaPlata, said. He was tall and thin but had big veiny hands that looked strong enough to crack a coconut.

"Just so you know, the Commonwealth Attorney is not inclined to press charges against you for discharging your weapon," the other cop, Billups, said. "Mrs. Turner is going to be fine and she doesn't want to pursue any criminal action. Since the gun was registered, you're in the clear as far as that is concerned." He was built like a fire hydrant and had a hairline that was retreating like Lee at Gettysburg. They sat across from her on a narrow love seat covered in a fading floral pattern. Lou Ellen sat in her recliner with her legs elevated on the foot rest. Her crutches lay on the floor next to the chair.

"Well, that's good to know. I mean since I was trying to save her life," Lou Ellen said. She shifted in the recliner and felt a bolt of pain shoot through her entire left side. She grimaced and let out a long guttural moan.

"Can we get you something?" Billups asked.

Lou Ellen shook her head. "Docs already got me on the highest legal dosage of Oxy. They say the bullet bounced around in my thigh, bounced off my femur, and came out near my ass. It's been two weeks and it still feels fresh. I think I'm going to be in pain for a long time. Might as well get used to it," Lou Ellen said.

"Ms. Lovell, can you tell us anything about the people who robbed the store?" Billups asked.

Lou Ellen shook her head again. "They were both men, I think. They both wore masks. And gloves. They had gloves on."

"You're positive they didn't get away with anything? The safe was wide open when the deputies got there," LaPlata asked.

"Just a few hundred dollars in petty cash," Lou Ellen lied.

LaPlata stared at her. His almond-shaped eyes seemed to be studying her like a child studies an ant right before he holds a magnifying glass over it.

"It's just strange. There were pieces in the display cabinets worth a few thousand dollars. But they didn't go for them. This wasn't a smash-and-grab. They specifically went for the safe and safe alone," LaPlata said. His eyes never left Lou Ellen.

"I guess they thought we had the good stuff in the back, I don't know. Look, I don't mean to be rude but I'm really not feeling too great. Can we finish this later?" she asked.

LaPlata turned his gaze toward Billups. After a few seconds, the big man nodded. Both detectives stood.

"Well, Ms. Lovell, if you think of anything, please give us a call. We will get to the bottom of this, I promise you that," LaPlata said. He handed her a business card with his name printed on it in small neat letters. She took the card but didn't meet his questioning eyes. She could feel them boring into her skull.

"Get some rest, Ms. Lovell. We will be in touch," Billups said. The detectives stalked out of her apartment.

When she heard the door shut behind them, she closed her eyes and sighed. She dug in the pocket of her lounge pants and pulled out a brown plastic pill bottle. She dry-swallowed two more Oxy-Contin. The bitter taste soon gave way to a languid turgidity that moved through her body with a stealthy determination. She leaned the recliner all the way back and tried not to think about the cops or the store or the pain in her leg.

Twenty minutes passed before her cell phone rang. Lou Ellen sat straight up, feeling her heart pounding like a pile driver in her chest. She pulled it out of her pocket and looked at the screen.

The caller ID said John Elevonone. John 11:1. The first mention of Lazarus in the Bible. Getting a phone call from Lazarus "Lazy" Mothersbaugh was never a good thing. Getting a call from him after you had let one of his fronts get robbed was terrifying.

She could ignore it, but he would just call right back and that would make things worse. As if they could get any worse. She pressed her finger against the screen then held the phone against her ear.

"Hello?"

"Well, well, well, if it ain't Annie Oakley herself," a reedy, high-pitched voice said. You could hear the mountains of Lynchburg and Roanoke in his speech. Some people would make assumptions based on that thick accent. Those people were foolish.

"Hey, Lazy," she said.

"Hey, Lou. How ya feeling? I hear tell you got a bullet that took a tour of your nether regions," he said. He laughed softly.

"Nah. Got hit in the hip and it came out near my ass." She heard him take a deep breath. Phlegm rattled through the phone.

"This a mess, Lou. A big ol' greasy killing hog of a mess," Lazy said. Lou didn't respond. "You done good by me, Lou. That's why I let you work that store."

"I don't know what happened, Lazy. Those guys they just came busting in and . . . I just don't know," she said. She didn't really know. She had her suspicions, but she didn't know anything for sure.

There was silence on the other end of the phone. A loud banging came from her front door. It sounded like someone was trying to hammer through the door frame.

"Yeah, ya do. Horace and Burning Man gonna ask you about it and you gonna tell them. I tell you, Lou, I wish it didn't have to come down like this. But if wishes were horses, beggars would ride," he said. The line went dead.

Lou Ellen turned her head in the direction of the door. They were still pounding on it. Lou closed her eyes. "It's open!" she yelled. Fuck them. If they were coming to kill her, they could open the goddamn door themselves. She heard heavy steps and then she saw them come around the partial partition in the hallway.

Horace was grinning with a smile that made him look like a jack-o'-lantern that had been carved by a Parkinson's victim. His salt-and-pepper hair was piled up on top of his head in a bedraggled, greasy mop. He wore an old Texaco T-shirt and denim jeans. His arms were covered in Nordic tattoos. Vikings and battle axes and skulls. Billy "Burning Man" Mills stood next to him. He was a foot taller than Horace and half a foot wider. He wore a white button-down shirt open at the throat and a pair of wrinkled khakis. He had lank black hair with wisps of gray that was parted down the middle. His Van-dyke goatee was still more black than white. His green eyes were flinty flecks of jade. If not for the scar on the left side of his face he would be considered a ruggedly handsome man. A burn mark stretched from his chin over his cheek up to his eye and around what was left of his ear. Lou knew he wore his hair long to obscure the scar as much as he could.

"Hey, Lou Ellen. How ya doing?" Billy asked.

"I'm alright, considering," she said. She realized Lazy had only called to make sure she was home and not in the hospital. Lou dropped her hand to her right side. The cops had her gun, but she had a switchblade that she carried with her nearly all the time.

"Yeah. Getting shot hurts like a sonofabitch. Feel like somebody sticking you with a hot poker all the way down to the bone," Billy said. He sat in one of the chairs the cops had retrieved from the kitchen. He leaned forward and let his hands hang loosely between his legs.

"Makes you think it's the most pain you ever gonna feel," he said. Horace tittered.

"Yeah," Lou Ellen said. Her mouth was desert dry.

"It ain't, though. There's always more pain," Billy said. He ran his hand through his hair and she saw the rest of his scar.

"Billy . . ."

"Shh. I just gotta ask you two things, Lou. Just two questions. Then we gonna be gone," he said.

"The cops were just here. I didn't say anything. You know I didn't," she said. She felt tears building up in her eyes and hated herself for it.

Billy smiled. "Aw, I know that, Sis. We watched them leave. They long gone now. But thank you for answering my first question," he said. The smile seemed to make his scarification more disturbing. It was as if the ghost of his old face was rising from the grave. Billy scooted his chair closer to her recliner.

"Now my second question is the humdinger. Who'd you tell about them diamonds? You know, the ones Lazy was using to pay for them girls?" he asked. He smiled again and the skin around his eye crinkled like crepe paper.

Lou Ellen felt her tongue squirming in her mouth. She could tell the truth. Just let it all out and hope for the best. Or she could lie. Just pretend she had no idea how those guys knew there was almost two million dollars' worth of diamonds in the safe. Or she could try and find some middle ground.

"I didn't tell nobody. But there's this girl that work there," she said.

Billy leaned forward. "Aw Sis. Not another girl with a pussy that taste like cotton candy and dreams," Billy said.

"I didn't tell her nothing. Not really. We just kinda hung around each other. She might have picked up on some things," Lou Ellen said.

Billy nodded sagely. He ran his right hand along Lou's left thigh. "Lazy got a friend in the hospital. She says a little to the left they could have hit your femoral artery." His hand stopped at her wound.

"Yeah," Lou Ellen said.

He squeezed her thigh. His hand closed on her like a bear trap as his thumb dug into the wound. The pain was a living thing that grabbed at her throat and choked off her breath. She instinctively pulled out her knife. Billy's left arm shot out and caught her wrist as she came up with it.

"Come on now, Lou," he said. He gave her wrist a hard twist and the knife fell into her lap. "What's her name? The girl who must have a pussy that taste like magic and star-shine?"

"Lisa," she wheezed.

Billy let go of her leg. He plucked the knife out of her lap.

"Lisa's the blonde, right?" Billy asked.

Lou Ellen nodded.

"That means it was the other one. The redhead. Jenny," he said as he sat back in the chair. The biscuits that held it together creaked. Lou breathed heavily through her mouth. "I didn't think you'd give the real one up. You a bad liar, Lou Ellen. You always had a soft spot for a fat ass. Lisa too skinny for you." Billy stood.

"No, Billy, don't hurt her. Please."

"If it was just a jewelry store, this could go another way. But them cops gonna start poking around. They gonna be looking at the books and seeing the math don't add up right," Billy said.

"I ain't gonna say shit," Lou Ellen said.

Billy frowned. "I know you good people, Lou. But them boys gonna lean on you hard. If it makes any difference, I told Lazy it should be me. Seeing as I done known you the longest," he said. He walked around to the back of the recliner.

"Billy, just tell Lazy I can explain. I can make this right," Lou Ellen said. She twisted in her chair, so she could see what he was doing behind her. It hurt like hell, but she contorted her torso and tried to look over the top of the chair. Her eyeballs bulged from their sockets as she strained to see. Billy pulled a rolled-up black plastic bag out of his back pocket.

"Nah, ya can't, Lou. Some things when they get broke, you can't put them back together."

He slapped the bag over her head and pulled it tight around her neck. Lou Ellen bucked up out of the chair and tried to stand as she clawed the bag.

"Can you get her fucking hands, please?" Billy asked. Horace ran over and straddled her hips and grabbed her arms. Horace thought he could see the outline of her nose in the dark plastic. A bubble rose and fell where he thought her mouth was. Lou screamed but the sound was dampened by the bag. Her screams became a desperate squealing. The squealing devolved into animalistic grunts that became increasingly desperate. Her gesticulations slowly became less frantic. Her grunts slowed and became nearly imperceptible gasps. A few minutes passed, and her legs stopped kicking.

A few more minutes passed, and she stopped moving completely.

A pungent stench filled the apartment. Neither Billy or Horace were too perturbed by this. It wasn't the first time someone had voided their bowels in their presence. Billy removed the bag, rolled it up and shoved it back in his pocket. Lou's head lolled to the right. Her tongue protruded from her mouth like a turtle's head from its shell.

Billy reached into his pocket and pulled out a handkerchief. He wiped his forehead and put the cloth back in his pocket. From his other pocket he pulled a flat silver flask, a pack of cigarettes and a book of matches. He lit one of the cigarettes with one of the matches and dropped it on the floor between Lou's feet. He hadn't put it in his mouth. He'd just held the match to the tip until a small cherry appeared. He poured the contents of the flask on the floor and the curtains. He poured some of it directly on Lou Ellen's body. The acrid smell of moonshine overtook the scent of shit that had filled the air.

Billy let out a sigh and gently stroked Lou Ellen's cheek.

"Dammit, Sis," he mumbled.

He tossed another lit match onto her body. The flame started slowly, shyly. Then it spread quickly up her leg. He tossed another match near the curtains. They went up like paraffin. Billy watched the flames dance across the fabric like zealots full of the holy ghost.

The flames reminded him of the snake handlers at his grandfather's church. Gyrating across the rough-hewn wooden floor boogying for the Lord.

"I guess we better get going," Horace said. Billy blinked his eyes.

"Yeah. You go see the redhead. I'm gonna talk to Lisa."

"I thought Jenny was the one."

"Yeah, but it doesn't hurt to cover your ass. Come on, let's get the fuck out of here. I don't want to watch her burn," Billy said. He pulled his sleeve down over his hand and opened the front door. He and Horace strolled to the Cadillac. By the time they left the parking lot and turned onto the street, the first plumes of smoke were just beginning to pour from under Lou's front door.

FIFTEEN

Beauregard sat in the Duster and tapped his fingers on the steering wheel. The skies were overcast, threatening to release a deluge of much needed rain. In the distance a water tower emblazoned with the name CARYTOWN stared down at him like an iron giant. An abandoned train trestle bisected the horizon to his left. All around him the remains of an old factory were scattered like the bones of dinosaurs made of brick and steel.

He checked his watch. It was five minutes after four. Ronnie was supposed to meet him at two on the dot. He wasn't surprised he was late for the meeting. He had been a week late getting the money from his "guy" in DC. The delay had made Beauregard's already desperate situation worse. His suppliers were blowing up his phone like a spurned lover. The mortgage on the garage was due in three days. Not to mention the deadline for Ariel's college registration was approaching quick, fast, and in a hurry. The nursing home staff was gleefully packing his mother's bags, anticipating her imminent removal.

"God, Ronnie, don't fuck me on this. I think I just might have to make you into a paperweight if you do," Beauregard said to no one. He checked his watch again. It was ten minutes after four. He closed his eyes and rubbed his forehead. He heard the rumble of a big-block engine. He opened his eyes and saw a black Mustang rolling across the pavement. The driver navigated the vehicle around cracks and potholes with the gentle ease of a new car owner.

The Mustang pulled up alongside the Duster. Ronnie Sessions grinned at Beauregard from behind the wheel. Beauregard lowered his window as Ronnie did the same.

"What the fuck is this?" Beauregard asked.

"What? It's a car, man. A BOSS car. 2004 Mustang."

Beauregard leaned out the window. "Have you been watching the news? All they been talking about is that someone died, and two other people were shot in a brazen jewelry store robbery. The police are on this like stink on shit and you go buy a new car," he said. He said each word slowly and distinctly like he was biting them out of the air and spitting them at Ronnie.

"It's not new. I got it used from Wayne Whitman."

"What you pay for it?"

"I got a deal. $7,000. He even threw in a set of rims."

"And you don't think broke-ass Ronnie Sessions throwing around money ain't gonna attract some attention?"

Ronnie rolled his eyes. "Bug, will you get that six-foot-long stick out ya ass? We did it! The cops ain't releasing any information cuz they ain't got no information. They chasing their fucking tails. So, relax."

Ronnie leaned over and grabbed two cereal boxes out of the passenger's seat. He handed them to Beauregard.

"Go buy yourself something nice. Take your wife over to Barrett's. Go have some nice quiet married people's sex at the Omni Hotel."

"Don't talk about my wife, Ronnie."

"Hey, I ain't mean no harm. I'm just saying Captain Crunch and Toucan Sam are holding $80,000 that belongs to you. Enjoy that shit."

"$87,133.33. It's supposed to be $87,133.33."

"It is, Bug. Jesus, I was just talking."

Beauregard put the two boxes in the back seat.

"Hey, man, maybe down the road we can talk about working together again. We make a good team. I can get somebody to replace Quan. I know how you feel about him. To be honest—"

Beauregard cut him off. "No. We done. And keep my name out ya mouth, Ronnie." He wound the window up and started the Duster. He hit the gas and tore out of the lot. The sky began to cry as he passed the water tower and turned onto Naibor Street. As he merged onto the interstate a sign to his left thanked him for visiting Cary-town, Va. He turned on the radio and settled in for the two-hour ride back to Red Hill County. Felt like the bear crushing his heart began to relax a bit. No one had seen him in the store. Only Ronnie, Reggie and Quan knew he had driven for the job. If his name ever came up, he knew who he had to go see.

And who would have to disappear.

Ronnie passed a box truck on his way down 64. He had Jenny's cut in the back seat and an overnight bag in the trunk. He didn't know about Bug, but he planned on partying like Tony Montana all weekend. Ronnie steered around a ramshackle SUV while taking a sip from a pint of Jack Daniel's. He put the bottle back in the cup holder and popped in an Elvis CD. The King's deep baritone rumbled through the speakers.

"That's what I'm talking about," Ronnie said. He took another sip.

Bug was giving him a hard time, but he had a point. The Ses-sionses were not known for their immense wealth. People would start talking if he spent too much money around town. Good thing he didn't plan on being in town much longer. He realized he had meant what he had said to Jenny. They were going to leave the coal mines and cornfields and crab pots of Virginia behind. He was going to go somewhere and spend his days drinking piña coladas and his nights getting his dick sucked by Jenny until the cash ran out or it was time to trade up. He didn't understand why Bug couldn't take one minute to celebrate. True, he had held out on him and Quan a little, but they were still rolling in enough dough to make it rain in strip clubs for the next three years. That black motherfucker wasn't even grateful Ronnie had let him in on the deal.

He put the bottle in the cup holder and pulled out his new smart-phone.

"Call Jenny," he said into the phone. He had picked it up the same day he got the car. The hands-free feature was like science fiction. Fuck a flying car.

He'd gotten back from DC three days ago after spending some time in the nation's capital with Reggie. They'd met Brandon Yang in Chinatown and gone to see his boss at a bar that catered to Chinese diplomats and immigrants. Ronnie had met Brandon inside just like Quan and Winston. Brandon was doing a year for mail fraud. He'd told Ronnie that the mail fraud beef was nothing. He worked for a guy that moved so much money as a fence for high-end merchandise, he stored it in coffins stacked six high in a warehouse he owned in Maryland. Brandon said he would be taken care of for keeping his mouth shut and doing his time.

He hadn't been lying. No one hassled him inside. He had a cell to himself. He had a cushy job in the prison laundry. Guards let him have two conjugal visits a month. It was like he was on a vacation instead of doing a bid. The only thing he didn't have was someone to play chess with. He was absolutely obsessed with the game. Ronnie approached him one day and offered to play him for some cigarettes. He'd lost, but he made Brandon work for it. They'd hit it off and when Brandon left Coldwater he told Ronnie to look him up if he ever came across something that might interest his boss.

He had done just that. When they went to see Brandon's boss, he had learned two things. First thing he learned was that Chinese guys liked to smoke a LOT. Second thing he had learned was that he didn't know shit about diamonds and neither did Jenny.

"I give you $700,000," Brandon's boss had said. Or more accurately, Brandon had said after translating for the old guy, who looked like a villain in a kung fu movie.

Ronnie had held on to the sides of his chair. Seven hundred

thousand. You could add up all the money everyone he had ever known had made and it wouldn't come close to that. If they were offering seven there must have been three or four million worth of diamonds in the box. He couldn't speak. His tongue refused to work.

They thought he was negotiating.

"Seven-fifty. Final offer," Brandon said after some more gibberish from his boss. Ronnie found his voice.

"Yeah. Yeah, that's fine," he said. For a fraction of a second, he wondered why such a small store would have that much in diamonds sitting in a safe. The bag of money they handed him forced that idea to flee like a startled rabbit. It didn't matter. With what they were giving him, he could pay Chuly, give everybody their cut, and still have enough to shit on a gold-plated toilet.

After the meeting, they hit the town. Drinking up and down the alphabet streets. Going to rooftop clubs where the waitresses walked around opening champagne bottles with swords. They'd eaten in restaurants with names Ronnie couldn't pronounce. They had even picked up some women who had turned out to be working girls. He and Reggie and Brandon had taken turns with all three girls. Ronnie had lived out one of his fantasies and snorted coke off the sexiest hooker's ass. They had partied like rock stars. And why not? He was in high fucking cotton now. No more counting loose change for gas. He wasn't Bill Gates rich, but he was far from poor. Even though the AC was on, he lowered the window. He let out a loud whooping rebel yell.

"Hello?" Jenny said.

Ronnie raised the window. "Hey, sugar bottom. I'm on my way to you right now. I feel like Santa Claus. Can I put something in your stocking?"

"You got the money?" Jenny asked.

Ronnie frowned at the phone. She sounded . . . strange. Like a kid who had dropped his ice cream cone, lost his puppy, and seen his dad get beat up all on the same day.

"Yeah, I sure do. I'll be there in like forty-five minutes. Maybe sooner. This Mustang got some kick."

"Okay." She hung up. She didn't even ask about the car.

"What the fuck is wrong with you?" he said, staring at the phone.

SIXTEEN

Beauregard got back to Red Hill a little after six. He got to the bank just before the drive-thru window closed. He deposited three thousand for the mortgage payment and another five for all the other bills. He left the bank and headed for the nursing home. He pulled in and headed straight for the administrator's office.

Mrs. Talbot was putting her laptop in a leather valise.

"Mr. Montage, how are you? I'm just about to leave for the day. Perhaps you can come back in the morning? I can help you arrange transportation for your mother. And I'll be more than happy to organize her oxygen deliveries at your home," she said. Beauregard could count every one of her capped teeth as she smiled at him.

"That won't be necessary," he said. He had already counted out $30,000 in the car. He put six bundles of $100 bills on Mrs. Talbot's desk. Each bundle consisted of fifty $100 bills. The smile on Mrs. Talbot's face melted away like the wax from a cheap candle.

"Mr. Montage, this is highly unusual."

"No, it's not. I've paid y'all in cash before. I've specifically paid YOU in cash before when my Mama has shown her ass up in here. So, could you please give me a receipt? I'll have the remainder of the money later this week. I don't have any change right now," he said.

Mrs. Talbot sat down and pulled out her laptop.

————

His mother was lying back against a pillow that was engulfing her head. A few cardboard boxes were stacked in the far corner of the room. A talking head chattered on from the television about the weather. The rain that had blessed Carytown was not headed to Red Hill. She was so still he almost thought she was dead. Her thin chest barely rose as she took a breath. He turned to leave.

"You gonna make me sleep on the porch?" she asked. She sounded weaker than the last time he had visited her. He went to her bedside.

"No."

"Oh joy, I get to be in the big house, Massa," she said.

"I paid the bill. Well, most of it."

Her eyes widened. "That was you?"

Beauregard frowned. "What was me?"

"That shit on the news. The jewelry store. When they said the robbers got away in a Buick Regal that jumped an overpass under construction, I knew it. I just knew it. Sounded like something your Daddy would have done." She started to cough ferociously. Beauregard grabbed the pitcher off her nightstand and poured her a glass of water.

"Don't you worry about that."

"You would do anything not to have me at your house, wouldn't you?"

"Mama, please. It's not that. I'm just trying to do what's best for you."

"Right. Right." She coughed again, and he gave her another sip. She did not say thank you. Beauregard smoothed her head scarf.

"They gonna find you."

"I told you don't worry about that."

"They gonna find you, and you gonna have to run just like he did. Leave your kids and your wife behind. Let them fend for themselves like your Daddy did to me."

"To us," Beauregard said.

She ignored his correction. "You thought you was saving him that day at the Tastee Freez. All you did was postpone the inevitable."

Beauregard flinched. "Mama, don't," he said.

His mother turned her head. The low fluorescent lights gave her a cadaverous appearance.

"'I'll save you, Daddy. I'll stop the bad men from hurting you.' And what did he do? Left town while they tossed you in a cage. Lord knows I didn't have no money for a good lawyer. You did all that for him and he just ran."

Beauregard's head began to throb. "You think he ran from me or the cops? He ran from you. He couldn't stand to hear your mouth one more minute," he said. The words left a foul taste in his mouth, but he couldn't help himself. No one knew how to push his buttons like his mother. If anyone else had talked to him like that, they would be counting their teeth in the palm of their hand. All he could do to his mother was try and strike her where she was softest.

"That's how you talk to your mother?"

"That's how you talk to me."

"When I die, don't sit up in church pretending you miss me. Just burn me up and toss me in the trash like you doing now."

Beauregard rolled his eyes. This was her fighting style. Attack you from the front, then pivot and spring a surprise attack on your flank.

"Good night, Mama." He turned and walked to the door. Before he could leave, Ella had another coughing fit. He went back and gave her some more water, but it didn't seem to help. He slipped his hand under her back and was shocked by how insubstantial she felt. He pulled her up and lightly tapped her between her shoulder blades. She nodded, and he let her lie back on the bed.

"I . . . should have picked a better father for you. But Anthony had the cutest smile I'd ever seen," she said. She was wheezing, and a thin line of saliva was hanging from her stoma.

"You want the nurse?"

She shook her head. She wrapped her bony fingers around his wrist.

"You could have been better than you are, but you spent too much time looking up to a ghost."

Beauregard felt a hitch in his chest.

"Not anymore."

"Liar."

Beauregard got in the Duster and pulled out of the nursing home spinning tires. He had one more stop to make, and he was dreading it.

Beauregard brought the Duster to a stop in front of a two-story white farmhouse that was quickly going to seed. The black shutters had faded to a washed-out greenish color. The porch was beginning to lean on the everlasting. Beauregard got out of the car and tramped across the yard. His feet kicked up dust devils as he walked. There was no grass or shrubs near the house. An El Camino sat up on blocks near the front door. An old brown couch covered by a tarp sat on the right corner of the house. Empty beer cans and cigarette butts littered the yard.

Beauregard knocked on the screen door. He didn't hit it as hard as he could because he was afraid it was going to fall off the hinges. He could hear Fox News blaring from somewhere inside the house. Shuffling footsteps brought Ariel's grandmother Emma to the door. A short stocky woman with jowls on top of her jowls. An unfiltered Pall Mall was hanging on to the corner of her lip for dear life.

"Yeah?"

"Can you get Ariel for me? I called her phone, but she didn't answer."

Emma took a drag on her cigarette. The tip glowed red like a piece of ferrous metal being melted. "Phone's off. You'd know that if you called her more."

"Just get her for me," Beauregard said.

"What you want with her?"

"I want to talk to her. I'm her daddy. No matter how hard you try to pretend she has the world's best perm."

"You coming around here every once in a while with your drug money don't make you a father."

Beauregard leaned forward and lowered his voice. "Go get my daughter. Now. I'm not in the mood to play this fucking game with you. Not today."

Emma blew a cloud of smoke out through her nostrils before turning away from the door. He heard her whisper "asshole" as she walked down the hall. He went back to the Duster and sat on the hood. Ariel came out a few minutes later. She was wearing a tank top and shorts so tight they would become a thong if she sneezed.

"Hey."

"Hey. Where's your car?"

"Rip needed it for work. And since my phone is off, he can't call me to pick him up, so I let him take it."

"He got a license?"

"Yeah, he just ain't got a car."

"Come here."

She joined him on the hood of the car. "You gonna give some static about that?"

"Nah. There are more important things than Lil Rip driving your car."

He reached into his back pocket and pulled out a bulky rolled-up brown envelope like the one you used to mail documents.

"One year of tuition at VCU is $24,000."

"Yeah. Plus, textbooks."

He handed her the envelope.

"What is this?"

"Twenty-four thousand dollars. I guess colleges don't take cash so open some bank accounts. Don't deposit more than $10,000 in each. The government will come asking questions if you do."

Ariel's mouth was agape.

"Where the fuck did you get this money?"

"Watch your mouth, girl."

"Sorry. Where the hell did you get this money?"

Beauregard laughed.

"Look, don't worry about that. Just don't let your Mama or your grandmother know you got it. I can't promise you I'll be able to do more anytime soon, but this is a start."

Ariel twisted the envelope in her hands. She frowned.

"Am I gonna get in trouble taking this money?"

"Why would you say that?"

She pushed an errant curl behind her ear. The breeze came up and knocked it loose.

"Mama says that you do things. Illegal things."

"Does she."

"Yeah."

Beauregard crossed his arms and looked straight ahead.

"You take that money and you get the fuck out of this house. Out of this county. You ain't gonna get in any trouble. Go and don't look back. Don't ever come back. There's nothing here for you. Not Lil Rip. Not your Mama. Not me. Your star is too bright for a place like this," he said.

"I don't know what to say."

"You ain't gotta say nothing. You my daughter."

He didn't say he loved her. He wanted to, but it felt wrong to say it now. She might feel obligated to say it back and he didn't want that. Just because he had given her this money didn't mean he had earned an "I love you" just yet.

Ariel let out a long sigh.

"And you my daddy," she said. She hadn't called him that since she had learned how to tie her shoes.

There didn't seem much to say after that so they both stared straight ahead with their feet on the front bumper of the Duster. They stayed like that for a while, neither one of them saying a word. They just watched the sunset and listened to Emma yell at the television. At some point, Beauregard felt Ariel's hand in his own. He squeezed it and sat there for a little while longer.

Once he had left Ariel, Beauregard decided to go out to the Walmart and pick up some Delmonico steaks, potatoes and some ice cream for dessert. He wasn't going to buy a car, but Ronnie had a point. He should enjoy some of the money. He usually avoided going by the Walmart because it meant passing Precision and he didn't have any desire to see all the cars that should have been at his shop behind their black-powdered aluminum fence. Kia did most of the shopping by herself. On the days he did accompany her he took her over to the Food Lion in Tillerson two counties to the north.

He turned onto Market Drive and dropped his speed down to 35 miles per hour. A mile from the Walmart he heard the shrill whine of sirens. He clenched the steering wheel and got ready to punch it. He looked up in the rearview mirror and saw a fire engine bearing down on him. He pulled over and let it pass. Two more followed the first one, sirens and lights blasting at full power. Beauregard pulled back onto the highway and continued to the store. He wondered if the trucks were headed to the Walmart. Had some bored high school kids called in a bomb threat?

"Goddamn," he said.

Precision Auto was engulfed in flames. Plumes of fire shot fifty feet into the air, setting the sky ablaze. The volunteer firefighters were valiantly battling the inferno, but it didn't look like they were making much headway. The Precision Auto Repair sign was melting on its fifteen-foot-tall pole. Beauregard studied his rearview mirror as he passed by the scene. The flames glowing behind him made it seem he was driving straight out of Hell.

When he got home from the store, Kia was sitting on the couch with Darren.

"Hey, where's Javon?" he asked.

"He asked could he stay over at Tre Cook's house. I didn't think you would mind."

"I don't. I was just asking."

"What you got there?"

"Got some steaks. Gonna make some potatoes au rotten," Beauregard said as he brushed Darren's head with the shopping bag.

"Eww."

"What, you don't want no rotten potatoes?"

"No, Daddy, that's nasty."

"Well, more for me," he said as he walked into the kitchen. Kia got up and followed him into the kitchen.

"You got paid?" she asked.

Beauregard put the steaks on the counter. "Yeah."

"No more, right?" Kia asked.

Beauregard went to her and enveloped her in his arms.

"No more." He kissed her forehead before releasing her. He cut open the packages of steaks and placed the meat in a bowl. He poured some seasonings in the bowl and filled it with water for a quick marinade.

"Precision Auto Repair was on fire when I went to Walmart."

"What? When did this happen?"

"I just told you. About an hour ago."

"Well, fuck."

Darren collapsed into giggles.

"What?"

"You know they gonna think you had something to do with it, right?"

The thought had crossed his mind, but he hadn't so he didn't expend any energy worrying about it.

"Yeah, but I didn't."

"I know you didn't, but they still gonna say it."

He walked back into the living room.

"So? You gonna peel these potatoes?"

They had dinner then sat on the couch watching a movie until Darren fell asleep. Kia picked him up and he snuggled against her neck.

"I'm going to put him down. Then I'm gonna be right behind him. You coming to bed?"

"In a few. Gonna check out the news." Kia cradled Darren to her chest. Beauregard thought she was going to ask him a question. He waited for it, but the moment passed. "Tell your daddy goodnight," she whispered to Darren.

In response to her request Darren gave him a lazy goodbye wave.

"Night, Stink."

The two of them went down the hall and left Beauregard alone in the living room. The news was the usual collection of local political stories blown up to Watergate proportions. Human interest stories that weren't all that interesting. A report about a fire at an apartment complex in Newport News. Beauregard was just about to cut off the television and head to bed when the talking head mentioned Cutter County.

"And new at eleven, authorities have released the name of the man killed in last Monday's attempted jewelry store robbery. Eric Gay, nineteen, of Cutter County was killed in the botched robbery. He leaves behind a wife and a young son. Our Ellen Williams spoke with Mr. Gay's widow Caitlin as she struggles to find the words to one day explain to her son what happened to his father," the talking head said. The screen jumped from the studio to a cramped trailer. A young white woman was holding a picture in one arm and a baby with an ecru complexion in the other.

"Attempted?" Beauregard said out loud.

As the camera zoomed in on the picture, it showed a young man smiling in his high school basketball uniform. He was kneeling with one hand on a basketball and the other hand on the floor. He hadn't had the time or the money to take any new photos that could be used on the air. When you were that age, you thought you had plenty of time for everything. There would be time later for a professional portrait with your wife and your new baby. Except later had been stopped in its tracks by a bullet.

"That's right, Frank. Caitlin cried as she told me how she is struggling with the idea of explaining to her son Anthony how his father died."

The segment went on for another five minutes, but Beauregard didn't pay attention. He gripped the arm of the couch so tight his hand began to ache. All he could see was Eric Gay's smiling face. The same face that had stared at him pleading for help on the side of the road.

He got up and went into the kitchen. He grabbed one of the beers he had bought earlier. He checked the sink for a bottle opener. When he didn't find it, he started looking through the drawers.

Why had the news reported the robbery as an attempt? He'd seen the box. Seen the way Ronnie held on to it like it was a life preserver in the middle of the North Atlantic. He might be running game about the amount of the cut, but he had gotten paid. So why was somebody lying to the cops?

Beauregard rifled through the forks and spoons. Nothing.

Why had Eric Gay been in the store? He had told him he was broke. Maybe someone had given them some money. Slipped $500 in a card for the baby. Maybe Eric had gone to get his wife a gift. A thank you for bringing his son into the world. He had wanted to do that for Janice when she had Ariel. He'd thought about doing it for Kia when she had given birth to Javon. By the time Darren entered the picture, other things seemed more important.

He opened the catch-all drawer. There were rolls of duct tape, a ruler, a device to open jars, and other miscellaneous items that tend to accumulate during the life of a household. A bottle opener was not among their number.

Eric and Caitlin had named their baby Anthony. In the book of baby names Janice had dog-eared while carrying Ariel, it said An- thony meant praiseworthy. When they found out it was a girl, they settled on Ariel because Janice liked a cartoon character with the same name. When he and Kia had the boys, she picked the names. He had suggested "Anthony" both times. A subtle tribute to his Daddy's memory. Kia had shot him down both times.

Now there was a boy who would never have memories of his daddy. He would grow up without a father just like Beauregard.

He hadn't really thought they would actually do it. Why the fuck had they named the baby Anthony?

Beauregard hurled the bottle to the floor. It shattered. Shards of glass flew across the kitchen. The beer followed the uneven curve of the floor and pooled under the table.

SEVENTEEN

Ronnie pulled into Jenny's apartment complex with the radio blaring and an empty pint bottle of Jack on the floor. The smile on his face became wider the closer he got to her door. He knocked three times, paused, and then knocked twice more. She opened the door a crack. Ronnie saw she hadn't unlatched the chain.

"You got the money?"

He could barely see her face through the opening in the door. "Well, hello to you too. You gonna let me in?"

"Can't you just pass it to me?"

"No, not really. I got it in these boxes," he said, taking the cereal boxes from under his arm.

"Cereal boxes?"

Ronnie grinned again. "If the cops stop me with nearly a hundred grand in cash, they gonna ask questions. If they see a back seat full of cereal boxes, they just gonna think I'm a big fan of breakfast."

"Whatever. Just slide the box through the door."

A scowl rippled across Ronnie's face.

"You got somebody in there?"

"Ronnie, just give me my money."

"Hey, it ain't like we married or nothing, I'm just asking. I mean, I was hoping I could spend the night, but if you got some dude in there, I'll go on down the road. Can't say I ain't disappointed."

He handed her one box then the other. Jenny snatched them out of his hand with startling quickness.

"You alright? You don't seem like yourself."

"I just got a lot going on right now. I'll talk to you later."

"If I was you, I'd keep an eye on them. You don't need to let your new friend know you holding something magically delicious."

She shut the door and locked it.

"Ain't that bout a bitch," he said under his breath. He whistled a low short tune and headed back to his car. Maybe the time to upgrade was now. Jenny was beginning to look rode hard and hung up wet anyway.

Jenny opened the boxes. They were both stuffed to the gills with cash. She sat them on the couch and went to the bedroom. She grabbed a few shirts and pants and threw them in an overnight bag. She went back into the kitchen and took her sugar bowl out of the cabinet. She'd hidden twenty or so Percocets in the bowl. A gift from Ronnie. She shook all the Percs into her hand and put them in a pocket on the side of the overnight bag. A wet lock of hair fell into her face, but she didn't bother moving it. The wail of an electric guitar made her jump like a long-tailed cat in a room full of rocking chairs. She looked down at the kitchen floor.

The man had finally stopped bleeding. The handle of an eight-inch butcher knife stuck out of his neck like the crank on a jack in the box. The guitar sound was accompanied by a low vibration coming from the pocket of his jeans. That was the tenth or fifteenth time his phone had gone off since 3:00. Jenny stepped over him, careful to avoid the puddle of blood that was surrounding his body, and opened her freezer. She pulled out the ice tray and placed three cubes of ice in a small freezer bag. The ice felt good against her right eye.

Her daddy had been a mean son of a bitch but the one good thing he had done was teach her how to fight. That bastard never pulled any punches with his mouth or his fists. Those hard lessons had proved lucky for her but bad news for the guy lying on the floor. She stepped over him again and went back to the living room. It took some elbow grease, but she got both boxes in the overnight bag.

Jenny went to the window and peeped through the drapes. She didn't see Ronnie anywhere. She grabbed her keys from the hook by the door. She went back to the window. Her apartment complex was laid out like a motel. A series of units with one big front window and a front door that faced the parking lot. She only saw one strange car and that was parked right next to hers. The car looked empty. Still, she decided to wait a few more minutes. She didn't want to pass Ronnie on the road. He'd follow her and pretend he didn't care if she had a guy at her place, then he'd try sweet-talking her. She couldn't have that. She might just tell him everything. No, she had to run. Running might make her look guilty to the cops but staying would get her killed. She'd seen the news. Lou Ellen was lying. Whoever owned the shop didn't want the police in their business. They were sending guys like the dead guy on the floor of her apartment with a mouthful of rotten teeth to handle it for them. Once she got down south, she'd call Ronnie and warn him. She did owe him that.

Jenny checked her phone. The guy had knocked on her door around noon. He'd punched her in the face at 12:15. He was dead by 12:30. It was now nearly 7:00. Six hours of sitting with his rapidly cooling corpse waiting to see who would show up first. Ronnie or Yuckmouth's buddies.

Almost as if on cue, his phone rang again.

"Fuck this," she said. She grabbed her overnight bag and left the apartment. She hopped in her car and started the engine.

"Breathe. Just breathe and drive. That's all you gotta do," she said out loud to herself. She tossed the bag in the passenger seat.

Checked the rearview mirror. Nothing. As she backed out of her parking spot the fuel light started to blink. That was fine. She had more than enough gas money. She'd stop somewhere in North Carolina and score some Adderall or something. Drive all night to Florida. Getting to the Bahamas shouldn't be hard after that. Money talks and everything else walks. She pulled out of the parking lot and turned onto Bethel Road. A fine mist of rain began to fall. Jenny thought that was symbolic. It was like the rain was baptizing her. She'd come out of this a new creature. She didn't have any AC in the car, so she was going to leave the window down until it started raining harder.

A black Cadillac Seville passed her on the two-lane highway as she headed for the nearest gas station. It was the only car on the road. No cops. No gangsters with butter yellow teeth. No Ronnie. Just the old Jenny on her way to a new life.

She was almost to the interstate when she noticed the Cadillac had turned around and was following her.

EIGHTEEN

"Wake up, sleepy head," Kia said. Beauregard opened his eyes. "Can you pick Darren and Javon up this evening? I'm gonna pick up another office job tonight."

"Yeah. Where does that Cook boy live?"

"On Falmouth Road."

Beauregard sat up in the bed.

"Falmouth?"

"Yeah. They in that subdivision," Kia said. She clipped on some earrings and closed her Rottweiler-shaped jewelry box. Beauregard thought that box was one of the ugliest things in existence. You had to lift the head to open it at the throat. You basically had to decapitate it every time you wanted an adornment.

"Okay," he said.

"We gonna be alright, ain't we?" she asked.

Beauregard spun until he felt his feet hit the floor. He grabbed her hand and brought it to his lips. He gave it a brief peck. "Yeah."

She turned and hugged him against her belly. He felt her hand on the back of his neck. He breathed her in and smelled the scent of her body mixed with her perfume and the remnants of the dryer sheets she used in the laundry. Even if they weren't going to be alright, he would never let her know.

Kelvin was already at the shop when Beauregard arrived. There were two vehicles in the air on the lifts. Kelvin was under one, a black pickup truck, working on the oil filter.

"Hey."

"Hey. You just in time. Doing an oil change on this one and the car keeps making a funny noise that's not a rattle or a clank or a clang or a ping," Kelvin said.

"Then ain't a funny noise, it's just the engine," Beauregard said.

Kelvin laughed. "I'm just telling you what the lady said. And we got a call from the Cedars Septic Service. Wanted to know if we could look at one of their trucks today. I told them we didn't take no crap."

Beauregard frowned.

"Fuck you, that was funny. I suspect we gonna be real busy this week," Kelvin said.

"Yeah. Precision caught on fire last night," Beauregard said.

"Oh, I didn't know if you knew. Sucks for them, but good for us."

"I guess," Beauregard said.

They did twelve oil changes, replaced eight sets of brake pads and started on the septic truck. By four, they were both soaking wet with sweat and loving every minute of it.

"Nice being busy, huh?" Kelvin asked. He had just driven a two-seat sports car into the back lot after adjusting its fuel injector. Beauregard was using an impact wrench to take off the back tire of an old Caprice. Before he could answer, they heard two vehicles pull up and the sounds of multiple car doors slamming shut. Beauregard stopped trying to remove the tire's lug nuts and turned to face whoever was coming into the shop. It wasn't the cops. If they had come for him, they would have announced themselves as soon as they got out.

Patrick Thompson and his father Butch entered the shop through the first roll-up door. Patrick was a thin wiry figure with a shock of bright blond hair cut into a shaggy surfer-boy style. Butch was a square block of a man. All hard angles and broad shoulders. He was bald but had a prodigious blond and gray beard.

"Pat," Beauregard said. He had known Pat Thompson before he'd become the competition. He'd seen him at Danny's a few times. Pat had a '69 Camaro that he liked to run on the back roads sometimes. They had never gone head to head, but Beauregard knew the Camaro had legs. His daddy used to be a truck driver for a long-haul company out of Richmond. A year and a half ago, Butch Thompson had stopped at a gas station to fill up his rig. While he was in line to pay for his fuel, he'd purchased a one-dollar scratch-off ticket. He'd done the same thing a hundred times in the past. The most he'd ever won was $700. That day he received a huge return on his investment. He hit for $400,000. He called up his boss and told him to send someone to pick up his load because he had just quit. He and Patrick had opened their garage a few months later.

"Beau. You heard about my place?" Patrick asked. His blue eyes bore a hole into Beauregard.

"Yeah."

"That's all you got to say? Yeah?" Butch asked. He was clenching and unclenching his hands. They looked like bear traps.

"What you want me to say, Butch?"

"Somebody say they saw a black guy running from the scene, Beau. I thought maybe you might know something about that," Patrick said.

Kelvin picked up a torque wrench.

"Why would you think I'd know something about that?" Beauregard said.

"Cuz you the only black guy who owns a garage that's been getting its ass kicked," Butch said. He took a step forward.

"You think I set fire to your place? Really?" Beauregard asked.

"I think you might know who did. The cops say it was deliberate. My dad told them to come talk to you, but I guess they didn't take us serious," Patrick said.

"Pat, I didn't have nothing to do with what happened to your place. I'm sorry for you, but I don't know nothing about it."

"You a lying black bastard," Butch said. His face was mottled with splotches of red just above his beard.

"What you say?" Beauregard asked. He let the impact wrench slip from his hand and held it by the air hose. It hung loosely by his side.

"You heard me. You know who did it. You sent them. Couldn't compete with us anymore. Then we got that contract. In three months there was gonna be a CLOSED sign on your door and we all know it," Butch said.

"The cops say they need proof to arrest you. I just wanted to ask you to your face," Patrick said. His eyes were red. He'd probably been up all night. Beauregard knew he would have been.

"I told him it was a waste of time. All you people do is lie and steal. And make babies you can't take care of. Bunch of fucking nig—"

Beauregard whipped the impact wrench up and out by its air hose. It flew through the air and smashed into Butch's mouth. The bigger man stumbled backwards, his hands covering the lower half of his face. His blond and gray beard was stained with streaks of red.

Beauregard snapped the wrench back and caught it in midair. He ran at Butch and clocked him in the forehead with the wrench. Butch fell onto his ass. He raised his hands and grabbed at Beauregard's shirt. Beauregard hit him on the top of the head. The impact wrench split Butch's scalp open like an orange peel. Beauregard raised the impact wrench above his head.

Patrick tackled him. They tumbled to the floor. A thin arm snaked around his neck and gripped him like a python. Kelvin came running over. He swung the four-foot-long torque wrench like a golf club. The head struck Patrick in the small of the back. Beauregard heard him cry out like a wounded fox. Beauregard shrugged him off and got to his feet. He kicked Patrick in the gut. Then he kicked him again.

"Please . . . ," Patrick gasped.

Beauregard got down on one knee and shoved the socket of the impact wrench in Patrick's mouth.

"I should break all your teeth. Make you eat soup for a year. Give you time to think. If I had wanted to put you out of business, I would have just caught you outside of Danny's one night and broken both your hands. Not burn down your shop," he said.

Patrick's eyes were wild. Saliva dripped down his chin. Beauregard took the wrench out of his mouth and stood.

"Get the fuck out of here," he said. Patrick rolled into a kneeling position. He held his stomach with one arm and crawled to his father. Butch was flat on his back and mewling. Patrick struggled to his feet. He grabbed his father by the arm and helped the older man off the floor. The laceration on his scalp was bleeding freely, making his face a crimson mask. His beard was nearly soaked through. The two of them limped out the door. Kelvin tossed the torque wrench to the ground. It sent an echo reverberating through the garage. He was breathing hard.

"Well, that went well. How much bail money you think we gonna need?" Kelvin said.

"They ain't gonna tell nobody. At least not the cops."

"You don't think so?"

Beauregard set the impact wrench on top of the tool chest. The socket was smeared with blood and spit.

"They were here trespassing. They said the cops told them to let them handle it. They won't feel too much sympathy for them. Besides, guys like that only talk about the fights they win."

Beauregard turned into the cul-de-sac off Falmouth Road. It was called, not surprisingly, Falmouth Acres. He drove past the lawns manicured to within an inch of their lives and the only sidewalks outside of the courthouse area. This was where money lived in Red Hill County. His old pickup stood out among the luxury cars and SUVs.

The Cook house sat at the end of the cul-de-sac under the shade from an enormous elm tree. Beauregard would not have built his house there. A strong storm could send a branch crashing through the bedroom like an arboreal missile. Money made you value aesthetics over safety, he guessed. He parked on the curb and walked past a brick column with a plaque that proclaimed the House of Cook was established in 2005.

The doorbell was a white button in the center of an arabesque series of swirls. He pushed it once and heard the theme from every old horror movie he had ever seen ring through the house. The door opened, and a slim, pale white woman greeted him. A sharp bob with razor-cut bangs framed her narrow face. She wore a long black sleeved shirt and black tights despite the heat. Beauregard felt a cool rush of air when she opened the door. A central air unit was working hard to keep the whole house at a comfortable temperature.

"You must be Javon's father. I'm Miranda."

"Yes. Nice to meet you."

"Well, come on in." Beauregard didn't move.

"Actually, I'm kinda in a hurry. Could you just get Javon for me? Please."

Miranda smiled.

"Of course. I must say my husband and I were so impressed with your son. He is a perfect young gentleman," she said. She went back into the house through an expansive foyer. A few minutes later, Javon came down the stairs.

"Thank you for letting me spend the night, Mrs. Cook," he said as she slipped on his backpack.

"Well, you're welcome. Tre sure appreciated you hanging out with him. He was glad to have someone to talk to about Claude Monet," she said with a smile.

"Well, you take care now," Beauregard said. He put his hand on Javon's shoulder and half guided, half pulled Javon through the doorway. They walked to the truck in silence. Beauregard pulled out of Falmouth Acres. He turned right and headed deeper into the county.

"Where we going?" Javon asked. Beauregard didn't respond. He turned down Chain Ferry Road then down Ivy Lane. The lane ended at the old public landing for the Blackwater River. Once they reached the boat ramp Beauregard stopped the truck and killed the engine.

"We need to talk," he said.

"About what?"

Beauregard gripped the steering wheel. Then he relaxed his grip and turned to Javon. "I'm gonna ask you a question and I want the truth. Do you understand me?"

"Yeah."

"Don't just say that because you think that's what I want to hear. I want you to tell me the honest truth."

"Okay," Javon said. He had his head down with his chin nearly touching his chest.

Beauregard closed his eyes and ran a hand across his face. He left his hand over his eyes. "Did you set fire to Precision Auto?"

Javon didn't respond. Beauregard opened his eyes and caught a glimpse of the river. The sun was skipping across its surface like stones. The window was down so he could hear the water gently lapping against the riverbank. His grandfather used to take him here to fish for catfish and carp. He wasn't that good at fishing, but it didn't really matter. His Granddaddy James, his mother's father, was a patient teacher. If he hadn't gotten sent to juvie, then he might have gotten good at it. By the time he got out, his grandfather was dead.

"I ain't never heard you talk about this boy Tre Cook before. But his house is within walking distance of Precision Auto. So, I'm gonna ask you again. Did you do it?"

Javon ran his hands over his face the same way his father had a few moments earlier. He turned and glared out the window. When he spoke, his voice didn't crack or waver.

"I was just trying to help. Mama told Aunt Jean we might lose the shop."

Beauregard punched the dashboard. The old leather split just like Butch Thompson's scalp. Javon flinched and pressed himself against the door of the truck. Beauregard grabbed him by his arm and shook him.

"What did I tell you? Didn't I tell you that you didn't have to worry about that? Jesus Christ, Javon, do you even know how much trouble you could get into? They could send you to juvie, and trust and believe you don't want that! What if somebody had been in there working? Goddamn it, boy, what was you thinking?"

Beauregard had never hit his boys. For that matter, he had never hit Ariel. His mother had slapped him around a few times and his father had gone ballistic. He didn't let his kids walk all over him, though. He demanded their respect, and when he didn't get it, he let them know accordingly. The desire to strike one of them for some transgression had never been stronger than his desire to assure them that they were loved.

Until today. A part of him (the part that loved the thrill of driving, perhaps?) wanted to slap Javon right in the mouth.

"I just wanted Mama to stop crying!" Javon yelled.

"What?"

"You don't know because you always gone. She don't cry in front of you. But whenever you ain't home, by the time she puts us to bed she cries. She was telling Aunt Jean on the phone that every time you leave, she scared the next time she sees you it gonna be in a casket. She always talking to her about she don't want you to do stuff that gonna get you in trouble!" Javon said. He was weeping now. Tears and words flowing freely in equal measure.

Beauregard let go of his arm.

"I thought if the other place was gone, you wouldn't have to do the bad stuff. I thought things would get better. I don't want you to die, Daddy," he said. He grabbed the tail of his T-shirt and wiped his nose.

Beauregard clenched his jaw. He moved his head around in a circle like he was taking in his surroundings for the first time. A nasty bubble of acid was trying to work its way up his esophagus.

"Javon, I ain't gonna die. Not no time soon. And even if I do, that still don't mean you gotta try and take over. You ain't the man of the house. You just a twelve-year-old boy. That's all you need to be. That man of the house shit will get you hurt. Trust me," he said finally.

"Mama said you did when your Daddy left. She said you did what you had to do," Javon said. His tears had slowed to a trickle. He sniffed, then let out a wet cough.

"Don't do what I did, Javon. I ain't nobody you should be trying to be like. I made a lot of mistakes. Terrible mistakes. The only good things I've done is marrying your Mama and having you and Darren and your sister. The things I had to do hurt a lot more people than they helped. I was trying to be something I wasn't ready to be. Just like you did," Beauregard said.

He could see himself in the driver's seat of the Duster. Thirteen years old. His foot on the gas. The horrified faces of the three men that had been talking to his Daddy.

"Are you going to tell on me?" Javon asked.

Beauregard snapped his head to the right. "No. No, I'm not going to tell on you. Was that Tre boy with you?"

"No, I . . . I snuck out by myself. I told him I was meeting a girl."

"The only people that know is me and you. And that's the way it's gonna stay. But you gotta promise me something, and I mean you gotta swear to me, boy."

"Okay."

Beauregard studied the horn in the center of the steering wheel.

"I ain't gonna tell you it's wrong, because you know it's wrong. You gotta promise no matter how bad you think things are, you won't never do anything like this again. You start down a road like this and before you know it you can't find your way back. You lose yourself. One day you wake up and you're just this thing that does shit and don't feel nothing. And that's the worst thing you can be. I can't let that happen to you. I'm your Daddy and it's my job to protect you.

Even if that means protecting you from yourself. Promise me you won't ever do anything like this again," Beauregard said.

"I promise."

Beauregard put his arm around Javon and pulled him close.

"I love you, boy. As long as I got breath in my body, I'm gonna be there for you. My Daddy wasn't always there for me. I ain't gonna do that to you." He hugged him tight then released him.

"I love you too," Javon said.

Beauregard started the truck, but before he could put it in gear, Javon asked him a question that stopped him cold. It was a question he had expected him to ask one day. In some respects, it made sense he would ask the question now, after his Montage blood had made itself known in spectacular fashion.

"What happened to your Daddy?" Javon asked.

Beauregard sat back in the truck and let out a mirthless chuckle.

"My Daddy? My Daddy was like a thunderstorm in a world of gentle breezes. That's the way he tore through life. That's the way he raised me," Beauregard said.

Javon opened his mouth like he was going to ask another question, but then he shut it and turned to the window.

Later that night, Beauregard sat on the porch drinking a beer. The crickets and the katydids were having a battle of the bands. The moonless sky was black as pitch. The temperature had dropped approximately one degree from a high of 97 earlier in the morning. Moths danced around the yellow porch light. Drawn to their death by the same thing that fascinated them.

Kia came out and sat next to him in the other plastic Adirondack chair.

"Javon is quieter than usual. He fell asleep with those ear phones on. He ain't come out of his room since we finished eating."

"Uh huh," Beauregard said as he took a sip of his beer.

"Anything going on I should know about?" she asked. She touched his arm and he handed her the bottle. She took a long sip, then handed it back. Beauregard answered her question with a question.

"You tell Jean I was doing a job?" he asked.

Kia crinkled her brow. "No, why you ask that?"

"Javon said he overheard you telling her I might have to do something bad to save the shop."

Kia bit her bottom lip. "I might have said something like that, but I didn't say it was a job. Now I've answered your question. You gonna answer mine?"

Beauregard took another sip. "Pat Thompson came by today. Accused me of burning his place down just like you said he would. We got into it."

"Did you hurt him?"

"Nothing some iodine and bandages can't fix."

Kia leaned back in the chair.

"You think they gonna press charges?"

"Nah. They was in the wrong. I know this ain't the end of it, though."

"What's that got to do with Javon? You know why he's so quiet, don't you?"

Beauregard peered into the darkness. The light from the highway danced down the road like ball lightning.

"Javon set fire to the Precision Auto," he said.

Kia shot up and headed for the door. Beauregard reached out and grabbed her wrist. He pulled her back down as gently as he could.

"He thought he was helping. He's heard us talking about how tight things are. Burning down the competition seemed like a solution," he said.

"Jesus, Bug, what are we gonna do?"

"We gonna protect him, that's what we gonna do. You know, I used to think I was a better man than my Daddy. I tried hard to be a better father. But it's like I gave my boys a sickness. The counselor in juvie called it a 'propensity for violent conflict resolution.' That's one way to put it," Beauregard said.

He finished his beer in one long gulp. He stood up and hurled the bottle into the woods. He heard it land somewhere in the brush.

"It's a fucking curse, is what it is," he said. "Money can't fix it and love can't tame it. Push it down deep and it rots you from the inside out. Give in to it and you end up doing five years in some hellhole. I once saw my Daddy beat a man half to death with a bar stool over the man's wife. What Javon did ain't really his fault. Violence is a Montage family tradition."

Red Hill County

August 1991

"It's gonna storm, Bug. See them clouds over there? It's coming hard and fast. Can't you smell it in the air?" Anthony said.

Bug leaned out the car window and let the wind slap him in the face. His Daddy was right, he could smell the rain in the air. It was a high sweet scent that suffused the atmosphere. In the distance a mass of dark clouds were gathering. They were full like overripe plums ready to burst.

"After we get the shakes, maybe I should go get some neck bones. Take you home and make some soup for you and your Mama," Anthony said.

Bug knew what that meant. His Daddy was planning on spending the night. That meant an hour of laughing and two hours of arguing followed by two hours of hushed talking in his Mama's bedroom. It also meant he got to spend more time with his Daddy.

They pulled into the Tastee Freez and his Daddy put the car in neutral. He set the parking brake and hopped out with a deft agility that belied his size. He closed the door, then leaned through the open window.

"Two shakes and a couple of greasy cheeseburgers. You want anything else?"

"No. Can I get a chocolate shake instead of strawberry?"

"Sure. You changing up on me," Anthony said with a laugh. He jogged over to the sliding window to place his order. A few other customers were parked to the right of the building. Carhops made trips back and forth, ferrying food and drinks to families in minivans and the odd station wagon. Bug heard the high-pitched laughter of the girl taking the orders. He saw his Daddy trying to poke his head through the window and the girl giggling like a maniac. A few raindrops began to hit the windshield.

He wished it could always be like this. Him and his Daddy riding the roads on a rocket with wheels. Watching the rolling hills blur as they flew past. The smell of gasoline and burning rubber soaking into their clothes. Just him and his Daddy surfing the blacktop. No destination in mind, just enjoying the drive. But he knew that was a daydream. Things would never be that way and he was learning to accept that. The truth was his Daddy was always a better father in his daydreams than he was in real life. That didn't stop him from loving him so completely it felt as inherent as the color of his skin.

Screeching tires made him turn around. A white IROC-Z skidded into the parking lot and stopped just inches from the Duster's rear bumper. Bug saw three white men get out and start stalking toward his Daddy as he came over to the Duster carrying the shakes and the burgers. The men walked past the window and Bug caught a whiff of liquor. It was bitter and mean like the green rubbing alcohol his grandmother used on her knees. Bug sat straight up in the passenger seat as the men surrounded his father. The biggest man was wearing a light blue tank top that showed off his multiple tattoos. The blurry edges and the pale black-gone-green ink made the tats look like the scribblings of a child. A bright, wine-colored birthmark stood out against the pale skin on the man's neck. His black hair was slick backed and thinning.

"Ant," the man said.

Bug watched his Daddy give the man a once-over.

"Red," he said finally.

"Get in the car, Ant," Red said.

"What this about Red? Huh? We done. We quits," Anthony said. There was a tone to his Daddy's voice that disturbed Bug. He sounded like a different person. He spoke in a flat, robotic way that seemed in direct contrast to his usual jovialness.

"We ain't done, you motherfucker. We ain't done by a long shot. My brother got picked up Tuesday," Red said. He spoke with a restrained ferocity that was frightening. Bug thought he sounded like a rabid dog growling through a fence.

"And what that got to do with me? White went out and got a Corvette and dropping c-notes at Danny's Bar a week after we did what we did. Sheriff ain't gotta be Matlock to figure that out," Anthony said.

"You the only one that could put any of us at the scene. He called me last night saying the cops told him they got a witness that put him at the payroll robbery. Now I know it ain't me. And it ain't Blue. So, who the fuck you think that leaves? Now get in the goddamn car," Red said.

Bug saw him pull up his tank top. He caught a glimpse of a wooden handle. He had a gun. The man had a gun and was telling his Daddy to go with him.

"Red. We can talk about this but not now. Not in front my boy," Anthony said. Bug watched as his eyes narrowed to slits. He knew what that meant too. That was the same way his father had looked last night in the bar. A man had told his Daddy to stay away from the man's wife or he was gonna catch a bullet. His Daddy had finished his beer, then picked up the bar stool and beat the man half to death with it. They'd left Sharkey's shortly thereafter. His Daddy had made him promise not to tell his Mama they had been in a bar and Bug had agreed that was something his Mama definitely did not need to know.

Thunder boomed from the east. The rain began to fall faster.

"Why not? He need to see what happens to snitches. Now I ain't gonna say this again, Ant. Get in the goddamn car."

Bug was lifting his leg over the gearshift before he fully understood what he was doing.

"I'm not leaving my boy here, Red. You gonna shoot me in front all these people?" Anthony asked.

"Try me, Ant. My brother staring down twenty-five years. Just try me."

Bug slipped into the driver's seat.

"I ain't no fucking snitch, Red. You want me to go with you, okay. But you follow me and let me drop my boy off."

Bug gripped the 8-ball shifter.

"You must think I'm a fool. I ain't letting you get behind the wheel of no car. The last thing I ever see of you will be your fucking tail lights."

Bug eased the clutch in and slipped the Duster into first. The engine idled like a quiet man clearing his throat.

"Red. Please. Not here," Anthony said.

Bug stared at his father. His father caught his gaze and stared back. His nod was so subtle it had to be an unconscious gesture, Bug released the parking brake.

"Get your black ass in the car. I'm not telling you again. Last time, Ant," Red growled. His face was emblematic of his nickname. Anthony cut his eyes toward the Duster.

"Whatever you say, Red," Anthony said.

Bug took his left foot off the clutch and slammed his right against the gas pedal. The leather steering wheel cover was slathered in his sweat. He gripped it as the Duster leaped forward. Anthony threw the cardboard drink carrier into Red's face and jumped to the left. Smoke from the rear tires enveloped the Duster as the engine howled.

The space between the Duster and the three men who had confronted his father was less than twenty feet. The Duster went from

0 to 50 as it covered that distance. Bug could hear screams through the open windows. The screams sounded womanish, but they came from two of the three men in front of him.

The impact was horrific. The whole car shuddered when he plowed into them. One of the men was launched skyward. Red and the other one disappeared under the front bumper of the Duster. Bug kept the pedal to the floor and rolled over them. He heard their bodies bounce off the undercarriage. It reminded him of the time his mother hit a raccoon in her old LTD. A hollow knocking that traveled the length of the car. He passed by the order window doing 60. He saw that the young white girl's mouth was a huge O as he flew past her. He hit the clutch and the brake while twisting the steering wheel to the left. The Duster violently stalled and skidded to a stop.

Anthony got up off the concrete and ran over to the three bodies sprawled across the ground. They seemed to be bleeding from every orifice. Blue had tire tracks across his forearms and chest. His head was twisted at an odd angle in direct opposition to the position of his pelvis. Timmy Clovis had flown straight up in the air and landed directly on his head. A red and pink fibrous mass was leaking out the back of his skull. Beauregard realized that was his brain.

Red Navely groaned.

Anthony knelt beside him. Both his legs were bent backwards at the knee like a bird. Red's chest was crushed into a concave on the right side. Blood bubbled out of his ears and his mouth. A swath of skin had been sloughed off the side of his head, exposing an angry red wound. Every breath he took expelled more blood that then splashed across his chin. There were tire tracks across his thighs.

"I told you not in front of my boy," Anthony said. He placed his wide hand over Red's nose and mouth.

"Is . . . . is he okay?" a tiny voice squeaked. The girl from the register had come from behind the counter. Anthony bent over Red's body.

"Go call 911! Go!" he screamed without turning around. He

heard the girl's feet pounding against the pavement as she ran. Red tried to move his hand toward his gun, but it didn't seem to be working correctly. He trembled once, then twice, then was still. The life drained out of his eyes like a light bulb slowly going dim.

Beauregard squeezed the steering wheel so hard his forearms ached. He could see a willowy plume of white steam pouring from under the hood. The hood itself was dented in the middle. His chest felt like an elephant was standing on it.

"Get out the car, Bug. No need to give the cops a reason to pop a cap in you when they get here," Anthony said. He opened the door and helped Beauregard out of the car. Beauregard bent over and placed his hands on his knees. He waited for a stream of vomit that never came. Anthony rubbed his back with his huge soup bone of a hand.

"It's alright, Bug. You go on and be sick if you need to. You ain't meant for this life. That's a good thing," Anthony said.

"They were gonna kill you," Beauregard said between dry heaves.

"Yeah, I think they had that in mind, Bug. Don't you worry, I'm gonna tell the cops it was an accident. Everything gonna be alright."

Four weeks later, Bug was sentenced to five years in juvie for involuntary manslaughter.

By then his Daddy was long gone.

NINETEEN

"Wake up, Ronnie."

"Lemme alone, Reggie. My head aching like a gnome digging his way out with a spoon," Ronnie said. His mouth tasted like the bottom of an oil barrel. If his memory served him correctly, they had drunk three bottles of Jameson last night. He and Reggie had consumed most of it, but the two Mexican girls had their share too. What were their names again? Guadalupe and Esmerelda. That sounded right. Maybe.

"Ronnie, please wake up."

They'd picked them up at Laredo's Saloon in Richmond. Brought them back to Reggie's trailer for a night of debauchery so uninhibited it would have made Hugh Hefner blush. The last thing Ronnie remembered was one of the girls sucking his dick like she had been poisoned and the antidote was in his nuts.

"Ronnie, wake the fuck up!"

It had been two weeks since the job and he wasn't slowing up one iota. For all his talk about white sandy beaches and blue skies, he wasn't in such a hurry to leave Virginia anymore. Jenny had bailed on him but that wasn't such a bad thing. The same day she dipped, they found the dyke chick burnt crispier than grandma's fried chicken. The way the news was telling it, the cops figured she and Jenny had been in on the robbery. There was no mention of any of their possible accomplices. The heat wasn't off, but it was turned down from broil to simmer.

"You should listen to your brother."

Ronnie's eyes snapped open as he reached for his piece under his pillow. He had given Reggie the money to purchase it legally. A Beretta 9 mm.

"Ah, it ain't there, brother. You might want to sit up for this."

Ronnie turned over so slow he might as well have been demonstrating plate tectonics.

Two men were standing on either side of Reggie at the foot of his bed. One of them had a nasty scar on the side of his face. He wore a white dress shirt open at the collar with the tail untucked. The other man was as wide as a refrigerator. He wore a blue blazer over a black T-shirt. The T-shirt barely contained his belly. He was the one pressing the barrel of a .357 into Reggie's ribs.

"Morning, Sunshine," the man with the scar and the Colonel Sanders facial hair said.

"You from Chuly? Because I gave Skunk the money. I paid in full, with interest," Ronnie said. The man with the scar shivered and laughed.

"Nah, we ain't from Chuly. And we ain't nearly as bad as Skunk Mitchell. Not really," the man with the scar said.

Ronnie sat up and let the blanket fall and cover his waist. Reggie's eyes were as big as dinner plates. Ronnie wracked his brain. Was there someone he had pissed off in the last few weeks that would send some boys to rough him up? He drew a blank.

"Look, I don't know what this all about, so why don't you enlighten me a little bit, Hoss," Ronnie said. He spoke to the man with the scar. He seemed to be the brains of the operation. The man with the scar smiled.

"Well, let me see how I can put this. You done fucked up, Ronnie. You done fucked up so bad you might wanna find your mama and crawl back in her snatch and try again. But since that ain't gonna happen, you need to get up, put your clothes on, and come with us. Be quick now. I'm trying to catch breakfast. You boys ain't got nothing in the cabinet but a cereal box full of money. Can't eat that, now can I?" the man with the scar said.

Ronnie had heard the phrase "His blood ran cold" before, but it had never carried much weight with him. He always thought it sounded like something some Hollywood scriptwriter had convinced himself was cool. Now as a chill settled in his veins, he understood the time-tested phrase. They knew about the money. That could mean one of two things. A: This was just some random home invasion that got lucky. That didn't seem likely. A rust-covered single-wide trailer was not usually the target of a crew of home invaders. These boys didn't look like hopped-up meth heads looking for an easy score. So that led to Option B. They were pros who had come specifically looking for him and the money. That was the option that chilled him to his bones. That option led to all kinds of bad conclusions. He decided to play dumb and see if these boys would let him in on what kind of game they were playing.

"Hold on now, I mean, what's going on, man? I don't get what's happening. You gotta give me something. Y'all rolling up in here like Wyatt Earp and shit," Ronnie said. He spoke in low soft tones and let honey drip over his words.

The man with the scar frowned.

"You just ain't listening." He pulled out a gun of his own and shot Reggie in the right foot. The tiny bedroom was filled with the ear-splitting cacophony of the gunshot. Ronnie jumped back and covered his ears. Reggie fell to the floor clutching at his right leg. The light breaking through the window highlighted his pale sweaty face.

"Shit, man!" Ronnie squealed. Reggie had fallen over and was lying in the fetal position. His moans were wet and reedy. The man with the scar pointed his gun at Ronnie. It was a .38 with a wood grip. It looked like a toy in his wide hand.

"You wanna get your clothes on? I was serious about that breakfast."

TWENTY

Beauregard hadn't been dancing in years. Not because he didn't enjoy it, but there never seemed to be enough time. Between dealing with the garage and the boys and Ariel and his Mama, spare time was scarcer than hen's teeth. When he had been double-deep in the Life, he and Kia would drive up to Richmond at the drop of a hat. They'd get dressed up, hit the clubs, and dance until the ugly lights came on. They would leave having spent more on spilled liquor than most people made in a week.

It had been so long Beauregard worried he wouldn't be able to find the beat. Yet here he was in the middle of Danny's, dipping and gyrating in rhythm with Kia. One arm around her waist, the other on her firm hip. The music thumping from wall-mounted speakers filled the bar with a tribalistic carnality. Beauregard felt it working its way through his body as Kia pressed herself against his crotch. Even after all these years, she still captivated the savage that lived between his legs. She was a caramel-dipped Aphrodite to his chocolate-covered Pan.

The song ended but the spell remained unbroken. He pulled her close and nuzzled her neck. The scent of her skin beneath her perfume was more intoxicating than the $500 fragrance she had bought that morning. She had also purchased a new outfit and gotten her hair done.

"Now, Mr. Montage, you gonna take me out and we are gonna dance and drink, and if you're lucky, you gonna get some A1 pussy tonight," she had said after her shopping spree. He hadn't needed much convincing. The money from the jewelry store job had given them some breathing room. Might as well enjoy it. Ronnie was a weasel, but he had been right about that.

Eric, Caitlin and little Anthony aren't enjoying much these days though, are they? Beauregard thought.

He'd given serious consideration to sending Caitlin some money. Not a lot but enough to help with the bills or buy a toy for the baby. He'd ruminated on it long and hard before finally pushing the idea away. Things were still too hot right now. No way he could go anywhere near Caitlin and Anthony. That didn't stop him from thinking about them though. Especially that baby boy. He'd grow up belonging to the same fraternity as Beauregard. The brotherhood of fatherless sons.

But he wouldn't be a member if you hadn't done your part to induct him, now, would he, he thought.

Kia rubbed his thigh.

"The way you was dancing up on me I think you want this," Kia whispered in his ear. Beauregard forced a smile.

"All the time and twice on Sunday," Beauregard whispered back. She giggled and kissed him. The taste of whiskey and bubble gum–flavored lip gloss filled his mouth.

"Yo, let's get some shots!" Kelvin said. He had his arm around the waist of a woman Beauregard had never seen before and didn't expect to see again. Kelvin had some disposable income as well. The garage was busy as a one-legged man in an ass-kicking contest. Beauregard would never admit it, but Javon had been right. Burning down Precision had helped. That saddened him something fierce.

"Okay, what y'all want?" he asked.

"Nothing too strong. I'm feeling those Blue Motorcycles," Kelvin's friend said. She was a tall drink of water with long brown hair highlighted with blond and a hard-earned natural tan. A few of the regulars glanced at them when they came in but not with any serious intent. They just regarded her as another white woman lost to the other side.

"How about Red Headed Sluts?" Kia offered.

"I know a few of those," Kelvin said. His friend jabbed him with her elbow.

"I'll get some Royal Flushes," Beauregard said. He headed for the bar while everyone else went back to the table. Beauregard leaned against the scarred railing that surrounded the top of the bar and raised his hand.

"What can I get you?" the bartender asked.

"Four Royal Flushes."

"Coming right up."

"A Royal Flush is the hardest hand to get in poker. Almost never happens," a man sitting to Beauregard's right said. Beauregard turned and gave him a nod.

"Yeah, that's what they say," he remarked. He wasn't sure that was what they said or not, he was just making conversation.

"Yeah, the Dead Man's Hand is more common," the man said. He moved his hair out of his face. Beauregard saw he was scarred worse than the bar top.

"What?"

The man smiled at Beauregard.

"Aces and eights. The Dead Man's Hand. Wild Bill Hickok was holding that when somebody snuck up behind him and blew his head off," the man said.

"Oh yeah, that's right," Beauregard said. The bartender returned with the shots. He placed them in front of Beauregard and slipped away. Beauregard gathered up the four shot glasses and started to leave.

"Personally, I wouldn't never sneak up behind a fella. If I was going to kill you, I'd just pull up and put two in your face. That's how they taught us in Iraq. Double tap," the man said.

Beauregard stopped and studied the man's ruined face. The man was still smiling. "Uh huh. Well, you have a nice night," Beauregard said. He gathered the shots and returned to the table. A new song came on the jukebox and some couples made their way back to the dance floor. Beauregard handed everyone their shots.

"Woohoo. I felt that in my toes," Kelvin said. His friend laughed and leaned into him.

"Damn, you trying to get me drunk and take advantage of me, Bug?" Kia asked. Her skin shimmered under a patina of sweat and glitter makeup. Beauregard tickled her chin.

"It ain't taking advantage, if you want it," he said. Kelvin burst out in high peals of laughter.

"Smart-ass," Kia said but then she leaned in and kissed him again. Beauregard kissed her back, then surreptitiously peered over her shoulder. The man with the scarred face was staring at him.

Beauregard dropped his eyes. He hugged his wife, then gave the bar a quick once-over. He recognized most of the patrons or had an idea who they were save for the man at the bar and two men sitting at a table near the far-right wall. They were both Beauregard's height but considerably wider. They were wearing blue blazers and black T-shirts. They both had a mug of beer in front of them, but they had barely touched them.

Beauregard studied their faces. They were exceptionally unremarkable. Flat doughy visages with a narrow slash for a mouth. The only thing that stood out about them were their eyes. Dead brown eyes like pennies that had been buried in the dirt.

Red Hill County was not a place that strangers visited often. It wasn't at the crossroads of any major highways. The interstate on-ramp was mainly an escape route for the locals. Unfamiliar faces were a rarity. Beauregard watched the two men at the table. They stared straight ahead or occasionally up at the ceiling. They never once turned their heads toward the bar. They never looked in the direction of the scarred man.

"Listen to your gut. The day you don't, it's going to be a shitty situation."

He'd overheard his father say that dozens of times. A crude saying but also an accurate one. His gut was talking to him now. Whispering to him that there was something up with the three unfamiliar faces.

Beauregard pulled out his phone and sent Kelvin a text.

Take the girls outside.

Kelvin picked up his phone. He read the message and typed a response.

What's up?

Beauregard's fingers flew over the screen.

Guys at the table and the bar. I need to check them out.

Kelvin sent back a long response.

You want me to send them home?

Not going to leave you.

3 on 2 is better than 3 on 1.

"Who you texting?" Kia asked. She reached for his phone. Beauregard grabbed her wrist and pulled her hand to his mouth and kissed it. She rolled her eyes and pulled her hand away. "Everybody you know is here," she said. She was grinning like a mad clown.

"Jamal bringing a car to the shop. I gotta go down there and open up."

Kia slipped out of her chair and into Beauregard's lap. She threw her arms around his neck.

"Noooo, you can't leave. We just getting started." She kissed Beauregard on the neck, but he thought she was aiming for his cheek.

"You drunk, boo. I'm gonna get Kelvin to take y'all home. It's midnight and we gotta get the boys. K, you mind taking them home and picking up Darren and Javon?" Beauregard asked.

"You sure?" Kelvin asked. The jocularity that had been in his voice earlier had evaporated.

"Yeah, I'm sure. I'll call you tomorrow."

"Bug, I'll ride with you," Kia said.

"Baby, you need to go home. You gotta work tomorrow. Go with Kelvin and them. I'll be home after a while," he said.

"What's wrong?" Kia asked.

"Nothing. Just gotta go open up for Jamal. One day I'm gonna get my own wrecker truck and we won't have this problem," he said. He tickled her chin again, but her face was slack.

"NO, something's wrong," she slurred. The last shot was hitting her. It had also apparently improved her lie-detecting skills.

"Nah, baby, it's okay. I'll be home soon," Beauregard said. He slipped her off his lap and stood. Kia rose and wobbled but Beauregard gripped her left elbow and steadied her. Kelvin and his friend rose as well. Beauregard kissed Kia on her cheek.

"See you in a few, boo," he whispered.

"You sure?" Kelvin asked.

"I'm sure. I'll see you at the shop tomorrow," Beauregard said.

"Bring me a doughnut when you come home," Kia said.

"Alright, baby. I love ya."

"You better," she said. She headed for the door with Kelvin and his friend in tow. Kelvin looked back over his shoulder. Beauregard didn't say anything. Kelvin followed the ladies out the door.

Beauregard turned around and went back toward the bar. As he passed the table with the two hillbilly hoodlums, he gave them a closer look. The one on the left had a bulge in his waistband on the right side. Beauregard wasn't shocked they were able to get a gun into Danny's. The bar didn't have a bouncer. The sign on the door prohibiting weapons was taken as a suggestion by most of the patrons. Beauregard walked past the scarred man sitting at the bar. He had a bulge in the small of his back under his white shirt.

Beauregard went to the bathroom in the rear of the building. He ran some water in the sink and rinsed his face. Three armed men he had never seen before were in a bar in his hometown. Had the Thompsons hired some out-of-town hitters? That didn't seem likely. Patrick and his dad were hands-on type of boys. If there was going to be any blowback, they would do it themselves. Beauregard dried his face with a paper towel.

He'd been watching the news off and on since he'd seen the report about Eric. The jewelry store manager had been found burned to a crisp in her apartment. Ronnie's girl had skipped town but she'd left a dead body behind. The police said that arrests in the robbery were imminent but Beauregard thought that was some high-grade horseshit.

"Someone's tying up loose ends," he said to his reflection.

That was the risk you took being in the Life. No matter how smart you were or how well you planned there was always the possibility that some shitkicker would show up at your favorite bar looking to double tap your ass. It was the Sword of Damocles you willingly placed above your head every time you pulled a job.

He took a deep breath and exited the bathroom. He grabbed an empty chair from one of the tables in the bar and pulled it up to the table of the two gunmen in cheap blazers. He sat down next to the one on the left.

"Can I help you?" Lefty said.

"That depends," Beauregard said. Quick as a cat he grabbed Lefty's gun with his left hand while grabbing Lefty's left wrist with his right. Boonie always said he had his father's hands. He pressed the barrel of the gun into the hard slab of Lefty's belly.

"Maybe you can tell me why you and your buddy at the bar been eyeballing me all night." Righty reached under the table, but Beauregard shook his head. "No. Put your hands back on the table, palms down. Do it now or I'm gonna start pulling the trigger and I ain't gonna stop until it goes click."

Righty's face bloomed as red as a circus balloon, but he did as he was told.

Beauregard's neck tingled. Someone was coming up behind him. He didn't take his eyes off the two gunmen. The scarred man pulled up a chair and sat down. He had a glass filled with some dark liquid.

"You a slick one, ain't ya? Although to be honest, a one-armed monkey could get the drop on Carl here. No offense, Carl," the scarred man said. Carl didn't seem like he took too much offense to anything. Even a gun in his stomach.

"Who sent y'all?" Beauregard asked. He didn't turn and face the scarred man. He kept the gun pressed against Carl's belly. Someone had played a bluesy love song on the jukebox. Couples were slow dancing on the old parquet floor. Bodies gently twirling in small elliptical orbits in time with the mournful notes coming from the speakers.

"Right to the point. But this ain't the part where you ask questions. This the part where you use your eyes and your ears," the scarred man said. He reached into his pocket. Beauregard pressed the gun deeper into Carl's flesh.

"Burning Man . . . ," Carl said in a low rumble of a voice.

"Don't worry, Carl, Beauregard here is a smart boy. He ain't gonna ruin your guts here for no good reason. I just got something on my phone he needs to see," Billy said. He placed his phone on the table and touched the screen. Beauregard cut his eyes downward.

There was a cell phone on the table. A short video was playing. The video showed the tail lights of a car leaving Danny's parking lot. Beauregard narrowed his eyes. The tail lights belonged to a Nova. Kelvin's Nova.

"We was gonna pinch you when you left, but you made us. We had five guys. The three of us in one car and two more boys in another. Word has it you a real wild boy with a mean streak. But when you made Carl here, I says to myself, well, now we gonna dance. So, I told my boys in the other car to follow your little friends there. Now I seen how fast you is. And goddamn if you ain't as fast as a knife fight in a phone booth. So you probably thinking you might be able to shoot me, Carl and Jim Bob," Billy said.

Carl winced.

"But," he continued, "if my boys don't hear from me in say, oh I don't know, five minutes, they gonna light up that car like the goddamn White House Christmas tree."

Beauregard pulled back the hammer on Carl's gun.

"What if I don't believe you? What if I just shoot the three of you and call my friend and tell him to punch it? That Nova has some get-up-and-go."

Billy smiled.

"I bet it does. But that's an awful lot of what ifs, ain't it, Beauregard? Come on now, like I said, you a smart boy. Give Carl back his gun and let's go on up the road. Got somebody that needs to talk to you, and he ain't the type that likes to be kept waiting."

Beauregard leaned into the gun and it dug deeper into Carl's flesh. He could shoot Carl, that much was a given. Could he get the one on the right and the one Carl called Burning Man too? Even if he got all of them, could Kelvin outrun the car tailing him? Like Burning Man said, that was an awful lot of what ifs.

"Tick tock tick tock," Billy said.

Beauregard thought about what Boonie had said. About the way men like him died. He didn't want to take Kia with him. That honor was reserved for men like the three seated at the table with him. Along with whoever was their boss. Beauregard shoved the gun back in Carl's waistband.

"Let's go," he said.

Billy tossed back his drink. He grimaced, then put his glass on the table. He picked up his phone and let his fingers slide across the screen. He put the phone back in his pocket.

"See, now Christmas don't have to come early."

TWENTY-ONE

They didn't blindfold him. That was a bad sign. It meant they didn't care if he saw where they were going. Which most likely meant he wasn't ever leaving once they got to where they were going. They didn't tie his hands up either. No need really. They had their insurance policy, after all.

Beauregard sat between Jim Bob and Burning Man. They were riding in a 2010 Cadillac CTS. A nice midsized sedan with a powerful 3-liter engine. The interior of the car was bathed in a ghostly pale light. LED lighting ran along the inside of the doors and along the floor. Just a subtle accent lighting, nothing too overbearing. Beauregard noticed the child locks were engaged. He had thought about hitting Jim Bob with an elbow, opening the door and pushing him out after he had relieved him of his gun. Shove the barrel into Burning Man's eye and suggest he contact his boys and call them off completely. He could see that plan was going to be foiled by well-meaning consumer advocates.

They jumped on the interstate and headed west. The Caddy sliced through the night. Beauregard felt his ears pop as they began to climb into the Blue Ridge Mountains that bisected Virginia at odd intervals.

Finally, they took an exit near Lynchburg. The off-ramp deposited them onto the oak tree–lined main street of some quaint hamlet tucked away near Peaks of Otter mountain. Dark green streetlamps played peekaboo with the wisteria trees up and down the street. A banner stretched across the front of an imposing granite building lined with columns proclaimed that the Kimball Town Fair was one week away. The car turned off Main Street and down an equally well-lit side street. The car stopped in front of a tobacco shop at the end of the sidewalk. It was the last shop in a short row of stores. A brick façade was interrupted by a huge picture window. A glowing sign above the front door said it was THE HOT SHOP. The neon sign in the window of the shop said it was closed. Jim Bob pushed the barrel of his gun into Beauregard's ribs.

"Try something. I want you to. Then I can pull the trigger until the gun goes click," Jim Bob said. He leered at Beauregard, showing his crooked teeth.

"Alright now, Jim Bob, you know Lazy wants to talk to this boy," Billy said as he opened his door. Jim Bob pushed Beauregard toward the same door. They all exited the car on the same side. Carl got out and before Beauregard could react, he punched him in the right kidney. Beauregard stumbled and fell against the car. He took a deep breath, coughed, and then stood up straight.

"Goddamn, you boys got two-inch peckers or something? Stop that shit. Lazy wants to talk with him. He can't talk if he throwing up and pissing blood," Billy said. Beauregard didn't detect any real concern for his well-being. Burning Man's only concern seemed to be not disappointing Lazy. Whoever that was.

"Sorry, Billy," Carl mumbled. Beauregard figured Burning Man must be this Billy's nickname. That struck him as oddly cruel, but then again you didn't get to choose your nickname. If you did, no one would refer to him as Bug.

Billy aka Burning Man knocked on the door of the smoke shop. A thin white boy with lank blond hair and a sleepy face opened the door.

"Y'all came back quick," the boy said.

"He didn't put up much of a fight. He here?" Billy asked.

The boy shook his head. "Not yet."

"Okay," Billy said. He gestured toward the interior of the store. "After you," he said to Beauregard.

Beauregard entered the store. The overhead lights were off but there were enough novelty neon signs and clocks on the walls to light his way. The signs and clocks all depicted scenes from old movies. Some Beauregard recognized, some he didn't. There was Rick and Sam at a piano from *Casablanca* against a red backdrop. A clock on the far wall above a shelf full of cigars was adorned with the maniacal grinning face of Richard Widmark as Tommy Udo from the original *Kiss of Death*, outlined with a cool blue chemical fire.

The kid who opened the door sprinted past Beauregard and knocked on a door behind the counter. A huge beast of a man opened that door. Jim Bob pushed Beauregard on through. The room was sparsely decorated. There was a cheap oak desk with a rotary phone sitting anachronistically near the edge. The walls were blank slabs of gray concrete. There was a wooden chair behind the desk. Three metal chairs sat in front of the desk. The spartan confines of the room stood in stark contrast to the garishness of the rest of the shop.

"Have a seat," Billy said. There was only one empty seat among the three chairs. Ronnie was sitting in the first chair and Quan was sitting in the second. Beauregard sat next to Quan.

"Bug, I'm—" Ronnie started to say but Beauregard cut him off.

"Shut your mouth," he said. Ronnie dropped his head. Beauregard crossed his arms. Quan had his head in his hands. His breathing was hard and labored. He was tapping his right foot like he was keeping time with the world's fastest rhythm section. A box fan sat in the corner moving the stifling air around. A single light bulb encased by a wire mesh cage shone down from the ceiling. A few empty plastic milk crates were stacked in the far-left corner of the room. Beauregard figured it had been a storeroom at one time. Now it was a shabby torture chamber masquerading as an office.

Both Quan and Ronnie had been smacked around. Quan's mouth was bleeding profusely. His white basketball jersey was covered with red splotches. Ronnie had a mouse under his left eye. His nose was swollen and crooked. Neither of them had been restrained either. There was obviously no need. There was no fight in them. Beauregard could see that as soon as he entered the room. Their stooped shoulders and downcast eyes told the story of their submission. If it came down to it, they wouldn't be any help.

Beauregard heard the hinges on the door creak.

"Well now, the gang's all here," a high, tremulous voice said. Beauregard felt Quan flinch.

A tall, thin man entered the room. He wore a neatly pressed pair of khakis and a black button-down shirt under a black corduroy vest. He was narrow in the hips with jagged angles for arms. His ruddy face was narrow and ended in a wickedly sharp chin. A dark pile of brown hair tinged with gray stood up on his head like he had stuck his finger in a light socket while wearing a bad toupee. He stood in the center of the room directly under the lone light. He grinned at them. A rakish smile that spread across his face like spilled milk. Huge teeth too white to be real filled his mouth.

"This here the Apple Dumpling Gang, huh?" the man said. He laughed at his own joke. After a half a beat, all of his men laughed as well. He motioned toward the chair behind the desk. Carl grabbed it and the man parked himself in front of Quan. He crossed his legs. A smirk had replaced his grin.

"I love movies. Don't matter what kind. Horror movies, crime movies, old movies, new movies. Hell, I even like romantic comedies. Love me some John Hughes. And Molly Ringwald? Whew whee," the man said.

"We so sorry—" Ronnie tried to say but the walking wall who had opened the office door smacked him in the back of the head. Ronnie pitched forward and landed on the floor in a heap. Jim Bob and Carl grabbed him by his arms and sat him back in his chair.

"But some of my favorite movies are heist movies. I love that shit, man. Something about a heist that goes down smoother than a twenty-dollar hooker gets me every time," the man said. He stood and turned his chair around. He sat back down and rested his arms on the backrest before laying his chin on his hands.

"You gotta tell me. How'd y'all do it? Did y'all sew stop watches in your gloves? What kind of engine was in that car? Who came up with driving off the damn overpass? That was some brass balls shit there, I tell ya," the man said.

No one spoke.

"Come on now, it's alright. Y'all can talk now," the man said.

Still no one spoke.

"It was a modified V8 with a nitro kit," Beauregard said finally.

The man winked at him. "Nice, nice. See, that's what I'm talking about. Heist movie shit," he said.

"Are you Lazy?" Beauregard asked. He heard footsteps behind him. He braced himself for the blow but the man in front of him held up his hand.

"Hold on, Wilbert. This fella here just reminded me I forgot my manners. My mama named me Lazarus Mothersbaugh on account of how I died during delivery and then came back to life once they got the cord from round my neck. But everyone else round here calls me Lazy. I think cuz they was too lazy to say my whole name," Lazy said. All his men tittered except for Billy. He was staring off into space.

"Now back to the matter at hand. If you boys had robbed any other jewelry store anywhere else, you would be sitting pretty as you please. But you robbed one that belonged to me. So that means you in some deep doo-doo," Lazy said.

He smiled but this time it seemed forced. Beauregard thought it was an actor's smile. Just another part of a performance.

"Any of you ever heard of me?" Lazy asked. Quan raised his hand. "Goddamn, boy, you ain't in English class," Lazy said. Carl laughed.

"You boys really screwed me over at that store. I was using it as a pay window of sorts. I got hold of some diamonds in a deal that we don't have to go into right now. Let's just say I'm a silent partner in some very interesting developments. But son, them diamonds better than cash. Easier to carry and impossible to trace. That comes in handy when you paying for two or three of them Mexican fillies from out West. Yessir, I had a nice lil setup out there. And you boys fucked it up good. Now the cops snooping around. And some of my transactions have gone south," Lazy said. He sucked his teeth and nodded his head. "But goddamn, the way you pulled it off, well I just gotta tip my hat to you. Now that girl, what's her name, Burning Man?"

"Jenny."

"Yeah, Jenny. She said you was the brains, Ronnie. You the one that put it all together," Lazy said. He pointed one long narrow finger at Ronnie. Ronnie's face was ashen. "But Beauregard, you was the one behind the wheel. Goddamn, that was some high-test driving there, boy." Lazy kept pointing at Ronnie, but he turned his head to look at Beauregard. "That wasn't your first time at the rodeo, was it?" he asked.

Beauregard didn't say a word.

"Answer him," Burning Man said.

"No," he said.

Lazy got up and walked around behind Beauregard. He bent down and put his mouth near his ear.

"I asked around about you, boy. They say you could outrun the devil on the highway to Hell," Lazy said. He straightened up. "But no matter how much I like your style, boys, and God knows y'all get points for style, I can't let something like that slide. I mean, you stole from me and now I must be compensated," Lazy said in a sing-song cadence. He sounded like a Baptist preacher during a tent revival.

He pointed at Wilbert. The big man left the room. He returned a few minutes later with five cereal boxes. He dumped the contents of the boxes onto the desk. Bundles of cash spilled across the desk like the bounty from a fall harvest.

"You boys must have had a good fence. Take your cuts and add them to what ol' Ronnie had left, you must've gotten something like $700,000 on three million. That's a good return," Lazy said.

Beauregard and Quan glared at Ronnie. Lazy burst out laughing.

"Lawd, he shorted y'all? That's a damn shame," he said. He walked around to face them. "Now we got Ronnie and Jenny's cut. Quan didn't have enough to really bother with, but we took it anyway. Beauregard, you lucked out. I ain't gonna have my boys roust your house looking for your slice. I suspect you ain't dumb enough to keep it on you. And at this point it don't really matter. Even if we had it all, y'all still be behind. Now if this was any day, y'all asses would be dead as the bacon I had for breakfast," Lazy said.

He sat back down in his chair. Beauregard felt this was all building to a "but." If he was gonna kill them, he wouldn't have gathered them all together for a staff meeting. Lazy wanted something. He wanted it bad.

"However, God has smiled on you today. Yessir, you fellas done crossed my path at a time I have need of some boys with a special set of skills," Lazy said. Beauregard recognized the line from some stupid action movie a few years back. "I know it seems impossible cuz I'm such a charming fella, but I'm having some problems with a boy from North Carolina. We having a disagreement about who runs what round these parts. And I got to give it to him, that boy been giving me all I can handle down there. But I'm gonna win. Cuz all he got is soldiers. I got family," Lazy said. He nodded to his men. They nodded back.

"One of his soldiers got himself a nasty meth habit. Now as fate would have it, the boy he owes is one of mine. In exchange for his debt, the soldier told me a lil secret. His boss got a shipment coming through the Carolinas. A truckload of platinum that ain't even supposed to be on this side of the country," Lazy said. He held his hands out in supplication.

"This where you fellas come in. You gonna get that shipment for me. Now it ain't gonna be easy. This ol' boy got lots of firepower and he don't give two tight fucks about showing it off. And if that soldier is right, this here shipment is a big deal for him. Losing it would hurt him something fierce. So, you know he gonna fight for it like a dog on a bone. But if you get it, well then, I'll call us even," Lazy said.

That's a lie, Beauregard thought.

"How's that sound, fellas? I guess y'all a part of the family now," Lazy said.

"You got the route and the time? Do you know how many cars he got riding with the truck? You say he got firepower, so I'm gonna assume he got cars riding shotgun," Beauregard said. He braced for the blow and this time it did come. A short rabbit punch right between his shoulder blades. He gripped the sides of the chair. A bolt of lightning ran down his back to his left thigh, but he didn't fall.

"Honestly, that's a good question, Beauregard. Really it is. But our family works like a real family. I'm your Daddy now. And you don't speak unless I tell you to," Lazy said.

He pulled on the backrest of the chair and leaned back until two of the legs came off the floor. He balanced there for a second before putting all four legs back on the ground.

"The other thing we don't do in this family is run our mouths. We ride together, and we die together. And we never ever snitch on members of the family. Ever," Lazy said. He ran a hand through his wild rat's nest.

"Beauregard, you wanna guess which one of your partners gave you up? Jenny told us all about Ronnie and Quan, but she didn't know shit about you. We wouldn't have never found you if one of them hadn't ran they mouth. I'll give you a hint. It's the same boy who been running his mouth at the strip club about how he had to drop some fool during a robbery," Lazy said.

Beauregard didn't respond. He didn't need the hint. Ronnie might have been a cheat, but he wasn't a snitch.

"Oh Jesus," Quan moaned.

"I doubt you gonna see him," Lazy said.

Billy pulled out his gun. A small black .38. He shot Quan in the face three times. Each report sounded like a cannon inside the small room. Beauregard felt warm droplets rain against the right side of his face. Quan slid out of the chair and collapsed onto his side. His head landed at Beauregard's feet. Quan's whole body shuddered. He let out one wet gasp, then was still.

"Goddamn, man!" Ronnie screamed. A ham-sized fist slammed into the side of his head. He went flying and landed against the desk. No one moved to pick him up this time.

"That boy was like a broke icebox. Couldn't keep shit. Fellas like that ain't good for nothing except target practice," Lazy said.

Beauregard didn't look down at Quan's body or at Ronnie's prone form on the floor. He stared at a spot on the wall behind the desk.

"Pick him up, will you?" Lazy said. Carl grabbed Ronnie and sat him in the chair again. Lazy scooted his chair forward until the legs were pressed against Quan's thighs.

"Here's the thing, boys. You owe me. So, you gonna get this done. Cuz if you don't, I'll kill everyone you love. I'll do it front of you and I'll do it slow. Maybe I'll have Burning Man light 'em up. Maybe I'll have the boys beat 'em to death with hammers. It don't really matter how, just know they gonna end up dead. And you'll join them. I promise you that. My word is my bond," Lazy said. He got up and put his hands on his knees. He locked eyes with Bug then turned his attention to Ronnie then back to Bug.

"I can see the hate in your eyes, boys. That's fine. Hate me all you want. If you wracking your brains for a way to get at me, let that shit go. If God couldn't kill me when I was born, you two ain't gonna do it now. You try anything funny and I'll make you choose which one of your loved ones get they throat cut first," he whispered. He stepped back and clapped Billy on the shoulder.

"Burning Man here is gonna give you the info on the route and the day and time. You gonna get a throwaway phone with one number on it. When it's done, and I mean as soon as it's done, you call that number. Other than that, I think we finished here," Lazy said.

"Get up," Billy said. Beauregard and Ronnie rose. Jim Bob pushed them toward the door.

"Get to walking, Rock and Roll," Billy said.

Ronnie blinked. His eyes began to water but at last he began to walk. Beauregard looked over his shoulder at Lazy then followed Ronnie out the door.

When they were gone, Wilbert and the kid got a tarp from behind the crates and wrapped up Quan's body. Carl helped them. After they had the body wrapped up, Wilbert turned to the kid. "Go get the van."

The kid jogged out the front door. Wilbert started gathering the rolls of cash. Carl moved the three chairs back to the corner near the crates.

"We could take that truck," Carl said.

"Yeah, we could, but then Shade would know we got a man on the inside. Let them boys try and get it. He sees a mixed-race crew he won't put it on us. He thinks all we are is a bunch of backwoods racist rednecks," Lazy said.

"Ain't we?" Carl said.

Lazy smiled. "That's beside the point."

The kid came back into the store. He and Wilbert carried Quan's body out to the van. Lazy crossed his legs. Carl leaned against the wall. He knew Lazy was about to pontificate.

"That truck gonna have more than a thousand pounds of platinum coils on it. We killing a bunch of birds with one stone. We keep our man on the inside. We put a dent in Shade's pocket. We gonna get back triple what them boys pinched. And when they bring us the truck, I'm gonna let Burning Man turn them into fucking candles," Lazy said.

"You always got a plan, don't you," Carl said.

Lazy smoothed his vest with his wide hands. "It's like my Daddy used to say. While they picking apples, I'm planting seeds."

TWENTY-TWO

The car dropped them off just off the exit.

"Here's the phone and the time and the route. You got a week," Billy said. He handed Ronnie a flip phone and a scrap of paper through the window. Jim Bob spun his tires as he pulled away. Gravel flew up and nearly hit them. It was late. Beauregard checked his watch. Nearly five in the morning. The sky was still dark, but sunrise was just around the corner.

"Bug, I didn't know," Ronnie said. Beauregard started walking. Ronnie trotted behind him. "I swear I didn't fucking know. How could I? Bug, what are we gonna do?"

He caught up with Beauregard and put his hand on his shoulder. Beauregard spun around and clamped both hands on Ronnie's throat. He dragged him off the shoulder of the road and down into a ditch bed. Ronnie grabbed at Beauregard's arms. He might as well have been trying to bend steel with his bare hands. Beauregard's biceps stood out in sharp relief under the sleeves of his shirt. He put his full weight on top of Ronnie as he squeezed the life out of him. Ronnie tried to scratch at his eyes, but Beauregard's arms were too long.

"You . . . need . . . me . . . ," Ronnie squealed. It came out in a garbled mishmash, but Beauregard caught it. Ronnie's eyes began to flutter in their sockets. Beauregard let him go and fell back against the ditch bank. Ronnie propped himself up on his left elbow. Rubbing his throat with his right hand, he coughed up a wad of phlegm and spit it on the ground. "It's just you and me, Bug. We need each other if we gonna get out of this."

"Shut up. Just shut your mouth and listen for a minute. You know he ain't gonna let us go, right? Even if we pull it off, he's gonna kill us anyway. Just like he killed Quan. Just like he killed Jenny. Just like he killed that lady that was the manager. You heard what he said about the cops. He cleaning this shit up. The only reason we still alive now is because he wants that truck. And he's scared of that guy he was talking about. That's our ace in the hole. The truck and his fear," Beauregard said.

"You got a plan already?" Ronnie asked.

"I been making a plan since he shot Quan," Beauregard said.

He climbed up the ditch bank and resumed walking down the road. Ronnie waited a few minutes before he fell in behind him. A tractor trailer passed them heading out of town at the same time Ronnie tried to ask Beauregard a question.

"What?" Beauregard asked.

"I said do you really think Jenny is dead?" Ronnie said.

Beauregard kept walking. "Yeah," he said.

"I was supposed to go to the prom with her when we was in school. I got expelled the week before the dance. I waited for her out in the parking lot after it was over. When she came out of the school, the light from the hallway lit her up from behind. She looked like a redheaded angel. I guess she a real angel now," Ronnie said.

Beauregard didn't respond. The sound of their footsteps on the gravel that lined the shoulder filled the space between them.

"This plan you got, do it include killing these motherfuckers?" Ronnie asked.

Beauregard put his hands in his pockets. "Yeah."

"They bad, ain't they, Bug? They some bad motherfuckers, ain't they?" Ronnie asked.

"They think they are. But they bleed like everybody else."

They got back to Danny's by eight. Beauregard gave Ronnie a ride back to his trailer.

"Give me the route information," Beauregard said.

He had parked his truck behind Reggie's car. Ronnie rooted around in his pocket and pulled out the scrap of paper.

"I'm going to call you tomorrow. We gonna need at least two other people. Can Reggie roll with us?" Beauregard asked. Ronnie shrugged, then slid his fingers through his hair.

"I dunno. He can drive. He ain't no good with a gun, though. And he wouldn't bust a grape in a food fight," he said.

"If it goes the way I figure, all he gonna have to do is drive. I'll call you tomorrow," Beauregard said.

Ronnie got out of the truck. He leaned on the car door. The passenger's window had been lowered all the way. "Bug, I swear if I had known that store belonged to somebody like this I would have never got y'all involved," he said.

The look Beauregard gave him made Ronnie shut his mouth with an audible plop. He stood up straight and backed away from the truck. He watched as Beauregard backed out of the driveway doing 35. When he hit the road, he whipped the truck around. He spun his tires as he drove off toward the horizon.

Ronnie went into the trailer. Reggie was lying on the couch with his foot on the armrest. It was wrapped in duct tape and what appeared to be an old T-shirt. Ronnie slammed the door. Reggie sat up straight. He was holding Ronnie's gun in his right hand. He swung the barrel around and aimed at the door.

"Jesus H. Christ, butt munch, put the gun down," Ronnie wailed.

Reggie blinked his eyes a few times. "Ronnie! Holy shit, I'm sorry. I thought it was those guys coming back," he said.

Ronnie held out his hand to Reggie. Reggie didn't move for a few seconds.

"Oh yeah. Here, I don't even know what to do with this thing," he said as he gave Ronnie the gun.

"Pull the trigger, dingbat," Ronnie said.

Reggie swung around and struggled to his feet. He hobbled over to his brother with unsteady steps. He threw his arms around him and squeezed him with unexpected strength.

"I thought you won't never coming back," he whimpered in his ear.

"What, and leave all this?" Ronnie said.

Reggie released him, and Ronnie helped him back to the couch. Reggie plopped down, and Ronnie plopped right next to him. They both leaned their heads back against the backrest in eerily similar motions.

"Ronnie, who were those guys?" Reggie said.

"Trouble with a capital T," Ronnie said. He closed his eyes tight. Sleep was creeping up on him like an assassin.

"How's your foot?" Ronnie asked.

"The bullet went straight through. It must have missed the nerves and stuff because I can still wiggle my toes. I cleaned it out with some peroxide and tied it up with the tape."

"I know it hurt like a son of a bitch," Ronnie said.

"I had some Oxy left. So, ya know. It's okay right now," Reggie said.

Ronnie rubbed his forehead. "Reggie."

"Yeah."

"How did they know the money was in the cereal boxes?"

"They came in waving guns, Ronnie. I . . . just blurted it out. I'm sorry. Is that what they wanted, though? The money?"

Ronnie snorted.

"Nah. They want everything, Reggie. They want everything we fucking got."

Beauregard parked next to Kia's car. The sun was up, and the grass glistened with dew. He got out of the truck and walked into the house. It was deathly quiet. He headed for the bedroom.

He slipped into the room without turning on the light. He was stripping off his shirt when the lamp on the nightstand came on.

"Where the fuck you been?" Kia asked. She was wearing one of his T-shirts and nothing else.

"Something came up," he said.

"And you couldn't call?"

"No," he said.

She knitted her brow as she appraised him.

"Bug, there's blood on your face," she said. She sounded far away, like she was speaking through tin cans tied with a string.

"It's not mine," he said. He pulled his shirt off and stepped out of his pants. He slipped out of the room and went to the shower. He took off his underwear and socks and let the shower run so the water could warm up. He stepped over the edge of the tub and let the water hit him full on in the face.

He was just starting to lather up when the shower curtain was pulled back so hard a few of the rings popped loose.

"Bug, what the fuck is going on?" Kia said. The water splashed over her face and chest, soaking the T-shirt.

"Nothing you need to worry about."

"It's got to do with that job, don't it? I told you! I fucking told you to leave it alone. Sell that goddamn car, but no, you wouldn't listen. Now you come in here after being gone all night with somebody's blood on your face," she hissed.

The hiss became a sob. Beauregard grabbed her and pulled her into a tight embrace.

"I'm going to handle it. I promise," he said. She pushed him away. He studied her face. She was still crying, but the tears were lost in the water that was raining down on them both.

"You always say you going to handle it. But I was here last night waiting for a call saying you was dead. You ain't handling it if I end up a widow," she said. "I know you was pissed at me for talking to Jean but it was true. Do you know how many times I've planned your funeral in my head? You gonna handle it. How can you stand there and say that to me with a straight face?"

Beauregard turned off the water. He stepped out of the shower. Kia took a step backwards. He reached around her and grabbed a towel. He wiped his face and chest, then hung the towel back on the rack.

"Because I always do," he said finally.

TWENTY-THREE

Kelvin raised his hand to get the waitress's attention. She came strutting over in her too-tight jeans and too-short T-shirt.

"What ya need, boo?" she asked.

"Two beers," Kelvin said.

"You got it, sugar."

She came back with two lukewarm bottles of beer. Kelvin grabbed his and took a long swig.

"You really think it will work?" Kelvin asked.

"I ain't got no choice," Beauregard said. He took a sip of his beer.

"Well, when we gotta be in North Carolina?" Kelvin asked.

"I can't ask you to do that, K," Beauregard said. The waitress played a blues song on the jukebox. Danny's sound system struggled to accommodate the deep bass coming through its speakers. There were only two other patrons in the bar sitting in the corner. He and Kelvin had just closed the shop for the day. Kelvin had suggested they get a beer. Once they got seated, Beauregard just let all the events of the last thirty-six hours spill out. He couldn't tell Kia and he didn't want to tell Boonie. Kelvin was the only person he could talk to. He hadn't been asking for his help. He just needed to vent.

"Nah, fuck that. If you think I'm gonna let you go on another job with low-rent Jesse James and his retarded brother, you done lost your mind. He the reason you in this mess," Kelvin said.

"It's my mess and I gotta clean it up."

"Beauregard, don't make me say it."

"Say what?"

Kelvin dropped his voice.

"I owe you. Not just for giving me a job. I owe you for Kaden. Let me help. I need to help you," he said.

"You don't owe me shit for that," Beauregard said.

"That's not how I feel. Let me do this," Kelvin said.

Beauregard finished his beer. He held two fingers up and the waitress winked at him from across the bar. A few more people trickled in just as a sugary doo-wop song filled the air.

"We got six days to get ready."

"What kind of resistance we liable to get?" Kelvin asked.

The waitress dropped off the beers. Beauregard waited until she walked away to continue.

"A lot, I think. I asked around about this fella. Seems like him and Lazy been butting heads for a while. You remember Curt Macklin? Got a chop shop in Raleigh? He said that most of the OGs and crews in the Carolinas and Virginia done fell in line with this guy. Lazy the only one taking a stand, and it ain't going so well for him. Curt told me Lazy sent some boys to a spot this fella was using to cook some meth. He sent them boys back to Lazy in a five-gallon bucket," Beauregard said.

Kelvin made a face. "What they call him?"

"Curt said all he ever heard them call him was Shade. I asked Curt was he really that bad. Curt said he was worse," Beauregard said.

"Why we ain't never heard of him before? Or this Lazy dude?" Kelvin asked.

Beauregard shrugged. "I guess the kind of shit they into don't really require wheelmen," he said.

"Like what?" Kelvin asked.

"I talked to a doughboy from Newport News I know. Did a run for him to Atlanta. He told me Lazy basically runs everything west of the Roanoke Valley. He owns a bunch of smoke shops out there. Some payday loan places too," Beauregard said.

"Legal loan sharking," Kelvin said. Beauregard nodded.

"The boy I know told me his real money comes from running girls up the DC-Maryland corridor. Services a whole bunch of them government and military types up that way. Said he supposed to be a college boy. Got a degree in chemistry or some shit. Controls the meth, heroin and pills coming in from West Virginia. Said he runs moonshine too," Beauregard said.

Kelvin laughed. "He must do that for old times' sake. Damn. So you caught between a wannabe Pablo Escobar chopping motherfuckers up and putting them in grease buckets and a redneck Walter White. When you fuck up you do it right."

Beauregard rolled his eyes. "If you don't want to get in this . . ."

"I didn't say that. I'm down. Besides, both of my girlfriends are gonna be out of town this weekend so I ain't got nothing to do," Kelvin said. He took a long sip off his beer. "You really gonna try and play them against each other like a chess game, huh?"

"It ain't chess. It's more like playing with a train set. We gonna put them on the same track and let them run into each other," Beauregard said.

"You think ol' boy gonna go for it?"

"I think this Shade is eating him alive. He wants to hurt him, but he also needs what's in that truck. He already had his back against the wall before we came along and robbed his drop bank."

"And how you plan on not getting caught in the cross fire?"

"I'm gonna get in touch with Shade and tell him when and where I plan on meeting Lazy with his truck. Then I'll drop it off an hour earlier. They'll both show up at the same time."

"Well, it sounds simple. That means something is gonna go to shit," Kelvin said. "Wait, what if Lazy gets the drop on Mr. Shade?"

"I got a rifle with a scope," Beauregard said.

"Well, damn. It's like that, I guess," Kelvin said.

Beauregard took another sip of beer. "Yeah, it's just like that. But first things first. We gotta get that truck."

"Yeah, that's gonna be the fun part," Kelvin said.

Ronnie sat on the couch with the door open. The AC had finally died a horrible death. Spitting out water and Freon like it had mechanical tuberculosis. Reggie was lying down in his room with his foot elevated. Ronnie could see the sun setting through the open door. Orange and red streaks sliced through the sky. Sunlight danced across the waxed surface of his Mustang. He hadn't driven the car since he got back from seeing Quan get his face blown off. The car only had a quarter of a tank of gas left. It was enough to get down to Danny's, but then what? He didn't have enough to pay for a drink, let alone get back to the house.

"Oh, how the mighty have fallen," he said. He sipped the last beer from the fridge, which didn't sound so healthy either. A week ago, he was snorting coke off some hipster chick's titty, now he was rationing his beer. The vibrating of his cell phone interrupted his sad requiem for the life he had just lost. Ronnie pulled it out of his pocket and checked the display.

"Hey, Bug."

"We on. Your brother okay to drive?"

"Well, kinda. They shot him in his foot when they came and scooped me up. He patched it up with some gauze and duct tape. He hopping around here like Peg Leg Bates, but it should hold," Ronnie said.

There was a heavy silence on the line.

"We'll just have to work with it. We leave for North Carolina Friday night," Beauregard said.

"Bug, you still ain't tell me what this plan of yours is. How we getting our money back?" Ronnie said.

More silence.

"Ronnie, there ain't no getting your money back. If this goes the way I think, we are getting our lives. You should have put some of your money somewhere safe. Not cereal boxes," Beauregard said.

The line went dead.

"Fuck you, Bug. That was a good idea," Ronnie said to the mute line.

TWENTY-FOUR

Beauregard adjusted the bandana around his nose and mouth. It had the image of a skull and crossbones printed on it. He'd seen the characters in some of the video games Darren and Javon played wearing a similar type of mask. He pulled the baseball cap down tight on his head. He'd adjusted his disguise at least a half a dozen times since Kelvin had texted him and told him he was in place.

It dawned on him that he was actually nervous. The sensation was so foreign to him that the realization was jarring. Usually when he was about to do a job a sense of tranquility came over him. The knowledge that he had calculated all the possible outcomes and prepared for any eventuality gave him a sense of peace.

He didn't feel any of that peace tonight. Tonight, he felt like an amateur. A virgin fumbling and tumbling his way to either ecstasy or agony. Six days. Six goddamn days to plan, get the necessary pieces in place and get down to North Carolina to execute the goddamn job. Beauregard adjusted the knapsack digging into his shoulders. He took a deep breath. A few mosquitoes buzzed around his face, apparently attracted to his warm breath and the promise of a big heaping gulp of his rich delicious blood. He waved them away and checked his watch. The hands glowed softly in the darkness. It was ten o'clock. Lazy's man swore the caravan would be coming through Pine Tar Road between ten and ten thirty. Swore on a stack of Bibles they were coming that way to avoid the interstate and overzealous deputies manning obscure speed traps. Although Beauregard wasn't sure how much anyone could trust the word of a hophead.

Locusts bleated in the marshy woods behind him. A rivulet of sweat ran down from his forehead and dropped into his right eye. He rubbed his eye with the back of his gloved hand, then crab walked across the dry, shallow ditch and edged up closer to the road. The sun had set two hours before but heat still radiated from the asphalt. Beauregard checked his watch again.

"Come on. Come on," he whispered.

Beauregard touched the butt of his .45. It was tucked into the small of his back. He knew it was there but touching it was reassuring. There hadn't been time to get any pieces from Madness. Just another example of how far he had let his standards slip when it came to this particular pinch. But this wasn't a normal score, was it? His desperation and Ronnie's greed had landed them all in a hornet's nest surrounded by vipers. Yet despite the startling lack of preparation and the sharp vicissitudes he had experienced in his fortunes since they'd knocked over the jewelry store he still planned on getting out of this alive. Lazy had made the same mistake a lot of people made about him. People like his own mother. Or the boys at Precision. The folks at the bank. Ariel's mama's people. Even sometimes his own wife. They all underestimated him.

His Daddy used to say when Bug set his mind to something he was like a boulder rolling down the side of a mountain. And God help anyone who got in his way.

The throwaway phone in his pocket vibrated.

Beauregard pulled it out and checked the screen. It was a text from Kelvin.

Here they come. Five minutes away.

Beauregard stood up straight and slipped the knapsack off his shoulder. He unzipped it and pulled out a road flare. He ignited the flare and trotted over to a shabby, rust-flecked gray 1974 Lincoln Continental. Once he'd explained the situation to Boonie the old man had insisted on helping to get the vehicle Beauregard needed for his plan. This was after he'd unleashed a ten-minute profanity-laden diatribe about Ronnie Sessions and the circumstances of his birth. He'd tried to keep Boonie out of this, but like many things lately, that hadn't worked out like he'd planned.

The pungent scent of gasoline emanated from the Lincoln in nauseating waves. Beauregard tossed the flare through the Lincoln's open driver-side window and jumped backwards. The car burst into flame with a loud WHOMP. Beauregard had diluted the gas just a bit so the car wouldn't explode but instead burn with a nice and steady flame. He slipped back into the woods, pulled a pair of night vision binoculars out of his pack, and resumed his crouch. He'd parked the Lincoln horizontally across the narrow back road. A standard non-interstate dual-lane road varied between ten to twelve feet wide. A Lincoln from bow to stern was roughly nineteen feet long. Cars barreling down Pine Tar Road would not be able to maneuver around it in the best of conditions. Now that it was engulfed in flames and blocking the road they'd have to stop.

At least that was what Beauregard hoped would happen. He texted Ronnie and Reggie.

Get in place. Ten minutes.

He put the phone back in his pocket. The light from the flames engulfing the Lincoln cast odd shadows across the blacktop. The burning leather and plastic sent black plumes of smoke up toward the quarter-full moon and the bluish black sky that served as its backdrop. Beauregard could see why they had picked this route. He hadn't seen a car in over an hour. Pine Tar sliced through several counties whose total population was less than one borough in Manhattan. It was a route he would have picked.

The sound of two vehicles approaching broke him out of his reverie. A pair of powerful LED headlights chased away the darkness. A white Econoline van crested the hill followed by a black four-door SUV. The driver in the van probably didn't expect to see a car on fire in the middle of the road at ten o'clock on a Thursday night. Beauregard watched as he stood up on the brake pedal and the van started to fishtail. The weight of its payload was throwing off the handling. Beauregard filed that away for later. The black SUV slammed on the brakes as well. For a second Beauregard thought the SUV was going to rear-end the van but the driver of the SUV had the advantage of better brakes and superior handling and stopped the vehicle three inches shy of the van's rear doors.

That was the one thing Lazy's man had definitely gotten wrong. It wasn't a truck that was transporting contraband for Shade, it was a van. Burning Man had called them the day after they had watched him ventilate Quan with that little tidbit of information. Their inside man had called them in a panic. Beauregard wondered what he was more afraid of, Shade or a lost hookup. When Beauregard had asked for the make and model of the van Burning Man had been incredulous.

"What difference does that make?" Burning Man had asked.

"I need the license plate number too," Bug had said, ignoring the scarred redneck's question.

"I kinda wish I could see what you planning, boy," Burning Man said with a chuckle. Beauregard made himself not crush the cheap flip phone into a thousand pieces. Lazy's inside man got them the info but it wasn't until this precise moment that Beauregard truly believed he'd gotten it right. The van was just as he had described it. A 2005 Ford Econoline with only driver and passenger windows. The type of vehicle you saw on the road every day and hardly noticed because it was so ubiquitous.

The driver of the SUV turned off his headlights but kept on his parking lights. Beauregard peered through the binoculars.

Three men exited the vehicle. They walked around to the front of the van, which still had its headlights on full blast. Even though it was in the high 70s two of them were wearing light, loose-fitting hoodies. Between the illumination from the headlights and the glow of the fire Beauregard could clearly see the bulges in their waistbands under their hoodies. The third man, the driver, made no attempt to hide his weapon. He carried an AR-15 in his wide mahogany hands. The triumvirate stared at the immolating car, then glanced at each other, then turned back to the fiery mess of melting steel and shattering glass that blocked their way. Staring through the binoculars gave everything an emerald sheen. Even the flames from the car seemed to give off a chartreuse radiance.

"Should we call somebody?" one of the hoodie-wearing brothers asked.

"Who the fuck we gonna call? Smokey the goddamn Bear?" the driver asked. He was wearing a Washington Wizards jersey. He had long dreadlocks that fell down his back in serpentine coils. Before the first hoodie-wearing brother who had asked the pertinent-if-somewhat-naive question could respond, a pickup truck crested the hill and stopped behind the SUV. All three men spun around and faced the pickup. The driver held his AR-15 down by his side and stepped into the shadows. The driver of the pickup cut the ignition and killed his lights. The driver's door of the truck creaked open and Kelvin hopped out. He was wearing one of his work shirts with the name patch removed.

"Hey, what the hell is going on?" he asked as he walked toward the men and the car, which was now completely engulfed in flames. The driver, Mr. Dreadlocks, stepped from the shadows brandishing the AR-15. He didn't point it at Kelvin but he wasn't letting it dangle at his side either. He held it at an angle across his midsection. Beauregard took a deep breath. He'd told Kelvin he had to really sell it. Make sure he sounded irritated and confused. However, it was a precarious balancing act. If he came off too calm they might get suspicious. If he came on too strong they might just shoot him on general principles.

"Who the fuck are you, man?" Dreadlocks asked. Kelvin made a show of noticing the gun. He backed up and raised his hands.

"Hey man, I don't want no trouble. I'm just trying to get home,"

Kelvin said. He let the bravado and annoyance slip from his voice and replaced it with wariness and fear. Beauregard thought he could earn an Oscar with this performance.

"Turn around and go another way, cuz," Dreadlocks said. Now he was pointing the gun at Kelvin.

Fuck, Beauregard thought.

He put his binoculars down and grabbed the .45. He aimed it at Dreadlocks. No one said a word. Beauregard could hear the crackling of the fire as it consumed the former luxury car, the hooting of a lonesome owl, the idling engines of the van and the SUV and the beating of his own fluttering heart. The locusts had lowered the pitch and volume of their serenade to nearly imperceptible levels.

Beauregard felt his stomach tighten like a boa constrictor was in his guts. He had two extra clips in his backpack if things popped off. He put his left hand on his right wrist and steadied his gun hand. He should take out Dreadlocks right now. Then take out the Hoodie Brothers. The flames were giving off enough light that he thought he could nail Dreadlocks for sure. The Hoodie Brothers might be more problematic. They were standing in the shadows.

The longer he waited the more likely it was that Kelvin was going to eat a bullet. He squinted but he couldn't see how much pull Dreadlocks had on the trigger. He was pulling about three pounds of pressure on the five-pound trigger of the .45 himself.

"Look, man, this is the only road that I can take. I don't know what's going on and I got no interest in finding out, but I got a fire extinguisher in my truck. If we can put the fire out we can push the car out of the way and we can all go on about our business. And my business got nothing to do with your business," Kelvin said.

Silence.

"We gotta get down to Winston-Salem by two," one of the Hoodie Brothers said. Kelvin shrugged his shoulders. The muscles in Dreadlock's forearms rippled like rigging ropes.

He ain't going for it, Beauregard thought. He started to rise out of the milkweed and heather on the side of the road.

"Look, my wife already gonna bite my head off because she thinks I'm cheating on her. Let's help each other out, man," Kelvin said.

"Are you?" one of the Hoodie Brothers asked.

"Am I what?" Kelvin asked.

"Cheating on her?"

Dreadlocks motioned with the AR-15.

"Get the fire extinguisher," he growled. Kelvin nodded and jogged back to the pickup.

He grabbed a slim red fire extinguisher from behind the bench seat. He went back to the car, pulled the pin and sprayed down the Lincoln. A whitish cloud of CO_2 enveloped the car, dampening the flames. Kelvin had to hit the car three more times before the fire went out completely.

"Let me see if I can put it in gear. Then we can push it. Be careful though, it's still fucking hot," Kelvin said. He gingerly reached his hand through the window, taking care to not let his arm touch the still smoking car door. Beauregard had left it in neutral but this was all a part of the act.

"Hey, it's already in neutral," he said. He stepped back and pulled his shirt over his head. He walked to the back of the car. By wrapping his shirt around his hands he made it into an ersatz oven mitt.

"We all gonna have to push it. It's a Lincoln. An old one. It's heavy as shit," Kelvin said. The Hoodie Brothers put their hands inside the pockets of their hood jackets and took a position on either side of Kelvin. Beauregard saw the door of the van open and watched as an amber-colored dome light came to life. A big beefy brother wearing a baseball cap with a broken bill started to get out.

"Get your ass back in that van," Dreadlocks said.

The van driver got back in but didn't shut the door all the way. Eventually the dome light blinked out.

"Hey man, it's gonna take all of us," Kelvin said.

"Y'all got it. I got faith in you," Dreadlocks said. He was still pointing the rifle at Kelvin. He stood between the van and the Lincoln.

"Tyree, this car heavy as fuck. Come on, man, let's just move it and get on," one of the Hoodie Brothers said to Dreadlocks. Beauregard inched closer to the road.

Tyree set the rifle down on the road. He took a position next to the Hoodie Brother on Kelvin's left.

"I ain't messing up my jersey," Tyree said as he placed his Air Jordan on the trunk.

"Hey, I feel ya. Alright, on three," Kelvin said.

"One."

Beauregard put the binoculars back in his pack and crept over the dry ditch bank. He crouched down until he was crab walking again. He inched his way up to the driver's-side door of the van. His rubber-soled shoes slipped over the gravel and asphalt like a sigh.

"Two."

Beauregard pressed his back against the side of the van.

"THREE," Kelvin exclaimed. The four men pushed and kicked the Lincoln. The screech of metal against metal filled the night as the brakes ground against the rotors.

Beauregard stood up and aimed his .45 at the driver. The man had a wide face with a light, almost tan complexion. He stared at Beauregard's gun like a bird staring at a snake. The driver's hand hovered above the horn but Beauregard shook his head. He pulled a piece of white paper out of his pocket with his free hand. He pressed the paper against the glass.

"TURN OFF THE DOME LIGHT. DO NOT MAKE ANY NOISE. GET IN THE BACK AND LIE FACE DOWN. IF YOU DON'T I WILL KILL YOU" was written on the paper.

The driver hadn't shut the door completely so Beauregard grabbed the handle and opened it slowly. He motioned for the driver to get in the back. The man slid his considerable bulk over the center console and lay down in the back of the van. Beauregard balled up the paper, put it in his pocket and climbed in the van. He saw that the man had followed instructions as carefully as a dutiful child. He shut the door softly then slipped out of his pack while still holding his gun. Using his free hand he retrieved two sets of handcuffs from the knapsack. He handed both pairs of cuffs to the driver.

"Handcuff one end of one set of handcuffs to one of the straps holding down the pallet. Hook the other end to the chain in the middle of the other pair. Then put that pair on. Do it quickly," Beauregard whispered.

"Are you gonna shoot me?" the driver asked. His voice was a tremulous whistle.

"Not if you put on the handcuffs," Beauregard said. He checked his watch. Taking control of the van had taken a minute and a half. They were right on schedule.

"That should do it, fellas," Kelvin said. The smoldering Lincoln was at a lackadaisical diagonal angle in Pine Tar Road's northbound lane. They'd moved it just enough so they could all slip by.

"Yeah," Tyree said. He retrieved the AR-15 and aimed it at Kelvin again. Kelvin held his hands out in front of him. He dropped his work shirt and took a step back.

Beauregard watched the scene through the windshield. All the saliva in his mouth instantly evaporated. His breath came in ragged bursts.

"Don't you do it," he murmured.

"Hey man, come on," Kelvin said. Tyree walked up to him and placed the barrel against his cheek. He pushed forward until the barrel was making a dent in Kelvin's face.

Beauregard planted himself in the driver's seat. He had the .45 in his waist but shooting through the windshield would throw off his shot. The van was a 6,000-pound deadly weapon if it came to that. Beauregard watched as Tyree pressed the barrel of his gun even harder into Kelvin's cheek. His whole body flinched.

"No, no, no, you gotta talk this motherfucker down," Beauregard said, not caring if the driver heard him or not. He saw Kelvin's face in the bright bluish headlights. It was terribly animated. His eyes were big as dinner plates. Snippets of the conversation reached him in muffled chunks. The words were indistinct but the AR-15 made the nature of Dreadlock's threat perfectly clear.

Beauregard shifted the van into drive. He could close the distance between the van and Tyree in less than three seconds. Which wouldn't matter because if Tyree pulled the trigger Kelvin would be dead before he hit the ground.

Beauregard clutched the steering wheel in a death grip.

"If I was you I would forget all about tonight. I see you again, anywhere, your wife a widow. Ya feel me?" Tyree said.

"Forget about what?" Kelvin said.

"Come on, Tyree, we gotta go," one of the Hoodie Brothers said.

"Be gone, homes," Tyree said. Kelvin put his hands down and picked up his shirt. He grabbed the spent fire extinguisher and walked around the three men. He glanced at the van as he walked back to the truck. He climbed in and shut the door. Beauregard's bandana rustled as he exhaled deep from within his chest.

"Get in the car," Tyree said. The other two men hustled back to the SUV. As he made his way back to the vehicle he slapped the hood of the van. The windows and the windshield had a dark, smoke gray tint. In the faded gloom of the North Carolina night, with the blinding LED headlights blasting his retinas, Tyree failed to notice Beauregard sitting in the driver's seat.

"Let's get on, Ross," Tyree said after slapping the hood. He climbed into the SUV. Beauregard put the van into gear and hit the gas. The caravan was once again on its way. Kelvin counted to fifty before taking off as well. By the time he'd crested the next hill the tail lights of the SUV were just red pinpricks.

Beauregard kept the van near 60 as they navigated the serpentine road that twisted through the North Carolina hills. The SUV stayed about a car length behind him with its low beams bouncing off his side mirrors. He put the gun in the knapsack with his right hand while steering with his left. Switching hands, he grabbed the steering wheel with his right and slid his left hand under the dashboard near the door. His deft fingers found the van's fuse box. He visualized the fuse box's specs. He'd memorized them from the Chilton repair manual. He could see the square black box in his mind with the different colored two-bladed fuses in three short rows that ran the length of the box. Beauregard counted to himself as his fingers slipped across the hard plastic rectangles.

One, two, three, four down. One, two, three to the right, he thought. He pulled the fuse for the van's brake lights out of its socket. He let it fall from his fingers and buried the gas pedal in the floor. The van lurched forward as the engine screamed. A sharp curve was coming up but Beauregard didn't let up on the gas. He took the curve at 70. He felt the back wheels trying to slither to the right as he turned into the curve. He wrenched the steering wheel to the left and gave the brake a love tap. Glancing in the side mirror he saw the SUV was now about six car lengths behind them. He grimaced but his bandana hid his own visage from him as he flicked his eyes up toward the rearview mirror. Once again he stomped on the gas. The van's engine squealed in protest but Beauregard spared it no quarter. The speedometer topped out at 125 and he intended to get within shouting distance of that in the next two minutes. The road ahead careened into another hairpin turn that forced him to slam on the brake with his left foot while keeping his right foot firmly on the gas pedal. The van drifted through the turn like a big man who was surprisingly nimble on the dance floor. He checked the side mirror. The SUV's headlights appeared after a few seconds.

Beauregard heard the staccato rhythm of gunfire explode behind him. He took his foot off the brake and committed all his strength to pressing the gas pedal to the floor. He checked the side mirror again. Another burst of gunfire exploded even as the headlights of the SUV

receded. Soon they disappeared entirely. The crew in the SUV probably assumed the van driver had decided to double-cross them and
make off with their boss's loot.

That was exactly what Beauregard wanted them to think.

A long stretch of straight road unfurled in front of him like a
black ribbon. He checked the speedometer. 90 mph.

Beauregard fished his phone out of his pocket. Steering with his
left hand he scrolled through his contacts with a quick downward
glance. When he got to one that said R1 he pushed the green "call"
button. Returning his eyes to the road he saw a chestnut-colored doe
step daintily out into the middle of the road.

"Goddamn it!" he grunted. Beauregard whipped the steering
wheel to the right while letting up off the gas but not braking. He
heard the pallet in the back groan as gravity pulled at it with insistent
invisible hands. Beauregard drove the van onto the narrow shoulder
of the road and around the seemingly oblivious deer. The front right
tire tried to slip into the ditch but Beauregard refused to allow it to
escape. He'd come too far and had too far to go for that bullshit. He
hit the gas and slammed the wheel to the left. The van fishtailed,
shuddered, then the front right tire found the road again and dug
into the asphalt. Beauregard did all this with his left hand while still
holding the phone to his right ear.

"What is it?" Ronnie yelled.

"Nothing. Be ready. Two minutes," Beauregard said. He ended
the call and tossed the phone in the cup holder. Another series of
hills were coming up in one hundred feet. He had driven this road
twice since they had come down yesterday morning. He took notice
of every divot, pothole and twist and turn. The details were burned
into his mind like a cattle brand. He checked his side mirror. The
headlights of the SUV were nowhere to be seen. They had the faster
vehicle but he had the better skills.

At the top of the second hill Beauregard saw a white box truck
had pulled out in front of him from its resting place on the widest

part of the shoulder. He eased up on the gas and grabbed the phone. He called Ronnie again.

"You have to keep it at 60. I'm coming in hot," Beauregard said. His words came out in short clipped bursts.

"I got it. You want the door down now?"

"Yes." He tossed the phone aside again.

Boonie had gotten them the pickup truck and two other vehicles for Beauregard's plan. The box truck he had to steal. He and Kelvin had slipped down to Newport News and copped it from a plumbing supply store on Jefferson Avenue. The van they were going to steal was fifteen feet long, six feet wide and six feet seven inches tall. The Akers and Son box truck was just wide enough, deep enough and had barely enough headspace for the job. Originally it had a roll door that slid up and rolled onto two metal slats attached to the roof. Beauregard had gotten rid of the roll door in addition to making a few more adjustments.

Ronnie had wanted to go in guns blazing but Bug knew that was a fool's run. He'd figured, correctly, that the crew protecting the van would be strapped with some heavy artillery. They didn't have the time or the money to get into an arms race.

Beauregard inched closer to the box truck.

Instead of rolling upward the door of the box truck began to open outward like the lid of a coffin. Slowly, torturously it continued opening until it was nearly parallel with the road. After a breath-stopping pause it continued opening until the lip made contact with the road. The rubber weather stripping he'd installed at the top of the door began to smoke as friction began to devour it. He only had a few minutes before the rubber wore away and sparks began to dot the night. The door itself was made up of threaded rod welded together in a cross-hatch pattern like a sheet of rabbit wire. He'd sandwiched that between quarter-inch-thick steel plates. Two-inch-wide support struts ran from the bottom of the door to the top. They stopped just three inches before the weather stripping along the edge of the ramp began. Kelvin had helped him hook up the hydraulic system that opened and closed the door. A toggle switch dangling from the steering wheel of the truck controlled the entire apparatus.

Closed, it looked like any other door to any other box truck.

Opened, it became a ramp.

Beauregard focused on the ramp. They'd hit another flat stretch. This one went on for just under three miles. Ronnie was doing 60. He'd have to get the van up to at least 65 to get inside the truck and then stand up on the brakes to keep the van from crashing into the cab. This was their best shot. In about three minutes the road became a roller coaster and stayed that way for the next five miles until it passed a desolate gas station.

He pushed the van up to 65 and aimed it at the ramp. He felt it then. Felt it for the first time tonight. The high, the juice, the symbiotic relationship between man and machine. The thrumming vibrations that worked their way up from the blacktop through the wheels and suspension system like blood moving through veins until it reached his hands. The engine spoke to him in the language of horsepower and RPMs. It told him it yearned to run.

The thrill had finally arrived.

"Let's fly," Beauregard whispered.

He hit the ramp doing 70 mph. The van rocked like a skiff on the open sea. Beauregard heard the driver moan from the back. Grunting, he eased up on the gas infinitesimally. He'd adjusted the ramp so that the dip between it and the edge of the bed was minimal but if he came in too fast he'd pop the front tires. Without warning the truck shot forward, accelerating violently. Beauregard could feel the ramp slipping from beneath his wheels.

"Fuck!" Beauregard growled. He let up on the gas as the ramp disappeared completely from beneath the van. The front tires slammed onto the asphalt like Fat Man and Little Boy. The van careened from left to right as Beauregard struggled with the wheel. Once he had it under control he fumbled for the cell. He hit the "call" button with his right thumb as he steered with his left hand.

"What was that?" Beauregard said when Ronnie answered.

"I'm sorry, my foot slipped. Fuck it, Bug, I'm sorry I—"

Beauregard cut him off.

"Keep it at sixty. I'm coming in again," he said. They'd missed their best chance in the long straightaway. Now more steep hills loomed ahead of them. Beauregard gritted his teeth as the van struggled to drag itself up and over while carrying him, the driver and the pallet of platinum.

Ronnie was trying to keep the truck steady but it was jerking, faster on the downhills, slower as it struggled up. Impossible to time it right in these short valleys.

No headlights in the mirror. Not yet. He breathed deeply. They had one more shot. It wasn't ideal but they didn't really have a choice. After this last hill the road flattened out again. Only this time it was a matter of feet, not miles.

As Beauregard descended the hill he saw bright orange sparks erupt from the ramp. The rubber weather stripping had burned away and the metal was making contact with the asphalt. The sparks looked like fireflies from Hell. Two hundred feet. He only had two hundred feet left before the road ended and they were back on a main highway. Two hundred feet to make this work. The main highway was forty miles of flat blacktop four lanes wide. Once they hit it the SUV would catch up with them. He couldn't outrun them on that stretch. Beauregard focused on the ramp. The van's powerful headlights lit up the inside of the truck. The interior of the truck reflected the light back at him. Through a hail of sparks, he saw the four sandbags he had attached to the wall to act as a backstop. A desolate gas station illuminated by flickering sodium arc lights zipped by his window. The yellow lights left jaundiced streaks behind his eyes.

One hundred and sixty feet now.

Beauregard flicked his eyes toward the rearview mirror. He saw the ambient glow of headlights rising above the last hill they had gone over. The SUV hadn't crested that hill yet but it would in a matter of seconds. It was either going to be now or it was getting shot in the fucking face.

One hundred feet.

Beauregard grunted and hit the gas. The needle on the speedometer shot past 70 mph and leaned on 80. He passed a green rectangular sign that told him Pine Tar Road was coming to an end.

Drive it like you stole it, right? Beauregard thought.

He slammed the gas pedal to the floor. As the speedometer hit 90 mph, sparks washed over the van like a wave of falling stars.

"There! There it is, goddamn it!" Tyree yelled.

He whipped the SUV to the right and pulled into a desolate, dimly lit gas station. The gas station was about a mile from the end of Pine Tree Road. Tyree slammed on the brakes and jumped out of the vehicle with his AR-15 in one hand. The Hoodie Brothers followed him. They kept their weapons tucked under their shirts and kept their distance from Tyree.

Sitting under the sallow sodium arc lights that sat above the gas pumps was the van. Moths darted around and under the canopy above the pumps, casting strange, fluttering silhouettes that danced across the surface of the van. Tyree approached it from the rear with slow deliberate steps. He pressed the stock of his rifle against his right bicep while he grabbed the rear latch with his left. The doors swung open with a horrid creak.

"Motherfucker," Tyree said.

The van was empty. No driver, no platinum, no anything. Tyree seized the rear door and slammed it shut. He opened it again and slammed it shut. He did this five more times. The seventh and final time was too much for the rear window. It exploded into a million pieces. Chunks of tempered, smoke gray glass rained across the concrete.

Tyree threw his head back and howled.

"MOTHERFUCKER!"

Inside the store the cashier was putting a 40-ounce bottle of beer in a brown bag for his only customer. They both watched with mounting concern as the man in the parking lot slammed the door to the van again and again. He and his customer jumped when they heard the man in the parking lot baying at the sky as the glass in the rear door shattered. The cashier peered out the picture window at the front of the store.

"That don't sound good. Don't look good neither. I think that one boy there got a gun. You think I should call the cops?" the cashier asked as he handed the brown bag to his customer.

Reggie grabbed the bag and his change.

"None of my business, man," he said. His voice quavered a bit but since the cashier didn't know him from Adam he didn't notice. Reggie unscrewed the beer cap and took a big swig as he left the store. A warm wind rose up out of nowhere. It stirred the napkins and clear plastic lids and cigarette butts that dotted the parking lot. He headed for the highway, walking at a diagonal amble away from the van and the SUV. He tried to take another sip of his beer but his hands were trembling and he spilled it all over his T-shirt.

"Hey white boy, you see who was driving this van?" a voice asked from behind him. Reggie stopped. His throat felt like it was closing in on itself. He gripped his beer bottle tight. Exhaling rapidly, he turned to face the trio of men standing near the van.

"Nope," he said. Tyree stepped forward. Reggie stared at the gun in his hands. The beer in his guts started trying to climb out of his stomach.

"You didn't see nothing?" Tyree asked.

"Nope, sure didn't," Reggie said. His wounded foot began to

throb. He began to tap it like he was keeping time with a beat only he could hear. Tyree took another step forward. They were only a foot apart now.

"You sure about that?" he asked.

"Yep," Reggie said. His voice had dropped to a barely audible rasp. Tyree stared at him.

A cell phone rang. One of the Hoodie Brothers answered it.

"Hey Ty, it's Shade. He can't get in touch with Ross. He wants to talk to you."

Tyree clenched the grip on his gun. He started to step forward again but stopped. He held Reggie's gaze for a few seconds before swallowing hard and holding out his left hand.

"Give me the phone," Tyree said. His voice had lost some of its menace.

Reggie nodded abruptly and started hoofing it down the road. After he'd gone about about two hundred yards a pair of headlights appeared behind him and lit up his whole world. Reggie stopped, turned and used his free hand to shield his eyes.

A bedraggled pickup truck pulled over to the side of the road. The passenger door creaked open like a crypt. Reggie limped over to the truck and climbed inside.

"Everything go alright?" Kelvin asked.

"Yeah. I did just what Bug said. As soon as I saw the truck and the van go by I pulled out and drove to the gas station. Those guys pulled up like two seconds after I got in the store," Reggie said. He took another sip.

"You didn't get me a beer?" Kelvin said. Reggie clutched the bottle to his chest.

"I didn't know you wanted one."

Kelvin laughed.

"Calm down, Hee-Haw, I was just fucking with you," Kelvin said as they pulled back onto the road.

TWENTY-FIVE

Bug sat in the van in the dark and waited for Ronnie to make the turn. It would be a left turn onto an old dirt lane choked with weeds and grass, just past a shuttered feed and seed store. The dirt lane climbed up a steep hill and crested in a flat meadow. Beauregard guessed a house had stood in the meadow at one time, but it was long gone. Nature had not yet reclaimed the spot completely. He'd found the place the day before riding around in the Lincoln with Kelvin while Ronnie and Reggie had lounged at the motel. He didn't put too much stock in fate or luck but it had been fortuitous to find this spot. It was nearly a mile off the highway in the middle of nowhere with enough room for the truck, the van and the pickup Kelvin was driving to maneuver in. This time of night no one would notice them unless they came looking.

Beauregard hoped no one came looking. He didn't relish killing anyone. At the same time, it didn't fill him with tic-inducing anxiety. It was messy. Murder was always messy. If it had to be done, you had to expect to get dirty and clean up as best you could. When they had found those boys that had done Kaden, old Chompy had cleaned things up for them nicely.

The truck stopped. The hydraulic pump wheezed and shuddered as the ramp lowered once more. Beauregard started the van and backed down the ramp slowly. He hit the ground, turned the wheel to the right, shifted into drive and pulled up alongside the box truck. He killed the engine and climbed out and leaned against the driver's-side door. The box truck's headlights gave the meadow an eldritch glow moments before they extinguished. A copse of pine trees surrounded the meadow. Beauregard heard the door to the box truck open, then slam shut. Ronnie ambled around the back of the van.

"We fucking did it!" he said. He held up his hand for a high five. Beauregard glared at his hand until Ronnie lowered it and let it hang down by his side.

"It's not done yet. We have to load the truck."

"So, what about . . . your passenger?"

"He ain't seen shit. We load up the truck and handcuff his ass to a tree branch. If he's smart he'll wait till we gone and use the cuffs as a rope saw to get loose," Beauregard said.

"You think that's a good idea? Leaving him like that?" Ronnie asked. Beauregard pulled his bandana down past his mouth.

"I said he ain't seen shit. Besides, it ain't like he gonna go to the cops."

Ronnie shrugged his shoulders. "Just asking. Shade's worse than the cops," he said. He put his hands in his pocket. Beauregard noticed the outline of a small pistol in the right-hand pocket. It sat there like a sleeping scorpion. Deadly and inert all at the same time.

"Uh huh."

A pair of headlights climbed up the overgrown driveway.

Kelvin pulled into the meadow, then turned the truck around so that the tailgate was facing the back of the van. He put the truck in park with a loud clang. He and Reggie climbed out and met Ronnie and Beauregard in the middle of the field.

"That transmission got about twenty more feet in it," Kelvin said.

"It'll be fine. Ronnie, get the flashlight out of the truck. Let's get the old boy out of the van and find a tree to tie him to. Then we can load up the pickup truck. It's eleven o'clock," Beauregard said. "I want us on the road by midnight."

"You know, I've been thinking. How would Lazy know if we kept a few spools for ourselves? I mean I know what you said but really, you think that motherfucker gonna miss two rolls? Shit, two rolls is enough for the four of us. I know a guy can get us a real good price," Ronnie said. Beauregard put his hand on Ronnie's shoulder. He let his thumb lie on Ronnie's collarbone. Katydids began to call to each other from the undergrowth. Beauregard buried his thumb under Ronnie's collarbone and pressed against the brachial plexus.

"OW! Damn, Bug!" Ronnie squealed. He leaned over and put one hand on his knee while trying to remove Bug's hand from his shoulder with the other.

"You don't get to talk about keeping anything. You don't get to talk about what Lazy might know or not know. The only thing I want to hear you talking about is loading up this goddamn truck. Now get old boy out the van," Beauregard said. He released Ronnie, who then stumbled backwards into his brother. Beauregard untied the bandana and held it out to Ronnie.

"Make him put this on." Ronnie gave Beauregard a long hard look and for a second Beauregard thought he was going to make a move. Beauregard felt something akin to relief that they were finally going to get down to it, but then the fire faded out of Ronnie's eyes.

"Fuck, Bug. It's just a thought. Damn. You got the fucking key to the cuffs?" Ronnie said. Beauregard took the keys from his pocket. He placed the bandana in Ronnie's left hand and the keys in his right. Ronnie closed his hands tight and stalked over to the van. He opened the rear door and climbed inside.

"Listen up. I'm gonna put a blindfold on you. Then I'm gonna unlock the cuff from the strap. You ever want to see big titties and fat asses again you do exactly what we tell you. Cool?" Ronnie said.

"C-cool," the driver said. Ronnie straddled the man as he lay on his stomach and tried to tie the bandana around the driver's head. The two ends of the scarf barely met as Ronnie tried to tie a simple knot.

"Goddamn you got a big head. Like a damn pumpkin," Ronnie said under his breath. Groaning, he pulled hard on the fabric around the man's eyes and looped it into a harsh, tiny knot.

He unlocked the cuff from the metal banding strap that held the rolls of platinum in place on the pallet. He stood and grabbed Ross by the collar of his denim button-down shirt and helped him to his feet. They executed a slow backwards shuffle until they hit the bumper.

"Alright, step down. Easy. I ain't trying to pick your big ass up," Ronnie said. The driver's foot hovered in space as he tried to find the ground. Ronnie let go of his collar and grabbed him by the arm.

"Step down. Now your other foot."

The driver placed both feet on the ground. Ronnie held him at a somewhat perpendicular angle. He turned his head toward Beauregard.

"Where you wanna do this?" he asked.

"Poor choice of words," Kelvin said.

Before Ronnie could respond the tiny knot he had tied unraveled unceremoniously. The bandana fell from the driver's face and floated lazily to the ground. The driver looked over his right shoulder directly into Ronnie's face. They locked eyes for about half a second before he twisted from Ronnie's grasp and took off across the meadow.

"Fuck me!" Ronnie yelled. He pulled a .32 from his pocket and starting firing at the driver. The man began to run in a zigzagging pattern. He reached the tree line and began crashing through the woods.

"Get the flashlights!" Beauregard yelled. Kelvin ran to the truck and retrieved two heavy-duty Maglites. He tossed one to Beauregard.

"Come on. Reggie, you with me!" Beauregard said. He took off for the woods.

"You heard him, dipshit!" Ronnie yelled. Ronnie lit out for the woods. Kelvin passed him like he was standing still as they headed for the pines. Reggie limped after them but his loping gait didn't have much urgency.

Beauregard clicked on the flashlight. The pine trees and wild azaleas appeared ghastly in the harsh yellow light. He threaded through the woods, ducking under low-hanging branches and jumping over the rotted trunks of trees that were dead when he was still in juvie. He stopped for a second and listened. He tried to ignore the insects and the animals and just listened for the sounds a fat frightened man running for his life would make. A part of him wondered if Ronnie had intentionally tied the bandana with a slipknot or something. He'd been so intent on killing the driver, maybe he'd done it to force Beauregard's hand? Beauregard shook off that thought. That was a chess move. Ronnie was strictly a checkers kind of guy. Ronnie Fucking Sessions. That should be his nickname instead of Rock and Roll. The man was a congenital fuckup. Couldn't even tie a goddamn blindfold right.

A sharp embankment rose in front of him, dotted with dying pines and sickly cedars. The sound of his own breathing seemed unbelievably loud, like a bellows in an old steel plant. His .45 was heavy against the small of his back. He pulled it and brought it up in his right hand while holding the flashlight aloft with his left.

He heard a crashing and snapping behind him and to the left. That was Ronnie, Kelvin and Reggie. He eyed the embankment again. Could the driver, who was two cheeseburgers away from cardiac arrest, climb such a steep hill in less than two minutes? Normally Beauregard would have said no but fear gave men wings. He started climbing up the embankment. He pushed himself and reached the top of the ridgeline in less than five minutes. He paused and took a deep breath. It came out ragged.

The first few notes of "Born Under a Bad Sign" echoed through the night. They were harsh and sharp, nearly robotic. Someone liked the blues and had the song as a ringtone. Beauregard's head snapped to the right.

Too late he realized the forest was playing tricks on him. As he turned the driver slammed into him. They landed in a thunderous heap with Beauregard on the bottom. His right wrist cracked against a root or a rock. Pain sprinted up his right arm and he felt his gun slip away. The driver's bulk crushed him into the ground.

Every inhalation was agony. As he grasped blindly for his gun he felt warm metal biting into his throat. He couldn't breathe. Calmly, almost abstractly, he realized the driver was using his handcuffs to garrote him. Beauregard let go of the flashlight, stopped reaching for the gun and pushed himself and the driver up off the ground. The two of them pitched onto their sides but the driver still held on. Beauregard's hands scrambled across the driver's face like a pair of tarantulas. His thumbs found the man's eyes as his chest began to burn and black spots began to dance in front of his face.

Beauregard jammed both thumbs in the man's sockets. The driver cried out like a wounded bear. He released his hold on Beau's neck in an attempt to protect his eyes. Beauregard rolled away from the driver. Taking in huge gulps of air, he scuttled across the forest floor on all fours. He ran his hand over and through the detritus. His gun. He needed his gun.

The beam from his flashlight began to dance across a few trees that were a foot or so in front of him.

Beauregard flipped onto his back just in time to partially block a blow from the driver. He had gripped the flashlight with both hands and was wielding it like a club. Beauregard tucked his legs up to his chest and kicked at the man while using his hands to block his strikes. He had to get to his feet. Forget the gun. On his feet they were literally on a level playing field.

A corona illuminated the man from the back as a volley of shots resounded through the forest. A fine mist of blood and bone chips filled the air between him and the driver. The man started to fall forward. Blood leaked from two wounds in the center of his chest. Beauregard caught the body as it pitched forward, the flashlight falling from his hands. He shoved the driver's body off to the left and squirmed to the right. His face and neck were dotted with droplets of blood. Ronnie and Kelvin stepped up onto the ridgeline. They were both holding guns. Kelvin was also holding the other flashlight. He stepped over the driver and held out his free hand to Beauregard. Beauregard gripped it and Kelvin pulled him to his feet.

"You alright?" he said.

"Yeah. Most of this is his blood."

"Man, why did he take off running? Did he think there was a buffet up here?" Kelvin asked. Beauregard shook his head. He felt a smile trying to spread across his face.

"I owe you one," Beauregard said.

"Nah, we just even now. You owe Ronnie one though. I think he was the one that hit him," Kelvin said. Beauregard peered over Kelvin's shoulder. He saw Ronnie looking down at the driver's body. He was humming a tune that Beauregard didn't recognize. Beauregard turned his attention back to Kelvin.

"Let's get back to the van and get loaded up. I want to be back in Virginia by sunup," Beauregard said. The plan was for him and Kelvin to drive the pickup. Ronnie and Reggie, by virtue of Ronnie getting all of them into this, would have to take the risk of riding in the stolen box truck.

Kelvin was about to respond when his left cheek exploded. Warm fluid splashed across Beauregard's chest. A sharp pain ripped across his right deltoid as Kelvin crumpled to the ground. Beauregard jumped backwards. It was a move born of instinct more than anything else. He felt himself floating in midair for what seemed like minutes before his body crashed into the western slope of the embankment. He tumbled head over heels as shots rang out from the ridgeline and bullets ricocheted off the desiccated trunks of diseased pine trees. Dirt and twigs and dead leaves found their way down his shirt and into his pants and into his mouth as his body careened down the side of the hill. The world was a swirling kaleidoscope until he flipped one last time. The wide trunk of an old pine tree rushed toward his face then there was just blackness.

TWENTY-SIX

For a moment Beauregard thought he was blind. The world seemed dim and full of shadows. He blinked his eyes and felt something warm and wet running down his face. He sent his left hand on an exploratory mission and touched his face. It was blood. He had blood in his eyes. A wound above his left eye had clotted but his rough fingers opened it again.

He wasn't blind. It was still dark. Beauregard sat up and immediately regretted it. Vomit raced up his esophagus and out his mouth. He leaned on his left side and let it pour out across the ground. He felt like he was trapped on a merry-go-round.

Taking a deep breath, he tried sitting up again. He didn't vomit this time, but he sure wanted to. An owl hooted at him from somewhere. He listened for any other sounds. Like people walking or voices commiserating about him. But all he heard were the usual sounds of the forest at night. He hesitated then sent his left hand on an expedition. Up his right arm. When his fingers found the gash, he pressed his lips together tight and groaned. The gash was about two inches long but not deep. The bullet had grazed him. He flexed his right hand. His fingers moved, albeit begrudgingly. He touched his forehead. A knot the size of a chicken egg was sitting just above his left eyebrow and a little to right of the laceration that had bled into his eyes. He checked his watch. The pale glow of its face was not enough to draw anyone's attention. It was two thirty in the morning.

They had chased the guy into the woods around eleven. He'd been out for more than three hours.

Kelvin had been dead for three hours. His cousin, his best friend, had been dead for three hours.

Ronnie Fucking Sessions. He should have seen that coming. He should have been prepared. He'd seen Ronnie's face when Lazy had spilled that money across his desk. That lean and hungry look that said Ronnie did not want to give up his hard-earned loot. Beauregard had seen that look and dismissed it. Foolishly he had assumed Ronnie's desire to live would outweigh his greed. What he hadn't counted on was that for Ronnie, a life without money was no life at all. Now because of his avarice and Beauregard's hubris, Kelvin was dead.

Beauregard closed his eyes. He had to get up and he had to get moving. Kia and the boys were in the crosshairs of a movie-loving hillbilly psycho. A hillbilly who expected a van full of precious metal to be delivered to him no later than Sunday night. His inside man would tell him that the van never made it. Lazy would then sit and wait for a phone call that was never going to come. Lazy would surmise they had double-crossed him. He'd send shit-kicking Freddy Krueger after him. Ariel was safe because they didn't know about her. But Kia and the boys had to get out of town. Beauregard reached in his pocket. He pulled out the burner phone. It was broken. Probably crushed in the fall.

"Shit," he croaked.

He'd have to climb back up the hill. The van would be long gone. He'd left the keys in the ignition. Another mistake. The pickup and the box truck would still be there though. Ronnie probably had the keys to the box truck. That was okay. He could hot-wire the truck. Or he could get the keys out of Kelvin's pocket and drive the pickup truck.

Grief as strong as an earthquake hit him, sending tremors throughout his whole body. He felt his esophagus spasm but his stomach had nothing left to give so he just dry-heaved. Groaning, Beauregard smacked himself. Hard. After a few seconds he did it again. The tremors began to subside. He rotated onto his hands and knees. Taking a deep breath, he pushed himself to his feet. The world around him shimmered like he was walking through a wall of water. Beauregard closed his eyes and steadied himself. One more deep breath and he began climbing up the embankment. Each step was like walking through molasses. He stumbled, caught himself and kept going. The closer he got to the top the slower he climbed. He knew what was waiting for him up there. He knew what he would see once he scaled this nondescript North Carolina hill. But he had to see it. Not just because he needed a set of keys.

He deserved it. Deserved to be confronted with the blank emptiness that would be etched on what was left of Kelvin's face. So, he climbed. He pulled at saplings and clawed the moist earth and climbed. He marched toward his penance with a grim determination.

Kelvin's dead eyes greeted him as he reached the top of the hill. His head lolled to one side and his mouth was agape. The wound in his cheek was a raw red crater. Beauregard could see jagged remains of Kelvin's teeth through the hole.

Beauregard dropped to the ground next to Kelvin's body. Ants were crawling across his face. Some trundled in and out of his open mouth. Beauregard grabbed his hand. It was like touching a piece of hard cold wax. Kelvin's fingers were rigid as stone. Beauregard tried to brush the ants off his face but his hands started to shake. He shook his head and steadied himself. The ants he cleaned off climbed back on Kelvin's face with the pitiless proficiency of a hive mind. Beauregard tried to close his remaining good eye but the lid refused to stay down. He lowered his head until it was lying on Kelvin's chest. The fetid aroma of fresh death was so potent he could taste it. He swallowed it down and dared his stomach to rebel.

"Once I take care of all this I'm gonna come back and bury you right. I promise you that. You should've never been here. You never owed me a damn thing," Beauregard mumbled into Kelvin's chest. A few moments passed. Beauregard's mind played him scenes from the past like a home movie spliced together from old 8-millimeter reels. Kelvin and him as kids souping up their bicycles with playing cards stuck in the spokes to replicate the sound of a motorcycle. Kelvin daring him to drive without lights through Callis Road knowing damn well Bug would do it. Kelvin in a tuxedo handing him a ring. Those moments and a thousand more like them slit his soul like razors and flayed it open.

Finally, Beauregard raised his head. He touched his face. The blood, Kelvin's blood, the driver's blood, was still dry in the corners of his eyes. He hadn't cried. He hated himself a little for that but there would be time for tears later. He reached into Kelvin's front pocket for the keys. He moved over the ground on his hands and knees turning over the soil searching for his gun. He found it a foot from where he and the driver had tumbled to the ground. He put it back in his waistband and slid down the other side of the embankment. As soon as he reached the meadow he saw how the box truck and the pickup were both listing to one side. Both sets of tires on the driver's side had been slashed.

"You think you slick, don't you, Ronnie?" Beauregard said.

When they had scoped out the rendezvous spot Beauregard had noticed a few houses up the road a piece. A few trailers and some single-story ranchers. Most of the homes had cars sitting in the driveway. A few of them even had garages.

Red Hill was six hours away. Depending on what kind of vehicle he boosted and how much fuel was in it, he could make it and only have to stop once for gas. He had a little over $200 in cash on him. That had him hitting Red Hill around eight, give or take an hour. He could have Kia and the boys out of town by nine. Boonie could patch up his wounds. Then he could deal with Mr. Ronnie Sessions and Mr. Lazy Mothersbaugh.

Beauregard walked across the meadow. He slipped among the pines like a wraith and headed north.

There was a paucity of cars on the road as Ronnie crossed the state line into Virginia. Reggie had reclined the seat and drifted off to sleep. He hadn't spoken a word since they had come down off the hill.

"Hey, you hungry?" he asked Reggie.

"No," Reggie said.

"You gonna be like this all day?"

"Like what?"

"Sitting there like the goddamn Sphinx."

"I just keep thinking about that day we went by Bug's house when he pulled a gun on you. Put the barrel right up against your guts. He was willing to kill you in front of his wife and kids for coming by his house without calling. I keep wondering what he gonna do to us for killing his homeboy," Reggie said.

"First, if I had known you was gonna keep talking that shit, I wouldn't have said nothing to you. Second, Beauregard is dead," Ronnie said.

"You sure he dead? Did you go down that hill and make sure his neck was broke? Oh, wait, I know the answer to that," Reggie said.

"You know what? Shut up. Go back to sleep," Ronnie said.

Reggie shifted in the seat and turned his head to the door. Ronnie pushed a button on the radio, but nothing happened. He stared straight ahead trying to ignore what Reggie had said.

"I got him. I know I got him."

Reggie started laughing.

"Oh, you know you got him? Do you? I'll tell you what I know. I know that you double-crossing Bug and that Lazy guy done killed us. You know that, right? You've fucking killed us. Bug is gonna come for us. He'll come for us and he'll kill us like cockroaches. And if he don't, then Lazy and his boys will. We are so fucking fucked," Reggie said. He crossed his arms and stared out the window.

"Reggie, that's not going to happen. Trust me."

"Trust you? Quan trusted you. Kelvin trusted you. Bug trusted you. Shit, Jenny trusted you. How'd that turn out for them?" Reggie said. Ronnie put his hand on Reggie's knee.

"They weren't my brother. Look, even if I didn't get him he probably broke his neck rolling down that hill."

"You always say trust you but you always just making shit up as you go along," Reggie said in a voice as placid as a frozen lake.

"Did you want to go back to being poor white trash? Huh? This van is carrying twenty-eight rolls of platinum. Bug said every roll is ten pounds. Even if we get fifty cents on the dollar that's enough money to get us out of Virginia and set up somewhere where every road ends up at the beach," Ronnie said. Reggie didn't respond.

"He was going to give it all away, Reggie. All of it. Three million dollars' worth of second chances just gone," Ronnie said. Reggie moved Ronnie's hand off his knee.

"We always gonna be trash, Ronnie. Money ain't gonna change that," Reggie said. Ronnie opened his mouth to offer a rebuttal to Reggie's assertion but none was forthcoming. The truth had a strange way of ending an argument.

They drove in silence for a few miles. Ronnie opened his mouth to say something to get Reggie's mind off their current situation when the burner phone started vibrating in his pocket. Ronnie almost ran off the side of the road. Why were they calling so soon? He checked his watch. It was a little after five in the morning.

"That's them, ain't it?" Reggie asked.

"Nah, it's *Who Wants to Be a Millionaire*," Ronnie said. Sweat spilled across his forehead like an oil slick.

"You better answer it."

"Shut up, just let me think, okay?" Ronnie said. The phone continued to vibrate. Ronnie drummed his fingers on the steering wheel. The phone stopped vibrating. Then almost immediately it started again. Finally, Ronnie reached in his pocket and answered it.

"Hey."

"Rock and Roll. I thought you was ignoring me. You almost hurt my feelings. Where's the van? My man say Shade is pretty pissed it didn't make it to Winston-Salem. He asking the boys that was guarding it what happened but he don't much like they answers. He pulling they teeth out until he gets some answers he do like." Lazy chuckled. "Now I've gotta say, you boys keep impressing me, but weren't you supposed to call me when the deal was done? I thought we had an understanding," Lazy said. Ronnie let that last sentence hang in the air for a beat before he answered.

"Here's the thing. That fella Beauregard? He stole the van."

"I know that. That's what I told y'all to do," Lazy said.

"No, you don't understand. We had the van and then him and some fella he had with him turned on me and my brother. He shot at us and took off with the van," Ronnie said. There was a heavy quietness that carried a weight through the cellular network. It seemed to make the phone cumbersome.

"Where you at, boy?" Lazy said. He spoke with a deep deliberate articulation.

"Me? I'm about forty-five minutes from my place. He left one of the vehicles we used behind. I guess that was lucky for us," Ronnie said. A line of cars passed him like he was standing still. He checked the speedometer. He was doing 70. The van was rattling like a washing machine full of bricks.

"Alright. You get to your place, you stay put. We gonna come out there. See if we can figure out where this old boy done run off to," Lazy said.

The line went dead.

"Why'd you tell them we were going home?" Reggie said.

"To buy us some time."

"We gotta go home eventually."

"No, we don't. We going to see your girlfriend out at Wonderland. I got a guy who can sell this shit, I just can't run up on him without calling first. We just need a few more hours," Ronnie said.

"She don't particularly care for you," Reggie said.

"I don't give a fuck. As long as she don't eat me, we be alright," Ronnie said.

Lazy put the phone down on his desk. Billy finished with a customer in the front of the store, then walked into the back office.

"Rock and Roll says that boy Beauregard took off with the truck," Lazy said.

"How you want to handle this?" Billy asked.

Lazy pulled out a pipe and filled it with a pungent wad of apple-flavored tobacco. "Call the boys you got watching they places. When Ronnie and his brother show up, bring 'em back here. Get Beauregard's people too. If he did run off with the van, he gonna try to warn his wife. We get her back here, he'll bring us the van. If he got it," Lazy said.

"If he got it?" Billy said.

Lazy lit his pipe and took a deep drag. "He might done run off with it. But he struck me as smarter than that. He also might be lying face down in a ditch and that Sessions boy might have it. Either way, we gonna figure it out. We might have to roast a few marshmallows over them, but we'll figure it out," Lazy said as he exhaled a bluish plume of smoke.

TWENTY-SEVEN

Beauregard pulled into the rest stop with the Jeep hidden inside a cloud.

Steam was pouring from under the hood and enveloping the entire vehicle. He had just crossed the state line back into Virginia. The clock on the radio said it was nine in the morning. The needle on the temperature gauge was so far in the red, it needed to file for bankruptcy. Beauregard parked the Jeep and killed the engine. He checked the rearview mirror before he got out of the car. The cramped single-wide he'd broken into had a surprisingly well-stocked medicine cabinet. Large and small bandages, peroxide, rubbing alcohol and some aspirin. The long-sleeve black shirt he had taken was too big for him and the pants were too long, but they would do for now. The Jeep had been a gamble from the start. A rust-covered relic with a severe oil leak and two bald tires in the front. It looked like a leftover prop from some apocalyptic movie.

Still, it had made it all the way to Sussex before it started giving up the ghost. Beauregard got out and popped the hood. More steam swirled around his head. The sickeningly sweet smell of antifreeze filled his nose. Beauregard waved away the steam. On the side of the radiator, he saw a plume of steam coming from a pin-sized hole. Beauregard looked around the rest stop. It was one of the larger ones on the interstate. A line of picnic benches sat under some huge oak trees. A brick building housed the bathrooms, snack machines and an information desk. Beauregard headed for the picnic tables.

The first three were bare. Nothing on the tables and nothing on the ground under them. It was just his luck to pull up to a rest stop with a fastidious cleaning crew. The fourth table was occupied by an Asian family eating their breakfast. Beauregard tried to put on a smile when he approached them.

"Excuse me."

The father appraised him with a wary stare.

"I hate to bother you, but do you folks happen to have some pepper?"

The father conferred with the mother silently. The looks they exchanged seemed to acknowledge that pepper was not a deadly weapon that could be used against them. The two children, a boy and a girl, both under ten, reached into their fast food bags and pulled out several pepper packets. The mother gathered them up and handed them to Beauregard.

"Are you eating breakfast too?" the little girl asked.

Beauregard smiled. "No, my car is running hot because the radiator is leaking. Some pepper will fix the hole for a little while," he said. She nodded her head as if she discussed emergency car repair every day.

"What happened to your face?" the boy asked. His mother shushed him.

"An accident," Beauregard said. He stuffed the pepper packets in his pocket.

"Thank you," he said. He headed back to the Jeep. Halfway there he stopped and turned around. "Say, you folks don't have a phone, do you?"

Kia was pouring milk for Darren's cereal when she heard the knocking at the door. Javon was still in bed. He'd been up all night drawing while she and Darren had watched a marathon of animated movies. She finished pouring the milk and slid Darren his bowl.

"Eat your breakfast," she said. She got up and started for the door. As she went to answer the door, her cell phone started chirping. Kia stopped and turned toward the bedroom. Then she looked back toward the door. The cell phone stopped chirping. She continued to the door.

"Mama, you forgot the cereal," Darren said. She barely heard him. She peeked through the diamond-shaped window in the center of the door. There was a white man standing on the porch. Two more white men were standing next to a late model LTD. The one on the porch was as big as her refrigerator. The other two were considerably smaller. The man on the porch was wearing a white button-down shirt and jeans. The two by the car were both wearing T-shirts and jeans. One had on a faded CAT baseball hat.

She opened the door a crack.

"Can I help you?"

The big man wrenched the door from her grasp. She stood in the doorway wearing one of Beauregard's T-shirts and sweat shorts. She was painfully aware of how they clung to her ass.

"You married to a boy named Beauregard?" the big man asked.

"Why? What's going on?" she asked.

The big man gave her the once-over. "Get your boys, y'all gotta come with us," he said.

"I ain't going nowhere with you and neither are my boys. Now tell me what the hell is going on," Kia said.

The big man turned to the two leaning against the car and beckoned them. Without warning, he grabbed Kia's arm and started dragging her out of the house. He moved with such astonishing speed, she was on the first step before she started fighting back. She scratched at his eyes and kicked at his balls. She got one grunt for her trouble. The white boy in the CAT hat brushed by them. Her heart shattered when she heard Darren start to scream.

"Mommy! Mommy! Mommy!" he howled as the CAT-wearing man dragged him out of the house by his thin arm. The third man went into the house as Kia and Darren were being forcibly walked to the car. Kia twisted and fought with everything she had in her, but it was no use. It was like trying to wrestle a mountain.

The big man stopped dragging her. He pulled her close and put his forearm around her neck. She felt something cold and hard against her temple. No one was moving. Kia craned her eyes toward the house. The third man was backing out of the house with his hands up. When he got to the bottom step he stopped.

Javon was standing on the porch holding a gun. It was a Beretta 9 mm 92 series. One of his father's guns.

The big man gripped Kia tighter.

"Now you just wanna hold on a minute and put that gun down. You don't want nobody to get hurt now, do you?" he asked.

Javon didn't move. He held the gun straight with his free hand bracing his wrist. "No, I don't. So, let my mama and my brother go," he said. He didn't stutter or whisper. He spoke with a loud, clear voice that was on the verge of changing.

"Look, son, you don't know what to do with that," the man said.

Javon never took his eyes off the big man. He clicked the safety off.

"Let my mama and my brother go," he said.

The big man was still trying to make up his mind how to handle this situation when CAT Hat raised his gun and mumbled under his breath.

"Fuck this shit."

Javon pointed the gun in his direction and pulled the trigger. The pistol jumped in his hand like it was alive. The man in the CAT dropped to a crouch. The bullet zipped over his head and shattered the headlight of the LTD. Javon kept pulling the trigger. He moved from the man in the hat to the man standing right in front of him. A red flower bloomed on the man's chest as he fell like a marionette whose strings had been clipped. He never even reached for his gun.

The big man pulled his gun away from Kia's head and pointed it at Javon. As soon as he did a bullet slammed into his neck. He pulled the trigger reflexively but without aiming. CAT Hat dived to the ground and crawled back toward the driver's side of the LTD. He raised his gun and fired over the hood.

The big man staggered back to the LTD. His gun slipped from his grip and landed in the grass. He fell into the car with his legs still hanging out of the door. CAT Hat jumped in the driver's seat. He started the car and pulled at the big man's shirt, dragging him further into the car. Bullets cracked the windshield as he put the car in reverse. The big man's feet dragged across the ground as they backed out of the yard and tore down the lane.

Javon kept pulling the trigger even though no more bullets came out of the gun.

"Javon!" Kia screamed.

"Javon, call 911!"

Javon kept pulling the trigger.

"Javon, call 911!" she screamed. Her eyes were bugging from her head. Her face and chest were covered with streaks of red. She was clutching Darren in her arms. It was then that Javon finally understood. He ran inside the house and went to his mama's bedroom. Her cell phone was on the nightstand. He dropped the gun to the floor. He grabbed the phone and dialed 911. His mother's screams echoed throughout the house.

"911, what is your emergency," a robotic voice asked.

"Somebody shot my brother," Javon said. He dropped the gun and started screaming too.

Kia sat in the waiting room directly under a television that was showing an advertisement for the hospital on a loop. The light from the fluorescent fixtures reflected off the white floor tiles. It was giving her a headache. Her eyes were stinging. She had cried all the way from the house to the emergency room. They wouldn't let her sit in the back with Darren. She stared at him the whole way to the hospital through a small window in the cab of the ambulance. The driver had tried to get her to put on her seat belt, but she ignored him. She had to keep her eyes on him. If she kept looking at him, then he couldn't die. She told herself that as they careened down the road. As long as she could see him, he wouldn't die.

Kia put her head in her hands. Her chest was a nest of knots that were continually tightening. Jean rubbed her back as she stared at the floor through splayed fingers. He was only eight years old. Eight-year-olds aren't supposed to die. They're supposed to make stupid jokes and refuse to wash off a fake tattoo their brother gave them.

"Kia."

She raised her head. Beauregard was running through the waiting room. He was calling her name. Not screaming it but using the full force of his deep baritone voice. When he came around the corner, he stopped five feet away from her. He looked like Hell warmed over. The left side of his face was one huge angry bruise. He had on a long-sleeve black Lynyrd Skynyrd shirt two sizes too big. A pair of oversized pants hung from his frame.

"Kia. What did they say?" he asked.

She glared at him. "You not even gonna ask what happened?" Kia asked.

Beauregard dropped his eyes. "I went to the house. I saw the bullet holes. I went next door. Linda told me. The car broke down. I would have been there, but the car broke down," he said. She could barely hear him.

"Men came to our house. Men that were looking for you," Kia said. She rose from her seat.

"I know. I tried to call but you didn't answer," Beauregard said.

"Don't do that. Don't you do that. If you hadn't gone off with that white boy pulling some goddamn job, you wouldn't have had to call," Kia said. She spoke through bared teeth.

"Kia. Let's go outside and talk," Beauregard said.

"Talk about what, Beauregard? About how you fucked around with some gangsters and they came to our fucking house? You wanna talk about how I told you to sell that goddamned car? But you wouldn't do it, would you? Because you didn't want to get rid of your dear Daddy's car. My son is on an operating table fighting for his life because you care more about a dead snitch than you do your own children. My other son is down at the police station because he had to shoot two people to keep them from taking his mama and his little brother. Do you get that, motherfucker? My son had to kill somebody today. But I guess you think that's alright. It's a Montage family tradition, right?"

Beauregard knew she was trying to hurt him. The only person who knew your weak spots better than the woman who raised you was the woman who shared your bed. But he took it. Took it like he had never taken it before because she was right. He had brought this horror down upon his family. But that didn't mean he didn't love them.

"They my sons too, Kia," Beauregard said.

Kia stepped forward and slapped him. Her tiny hand caught him flush on his bruised cheek. Flashing lights appeared in front of his face. For a moment he felt something cold and alien bloom in his chest. He raised his right hand and curled it into a fist but only for a split second. He deserved that. That and so much more.

"Not today they ain't. Today they my sons and I've got to protect them. Protect them from people like you," Kia said. She pressed her body against his. Her limbs felt like steel wires. Her breath smelled of smoke and stomach acid.

"Kia, I'm not people. I'm their father."

"Go," she said.

"The car broke down. I would have been here, but the car broke down."

"GOOOOO!" she shrieked. She pounded on his chest with her

fists. When he tried to put his arms around her, she recoiled like he had the plague.

"GET THE FUCK OUT!"

"No, Kia please," he said as he reached for her. She shrieked again. A raw guttural howl with no discernible words but in a language that was clearly understood.

Jean got up and pulled her into her bosom. Kia went limp in her sister's arms. Jean guided her back to her seat.

"Beauregard, just go. I'll call you when we hear something," Jean said.

He turned around in a near perfect 360-degree circle. The intake clerks, the nurses, the janitors, other patients, they were all gawking at them.

"The car broke down. I would have been here, but the car broke down. I fixed it and I came straight to the house. I fixed it," he said under his breath. He said it again as he headed for the sliding glass doors. And again, as he walked toward the rust-covered Jeep sitting in the parking lot with a screwdriver jammed in the ignition. Beauregard got in and slammed the door. He began to scream and pounded his palms against the steering wheel. Every muscle in his body worked in concert with his diaphragm. His chest began to ache as he arched his back and howled. People walking across the parking lot lowered their heads and looked away as they hurried past the Jeep. The sound coming from that battered vehicle needed no explanation or translation.

It was the pure and unmistakable sound of despair.

TWENTY-EIGHT

Boonie unlocked the door to his house with one hand while balancing a six pack in the crook of his free arm. The sky was filled with streaks of magenta as the sun dipped below the horizon. As he stepped across the threshold, his guts jumped up into his mouth.

Beauregard was sitting in his leather recliner.

"Jesus, boy, you scared the shit out of me. What the hell are you doing in here?" Boonie asked.

Beauregard raised his head. "I fucked up, Boonie," he said.

Boonie closed the door and got a good look at him.

"What the hell happened to your face?"

"You was right. About Ronnie, about everything," Beauregard said.

Boonie sat down on the couch that was perpendicular to the recliner. "Talk to me," he said.

Beauregard gingerly ran his hand over his forehead. He told Boonie everything. The jewelry store, Lazy, the van, Kelvin, everything right up to what happened to Darren. Boonie listened quietly, never once interrupting or asking any questions. When Beauregard was done, Boonie got up, went into the kitchen and returned with a mason jar. He unscrewed the top, took a sip, and sat it on the coffee table between them.

"I'm so sorry, Bug. What you want us to do?" Boonie asked.

Beauregard turned his head and leaned his good cheek against the side of the chair. The surface was cool. Boonie's central air unit was working overtime.

"You know, I used to think of myself as two people. Sometimes I was Bug and sometimes I was Beauregard. Beauregard had a wife and children. He ran a business and went to school plays. Bug . . . well, Bug, he robbed banks and armored cars. He drove 100 miles per hour on hairpin curves. Bug threw the people who killed his cousin in a car crusher. I tried to keep them apart, Beauregard and Bug. But my Daddy was right. You can't be two types of beasts. Eventually one of the beasts gets loose and wrecks shop. Rips shit all to Hell," he said.

He grabbed the mason jar and tossed it back. When he sat it down, nearly half of its contents were gone. Tears leaked from the corners of his eyes.

"They shot my boy, Boonie. They shot my boy because Bug fucked up and Beauregard wasn't there to fix it."

"We gonna fix it, Bug. You just tell me what you want us to do," Boonie said.

Beauregard sat forward. "I'm gonna fix it. I might need a few favors."

"Anything," Boonie said.

"I parked up the road back down by that old house on Carver's Lane. I need to get that car to the yard and get rid of it. Then I'm needing to borrow a vehicle. Can't make no moves in my truck."

"Okay, no problem. But what we gonna do about this Ronnie and Lazy situation?" Boonie asked, his voice full of malice.

Beauregard smiled. It didn't go much farther than the edge of his mouth. "We ain't gonna do nothing. I'm gonna find Ronnie and get that van back. There's only two places he could be. He can't just roll up on somebody to move that much swag. The way he moved them diamonds, I know he got a connection, but it'll take a couple of days to set up a deal. I don't think he's dumb enough to be at his house.

So that leaves Wonderland. Once I get the van back, I'm gonna call up Mr. Lazy."

Boonie grunted.

"You can't go up against these boys by yourself. Them fools up at Wonderland ain't shit, but this Lazy fella is bad news."

"I already got Kelvin killed."

"And I ain't gonna let you get killed. Anthony was like a brother to me, but you done become like a son. I can't just let you go out here all alone like you some fucking cowboy. Your family needs you. Hell, I need ya, you stubborn son of a bitch," Boonie said.

Beauregard leaned forward and stared in Boonie's eyes.

"I'm already gone, Boonie. I know what you think my family needs, but I'm gonna tell you what I need. I need for you to do for my sons what you did for me. Be there. I think I understand why Daddy left now. Beauregard and Bug are the same person. And that person ain't no good for a family."

Boonie snatched off his cap and slapped it against his knee. "Stop talking that crazy shit. You they father. You're Kia's husband. They need you. You leave, and you make the same mistake Anthony made," Boonie said. Spittle flew from his lips.

Beauregard stood. Boonie stood as well although it took him a bit longer to get to his feet. He jammed his stained cap back on his head.

"You don't want to help me then I'll go," he said.

Boonie crossed his arms. "I would do anything for you. You know that. But I saw what Anthony leaving did to your Mama. What it did to you. I know he thought he was making the right decision, just like you do. But you were both wrong. Bug, look around. You the closest thing I got to family these days. Don't do this," Boonie said.

"This thing inside us. This thing in me. The thing that was in my Daddy. It's like cancer. It gotta end with me, Boonie. Kia ain't like my Mama. They won't grow up fucked-up like I did. Javon ain't going to juvie. He'll get off with self-defense. And if Darren pulls through . . ." Beauregard swallowed hard. "When Darren pulls through, he and his brother and his sister are going to grow up and get out of Red Hill. They are going to go to college and fall in love. Have kids of their own. But the only way any of that happens is if I get ahold of Ronnie and Lazy. Now if you can help, I appreciate it. If you can't, then get out the way. I'd appreciate that too," Beauregard said.

Boonie breathed deeply through his mouth. His eyes moved past Beauregard to the wall behind the recliner. There were old photos in cheap frames on the wall. Boonie and his wife. The first day at the scrap yard. Him and Anthony posing next to Boonie's '67 Mercury Comet. His eyes moved back to Beauregard.

"Let's go move the car. Then we can get straight on everything else," Boonie said.

"Hey, Mama," Beauregard said.

His mother trembled as her eyelids quivered. They rose slowly and Beauregard could see her mind working as she struggled to focus.

"You look like hell," she said finally.

Beauregard chuckled. "I know."

"What time is it?"

"A little after nine."

"They let you in after visiting hours?"

"I didn't give them much of a choice."

Ella gave him a long sideways glance.

"What's wrong? Did they tell you I only had a week left?"

"No. Hey Mama, you remember that time we picked all them blackberries out back of the trailer? We must have picked a gallon. Daddy came by later, brought me that knockoff G.I. Joe action figure. I think it was called Action Man or something? He stopped by with that and he helped us pick some of the blackberries. Then we went inside, and you made that cobbler. Remember that?"

"They must have told you I'm gonna die in an hour," Ella said. Beauregard threw his head back and laughed. Ella shivered.

"God, you sound like your Daddy," Ella said. Beauregard stopped laughing.

"Nah. I was just thinking. It wasn't always bad. You know with you and me and Daddy. That day was nice. Wasn't often we got to act like that."

"Like what?"

"A family," Beauregard said.

Ella stared straight ahead.

"You running, ain't ya?" she said.

"Now why you say that?"

"Mothers know their children."

"I'm not running. I just gotta take care of some things."

"Huh. That's what he used to say. Then one day something took care of him."

Beauregard got out of his chair. He went to his mother's bedside. He leaned over the railing and kissed her on her forehead.

"You can be as mean as a rattlesnake dipped in arsenic sometimes, but you're my Mama and I love you," he said into her ear. "I don't expect you to say it back." He gently ran his hand over her brow before heading for the door. Ella watched him walk out and turn down the hall. She licked her dry lips.

"Goodbye, Bug," she whispered.

TWENTY-NINE

Reggie took another hit. He hadn't done coke in a long time. He preferred the languid honey-drip high a taste of heroin provided. However, beggars couldn't be choosers. Ann had coke, so he did coke. As soon as it hit his bloodstream, he remembered why he didn't like it. Every inch of his skin increased in tactility by a thousand percent. Even the strands of his hair seemed to be receiving sensory input. Ann took the vial from him and poured out a thin line on the back of her hand. She snorted and immediately started rubbing her nose vigorously.

"Goddamn Almighty! That shit is potent," she said.

"Uh huh," Reggie said. His heart was Irish clog hopping in his chest.

"Come on. Let's do something. Coke makes me horny."

"What, you hungry?" Reggie asked.

Ann crinkled her nose and grabbed his crotch.

"No, I'm HORNY. We can eat after," she cooed.

Reggie let her pull him on top of her. As he was letting her slide his pants down, he heard a commotion out front. That wasn't unusual. Wonderland was nothing but one long commotion with momentary respites of peace and quiet.

Whenever Beauregard came up to Wonderland, he marveled at how the name had stuck. He couldn't believe any of the inbred zombie tweakers that hung out up here understood the concept of sarcasm. To them, it really was a Wonderland. Beauregard thought a better name would be "Lost All Hope Land" or "Crabs and Syphilis Land." Secreted deep in the rolling hills of Caroline County at the end of an oddly scenic drive, Wonderland was an oasis of sorts. A collection of four double-wide trailers connected to form a two-legged T near a picturesque lake. Wonderland's pastoral location was at odds with the entertainment it provided. You could indulge a wide variety of vices at Wonderland. The ones that were the most popular were the old favorites. Sex and drugs with a splash of white lightning thrown in for good measure. He hadn't bothered going to Reggie and Ronnie's place. Ronnie was a lying, double-crossing piece of shit but even he wasn't that stupid. He might have thought he'd gotten rid of Bug, but he knew he still had Lazy to contend with. There was no way he'd go back to their trailer. He'd want to go somewhere he felt safe. Somewhere he could relax while he tried to unload the platinum. Somewhere he could celebrate outsmarting both Bug and Lazy.

Wonderland definitely fit the bill.

A menagerie of cars and jacked-up trucks were parked off to the right near the base of the mountain. Reggie's car was parked next to a truck with a Dixie flag in the back window. A honky-tonk standard was blasting out of one of the windows of the mobile home monstrosity. Back in the day, a place like this might be called a shot house. Nowadays, shoot-up house was a more apt description. Beauregard tucked his .45 into his waist and stomped over the moss and grass to the foot of the T where someone had fashioned a crude front door.

A thin man sat on a stool near the door sipping from a flask. He gave Beauregard a long hard look.

"What's up, Hoss?" he asked.

"What up, Skeet," Beauregard said.

Skeet sipped from his flask. "Long time, no see. If you looking for Jimmy, you out of luck. He got picked up. Doing two years in Coldwater for possession with intent," Skeet said.

"Nah, I'm not looking for Jimmy," he said.

A short wide man with a Dixie flag baseball cap and a face like a gravel road ambled over to the door. He was holding a red plastic cup full of liquor. Beauregard took in the scene. The first trailer served as a bar and lounge. A raven-haired beauty named Sam was standing behind a bar made from an old sheet of plywood and some milk crates. Near the bar were five or six ragged beanbag chairs. A few people were splayed across them like dolls. The rest of the denizens were sitting around two different plastic patio tables. A long-haired hipster in khaki shorts and sandals was chatting up Sam near the bar. No one was really paying attention to the naked girl dancing on the stage made from an old high school cafeteria table. A neon Coors sign hung on the wall behind her. It gave her skin a devilish red glow. The rest of the lights were turned down just low enough so that you could still find your crystal meth if you dropped it. A pungent scent filled the air. It was a witch's brew of weed, whiskey and body odor.

"Sam running things now?"

"Might could say that. I mean she is his sister."

"How's that working out?"

Skeet shrugged. "Alright. Most people just go on like Jimmy still here."

"Uh huh. Look, Skeet, where Ronnie and Reggie at? I saw Reggie's car outside."

Skeet's watery brown eyes flicked left to right. He hesitated before answering. "Well, Ronnie left a while ago. Reggie in the back," he said.

"Thanks."

"What you want, boy?" the man in the Dixie hat said. His words came out sideways.

"Nothing," Beauregard said. He moved past the man. Dixie Cap reached out and grabbed his arm. Beauregard looked at the hand on his arm then at the hand's owner.

"Can't we have one place without you poking your head in it? Goddamn, y'all done took over the White House," Dixie Cap said.

"If you don't get your hand off me, I'm gonna feed it to you," Beauregard said.

"Bobby, get on now," Skeet said. He hopped off the stool and removed Bobby's hand from Beauregard's arm. Bobby mumbled something, but Beauregard ignored him. He threaded through the first trailer until he came to the intersection of the T.

Left, or right? Beauregard decided it didn't matter. He had to be in one of the rooms back here. Jimmy Spruill rented rooms at the top of the T an hour at a time. Just in case you wanted to get high in private with your soul mate for the night. Back here Wonderland gave up any pretense of civility. The four trailers attached end-to-end were a smoked-filled Tartarus awash in dying embers and used needles. No one looked up from the belts they were tying off to acknowledge him as he passed. The layout of the bedrooms changed as you moved from one trailer to the next. Sometimes they were on your right, then they were on the left. None of them had doors. Instead they sported beaded curtains or sheets draped over a compression shower rod. When Beauregard peeped in, he wasn't admonished. A few times he even received an invitation to join the festivities.

Reggie was in the last room in the last trailer. His pale white ass was pistoning up and down on top of the big girl that had been at his trailer a few weeks ago. His pants were bunched around his ankles. The woman opened her eyes and stared at Beauregard over Reggie's shoulder.

"Baby," she squeaked.

"So . . . close," Reggie panted.

"Baby, somebody here!" she squealed. Reggie froze in midstroke. Beauregard stepped in the room and grabbed Reggie by the hair. He pulled him off the big girl and slammed him face first into the wall. When he pulled his head back blood was pouring out Reggie's nose and chin. He slammed his face into the wall again. It left a bloody Jackson Pollock painting on the wall.

"Hey, Reggie, pull up your pants, we gotta talk," Beauregard said.

Reggie pulled up his pants as Beauregard held a wad of his hair. After he had covered his narrow ass Beauregard dragged him out of the room. The large woman was struggling to get out of the bed. Her prodigious breasts spilled across her belly like an avalanche.

"You let him go!" she screamed. Beauregard ignored her and dragged Reggie down the hallway. Reggie tried to claw at the walls, but he could find no purchase. Ann finally got up and tossed on a T-shirt. She waddled after Beauregard and Reggie as fast as she could. When Beauregard reached the front lounge area, Skeet hopped off his bar stool.

"Yo Bug, what the hell?" he asked. Bobby jumped up from his beanbag and launched himself at Beauregard and Ronnie. Beauregard figured he'd been spoiling for a fight ever since he'd seen a brown face walk through the door. As Bobby hurtled toward them, Beauregard pulled the .45 out of his waist. He flipped it so that he was holding it by the barrel and slammed the butt into Bobby's mouth and jaw. His Dixie flag baseball cap flew off as his head snapped back. Beauregard herded Reggie to the side as Bobby fell into one of the patio tables. Drinks went flying as the table collapsed under his weight. Beauregard wheeled around with the .45. He panned across the room with the business end.

"Get him!" Ann screamed.

"I'm taking him out of here. Anybody got a problem with that, say something," Beauregard asked. No one spoke. Beauregard backed out the door with Reggie, shirtless and crying, in tow.

"Y'all just gonna sit there? Some friends you are!" Ann screeched.

Sam poured some moonshine out of a large plastic jug into a mason jar and handed it to the hipster. "Can't argue with a .45," she said in her throaty voice.

The men who had been sitting at the demolished table floated over to the bar. Conversations that had been muted returned to their normal volume. The girl onstage stepped down and another skinnier girl took her place. Skeet and a few other guys helped Bobby up and gave him some paper towels for his bloody mouth. After a few minutes, it was like nothing had happened. And for all intents and purposes, nothing had.

Beauregard turned off of Route 301 and navigated the narrow back roads that led out of Caroline County and back to Red Hill. He hugged the white line as he drove down the single-lane road masquerading as a double-lane highway. Reggie lay in the passenger seat with his face pressed against the glass. Neither he nor Beauregard spoke. There was nothing they needed to say.

Beauregard turned onto a gravel-covered road. They passed a cell tower surrounded with bright new chain-link fencing that shimmered in the truck's headlights. Beauregard turned off the gravel road onto a narrow driveway covered in cracked asphalt. The driveway led to a clearing where the remnants of an old factory held court like an ersatz Stonehenge.

"Get out. Don't run. I'll shoot you in the back," Beauregard said.

Reggie climbed out of the truck. He took off running as soon as his feet hit the ground. He headed for the woods surrounding the clearing. Beauregard shot up in the air. Reggie dropped to the ground. Blades of grass scratched his chest. He felt a hand grab him by his hair and pull him to his feet. He let himself be dragged back to the truck. Beauregard pushed him against the passenger door. They locked eyes for a moment.

Beauregard punched him in the stomach. Reggie doubled over, then fell to his knees. He made a wet gagging sound. Beauregard thought Reggie might throw up but he didn't. He made some more gagging sounds then raised his head. Beauregard dropped to his haunches so that they were eye to eye.

"I'm only gonna ask you once. Where is Ronnie?"

"I didn't know. I didn't know about it. I would have never gone along with it," Reggie wheezed.

Beauregard put the .45 in his waistband near the small of his back. He grabbed Reggie's left hand with his own. Using his right hand, he opened the passenger door on the truck. By the time Reggie realized what he was doing it was too late to struggle.

Beauregard gripped Reggie's wrist and forced his hand against the door frame. He slammed the door shut on Reggie's hand.

Reggie's mouth filled with hot stinging bile and this time he did vomit. It dribbled over his loosened teeth and down his shin. He screamed. He kicked his feet. He swallowed some vomit, then threw it up again.

"Where is he, Reggie?" Beauregard asked. A slight breeze moved the grass in the clearing. The blades undulated like waves in a lagoon.

"I . . . don't . . . know," Reggie said.

Beauregard pulled the door back and slammed it on Reggie's hand again. Reggie threw his head back and howled. His eyes widened to the size of silver dollars.

"Don't . . . make me tell. He's my brother. Don't make me tell. You're gonna kill him if I tell," Reggie cried. Fat tears rolled down his cheeks, cutting tracks through the blood on his chin.

"I'm gonna kill you if you don't. They came to my house, Reggie. They shot my son. All because Ronnie couldn't stick to the plan. I don't want to hurt you any more, Reggie. But I will. And I won't stop until you tell me where he is. You pass out and I'll wake you up. Once this hand goes numb, we'll start with the other one. Then we move to your feet. Then your dick. I'll feed you to this truck piece by piece," Beauregard said.

"I'm so sorry. I didn't know what he was gonna do."

'I know you are, Reggie. I know. Where's Ronnie?"

Reggie's Adam's apple bobbed up and down like a fishing lure.

Beauregard pulled the door back.

"Wait!" Reggie begged.

"I don't have time to wait, Reggie."

"Please. He's my brother."

"And Darren is my son."

Neither man said anything. As the seconds ticked by, a dog bayed in the distance.

Reggie hung his head. "He went over to Curran County. Other side of the hills here. Crashed with some girl named Amber Butler. I think she lives off Durant Road. I don't know what he did with the van."

Beauregard stood.

"Alright. Alright," he said. His tone was robotic.

Reggie looked up at him. His eyes were red and rimmed with tears.

"I'm scared, Bug."

Beauregard pulled out the .45.

"Nothing to be scared of, Reggie. Just close your eyes."

Beauregard got back to the salvage yard just before sunrise. A man-sized blue tarp was on the back of the tow truck. The office was locked, but he knew Boonie kept a spare key in an old Pontiac next to the main building. Once he had retrieved the key, he went inside and grabbed another key from the rack to the left of Boonie's desk. He went back outside and grabbed the man-sized tarp off the back of the truck. Beauregard hoisted it up on his shoulders with a deep groan. He stomped around the back of the office and headed for a dilapidated Chevy Cavalier. He used one hand to unlock the trunk with the key he grabbed from the rack. He dropped the blue tarp into the trunk and slammed it shut. Once that was done he went back inside the office and locked the door behind him. He scooped his phone off Boonie's desk as he headed for the couch. He had one text message. It was from Jean, not Kia.

Darren came out of surgery. They got the bullet. Still touch and go.

Beauregard flopped onto the couch. He pressed the phone against his forehead. Darren was finally out of surgery. Darren, who loved to giggle at the absurdity of curse words. They had pulled a bullet out of his baby boy. Beauregard's eyes began to burn. He buried his face in his hands. Sadness and guilt hovered around his heart like buzzards. He wiped his eyes and pushed those feelings away.

They could have his heart when this was over.

THIRTY

Ronnie bent over and lit his cigarette on the burner of Amber's stove. He inhaled deeply and let the smoke fill his lungs. Cancer never tasted so good. He went to the window, pulled the vanes of the blinds down. Nothing. Just darkness. He let the smoke in his lungs billow out of his nostrils. Amber had just left for her shift at the hospital. He'd asked her to cop him a few Percs, but she had blanched at the request.

"Ronnie, I ain't into that no more. I got my RN now. Can't fuck that up."

"Hell, get me the extra-strength aspirin then. I need something," he'd said. He'd take whatever he could get. His nerves were as raw as a bedsore. He'd tried Reggie all day and couldn't get him. His phone wasn't even going to voice mail. Just rang a few times and disconnected. He took another drag on the smoke and let the smoke flow from his nostrils and mouth. Lazy had been blowing up the burner phone so much that it finally ran out of minutes.

Ronnie knocked some ash off his cigarette into the sink. Amber had her own trailer at the end of a long driveway, just like Reggie. The driveway was bordered by a cornfield on one side and a thin grove of walnut trees on the other. Hard for anyone to sneak up on him. Not that anyone should know where he was. Unless they got to Reggie. But Lazy didn't know anything about Wonderland. At least Ronnie didn't think he did. Ronnie inhaled again. He might need to ride up to Wonderland. Grab Reggie and make for the West Coast.

There was nothing in Virginia for them. Not anymore. He couldn't even—

An engine was revving outside in the dark. Ronnie went to the window again. He didn't see any headlights. He ran to his bag and grabbed his gun. He stubbed out the cigarette on the linoleum and cut off all the lights. Breathing hard, he peeped through the blinds. The engine was close. He could almost feel the vibrations as it revved again and again. Ronnie sucked his teeth. Could he make it to his Mustang? It was at least ten steps from the front door to the car. He licked his lips. The engine stopped revving. Now it was a high metallic whine. Ronnie opened the blinds a crack.

"Oh fuck!" he yelled. He ran for the back door.

A wrecker truck was racing toward the trailer with the headlights off. As Ronnie ran through the kitchen, the truck rammed into the trailer. The front wall imploded, showering the interior of the mobile home in glass, metal and wood. The roar of the engine filled the structure. The impact threw Ronnie into the fridge. The door handle caught him in his right side like a kidney punch. He bounced off the fridge and headed for the back door.

Ronnie kicked open the back door and took the rickety wood steps two at a time. He was almost on the ground when someone grabbed the door and slammed it into him. He lost his balance and fell to the ground. The gun leaped from his hand and disappeared into the darkness under the trailer. Ronnie rolled on his back and used both his feet to kick the door back toward whoever had grabbed it.

The door rocketed back into Beauregard's face. He felt something in his nose give way. Blood and snot poured from his nostrils and down his face. A piece of his incisor tumbled down his throat. He stumbled backwards and landed against the back wall of the mobile home. He pushed off and stepped from around the swinging door with the .45 leading the way. He caught a glimpse of Ronnie's form running into the cornfield next to the trailer. Beauregard ran back around to the front of the trailer. When he reached the truck, he removed the crowbar he had wedged against the dash and the gas pedal. He hopped in and jammed the truck into reverse. Backing up, he flicked on the headlights and the running lights. There was only one beam of light on the passenger side illuminating the dark. One of the headlights must have been damaged in the crash. One would have to be good enough. He shifted into first and floored the gas pedal.

Ronnie was leaving a trail in the dry cornstalks a blind man could have followed. The headlight cast animated shadows as the truck bounced over row after row. Ronnie was running straight ahead, leaving broken stalks in his wake. Beauregard shifted into second and closed the gap. Ronnie must have realized the futility of trying to outrun the truck by sticking to a linear route. He slashed to his right. Beauregard figured he was heading back to the main road. Maybe get across the highway into the woods. Or maybe he was just running with no idea where he was going. Terror had a way of making smart men stupid.

Instead of wrenching the steering wheel to the right, Beauregard stood up on the brakes and wrenched it to the left. The back end of the truck skipped across the rows like a stone across the water. Ronnie saw a wave of dirt and cornstalks flying toward him a second before the back of the truck crashed into him and sent him flying like a softball.

Beauregard felt the truck make contact with Ronnie's body. It was like hitting a good-sized buck. He put the truck in neutral and shut off the engine. He grabbed his gun and climbed out. Standing by the truck he heard moaning coming from the west. Beauregard walked through the brittle stalks dried almost to dust from weeks without rain.

Ronnie was lying on his back with his legs twisted into odd angles. Even in the dark, Beauregard could see his jeans were stained. Fluids were leaking out of Ronnie Sessions at an alarming rate. He was trying to scuttle backwards but his arms failed him. Beauregard let the gun dangle at his side. He wiped his nose with the back of his free hand. His own blood looked like oil on his skin.

"Ah Jesus, Bug, I fucked up. I know it. I'm sorry. I think I done broke my legs," Ronnie said. His salt-and-pepper goatee was stained burgundy by the blood bubbling out of his mouth.

"No, you didn't. I broke your legs. And you're not sorry. You just sorry I caught up with you," Beauregard said.

Ronnie took several deep breaths. "I am, Bug. About the job, Kelvin, everything."

Beauregard stepped on Ronnie's shin and let his full weight press down on the shattered bone. A strange sound came out of Ronnie. It was half scream, half strangled groan.

"You don't get to say his name. Are you sorry about my son too? They came to my house, Ronnie. My little boy is laying in a hospital bed fighting for his life. You sorry about that too?" Beauregard said. Ronnie's eyes rolled back in their sockets then focused on Beauregard. Beauregard dropped to his knees beside Ronnie's body. "You just couldn't stick to the fucking plan, could you?"

"I couldn't go back to being poor white trash, Bug. I could take being trash. I just couldn't stand being poor again," Ronnie said.

Beauregard shook his head slowly.

"Where's the van, Ronnie?"

A thought sliced through the fog of pain clouding Ronnie's brain.

"You found Reggie, huh? Did you kill him, Bug? He didn't know what I was gonna do. Did you kill my brother, Bug?" Ronnie asked.

Beauregard didn't say anything. All Ronnie could hear was his own labored breathing. Ronnie blinked his eyes hard three or four times. Tears ran away from the corners of his eyes and sluiced through his crow's feet.

"The van, Ronnie."

"Hey, Bug? Fuck you."

Beauregard shot Ronnie in the left knee. Ronnie opened his mouth wide in a rictus of agony. Beauregard got to his feet.

"That was for Kelvin."

Beauregard shot Ronnie in the other kneecap. Ronnie vomited, choked on it and vomited again. Beauregard pushed Ronnie's head to the left with his foot to clear his airway. He didn't want him to pass out.

"That was for Darren," Beauregard said. "I'm gonna ask you again. Where's the van, Ronnie?"

Ronnie craned his neck to meet Beauregard's gaze. "Why should I tell you, Bug? Ain't ya gonna kill me?" he rasped.

"I can hurt you a lot more before that happens," Beauregard said.

Ronnie closed his eyes. Beauregard could see movement behind his lids like he had entered a REM state. Moments ticked by as Beauregard waited for him to answer.

"I don't have time for this, Ronnie," Beauregard said. He stepped on Ronnie's right knee and ground his heel into the bullet wound just above his patella. Ronnie screeched and sat straight up at the waist like a vampire in a coffin. He pawed at Beauregard's thighs. Beauregard kneed him in the face. Ronnie fell back onto the dirt with his arms outstretched. His fingertips brushed against a few downed cornstalks. When his eyes opened Beauregard could see there was no more fight left in him.

"It's down at my granddad's old place. Crab Thicket Road. Bank owns it, but nobody wants to live out there in the middle of no-fucking-where," Ronnie wheezed. "Jesus, it's a fucked-up world, ain't it, Bug?" he croaked. Blood was flowing freely from his mouth now.

Beauregard turned his head and spit out a globule of blood and saliva. He put his foot on Ronnie's chest and aimed at his head.

"The world's fine, Ronnie. It's us that's fucked up," he said.

Beauregard got back to the salvage yard around midnight. Boonie's truck was still there when he pulled up to the office. Boonie met him as he climbed out of the wrecker. He stood in front of the office door with his hands on his hips as Beauregard pulled a green tarp out of the truck. It tumbled to the ground with an audible thump.

"You find out where the van is?" Boonie asked.

"Yeah," Beauregard said.

Boonie sighed and tugged at his hat.

"We can put him in the Cavalier with his brother. In an hour, they won't be nothing but a big-ass paperweight," Boonie said. He squinted and studied Beauregard's face. He gestured to the busted headlight and the cornstalks stuck in the grill.

"Looks like he didn't give it up easy."

Beauregard caught a glimpse of himself in the driver's-side window.

"I'm glad he didn't," he said.

THIRTY-ONE

"That'll be $87.50, ma'am," Lazy said. He slid two cartons of Marlboro Reds across the counter. The old woman set the bag with her oxygen tank in it on the counter. She pulled a hundred out of the pocket of her yellow polyester pants and handed it to Lazy. As he was counting out her change, he heard a shrill whistle echoing from his office. He handed Mrs. Jackson her change and went into the back office.

The burner phone was ringing and vibrating on his desk.

"Hello?"

"You want the platinum? I got it. You come on down here. Just you and the boy with the scars and somebody to drive the van. It's a little after two. I figure y'all can make it down here by five. After five, I drive the whole fucking thing into a lake," a voice said.

"Is this the missing Mr. Beauregard? I thought Ronnie had this phone."

"He don't need it no more. I'll text you the address," Beauregard said.

Lazy chuckled. "Beau, I don't think you get how this works. You don't give me orders. You don't tell me where to go or what to do. I do the telling, son. If I say bring me the van, you bring me the goddamn van. If I tell you to eat a shit sandwich, you eat the goddamn shit sandwich and ask for a glass of piss to wash it down. That's how things work around here," he said. He heard Beauregard breathing on the other end of the line.

"I don't think you understand. You need this more than I do. And trust me, Lazy, you don't want me coming up that way. You sent men to my house. Threatened my wife. They shot my baby boy. We meeting someplace neutral so we can be quits with this. I come there and I'm likely to kill everything I see. You want the address or not?" Beauregard said.

Lazy squeezed the phone. "Fine. Send it on, boy. We'll have a little conversation when I see you," he said.

"Five o'clock," Beauregard said. The line went dead.

Lazy watched a narrow crack slither across the screen on his phone as he gripped it tight.

Beauregard closed the flip phone and set it on Boonie's desk.

"He going for it?" Boonie asked.

"He ain't got no choice. Shade is kicking his ass. He lost the jewelry store. He needs this," Beauregard said.

"You think this gonna work?" Boonie asked. Beauregard rubbed his wide hands on his thighs. His legs were still sore from the fall. The pain made him wince but it also made him feel sharp.

"I gotta make it work," Beauregard said.

He got up out of his chair. Boonie rose as well. He slipped from behind his desk and stood in front of Beauregard. A second passed, then another and another. The moment stretched on and on until it collapsed under the weight of its own tension. Boonie threw his arms around the bigger man and squeezed him tight. Beauregard squeezed him right back.

"It's alright. Everything's gonna be alright," Boonie said.

"No matter what happens you make sure Kia and Ariel and the boys get what I left 'em," Beauregard murmured againt Boonie's cheek.

"Don't you worry about that. Go handle your business, boy," Boonie said.

He let go of Beauregard, stepped back and rubbed his eyes.

Beauregard nodded then headed for the door. He opened it and paused for a moment. The afternoon sun carved an elongated shadow around him.

"I loved my Daddy. But you was a better father to me than he ever could have been," he said. He stepped through the open door and closed it behind him.

Beauregard went to the hospital after he left Boonie's. He headed straight for the ICU department. A tall, gaunt nurse with her chestnut brown hair pulled back into a severe bun was standing at the nurses' station.

"Excuse me, what room is Darren Montage in?" he asked.

The nurse looked up from her clipboard. Her light green eyes were hard. "Only immediate family can see him, sir."

"I'm . . . I'm his father."

"Oh, I see. He's in room 245. He can only have visitors for fifteen minutes," she said. She returned to her clipboard.

Beauregard entered the room like the floor was made of lava. The pungent, antiseptic odor of the hospital was even more concentrated in the ICU. It was like the whole area was dipped in Lysol.

Darren was lying on his back in the middle of the bed. The head of the bed was slightly elevated, letting the overhead lights illuminate his face. It gave him an otherworldly countenance. Beauregard knew he was small. The last time they had taken him to the doctor for a checkup they said he was a bit undersized for his age. In the middle of the hospital bed, hooked up to tubes and machines, he looked positively miniscule. Like one of his action figures. Beauregard approached the bed. He took his son's impossibly tiny hand. It was cool to the touch. The machines beeped and hissed like some Rube Goldberg contraption.

"I never wanted any of this for you. Or your brother or your sister. But I brought it to you. Somebody else might have pulled the trigger, but I did this. I gotta own that. I hope someday you'll know how sorry I am. No matter how things go today, I don't think I'm ever going to see you again, Stink. So, I wanna tell you I love you. A father who really loves his children doesn't do anything to hurt them. He doesn't put them in harm's way. Not on purpose. He ain't an outlaw or a gangsta. It done took me a long time to realize that," Beauregard said.

He leaned over the railing and kissed Darren on his forehead.

"I'm never gonna hurt y'all again," he said.

Ariel was trying on sunglasses when her phone rang. She checked it, didn't recognize the number and hit end. It rang again a few seconds later. It was the same number. She groaned and answered it this time.

"Hello?"

"Hey," Beauregard said.

"Hey. You get a new phone?" she asked.

"Yeah. What you doing?"

"Me and Rip at the mall. What's up?"

"Uh, nothing really. You ain't spending that money, are you?" Beauregard asked.

"No. Me and Rip just hanging out. We both off."

"Oh. Well, I just wanted to tell you something."

"Tell me what?"

Beauregard waved a fly out of his face. The van didn't have any AC anymore, so he had both windows open.

"I love you."

Beauregard heard the indiscernible din of disembodied voices on the phone. The aural flotsam and jetsam of a large American mall. The cacophony of hundreds of footsteps. Everything but his daughter's voice.

"I . . . I love you too, Daddy," she said finally.

"I gotta go, baby," Beauregard said.

"Okay," Ariel said.

The line went dead.

Beauregard put the phone in his pocket. He climbed out of the van cradling the double-barrel shotgun in the crook of his arm. Fluffy cumulus clouds rolled across the sky, obscuring the late afternoon sun. He walked to the front of the van and leaned against the hood as he watched a long black car wind its way down Crab Thicket Road.

THIRTY-TWO

The Caddy came to a stop fifteen feet in front of Beauregard. It idled under the setting sun like some predatory beast growling at its prey. The passenger door opened, and Billy climbed out. Both rear doors opened next. Lazy and a man Beauregard didn't recognize got out and stood beside the car. Lazy was wearing a light tan golf shirt and white pants. His wild hair looked like a woodland creature had made a nest in it. He was grinning at Beauregard. He started to walk forward but Beauregard pointed a shotgun at him.

"That's far enough," he said.

"Well here we are, Bug. This supposed to be a showdown? Like in—"

Beauregard cut him off. "No. No, it's not. It's just me giving you what's yours and you leaving me and mine alone."

Lazy let his tongue slide over his lips.

"Where's Ronnie and Reggie, Beauregard?" Lazy asked.

"Nowhere you gotta worry about," Beauregard said.

"Now see, if that's how you treat your partners, how can I trust you? How do I know you ain't replaced all the platinum with aluminum foil?" Lazy asked.

"Come take a look. Just move slow," Beauregard said.

"Check it out, Burning Man. See if we all gonna go home happy," Lazy said. Beauregard kept the shotgun trained on Billy as he walked backwards. Billy followed him at a relatively safe distance until they reached the back door of the van. Beauregard gestured toward the door with the shotgun. Billy gripped the handle, then looked back at Beauregard, whose slick brown face was unreadable. Billy opened the door while simultaneously jumping backwards.

"You can't blame me for being jumpy," he said. Beauregard didn't acknowledge him. He poked his head around the swinging door. There in the back of the van was a pallet of metal coils five or six levels high. Billy closed the door and walked back to the Caddy. Beauregard followed him, listening to their feet crunch on the dry dead grass. Sweat was pouring down his face but he didn't dare wipe his eyes.

"Well, what you say, Burning Man?" Lazy asked.

"It's in there," he said.

"The keys are in the van," Beauregard said as he began to back away.

"Hold on. I can't just put a member of my family in that van on your word," Lazy said.

"What you saying?" Beauregard asked.

"I'm saying why don't you start the van up for us? Make sure this ain't like the beginning of *Casino*," Lazy said.

Beauregard didn't move.

"Or do you have a little surprise fixed up for us in there, Beauregard?" Lazy asked. A few crows cawed as they flew overhead. The clouds had parted and now the full fury of the sun was bearing down on them.

"Fine," he said. He used one hand to reach through the driver's window and cranked the motor. It came to life with a cough and a sputter, but it finally caught and turned over. It idled as rough as a rock polisher.

"Shit, is it gonna make it down the lane?" Billy asked.

"It'll make it just fine," Beauregard said.

"Alright then. Sal, go on get in and follow us back home," Lazy said.

Beauregard stepped back and to the left. The man Beauregard didn't recognize was wearing a white wife beater and blue jeans at least one size too small. He climbed in the van. "This got AC?" he asked in a squeaky tin whistle voice.

"No," Beauregard said.

Lazy appraised him with his hands on his hips.

"You know this ain't over, right? We gonna see you soon, son," Lazy said. He winked at Beauregard.

"You wanna come for me, then come on. This . . ." He nodded at the van. "Is so that you leave my family out of it. What we got going on is between you and me. Don't worry, I'll be around. But I think you gonna have your hands full with Mr. Shade and his folks for a while," Beauregard said.

"I just might. Don't worry, though, we ain't gonna forget about you," Lazy said. He got back in the car. Billy used his thumb and forefinger to make a shooting motion toward Beauregard as he climbed back in the passenger seat. The driver put the car in gear. He backed up into a clutch of honeysuckle, then turned around and headed down the driveway. Sal followed them. They crept through the brush and over the potholes at a snail's pace.

Lazy pulled out his cell phone.

"When he leaves, follow him. Then grab him and bring him and his family to the store. We gonna make this last over a three-day weekend. Don't fuck around with this boy. Go in there with guns blazing. Don't let him get the drop on you," Lazy said. He ended the call and put the phone back in his pocket.

"You want us to give them some backup?" Billy asked.

"No. We need to get this van back. I got some bills I gotta pay and I want you with me," Lazy said.

"You sure they can handle it?" Billy asked.

"They better," Lazy said. He sat back and gazed at the cedar trees that lined the driveway. Billy turned on the radio. He kept spinning the dial until he found a country song. Not that slick Nashville shit but a real country song with some steel guitars and a whiskey-soaked melody.

Beauregard watched them ease their way down the lane. The setting sun bathed the vehicles in a soft magenta hue. He pulled out a cell phone and brought up the number to the burner Lazy had given Ronnie. He was a practical man not overly enamored with irony. That being said, he thought it was kind of fitting he'd used that phone as the trigger for the bomb.

He'd never made a bomb before, but it wasn't that difficult. In a way, it was like the ignition system in a car. He'd called Madness and received an over-the-phone tutorial. After a quick ride to the hardware store and some experimentation, it was ready. The convoy reached the end of the driveway and paused.

Beauregard pressed send.

The explosion didn't look like a mushroom cloud, but it was still impressive nonetheless. One minute the van was there, the next it was an exponentially expanding ball of fire. Despite the van being a good eighty feet away, the concussive force hit Beauregard like a sledgehammer. His ear popped so hard he thought he might have ruptured his eardrums. He saw the van explode a split second before he heard it. The shotgun was knocked from his hands as he landed on his ass. Luckily it didn't discharge. The world was a twisting piñata that made him nauseous. He closed his eyes and tried to find his equilibrium. Transitioning from his behind to his hands and knees, he heard the sounds of suffering over the roaring of the fire.

They weren't dead. They might be fucked up, but they weren't dead.

An overabundance of saliva was filling his mouth, but he didn't throw up. He took a deep breath and pushed himself off the ground. He shielded his eyes with his hand as he peered through the fire. The back window of the Caddy was gone. The lid of the trunk was bouncing up and down like a stripper on the pole. The bumper was missing in action. It was a testament to American engineering that the car was still moving. It paused for a moment as the driver's door opened and a body was pushed out onto the ground. The door closed and seconds later Beauregard watched as the back wheels kicked up clods of dirt and dead grass as the Caddy sped down Crab Thicket Road.

"Shit," he mumbled. For his first foray into bomb building, the complete annihilation of the van was impressive. However, the van was only half the equation. He'd intended to get the Caddy too. Whatever his intentions had been didn't matter now. He couldn't let them get away.

He scooped up the shotgun and headed to the barn. It sat in the middle of the heather and goldenrod like it had dropped out of the stratosphere. The paint on the doors had faded long ago. There was only the suggestion of crimson on their surface now. Beauregard wrenched the doors apart.

The Duster sat in the shadows of the old barn like a dire wolf in the recesses of a cave. Beauregard tossed the shotgun in the passenger seat. He climbed in and fired up the engine. It roared to life, stirring up the decades of dust in the barn. The duals played a concerto as he shifted it into gear and burst out of the barn. He skirted around the remains of the van, rolled over the body in the grass and hit the blacktop doing 40 mph.

"Get us the fuck out of here!" Lazy screamed. Glass and blood littered the back seat. The lid of the trunk bounced up and down like the mouth of a huge puppet. The car swerved from one side of the road to the other but it never slowed down.

"He can't catch us!" Billy screamed back.

Lazy took a look out what was left of the back window.

The Duster was bearing down on them like 2,000 pounds of thunder and steel.

———

Beauregard closed in on the Caddy, a shark zeroing in on a seal. He shifted into fourth. The front bumper of the Duster kissed the empty space where the bumper used to reside. The Caddy lurched out of his reach. The Caddy's one remaining tail light glowed like the eye of a demon as it braked for an upcoming hairpin curve. Beauregard crushed the brake and the clutch and drifted through the curve right behind the Caddy. As he drifted, he leaned to his left.

The rear window of the Duster shattered. Shards of glass rained down on his back and shoulders. He held onto the steering wheel, but the Duster tried to get away from him. The rear end fishtailed like it was salsa dancing. Beauregard downshifted, regained control, then hit the gas again. He gave the rearview mirror a quick glance. There was a baby blue Mazda chasing him. A man was leaning out the passenger window with a pistol. The three-vehicle car chase turned onto Route 603. An eight-mile straight stretch that bisected Red Hill County. The man in the blue car fired at the Duster again. The passenger-side mirror disappeared.

Beauregard slammed the clutch, hit the brake and shifted into reverse. He then immediately released the clutch, hit the brake again with his left foot, and floored the gas pedal with his right while twisting the steering wheel to the left. All this fancy footwork resulted in the Duster spinning 180 degrees. He was now going backwards at 50 miles per hour facing the Mazda. The driver of the Mazda hit his brakes as he braced for an imminent collision. The passenger was thrown forward, then he fell backwards.

Beauregard grabbed the shotgun with his right hand, transferred it to his left, and wedged the barrels between the side mirror and the door frame. He adjusted his aim to the left and fired both barrels at the blue car. The recoil made the gun jump from his hand. It fell out the window and clattered onto the road.

He'd aimed for the driver, but his shot had gone low and punched a hole in the grill. Steam began to billow from beneath the hood. Moments later the hood popped up like a jack in the box. Beauregard repeated his previous machinations and spun the Duster another 180 degrees. As he was completing his revolution, a trash truck blew past him in the opposite lane, nearly clipping the front of his car. The trash truck swerved to its right just as the blue car drifted into its lane.

Beauregard barely heard the crash in the rapidly receding distance. The ringing in his ears was relentless. He shifted into fifth gear. The Duster's tires clawed at the asphalt. He pulled into the passing lane and pulled alongside the Caddy. He caught a brief glance of Burning Man's ruined face before a minivan forced him to slow down and drift back into the northbound lane. Burning Man's reflexes must have been dulled by the explosion. He fired his gun out the window of the Caddy, missing the Duster entirely and shattering the window of the minivan. The van ran off the side of the road and into the ditch. The landscape changed from dense undeveloped woodlands to wide open fields. Beauregard shifted back up into fifth. He pulled alongside the rear quarter panel. He swung the Duster into the Caddy at over 90 mph.

Billy saw him coming in the rearview mirror. When the Duster slammed into them, it felt as inevitable as the setting of the sun.

That motherfucker sure can drive, he thought.

Beauregard watched as the Caddy fishtailed across the highway. Burning Man tried to maintain but he wasn't a wheelman. He overcorrected, and the Caddy ran off the road, hit the ditch and somersaulted through the air. The Caddy crashed into a fence surrounding a pasture. It rolled a few more times, sending a few cows scampering for cover. It came to rest upside down with the wheels still spinning. Oil and gas were pouring from the hood and spilling across the ground. Beauregard skidded to a stop, backed up and drove down the service driveway next to the pasture. He guided the Duster through the ruined fence.

He stopped a few feet away from the Caddy. He didn't shut it off, just put it in neutral and hit the parking brake. He pulled his .45 from the glove compartment and got out of the car. The cloying scent of engine coolant mixed with the raw, mean aroma that surrounded bovines in the middle of summer. Beauregard trained his .45 on the upside-down driver's door. He took quick shallow breaths as he inched his way to the door. A tanned arm stretched out the window. The hand was lying on top of a cow patty. Beauregard kicked the arm. The rest of the body slipped out of the driver's seat and collapsed in a loose tangle of limbs against the headliner. Burning Man was extinguished.

Beauregard moved to the back seat.

A fusillade of bullets ripped through the rear door. Beauregard felt two sharp scorching pains to his forearm and the lower section of his thigh. It felt like someone had hit him with an incredibly hard, incredibly tiny hammer. A red-hot hammer that burned him to his bones. He stumbled and fell to the ground. He landed on his side. His head and neck were slathered in cow shit. Where was his gun? He must have dropped it. The rear door started to creak open. Beauregard pushed himself off the ground and dragged himself back to the Duster.

Lazy fell out of the back seat. His left arm was twisted like a bread tie. He scrambled to his feet and leaned against the Caddy. He raised a Desert Eagle .380 and scanned the field.

"Where you at, boy? You hiding behind that car? I got you, I think. I heard you squeal, boy. Give me a minute, I'm coming to finish you off. I told you God himself couldn't kill me, how the fuck you thought you was gonna do it?" Lazy screamed. He blinked his eyes. Lights were flashing around his head like fireworks. The .380 was so heavy in his hand. If he wasn't leaning against the car, he felt he might topple over. His adrenaline was beginning to wear off. Pain gnawed at the edge of his perception. Racing up his arm and across his back. That was alright. He could handle pain. Just like he'd handled Beauregard.

He heard the engine of the red car rev up like God screaming at Moses on Mount Sinai. His damaged ears felt like they were bleeding. He saw Bug pop up in the driver's seat. Lazy brought his gun up and started pulling the trigger.

Beauregard ducked down until his chin was on the steering wheel. One bullet punched a hole in his windshield and sailed over his head.

Beauregard slammed the gas pedeal to the floor.

The Duster plowed into Lazy, trapping him between its grill and the rear of the Caddy. The Caddy spun like a merry-go-round as the Duster rammed into it. Lazy disappeared under the front tires. Beauregard felt the car bounce once, then twice. He moved his foot off the gas. He pushed in the clutch, put the car in reverse and backed up. The car bounced once, then twice. Beauregard hit the brake and the Duster stalled.

Beauregard fell back against the headrest. There was numbness in his right leg that was now spreading to his right side. His left forearm was missing a chunk of flesh the size of a quarter. Blood raced down his arm and entwined his fingers. There was a hole in the right leg of his jeans that was weeping red tears. He took a deep breath. The world seemed to be contracting and expanding at the same time. He closed his eyes. He let his hands run over the polished wood grain steering wheel. Along the leather seats. He caressed the 8-ball shifter.

"You ready, Bug?"

Beauregard rolled his head to the right. His father was sitting in the passenger seat. He was wearing the exact same clothes he had been wearing the last time Beauregard saw him. White ribbed tank top under a short-sleeved black button-up shirt. A pack of cigarettes in the breast pocket. He grinned at him.

"Come on, boy. You ready to fly?" his father asked.

"You're not real."

His father blanched. "Boy, what the hell you talking about? Shut up that fool mess and let's go."

Beauregard turned his head and looked straight ahead. He heard sirens coming from the northern end of the county.

"You're not real. You're dead. Probably been that way for a while now. I never stopped loving you, though," he croaked. He closed his eyes again and started the Duster. When he put the car in gear, he opened his eyes and glanced toward his right. The passenger seat was empty. Pushing the gas pedal was agony, but he bore it. Beauregard drove across the pasture. A few cows stared at him as he passed. The Duster turned left onto a dirt lane at the back end of the field. The lane went from red clay to gravel. Beauregard got to the end and turned left onto a narrow blacktop back road. Soon the sirens were just faint horns playing a mournful tune to an audience of beasts.

THIRTY-THREE

Kia entered Darren's room carrying a teddy bear with a GET WELL balloon tied to its arm. The machines that monitored his vitals beeped and hummed as she sat down in the chair near his bed. She placed the teddy bear next to his slight form and took his tiny hand in hers.

"He's gonna make it," Beauregard said.

Kia didn't turn her head to look at him. She didn't even acknowledge him. Beauregard was standing in the far corner of the room. The glare from the fluorescent light over Darren's bed gave his son a ghostly countenance. He moved from the shadows and pulled up a chair to the opposite side of Darren's bed. The steady pulse of the EKG was comforting to him. It meant his son's heart was still beating. Seconds turned to minutes and neither of them made a sound.

"You were right. I should have sold the car," Beauregard said finally. Kia swallowed hard and wiped her eyes.

"You ain't never gonna sell that car," she said.

"You're right. I told Boonie to crush it," he said. Kia looked at him then.

"What do you mean, 'crush it'?"

"I told him to get rid of it," Beauregard said. Darren's eyes were closed but his lids twitched. Quick spasmodic movements that teased Beauregard's heart with the possibility of seeing his son open his eyes.

"I don't believe that," Kia said.

"You don't have to. It's getting done though. Probably happening right now," Beauregard said.

"Why would you do that to the Duster? You love that car," Kia said. Beauregard interlaced his fingers and stared at the dull linoleum floor.

"The men that came by the house, they won't be coming back," Beauregard said.

"You don't know that."

"Yes, I do."

Kia looked at him then. She made a noise that was halfway between a sob and a laugh.

"So, you took care of it," she said. Beauregard rose from the chair. He went to the window and stared out across the hospital parking lot. The setting sun was an orange beacon in the hazy sky.

"A man can't be two types of beast," Beauregard said.

"What the hell do that mean, Bug?" Kia asked. Beauregard let his head hang.

"When my Daddy ran off, I felt like somebody had put my heart in a vise and kept tightening that motherfucker till they arm got tired. It ruined me. And my Mama, she couldn't help because she felt like him leaving her was worse than him leaving us. I can't say I blame her really. My Daddy was the kind of man who left a big hole behind. It was easy for her to fill that hole with hurt," Beauregard said. He turned and faced Kia. She saw his eyes were rimmed in red.

"I couldn't do that. I just couldn't let myself hate him. So, I made him into my hero. I pretended that he wasn't a gangsta or a drunk or a bad husband or a bad father. I got out and I fixed that Duster up. I'd ride around and I'd tell myself that even if he was all those things it didn't matter because he loved me. But it does matter. It matters a lot. If your Daddy is the kind of man that can run people down with a car or shoot 'em in the face, it matters a whole hell of a lot. And there's not enough love in the world to change that," Beauregard said.

"Bug, you ain't your Daddy," Kia said. Tears danced on the edges of her eyes.

"You're right. I'm worse. My Daddy never lied about who or what he was. He owned it. I was the one who put him on a pedestal. He never climbed up there. But me? I lied all the time. I lied to you. I lied to myself. I thought I could be an outlaw part of the time and the rest of the time be a daddy and a husband. That was the lie. Truth is I'm an outlaw all the time. I was playing at being a good man," Beauregard said.

"What am I supposed to do with that, Bug, huh? You want to me to make you feel better? Tell you never mind what's happened, you are a good father and a good husband? Because I can't do that," Kia said. She squeezed Darren's hand. Beauregard moved to Darren's bedside and touched his other hand.

"No. No more lies. All I gotta do is look around and see what kind of man I really am. Ariel is dating some fucked-up gangster wannabe. Javon had to kill a man on his own front step. Darren laying here fighting for his life. You've had to watch it all go down. Kelvin is . . ." Beauregard's voice cracked.

"What about Kelvin?" Kia asked. Beauregard didn't answer.

"I can't keep doing this to y'all," he said. He walked over to Kia's chair and put his hands on the backrest. He watched the muscles in her back roil under her shirt. He could feel her body stiffen even though he wasn't touching her.

"Boonie's sitting on ten rolls of platinum for you. He gonna sell them and split it between you and Ariel. He gonna take over the note on the garage too. When I get settled I'll send you some more money," Beauregard said.

He moved to the door. His hand had fallen on the handle when he heard Kia's voice.

"So, you just running, is that it?"

Beauregard stopped in his tracks. The handle in his hand felt as heavy as a bag of bricks. He licked his lips. He spoke to her without turning around.

"You told me to go."

"I know what I said. You ain't gotta tell me what I said."

"What do you want from me, then? Tell me what you want, Kia."

"It ain't just about me or you, Bug," Kia said.

Beauregard laid his head against the door. Its polished wood surface was cool against his skin. He turned the handle a quarter inch. The door opened a crack.

"I know you telling yourself what you doing is for the best, but is it? Or are you just taking the easy way out?" Kia asked.

"You think this is easy for me? You think walking away from you and the boys is easy for me?" Beauregard asked.

"Look, I can't make no promises about you and me. But if you stopped doing gangsta shit I'd never keep you from the boys. You walk out that door and I won't have to. They'll hate you all on their own. I can promise you that," Kia said.

"I can live with them hating me if I know they're safe. If they around me they won't be," Beauregard said.

"You really believe that? Then do what your Daddy couldn't. Stay. Change," Kia said. Beauregard opened the door. The hallway was full of doctors and nurses hovering around all kinds of equipment. A few patients tethered to IVs were moving past the staff like forlorn zombies.

"I love you, Kia," Beauregard said. He stepped out into the hallway.

"Bug!" Kia shouted. He whirled around, afraid something had happened to Darren. Kia was standing near the bed with her arms crossed across her chest.

"If you're gonna go . . . do you have to go right now? Like, right this minute? Jean's bringing Javon up here in a little while. They let him go. I don't think they gonna charge him. He's been asking for you," she said. Beauregard stepped back into the room. Kia stared at him hard. Her eyes shined with a light born of fury and despair. He didn't know what to say. He waited for his father's voice to share some pithy words of wisdom but that wraith no longer spoke to him. He was on his own.

"You sure?" Beauregard asked.

"No. But I don't want to be here alone anymore," Kia said.

Beauregard went back to his chair. He sat down and enveloped Darren's small hand in his own. Kia sat down and did the same thing on the other side of the bed.

The dying light of day cast their shadows against the far wall. Their silhouettes overlapped, entwined like lovers. Silence filled the spaces between them. Kia lowered the railing and lay across the foot of Darren's bed. Beauregard studied the back of her head. The gentle slope of her neck.

After a while she let out a sigh.

"You're never really gonna change, are you, Bug," she said. The statement came out flat and listless. Some might say hopeless.

Beauregard closed his eyes. Faces rushed at him out of the darkness.

Red Navely and his brothers.

Ronnie and Reggie.

Lazy.

Burning Man.

Eric.

Kelvin.

A dozen other faces floated up from the river of his memories, their mouths slack, their eyes glazed over. Their last words wasted on pleas of mercy. Their last breaths becoming a death rattle in their throats. Other faces joined them, accompanied by the squeal of tires and the shriek of bullets.

Wives he had made widows. Mothers who waited in vain for their sons to come home. Sons who would never see their fathers again. All those faces, all those lives, nothing more than earth, ashes and rust now.

Finally, he whispered, "I don't know if I can."

ACKNOWLEDGMENTS

It is said that writing is a lonely endeavor. This is only partly true. I have been blessed to be surrounded by an incredible group of friends and family and fellow writers who have supported me, cajoled me and when needed given me a swift kick in the rear during this journey.

First and foremost I'd like to thank my agent, Josh Getzler, and all the great folks at HG Literary. Josh was the first person to believe in *Blacktop Wasteland,* and he has always been its fiercest champion. I'm forever grateful I stopped and talked to you in that hotel hallway in St. Petersburg.

I'd like to thank my editor, Christine Kopprasch, and everyone at Flatiron Books. You have been my own personal Virgil through this Divine Comedy. Always supportive, always insightful and always, always trying to make me a better writer.

I'd like to thank some of the people who gave me invaluable advice as *Blacktop Wasteland* moved from an idea I rambled on about to an actual book: Eryk Pruitt, Nikki Dolson, Kellye Garrett, Rob Pierce, you are all talented writers who were generous with your time and your wisdom.

Finally I'd like to thank Kim.

She knows why. She always has.

S. A. COSBY returns with . . .

RAZORBLADE TEARS

Coming July 2021

<u>Available to order</u>

HEADLINE